P. ... ...KS 1994

Let the River Stand

Vincent O'Sullivan is a major New Zealand writer. An award-winning short-story writer, he is also highly regarded as a playwright, poet, critic and editor. He has edited a number of major New Zealand anthologies. After spending part of the 1980s in Australia, he currently lives in Wellington, where he is Professor of English at Victoria University.

Thanks for a memorable holiday in Canada

May 1995 be a great year for you

Let the River Stand

Vincent O'Sullivan

PENGUIN BOOKS

PENGUIN BOOKS

Penguin Books (NZ) Ltd, 182–190 Wairau Road, Auckland 10, New Zealand
Penguin Books Ltd, 27 Wrights Lane, London W8 5TZ, England
Penguin USA, 375 Hudson Street, New York, NY 10014, United States
Penguin Books Australia Ltd, 487 Maroondah Highway, Ringwood, Australia 3134
Penguin Books Canada Ltd, 10 Alcorn Avenue, Toronto, Ontario, Canada M4V 3B2

Penguin Books Ltd, Registered Offices: Harmondsworth, Middlesex, England

First published in 1993
3   5   7   9   10   8   6   4
Copyright © Vincent O'Sullivan, 1993
All rights reserved

Typeset by Egan-Reid, Auckland
Printed by Australian Print Group, Maryborough, Vic.

The assistance of the Literature programme of the Queen Elizabeth II
Arts Council towards the publication of this book is gratefully
acknowledged.

For Syd

After the lunchtime sandwiches on the white plate, after the crumbs and the specks of cheese sucked up from her wetted finger, she folds her hands and leans back in the orange cane chair which is only hers, which from time to time she picks up and moves and resettles so that she is always in the fall of sunlight, as she moves from the shadow wing that spreads from the high wall and follows her. When the sky's space is hugely bright the cane chair shines in its lacing strands. She rubs her fingertips on the small greasy bumps, licks her finger and rubs the shine. Clouds already pile towards the afternoon. Then it will be corridors and the rec room, the thick corners of shadow and the pyramids of light beneath the green shades, the brimming yellow cones she moves her hands slowly into and out from, into the treacling light her fingers spread across her skirt, the furred and yellow smell that is wool and burning pine and sometimes piss, and the shadow rolls up her arm like a pushed sleeve, in and out until her arm is tired.

Sometimes in thinner light towards the evening the cake plate floats there not on anything until you touch. The mushy cake packs up between her teeth and her upper lip. Ugh!

There is a sound, a pushing towards a word which is never clear.

'What's that, dear?'

'What's that she said?' Excitement and pointing along the chair, the path, the winter rec room, jabbing at the single, the maybe word. Then her hand tapped nicely, 'Yes? You want to say?'

The moving wing this outside day begins to fall from the wall. The cane strands licked with sun, so shiny. The big white wall and this stretching dark. There is something she does not quite hear but strains towards. Her left leg kicks out involuntarily and her cup is an open mouth on the grass. Running then, the white clothes running, stooping, light licks along nurse's hair who picks up the cup, who strokes her arm, laughing, *everybody laughing*, not to worry, *telling her*, no harm done.

7

The wing thickens, over all. The sun undoes. First drops of rain squash fat pennies along the path.

Her head tilts out again towards the word, her wanting it, her pouted lips raised like an animal's, the word, the bellow, held . . .

ALEXANDER MacLeod bought the farm two miles south from the Pukeroro turnoff when already he was well past middle age, and still three years before he settled on finding himself a bride. He bought from a family whose two sons had enlisted for the war, although only one of them was of legal age, and it was the elder who survived, coming home from Messines with his left leg for ever stiffened in a surgical boot. MacLeod picked the land up for a song, a scrubby underworked block that became the best farm between the town limits and the line of low pretty hills that reminded everyone of England, except those who actually had seen what English hills were like. It was a generation before anyone else in the district would believe there was money in mixing dairy stock and cattle; two generations until the same excellent farmland was broken up for Australians to invest in horse studs, and the fashion set in for ten-acre blocks where the daughters of dentists could trot their ponies. It was 1919. Every farmer in the district admired him and not one laid claim to being his friend. He experimented with different grasses and alternated the feed he gave his herds. He handled animals they said as if he had moulded the bloody things himself, the way the beasts fitted and moved beneath his hands when he tended or doctored or simply directed them, yet with never a word of warmth or affection from the mouth that was a level slit beneath his grey moustache.

The year he was fifty-six and felt at last that he had things set up tidily enough to marry he chose a woman a little more than half his age. She was said to be good-tempered and intelligent, but as everyone knows those are the qualities a man comes to appreciate in time rather than ones that infatuate and spur him on. They said she was attractive enough on a good day but as she was knocking six feet in height there was no great competition among suitors. So when the offer was made the girl accepted. As one of her shorter sisters reported, Emily Fraser admitted it may not have been a match that set her on fire, but it was better to be *anyone's* bride across at Pukeroro than to wither for a lifetime in the family house, even with a river view and a library full of books.

After two years she conceived their only child.

'He'll be Alexander too,' MacLeod said.

It was not a thing to discuss with Emily but a fact to be announced. In the evenings before the child was born he sat across the hearth from his wife and watched her tall figure thicken with investment. They spoke sparingly to each other even from the first. It was said that from the day his wife informed him he might add paternity to his other successes, MacLeod began visibly to diminish with such unexpected contentment. By the time the boy was born his father seemed to have aged as if in deference to this last and unexpected bonus. He held the boy in the trough between his clenched knees and moved his calloused fingers over the pulsating head and tiny ribs. In those first few weeks there was a flickering between the parents which each knew was stronger than the sporadic and silent couplings that had set it off. Soon enough one of them no longer remembered even that.

To avoid all chance of confusion, the child was addressed as Alex from the day he was born, although from a kind of mild mischief his mother would sometimes say to MacLeod, 'Look here at young Ecky, will you?' (In time the name would be written up in gold lettering with slanted shading above the entrance to the Empire Hotel as 'A. and E. MacLeod. Licensees'.)

When his legs gave out for reasons his doctors never quite understood, MacLeod sat by the range which seldom burned with more than a handful of coal, or on the back verandah where the army blanket across his knees was spread with papers on which sketches and calculations moved in his last and almost frenetic dream, for he fretted now that he would not have time to complete his work. His laboured figures and sketches clotted into unreadable knots, driven by his conviction that all milking-machines worked solely on the principle of suction and pressure, but none of them paid adequate attention to one obvious yet paramount fact, the natural elasticity of a cow's tits. There was a sheet of paper covered with intricate sketches, and half a dozen drawings of udders, on the clip-board that Emily MacLeod took from her husband's knee on a February afternoon at four o'clock when she knew he was dead by the gathering veil of flies.

Young Alex grew tall and pale and thin like his mother, which distressed her although she spoke of it to no-one. She assumed without actual evidence that darker, wirier men had the lion's share of life. Her son's face also shared the same disposition as her own to look melancholy, if not actually sulky, unless a deliberate effort was made to convince this wasn't so. There were the same delicate long-boned features and eyes that were taken as penetrating or vacant pretty much on the hunch of whoever looked into them. Does he see a great deal, people would often enough wonder, or doesn't he know shit from clay?

They asked it because his dark eyes seldom shifted from their faces, yet his chinaware face confronted them without expression. As a child it was said that young Alex took everything in, as though behind the steady lift of his eyes there was some kind of reservoir where intuitions floated to make a certain kind of grown-up uneasy. Others confidently said the boy was thick as pig-shit. If anything got into that head it would need to be hammered down to stay there. The young girl in the farm cottage heard her father say that once. She had suddenly in her mind the grotesque image of the boy with his long head like a post with nails rayed about it in a circle, a crown, and his face was carved and set as in the ornamental poles at the top of the American chapter in *Geography for Schools*.

For a while he was nicknamed Ghost. The name lapsed almost as soon as it was clear it did not disturb in the least the tall self-absorbed boy. His mother said to relatives how he took after her own father. She said, 'We were always a rangy brood.' The brother-in-law to whom she last said it sat with one knee slightly lifted and clasped between laced fingers. He refrained from adding the other adjectives that came to mind as he remembered that anxious intelligent man who said he would be quite willing to die when he had re-read Gibbon, which was almost true at the time of his demise.

The boy was hopeless at sport, apart from a straining competence at soccer where his long reach and sudden darting movements made him an erratic goalie. But that was in a time when schools thought only of the higher gifts of rugby, and soccer was little more than an aberration, a game played occasionally during physical education or by the bloody no-hopers who might as well be girls.

The retired provincial forward who coached the school in rugby, and was accorded the reverence that in more exotic societies would perhaps be given the shaman who had scaled the holy mountain and talked with God, did his best for Alex as he did indeed for any boy. Until at the end of several weeks into the season he said one afternoon to the gangling boy quivering with cold, swaying on pea-stick legs against a scattering gust of rain, 'Look, lad, you might be better off sticking to running or something, do you reckon? You're not cut out for this lot.'

The coach meant he had done all he could, there was not a thing there that was salvageable.

Nobody tried to organise him again. On the school's compulsory sports day at the beginning of every year, it seemed he might at least give the high jump a go. But it was as though his left heel was weighted with lead, trailing and raking at the bar, failing to clear the height that boys not up to his shoulder floated across with ease. 'Useless,' the kids called out. The only race he attempted to run in was the half-mile. He had no style and no pace and came in behind the leaders, but he was no more tired at the finish than he was at the beginning. He told his mother, 'I'm just getting into the swing of it when it comes to the end.' As he thought more on it he said, 'If they had marathons or something I think I'd be right.'

He was just fourteen. After the race he had gone across to his mother at the edge of the field. Unlike most of the parents who chatted in clumps and called out for each other's offspring, she was a figure by herself. She held her son's pullover across her arm. She made him put it on at once. She told him, 'Over-exert yourself like that and you're chesty in no time.'

There were precedents enough in her own family to justify her concern. But the boy's health seemed to hold out for all the genetic hazards his mother could draw on. As they said in the school staffroom, apart from being a born comedian when it came to sport, anyone who tangled with young MacLeod was asking for trouble. He was so much stronger than he looked. 'He'll never be anyone's dreamboat, mind,' one of the women teachers said. The headmaster glared from his papers but said nothing. He took in the overweight woman and the beefy phys ed teacher who sat beside her, their lunch papers overlapping. They had been having illicit sex for several years. The older man thought, well, there are dreams and dreams, aren't there?

Alex sat at the back of the classroom, in front of the large oil-cloth chart of England's kings and queens. If he sat anywhere else he was an obstacle for other pupils. He was glad that he stayed at school, and was not sorry that jobs were so hard to come by. He helped of course at home but that was scarcely work.

He did not remember when his father died, but knew how the farm had run down under a series of managers. Whenever he said to his mother, 'I can help more round the place than I do, you know', she reminded him that there was the manager. As long as he was there they should leave it to him. 'We don't want him to think we're interfering.' She meant the only manager probably in the whole North Island who ran a farm with one arm. The other had flapped and torn for several seconds in the mill ten years before, the forearm and its hand already thirty feet away on the streaming belt before the power had been turned off. She had said against her brother-in-law's accusations, 'What right do you have *not* to give a man like that work?'

The day he applied for the job, the manager's black sleeve was folded neatly back across itself and the cuff fastened with a safety pin just below the elbow. He said he had farmed or at any rate worked on farms for fifteen years before he went to the mill for better money. He said if Mrs MacLeod wasn't embarrassed by his crook wing then she'd never be able to tell by anything else that there wasn't an able-bodied man taking the place in hand, she could put her last quid on that. He looked cocky and pathetic and tried to hold her eye. She had given him the job at once, before he mentioned his children and his pregnant wife, so how was she taken in, she used to defend herself, he hadn't even played his trump card? It was only a matter of years in any case before Alex would be ready to take it on himself. Out of his father's tight-souled skills and enduring silence there must surely be the makings of a farmer somewhere in him.

The boy's life was simple. He rode his bike to school and back, and helped morning and evening with the milking. He grew more unwieldly as he approached his middle teens, and as the headmaster once told his mother, her boy would never be one for making friends easily.

'Is that a problem?' she had asked.

His school reports said that he was 'a hardworking and trustworthy boy'. The best of his teachers thought without committing it to paper that if you ever wanted a specimen of tomorrow's average bloke, then you needn't go past young MacLeod. He was a decent boy, but dull. He would never be troubled by imagination. Mrs Scott the music teacher said if western civilisation depended on that boy getting three notes in succession right, then it would be the Visigoths and Attila again overnight. He was told he could step aside from the school's singing in a local competition much as he had been pointed to the sideline in sport. 'We don't all have the same gifts,' Mrs Scott told him kindly. The boy looked steadily at her from the advantage of his height, and she was the one who felt embarrassed. When she tried to explain this exchange to the one staff member with a university degree, a young fellow who in two years' time would set off for Europe and never return, he looked at her oddly, puzzled that it mattered to her. 'He's the raw material his country's built on. Do you expect miracles or something?' He detested the fattish raw-faced woman in front of him rather more than he did the gawping boy.

The same young restless teacher one day attempted to draw his charges on what they would prefer to be. Forget, he wanted to tell them, what is the inevitable case, that most of you girls will be married or knocked up by the time you are twenty and the boys will slog it out for a lifetime to keep your wives and your families in what you will convince yourselves is at least a semblance of happiness. He felt sorry for them, and superior. But he smiled as he asked them and held back his distaste, because he quite knew that his degree should confer a little tolerance for this bumbling shuffle of adolescence he was paid to herd and muster. He looked down at the untidy rows and thought while he quizzed the class on their ambitions that already there was somewhere a café, a striped awning, very possibly a *chic* foreign woman who watched his every move, and that he would think back on now with some wry nostalgia. He would test where he was against all this.

He considered the provincial faces, the stubby fingers moving shyly across sprouting bosoms and inflamed pimples. He waited. 'Well?' Stevie Battich said he couldn't say no to his own fleet of fishing boats. Toss O'Brien knew exactly the car that he would drive, the figure he would cut. When the girls moved on to their fantasies of smooth-haired nurses and elegant secretaries, and a few of the smarter ones began to have the teacher on – little snot-nosed Pai Weston from Matangi for instance saying he wouldn't half mind being Bishop of Aotearoa – Alex sat stolidly with what his mentor thought of as his Easter Island mug, and felt no urge to speak. His long hands rested on the desk in front of him, the domes of his wrist bones high above his navy-blue cuffs. He said when the teacher pressed him, 'I don't know that I fancy anything that much.' At which Toss O'Brien leaned across the aisle towards him saying, 'Just going to love them and leave them, that the story, eh Alex? Making a living from the girls?' (Christ, Dick would say when he remembered that. I was in the class next door and you could hear the racket through the wall. O'Brien was a strutty little rooster with curly hair and everyone's favourite and he used to give Alex regular arseholes. He was sorry he ever said that one though, a bit later on.)

Alex waited until the guffawing died down. Mr Cox could see it hardly touched him how the others jibbed at him. The boy let the quiet return in its own time, then simply repeated what he had first said. 'It's just like that at the moment, that's all I mean. Nothing that I fancy.' And because it was then so clear that no amount of shiyacking was going to touch him, the class laid off. That day and the months that followed. Which meant he continued to grow and to work on the farm and read slowly and sometimes aloud some of his mother's books, and that was about it. The newspaper and the wireless kept chorusing there were harder times ahead. He would stay on at school the next year, because again there was nothing a boy could leave to do. Some of the kids did leave, though, the ones whose parents grew hot at the thought of education encroaching further than it had ever gone with themselves, who were bitter at the narrowing chances of a world that tricked them once too often. There was nothing books held out for them.

His mother watched Alex growing, brooding, from where she sat at the side of the range, from where she had watched his father wither into himself and away from everything else. As if to defy that frugal departed spirit, she leaned forward to feed the red embers between the bars, opening the iron door to pile in cones and lengths of sawed pine. She kept the range burning even through the summer. The cones flared brightly and swiftly and sank to blue-grey ash. The lengths of wood often hissed with the exuding gum. She sighed at the heat she had craved for years when her husband had measured it by the foot. Her boy sat most evenings at the kitchen table, his knuckled fists holding his awkward ears flat against his head. In the winter his ears glowed a savage meaty red where his fingers scuffed at their chilblains.

She encouraged him to keep at his schoolwork. At times she deliberately, and she hoped casually, spoke of her own father, his student days in that other Cambridge before the end of the century. She repeated some of his stories, the honey of fifty years' second-hand nostalgia sweetening the simple enough events of a careful student life. She mentioned another friend who now lived back in Australia. He too had been a lawyer. She told Alex, 'That is an enticing world.' She meant in the swim of life, close to the grain of real events, where Emily Fraser herself had never been. She tried to direct her boy away from the crude prejudices that surrounded most of their neighbours, the assumptions that grew thickly and raggedly as a hawthorn hedge. She said sometimes, and laughed, 'A leaf from Mr Wallace's book.' She said to him as well, 'You don't need to believe everything you hear Uncle Art say.' She meant when her sister and her husband came across from their own farm at the foot of the Maungakawa. Her brother-in-law who crumbled cake before scooping it up in the palm of his hand for a moment apparently fixed across his face like a nosebag on a horse, then the cake sprayed back as he raged against the country's drift to Bolshevism. 'I know what I'd do,' he said, the crumbs now across his shirt front so that he brushed at them urgently as though they might be bees, 'I'd give them the bludgers' paradise they're on about, all right. I'd give them barricades!'

The boy said nothing when the sisters sat in the sitting room, waiting for the man's irritation to wear itself out. Then 'More cake?' he would offer, his height accentuated by the gloom of the blind-drawn room and the sense it always carried of quiet, order, an almost unused repose. He stood there with the cake plate extended, the gold-scrolled edge the merest glimmer in the trough of shadow between himself and his uncle. There was as little likelihood of irony in his words as there was of his deliberately pouring tea across this visitor's foot. But later in the week when his mother proffered her advice, Alex smiled at her, the slow lift of first one side of his face that momentarily might be mistaken for a sneer. It was rarely he smiled so directly at her, at anyone. 'I haven't believed a thing he's said for years.'

It sometimes puzzled his mother that Alex's only friend was the farm manager's daughter, a mite of a thing with fuzzy hair and a face so freckled it seemed sprinkled with sand. Her eyes were small and brown. She looked at you with her eyes half screwed up, as though a few feet were miles off. Mrs MacLeod found the girl plain enough without that, the eyes that reminded her of raisins.

The girl was a couple of classes lower than Alex. She would come across some nights to the farmhouse. Her own home, although bigger since two rooms were added for her one-armed father's increasing family, was always called the cottage, and continued to seem small. She timed her visits so she was there after Alex had come in from milking and had his tea. Her excuse was different each time. It could be a message from her mother, or something they wanted to borrow, or a query from her father about tomorrow's work. But once there, her reason was single enough. 'Read a bit of it to us, Alex,' she said. She handed him the dark green book with the burnished lettering and drew from between its pages the old bookmark that must have remained with it for decades, since a twenty-year-old Alexander MacLeod had sailed from Strathclyde with his dozen volumes tucked in between his shirts. Scott and Stevenson and Galt. They were a parting gift from his aunt. The strip of card in each volume was foxed with gingerish specks. Beneath the drawing of a long-gowned woman there were set out the incentives of the Scottish Benevolent Society. On the back of the card the girl liked to hold as Alex read there was a faded nest of figures where presumably his father had checked the promises on the other side. And the girl sat on the lid of the hammered brass coal-box as Alex read aloud the first piece of real fiction she had ever heard, at the end of which a villain's head was stepped on by a perfectly obedient elephant. Her eyes snapped with the excitement of what life might be like in other places, away from the cottage with its outside dunny and a father who belched without saying pardon and a mother who disliked cooking and housework as much as she was irked by the two children under five who were palmed off whenever possible on their older sister. She hated with her small but total passion the family she was fated to. Yet across one paddock, as close as that, there was the old house with its long verandah and inside the table with its crushed-velvet cloth the colour she imagined spilled wine must be and two dark-stained stands in the corners of the room with large richly patterned china pots from which the leaves of aspidistra drooped down cool and shining. From wire baskets on the verandah there hung delicate damp veils of maidenhair fern. On the walls of the long passageway were pictures she could look at for ever. One was of a nun standing in a doorway, watching a mother play with a little girl. Another was so sad the feeling she had as she looked at it seemed inexhaustible. There was a doctor sitting near a cradle, his chin in his hand, and you knew from the crying lady and the man who stood behind her that the child was going to die. The girl said, 'I want to cry too when I see that.'

'It's just a picture,' Alex said to her. 'It's like a book, you can feel sad if you want to but you know it's not real. So you can enjoy being sad as well.'

The girl looked at him then, held him with her steady frank stare. 'I like this place more than anywhere I've ever seen except

18

for that hotel in town.' She stopped, as if even that had confessed too much.

'Have you been inside?' Alex now who was fascinated, hoping the girl would tell him that she had.

'When Dad was looking for this joker who was supposed to be out here haymaking. There were carpets on nearly every bit of floor and pictures right along this high dark hallway thing when you went inside.'

'What were the pictures?' Alex said.

'You couldn't tell properly because the way the light was falling across the glass. Horses, mostly.'

'What else?'

'In the hotel?'

'That you saw.'

'There was a pot plant, it would have been too high just about for a room like the ones at home, anyway. It was in a corner so dark when you first came in from outside that you had to look for a bit to make it out. In this big brass pot thing that glowed like it had a light in it. And an elephant.'

'What?' Alex had closed the book with his finger left there for a bookmark.

'At the top of the stairway, that big flat bit where the stairs sort of change direction.'

'The landing,' Alex said.

'Is that what it's called?'

'That flat bit is.'

'It was standing there. It must have been nearly as high as that table where you are. The trunk was curled up in a hook and it had this yellow cloth across it.'

'An ornament?' Alex said.

'And high curved-up tusks.'

Alex said, 'Sounds a funny thing to have there.'

'It looked good.'

Then they sat there, each suddenly surprised. Alex's ears scalded, he felt they must be sticking out a mile. And the girl knew how small she was compared with the others at school, she didn't have a sign of a bosom yet. Even friends in her own class stopped talking about titties and pinny pains and things when she came up, as though she were a kid who would go off and nark. She knew now as she watched the boy riffle the edges of the book that they might wait like that for ages, beneath the leaning doctor and the father in his shirtsleeves, if she didn't say something first. So she told him, 'I suppose that's why I liked the last one.'

'What?' he said again.

'The last book you read.'

'*The Surgeon's Daughter*?'

'Why I liked the bit about the elephant.'

Alex's face split with a laugh that surprised her. Then she laughed too. It was a joke she hadn't meant to make and she was grateful for it. She liked to make him notice her like that. Then she couldn't stop herself. She was gabbling on, she knew it was that, but each detail of the hotel that had set in her mind for eighteen months now moved freshly for her. She wanted him to share it and she wanted him to keep grinning at her while she catalogued the treasure. There were red-hot pokers, she said, they were placed on a shelf beside the place where you signed the book if you stayed at the hotel, the book was as thick as this, holding her thumb and forefinger as far apart as they would go. The flowers were in this enormous polished vase that turned your face back at you stretched wide like a balloon. She had looked into the dining room and what she remembered was the stiff fall of the starched cloths. It was as though they were carved, she said, that's how stiff they were.

'What else?' Alex said.

She talked so quickly she laughed at herself, at the fun of talking about the picture in her mind. The clean waxy smell she remembered from where the boards at the side of the red carpet were polished so the light skidded all over the place. There was a shining black balustrade leading up the stairs to the bedrooms, she supposed, and carpet rods that were brass and polished too at every step. Everything, she said, sort of glinted out at you. There had been a woman with a swelling at the side of her neck who wore a bunch of keys on the belt round her waist. The keys leaped at every step she took. She had walked down the stairs and the clump of keys sprayed out ahead of her then fell back with a soft clashing against her skirt. But the girl stopped there. The keys were something she could not explain, her sense that they were indeed a kind of charm, and thinking of home after that was to go somewhere small and cold. You couldn't begin to explain it. Instead she stood up suddenly, shaking her frizzed head. 'I'll have to get along. Mum'll be carrying on like anything that I've been even this long.'

The girl ran across the paddock between the houses, her feet chilled with the wet flicking of the grass. She stepped onto the edge of a concrete trough to help her across the wire fence. Her face was still hot from her talking. She wondered if her cheeks could possibly be as red as they felt. Because he had answered when she said that about having to go, 'Then we'll talk about it again another time. I like it when we talk about that.'

The hotel was not talked about again. Yet for years there would be the ghost of its silver trays and the clash of its keys and the odour of polish rising from the dark gleam of the floors. There would be that enchanted building just as there was the bride whose brother made her marry when she was unwilling and the dark lovely Rebecca and men who toasted the king across the water and sighed into their goblets, those stories Alex read to his mother and to the girl as well whenever she cut away from the babies and the chores long enough to hear them.

At school she and Alex seldom spoke more than to greet each other. But that was all right, the girl thought, school was another world. He remained her friend in the true one, the one they never spoke of, among the royalists and the crusaders and the glints from the brooding vases. For Alex it was more matter of fact. He liked it, however, when the girl came across the farm, and he would sometimes turn down the corner of the page at the best pieces as he read. He would keep them to go back to because he knew, always, what bits would please her.

On September the tenth, the week of Alex's sixteenth birthday, a shack at the end of the clay crossroad was lived in for the first time since the Great War.

Alex first knew of it hearing his mother ask the manager, 'Who's down in that old place then? Have you seen them yet?' The manager stood tamping the smoothed stump beneath its flutter of empty sleeve. From the distance, Alex thought, it's as though he's stroking a kitten you can't quite see. He had read of servility in those long small-printed stories, and he supposed in its way this must be what was meant, the hired man speaking carefully to his mother, his head nodding as she spoke, eager always that she agree with him. He laughed and said, which place was it, exactly?

His mother told him again. 'You know it, Stan, that place not far from the river? Used to be people called Lomas lived there, years back.'

'The old boy who went nuts when his son didn't make it back?'

'It was a sad story,' his mother said.

The manager, who felt uneasy when women reminisced, drew them back to the present. 'Whoever it is, they've got themselves a job knocking that place into shape.' He could visualise it now, the scraggy tumble of gorse and thistle and ragwort and macrocarpa, the house that had been rough enough on the eye even when it was built and was now twenty-five years later a smear of rusted iron and ochre-coloured weatherboards as you drove past.

'Is there even enough land there to farm it properly?'

'Maybe thirty acres, missus. No one can make a go of that.'

'Old Lomas had family money. It wasn't farming I suppose made him stay on there in those days.'

The manager's fingers edged through to the fleshy surface beneath the cotton sleeve. He laughed, exposing his stained bottom teeth. His opinion of the new people was that they couldn't be much chop. 'Fancy taking a family into that dump. Can you imagine who'd do that?' And he said to his young nephew who stood a little back from the adults, fearful that this talk would turn to the farm and so go on interminably, 'No kids turned up at school yet have they, Dick?'

And the boy deferred across the space between himself and the taller boy, 'They haven't, have they, Alex?'

Dick was the girl's first cousin. He liked to explain much later that he used to be in the next classroom to Alex and sometimes they kicked about together but he wasn't actually what you'd call his cobber, not at that stage. Alex didn't have cobbers. But he was

Bet's cousin and the only one in the know about how she and Alex got on together, like. 'No one else knew she was gone on him because she was always knee high to a bloody grasshopper until she was pushing twenty. I'm not having you on. No bigger than this.' He held his palm level less than five feet from the floor. He liked the details that set distance between those days and where he was as he told it. He liked being the only bridge from then to now. 'But she had her sights on him, don't worry about that one. Through all those bad years she told me once she never thought of them except together, sooner or later.' As he speaks of it his eyes take on a puzzled squint. 'I know I saw only the tip of the iceberg,' he admits. 'I'm not making out for a minute I really had the hang of them, let alone bloody Princess.'

He means he is back at the beginning, at the moment of fracture when a simple story breaks into two stories that are nothing like each other yet can never move apart. When the new girl first arrived, the tall girl whose hair could switch from gold to within a shade of black depending on the light she walked through. He will say, retelling it, 'She had so much class, that one, the rest of us just stood there like and gaped.'

The new girl set herself apart by everything she did. It took only a couple of days for the school to know her old man was silly as a chook. You only had to see the way he drove her up to the school gates on the back of his clapped-out tractor, sitting there at the wheel with a balaclava covering half his face and his hands in matching khaki mittens, although it couldn't have been cold because he wore shorts and cut-off gumboots. And the girl stood up there behind him, one hand balancing herself on her old man's shoulder. That first morning she stared directly back at them when the playground stopped its milling and haring about and the kids raised their heads and looked at her as dumbly as cows disturbed at their grazing. You might expect at any moment they would break out and yell at her and give her the treatment. But they were held back by what Dick later said you could only call her shining, her height and her white dress and her hair lifting slightly with the slow movement of the tractor, and more than these, the total sense of command he can find no word for. She stepped down from the metal bar at the back of the tractor without saying a word to her old man. Nor did he speak to her, or so much as turn his head. He wheeled the tractor back down the road he had come, to where the asphalt petered out into dust and grit during the summer term and clogging mud in winter. The man's head, round and squat in its knitted cover, jogged with the grunting movement of his machine. His outline wavered in the oily fumes that rose behind him.

The girl must have come those three and a half miles to school standing erect and grand on the jolting bar that at home dragged about the flat-top tray and the cans from which he fed the pigs, riding there as though on a chariot and not behind a half-wit father on a vehicle so antiquated most of the kids had never seen one like it. Dick telling the story always got to that. 'We knew from the minute we saw her, mind, there was something special about her, something crazy.'

She had viewed them from the height of her pig-bar with what they could not call dismissal or total indifference because until then none of the kids who looked back at her even knew how to spot or label such things, and now she stood at the entrance to the school without glancing to her left or right. Some of them thought, so she doesn't know what to do, eh? She'll have to ask us at least where she has to go. But after her few moments of hesitation she walked directly to the school steps and into the main entrance which pupils were not permitted to use, and they heard the sharpness of her knock against the headmaster's door. But sooner or later she would have to go into one of the classes. There'd be time enough then to sort her out. Arriving at school like that, dolled up in her white dress among all the rest of them in uniform. The first of the mob to speak said, 'Is that how bitches come to town?' The playground whooped with its release.

Inside she told the headmaster, 'I'm Barbara Trevaskis. We've just come up here to live.'

For days the school talked about little else. She was polite when anyone spoke to her, yet there was such aloofness in her only a few of the more confident girls, the ones the teachers branded as brazen, came up to draw her out, to define her at least in terms they might understand. They felt only her remoteness. She was as different, as set apart, as if scarred by the sharpened stones of some primitive tribe. The other girls wore gym frocks and carried cardigans but she wore day after day her white, ill-fitting dress. It was spotless and ironed and that alone made wherever she happened to be the centre of the school.

'She must have two or three that look exactly the same,' one of the girls said.

But Toss O'Brien's sister put her right. 'No she hasn't. I looked at the hook and eye at the back of her neck the first day she was here, the way it's sewn not quite straight. It's the same one every day all right.'

'That means she must wash it every single night.'

'And dry and iron it and all. *Overnight.*' The thought appalled them.

The headmaster had said she could come dressed like that for a week, say, until her father had time to sort things out. He smiled at her and made it clear that he quite understood when you came from another district you didn't always have what a new school expected you to wear. He shifted the leather-edged blotter in front of him, lining it carefully with the edge of the desk. The girl answered so briefly to anything he asked that at first he thought it was impertinence, then shyness, although there was nothing else about her that marked her as hesitant or awkward. When she was talked of afterwards, after 'the incident' as the staffroom cloaked it, there was not a teacher who could bring to mind even one occasion when she had spoken out of turn. Someone would say, 'But she was only here a couple of terms.' And it would be the headmaster who came back, 'Have you known any other pupil that wasn't here long enough to get the hang of?'

That first morning he looked at her with her hands held demurely in front of her, her head tilted slightly, the curtain of hair obscuring half her face. Was she having him on, this little-girl stunt? She made him think of ivory.

'Did you like your last school, then?' he encouraged her.

She told him the name of it, a place so small and so far south he could not have pinpointed it on the map to within fifty miles. She smiled back at him, directly, but that was all she said.

Did she have any kind of document, then, some note perhaps from her former head? The girl placed her hand for a moment against the side of her hair, lightly, as though she touched at some animal she was unsure of, and shook her head.

'So you didn't like it, then? Surely you can tell me that?'

As if the school itself were not the point, she said, 'Down south. I'm glad to be away from there.'

'And your father farmed there too, did he?'

Again it was not the question she chose to answer. 'There was just tussock and a few houses and the mountains you never got away from. There was snow that made the river high. Last year the school had to close because of it.'

The headmaster concealed his irritation. He was surprised after her first monosyllables that she took that sudden turn for what he thought of as 'feminine talk'. She had made him think there was a kind of clarity about her when she first came in. He hoped now she didn't have the kind of mind his wife possessed, priding herself on not conceding a thing to logic, mistaking for insight the fact that coherence survives in spite of how we mangle it. He observed how the girl's hands, her arms, were already those of a woman.

'We hope you like it a bit more here, then,' he said in his jaunty voice that he knew the girl would see through at once. There were so few moves you could make, though; you weren't in the teaching game for long before that came home to you. He said to her, 'Trying's half the battle I suppose, isn't it?' The vague image in his mind of clashing weapons, the badly drawn charging armies in those annuals that were so popular with the boys. He knew the absurdity of pep-talk, but he knew teaching could not survive a day without it. The hogwash element – absurd and yet inevitable. He stood up from behind his desk.

'Well, Barbara. We'd better find you a class, seeing that's what you're here for.' He walked with her down the corridor and left her with Mr Simpson. Something for that smart young man to think of.

When the bell rang she joined the rows behind the marked line where the classes assembled. As they stood waiting to be marched inside, a brief swirling breeze picked up and fluttered the gym frocks of the girls, ran across the shirts of the nudging boys. The light hairs stiffened on Barbara's bare arms.

One of the girls said loudly, 'It's a tennis frock she's wearing.'

Another answered her, louder than she needed, 'You simply wear what you've got if that's all you've got.'

On her second morning Barbara took a mustard-coloured cardigan from the schoolbag she tucked between her feet and the side of her desk, although bags were supposed to be left on the pegs out in the corridor. As she leaned down to fetch it out, Toss O'Brien reached across from the parallel row and ran one finger with its dirty nail along the inside of her arm. He followed the vein that traced from her forearm to her wrist. His own arm brushed against the front of her dress. Then he turned back towards those behind him, grinning at their approval. Barbara laid the cardigan across her shoulders without putting it properly on. She had already sat there for the first hour with the gooseflesh stippling her arms. 'She's so special she doesn't like to let on she even gets cold.' A girl's voice from further down the room.

At lunchtime she sat on the girls' bench along the outside of the school hall. She opened a piece of newspaper and ate the one sandwich it contained, an uncut slice the width of the loaf. She sat several feet away from the nearest other girl. It was done so naturally even the dullest could see she chose to be there, they were not expelling her. So the first thing they knew of her for certain was simply that – it was all one to her whether Toss O'Brien ran his finger along her arm or not, whether the girls ignored her for the fifty minutes of the lunch break or came up at last to speak to her, as a cluster of them did.

'Are you any good at basketball?'

She glanced up at them, folding the scrap of newspaper would you believe it back into a neat square.

'With your height and that we thought you might be.'

'No,' she said.

The girls waited, expecting more.

Moira Barnes edged forward until she stood directly above her, so that Barbara sat in her shadow. 'Is that the truth?'

So she informed them, 'When I'm not actually at school I have to be at home. I can't get away on Saturdays.'

There was silence for a moment. Then one of the group laughed and said to her, 'If you've got to clean that place up you've moved into, then you won't get out till you're fifty.'

A more kindly girl tried to cover up. 'At lunchtimes and that, we mean. We play at lunchtimes too.'

'There isn't time then either,' Barbara said. She looked up at them for the first time.

'Of course there is. We just told you we play.'

'Not if you think about it,' Barbara said. 'There isn't time.'

So the girls went off and said she was a stuck-up slut, did you see the way she half smiles and looks at you under her lashes like she's in the pictures or something? They said what a pain in the neck she was and it was a good thing anyway that she didn't want to play, who'd want to be on her side? Those tall ones weren't great shakes at basketball anyway, you always thought they would be then they turned out duds. 'Moira's the best goalie in the school and she wouldn't be up to that one's shoulder.' They left her, as she wanted to be, alone. They made out none of the boys were taking any notice of her either. (Which was just so much bulldust, Dick says. The boys' playground was like a field of asparagus, if you took his meaning.)

The one girl in white among the others in their black, her gift for stillness when they became agitated and clumsy and aggressive was a thing so unusual she disturbed them. 'Who does she think she is?' they asked. What they meant was, 'She knows very well, but do we?' It was the certainty of a mountain above its foothills. (Which among her semi-articulate and confused peers would have been pretty talk indeed. But it was how Alex chose to put it years later, the image he used the one time he spoke about her at length to Dick. Which would be a quiet weekday afternoon and his friend sitting on the high wooden stool across the bar, taking it on himself to raise her name. 'That first week the Princess turned up at school, Alex, remember? And there wasn't another girl could stomach her?'

Alex would say that then, about the mountain. His fingers flipped the bones on their black cord. In the silence between the two men there was the hard distinct clacking as the bones slapped on one side of his hand, then rose and flicked and slapped against the other. But that was as much as he said. And Dick watching, hoping he might say more now that someone had mentioned her straight out. And his telling it later, 'It was no go, see. Alex just sat there swinging that thing as if he's some Indian with his prayer gadget or something, swinging it and looking past me to the corridor at the pot plants and the copper urns and things, then he did say something. Know what it was? He said *better not to talk about her again*, eh? You know the way he says things so quiet and yet it's like a guillotine that's cracked down?'

'Was it Madam?' someone will ask. 'I mean was it for her sake he wouldn't talk?'

Then Dick giving his look that accentuated the odd sloping of his eyes, the impression from that and his cracked chapped hands resting on the edge of the bar of an alert and ageless lizard. And he will say, 'You're never going to understand the first thing about that story unless you get the hang of one thing. Where Alex lives now, I mean running the bars and all, pleasant and quiet like you lot know him and never giving much away and being so polite to Madam and genuinely liking her too, loving her I suppose, well *that* life, see, and all that about the Princess, they just don't touch, that's what you've got to understand. It's like a bloke who comes to a new country, see, but stays living in the other one as well.' Dick pauses and hitches at his waist, a habit since he was a boy. 'I'm not saying he's unhappy, mind. I'm not hinting that for a second.' But that talk is twenty years away, when Dick likes to cast himself back to now, to the square of playground asphalt and the green expanse of the sports field and the years when his parents spoke hardly of anything but money and jobs. And to his favourite story from then. 'Did I tell you about the dog?')

The desire to inflict discomfort on Alex was something the school exhausted about a year before the new girl arrived. Suddenly there was no one getting at him about his ears, his height, his indifference to almost everything and everyone except perhaps that stunted kid whose father worked on his old lady's farm, and the kid's weedy cousin, next thing to a mongol that one, ever looked at him *properly*? But there was a compelling reason for their laying off. In less than a year the boy who had been scorned by the rugby players as weak as piss and hopeless as a girl became one of the strongest in the school. He continued to knock into desks and fumble a ball if it chanced to come his way, but his body took on the tension, the resilience, of a coiled spring. When a craze for wrist-wrestling swept the school, Alex found he could force with apparently little effort, and in a matter of seconds, any rival to his side. That there was more than merely strength was brought out by the dog.

In the middle of the term when Barbara arrived, a distempered mongrel ran terror through the playground. It was first spotted hanging about the gates and snarling, then once the playground had emptied it ran and circled in the centre. The dog bared its yellow sloping teeth at the windows where the classes called and yelled to it. The animal's tremor excited the children beyond the command of teachers that they go back to their desks. 'You die, you know, if they bite when they're like that.' The news flew about that the headmaster had phoned a farmer to come immediately with his gun. No one wanted to miss out on that. Some of the standard six boys were swinging school jerseys from the window, others biffed bits of chalk at the puzzled gaunt creature that at first cringed back when the chalk skipped on the hard surface in front of it. When one piece grazed against its lowered skull, the dog braced its legs and raged back at them. Its half-bark, half-howl fluttered the rows of faces behind the glass.

Then the dog began to pace the playground, trotting to the post at the edge of the marked-out basketball court, trotting back to the centre. Its hind legs shivered as though with cold. When its rump grazed against the post it turned, snapping at its own movement, before slinking towards the steps that led up to the classrooms. Its saliva dripped as it moved, a silvery viscous string flicking back and catching against its leg. Then it stood in utter quiet, looking for those few seconds with almost an expression of bewilderment, while the faces above it flattened against the windows, silent now in their anticipation. The farmer must be on his way by now, his rifle slanted across the seat of the car beside him. Then the dog levelled its neck so that from flank to dripping muzzle it appeared as one straight line. It began a low vibrating howl that sent the classes to a frenzy. In two of the classrooms the teachers were shouting for silence, but theirs were voices from the back of a colosseum, calling for reason once blood was on the loose. The taut dark body began to quiver, the throat tilting slowly higher with the sustained note not of aggression so much as the reverse, an extended and morose plea. Then it set forward again with an oddly stalking movement, a bird dog's slow and intuitive approach to a stretch of quiet water. And then it stopped. Its head had turned towards some sound. For an engine momentarily had idled, then revved again behind the hawthorn hedge between the playground and the public road. A fresh cry went up in the classrooms. 'That must be him! He'll have the gun.'

But instead of the summoned gunman appearing between the concrete pillars and the wrought-iron arch above the War Memorial gates, there walked the frizzy-haired girl whose mother had pleaded ill that morning, who could come to school only after the babies had been attended to and the doctor called. It was the doctor who had dropped her off after his visit. Bet had sat sullenly beside the doctor because she was confused. She resented the doctor's reprimanding her mother, yet she knew he was correct, that there was as much drama as illness in how the woman behaved. She received without answering him the doctor's attempts to jolly her along as the car whose walnut dashboard she longed to stroke whisked them between the hedges and the paddocks. As he stopped outside the school he was telling her she must not let anything at all interfere with her schooling. She understood that, didn't she? Not her mother or anybody?

'Yes,' Bet had said.

She glanced across at him, saw the hairs stiff like fuse-wire springing from his ears. His hands too were coated. She disliked the soapy smell of him. He was a man who loathed the way so many of the brighter girls simply dropped away at about this age, taken from schools by families who would never understand that while peasant was a word left behind in the countries they or their parents had come from, that word's defining marks were set on them ineffaceably as scars. 'You're a clever one. Remember that.'

She had looked down at her own hands with their squat bitten nails. Because she had scarcely grown for several years, the gym frock which was third-hand when first she put it on was now a rubbed bluish-green. Her fingers were red from the cold water in the wash-house. She detested those coarse immature hands. As she left the car and thanked the doctor for the ride, the man felt

31

the child's embarrassment and anger pour across to him. He said, 'Here. Just a minute, Elizabeth.' He handed her a shilling which she stretched out her palm to receive. He winked at her as though she were nine or ten. She then slammed the door and waited at the side of the road until he drove off, the long damp grass near the culvert brushing against her legs. She felt a welling rush of shame, deeper than her dislike of her mother, than the coin enclosed in her fist. The row of hawthorn blurred in front of her as the tears she also hated rose against her will. She had not thought to find a handkerchief before she left home, and she put one finger in the front of her cardigan and raised it to rub the wool across her face. She knew her arriving late would stop the class's progress and swing its tribal heat towards her when she entered. There was nothing else for it. She could not hang round out here until playtime, someone surely would see her. There seemed so little choice in anything. She swung her schoolbag savagely and high against one of the grey stone pillars. She rubbed again at her eyes, this time with her closed hand, and walked between the gates.

Alex watched the dog's movements with the rest of his class. He took in silently the slate-covered animal's erratic indecisive will, its pulsating with life as vivid as his own, but dangerous, mad. It must be only minutes now until its killer arrived and its sad, sweating body convulse to death. It was the simplicity and enormity of that which Alex pondered on. In a playground where nothing like this was expected to occur, the death would be so much more dramatic than the slaughters so many of the class were familiar with in the yards at home. Its expectation held their faces against the glass.

Alex went from the room without being observed. He ran down the corridor to the double doors which opened to the shallow flight of steps. It was not the speed or the courage even, at first, but the unexpectedness which caught those in his own class and the younger children as well, which held the headmaster's voice from calling out until the angular figure of the boy had dashed across the asphalt. The dog fell heavily beneath his weight, the double impact of the descending knees. The wet muzzle slammed flat to the ground, the boy's hands at once straining at the throat. The dog's jaws beneath such pressure were clamped, incapable of tugging to left or right. And the grey body lay equally imprisoned beneath the boy's rigidly set knees. There was a moment of utter stillness, the dog and the boy poised as though holding some deliberate pose.

'MacLeod!' The headmaster had found his voice. He bawled to him from the half-opened window. 'MacLeod!' The boy and the dog still briefly but intensely carved, immobile, while the voice volleyed across the playground. To Mr Simpson's mind in a neighbouring room there was the momentary suggestion of tableau, some hovering depiction of moral strength and animal force. Then the racket broke from the line of classrooms as the stunned dog gathered its force. One rear leg scrabbled free and stroked repeatedly down the back of the boy's thigh, a run of blood drawn on the pale skin. And it was then that some of those ranged along the windows noticed as the dog bucked its haunches free, the dense muscular lurch as the back legs gained their purchase although its head still ground against the asphalt, noticed that Alex's mouth was moving. He was not shouting but simply speaking, and they saw the girl he was talking to. She stood partly concealed by one of the pillars at the gate. Her schoolbag trailed from her hand, she was caught in the dappled jig-sawing of light beneath the ghost gum that spread above the memorial arch. The girl was sloughed with shadow and with light. Her own lips opened but no sound managed to issue from between them, or none certainly that carried to the straining and kneeling boy who talked across the dozen yards at her. He told her to run behind the goalpost and along to the side door. 'I've got him,' he assured her. 'You move fast as you can.'

Then with renewed vicious energy the dog whipped itself onto its feet. It was clear to those who watched and hollered from the classrooms, as it must have been to the transfixed girl and perhaps by now to the boy himself, that the dog's desperate twisting must break him loose. But the hands with their taut raised tendons viced the mongrel's head back against the ground. An expanding ribbon of blood which only Alex could see had begun to ooze from the dog's mouth and nostrils. I must have got his ribs, he thought, his ribs have gone. The animal's lips were raised above the rake of its teeth, the long blue tongue reached over the blood and mucus.

Then, as if her will were suddenly released, the girl broke from her immobility and ran towards the side of the building, her sandals clapping against the asphalt. She was so close beneath the windows that her cap of frizzy hair was only inches from the hands that gripped the ledges. But as she ran the dog lurched and yelped and lunged itself from between Alex's scraped and bleeding knees. It flowed out like a dark shadow from the boy's control. But it did not pursue the girl. It wheeled to face him. Alex's head turned from the dog to the girl who was twisting now at the knob of the green wooden door into the corridor's still vastly distant safety, then back towards the dog. He heard the door bang somewhere behind him. He felt a sudden weakness, standing alone in the middle of the playground.

The dog confronted him from four or five yards distance, the purple gums exposed above the slow guttural snarl, its teeth snapping with a puzzled awkwardness against the increasing spate of blood. It began to move forward, but staggering now in its abating rage. Its pierced lung dragged attention from the adversary in front of it. The dog stopped, a perfect target.

Two shots clapped close together through the morning air. At the first the dog's foreleg shattered. The impact spun it sideways in a howling arc. There was then a flattened thud as it landed upon its side, the second bullet entered below its jaw. A man stood a little back from the gates, a rifle levelled in his hands. He motioned with the barrel for Alex to remain where he was. Then he walked over to where the dog lay in its broad dark stain as on a carpet. He placed the muzzle of his gun a little forward of the animal's ear. The head lifted slightly with the blast. A tiny crater remained there in the asphalt, a delight and warning to the school.

Alex wished he could have saved the dog from the shots.

Often before the morning bell and again during the lunch break, Alex stood leaning against the Anzac gum. He liked its touch confirming roundness behind his back, the stirring of its strips of loose bark, silvery on one side and rasping brownish-red on the other. He preferred to stand there by himself, watching whatever went on in the playground. If the little red-haired bloke from a lower class came across and nattered to him, well that was all right with him. Not that Dick Norwood had much to say, although he could take the whole of lunchtime to say it.

Alex leaned with his hands behind his back, flattened against the skin of the tree. His eyes moved across the school yard or out along the straight and usually quite empty road towards the patterning of farms that came, after several miles, to the bland rise of hills. He nodded when it was necessary. He answered in a few words when Dick paused from his flow of chat and quizzed him, 'That's right, wouldn't you say, Alex?' Young Norwood's face lifted to his taller friend the identical eager deference he would use those decades later in the bar.

After his seeking out the dog, Alex was left even more to himself. The distance of his schoolmates was tempered now with dumb respect. Some of them said 'old Alex' when they spoke of him, hinting at an intimacy none of them could claim. But the gangling classmate who had done what none of them would ever do, who in that combination of absurdity and courage had run out to sit on top of a crazed dog, and so clearly done it to keep the animal from a plain and silently terrified girl, was neither grateful to those who spoke to him nor bothered to ignore them. When he answered them briefly his voice, as a few of the girls began to notice, was now more measured, more precise, than any of theirs. If they came as far as where he stood at the tree, his eyes continued to rake behind their shoulders to the movement in the playground or to turn from them completely to look down along the road. He didn't give a bugger either way.

The headmaster was the first one to phrase it like that. He watched across from his office one sweltering November morning as two boys approached young MacLeod. Whether they merely wanted to talk to him or ring him in for some game for which they needed an extra man, the head could not tell. But it was clear they meant no more to him than a wasp passing a couple of feet from his ear. 'He's a rum one all right,' he said to the new maths teacher. The boys ambled off and left him, a bizarre enough figure with his height and his black school shorts and his shirtsleeves rolled down from the early sun. The boy's head tilted back and he stared up to the branches above him, their trailers of loosened bark. Then the head surprised the young teacher with his directness. 'He doesn't give a bugger, that one. Once you've caught on to that, there's no great mystery about him.'

Alex thought he could look at those dangling strips, their easy constant stirring even when there seemed no breeze, and never tire of it. He picked a fragment of split bark from the trunk and bent the springy crust between his fingers until it snapped. When the bark first lifted away you could see the moist living body of the tree. You touched it and it was tacky, like touching a sore. He was glad that little joker was leaving him alone for a bit. He preferred this standing by himself.

Dick Norwood sometimes saw Alex when he went out to his cousins. On the long stretch before they turned into the rutted drive and jolted the cattlestop, his father would say with an amused contempt that Bet's old man couldn't weed a turnip patch without making a balls of it. 'When you think what that place used to look like when old Ecky was running it. Look at it now, for Chrissake!'

Dick's mother defended her relative not from principle but from the long habit of crossing what her husband said. 'His widow doesn't seem to notice it as much as you do, then. She's never said a word against the way Stan runs it.'

Dick's father snorted at her defence. 'If she can't bloody see, then she's got the perfect man for the job.'

Mrs Norwood stirred fatly on the seat beside her husband. 'I'd like to think,' she almost always began. Her husband finished the sentence for her. 'Like to think how I'd manage a farm if I had only one mit, that it?'

'It's not as if it doesn't come into it.'

'He's got so much mileage out of that stump of his I don't know why you don't offer him a bit of my help too one of these days.'

Then Dick would wait for the rapid snip of his mother's purse. 'You always have to take things too far.' Her handkerchief in her hand, dabbing at her eyes.

'Perhaps that's the advantage of two arms,' his father said. 'Stops you believing bullshit when it's right under your nose.'

'In front of Dick, if you don't mind,' his mother chipped, looking from her window rather than glance at the man beside her.

Then sooner or later his father would say it. 'Sorry.' His head held rigid as he glared ahead, the vein in his neck swollen with irritation. 'Sorry I forgot to tell you, Dick, your uncle's the best frigging farmer between here and the coast. Just I get a bit confused by all that dock in the front paddock and the odd rooted fence and a scab or two on those cows. I seem to miss the great job he's doing apart from a few small items like that.'

In the back seat Dick would wait for the bickering to flare again on the journey home. Once they were back his father began the milking and his mother clattered her hurt feelings in the kitchen. There was a picture of the Sacred Heart beside the *Star* calendar and his mother frequently raised her eyes to it, to the yellow-robed man holding his heart in the palm of his hand in a way that made Dick think of a cricketer cradling the ball as he walked back to take his run. He watched his mother look at the picture, the complicity with Jesus. We know what suffering is don't we, that meeting of the eyes seemed to declare, us two, eh? But for all the rowing on the way home and the boredom of his auntie's illnesses when they were there, Dick waited for the days when his mother said they had better call across, they hadn't seen Stan and Madge for three or four weeks. His mother whisked at basins and there was always a tin of food they took over with them. 'Don't take your own with you,' Dick's father said, 'you'll wait till doomsday before you get afternoon tea at that place.'

'The woman's not well,' his mother said.

'You wouldn't be either if you knew someone like you. All your baking done for you. Your kids looked after.'

While the grown-ups sat in the small sitting room that made Dick uneasy with its smell of his aunt's embrocation, he and Bet walked round the farm. They deliberately skirted the old house, hoping Alex would see them and come out. The girl said how she sometimes heard him reading aloud while his mother sat almost on top of the kitchen range. 'You'd think it was always winter in that place. The stove's on all the time.'

'Is she sick or something?'

They watched the long verandah and the windows with their levelled holland blinds. If Alex saw them he came out to talk. For Dick it was like waiting for a hero. He could not see the door open or the tall figure step round from the garage without seeing the sudden dash across the playground, the slavering of the mad dog pinned to the ground. And his cousin now spoke of Alex with a sureness that surprised him, as though there were bits of life that were theirs and no one else could touch them. Yet she never spoke of that morning at school, and Dick did not ask her. What was there to say about it? About those terrified yet exalted minutes between her gathering the bag she had swung against the gate and sighting the wet-mouthed and restless dog, between that and her sliding against the polished corridor inside the door, the lurch into darkness and the smell of disinfectant and the double ringing of the gun from far away, outside. The rest of the school may have watched and called out and seen the minutes of drama, those kids who thought they knew and argued on what took place, but they had not been *there*. They had counted by the usual tick of watches. Not like her and Alex by the flow of blood. There was never to be a way of explaining that. It became a possession as certain as her own limbs, an intimacy between herself and him. The trick was again to get inside that privileged dome where time and shapes and the pounding of their hearts was something so separate, so remote from where others might ever come. Only the two of them now that the dog was dead, although that sinister force had been there too, sharing that extensiveness of space and the pure catch of time that was like looking through a glass of water, things the same yet seen as though in some kind of ordained and sudden clarity. Whatever happens now, Bet knew, nothing can alter that.

The two boys stood beneath the gum. The small one moved constantly as he talked, the other could stand for ten minutes with one foot rested, as his hands were, against the Anzac trunk.

Alex watched the slopes of Pirongia, the half-farmed, half-bushclad mountain that came forward and receded according to the weather. Almost always now he thought of one thing, while Dick gabbled on and Alex provided the monosyllables, the grunts, the occasional query, that showed he followed his friend. When Dick talked of the new girl Alex only then bothered to look at him directly. 'What do you know about her?'

The spattering of freckles, the broad gap-toothed grin, struck Alex as being a child's drawing of a face.

'Shit, who knows anything about her, do you reckon?'

Alex thought of how she first arrived. He went back and back to that. He had held the raised lid of the desk in front of him, the neat stack of books beneath his other hand, and then his casual glancing across the yard. That was when he saw her. The slight rise of her breasts, her hair pouring out behind her. He could for the moment see neither the tractor nor the man who drove it. For those first seconds he did not comprehend what he was looking at, the strange half-figure skimming above the hedge. Only where the tall hedge thinned near the school gates did he see the grey machine and the man in the balaclava, and the full length of the girl who stood on the metal bar, balancing herself with her hand on the driver's shoulder. He saw how she stepped down without speaking to him, without turning. As she stepped to the road, the girl's hand held her dress close in against her legs, avoiding the brush of the large back tyre. This morning he had watched again, as he waited and watched each morning now, as the tractor bore her along the road. It made him think of pictures from the Great War, that dark grunting machine, the concealed face above the wheel. But the girl made the picture seem so queer, her breasts level with the man's head, her hand touching his shoulder so clearly for balance, so clearly with disdain. The man stopped without cutting the engine. Then the tractor was turned and dwindled back towards the crossroad and the hills. The girl stooped momentarily, tying a loosened shoe lace. She was not aware that the two boys watched her from their camouflage of light and shadow beneath the gum. She saw them as she walked past into the playground, but neither they nor she spoke. Dick resumed the details he had been handing out, the factory he said they were going to build out there just along from the Bruntwood store. He provided figures and dates because his own father supplied the dairy company, so of course he knew. He said it meant the farmers round that way could take their own milk in, there would be no need for the truck to call each day to pick up the cans.

'It's called modernising,' Dick said.

'Yes?'

'Well it must be, musn't it? Stands to reason.' The boy used the same phrases as his father.

Alex watched how the girl's right hand came across to her left wrist and pushed at a loose silver bangle, wedging it firmly higher along her arm. She picked up the small square case she had placed on the road when she first stepped down. She walked through the gates and across the milling front playground where the kids slowed in their games and halted as she walked between them, her white dress disruptive among their uniforms. Alex watched her touch the shoulder of the dress. The bangle slipped loose and she pushed it again. There was nothing else he wanted to look at except her.

Some days later Dick said, 'That joker brings the girl on the tractor, you know?' Bringing her, Alex thought, as though on a chariot. 'They reckon that's not her old man after all, know that? It's her uncle.' He allowed his facts to tumble out. Her parents were dead, see, the joker in the balaclava was the only one to look after her. And the story went how he did that not because of family feeling but because somehow there was money enough in it for him to buy those lousy acres down near the river so long as he took the girl as well. 'Not lousy even so much as just shagged,' Dick said, 'because no one's given a stuff about them for years. You ignore the land like that it knocks the shit out of it.'

'So they say.'

'There's no *saying* about it, Alex. It bloody does.' And he said, you wouldn't believe it, would you, but in the middle of all this, the best dairy country in the world, mind, that mad bugger was running *pigs*!

Later in the morning, in the minutes between a change-over of teachers, Alex heard two of the girls confiding loudly enough for him to pick up their strictures. For the second time in an hour Alex heard how that oddball who drove her wasn't even a cow cocky's foot. Ailsa Blackie's own father had said he was putting pigs in the haybarn. Where the hell was hay going to go if the moron ever got round to making any? And the other girl, fat Moira Barnes, said with the scandalised intonations of her mother, 'And you know that blackberry that's run all over the driveway like coils of wire or something for years? He hasn't raised a slasher to it and they've been there now for over a fortnight.'

'Shouldn't have the place then, should they?' Ailsa said.

They were silent at the enormity of it. The thick loops of blackberry across the wasted years, high as a house by now, running from what once was an orchard as far as the outside dunny a few yards from the back door. 'You'd need the slasher to go out to pee!'

So that was the story after her first ten days at school. The recurring fact was that the crazy blighter with his balaclava over his swede on warm days as much as on cold, who drove his antiquated tractor right into Cambridge to buy his groceries and hardware, creeping all that distance along dirt roads then the miles of tar seal when he could have bought most of the stuff at a store only a couple of miles from where he lived, he was only her uncle, *if that*. There was no hot water of course in that shack of theirs and no telephone and if the electricity worked after the years of its desertion that was not because the man had been into the department office and made it legal. Toss O'Brien's father worked for the department and he would be the first to know. They were sending an inspector out anyway, they had the length of that joker.

The class could go on for hours about *that* place. There was a copper in a lean-to that had no walls to it, ever heard of that? It was supposed to be the wash-house. 'You'd only call it that if you'd never seen what a real one looked like, mind.' But most of what they said was guessed at. There was no real way of telling what went on behind the front paddock with its generations of gorse standing higher than a man, its grey roots thick as forearms. Behind its protective massing no more than the rusted pitch of the roof could be spotted from the road. Neighbours said the new bloke was leaving the gorse out the front there on purpose, as though its defensive wall was important to him. He had slogged away though at the paddocks between the house and the steep clay bank to the river, there was nothing wrong with the way he was clearing those. But he also ignored the house itself as much as he did the gorse facing the road. His hammering and his clearing and his long hours of work were in the service of his pigs. Ailsa Blackie had heard her old man say, you're not going to believe this to her mother. 'I just seen him down near the end of his drive there with these two billies full of blackberries, so I said, in for a spot of jam are you? No he said, I don't go that much on jam. So I waited and he saw I wasn't driving off and after a bit he said he was collecting them for a sow that had gone crook on him. Can you believe that? Collecting blackberries for a bleeding pig!' Ailsa had watched her father tell the same story to another farmer and she said he was so angry while he told it that the vein stuck out on his neck like a bit of cord. He was hitting the flat top of a fence-post with his opened hand. And when he brought up the new neighbour again that night at tea he had slapped his hand down in that same way and so hard on the table that the knives and forks leaped all over the place. 'Christ all bloody mighty,' he shouted, and his wife had raised her own hand to stop the kids from moving. 'What do we have to get scum like that in the district for?' He saw the billies heaped with the dark sweating fruit.

Dick reported at the Anzac tree that there'd been ructions at home about the new people too. 'Well thank goodness there's a few farms between them and us,' his mother had said. She disliked the fact that the man in his damn fool get-up and that stuck-up daughter just breezed in like this, upsetting the whole district, but she was blowed if she'd go along with her husband either, getting a proper snitcher like that from someone else's report.

'As if it matters a stuff whether it's three farms away or ten,' Dick's father said. 'Or next bloody door.'

The boy watched a thread of saliva leap across his father's chin and the back of his hand sweep after it. 'Larsen says that kid thinks she's Lady Muck to top it off, like. That's right, isn't it, Dick?'

'I don't know,' the boy said.

His father turned on him. 'Does anything ever get through to you? *Ever?*'

'Just because he doesn't get a set on people.' His mother was patting at the sandwiches for tomorrow's lunches.

'Dressing up like none of the other kids. Travelling by first-class tractor!' He laughed curtly, looking at the wife who did not look back. 'And then her old man turning on Eddie Larsen?'

'It's not as if he was asked to call,' Dick's mother said. 'He was

42

out for a snoop, you know that.' Her heart pelting as she said it.

'A neighbour does the decent thing and passes the time of day and that bastard just turns on him.'

'That's the Larsens' problem, then.' The lunches rustled as the woman wrapped them in newspaper.

The boy did not tell them the other things he heard at school. That Toss O'Brien said he wore that balaclava thing because his chin was shot away and he didn't want the world to see that the bottom half of his face wasn't there. Or the rumour he'd knocked up a schoolkid down south sixteen years ago and Barbara was the penalty he had to lug about with him for ever. Ann Larsen put it around he was loaded as well, they shouldn't be taken in by that poverty stunt he pulled. Ann Larsen had been the best looker in the school until that new bitch came on the scene. How did she know that? Bet had asked. Because the people in the Cambridge shops would tell you, that's how. When he took his money out it was a wad as thick as your wrist. Toss's old man had said he was having the lot of them on, he was making tits out of everyone.

Dick's father went to the opened back door and spat into a clump of hydrangeas. He lit a smoke and looked across at his own immaculate yard that was understocked because money was so tight. The arse had fallen out of farming, you just hung on hoping things would pick up. But he was damned if he would farm badly because of that. He was proud when he looked out at what he had, what he'd made for himself. He used to tell the kids if they found a weed on the whole place that he'd overlooked he would give them five bob, and they scoured about without ever getting sixpence from him. The fences and the sheds and the whole place – square and straight as if every inch was set against a ruler. He thought why the hell do women always pull that argumentative line? To stick up for a no-hoper? There was no point trying to talk when Grace was on that tack. He heard her banging a cupboard shut with a jab of her knee.

Why did he have to go on like that about Larsen, she was thinking. She felt the fair man with his blue eyes that went through you clean as steel through butter. Sometimes it would be months and she'd not hear a thing, then twice a week that clicking on the party line that made Tom ask what kids were skylarking round with the phone and she would sit not dropping a stitch or missing a whisk with the baking spoon and she knew she would be there all right for him, in the barn on the deserted farm at ten the next morning. Her mouth felt as though it was drying on her when she thought that might stop.

Her husband called in from the doorway. 'Do you have to slam round like a trollop or something?'

'Yes I do!' she bawled back at him.

Dick sat with his hands pressed hard between his knees. He looked at the picture with the cricket-ball heart, the remnant his mother kept of the church she no longer went to. Don't let them start, he was asking the picture. The man with the mild face looked down at him. But then his mother was crying and that was always a good thing. It meant that the shouting would die down and after a bit Dad would talk quietly to her, they would talk for a while like they mattered to each other. Dick waited for those times as the best of all. And while he and his sister slept in the adjoining room the man would strain above the crying clasping woman. 'There,' he would tell her. His calloused palm passed over her forehead as he breathed against her ear, smoothing her cheek, caressing her. After he had moved from her and grabbed as he always did the fistful of blankets around his shoulder, she would lie and think then of the other man.

It was nearly always on a sale day the clicking phone signalled for their assignations. She would be breathless by the time she followed the river bank and kept to the cover of the trees along the intervening farms. She carried a sugarbag that she could say was for pine cones, supposing a neighbour intercepted her. Larsen was never there before her. In the high mustiness where the daylight knifed in slivers between the contorted boards she felt the sweat running in her palms, between her breasts, as she waited. She knew he was near when he twanged the only surviving strand of wire in the last fence he crossed. It was the one joke between them. The square of light when the barn door opened set him there in black solid outline, then the day was blocked away with the drawn door behind him, and she heard his boots scuff across the floor. She had released the hooks at the back of her brassiere before he came. She felt the velvety push of blood inside her ears, the fear that he might tell her, as at times he did, that this would be the last time. He might turn her then and force her down across the canvas cover he had brought with him the first time they agreed to meet. Or tell her to stand there in the gloom that lightened once their eyes were set to it, ordering her to walk there totally naked while he watched her. Or simply say to her as her arms crossed and she began to lift her dress, 'No, don't.' He would raise the dress himself. It was never the same two times in succession. He had never kissed her quietly before they began nor handed her things once it was over. And those nights she would lie with what she supposed was disgust for the thick weight of the man she had married. She felt with a brief spasm of panic that he was one side of a trap. Larsen's lean pale body was the other. She would say into the dark space of the bedroom, 'Sacred Heart help me. Make him not stop yet.'

Dick's mother held her knee tight against the cupboard beneath the sink. I'm all het-up, she was thinking. How much longer can I last? She thought how she was not stupid, she was not an absurd dim-witted woman like Stan's wife, was she? Yet why were her own feelings such a puzzle to her? Why could she not decide even where desire and revulsion branched into different things? Two men, she thought, there are always two men. And she knew she would do anything if Larsen demanded it. Yet she had the image of her mind, of some part of her anyway, moving always above her body, above what she did, independent of them both. Something in her like the scraps of pumice you saw moving downstream on the dark flashes of the river.

Her husband banged in from the porch. He stood at the kitchen table and tapped at the spread scraps of wood, at the two small knives Dick used for carving. He called through to his son in the next room. 'If you've got nothing particular against tidying up, do you reckon you might do a bit of it?' He turned over a thin piece of wood, the sliding top of a pencil case that Dick had worked with a series of carefully interlinked stars. At their centre a larger star rayed out, its narrowing points slipping between the other shapes to the edges of the wood. Dick came through from his own room.

His father said, 'Are they making you do that at school?'

The boy gathered the pieces of wood and his knives, wrapping them in a strip of old velvet he had salvaged from a tossed-out cushion. 'No. Just 'cause I want to.'

His father watched the pieces being wrapped away. The boy had a knack, he supposed. 'As long as you don't bugger round with it too much, eh?'

The woman at the sink stood sure of herself again. She ran water across her hands and dried them on a teatowel. They came and went as quickly as that, her moods, her gulfs of panic. She felt lucid and in control. She said, knowing how boldly she tempted her own feelings, 'Dick's carving that for Ann Larsen, that's what he's doing.' She laughed at the nonsense of it – pint-sized Dick and Larsen's daughter! Her husband laughed too, the boy wheeling away, flushed and tongue-tied from their amusement.

'Is that so, is it?' his father said. 'Go for blondes, do we?'

Dick went to his room and closed the door. Why do they think I have to be doing it for anyone? That had never occurred to him before. You just carved because you carved.

In the kitchen his mother began the pastry for tomorrow's pie. She knew Tom had simmered down. Get a laugh from him like that and things came right. He put his hand out as she passed him and lifted one of her breasts. He said, 'Little blighters don't waste time these days, do they?' He thought of himself and Grace down the river near the golf course when they weren't such a hell of a lot older than Dick was now. He couldn't believe his luck when his hand had got under her frock and she hadn't told him to stop. Not even when it was right there. He drew Grace close against him, but both her palms were pressing against the front of his shirt.

'The kids could come in any minute,' she said. 'You'd better wait, eh Tom?'

'There's no great mystery about us,' Barbara said. She stood at the fence near the road. One bare foot was on the bottom strand of wire, her hands rested on the lichened timber of the post.

Her eyes are kind of gold, that's the strange thing, Alex thought. You think they're brown but they're not. His own hands moved on the rubber grips of his handlebars. Not brown but actually gold like light was shining from behind them.

The grips were slippery in his hands. He was unsure of what else he could say, but he was not afraid of her, which was something. Just about everyone else was, he knew that. 'They're just shit scared,' Dick said, 'that's why they run her down.' Nor nervous either, not even with his heart belting away he knew he wasn't nervous.

The sun was too hot on the back of his navy-blue shirt. It had been hot that morning too, when he stood behind her in the ranks and was inches from the deep colour of her skin and he saw how it paled where she raised the weight of her hair with one hand. The paler skin and the tendrils, the wisps of her hair, at the back of her neck. He saw there was a pulse beating rapidly at the side of her throat, directly above the neckline of her dress. She had turned and knew they were looking at her, but Alex was the only one whose eyes she met. He knew by the vein that she was nervous too. And when they called her snobgob because she spoke differently to any of them he knew that what they thought was Barbara being so God-almighty pleased with herself was so very different from that. It was her knowing how to keep control. She put a fence round all of them and he was the one who knew. He thought, I shall tell her that one day. I already know that much about her.

He smiled down at the chips of gravel on the road that he sliced across with the front tyre of his bike. She was telling him now of how they left the south. How the man had money enough to buy a farm like this but that was all. 'We're rabble,' she said. She liked saying that. She smiled too.

'Of course you are.'

Barbara said there were no other relatives, see.

'Who is he then?'

'Who?'

'Him.'

He waited, but she said nothing. Then he handed her the books that were his reason for coming. Whatever she does, she is there, quiet at the centre of it. Close and directing you from the distance at the same time. He had thought that a dozen times. Her voice gave the impression of *stepping down* – that was what he meant. As when her hand left the man's shoulder and her foot descended to the ground. He thought of a phrase from history class, 'she took possession'. She did that whenever she began to talk, that sense of her having decided to come down, to let herself be seen. Alex thought, I understand that about her too. That is why so many of them hate her. 'Have you got any books at home?' he asked her. And she said, 'If you bring me some.' That was how she was. You came towards her only if she wanted you. She never turned her face to you without you knowing for certain she had decided she wanted to.

Alex felt the cushioning of the tyre against a larger stone. He prodded the wheel in closer, then drew it back. He felt that he stood for the moment in a particular clarity. He thought, I am the only one who knows by the ticking in her throat, which even she cannot control.

It took over two weeks at school before he spoke to her. He did not approach her, nor even to any casual observance take much notice of her. Dick was the only one who picked it up. He said, 'You hardly take your eyes off her, know that?' And Alex said to him the one unguarded word he was to say to anyone, ever, about the girl. The word young Dick was not to understand, and felt embarrassed by. 'I'm enchanted,' he said. (Barbara tells him later, giving him back his green-covered Walter Scott, that she knew he would like that stuff, he was like someone from one of those books himself. 'Keeping them at bay,' she says. Teasing him. His silence, she means, his defence of her at the edges of gossip and conjecture and obscenity. He will say, 'You're having me on.' Her tongue moving across his chest. She is laughing when he tells her in that case she is Cinderella, she lives in a hovel, there is only one person she shines for. It will be her turn then to tell him, 'Come off it, now.')

Barbara watched the boy's playing with the movement of his bike. She told him more about their coming north, and how the man himself said even now, with a farm of their own and his mad farming that soon enough the district would reluctantly concede, acknowledging the pigs that against all their predictions and hopes would flourish, that they would not be there for ever. She said he was talking already that they might have to move on.

So Alex told her then with his ineradicable blustering truth,

'They reckon, you know, he couldn't bale a calf properly. That's how much he knows about it.' He put his weight on the handle-bars and the girl slapped an early mosquito that rested on her leg. They both turned to look at the man who was still there, in the driveway thirty yards up from the road. When he saw he was stared at, he placed two fingers in his mouth, whistling the girl up like a dog.

'He can whistle anyway,' Alex said.

'Only I'm not trotting off, notice?' They said nothing then for quite some time. She removed her foot from the strand of wire. But then she went. 'Come over again, won't you?' She walked along the drive with its middle strip of grass bent over and soiled by the constant passing of the tractor. The unpainted house was almost concealed behind the gorse and macrocarpas. The man waited for her at the top of the drive. He was hooded even now with his balaclava, although he was at home and the sun burned fiercely.

Alex waited for the girl to draw level with the man. Then again he slid his hands down the warm flow of the handlebars. He set off along the sandy surface towards the crossroads. A fine narrow spray like the streaming of an egg-timer rose from his front tyre.

Later Alex put to the girl, 'Why did you go when he whistled at you? Are you scared of him?'

'*Scared?*' He whistled, Barbara said, because he was the one who timidly refused to come closer to where they talked. It was his signal that he had the copper boiling in the lean-to as she instructed. 'He lights it and keeps it going when I tell him to. I don't like collecting wood for it because I don't like spiders.'

She repeated so Alex would know for certain, 'He whistles because I've already told him to.'

There was a half mile of poplars along the last stretch towards home. The road here was surfaced, and against the endless sibilant movement of the trees Alex's tyres hummed as he leaned over the bars and stood to pedal. He was thinking of Barbara crouched in front of the copper with the sky open to either side of her, watching the flame eat at the dry wedges of pine. She is doing that this instant, he thought. Because he had questioned her on how long it took, on precisely what she would be doing so he would know at the exact time. If he knew about her like that, it was a way of still being with her. Crouching as she had said for maybe ten minutes, watching the flames tent across the piled wood, then cutting the yellow soap into slivers with a kitchen knife whose bone handle had been scorched on the stove, then lifting the pole which she prodded and stirred in the vat of sheets and clothes. It was something Alex would never see her do, yet it was vivid in his mind, the girl so unlike the white-dressed figure at school, in her green home skirt and bare legs and a fawn blouse with its sleeves rolled back along her forearms, raising the pole and lowering it with the identical action with which she might push a shallow punt away from the wet bank of the river, easing the silent craft into the will of the current. Her breasts rode high with the lifting of the pole, her hair swung forward with the sideways leaning pressure. Steam worked in drifts about her raised bare arms, the swaying curtain of her hair.

It took twenty minutes for him to cycle from Barbara's place to home. He changed into dungarees before going down to the shed. As he entered he nodded to the one-armed man who was already at work in the clatter of the machines. The manager moved quickly, half-bent between the stalls as though there was such urgency that there was not time for him to walk erect. His bad arm was in a leather holster that he wore only in the shed.

Alex rubbed the disinfected cloth across a cow's bag and slid on the gulping cups. They were one of the first farms to milk entirely by machine. The metal sheaths were heavy, the long brown hoses leading back to the separator like fat interminable worms. From a shelf at the side of the shed a radio blared out, adding to the racket of the job.

Between one animal's exit and the next's shambling entry to the stall, Alex swilled the cups in a bucket of water. Replaced, they chugged and gulped. Always above the shed's rhythm and clatter he was conscious of the sweetish reek of the milk and the warm gut smell rising from the cows' droppings and the dull glimmer of metal rods. She had looked at him so directly before he left, before she turned to the figure whistling at her. 'You'll come back?' she had said. Her words kept on at him as he drove the animals into the stalls, as he stooped beneath them with the large grotesque hand of the milking cups. He yelled at the ones that held back and slapped at their haunches with his opened palm. He leg-roped the stroppy ones and with the tractable he spoke and patted, rubbing his fist on the large bone between their eyes. When the job was done Stan tinkered at the dials and wheels out the back of the shed. Alex hosed the gear with boiling water, and with cold he scoured the yards while the manager clanked awkwardly with the large metal cans. Then the herd was in the paddock again, their casual ageless movement across the line of the sky.

His mother said when she had switched off the radio, 'No reading tonight then, Alex?' They had done the dishes together and sat as they usually did at either side of the range. His fingers were clasped around his crossed knee. She thought, his hands are already those of a farmer, they are raw and swollen with his father's work and his grandfather's too, she supposed, and God knows how many before that. She knew so very little of her husband's forebears.

'I just feel like sitting on here quiet for a bit.'

The woman took up the shawl in which her knitting was wrapped. She spread it open on her lap, holding up in front of her an almost completed sleeve. She leaned across and rested it along her son's arm, drawing its sides together until they met. She then let its long softness coil on her knees, and began with the heavy needles that worked against each other in a rapid soft clashing while neither she nor the boy spoke.

She thought how something must be on his mind. It was inevitable, she knew, that at his age there would be parts of his life he chose not to speak of with her. She supposed he must now or very soon be troubled by what troubled them all. Yet she knew she supposed that on so scant experience – there was little enough in her own life she could call as witness. Which was that men were prodded towards women, towards sex, they were obsessed by it for thirty, forty years. Doubtless some women too. Mrs Norwood who confided in her. That schoolfriend of her mother's who left four children for a man who could scarcely read or write. She had gone with him to a mill town near Kaipara and after two years he had died. The woman came back and took up with her family and was what even her mother called 'exemplary', except the district thought her husband a fool and the woman herself unspeakable. You heard stories like that. That woman had told her mother there was nothing she would not have done for him, she would have starved herself to keep him fed. 'Those were her words.' Her mother always finished the story there. She meant, 'That is what the flesh will do, God help us.' It was strange how Alex's mother often thought of that. As a girl she remembered the thing was told discreetly and the ladies had picked at their gloves in whatever it was – incomprehension? Horror? She had thought not of the deserted children or of the dense loneliness of the bush where the woman had gone to live, but of a darkened room, what she knew was at the centre of all such stories. Yet from where had she derived even so much comprehension as that? A room thick with mid-summer and a woman in her stays and a man vaguely naked who waited for her to turn towards him, her clothes hissing, crumpling, until she stepped from them, free. He was a Yugoslav, the man. He died because a tree had broken both his legs. He had lain on a cart for fourteen miles and talked to the woman and held her hand. The women who spoke of it and paused and moved a teacup on its saucer, they must have sometimes seen it in their minds too, mustn't they, the young girl had thought. The dark room which is the one reason men and women run off together. But the idea of discussing such things with Mr MacLeod! He had disliked her undressing in front of him. The memory stayed with her of that. Her arms crossed, lifting above her head the brown velvet dress she had worn in the first week of their marriage. She had laid her dress and then her petticoats across the chair before she turned to face her husband. Her breasts, which were fine – her sisters envied her that and perhaps nothing else – appeared to him as she believed he would want. He had said to her, 'There's no call for that.' Yet she knew she might have spoken of such a matter to Mr Wallace. They might have talked the world away, mightn't they just!

Mrs MacLeod clashed her needles more sharply than usual.

Alex looked across at her. Her yellowish skin was looser, he was sure, than even a few months ago. Sometimes she would lean back in her armchair and close her eyes. Her eyelids then made him think of delicate shells. Just getting old, she joked with him, when she saw him watching her rest.

'Give the fire a stir, love,' she asked him now.

Alex dug with the short iron poker between the bars. The jammed pieces of wood tumbled and the flames rose, their reflections leaping out along the legs of the table. For those seconds of brightness his mother's skin became younger by decades.

'That's better,' she said. The boy moved his own chair further back. The evening was warm enough as it was, without the blaze. Across the paddock the manager would be sitting in his shirtsleeves, his untidy wife dabbing at the hollow of her skinny throat with the same cloth that she used for drying the dishes and wiping across the babies' mouths. Alex had seen her do it, and his stomach turned.

His mother said, 'You'd think I'd been chopping wood all day.'

Alex looked at her. 'Oh?'

'I'm that weary, I mean. I'm that worn out.' She laid the knitting across the opened shawl and clasped her hands. There was such endless pleasure, wasn't there, watching the rise and fall of the flames behind the black fence of the bars? The sudden collapse into glowing shards and occasionally as now the greenish film licking over some tiny pocket of gas. Mr MacLeod would have known exactly what. Em, he used to say to her early on, one of the miracles of nature is that a woman can live thirty years and know scarcely a thing.

Emily MacLeod eased the cushion behind the pain that flowed from above her hip.

'All right?' her son asked her.

'Stiff with age. That's all.'

'You?' Alex said. He looked at her warmly.

'Even me,' she smiled back.

They spoke quietly to each other. 'Tennis in a month's time,' Alex joked.

'I'm sure,' she said. 'A pair of athletes like ourselves.' He is bones and height and skinniness, his mother thought. The image of his father at that age if you put against him this instant that

53

faded reddish photo between the pages of the Bible. Yet he's really our side, isn't he, every inch of him? He is soft and deep and puzzled at what goes on.

It was the boy now who closed his eyes. His legs were stretched out towards her, his shoes inches from her own feet. His head turned a little, emphasising the long flow of his face. She could see Mr MacLeod as he lay for the last time. She thought of it without morbidness. She had stood, hadn't she, and looked down on him for several minutes. He was almost comical with the tucks and pleats of satin around his head, his hair for the first time in years so carefully flattened back, that little tie he wore with the dark suit. When the others left her discreetly to her grief, as they had been schooled to believe it must be, she admitted how his lying there, so carefully prepared for his enduring compact with the earth, meant so little to her. She had looked mostly with curiosity at what utter stillness is. But she took the sequence of condolences as Mr Wallace would have wanted her to, as parts of truth that became untrue only when cut off from everything else. For nothing is true except as it relates. He had told her that on the lawn while they watched the cricket. There is only one sin finally, he said, and that is cynicism. To think that all the human spirit works for is a game not worth the candle.

Emily MacLeod thought how her mind was a clutter tonight, certainly. Coffins and a twenty-year-old picnic and her boy growing up and goodness knows what else. Perhaps she would try to sort it out a little in the old notebook she had again taken to writing in. She broke in on her son. 'You wouldn't fancy a cup of tea?'

He opened one eye at her. '*You* would,' he said.

'Only if,' she said.

'You're a crafty one.'

Alex ran the tap and heard the high whining hum in the pipes before the water flowed. 'It's been like that a lot lately. I thought Stan was going to look at it?'

'Poor old Stan. He's always got enough to keep him going.'

'There's that big dark fellow does odd jobs for him.'

'Mr Burke?'

'Stan could ask him to have a go.'

He carried the kettle to one of the black holes on the range. He stretched in front of his mother. 'Excuse me, miss.'

'Your grandfather was just as bad. He talked tough but when it came to doing things. He'd have raged about Stan not getting on with those odd jobs but he'd never sack him. He'd still be here when no water was coming through at all.'

'Not rambling again, are we?' Alex said.

His mother laughed. There was a piece of gold in one of her teeth that Alex liked to see when she was amused.

'I must be asleep on my feet,' she said. 'All the sense I'm making tonight.'

'Gone in the swede,' Alex said.

'I beg your pardon?'

'It's what they say at school. Means not the full quid.'

'Thank you.'

He said, 'It's what Dick and the others say about that new girl's father. He wears this knitted thing over his head all the time. You know, I've told you about him?'

'Barbara's father?' she tested.

'Yes,' he said. The tea-measure clacked against the side of the tin.

'And she still wears her white dress, does she? All the time?'

When he did not say yes but, 'Wears white? I'm not sure. Yeah, I think she does', his mother knew. She is the one, then. For what is the point of little lies like that, except defence? She wrapped her knitting things away and laid them beside her on the floor, on the black notebook with its now rusted clasp.

She watched the boy's moving at the bench, the awkward strength which one day she supposed would be admirable, and that softness that would be there too, she hoped, to temper, to make fine. Her mind returned to what she had been thinking earlier on. He will experience soon enough what is almost as common as birth or death, yet like all of us he will think it so unique, so much a treasure of his own. She thought of Mr Wallace's phrase when they had watched one night her sister and her almost-husband a week before their marriage. 'The shimmer of the peacock's tail,' Mr Wallace had said. It was not to her, of course. The men were holding their dark glasses of port and she was pouring coffee at the small table inside the dining room door. Her father snorted, and asked with his rather theatrical cynicism, 'You don't mean the music of the spheres and God's will as well?' 'The very same,' said Mr Wallace.

She thought of Mrs Norwood who broke down and cried to her, whose fine shoulders she had stroked in crude animal comfort as the woman said through the tangle of hair she lifted from her wet cheeks, that it was all right for someone like Mrs Macleod, people like her who could think straight. 'You've never known what it's like, a hot coal burning into you and not being able to bear the idea that the burn will stop.' And humbly Emily had thought, the woman is quite right. I must accept that reprimand as just. They are to be envied, the rash ones, the true believers.

Alex handed his mother her tea. He hoped that tonight she wouldn't ask him to read. He sipped his tea, he was seeing again the girl's naked foot on the piece of wire that pressed her flesh back whitely and the man in his khaki hangman's hood whistling her up from along the drive. She had walked slowly back to the house. There was a patch half-way along the drive where only her shoulders, the long glitter of her hair, showed above the muddled green and yellow of the gorse. She had taken a loaf of bread from a tin nailed to a post a few yards from where they had spoken. He had seen her raise the loaf and set it against her mouth. As she sometimes raised a book at school with its dry edges against her lips. The man had held out his hand and she put the loaf of bread in it.

She had walked towards him very slowly. There was a distinct enjoyment in her making the man wait, Alex had understood that. She was saying to the man, wasn't she, that she was down there to talk to her friend, not to fetch something for him? The spill of shadows from the macrocarpas had flowed over her, for a second her flesh was a kind of hazy blue.

She had said when she first saw him at the end of the drive, when she came down to speak with him, 'I knew you'd come.'

'Why?' he said. 'How did you?'

'Because of Monday,' she said.

'Monday?'

'Because you held Toss O'Brien so I could stand on his hand.'

When she said that her tongue moved across her lips, wetting them.

Alex felt it clearly as a physical blow that the girl was odd. 'Odd' was what his mother said when she meant someone thought so differently from yourself that you could never come to the same point, live in quite the same world. Yet he knew utterly what she meant. He knew they had moved into a different mode, their speech both code and clarity beyond what words were meant to do. It was as certain as an actual jolt. The sweat sprang inside his shirt, and he took his hands from the rubber grips.

'I think of that all the time,' she said.

'I didn't mind doing it.' His eyes now on her legs, her shirt, avoiding the look she wanted him to return to.

And she waited again until she knew he would not take his eyes from hers and she told him, 'It was good you holding him for me. Wasn't it?'

It was then he heard the axe ring clearly and briefly from the top of the drive and saw the man who now in the honed silence was standing there watching him. It was then she began to tell him, 'There's no great mystery about us', and told him more than anyone else could know about her, smiling at him, tormenting the man with the covered head.

Later in the week, from where she was making scones at the kitchen table, Alex's mother remarked, 'I hear there's been some trouble at school?'

He sat at the other end of the table, his books beside the vase of bronze beech leaves pushed from the centre of the table to one side. An atlas lay open in front of him, his finger resting on the scale at the bottom of a continent. He attended to her without looking up. 'Trouble?'

Always they had spoken so openly with each other that her sister had been shocked, hearing them discuss what bull the cows should be put to, what state the finances of the farm were in. Now Emily thought, perhaps we have come to something at last where we are on other sides of a chasm. Alex tapped his pencil on the map in front of him. He anticipated her. He said, 'You mean that business with O'Brien?'

The woman wrapped the scones in a linen teatowel. 'I may have got it wrong.'

'Wrong from where?'

'Whom.'

'Whom, then?'

'Bet's mother mentioned it in passing.'

'Oh, Bet's mother!'

His mother smiled and tapped his wrist with the wooden spoon that lay beside her. 'I didn't say we talked about nothing else. It really was in passing.'

Alex disliked the woman whose house smelled always of milk and drying clothes and boiling cabbage. He found it easy to dismiss her or whatever she had said.

He kept on at his map. He filled in the capitals of the states and the dates of their establishment and, in brackets beneath, the names of the first governors. *Macquarie*, he printed, *Philips*. There was a pleasure in lists, in these neat packages of history. He knew they told you nothing about how even one single life had been lived, but he enjoyed them all the same, tied up and marshalled much as the pages of the atlas were divided and coloured in. Henry and Mary and Edward and Elizabeth. He could learn those lists off easily. *Heritage*, the teacher drummed at them. He showed them a painting of Agincourt. You're part of that, he tried to tell them, all that's part of you. And when the class discussed Anzac Day earlier in the year, Mr Adams had needed to turn away and look out the window. There were wall charts the class had made, pictures of the King and General Haig and Kitchener's big pointing finger, and the scenes the pupils had drawn of taking ridges and jumping from landing craft and the Turk bullets slapping up the water into finely drawn spouts. O'Brien had asked the shy, easily emotional man, 'Wasn't it the English though who mucked us up? Wasn't it more things just going wrong than us being brave for the flag, like?' He had known this question would offend. Mr Adams looked at the boy as though he had inflicted a personal hurt. 'Have I taught you nothing?' he said.

Alex liked history because it was so simple, as of course real things could never be. It was never reigns and decades and thinking of people by the millions. It could never be like that. It was one person putting a cake in his mouth, and another stabbing a stranger with a knife, or someone looking at a girl's foot standing on a wire fence. It must always be like that. *Me* at the centre of all that whirls and flows. When Alex let his mind sink into the rush of time and then draw back to himself, examining the minute patterns on his palms, his fingers, his own inexplicable identity, there was this feeling of such intensity, a buoy riding yet fixed on a pouring tide.

'Well? Not answering your old mum?'

The boy screwed the top of the green Onoto pen that had been his father's. 'She'd never get something right, well would she?'

His mother took her knitting from the shelf beside the wireless. 'I'm hardly to judge that, am I?'

'It was simple,' he said. He tried to make it true and understandable for her. 'They give her a rotten time because she's different. Because she doesn't dress the same for one thing. Because they think she's stuck-up when she can't be bothered with them.'

He waited for his mother to look up at him. 'And?' she said.

'And O'Brien tried to get smart with her. That's all there was to it.' He smiled at his mother's seriousness. 'You'll have to take my word for it. Mine or Bet's mother's.' Toss who was ahead of Alex as they came into the classroom when the bell clanged for the end of lunchtime. O'Brien in front of Alex and Barbara in front of him. Then the small dark-haired boy who reminded Alex of a weasel or a stoat, clever and darting and sly, slipping his hand beneath the girl's arm and grabbing at the swelling of her breast. He grinned at the line of shocked and delighted schoolmates. 'See if Lady Muck's got charlies.'

Then as though a magnet had drawn beneath a pile of filings, the class instinctively moved back. A space opened that left the three figures inside an arena, the girl and Toss grinning towards them all and the tall youth who for the moment was quite still, the only one who understood what there was to do. Then the small handsome boy sensing what was moving towards him. 'Ask her,' he said, pointing to Ann Larsen. 'I did it for a bet, eh Ann? That's all I meant.'

Alex leaned rather than stepped forward. So quietly that not all

59

of them were sure what he said, as he told O'Brien before his hand had reached him, 'She's a princess to shit like you.' Alex in his coldness quite as much surprised as those who heard him. Two words he never used, drawn from him as if without his knowing, without consent. Then the movement of his arm was slow and deliberate. He took the arm which O'Brien had raised and held across his face. He looked towards the girl as though only she might now do something to protect him. But the girl was looking past him, watching Alex.

The arm was wrenched up behind his back so sharply that in the interval before O'Brien jerked forward and let out the first of his bellows, those who stood in the rough circle about them heard the clear click of bone. O'Brien lurched forward so that he fell on one knee. Alex took the one step that was needed for him not to lose the pressure he enforced. The boy called out again, a wordless whimpering plea. He thrust out his left arm, taking the weight of his body on his splayed-out hand.

There was a film of sweat along the taller boy's lip. And again he leaned his weight into the kneeling figure. O'Brien's breath rasped from him. Through the tears of humiliation as well as pain he pleaded again, 'It was for a bet, Alex. Alex!' The girl then moved for the first time. With that smooth fixity to her face that had made the headmaster think of a graceful polished mask, she placed the heel of her shoe on the boy's spanned hand.

'Call her that,' Alex told him quietly. 'Call her Princess, eh?'

The boy arched over, his cheek now pressed against his knee. Alex moved the pressure of his hold so that O'Brien was obliged to swivel slightly, a kind of obeisance in front of her. Above the boy's gasping she looked across at Alex. She balanced on the hand beneath her heel. It was so brief, Alex thought later. It could not have been more than seconds. But Mr Simpson had grabbed at his shoulder, needing to reach up to him, yanking him back. 'What in hell's going on with you barbarians?'

He was wrenched without relinquishing his grip. He saw the master's mouth opening and shouting at him, the flush of the man's face although his words remained remote, coming at him as if through glass. His own words too seeming somehow beyond him, his repeated order to O'Brien, 'Say it! Say it!' Then the other boy's blubbering and snot and fear, his slobbered repetitive chant, 'Princess. Princess.' Alex's own breath went from him in an exhalation of relief. He knew the silence of the class was part too of O'Brien's confessed subjection. They were watching still under compulsion. It was all right now to let them go.

'My God, MacLeod!' the teacher was saying. The man assisted O'Brien from the ground. Alex stood back as though it were hardly his business any longer. Barbara walked to his desk. She and Alex had not spoken to each other, each seemed less obviously touched by what they had done than the rest of the class. For the rest had moved now into a club of hysteria, shouting and calling out to O'Brien, more malicious in their savagery than Alex had been in his. Mr Simpson yelped at them from the raised dais of his desk. O'Brien was sent off to the school infirmary because of his hand. The girl's heel had broken the skin to the size of half a crown, a brilliant welling of blood where a wedge of flesh hinged back like the broken skin of a peach.

But Alex put it simply for his mother. 'The way he spoke to her and tried to touch her. Someone had to stop him.'

'But you needn't hurt him though?' his mother said.

'Yes. Someone had to.'

His mother held out to him the limp hank of wool for her to roll into a ball. His levelled palms faced each other as he slipped the soft strands across his fingers and moved his arms apart. She knew the boy had no more to say.

Her fingers blurred as the ball thickened in her hands. When she fumbled for a moment and the wool sagged between them, he gave the brief laugh that she knew was the surest thing he had taken from his father. Yet when had Ecky MacLeod ever been moved, she wondered? Ever hurt a man purely from passion? But passion is choice too, no matter how we like to say 'swept away'. It was a beam that lit up some people she supposed, and failed to touch others.

She held the completed ball of maroon wool in her hands. She thought how she tried as honestly as she could to think about things without confusion, without 'sentiment', as they used to say, blurring and confusing them. But did she know so very much more than her husband, if it came to that? Oh, she had *wanted* life to be clear – but if it hadn't come about, what was the point then of trying even? And she thought now of her confused passionate son; she would not deprive him of that passion, even if she could. That road to Damascus where not God necessarily but *something*, sex or rage or compassion or simply one's utter certainty of right, fell on one like an axe, turned life so suddenly about that west faced you from where you thought was east.

Alex laughed again. 'Now they all call her Princess, you know that?'

'As a joke?'

'No fear it's not,' Alex said.

He thought, it's like they had all been waiting for that word, because it made them understand what they only guessed at before I made them use it. She walks through them and above them and they know that, they have their word now that says how they know it. They have a name for it and I gave it to them. *Shit* was the word that smeared O'Brien and whoever disbelieved.

Bet confided to Dick by the concrete trough at the paddock's edge. She tried to pin it down, to explain the other girl. Dick waited and stirred the black water with a peeled stick of pussy willow. He supposed Bet must hate her because Princess now ruled Alex as if he were a dog, a foxie that panted and waited to be called. But his cousin said nothing of that. Instead she said, 'It's that dress. She's never going to wear another one, you know. She *wants* to feel queer.'

'Queer?'

'Out of it.'

Bet gave that smile of hers that sometimes made you think she was wincing. 'She's got her spot of sunlight now and nothing else matters.' Because they'd heard at school how the headmaster had sent for her again and said what about it then, what about that dress?

In his office the headmaster noticed again how the girl's eyes seemed to change colour if you altered your angle of looking at her. The way you might see a cat's change. Quietly he said, 'Now come on, Barbara, what about that gym?' And she had answered him just as politely. She said that there was nothing in fact to explain beyond her uncle saying he could not afford it. As well as that, they might not be in the district for all that long. That too was something the man had not decided.

'I quite see that,' the headmaster said. But he was sure Barbara would see his problem too. 'I think you're more – '. He paused on the word mature, preferring to take up another. 'More sensible than most of the girls here. You know how easily jealousies begin. How easy it is for people to be marked out. I think you understand what I mean?'

Half an hour later in the staffroom the head would say to Mrs Scott she had damned well sat there, cool as you like, leaving it up to him to explain *himself*. You'd have thought he was the one being hauled up. He had decided then on a certain curtness.

'There.' He placed between them on the desk a brown paper bag. It was a gym frock his wife had washed and pressed and folded. With it was a short-sleeved summer blouse. The girl said, 'It was kind of you to get it for me.'

'My wife's the one who got it. No one else of course need have the slightest notion of where it came from.'

Barbara sat upright in her chair. The headmaster took a cigarette from a packet, lighting it, discarding the match, slowing the sequence to allow her whatever time she needed.

She said, 'It won't fit.'

The headmaster laughed at her certainty. 'I think you'll find it does.'

'No.' She shook her head. 'I can't see it ever fitting.'

Mrs Scott stirred her tea at the communal table. 'You told her you wouldn't put up with insolence?' She lowered her voice. Further along the table Mr Simpson turned the pages of a book about the cave drawings at Lascaux. Beside him the new maths man tapped one finger lightly on an exercise book spread out in front of him.

'Of course,' the headmaster said. In fact he had told the girl, 'There are less than a few weeks to go this term so I'll give you that time to make up your mind. But next year, you understand me?'

'Next year?' the girl repeated. Then, rather oddly, they had smiled at each other. She left the room and closed the door. The headmaster allowed himself the rare luxury of speaking aloud to himself. 'Clever bitch,' he had said.

Alex continued to watch her across the playground, continued to think of her. He would elaborate to himself, you can imagine a river if you like, and there's two rocks that stand out from it and there's nothing between the shores to break the mirror of the water, only those two rocks, and we are like that. Because water means nothing to the rocks and everyone here means nothing to us. It doesn't matter if we never talk at school or she sits over there and I stand here by the tree because we know. He would tell her, 'I look at you most of the time but when I don't it's much as if I still do anyway.' She would tell him back, 'I know that all the time.'

They stood on either side of the red mail tin nailed to the post. Now that this too was in its way a ritual, a certainty of implications, they could easily enough go for minutes without speaking. Until she would finally say, 'He wants me to go now.' Alex frequently saw the man with his covered head slip rather than move between the buildings, carrying wood into the lean-to with the copper. She saw Alex looking at him. She said, 'He hates you watching him.'

'I hate him too,' Alex said.

Dick continued to tell him more than he learned from her. He now knew that her uncle was providing luxury for his pigs in the renovated barn. The man had bought a huge sow from Ohaupo and a boar one-third its size. He had bought up a dozen porkers, thinking he could make money from bacon at a time like this. Dick repeated his father's words, the bastard was stark-staring. 'What's more his boar's so bloody puny he can't make a go of it. Larsen or even the old man could jack up borrowing one for him but he's so off his rocker he won't even talk to them.'

The last time Alex rode towards her she was already there at the fence. She stood barefooted in the skirt whose hem she had raised to her knees. Tall stems of grass swished against her legs when she stepped towards him on the road. She held up her thumb, directing him to look behind her.

'I've seen it,' he said.

On the other side of the drive a board from an apple crate was nailed to a macrocarpa. In black paint was written 'KEEP OUT, EVERYONE'.

'That's for me, is it?'

'It's for everyone.' Barbara leaned to him and touched his hand. Her hair was flecked and brilliant with the light. Then she said what she had not so much as hinted at before. She said, 'Put your bike there under the hedge. Walk back up with me.'

'He wouldn't if he knew,' Bet said, 'he wouldn't want to be her friend.'

Always his cousin spoke so quietly, and now Dick had to strain to hear, to cut out the whine of his aunt's voice that came through to them from the sitting room. He heard his mother's deep laughter that always sounded dark against it.

The boy sat back from the table where the chinese chequers board was set between them. They had played three games and Bet had won them all. He said, 'Shall we walk outside a bit to see if Alex is at home?'

'The babies might wake.'

'What's that got to do with it?'

'I'd have to pick them up.'

'Don't talk nonsense,' Dick said. 'The house is crawling with women.'

She said again, 'He wouldn't if he knew.'

Dick leaned closer across the table. His cousin picked up one of the ball bearings that were the men on her side of the board and chinked it against another. 'They reckon her uncle shags her,' she said. 'If he is her uncle, that is.' Her head tilted over the board but her eyes looked up at him. The whites were bluish, startled. He felt his cheeks burn at what she said. Bet kept tapping one steel bearing against another. From the front room there were the women's voices, the movement of their cups and saucers. Both sounds seemed to arrive from a long way off.

'How does anyone know?'

The girl picked up several of the balls and let them pour into the palm of her hand. 'Not that it matters much.' She reached across and took Dick's men as well. They were made of painted clay and fell more quietly into the old chocolate box where they were kept. She pulled a chair across to the heating cupboard, standing on it to shove the box and the chequers board onto a high shelf. Dick was thinking, shit, he wouldn't mention that story to Alex, not for a hundred quid. He'd kill you just like that, I reckon. The way he never takes his eyes from her while he's leaning there at the Anzac gum picking off those chips of bark and Princess is sitting by herself, always, not giving a stuff about anything except that Alex is watching, that the other kids all know that he is watching, that the pair of them don't give a stuff for anything. And then when the bell goes the way he hangs back until they're all inside, guarding everything she did, watching no one steps out of line again.

'Shall we go outside then?'

'No.' Bet put the chair back at the table. 'It's too late now.'

'It's still light out there.'

'It won't be for long.' Alex would come out if he saw them in the paddock, he always did.

Oh how she wanted to go out into the late evening and the warm rising smell of the earth and that lovely flicker as you stood under the trees and the late birds whisked in past you! And the windows yellow across at the farm house. She knew Dick guessed at her confusion, at the lie about Barbara and her uncle that she so wanted to be true. She took up the large kettle from the range and banged it beneath the taps. 'The old bags in there'll want more tea, anyway.'

'I'll leave the bike here,' Alex said. He slid it under a tangle of convolvulus that formed a natural tent beneath the trees.

They walked together up the drive. Alex stooped to pick up a handful of small stones which he jogged between his hands. The swish of the long grass flicked at their legs, the stalks of paspalum smearing faint black lines across their skin. The paddocks, the trees, flashed here and there from the quick shower an hour before.

They stopped at the high swirling loops of blackberry. Drops of rain that gathered along the stems were running with light. Then through the tangle Barbara saw the quick greyish movement of a young rabbit huddling back. She raised her hand to Alex to stay quiet. She crouched a few feet from the tuft of pale fur, its eyes like large black beads. She wondered why it didn't make a run for it, surely a rabbit could cope with a bit of blackberry? Then she saw its hind leg buckled loosely at its side. The girl stood again, turning to Alex. The planes of her cheek were flushed, her hair poured with the light. Alex looked at her and his breath caught. They stood now in the rapid brilliance that can fall from a sky crossed all day with showers and intermittent fleetings of sun. When Barbara stretched out her hand to point, the fine hairs along her arm were molten. She took Alex's hand.

The girl drew him down to the darkened space inside the whirled stems. He saw the creature that quivered in the dimness. His own arm went down towards it, slowly as into a trough of cold green water. The rabbit stirred then scrabbled with its good hind leg. The hooked stems rasped against Alex's arm. But his hand plunged accurately and then withdrew, blood lined along the ridge of his thumb to above his wrist, another scoring his forearm. In his fist he held the palpitating scrap of life. He raised it gently, his tongue clucking with the small sounds of sympathy and comfort. He turned his hand, examining the leg that trailed from the rabbit's side. There was no sign of a wound. The girl put her index finger to where the head hunched into the pulsing body. She ran her fingers along the ears flattened on its back. 'They always feel so cool, the ears.'

'There's nothing we can do for it,' Alex said. His other hand now spanned it completely. 'It won't last long like this.' He walked to the lean-to wash-house and turned his back to her. She saw the quick jerk of his arm, heard a sound like a felt ball plopped against wood. He came back to her and without showing her the death he carried in his hand, he lobbed the small body back into the tangle of stems. The leaves stirred and sprang back.

Barbara's voice was matter of fact. 'It was the only thing to do.'

That then was the first time Alex went with her inside the fence and as far as the jumble of shacks at the side of the unpainted house. He saw the large barn which the man had turned into his pig palace, and the smaller garage they walked to and paused in front of. There was the catching smell of chaff and dried-out pine and decaying sacks. From a huge bag she took up a handful of chaff and let it stream loosely from the funnel she made with her fist. 'He only gives them the best.'

Alex caught the flicker near the barn door, the quick melting into its gloom that must have been the man. Then through the long dim tunnel at the far end of the barn the double doors swung back and he stepped out, several screeching pigs bumbling at his side. The stooping shape, the battering eager animals, were silhouetted against the light like shapes cut from paper. It struck the boy that what he saw was a kind of heavy furtive loneliness, the man with his pigs now streaming across the paddock, he and Barbara over here, so remote from him, so despising. He thought of the utter strangeness of that uneasy man sharing a house, a table, presumably at times some attempt at conversation, with the girl who disliked so much as mentioning him.

He rubbed his hand against the rough serge of his school shorts. The sting of his cut dragged him back. That and the sound of Barbara's foot scuffing in the spilled grains and the continued high squealing of the pigs drew him back from his expanding sense of confusion. But then Barbara was touching him. She took his wrist and raised it. The man had turned a tap above a cut-down drum and gone back into the barn. The door was still half open so he may have seen them from where he stood. It was too dark inside to see him. She held Alex's wrist on her palm as though balancing its weight. Then she raised his arm further, the scratch with its thread of blood beneath the movement of her tongue. It was a sensation that stayed with him for days. It was there in his mind whatever else he was doing or compelled to do. Her mouth was hot on his arm. The slow circling of her tongue, her drying her own spit then with her cheek stroking along his arm.

'A bloke like that should be horsewhipped,' Dick told him. Three days later, at the tree.

'Is that what your old man says?'

'Of course it's what the old man says. What everybody says.' Because when Ann Larsen's father went across the second time to say he wouldn't have the pigs rooting through his property like some of them were doing, that crazy bastard stood on his tumbledown verandah sweeping a gun level with his hips. 'Like some old joker gone mad in the pictures,' Dick said. He spoke through his wool thing, he told old man Larsen he'd better piss off or he'd cop it. He said, you think I won't do it then you're wrong about that too. He tilted the gun up, Larsen says, to a fucken magpie at the top of the pines thirty feet away, say. Next thing there's a bang so close to Larsen's ear he thought he'd got it himself. And there's this splash of feathers drops down a stone's throw away. Much as to say I want to shoot a thing I shoot it, right?'

'If he doesn't want to see people he doesn't have to.'

Dick's face crinkled with exasperation. 'You just can't do that, Alex. Come into a place and make your own rules and go round dressed like a bank robber and swinging a gun at people into the bargain. You can't do that.' And he continued with his story of the gun leaned against the rail of the verandah and Larsen running down the side of the shed out into the open of the paddock, making hell for leather to the boundary fence, humiliated by a mad man. Larsen vaulted one of the posts, then turned to look back to shout his abuse from his own land, and the words bounded back from the river gully. 'So that's when the bastard shot again,' Dick said. 'Larsen's back on his own property, mind, and he sees him pick up the gun and this time he makes a chip from the post Larsen's just got over fly up near his shoulder.'

Behind the man, Alex was thinking, behind him and above the gun put down for the second time and the hot odour of the shot, that raggedy mounted stag's head hanging at an angle from the wall beside the back door. It must have been there all the years the place was empty. One eye was gone, a dribble of straw from the hole where sparrows had worked at the stuffing. Barbara had seen him look at it the first time she took him to the top of the drive. The dead mutilated head above the rotten boards of the verandah where the man soon enough would stand in Dick's story, the rifle swinging, accurate, level with his belt. He had asked her, didn't that head there give her the creeps? 'One time when you're here, then,' Barbara had told him, 'we'll take it down the back and burn it.'

'Burn it?'

'Give it a crown of flames.' She had laughed at the fun of it.

'There's a place behind the trees.' Her upper lip lifted to show her pale gums, her splendid teeth.

She led him down from the back paddock to the river. There were pines and native trees, mostly puriri and matai. Where the farm ended the river swept into a broad slow bend. On the ridge of the clay bank the trees followed the river's curve. This was the paddock the man had worked on – two paddocks, in fact, for he had uprooted the rotten fence-posts that formerly divided it into two, believing the more space his animals had to run in the healthier they would be. He had slashed at gorse and ragwort and the head-high stands of willow that the years of neglect had allowed to move across the farm. He burned huge stacks of dead and living wood, the mounds of weed and wrist-thick gorse, and new growth sprang green and manageable in their place. His fires had burned for several nights and the pines jigged in their flames. He then worked at restoring the barn and setting the former cowshed to the new demands of sties. The fences that mattered more to him after Larsen's intrusion he worked at with close-meshed wire and new posts. It was as if he knew by instinct that nothing would enrage his neighbours more than the work he put into his farm. Yet worse than that, he left the front paddock as it was, the jumble and disorder of fifteen years. By the same indifference the house remained unpainted, the walls of the garage sagged. Of all the things about the crazy bugger who couldn't as they said farm a flowerpot, who probably couldn't slice bacon let alone cope with a whole pig, that was the worst of his offences – his indifference, his not having, as the district sometimes said, the pride of a bloody hori. Dick had heard his mother speaking with Larsen down in Cambridge. She had said, why did it worry everyone the man didn't do the expected thing? Larsen had sworn there in the main street. 'Expected my arse,' the tall fair neighbour said. 'He doesn't do the *normal* thing. Isn't that enough?'

The girl said as they stood above the dark bar of the river's current, 'Give me one of those stones.' He picked up a handful from the lip of the bank. He passed her several and took up more. They aimed at the fragments of pumice floating downstream.

'They've come maybe a hundred miles already,' Alex said. 'If you go to Taupo you see pumice lying on the beaches. Chunks as big as rocks.'

They sat then beside each other. Their legs touched as they hung above the shallow cliff. Still they watched the drifting grey blobs and the quick restless indentations on the water, the scratchings of breeze across the surface.

She said, 'He oils his gun every night.'

'Your uncle?'

'He can take a tin and throw it as far as he likes and hit it just before it touches the ground. Then he hits it with another bullet before it stops spinning from the first. The tin jumps like it's alive. He does it whenever he sees anyone looking from the other farms.' Then she ran her tongue along her lips. They shone wet, Alex thought, as when the tide slips back and you see that shine on wet sand. She watched him looking at her.

Alex touched the side of her mouth. 'You get little hollows when you smile like that. You never see them any other time.' His hand fell and his fingers brushed against her arm. He put his head closer towards hers. He heard the pounding in his ears as though some engine came behind him from across the paddock, a rush through which he saw in such clarity the fine parting in the centre of her hair, the falling of its rich mass, the vein that ticked in her neck. There was nothing in his mind now but his wanting to touch her, to draw her towards him. Both his hands moved down her arms and took her wrists. She put her tongue on his. Then she said so quietly it was as though she expected it might be overheard, although they were a hundred yards from the house. 'What if he's looking now?'

Alex saw that he gripped her so hard the skin paled at the edges of his fingers. He said, 'I didn't know I was squeezing your arms so bad.'

Barbara brought him back, demanding the answer he had failed to give. 'What if he is?'

'Watching us?'

'Watching us this minute?'

He said, 'Did you think I'd be scared?' But he took his hands from her and without speaking they rose and began to walk back towards the scarred unpainted house he had not and would never

71

enter. For when they met on the farm it was always to be like this, walking down to the river and standing, sitting, above its darkened flow. Then walking back. It was their simply moving together which formed their closeness, more than what they said or where they were.

For a moment, in the middle of the paddock, she touched Alex's shoulder, her fingers then sliding down his shirt. He thought how it seemed so clear and obvious, this feeling they had for each other. Yet the clarity itself had become a puzzle. She would not have stopped him, would she, had his hands moved from her arms to the swelling of her breasts, or if he had opened her blouse to lay his hands on them, to kiss them even? As she accepted it that he move his mouth along the wet shining of her lips. And he knew she wanted the man to be watching too, squinting at them from the barn.

He rode quickly home down the crossroad, rising on the pedals when he came to the section that was sand. The girl's arms, the soft pressure of her thigh beneath the cotton skirt, her tongue slipping against his own, tied him to her while he cycled home and through the milking and then again in the evening when Bet came across with the parcel of wool her father had picked up in Cambridge. Or rather he had waited at the side of the car while Bet herself had gone into the shop with her envelope of instructions and money. The girl said now as she gave the parcel to Mrs MacLeod that her mother wanted her back at once. She moved quickly from the kitchen and across the farm.

'Is there something wrong with Bet?' From the window the woman watched her scamper to the trough where she climbed the fence.

'Is there?' Alex said.

'She doesn't come over here anywhere as much as she did.'

'You know how much she has to do over there.'

His mother did not pursue it. She untied the parcel and matched the wool against that she already had. She saw him sit at the table, turning the teapot in circles on the cork square beneath it. He thought of in the pines. He had looked at her and the light corrugated across them both and behind her the trees had been black, she was like something painted wasn't she on a background so purely different from herself. *It is not a matter now of what it will be like, it is only a matter of when it will be.* He watched his mother's slow movement about the kitchen, her yellowish skin, her grey-haired leaning above the wools. She too was there at the edge, like the man shifting behind the kitchen window when they had walked back down the drive. He and Barbara were the centre. There was only that and the edges so far off, the figures moving further away. Stopping to pick up stones from the bank, putting them in Barbara's hand. Her tongue slipping on his own. The black pull of the current below them with their stones breaking the placid surface, the buoyant chunks of pumice rocking in the wash, their rapid drift downstream.

His mother replaced the metal ring on the top of the range after feeding cones into the fire.

'Yes,' he said to her, 'I'll make fresh tea.' Barbara letting him rub against her skin and leg close against her own. The arc of her arm when she skimmed her stone across the black flat surface. He thought, we are not even each other any more. We are only both together. Picking up the stones and handing them to her and their frail quick reception by the water, and the grey small fragments that she aimed at still far out, floating and swift near the middle of the stream.

(As Dick will always remember it, the story begins with heat. The last week before the December holidays when the temperature levelled in the high eighties. 'After she's been at school for two terms and Alex in his high and distant way was her bloke all right, no one questioned that. But even with me he'd hardly say a word.'

Dick might lean forward now. If he's taken a shine enough to tell you this much then he will tell you more. But you know he is coming to a more important part, he is not simply yarning. He speaks now with a kind of lumbering awe, he is at an episode beyond his comprehension. He commemorates it still a generation later with the strangest source he can turn to, to the awkwardness of religion. 'There's that bit in the Bible, you know that bit? They used to hammer it into us those days. Jesus was your cobber sort of thing, and charts and what have you up on the walls and Himself there and his offsiders in all these pictures. But there's this picture too. It pissed me off, that one, because it didn't seem fair. A crowd hanging round a pool because an angel was supposed to show up any minute and if you got to the pool before anyone else did you got the drop on the lot of them, see, you were home and hosed. But if you were one of the left-overs, mind, which just about everybody was, then you were just shit out of luck.'

'So where's that get us?' someone asks.

Dick sips at his beer. He sometimes eases the pressure on his lower plate so his face bulges grotesquely. Again so absurdly a boy fancying he has some secret. 'They were like that, see? Alex and Princess were. As if the rest of us, the kids at school and the grown-ups at home, were those poor buggers round the edge of the pool that weren't even in the running. They knew the pool was theirs and the angel and bloody everything else was too, they were the shining ones. Know what I mean?'

'And you were in on it, eh?' Someone winks over his head, but Dick is undisturbed.

'All I'm saying is we knew something would happen. We knew it had to. Madam knew that more maybe than any of us.'

He thinks how things happened so quickly, the links of a chain pouring through your hands and you know the speed of it all right and its weight all right but there's not a chance in hell you can control its flow. There was so much, he tells you, in those last few days. Alex's mother died on Boxing Day and was buried two days later, on an afternoon when a freak storm cracked down from Maungakawa and the mourners at the cemetery along the Morrinsville Road had left the cars in their summer clothes and minutes later ran back to them drenched through. Then the district hardly had that death off its hands when Dick's own mother was taken into casualty, then for months was confined to a home where at visiting hours she would look at them speechless and wrap her handkerchief round her finger and bite on it to stop herself crying. A breakdown, the doctors called it, a mental collapse. They told that to Dick's old man while he stood with his hat in front of him, edging it round by its brim. The party-line telephones kept whirring like great wounded wasps, the wires running with the news about Alex taking off, and the fight the night before that at a party over at Tai's place where the Maori's old man had gone for Larsen with a pitchfork because the blond tall man was feeling the old wahine up in a shed out the back. 'Pins him to the floor they reckon with a pitchfork through his bum!'

'Well someone had to do it,' another voice puts in. 'Larsen was at it all over the district.'

A laugh goes along the men at the bar. 'They don't make rooters like old Larsen any more!'

'But that's run of the mill to the rest of it,' Dick says. 'That's just a bit of snatch on the side, and that happens anywhere, the husband doing his block.'

'The rest of it?' someone asks. Someone who doesn't know the story.

'Alex and Princess. And finding the other bloke when he's dead. And the whole business with the car.' And Dick knows when he gets that far with the story that there's gaps in it from here on that no one is going to fill, only Alex can do that. And you might as well ask the grave as ask Alex for an answer.)

Young Alex's aunts remarked that it was unnatural for the boy not to cry. Because he had shown no more sign of grief than if the coffin he helped to bear from the church then threw the first handful of earth upon where it lay between the clay walls, they said it might as well have been the coffin of a stranger. They said how it never does to pent up grief.

Outside the church he had taken the pressure of the women's cheeks against his own, the soft layering of their hands upon his sleeve. In the first car behind the hearse he sat between his mother's sisters. One of them took his fingers in her black-gloved hand. He looked ahead, between his two uncles in the front seat, to the long black car. The wreaths were level with the windows. Then again at the cemetery, in the few minutes before the breaking of the storm, he shook hands and repeated thank you, thank you. Until the prayers had already begun. As the first huge drops splashed on the pages of the minister's opened book the collection of relatives and friends looked apprehensively at the sky. Within seconds the rain pelted on them. The minister raised his long black skirt and tucked the prayerbook beneath it. He then said quickly the necessary words, the committal to earth and to eternity. They rushed through the Lord's Prayer. Some of the older folk already had turned and were scuttling across the patch of lawn and the gravelled path towards the parked cars. *Amen*, Alex said. The rain ran and broke across the polished wood of the coffin. Then the men stopped to slide the two thick boards from beneath it, playing out rope handful by handful as his mother was lowered from them all. The silver strip of metal with her name blurred under the slipping beads of water. The downpour plastered his hair against his forehead, his collar had become a wet noose.

Once more in the car his two aunts leaned together and Alex sat near the door. The women turned to look through the rear window at the slanted driving of the storm, at the gravediggers now running along the path to shelter inside a wooden hut. Alex took a handkerchief from his pocket while the women waited to see if he cried. He ran the cloth across his face, between the stiff collar and his chafed skin. They said to each other later, if you hadn't been so close as they were then you might have mistaken that dabbing at his cheeks for grief.

The car pulled out from the cemetery entrance onto the main road. One of his uncles cupped a match between his hands and lit a cigarette. Then he half turned towards the back and said, 'Well we couldn't have got a worse day for it.'

The aunt beside Alex said, 'It's a shame when they can't finish the prayers properly.'

Her husband who was driving said, 'Not that it matters one way or another in the long run.' And not that Emily would have minded either. They were silent until the car lurched at the rail crossing on the edge of the town.

The storm passed as quickly as it came on. The sun sparkled and dashed off the shrubs on his aunt's lawn. At the back where the ground was dug over for the vegetable garden the earth steamed. The men went out onto the verandah. They drank tea and then scotch while the women sat in the darkened sitting room inside. Bet and her mother had come in from the farm. Before the mourners arrived back, they buttered scones and set out the tea things on the table. They had the fires lit so that soaked clothes would dry out while friends and neighbours talked. There was something strange about fires in mid-summer.

Alex stood among the men. The uncle he cared for most came to him with a small glass in his hand. He said, 'Get this into you, lad.' The boy took the biting warmth at the back of his throat. His uncle quietly offered to run him back to the farm whenever he gave the word. 'Back home or stay here, whatever you want. It's up to you, Alex.' He said, 'Perhaps I'd better wait until a few of them have gone.' So an hour later there was again the handshaking and grasping embraces from the women, the calling out from one group to another at the sides of cars and across the stretch of front lawn.

The late afternoon was now humid. Some of the men had removed their jackets. They stood in their white shirtsleeves and dark waistcoats. The heavy women delicately touched their throats with the wads of their handkerchiefs. We musn't leave it so long, they were calling. Why is it that only when one of us dies we get together?

Alex went home when the manager called for his wife and daughter. The one-armed man had come to the funeral, then gone back to get the milking out of the way an hour earlier than usual. The first time he had broken routine for years. And although he was there alone he had not switched on the wireless while he milked. The clatter of just the machines was almost a kind of silence. One had to show it somehow, some small thing by way of respect.

He had looked across to the farmhouse with its drawn blinds, the stillness of any place when you know someone there has died. And when he drove back to town he knew he could think of nothing to say to the boy whose mother he had worked for now for the past eight years. He was afraid to think too far past today. Lose a job like this, there wouldn't be another. He waited at the wheel of the car until the business of grief was concluded on the footpath. Again Alex's aunt pressed him to stay in town with them, for a night or two at least? She turned to a quietly spoken cousin from Auckland, the woman Alex knew had been a favourite with his mother. 'Don't you think he should stay on here for a bit?'

The other woman rested a hand on each of them. 'If he wants to go back, let him.'

The women waved to the car as it moved off.

It was hot and clammy as they drove back home. There was the smell of wet humid hay, the sky was the colour of slate behind the mountain.

'In for another dousing,' the manager said. 'It's already ruined the hay for a few of them.'

Stan and Burke, the casual labourer, had got their own hay in the week before. Alex knew he was drawing attention to it, expecting his approval, while the manager was thinking God knows what the boy's got in mind, you'd need a winch to drag anything out of him. The old lady – she was the softest touch you'd ever come on. He had thought when the clouds opened up there at the graveside and the minister rushed through the last bits of the praying and the mourners took off back to their cars like it was only the races they were at, 'You deserved a better send-off than that one, missus.'

They stopped on the way back to pick up the twins from Dick's place. Dick's mother carried them out, a bundle on each arm. The boy began to whimper as soon as he saw them. Bet took him to her knee. 'Hush now,' she told him. 'You hush you'll get something good when you get home.' She hated it that there was noise in the car for Alex.

The manager said wearily, 'They should be all right being left by now, shouldn't they?'

Dick's mother leaned forward to the car, the thick swing of her black hair obscuring half her face, her flesh-smell sweet and close. She put her hand through the opened window to rest on Alex's shoulder. 'You feel like a bit of company with Dick or anything, you just come over, won't you?'

'Thank you,' Alex said.

Behind him Bet felt inside her cardigan pocket and found a rusk for the fractious child on her knee. Her mother turned sharply. 'Giving them biscuits every time they want one! Bloody spoiling them.'

Dick was standing beside his mother. He raised his hand to Alex as the car turned back into the road. Alex nodded back.

At the farm Alex unlatched the gate for the car to drive through. He then swung it back, slipping the looped chain around the supporting post. He walked after the manager's car as it followed the loop from the cattlestop towards the cottage. He heard the children bawling when Bet lifted them from the car and set them on the scuffed earth outside the house.

Their mother presently was shouting at him. 'You coming over for tea?' The same strident voice as when she went for the kids. He raised his arm in a slack wave and shook his head.

He saw Bet turn to look at him, checking a movement which may have been an attempt to wave across, to say to him what she then knew could not be said. She reached instead for one of the babies who had sprawled at the raised edge of the path inside the gate.

Inside the empty house, he smelled the odour from his still damp suit, the same pungency of wet cloth as from under a hot iron. He loosened his black tie and raised its loop over his head. He walked from the house into the warm reek of the cows that came to him from across the fence, where they ambled then paused a few feet from where he stood. The gritty crunching of their cuds was the only sound. He stepped over the stile that his father had built before the boy could remember. The grass beneath the apple trees at the side of the house was lush and dragging as he walked through it. A few late bees worked over the clover that grew so thickly at this side of the house. His mother loved the untidiness of summer, the way within a couple of months the dead sticks of the fruit trees and the low muddy grass sprang to all this, the profusion she liked to walk among, the dozen scents she unravelled.

As Alex moved there rose the smell of crushed mint that he disliked. He stopped between the trees in the late greenish light. He looked at the packed globes of fruit and the pale leaves, the moss that spread its maps on the oldest of the trunks. He thought how always there had been this stillness in here. It is like being inside a photograph that is already taken. Outside this one spot there is racket and confusion, there is the endless wrangle across at the cottage, there is the birth and death of animals and endless shit. The boy closed his eyes in the heavy odorous press of fertility. The feeling of composure that was always here among the trees, where his mother came and stood some nights before she went to bed, rubbing in her hands the snapped-off leaves, the fragments of rosemary, before raising her opened palms to her face. His mind drifting now towards hers, which is no longer there. Her fingers blind and silenced, he cannot imagine that. Like not ever been.

His eyes took in the mass and detail of the orchard. He ran his outstretched hand along the side of the house, across the surface of the boards. That is the feeling of chalk as well as of paint, he thought, and of painted wood warmed in the sun, and so even the feeling of the sun. I have only to do this, to touch a piece of board, and everything flows out from that. There is nothing we don't link up with just by touching on one thing. He stood as the centre towards which all things poured. As if her share of it was now added to his own.

She had said 'Goodnight, Alex' and kissed his forehead and gone through to the sitting room to check the lock on the french doors that stood open through the day, and to wind with the flat black key the chiming clock on the mantelpiece. But at night if you lay awake you heard not only the resonant and elongated striking, refining down to where the silence again stretched out, but the low whirring too before the first stroke chimed, the sound his mother said was like time clearing its throat.

He had sat on when she went to bed. He heard her moving about in the bathroom. There was the sound of her bedroom door closing, then the quiet about him in the kitchen. He pressed his feet on the metal edge of the range and tilted back his chair. His eyes were closed. Barbara was in the paddock looking at him and there seemed nothing behind or around them while they watched each other. They were heaving stones. Below them the water slipped between its sombre banks, the black surface erupting in small bright sheaves as the stones impacted. A kingfisher dropped away to their left, a swift blurring pellet until it shot from the dark backing of the trees to open sunlight along the middle of the river and its vivid sheen flared out. The shadow took it again as it swerved into the pines on the other bank. He had smelled her sweat, that close, the damp moonstains at the armpits of her blouse. They had lain for a time quietly together, looking at the scud of sky above the trees. She had brought her hand across to lie open-handed on his chest. She had moved it slowly down.

The cat leaped to Alex's lap from the top of the wood-box. His eyes snapped back to the kitchen's glare, yellow as butter. Ten yards away in her room his mother crossed to the double bed her husband had made in the weeks he prepared for her arrival, fashioned it from rimu and rewarewa, the smooth grain of one and the honey-coloured fleck of the other set in alternating panels that had struck the new bride as the ugliest bed she had ever seen. She took up a book from the table beside her bed, let it rest on the bedclothes, then placed it back without opening it, too weary to begin it. She laid it on the thick notebook Mr Wallace had given her goodness how long ago now, with its faded marbled edges and her gold-stamped name worn so indistinct that only by tilting the book against the light might the lettering be read. She set the edges of the books neatly square against each other. She switched off the bedside lamp in its warm plum-coloured shade.

She could see a bar of moonlight beneath the level of the blind. She heard young Alex slide his chair along the floor, the chink of china as he poured milk for the cat and opened the back door to set the saucer near the mat. It was perhaps ten minutes later that she died.

And now Alex came in from the late blur of the orchard and its crammed odours, and stood in the empty house.

'*It is a matter of constant surveillance, constant hope.*'

Doctor puts down the hand he has been holding, lays it along the arm of the orange chair.

'*After how many years is it?*'

'*Almost seven.*'

'*Isn't that too long to expect recuperation?*'

Doctor says, 'Time is not the factor we think it, not precisely, that is, in our accustomed terms. One thing this work will teach you is the relativity of time. We can test response to stimuli, organic normality, what have you. But as long as speech is lost what we are in fact testing in any sense other than mere medical data is quite beyond our guessing.'

'*Sounds appalling.*' *The group turns towards the trainee who always says too much. In two days she had said enough for Doctor to answer her by name.*

'*That may be, Miss Harris. Or it may be pure bliss. It may even be pretty much what it is for the rest of us.*' *His hand in an arc including all of them, their normal ways. They smile, some of them, at the very idea.*

Her eyes are holding theirs without apparent fear or interest.

'*Speech, you said, didn't you,* almost *completely gone?*'

'*An occasional word. A few times a year one of the staff hears it. We might as well say by pure chance.*'

'*Coherent, are they?*'

'*Single words are always potentially coherent. Or incoherent. Again, how can one speculate without a context? And they are seldom clear enough to catch.*'

Doctor's hand had been resting on her hair. He says there is no doubt of mental awareness to a considerable extent. A favourite chair, for example. A favourite place in the garden. Certain repeated arm actions that must have some significance. He smiles at the group. A marked passion for cakes.

82

'For what?' A tall serious young man leans towards him.

'Cakes.'

The group quietly snigger.

'Also a preference for certain staff, a strong dislike for at least one other patient. I can't offer you reasons.'

Miss Harris sees the tall young man take a note on a pad he carries. She will sit next to him in the bus.

Doctor then lifts the hair away from the scar that runs for several inches, from the temple, across the upper cheek, a pink broadening smear to behind the ear. His fingers indicate the length of metal sliver that penetrated the brain.

Mr Wallace has given me this notebook for my twenty-third birthday.

He called when no one was expecting him. It was at ten o'clock this morning, while I was baking scones with Nan. It is the first day of harvesting, so I expect we worked more eagerly than we will by the end of the week. He came in through the back verandah and was beside us in the kitchen before we knew he was there. Nan was singing a love song from her Thomas Moore album! She says the finer feelings always elude me, because I don't find her songs as moving as she does herself. In any case my arms were half covered in flour and I wore the old checked apron which Mother wore so long ago it is one of my earliest memories. I remember her standing at the table exactly as I was standing when Mr Wallace came in, and I am in a wooden pen in the corner of the room. My hands are gripping the rail to keep myself balanced and Mother is singing too, although I do not remember what it was. With Mother it would probably have been a hymn.

My hair had fallen loose during the baking. When I saw Mr Wallace I at once raised my hands, but it was before I had wiped the flour from them, so that he laughed at the mess I made. He said, 'Here, you've done yourself up for a war dance.'

He took up a cloth that lay across the back of a chair and dabbed it across my neck and cheek. I felt that my face must be flaring. I told him I could manage, then simply made matters worse. I took the cloth and wiped the flour from my hands as well, but while I was doing that I somehow knocked the pin from my hair, so that the lot of it tumbled down. Nan of course had stopped her singing the minute Mr Wallace came in. She looked as she has always done, as though freshly varnished, every hair so in place she is like a painting. She said to me as only a very tidy person could,

'Oh Emily, just *look* at you!' She made me sit down and put my hair back into place as though I were a child. I think it irritated her that I seemed not to care quite enough. 'Never let a man see you as though you were not expecting him' – she would tell me that after our visitor had gone.

'Ah,' Mr Wallace said. 'Why put it back up, Emily? It looks fine the way it is.' He stood there so at ease, so full of fun, that I laughed with him. Nan seemed so fussy and embarrassed you would think *she* was the one found unprepared. Or that Mr Wallace was Sam.

Mr Wallace rather teased us both. 'Shall I go out and come in again, and knock as I should have?' Later Nan complained that anyone else of course *would* have knocked. She said he barged in here like one of the family. But while he was standing there she smiled at him too. She pinned up my hair and patted the sides, much as though she were saying, there, I was now in a fit state to talk to a man, thanks to her. And to Mr Wallace she said, 'If you *will* come when we're playing at cooks.'

I noticed, as I suppose I always do, that both of us were taller than the man who chatted with us. He turned to me and I noticed (something else I always do!) those odd glints in his dark beard, like pieces of copper wire. Otherwise it was so black that Nan for one says there can be but one explanation. She also thinks it an affectation for a man who is only forty to wear a beard at all. No one had done that for years. I was thinking these things when he drew from behind his back the hand that had been there since he entered, even while he had dabbed at me with the cloth. He gave me this book, wrapped in dark blue paper and tied with a piece of string. He said, 'You'll have to excuse me that. I don't have a feminine hand when it comes to such things.'

There is something ironic in much that Mr Wallace says. It hovers there behind his words and it is impossible quite to pin it down. Nan insists it is a kind of condescension. A way of speaking to women which implies that he, after all, is really in control, but he will humour us for the time being. I have said to her, but surely he turns it against himself as much as at anyone else? Yes, she says, that is simply part of his confidence. I have a fear occasionally that I may become like Nan, who says things with such certainty but has no idea of what she really means. When I write in this book I must try to be dead straight.

So what do I mean about Mr Wallace? To begin with, I think that when he is agreeable it is very simply because he wants to be. He is not at all like Father, who has what people call lovely manners, but has them only for certain reasons. He has been trained to have them, and he knows how successfully they work. But when Mr Wallace takes notice of someone, say, whom everyone may have overlooked, he does not give a pin about being polite or even being charitable – which Father insists on as a *duty* and so is hardly what St Paul had in mind. (I must remember always to put this book where Father will never find it!) No, Mr Wallace would be kind by instinct. He would not even know whether anybody noticed that he was so.

I took his present, and covered with the business of opening it that I was confused. Nan stood beside me. She said to him, 'How extraordinary that you know!'

Mr Wallace laughed again. He was enjoying that we were both surprised. He said it was difficult to visit a house with young people in it and not know about birthdays.

'It must have been Frances who told you,' I said. 'She believes she *has* to tell everything to everyone.'

In fact I had heard her informing him several days before. She was sitting on the side verandah, where the shelves of maidenhair and aspidistra make it seem a kind of grotto. She was working the pattern on the cloth which she gave me this morning. The Irish girl who was here until last week had taught her how to cross-stitch, so Frances was desperate to show off her newest skill. She is scarcely twelve and already she is so unlike Nan and myself. She is so flamboyant and unrestrained. Needless to say, she is the one who irritates Father most. She will also be pretty, which divides the family neatly into two who are and two who are not. My hair will pass muster, and in the evenings can look very nice indeed. Nan's smile and figure are enough for some men to find her attractive. But an utterly honest eye would find us both homely. Frances will be of quite another order, although never on the scale Mary was.

'Oh, Frances,' Mr Wallace laughed. 'She asked me when my

own birthday was. She was to cross-stitch me a handkerchief.'

Nan said, 'No wonder Mother is speaking of boarding school.'

'One hopes not *that*.'

I know he watched me carefully as I opened his gift. The book delighted me. I touched the leather cover and the gilt clasp and held the book sideways so that the marbling ran with light. It made me think of oil on water, the swirling of the colours. Then I clutched it to me until I realised I must look like a little girl. I didn't want him to think I was performing in some way for him. But I was touched that he had given me a present at all, and what he had chosen I thought so handsome. I love the creamy feel of the pages as I pass my hand across them.

Mr Wallace said, 'It's not a diary, you'll notice. There's something too accusing in diaries when you see you've skipped a day.'

'It will last for years,' I said. I bent the pages back and they whirred as my thumb loosened them.

'Ah, the years!' he said, meaning the flowing of the pages. But we laughed as he said it. Had Father said the same thing he would have expected us to be moved.

I thought, how long would it take to fill a book like this, with my small handwriting? And now I am at the bottom, already, of the third page.

I am glad Mr Wallace made it so clear this is not a diary! I could never sit down each evening and think my life so interesting I feared I might forget we had visitors for lunch, and beef for dinner and the groceries delivered from town. Although diaries seem to have become a thing lately. Nan has kept one consistently all this year, a little fat red-covered one which she said was to help her get over her grief. I would have thought there was nothing more likely to make her think of it so often. Every day, she says, she asks herself what *precisely* her feelings are at this point in her life. Even Frances began one at New Year. For a few weeks the dear girl made a great show of sitting with it open on her lap each evening. Father said she was as likely to persist with it as any of the rest of us were to read Gibbon. I remember Mr Wallace pouncing on him for that. 'I should certainly hope they wouldn't waste their youth doing any such thing.' Father had looked at him sharply for a moment. Mother made that fluttering fluting noise, like a kind of confused dove, which she does whenever she feels her husband has been crossed. I suppose she has seen him so often break out into irritation, and that sound is something of a little last-minute prayer. Fortunately Mr Wallace amuses him or he would not be asked to visit us so often. So rather mildly Father admitted there were indeed other books we could be reading. 'Although they never do.'

'I'm reading *Uncle Tom's Cabin*,' Frances said.

'There,' said Mr Wallace. He held out both hands as if to say, what better example could you have?

Father ran his hand over her hair, in a way that he had seldom done with the rest of us. 'Well you might,' he told her. 'The country's so full of liberal rot you might as well bone up on all you can.'

At that Nan looked down at a glove she was mending. You could tell she was terrified that Father might begin on political schoolteachers and their corrupting influence. The decline of the young is one of his favourite themes, although he will go so far as to admit that there are exceptions. Sam for the time being strikes him as 'solid'. But Mr Wallace came to the rescue there as well. He turned Father back to Gibbon, which is like turning a bull back to its favourite paddock. The men were at once chatting about Basil the Second, and that marvellous annotation. When Mr Wallace said some phrase in Latin, Father was so diverted that at last he took his handkerchief from his pocket, brushing it against his eyes. 'Mind you, that'll go too,' he said. 'That will go with the rot.'

I expect he meant that no one would learn Latin. I have heard Father say that if there was a son in the family he could educate him better at home, in two hours a day, than by sending him to that damned school in town for a year. When he says that he usually taps the glass panel in front of the bookshelves where he keeps his student texts. 'They'll all make a bonfire of course one day,' he says. He so seldom takes any of them out that I wonder why he thinks a son would be avid to get at them. If Father does read in the evenings it is either newspapers from Auckland or some journal he subscribes to from England. I know, even as I write this, I am too critical of him. There is little enough harm, surely, in a wealthy solicitor wanting his family to believe that his real calling was to be a scholar.

I have asked Father several times will he teach me Latin. It pleases him that I ask, but he has always put it off and now he says it is too late. 'If you don't imbibe it from the age of nine or ten,' he tells me. And he opens his closed fist with a kind of puff, as though what flies out is the chance I shall never have and the fault somehow is my own.

It is curious how everyone believes Father when he talks like this. As they also believe he is disturbed whenever he says he is, and that he is truly angry when he raises his voice. Mother you would expect to, but why anyone else? It would be unbearable for her to know that once you take Father's little performances away you have taken half the man. Since he was twenty-three years old and a clever young man at that other Cambridge, the English one, he has done not a single thing except grow rich, marry and get himself four daughters who are already or about to be as tall as himself – his 'twenty-four feet of female issue'. He called us that to Mother once during an argument. He said it as he drew her chair back for her after a squabble that had lasted the whole meal. He remembered even then that manners were his strong point.

For all their bickering, though, Frances is the best with him. She simply will not be intimidated, unlike the two older girls who fear him still quite as much as they did when they were children. That is why I despise Mary so much. Now that she is married and living thirty miles off, and happier so she tells Nan than she ever expected to be, she still felt that she must name her first son after Father, whom she has never liked. When I think of her doing that I think of a woman who is in the open air, say, who has freedom and fulfilment and can walk whichever way she wishes, but turns her back on that and goes back to a prison, because liberty has frightened her and Father's name is on the padlock.

I have said how Mary was the one of us who was beautiful. Height with her was a gift, because she carried herself so well. Her bust is perfect and her hair the kind that flares red in artificial light and gold in sunlight. When she lived at home men kept coming to the house as though compelled. I was Frances's age and I adored her. I understood quite perfectly as they leaned over her, or looked in that way which for all the polish in the world remains what it is, so savage and demanding that I do not know why women take it for something else. Or in summer when she was dressed for tennis – so dazzling she could have commanded them anything. Yet in all that loveliness there was a centre which was not only conventional but silly.

But why on earth all this about Mary!

I am surprised how one comes to seem someone else, the minute one begins to write. This is certainly not what I sound like when I talk, and it is hardly what anyone would expect from 'the easy-going one' in the family. Mother describes me as that when she means I am not the ravisher Mary was, nor the soulful type Nan is, nor the charming tom-boy young Frances will probably be for several years yet. I am *good-natured*, which is always a phrase to watch out for. People say it as though it were the very last gift, when the fairy godmother had run out of everything else. And here I am pinning labels so eagerly on all the others, making a cake stall out of the family! I don't altogether like the person who is writing this.

But isn't this pretty much what Mr Wallace warned me of? On the night of my birthday he said in those few minutes we were alone together in the sitting room, and I had taken up his present again to run my fingers across the feel of the leather, 'The thing is to write with utter honesty. If you know you're the only person it's written for, there's no need for anything else.'

Even so, I said, I thought to write even *tolerably* honestly about oneself would be hard. I asked him did he keep a journal himself?

He put his hand for the merest second over mine. 'When I was a student in Sydney and about to reform the world, I believed I owed it to other generations. To write. To give them my thoughts. Nothing cuts you down to size more quickly than realising you don't actually have any!'

Nan and I share a bedroom. This is only since what Mother keeps referring to as her 'heartbreak', when it was thought that if there was one thing which should never be permitted, it was that Nan be left alone. And now two years later I am still here. My sister is propped up in bed writing, even as I sit a few feet away writing this. The difference is that she is composing a letter to her fiancé, and I am merely recording that is what she does. Sam is a year older than Nan. She met him at a picnic a few weeks before last Christmas, when Mother was convinced she was permanently inconsolable. I want to write about the picnic.

We had been asked across to friends at Whitehall. The homestead was near one of those outcrops of rock that can make it seem like paintings of the Wild West. Not far behind the house there is a thirty-foot rise of smooth reddish stone, and behind that a larger outcrop again. Sloped along its sides is a plantation of black pines.

Since the end of the war there has been a craze for picnics. The plan was that we arrive for lunch and return in the late afternoon. Father likes to drive his Wolseley with the hood folded back, while Mother sits beside him in her motoring hat and scarf as primly as if we were in church. This meant we would flash past guests in slower vehicles because Father is not much interested in any speed except the fastest. He raises his gloved hand grandly, and the horn keeps up its goose-cry. He also likes to be standing near the car when other guests pull up. He pats the bright yellow bonnet and pronounces it sound British stuff. He pats it the way you see men pat the neck of a horse, or a beast they're rather proud of. So when Nan said about this picnic that perhaps she would prefer not to go, Father said simply, 'Nonsense', and that was that. I remember she left the room in tears and he said to Mother that he could sympathise with grief, God knows, but the way that girl went on was morbid. He said we would go as a family, he would drive as a Father should with his daughters behind him. So we travelled on a clear Sunday morning with Mother's little silver bottle in her hands, ready to inhale when the dust and the numerous bends made her feel unwell. Frances sulked because she had been reminded she was a girl and not a larrikin. There was to be no yelping about with children younger than herself, or going off climbing rocks with the boys. Nan wore a black ribbon threaded through the throat of her white blouse, and carried a book should she feel like being alone. It was assumed I would work in with the other women, help brew up the large enamel pots of tea, place the paper doilies on the plates before they were handed out. Which was what I did.

And so to the Careys. Father at once joined the men who stood among the parked cars on the lawn. Mother stepped up to the long handsome verandah to be with the older women and, better still, with those who were delicate. That word *delicate*. It is Mother's favourite. It approves of china or furniture or a girl's complexion or kindness in a man. It means people who are aware of Mother's suffering, and especially it covers her own health on most occasions. Its opposite in all of those examples is *coarse*. I have heard her refer to a neighbour's wife as 'coarse' because she helped her husband on the farm only a month after her confinement.

No one will ever explain to Mother that to think as she does, to have everything so neatly in its place and to fear whatever is vital and sprawling and unpredictable, is the cowardice that only Father's money could afford. I think of her sister in the long steep street in Auckland, its sloping down to the park and the gasworks, and the houseful of my cousins who work in shops. They are more intelligent than us but they do not lay claim to our delicacy. One of them is engaged to a man who works for an auctioneer. He has a motorcycle with a sidecar and at weekends they drive about the country. Lizzie has told me how they go to those dark beaches an hour or so from the city. I can feel her long scarf flapping behind me when I think of it – such marvellous freedom. Mother and Father could hardly express their disgust when they heard of it. I said to Nan that they have no idea that their world – *our* world, because it is mine as well – is breaking up. There is nowhere else for our kind to turn to now, unless we change.

Time does not stand still. This I'm sure is why Father is so often angry. I have heard Mr Wallace say to him that the war has altered things for us all. It is not only Europe that can never be the same. I could feel my blood beating faster while Mr Wallace talked. 'You cannot tell young men to go and kill other young men, you cannot tell them what a privilege it is for them to die for *us*, then tell them the sort of lies we are telling them now.'

'What sort of nonsense is that?' Father demanded.

Mr Wallace did not answer him directly. He said, 'Your friend Massey is good with flags and our Higher Duty but he's out of his depth when it comes to how young men feel.'

Father bridled at the prime minister being brought into it. 'Hardly a *friend*,' he said. 'Have you ever heard his accent?'

'You vote for him.'

'He's a bulwark. He's not bloody soft on revolution the way you are, Wallace.'

Mr Wallace roared out his laugh. Then Father saw me at the doorway of his study. He was afraid I may have heard him speak discourteously. He made great play of laughing too, opening his box of cigars and edging them across his desk. 'They're good,' he recommended them. But Mr Wallace said before he took one, 'The world's run out of obedience, Leonard. There has to be something new.'

'There's nothing new in wanting to arm the natives,' Father could not resist. But he said it so that both of them knew it was a joke. It was also teasing Mr Wallace for giving the time he did to arranging classes for adult Maoris. It amused Father enormously to think of trying to make shearers read William Morris at the end of a day's work.

'That's not quite the story,' Mr Wallace said. He takes Father's banter in very good part. And I stood in the passageway outside the study with my cheeks burning as if they had been slapped. The excitement of talk, of *discussion*, is perhaps what I envy most about men.

Always with ideas, and with politics, which seem so often to be ideas distorted with vague examples, I know I go like someone along a dark corridor, quite unsure of my way.

Father was in his element at the picnic. He was with the men standing among the cars. He was unscrewing the top from his hip-flask in its tartan bag as I went to fetch our basket from the back seat. He was in mid-flight. 'They demand wages the country can't sustain. They do their bit for their country then expect easy street for life.' Because he was a lawyer and his words were educated, the farmers he spoke to felt sure they too were right, that the men in the cities, the men back from the war, wanted only to live at their expense.

I took the basket to the trestle tables at the side of the house. Mother stayed in the cool of the verandah and Nan walked slowly towards the paddock at the back, where the grass had been mown short for a cricket pitch. Young men with their shirtsleeves rolled up, and a few of the older men who had removed their waistcoats, were running up bowling, or chasing the ball when it was hit. Frances already was running about with a mob of young boys.

I saw Mr Wallace on the far side of the paddock. He was pushing a wheelchair. It was a young man who had been in Mary's class at school who had lost both legs in France. I had heard Mother say that he had become an atheist and broken his family's heart. Nan was also at the edge of the field. She stood with some other women and when the batsman struck out squarely and the ball flew towards where they stood, the group broke up and scampered. They shrieked and pretended panic, which meant Nan ran slap into a tall man who was standing behind her. She lurched back and he balanced her with his hands. (From such little beginnings, as they say!) I noticed that she was touching the black thread at her throat. With her rather slow lovely smile, it makes her seem somehow so vulnerable. Soon the man fell into step beside her. They sauntered down towards the creek, to the trees where Mr Wallace now sat on a smooth piece of rock beside his friend in the wheelchair.

This may sound as though I do nothing but stand and spy. In fact I was busy helping arrange the tables, with time for only an occasional glance to the paddock with the players. But how little time it requires to take in what goes on between people! I remember the cutlery twinkled in a heap and I began to sort it out. But I saw Mr Wallace light one of his slender cigars and then lean back. I thought he may have been looking across at me, but of course he could just as well have been glancing at any one of a dozen of us. Among my other 'determinations' is that I will not read signs with the eagerness my sister does. It is amazing how often over the years I have seen her titillated by what to me, at least, was no more a 'sign' than a leaf falling from a tree. Although even as I write this, I admit there is something in Mother's declaring I am quite unromantic.

(Now I am in brackets again, which Father believes is a sign of shilly-shallying in *any* writer, I might as well set down that it has taken me three evenings so far to set down this much about the picnic. I am trying to set it out as exactly as I can, and with as little 'dressing up' as I can manage. Yet it is strange how it becomes a sort of story-telling in spite of myself. Back then to Emily!)

I carried plates of food and cups of tea to the elderly women in the shade. I moved backwards and forwards between the kitchen and the long tables outside. Father spoke kindly to me when I asked him what he would like me to bring. 'Whatever you choose for me,' he said. There was no one near him, this was Father being gracious *personally* to one of his daughters. 'There's no one who knows my tastes better than that Em.' And when I returned to him with his plate of sliced ham and pickled onions and tomatoes, he said, 'Make sure you don't spend the day working, do you hear that? Make sure you enjoy yourself.'

There was now a farmer beside him, an Irishman who is what Father calls 'thick-tongued' when he takes him off at home. 'That's right now,' he agreed with Father. 'All work and no play, you know what they say about that.'

I thought if only I had a job like my Auckland cousins, even working in a jeweller's shop as Lizzie did. I don't know if there is anything that would please me quite so much. But Father sees no point in work except to get money. And as he has quite enough of that, it follows *ipso facto* – isn't that what he says? – that when I say I would like a job, he believes I am being perverse. He asks what it would give me that I don't already have.

After lunch the cricket match continued, and the men now seemed to take it more seriously. Father and his friends applauded loudly. Groups of women sat near the willows that lined the creek. The huge boulders on the hillside shimmered in the haze. It was about then, when enthusiasm or relaxation had set on almost everyone, that Mother was certain she wanted to go home.

I could tell how Father was irritated. He tugged at his fingers behind his back, making his joints crack as he said to the little Carey girl she had sent across with the message, 'Tell her I'll be there presently, will you do that for me?' He fished into his trouser pocket and gave the child a coin. When she turned it in her hand and exclaimed 'A shilling!', Father told her, 'For being a good girl.' He followed across the lawn. Then as though a knight entering an arena, the scarf already tied about his lance, he placed his hand on the back of Mother's chair and leaned forward – solicitously, don't they say?

I walked towards the hillside and the great exposed pieces of rock. Some of the children were clambering among them. Their figures were small against the sky when they climbed out and stood on the smoothly levelled tops. I heard Frances's voice, so buoyant and gay, among the shouting and the calls. I loved looking at the hillside, the immobility that had been there for ever, the whooping and hopping of the children across it for so brief a time. The rocks so everlasting, the children just for today. (*Ah now!*, I can hear Mr Wallace say. He thinks 'feminine' thoughts like this take one too much into oneself. What we need today is action!)

[Against her observation about the rocks, and in a more mature hand, Emily MacLeod had written, 'Only *18* years later and how wrong I was! Thomas Carey, who is mentally unbalanced with his debts, believed he could make a fortune from selling the coloured rock for ornamental fireplaces. The outcrop I wrote of then he has half blasted away, and not one order for a fireplace has been received.']

One of the girls from the house, a friend of my sister's rather than of mine, came to say Nan was staying on and could get a ride home later. Wouldn't I stay on too?

My sister waved to me across the paddock, beckoning me to join her where she sat with that same tall man and several other friends. Mr Wallace raised his hand as well. I gestured to the drive at the front of the house, where Mother already sat solidly in the car. Father was crouched, peering beneath a mudguard. I said to the girl that I had better go. 'Father won't be able to cope if there's anything needs doing at home.' I said it lightly. Yet I wanted them to think that I went from daughterly duty rather than because I simply wanted to go. I was glad that the chance had come along.

The country is so lovely in summer at that time of day. To sit in the car, open to the late light and the rushing breeze and it all being gathered in towards one – oh, I enjoy that. How the shadows fling out in broad pools as Father races along the roads, the sun brilliant and chipped behind the trees. People called goodbye, and cadaverous Mr MacLeod made a point of coming to the side of the car. Mother waved gracefully, a little too deliberately so, and Frances shrieked at her friends until Father ordered her to be still. We set off between the oaks that are sixty years old, great feathery giants. The story the Careys tell is that they were planted in the same year as the last European was killed in the district. The man is supposed to have crossed the boundary line at Maungatautari and was murdered with his own pocketknife. They say had he not been drunk the night before, then he might have run away as his two companions did. As the unfortunate man's name was Sullivan, there is a moral in it all too good to miss. Father likes to repeat the story which he calls an *exemplum*, and the Irish, excessive drink and the unreliable natives are despatched together.

Once at home, Mother went directly to bed. I cooked Father steak, which we ate in the kitchen. It is a habit we have got into when, on very rare occasions, there are only the two of us. There is a sense that we are doing something out of the ordinary, and are somehow closer than usual. It makes him sometimes reminisce about living in 'digs', as though to be out of the dining room and its polished reflections allows nostalgia its rein. As it darkened Father lit two candles rather than switch on the light. He was more than usually jovial because during the afternoon he and Mr Carey had decided on buying a racehorse. Carbine blood, he told me, on the mare's side.

'Is that good?' I said.

'Ask me after the Cup in three years time. We mightn't ever have to work again.' He recalled an acquaintance who had won the big race at Auckland several years before. 'A horse with no class at all to speak of. I think they picked the sire's name out of a hat. We'll use the same man to train our one.' Then he told me they would call it Caius. After his college. I said was that making up for not having a son to send there? I thought he might think that rather abrasive of me. But he thought it rather witty, a thing which always surprises him in a woman. He then paid me the compliment of talking with me as he does with Mr Wallace. He insisted that I fetch an Australian claret from the rack in the dining

97

room, and that we share it. That is not the same thing as having half each, mind you. But it was a gesture I was grateful for. He told me as though I had never heard it before about his friend the philologist who was sent down for swiping at a bystander with the processional cross at Easter. 'He was in High Church stuff up to his elbows. Pusey and Faber and Newman and the rest of them on his walls where the rest of us had real pictures, as we thought.' He laughed as he told me.

The girls did not come back until after ten. Father opened another bottle and was grateful when I questioned him about being a boy from the other side of the world, thrown in amongst all that. The buildings and the talk and the study which must have been such a privilege to do. His chatting on about it I suppose was part of my own dream. *Away*. The candlelight made him look younger, as it does with anyone. And as I had drunk more wine than is usual for me, I felt strangely moved to see him happy like this. Because Father's life with Mother must be as unendurable as a man might know, to live with a boring invalid one once thought so essential to one's life.

[Another note, again in the older hand but in a cheaper ink, which has faded brown against the earlier script's Indian black: 'I am less sure now than I was then. From their graves, the voice of each seems to state their defence more strongly.']

I laughed at his stories and encouraged him. I thought how at least for now, for this hour and a half, we were not father and daughter so much as we were friends. When he fell into different voices and in one story stood up to mime the parts, I saw flicker up what he must have been when he was a young man. I saw more clearly than I usually do the charm that people speak of, not its shadow which is only habit. Then quite suddenly his mood altered. He raised both palms outwards. It made me think of a man in a row of black minstrels. 'Ah,' he said. 'All that. All that.'

'That?' I said.

'Might as well be a thousand years ago.' He picked wax from the edge of the candlestick. 'I saw Gladstone at Victoria Station one day. Giving a dog something from his pocket. A piece of sugar or something.' He then mentioned other names as in a litany, names that even I recognised.

He said, 'It's like telling a story about someone else.' And he spoke with dismissive contempt of his own father. 'Made a mint from furnishing the Waikato troops. A kind of peripatetic grocer. He boasted he could deliver tea and sugar inside the barricades.' Father snorted. 'But you've heard all about him?'

'Yes,' I said.

'His dream was to send his son over there to be educated. Cut a dash in a country where he couldn't earn a living for himself.'

'He sounds very – attached,' I said.

Father went on, 'I lived his life for him, a son can't do more than that. His cousin who was a cleric got me into the university. His money got me my profession. This table we're sitting at was his. So was the one in the dining room – after he had gone up in the world. There's not a thing I have ever done that he would not have wanted.' Father tipped the bottle to drain the last dark drops.

I should have said to him, 'But Father, isn't that what you are doing with us?' But in my cowardly way I did not. Perhaps at that moment and never again he may have conceded that what I said was so. I mean *just*. But it was not only cowardice, my not speaking out. I realised I would not be playing by the rules. For I picked up with the certainty of instinct that what Father was saying was his code for something else. Although I cannot explain how I could be so certain, I was sure beyond doubt that it was not even his father he spoke primarily against. But Mother. He was telling me of disgust and of a wasted life.

Father let his opened palms fall flatly on the edge of the table. It was the action of a man who accepted his fate as final. I thought then how my one obligation now is that he shall never regret how he tried to speak to me.

He brushed his hand against my hair, and said why didn't we sit in candlelight like this more often? 'There's as much peace here, like this, as we're ever likely to find.'

I said the open air must have tired me, I really must go to bed.

[On the opposite page: 'I have read this section while young Alex turns and sighs with a chill he has picked up. When his hair is wet with perspiration and clinging to his forehead, he makes me think of his father coming in from the rain. And I think now what I wrote then must be more of a story than I intended. I mean the sentences that I put into the mouths of Father and Nan and the others. My memory cannot have been that exact. Not anywhere near so. I presume I was following some instruction or other from Mr Wallace. I remember – dimly enough – one opinion of his, that if you did try to record what people said, tried with honesty and no attempt at 'frills', then the *gist* of the truth would be there, whatever else you missed out. There must have been something in what he said. I haven't looked at these pages for years, and I am amazed at how like Father they still sound!']

It is several days later but I have not had time to 'tell all', as Nan likes to say in her letters. So I go back to the day and the night of the picnic, because already they seem some kind of pivot. (I would hate anyone to ask me what *exactly* I mean!)

I left Father in the kitchen. I lay in bed with the light off, although it was not at all late. There was such luxury in having the room to myself. It made me realise how much my life and my sister's are woven together. Singing or sulking, it hardly matters which, Nan is always there. In fact a houseful of women, all the time, yet all our activity circling about one male presence we think of mainly in terms of cajoling or placating. Whenever I hear in church some bland phrase like 'the house of the Father', I think quite naturally of ourselves out here.

The blinds were raised as I like them to be but as Nan swears keeps her awake. The moon was almost full and the trees set hard and dark against the sky. The slow *hush* coming in at the open window from the pines. Mother says it is like the sound of the sea, and so must be listened to because it makes her think of something distant and sad. 'The sea!' she says, raising one hand. For ten years in fact she has cried off going to the coast, as Father suggests we might, because of the discomfort of summer at the beach.

Yet I love them, I often enough think to myself as I lie awake. Beautiful senseless Mary and romantic Nan and Frances who will not be like any of us. And Mother who is bored and boring, her soul a pampered puppy lying in a basket. As I write that I harden myself to believing there is virtue in telling the truth. It is only truth which may be unkind, not myself for thinking it! And I tell myself too that the more clearly I see their weaknesses, they must of course see mine. I think of how my own mood changes several times a day, no matter how uneventful it may seem to someone else. Something said to me in passing, a book I am reading, a half-rotted bird at the side of the drive – things as incidental as these can swing us on ourselves, like the turning of a tide. Why do we expect consistency when it so goes against nature? Everything in our background teaches us, of course, to deny such a fact.

Naturally such profundity was not limited to that night! My mind tends to go over and over a few worn tracks like this. I am reminded of one of Father's trotters, round and round the same circuit, and such a jangle when it passes!

And now here is the story of another life. Nan came in at half past ten. I closed my eyes but she dropped her shoe, saying 'Shh' aloud to herself. So I did what she wanted and spoke to her. She crossed the room to sit on my bed. Her face and arms were a lovely pink from her day in the sun, although tomorrow she would be smothered with layers of balsam cream. I raised my hand and laid my fingers against her cheek. 'Scorching,' I told her.

'Yes,' she said, 'I never learn, do I?'

She took my fingers and pressed them as sisters are meant to do at moments of confidence. Yes, she had met this marvellous man, a schoolteacher near Hamilton. She laughed and shook out her hair, and the young man who had died in France two years before, of gangrene after a leg had been removed, was buried at last.

In time I learn how he fishes on the river and reads books in French, and because he is 'cultured' Nan leafs through books which he lends her. She sits through the afternoons with the books beside her on the sofa. She takes them up and puts them down, smooths their pages in her lap. She reads for twenty minutes, for half an hour. Then she says if one of us walks into the room, 'You know what Sam says about this way I have my hair up? Well, he wants me to wear it down.' And my irritation again is not with her so much as with all those things that have made her, have made us, the way we are. (Have made *me*, is what I really mean.)

I look at that phrase I have just used, 'those things'. How imprecise it is. And I must not make excuses for it. I remember Mr Wallace saying how there is no half way with honesty. To stop short of where it leads is not to be honest at all. So without being *trained* to think, without understanding how money works, for example, or knowing another language, or even without much idea of what life is like in Auckland, I try to think past my confusions. Everything in my life has steered me towards being a replica of Mother. To organise a tidy house, to live 'decently', to ensure family comfort as Father does its security, is to live out one's allotted part. Or Mary's certainty that to give her loveliness to her husband is all that life requires. So I come back time and again to what I do *not* believe – all that, for instance – yet am not quite sure what I do.

Last week when Mr Wallace was here we strolled around the edges of the tennis court before dinner. I told him about a book that Sam had given Nan which bores her to tears. It was about a woman who wanted freedom to become an explorer, if you please. He said in his slightly sardonic way, 'Even with the vote and the rest of it?'

I said, 'You mustn't humour me, Mr Wallace. I take it more seriously than Nan does.' I smiled as I said it, because he is the one man who would not have made such a mistake.

'What would you have, then?' he said.

'I would like a job,' I said. What could be more simple? Yet to say it outright to someone who understood! There was an elation in knowing that Mr Wallace listened to me, as though my saying it was half way towards possessing what I wanted.

We had stopped on the far side of the court. The lines had been chalked that week, and were squarely vivid in the late evening light. Behind us was a tall clump of camellias, a mass of dark shining leaves now that it was nearing the end of summer. In September the white and pink blooms were as exquisite as if they had been painted. I touched one of the thick smooth leaves and felt the blood coursing through my ears. Mr Wallace's hands were running along the canvas border at the top of the net, his face turned towards me. He had said nothing after I finished speaking.

I looked over towards the house. Mother and the girls were moving in and out of the dining room. Father came in and poured himself a glass from the decanter on the sideboard. He replaced the stopper and left the room. Frances came in alone, looked for something she could not find, and flicked the rim of the crystal fruitbowl before she too went out. For a few minutes the room was bright and empty and expectant. It seemed we were looking across to a stage. And then I said, 'Oh, I expect it is all talk finally. It's a happy enough world when we look across at it now. In a few minutes' time we'll be at that table, we'll eat and drink, and we shall be the centre of our universe. That is the last and strongest thing Father's money can buy. It can make us *believe* in what it buys.'

Again I felt that Mr Wallace was looking at me, looking *up* at me. (I am hardly ever with a man when I do not feel my height.) I knew at once there was a new tension – I can't think of what else to call it. Perhaps I half expected him to kiss me. (There – even *that* is written down.) Yet while I considered that and waited for it, my mind moved further back, as if to observe what I thought. So while I felt the vein beating so thickly in my neck that I turned a little from him, while my fingers slipped against the dark glossy leaf, I pondered too whether it would be a bad thing if Mr Wallace did.

What I mean by that is very simple. I knew that if we kissed, if he drew me closer to him as I wanted him to do, I would at that same moment lose him. Because we would never speak so frankly with each other again. I would be a woman in the way that means he wanted to make love to me, and for me he would be a man in quite that same way. Yet I doubt that people are ever totally open together again, once they are set as lovers. By then there is too much given, and too much to lose. After our bodies have come into it, I suppose I am saying, it is that much more difficult to say, 'Come, let us exchange our minds.' I could not lose that with Mr Wallace. So I turned and we began to walk back along the edge of the court. As he took up his step beside mine, his fingers brushed against me. I willed him to keep on speaking, since for the moment I could not. Knowing at the same time there was something so absurd in what I thought, it came on me as intensely as physical pain. I was so confused, and yet the confusion too had intimately to do with what I wanted, which is to understand myself.

From across the court I heard the chinking of cutlery as Frances fiddled at the table. We walked in silence. We knew that we had been on the brink of where we had never been before, and it was I who had drawn back. I had taken Mr Wallace back with me.

Twenty minutes later, after the celery soup, Father was standing at the head of the table. He carved the joint of lamb which he pointed out was in his care from the moment of conception until now, steaming and succulent on our plates. He had supervised its breeding and its killing, he had looked in on its baking even to the sprigs of rosemary he had handed to the cook.

I have been over and over our walk, the dinner, the conversations. During most of the meal I was silent, which allowed Frances to frolic and Nan to glow. The men were in good humour and Mother smiled, the matron at her table. My own mind was full of how I had acted like a fool. What was wrong with me that I had actually believed I could not hold feeling and mind in some kind of balance? Why had I thought a woman was capable only of one or the other, or of one in sequence with the other, but not together as a rational, feeling being? And now I hate even the words I used to think about it, this chopping up of life into 'mind' and 'body'.

When Father spoke to me I smiled. I affected a distant interest which was false. It covered my anger at myself. I listened to my sisters responding to Mr Wallace's teasing and to Father's attempt at epigrams. Mother from time to time put in a word of no consequence. So the old game went on. The blue pattern of my plate blurred in front of me, the reflections on the cutlery lengthened and brightened through my tears. I thought what I now write down, that for all my saying how there is nothing more important than to understand, I could not have made more a botch of it.

I lied and said I had a headache. I said they mustn't mind if I went to bed.

This is some months later. Two things now dominate everything else in the house. One is Nan's wedding, and the other is that Father has lost money because of Mary's husband.

I look from our bedroom window and see how the leaves are

falling. Look out quickly at the line of chestnuts to the main road, and it is as if the trees have been scorched. We have had so little wind this year that the leaves stay on and on. We have had a run of frosts, and the days are cold and clear.

Nan is away this weekend at her fiancé's. Father has gone to Auckland to consult with other businessmen who have lost money on the same enterprise. Last night he and Mr Wallace sat up late in front of the fire in his study. Mr Wallace asked me was it the thought of winter that made me melancholy, so I suppose I must appear rather plain and grim. But he asked it wryly; it may have had some joking edge to it that I did not pick up. He has been down south for a month, visiting political friends. But he does not say much about that, not in any particulars, because of Father. He sometimes refers to men called Webb and Holland, and Father at once goes silent or cracks his knuckles.

Earlier we had talked together in the study while I lit the fire, and before Father came in we sat in that lovely atmosphere of leather and bookshelves and the firelight quivering through the room. Mother was upstairs, Frances was still out, late as it was, with her pony. I said, 'It seems such a time since we saw you last.'

He took his watch from his pocket and wound the ribbed knob on the top. He was seated in front of the fire, rocking slightly towards me, then away.

'Working away for the revolution,' he said.

'Don't tease,' I said.

'A fact. Give or take a little.'

'Then I wish you'd tell me more about that, too,'

'*Too*? What else am I holding back?'

'I wish that I knew more about it. I know it's time to level things out – between classes and people, I mean. But even a child knows that much.'

'It's only fine print once you've agreed on that.'

'No,' I said. 'It's still looking through a frosted window.'

There was that clear metallic snap as Mr Wallace closed his watch. He said, 'I don't quite know what that means.'

'How the ideas *work* – that's what I want to know.'

I waited a moment and the cones crackled behind Mr Wallace. 'Yes?' he said.

'You'll say I'm being fanciful again, but to me – to people living the way you know we do out here – well, ideas are just like trees or scenery or whatever that you see in a play. You know what they are and yet you don't believe they're real. You understand what I mean?' Then I laughed at myself. How it takes so little of Mr Wallace's company to set me off like this. 'I do harangue you, don't I?'

He told me if I really did want to know, it was easy enough. 'There are books – pamphlets – plenty of material.'

'But who knows about them except you? I have never met anyone else.'

He told me there were far more people who thought as he did than I realised. There was a group that met once a week in Hamilton, for example. They were teachers and railway men and shopkeepers. As well as men like himself.

'People who are rich?'

'Money doesn't stop you thinking.'

'And your friends down south?'

'Miners, workers. You mustn't think they are not intelligent because they work hard.'

'And they tolerate you?' I knew my question was provoking, but suddenly I wanted to sting him, hurt him. He looked down at me sharply, where I knelt between him and the fire. 'There are men there who went to gaol rather than fight in the war. There are miners from the West Coast who can speak and reason better than someone like myself. There are others who believe with such passion that to talk to them is like this.' He held his hand across me towards the fire. I saw his palm glow, the fire leap at the ring he wore. 'If I can help people like that in however small a way, then there's some purpose to it.'

It was not like Mr Wallace to give himself away so directly. But I was not prepared to lose where we were for the sake of good manners. So I kept on. It was important that I knew.

'Purpose to your life?'

'If you like,' he said. 'If we must come totally into the open.'

I tried to imagine him among the only 'workers' I knew – the men on the farms, the ones who felt awkward if Mother spoke to them and who laughed too easily when Father jollied them along.

Then I knew I was thinking of it as Father himself would have done, that I was Father's victim as indeed he wanted me to be, in a sense. I could not think of them as being like ourselves.

I said, 'You mustn't mind my trying to find out.'

And Mr Wallace said, 'My dear Emily, you can ask anything you want.'

He sat forward in Father's leather chair, his arms folded, his voice closer to me than it had been even that evening on the tennis court. I felt the warmth begin to rise in my neck, my throat. But I listened carefully to what was more important than that. Some of it I had heard, of course, but in such a different way. Father sometimes slapped down his folded paper on the table and railed at the workers forming groups strong enough to defy the men who paid them. When Father spoke of them, they were advancing figures carrying flares, come to burn us out. It excited me to see his anger. Yet now Mr Wallace said very quietly, 'It comes down to whether we believe one man owns more than another because of a pre-ordained right. Say yes to that, and everything else follows – everything that you have here, that I have myself. Say no, and quite another world follows.'

He moved his head slightly towards one wall and then the other, meaning all this must go, my world as much as his. And it struck me there was also something curiously sad in his movement, in the way he looked older in the firelight than he did when we spoke by day, and that as he spoke, what attracted my attention most was the ring that glinted on his moving hand. I said to him, yes, I could see the endless chain from where we sat, from the comfort of our lives to the people who paid rents to Father and beyond to those who paid them in turn, until we came to those who had nothing to give except their bodies, who must sell themselves. But Mr Wallace disregarded that. He said, 'Once you decide that the way we live is based either on deception or force, then it is only a matter of deciding *how* you will have things changed.'

I think he waited for me to ask him more about the theory of this world. Instead, I said to him, 'And where will you fit in? How much will you give up?'

'I don't know yet how much.' I felt his hand first on my

shoulder, and then his fingers spanning my neck. The physical joy
of it was oh so clearly inseparable from the excitement in my mind
at what we had spoken of – the smashing of the room we sat in. I
thought while his hand moved across my shoulder and onto my
breast. If only he would say that out loud! If he would ask me to
smash it with him! His lips were on my throat then on my cheeks.
I smelt tobacco on his breath and felt the rasp of his beard across
my face. He was the first man who had kissed me. Then we heard
Frances calling out. Mr Wallace quickly stood and stepped
towards the fire. He rested his elbow along the mantelpiece and
tapped with his ring on the marble ledge. Frances swung open the
door and snapped on the lights.

'You can't see properly with just that fire, can you?' Her cheeks
were flushed with the cold air she had been riding through. She
still carried her crop and cap in her hand.

Mr Wallace smiled at her as he always does. 'Idly chatting
away. And I suppose I've quite stopped your sister getting on with
her work.'

'Work's right.' Frances tapped my arm lightly with her crop.
'I'm the one who has to go down to the kitchen and give a hand.'

The sudden light had thrown us back to where we usually were
– to dutiful daughter and family friend. I wanted to tell him what I
could not dare to say in words, in case he took me for extravagant.
I longed to tell him as I saw him standing there after Frances went
from the room and he moved a small marble ornament along the
top of the mantelpiece. His head was bent and he looked tired, I
thought, his eyes were hooded as he watched the small carved bear
between his fingers. What I wanted to tell him was not political
even, it had nothing to do with the words like 'federation' and
'workers' co-operative' that he and Father discussed, and that
Father spoke with a special venom. It was simply an image that
came into my mind. I wanted to say how I saw Father crouching at
the damp entrance to a cave, looking back onto the scraps of
rotting hide, the piles of bone, he had stored and treasured. While
we – Mr Wallace and I – we were facing day.

[In that other ink, on the blank facing page: 'How grand!']

Father came in a little later. I obliged him by taking up the
empty coal-scuttle and leaving. Before I was out of the study he

had already begun. 'There's not a chance of salvaging it. Not now.'

'No collateral?' Mr Wallace asked.

'Not a skerrick.'

I heard Mr Wallace's ring beating again against the mantelpiece before he said, 'Quarries are always risky things. There was that man Murphy at Eureka.'

As I hesitated just beyond the door, Father was saying, 'My daughter has married a fool incapable of licking a stamp, and it has cost me eight thousand pounds.'

I went to Mother's room. She lay with a handkerchief folded like a bandage around her fingers, which she then dabbed at her lips. She said, 'Her father will never forgive her for this.' For once there was real drama for her to weep to. I looked at her swollen eyes, the trickle of saliva at the corner of her mouth. But I touched her hand and pointed out that Father losing an investment was not going to put us on the streets. I said it gaily enough. And Mother said, had I forgotten how Father had given us everything? I should be a comfort to him, rather than joke about it.

'I'm trying to say there are things besides money.'

Then she said, 'Do you think he doesn't feel shame a lot more than the actual money part of it? A man respected by everyone in the district for a lifetime and then humiliated like this?'

It is now late and I sit in my own room. I have drawn the curtain back. There is a thin moon and the softest pricking of rain against the glass. Our mornings of brilliant frost are over, then. Yet it is so still. Occasionally I hear a swishing, so faint I am then uncertain if indeed I did hear it. I suppose it is a chestnut leaf just outside my window, brushing against the wall. I feel how warm my cheeks are. I am still excited by my talk with Mr Wallace. I am pleased I could think intelligently about what he said, and accept so easily his kissing me. When his hand moved from my shoulder and across me I was nervous but not confused. If he had touched me more I would not have minded. (There! It has taken me an effort to write that!) I think about the new order that we have no choice but to accept and then give our loyalty to. Although I know there is a danger in taking that too dramatically, as there is in thinking that if once I were away from here, away from the house and the family and the awful limitations, then I would be plumb in the centre of *Life*. I know that isn't true. But it is true that both those facts exist, and are very close together – the fact of what the world must one day become, and the fact of living more completely than I ever might do here. I quite know too that there is a kind of rhetoric in words like 'the future' and 'the people' and 'somewhere else'. There is that flare about them which is the wind slapping at banners, flags streamed out against the sky. That kind of excitement. But I know too that I am convinced of it when I am *not* excited. I do not have to be bored, or talking with Mr Wallace, or drudging in the kitchen, for me to hope for it. It has nothing to do with whether my cheeks burn, or a man wants to kiss me, or with the pleasures there would be merely to escape from Mother, Nan, Arthur's quarry, etc., etc. The truth is always there, whatever one's reasons for needing it.

[On the page facing this, and written much later, a long note in pencil. The writing is far less careful than usual, as though it were written quickly: 'Mrs Norwood has come to see me again. It is the third time in three months. The first time she talked to me about herself and Mr Larsen it was touched on carefully, almost like a naughty child owning up and then relieved she could cry. But now she speaks to me in the language she and the man must use together. My instinct is to tell her not to use such words in my house. Then of course I realise that I am being Mother all over again, that I am setting up my delicacy as the standard all must be judged by.

'She told me today that she loathes herself. When her mind is not actually set on rutting, as she says, then her feeling is one of disgust. I give her tea and tell her to take her time telling me, she knows I am her friend and she need not apologise to *me*. While the truth is quite the opposite. I mean we are not friends at all. I find her so heavy, so physically dominant. Her speech is so limited and imprecise that it takes considerable effort for me not to show how it irritates me. But none of that is to the point. The woman suffers more deeply than anyone I have ever seen. When she compares herself to an animal, to something that has no will, I see her move with that reluctant, unfathomably pitiful slouch of a beast confined to the few feet of its stall. There is not a thing I can say to help her.

'What strikes her now that Mr L says he will have nothing to do with her is that she believes in God in order to make bargains with Him. To say 'Give me Mr L and let my family die', to try like that old story to exchange her soul for what she wants. I say very little, which the poor woman takes as a sign of my sympathy, but I am out of my depth. There is one part of her that so desperately wants to be punished, to suffer for what she does. Another would go through fire for those few spasms, I suppose, that rule her so completely. I used to believe that everyone who had experienced 'love' with a man had been to much the same place. With differences, of course, but on the same scale, as it were. I now see how very ignorant that was. This woman is as far from anything I have apprehended as we both are from the moon.

'It is 11 years this week since Mr MacLeod died.']

Well, the wedding is over. Everyone (at least all the women) exclaimed when Nan walked into the old church on the corner of the main road, where the polished timber seemed darker for the great banks of flowers set at the sides of the altar. Frances and I walked a few steps behind her. Mother, her handkerchief at the ready, stood beside Mary. And next to her, as grave as if he had been carved on a coin, her husband who had caused the family such pain. Later in the day, after the toasts and the wine had done their work for peace, Arthur and Father made up. Or in Mother's words, the breach was healed. Mary cried when they shook hands. She kissed Father's cheek and squeezed her husband's hand at the same time. Mother, who was watching, was overcome. She said if they only knew the happiness they gave her. Frances was sitting beside Mother. She raised her eyebrows slightly when she caught my gaze. And Father patted Mother as he would a nervous horse, that manly mix of authority and comfort. But he looked pleased when Mary took his arm and they moved into the room where the dancing was under way. The string band took up that waltz from *The Merry Widow*. The guests applauded, or called out amusing things, as he and his daughter took the floor. Which was Arthur's cue to go and sit with Mother. She had said 'Ah!' when the music started up, and now she closed her eyes as well, rocking very slightly to the rhythm. 'My favourite,' she said, 'did someone ask for it?' If only her chest were up to dancing herself, how she would have loved it! 'But that's not to be, I'm afraid, Arthur.'

So the afternoon and evening passed. Handsome dresses and witty speeches, and music and much drinking. The bride and Sam drove off and we girls, and all the guests, lined the drive from the house. Mother and Father stood arm in arm on the verandah. I was moved myself. My eyes blurred while the wheels of the car flickered them away, and I thought how trivial it was, how mean-spirited, to look so eagerly as I did for the small follies all of us have.

'See you soon!' Nan called out. She gave a special wave to me, and I raised both my hands in waving back. I heard Mr Wallace's laughing just behind me. And Frances, so boisterous and chubby and uncaring for sentiment, was the one who turned and ran inside in tears.

Back inside, Mary sang two English folk songs and 'The Snowy Breasted Pearl'. She looked so grand, so stunningly lovely, that we believed we applauded her voice.

I sat with my cousins from Auckland whose 'commonness' Mother was a little on edge about. I said to Lizzie who works in a jeweller's shop, 'Can I come up to stay for a while soon?'

'Oh, do,' she insisted. It was ages since they'd seen me, she said, really seen me. I like her frank grey eyes, her mass of tumbling black hair.

I told her, 'If you knew how I envy you lot up there. All that living to get on with.'

'Lord, try getting into town every morning by nine o'clock and see how you like living.'

'Doesn't Tim pick you up? I hear he's got a car these days.'

'He adores the thing,' she said.

Lizzie's sister came in on that. 'He's even painted that white strip round the tyres, you know? Paints it every mid-week so it dries out spick and span for the weekend.'

'Do you wear goggles and all?' I asked. I was thinking of Father, honking his way through the country roads.

Both the girls laughed at the idea of it. 'It is a closed motor, silly.'

Then, as drearily as Mother would have said it, I heard myself remarking, 'Tim must be doing very well?'

Lizzie clapped her hands at the very thought of it. 'Apart from the car and my engagement ring we haven't got a brass razoo between us. That's what makes the parents so mad. "Don't think you can live on love for ever".'

Her sister said, 'Not that they've got a bean themselves, mind.'

'On to the voice of experience and caution, are we?' Tim said. He had come and stood behind his fiancée, resting his arm about her waist. He is small-built and dark and more fun than all of my male cousins together, who are a sombre lot. He is Irish, which worries them a little, although the fact that he drinks hardly at all, and has a steady job, almost makes up for that. As if *he* could judge anyone, Father says of Lizzie's Dad. That whole outfit enjoys life too much to make a success of anything.

Tim now spread his arms and said to Lizzie, making sure that his future father-in-law would hear, 'Well, girl, tell the old folks we're expecting a turn quite up to this one.' He said it with good-humoured irony, yet with such an edge that what his opened arms included was at once diminished. He grinned at Lizzie, directing her to take in everything about her, the house, the music, the wedding cake on its four squat silver pillars, the whole feeling one had on looking about that life was *solid*, to use one of Father's favourite words. The way Tim looked about implied that if indeed there was a Rock of Ages, then we were standing on a fragment of it. And if anyone fancied asking, 'But how about a bit of *spirit*, a touch of soul to go with it?', then the furniture and the cutlery and the stocked cupboards and the flattering mirrors all answered, 'Spirit? What about it? Tell us where it is and we'll order a hundred-weight.'

I felt all this in that quick exchange between my cousins. Lizzie's father answered Tim, 'It's leaner times up our way, young fellow. You'll be lucky if there's lemonade.'

I watched Lizzie lean forward, so easily and naturally, to take Tim's hand again when he removed his arm from her waist and kept up his joking with her father. Her hair swayed as she moved, the bright light running mazes in it. She tugged at his hand. 'We'll look after Em, won't we, if she comes to stay?'

Uncle Fred looked at me. 'No running amok after 4 a.m. We do have rules.'

I told Lizzie why I wanted to come. I said I knew Tim was in the Labour Party, wasn't he? I wanted to attend some meetings.

'You mean you're joining up?'

'I want to know what it's really like.'

'But that's marvellous, Em!' She told me how Tim was on the committee for Auckland West, I could meet as many people as I liked. 'Of course Dad has him on about talking like a socialist and then riding round in a better car than Massey's.' She tugged again at her fiancé's hand. 'Dad says you're a spy in the ranks, doesn't he, love?'

Tim said, 'Give us ten years. We're the obvious thing for this country.'

Father had joined us and took him up. He smiled to show he made light of it, but I noticed how one hand was turning a coin in his trouser pocket. Oh, I knew all the signs! I knew he was holding himself back, because of courtesy, because of the wedding. 'Give you lot ten years, Tim, and there won't be a man with his own land in the country. Bright young chaps like you – what do you have in common with lay-abouts and reds?'

Lizzie jumped up to kiss Father on the cheek. 'Uncle,' she said, 'we won't be happy until we have all your sort behind bars.' She knew how he loved the young to fuss at him.

'Come on, girl,' he warned her, dabbing at his cheek. 'You're gagging the truth with those tactics.' But he allowed himself to laugh off the impending doom of Labour. He was content with telling them, 'There's this too of course, Tim. I've seen you young bloods on the ran-tan before this. Give you a few years and you'll make *me* look like a radical.'

One of the hired waiters came round with fresh glasses of champagne. The 'young ones' took to the floor again. I danced with one of our neighbour's sons, who tried to speak with his lips together because he had snapped off most of a front tooth in the first rugby match of the season. I said I heard he had a hard time down at Taupiri.

'They never play clean over there,' he said. 'Ever hear anyone say they do?'

But the dancing was fun. Frances said she could never hear enough. There were a dozen or so of us who urged the band not to let up. Most of the girls were wearing long strings of beads that flew about when we danced the new pieces. Tim said it was like trying to dance in a roomful of scimitars. Then there was a shriek from another of the cousins. We turned to see her with both hands clutching at her throat, red beads cascading down the front of her white frock. The beads bounced like hail as they hit the floor. And so the wedding finished with us all on our hands and knees, groping in corners, bumping against each other, calling out like children as we scrambled to recover the rolling beads. We then flopped in the chairs along the side of the room.

'That's that,' Lizzie said. 'I couldn't move now if you paid me.'

'That'll come too,' Father called at her. 'Tim's mate Holland will pay you for less than that.'

Lizzie sighed and rolled her eyes at him. 'Will you be a dear, Uncle, and just put your whip down for a little?'

Behind me, I heard Mother say to her sister-in-law, 'She gets away with too much, that one.'

'Don't they all?' my aunt said.

The next afternoon, after our relatives had left, and we sat in the small conservatory in the surprisingly warm late sun, Father said benignly, 'One thing I'll give your brother Fred, it doesn't seem to worry him that he hasn't made his mark.' He means that they live in England Street in Freeman's Bay, that Uncle Fred is a carrier for a timber yard, that his daughters work and do not sit about, year after year, as we have done. And now that he was onto his views about life, Father added, 'If we judged ourselves, mind, I suppose there would be no failures in life, would there?' And Mother, philosophical too, said, 'A wife who cares a little more than Fred's does always helps.' And when I said, trying to keep my voice level and bantering, that not to be well off was not necessarily to bear the mark of the beast, Father patiently said nothing and let his cigar smoke drift across the banked greenery about us. But Mother reprimanded me. 'As if we're not all quite tired enough without that kind of silliness.'

It has taken me over a week to set down some of the things that happened on the day of the wedding. I have read it over tonight and have thought yes, it was like that, and yet not that way at all. I suppose what I want is impossible. Words make me think of tracing paper, of how you feel so sure when your pencil moves across what is underneath that you will be left with something very much the same. Then you move the paper and of course you see how different it is! Yet I go on expecting the real thing, oddly enough, even when I know my tracing isn't up to much at all.

My sister and Sam are back from their honeymoon. I have been given a jade paperknife, and for Frances they brought from Rotorua a glass phial of coloured sands set in different layers. They stayed here for one night when they came back, which allowed Mother to cry afresh, and now they have gone on to their new home. So again I have my room to myself. It is strange how often when I think of Nan I remember her before Tom left for the war, and how I would sit at this window near my bed and see them walking down the long stretch of the drive. Tom loved walking. Once they set off for the top of Maungakawa, and in the late afternoon Nan had to use a farmer's phone to call Father. Her feet were so bad she could not make it home. I liked him so much more than I do Sam. He walked with his hands clasped behind his back, his chin a little in the air. After dinner Nan would sit at the piano with her Thomas Moore *Melodies* and he would sing in his light tenor voice that made every song seem sad. Yet there even seemed nothing sad about his going away, apart from the expected tears the day he left. It was inconceivable that anything bad might happen. There were long spells when Nan would brood, but that was simply a matter of waiting between mailboats.

He wrote her long amusing letters and for New Year 1917 he sent me a postcard made of very fine muslin, embroidered with the French and British flags and the words *To a Dear One at Home* worked in coloured threads. Round the edges of the card there was a border of lace. On the back, in pencil, he'd written, 'We go up to the Front tomorrow or the next day. I think of you a great deal over here. Love T.' I kept the card on my dressing table until a few days after we knew that he was dead and Mother said to me, didn't I think it would be tactful to put that away?

There is a small photograph that I have kept in the drawer with the card. For once he is not smiling. He looks straight at the camera with his face turned slightly to one side, as though he has just begun to move away and yet is looking back. Several times in these last few weeks I have imagined him just like that, in those last few minutes when you fall asleep and images come into your mind without being called. I talked once to Mr Wallace about spiritualism or whatever one wants to call it. I said there was nothing I hated more than anything like that, where feelings lose their edges and blur into a kind of fog. I admit my irritation has something to do with Mother's sister and her books by Mrs Besant that she tries to get us to read. But I stress all this to myself because I believe if we do not try to be rational then we can only slide into one nonsense or another. It is something Mr Wallace and I agree about entirely. So Tom being in my mind so much, especially since the wedding, has nothing to do with the 'spiritual'. Once I have even heard myself saying his name aloud, although – the oddest thing – I heard the word first, before I realised that it was my voice that said it. I suppose someone might say I am jealous of Nan and that I want her to seem like the betrayer. I do not believe it for a moment. I think more simply that nature is forcing me to set my feelings towards some man, and the dead man comes from inside myself to remind me of life. To remind me of time, how much or little there is of it.

It is several days since I wrote that.

This morning I took the photograph from my drawer and tore it up. First I looked for a long time at the face above the uniform, above the leather strap running across one shoulder and Tom's hands hooked in the sides of his belt. That is the man who loved my sister, who my sister loved so deeply in return that the evening Father answered a phone call from his parents, then spoke first with Mother by herself, then with Nan behind the closed door of his study, we heard not her crying but the banging of things, the heaving and the impact of the paperweight and the marble pen-holder and the silver-topped inkwell from Father's desk as she, the most placid of us by far, raged at what she had been told. She shouted not only that no one else in the world mattered to her one bit but that she too wanted to die. She shouted for death that night until Father had her drunk enough on brandy for her to fall asleep.

I had that awful presentiment of time which begins to press so heavily until it is like a great smooth stone you have your hand against. Yet how vague it is, too, to say it like that! For a long time I held the photograph in my hand. I moved it slightly and it sheered with reflections running across it. Then again he would look at me. Tom sits in a studio against the blurred rising of a painted cabbage tree, a canvas hillside. I try to hold some sense of time, but it flows from me as if I tried to cup water in my fingers. It eludes me and frightens me. I hate that feeling of mystery as Mother hates pain and Mr Wallace hates injustice and as a few, I suppose, hate God. I said over to myself, 'There is nothing that matters except to understand.' Then I took the torn pieces of the photograph with me to the kitchen and raised the plate of the range. I sprinkled them down into the fire.

This is four months later. So much for Mr Wallace's advice to know oneself closely, day by day!

Today I saw that Father has gone back to reading one of his old books. It is by Procopius, and of course I do not understand a word of it. When I asked him, he said it was the story behind other stories, the only kind that counts. There is another person's name on the fly-leaf, and the date beneath the name is over a hundred years ago. Father has been talking of 'solid reading' for as long as I can remember, so I am glad that at last he has the satisfaction of doing it. More and more, since Nan has married, Mother spends her time upstairs. Father sits with his glass of whisky and sighs across the fireplace. He puts his feet on the edge of the coal-scuttle and frequently drops to sleep above his secret stories.

Mr Wallace too has gone. He last came on a day when it poured with rain. I took his coat at the door but he refused the towel I offered to bring him for his hair. He dabbed at his forehead and beard with a handkerchief. He raised his arms above the range to dry his cuffs. He then sat at the kitchen table and looked about for Frances.

'The girl's not out riding in this, surely?'

'She's over at Nan's for the night. I am the sole daughter left.'

'Like all the fairy stories,' he said.

'The duckling, you mean?' I tried to make light of it.

'The one all the good things happen to.'

'Shall I know when they begin?' I said. I may have sounded more sardonic that I intended. For Mr Wallace swung towards me, his face not only solemn but almost distressed. 'Emily!' he chided me. But then he paused, so clearly changing his mind from whatever it was he had intended to say to me. Instead, his hands fell palm downwards onto his knees. 'Father? He's in, though, isn't he?'

'I'll bring you through some tea?'

'Ah, please.' He went along the corridor towards Father's study. Then he came back to fetch his coat from where I had hung it behind the door. 'In case I slip out the front.'

'Then you won't be here for dinner?'

'Not tonight, alas.' I brushed down the coat, although he insisted I go to no trouble for him. When I handed it to him, and his fist closed around the collar, the dark red stone in the ring he wears caught at the fire from the opened front of the range. He returned to the darkened corridor and I closed the kitchen door.

Later, at dinner, Father said, 'He is leaving for Australia.'

'Australia!' My voice rose in a way that I detest, a female shriek of surprise.

Father spoke to Mother and myself. 'He preferred not to say goodbye directly. He hopes you'll excuse him for that.'

'Is he ill?' Mother wanted to know. Her tone had the implication, is he too one of that select band?

Father answered her curtly. 'He simply prefers a change of scene.'

'What about his business?' I said.

'Investments travel lightly,' Father told me. 'Not as if he needs to earn a living, as most of us do.'

I was about to say, 'And his work for the movement, though? What of that?' But I refrained. There was only the clatter of our spoons against our plates. Father poured his usual claret, and a smaller amount for me. I think he will miss Mr Wallace very much. There would be no more jokes in Latin, or the references that delighted them both, and that I longed to understand.

It isn't quite a year since Nan's marriage, and a matter of months since Mr Wallace left, but it now seems so clear that between them they helped keep Father buoyant. Since they have gone, he has begun to sink. More often than not he is morose. The car may stand there for days without his bothering to drive into town. I say things like, 'You'd hardly think Nan had ever left home, the way she and Sam drop in here nearly every weekend.' But the fact is that Father has become old. He is worrying again about the money Arthur lost. The spirit, as we say, has drained from him. Last summer he would hit the ball around with us on the tennis court, and now he will hardly walk to the end of the drive. Yet he is still, I think, such a handsome man. Sometimes when I look at Mother I think how different it can be with women. How time punishes the stupid by removing everything else.

At last, Tim has sent me the book from Auckland which he promised at the wedding. Lizzie's letter says it is an easy way to see what the Party is working for. It is so very much drier than the William Morris books Mr Wallace loaned me. But I see of course that it is far more useful. When I have finished this, and if I am still interested (I think they believe up there that it's simply a fad, my saying I want to know about Labour), then Tim will send me another book by a man called Parkin – or is it Larkin? Lizzie's writing is dreadful. Both of them say it entirely changed their way of thinking. There are also a couple of pamphlets they sent me, written by people they know. 'Watch this man,' Tim has written under one of the names.

Now that I no longer have Mr Wallace to talk with, I can see I have very little head for theory. Worse than that, even as I follow it, and grasp it point by point, I am actually bored by it. What it comes down to is that I cannot think in any useful way apart from people. I am surprised this has never come home to me before. One part of me, I find, is almost sceptical as I read those endless 'plans for the future'. Another part, that I so want to carry the day, believes how certainly it *can* be done. I am like a child waiting for Christmas, the way I count the days until I go to Auckland. I keep telling myself I must not expect some sudden illumination. As Tim wrote to me, what Labour needs most is people who believe beforehand, not those who cheer when the speeches are over. So I say to myself, I must first work this out alone and commit myself only because I am convinced. Yet oh, to walk into a hall, to know that here there are a hundred people, two hundred people, who believe and work for the same thing. That is what I want to have. For once in my life to feel I belong where I choose to be.

And I have told Father exactly why I want to go! Nothing tells more about how he has changed these last few months than the way he accepted it. He says that most of us have thought there is a new world round the corner, at one time or another. He says any man who hasn't is a fool. I joke with him, delighted that he can no longer be bothered to fly into a rage.

In my slow way I am learning perhaps something else about politics. Last week in Father's shelves I found a book by a Spanish saint of centuries ago. (The book had belonged to Father's mother, at a time when Anglicans were so close to Rome, as I've heard him say, that you would hardly know if you went into the wrong church by mistake.) This saint sounds quite crazy yet splendid, so certain of God yet so full of common sense. Her world could not be further from mine, nor aspects of it more repulsive, yet I read on and on. At the end I liked to think that I knew her. And I came to see that integrity can exist inside any system, and it is perhaps that more than anything I want to get closer to when I go to Auckland. The system, I mean, may be just the kind of room you sit inside. That fanatical church for her, the Labour Party for Tim and Mr Wallace. But to do things decently, to look with as steady an eye as you can, that still comes back to who does the looking.

Mr Wallace will not be back. I mean, *ever*.

There is something Father is on the verge of telling me, yet draws back from. He says only there is no point talking about it, or expecting to see him again.

'Is he well?' I asked.

'Oh yes. There's nothing wrong like that.'

Father burned the letter he had received from him, because I saw a fragment of envelope that survived the grate, the red Australian stamp in its corner. Frances says she doesn't believe for a minute that Mr Wallace won't return. He has promised her a book about riding so he is bound to keep his word.

[Opposite this last entry, written apparently at random as the book fell open: 'Mrs Norwood has told me today she expects she will go mad and kill herself. I could only stir my tea and wait for the words to finish spilling from her. I did not believe it when I told her she might be depressed because of the long winter, or because times were hard for everyone, and that spring would pick her up. She pauses while I talk but does not listen. She waits until I have finished so she can begin again, over and over the same few facts. After her last visit I did in fact fear that she might do herself some harm, but I know now that this is the last thing that will happen. I think of the cow that fell into the culvert the year after we were married. One of its hind legs was hooked and broken on the side of the ditch while its great weight dragged its body down into the hole. It took three days to die. Mr MacLeod tried to free it with ropes and with a tractor, although when the tractor moved the ropes bit hard into its flesh. I asked him several times to kill it, but he kept believing it might be saved. It was too valuable to throw away. Mrs Norwood is like that. And she *loves* the ditch that drags her down with her own weight. She would rather have the bellowing than silence, the pain than nothing at all. I watch her as I used to watch the cow, until it becomes unbearable. She cries when she leaves me, and tells me I am the only person in the world she has to talk to. I pay her for the eggs which are her excuse for calling in, and give her an old jersey of Alex's for her own boy to wear. He is such a mite, it was a foolish gift. She walks away, heavy, solitary as a beast.']

There is one blank page, and almost eighteen years, between the last time I wrote in this book, and my writing in it now. I do not quite know whether it is absurd, or simply sad, to put it like that. One blank page for eighteen years!

I have found the book in the bottom of my mother's sewing basket, which is almost the size of a small trunk. On the day I left home for good, to come and live here on the farm as Mrs MacLeod, I packed it with sheets of music and placed the notebook on the very bottom. As my husband had no piano, and was less likely to get one than any man on earth, the basket was put high up in a cupboard. A few times I have taken the basket down, to hunt out pieces Nan has asked me to find, and once to see if there was a photograph there of our grandparents. Frances had written from Australia, asking would I find it for her. That was five years ago at least. She said about her son, 'I don't think he will believe we actually go back that far, until he holds their photos in his hand.' I found it for her and posted it off, a faded square of cardboard with two stiff adults sitting side by side and a child on each parent's lap. Even then I put away the basket without digging deeper than the large legal envelope that held several dozen photos. Until last night, when the manager's girl came across.

I think young Bet comes mainly to see Alex, although that for the moment is neither here nor there to him. She has got hold of a tin whistle because, as she says, she has about as much chance of ever having a violin as she has of owning an elephant. Alex had told her that I have some old music somewhere. She has learned somehow to read music, and now she wants to try herself out. 'Then you must know music?' she says to me. She looks at one like a comic doll. I said I had not so much as played a note since a long time before she was born. But the girl insists. I could still help, like, couldn't I? Just the things in the music she doesn't understand?

'I'll try to, Bet,' I promise her. She is a curious wee thing, with an enormous mop of hair that drives her into herself with embarrassment. She likes to come across when Alex is reading to me. She sits at the table with her knees tucked under her and her chin in her hands. Her eyes scarcely move from Alex's lips.

There was one sheet of music that brought the past back to me with a rush, a feeble enough tune by an Auckland composer called Charles Harrop. Printed on its cover is a dedication to my cousin Lizzie. The moment I saw it I remembered Tim teasing her about it in their small Ponsonby kitchen. He laughed while Lizzie tried to tell me, 'He's the organist at the cathedral and he's a bit soft on me.' I remember Tim so clearly, flapping the sheet of music at her like a wing. 'A bit?' he shouts. But Lizzie laughed too; she said Tim went on like Bluebeard, didn't he? I put the piece among the others for Bet. And I thought of Tim who is no longer so lithe nor modest, and a Member of Parliament. The last time Mary and Arthur were in Wellington they all met by chance on the cable car and Arthur had turned on his heel and walked away, refusing to shake hands.

I smoothed out the sheets and read the words which Mr Harrop had also written himself, the moon on Auckland Harbour's furthest reach, the track of fire to where he stood at Shelly Beach. I thought of the night of Nan's wedding, and I was to go to Auckland to stay with them, to 'come out' as it were in their world of socialism. I had been so excited at the thought of it. And I never went. Because there was a sequence of events that nothing could alter. Mr Wallace, as I feared, did not come back. Then six months after he left Father suffered his first stroke. Within months of that Mother died as she would have liked, painlessly but with drama. Within twelve months Mr MacLeod, if not quite on a white horse, at least came along with a key that turned the right locks. Frances went to live with Mary, and the family house was sold. Strange, how I can write in a few sentences the most important events in my life. And how unimportant too, as I think of them from here. Because 'happiness', if one wants to use such a word, is *here* with Alex and myself.

Now that I have begun again, I might as well write it down. I have been reading over (again!) what I wrote those years ago. How it seems to stop so suddenly. And how often I wrote 'of course', 'in fact', those little hooks that try so hard to straighten things when we want life to follow a neat line. And how severe I was on Mother, for taking herself as seriously as the rest of us took ourselves! And how often I used exclamation marks by way of excusing myself some observation!! Well, one is I suppose what one writes and says and thinks at a particular time. How keeping a journal like that *fixes* one. I mean, I have this sensation of life flickering on and on, and only writing holds the image of what that flicker was.

It is strange how much I have lately been thinking about the family (emphasising, of course, my own part in it). If I were asked to put down our story without emotion, as though I were writing for someone else who wanted only to know bare *fact*, I would say this:

There was an eighteen-year-old girl who came from Dorset to Hamilton, where her husband was an importer of barrels, dry goods, glassware, whalebone for corsets and various items of hardware, during the years when the British and the Maoris were at war. He then found there was land for the buying. Their son became a clever young man whose father went to the expense of educating him in England and so divided him in two halves that were never again to match. He returned to marry a girl in the same church as they had both been baptised. His wife's people also owned a shop, which in her later life she described as much grander than it was. The girl who grew up in the odour of flour sacks and bulk sugar later behaved as if she could not have scooped a spoonful of molasses without instruction. There were four daughters to the marriage. The first was beautiful and not at all clever; the second was not so handsome but a little cleverer; the third was the tallest, plainest, and at one time believed herself to be the cleverest of them all. The youngest, more independent than the rest, went, as all the relatives said, 'completely off the rails'. Shortly before the death of her parents, she ran off with an Australian jockey from a house trainer's near Leamington. For two years that third daughter nursed her father, then married a man twenty-five years her senior. He was kindly, but too remote for it to matter. There was a child who was tall, sensitive and hardly bright in any way his grandfather would have admired. As a widow, his mother kept on the farm and paid a manager more than current wages because she felt guilt at paying a man at all. She saw her two older sisters several times a year but did not have much to do with her neighbours, whom she found coarse or narrow in their views, and they in turn saw her only as eccentric. Her younger sister, who was her favourite, she has never seen again, although once a year she receives a card. She has never learned deeply about politics, or anything else, as she had once hoped. She spends her time gardening, listening to the wireless, watching her son grow up. Her health fluctuates, but she does not believe in fuss. Nothing is clearer to her now, as she approaches her mid-forties, than it was when she was a girl and quite wrongly believed that as one grows older everything falls into place.

June 3rd. This morning a gum tree blew down near the boundary fence. Fortunately it fell into the paddock and did not damage the fence. At breakfast Alex asked me had I heard it fall. It happened just before first light, while I was sound asleep. He has already been down to see it. One of the steers, the one with a wall eye, had been caught beneath it as it sheltered against the storm. Later the manager came over and said we could sell the hide for twelve shillings. Oddly, it seemed there was no mark on the beast at all. Burke will skin it this evening.

August 9th. These last couple of days the air has been ringing with the sound of axes, and there is that distant panting noise of a saw, like an animal. The manager has hired a swaggie to help Burke clear away the tree. When I said, wouldn't that work be too hard for two men who were getting on, he explained there are now so many on the roads, he was doing them a favour. I had believed from what Mary's husband told me that times were getting better. I said that to Stan who tugged up his belt with his one hand and laughed at me. 'Don't you believe it, missus,' he said. 'Getting better!'

I walked to the gate at the edge of the orchard to watch them, one bending forward as he thrusts the saw away from him, the other coming upright as he draws at the other end. It was rhythmical and lovely to watch. Then they stopped for a smoke, sitting on one of the branches that lay level with the ground. They chatted together until they noticed I was watching them, and then they seemed subdued. I wanted to let them know I wasn't spying on them, so I moved away behind the hedge. Almost at once I heard them again at the saw.

Soon enough I shall have to prune the fruit trees. I love that smell of sawn wood and living sap, the pale wounds that will spring with new life. We stack the pruned pieces inside the wood shed, at the side of the pine lengths the manager cuts us each summer. At the beginning of each winter Alex tries how drily the pruned cuttings snap. Year after year he says, 'I reckon we could burn that lot now, Mum.' He has said it since he was a child, and we joke about it as a kind of ritual that brings winter in. The first days of frost, in April. Sometimes we have a run of biting mornings and perfect days and the sky is such a delicate rose and grey in the last of the evening light. Alex tucks crushed newspaper into the tangle of branches and cuttings, and the little tongues of flame leap up between them. We both love it, the beginning of winter, although we use the real fireplace seldom enough. Mostly we sit in the kitchen, in front of the range.

But this is rambling. I seem to be writing for the mere pleasure of putting down what I like to think of. If only I had kept it up, when there was more to write of!

September. I don't know why I haven't jotted down before that, the new cycle has begun. Last week I had vases stacked with snowdrops, and violets set in between them, the way they grow beneath the sycamores out front. They are the messengers our ancestors must have lived with for thousands of years, that say the dark battle has been fought out and won again. And today Alex brought in some early camellias. He took the flat Chinese dish that Mother had before she was married. He plucked them from their stems once the flowers were floating on the water. I said when I saw them in the middle of the table, 'Alex, but how lovely!' He told me he had seen a picture of flowers arranged like that in a book about Japan. They had different ways of arranging flowers, he told me; this must be about the simplest of them. But then the girl from the cottage came over, so we spoke of something else.

I am again so tired that I am in bed by nine.

September – 14th, is it? I think Alex senses that these days I am not quite one hundred p.c. (one of Father's phrases!), and his reading aloud is something he can do that pleases me.

The girl from the cottage is here whenever the poor dear can get away from all that she has to do at home. I am amused at how she always has some excuse as she taps at the door, some invented query that is her reason to come in, which of course she could do any time she likes. Sometimes she carries a piece of music. 'What happens here?' she says. Her nail-bitten fingers prod at a line quite beyond her skills or the pathetic verve she attacks it with. I said to her, why don't we start on music *properly* then, from scratch? Go over all this theory you know again? So we have begun lessons together. I have asked Mary to keep an eye out in Hamilton for a piano, a cheap second-hand one that would quite be up to our humble needs. The girl is worth the effort. She is quick and nervous as a cat. I cannot help noticing that her mind moves much more quickly than Alex's, although there is always a certainty in what he does, which the girl does not have. It is as though what he decides on even spontaneously were the end of a process, the *inevitable* end.

For the third year in a row the wisteria is a disappointment. When we first came it fell in cascades from the top of the Douglas fir outside the front verandah. Its root is thicker than a man's body, and it must have grown there for fifty years. But now, when it should be in full bloom, it hangs like strands of rope with only the occasional burst of colour. But the two rhododendrons on either side, as though to make up for it, are perfect. One of them is so deeply coloured it is near magenta. The other began its flowering about a fortnight later, and is now opening into broad trumpets so delicately pink one almost sees through the petals. I brought an armful in today and stood them in jam jars round the kitchen. It takes no more than a day or so for them to lose their crispness, but they bring such gaiety inside. They shout out, *Life*!

Oct 10. That tiresome woman married to the manager bored me today for over an hour. She came to borrow a measuring tape, she said. In truth it was because it is Saturday, and Bet is there to mind the twins and bring some order to that wretched house. I think back to what I used to hope for when I talked with Mr Wallace. I thought then how there must come a time, surely, when the waste and selfishness would go from families like our own, and the grinding dullness from those like the people in the cottage. Well, they may still. But what I was hoping for then was hardly politics. What I was hoping for was something different from what human nature is. I was dreaming for a wand.

Oct. Bet has missed her first music lesson since we began. There is something I think going on at school that I do not quite understand. I know Alex has been in some kind of trouble, but clearly he prefers not to tell me about it. At least *he* is certain that he is right, whatever it goes back to. I suppose I am placing a good deal on that, but I am sure he is *solid* (Father's word, again!).

Oct 20. A letter from Frances, who hopes to come across early next year. More than any of us, I think, she has kept alive, in spite of the doom our relatives liked to foresee for her. I must try to tell Alex more about her. I know Mary and Nan find him almost impossible to talk to. The living spit of his father, I'm sure they think that. So I would like Frances at least to understand him should they ever meet. He is not unlike her, her slightly oblique manner that so irritated the family, her coming at things from angles one did not expect. I want her to like him – that no doubt is what I have in mind. I wish she would bring her own boy across with her, although she says nothing of that being in her plan.

I have been thinking about the others of us – of Mary and Nan and myself, and how we are close but never deep together. The older we get, the more we move apart. When we talk of the old days at home, of our parents, of before any of us were married, there is a kind of camaraderie between us. A kind of nostalgia, anyway, that we can hide in, and so not bother ourselves too much with what we have become. The past has become a handy way of not talking about ourselves.

November. I am certain Alex is in love. So the absurdity, the loneliness, begins over again. For the next how many decades! How many of us realise, even at the end, that whoever we loved, whoever we wanted to love or loved us back, was no more to do with us than leaves decide to fall. The *season* is all that matters. Our blood compels us one way, 'morality' takes us another, the only certainty is that we shall be confused. I am not writing that with regret or bitterness, mind. But already I see how the grief has begun, at the same time as the joy. And I can tell young Bet is distressed. She still comes across, but less often, and at once regrets her coming. She then casts about for an excuse to leave as soon as she can. She finds her few words then dashes off. I notice she tries to hide her hands that are raw from the work she does at home. I feel such pity for her, and cannot say a thing. Her smallness is to her what once my height was to me, a constant rider one cannot throw for a minute.

Alex has finished *Ivanhoe*. When he read the last lines, I felt sadness. The book itself does not interest me very much, and I wonder at how those cardboard figures still move young people with their simple unconvincing world. But it was mid-winter when he began. Now there is summer lushness along the drive, thick grass springing in the paddocks, the fruit trees in their new leaves. Everything looks as though it is being licked by green, the way the fire licks over dried sticks.

It seems I need other tests. The sooner, as the doctor says smiling across at me, the better, isn't that so?

The usual Christmas cards are coming in, the signals that tell us how lives go on that have grown so far away from our own. Apart from Frances, none of those I write to do I miss by not seeing. Yet it is so good to hear from them, and a few, like Lizzie's note, are warm and funny. I see her lovely figure and her dark hair, stooping after the bouncing red beads.

Mrs Norwood has phoned me, again in distress. I did not ask her to come round, she is so exhausting. What is there I can do to help her? Loving. Rutting. And I write those words, one of them so 'sacred' as we are taught from the time we are children, the other I have never actually said because of its crudeness. How close or far apart are they, in fact? We so love the boundary lines between things, don't we? I think of those hopscotch squares we drew with chalk on the front verandah at home, Mary red in the face as she ordered where we could hop to and where we couldn't. Our games are so serious! This is said, admittedly, by a woman who is tired of watching them.

Dec 22. Frances has written again, to say she cannot come for at least another twelve months. I am so sorry for that. She says it has to do with the orchard she owns, and needing to supervise new buildings. She does not give many details. She says Alex must have used up all that was left of the family height. Her own son, in any case, has not inherited any of it. But he makes up for it in politics, she says. He is already a firebrand. She holds *me* accountable for that!

I have decided for next year to set myself one complete entry each week. (So, Father, I shall have method and order after all these years.) I mentioned it to Alex, who seemed amused at the idea. No more *Ivanhoes*, he said, we could take to reading from my diary. I laughed with him, and did not quite know how to explain that it seems important, even this late in the piece, that I can hold in my hand the shape of one whole year.

28 shillings for the ham Mr Larsen delivered this afternoon! I said that perhaps with a new man in the district they might not be so expensive next year. Pale men like that find it harder, I think, to hide it when they are angry. *Him*! he said.

'*Six days.*'

'*How many?*'

'*Six.*'

Doctor feels the stomach, stretched taut like a drum.

'*Laxatives?*'

The nurse holds up a small box for him to confirm for himself. She says, 'She's usually healthy as a horse.'

'*Argh!*' *Then again, as the head turns from one to the other, the fruitless effort at speech.*

Further down the infirmary the tall male nurse says, 'Listening to Einstein again, is he? Why not give her enough jig-saws and she'll make us a bomb. If she's not too preoccupied shitting herself after what Nurse there has been pumping into her.'

Nurse Harris caught the quiet words. She would ask to be shifted before much longer, she knew that. She wasn't putting up with him for much longer.

Doctor leaned closer, touched the woman's arm. But there was no further sound. He said, 'The secret of this work is patience, Nurse. Every skill finally gets down to patience.'

The male nurse slapped softly at the side of his face. 'Wake me up someone, will you, when he tells us something new?'

The patient nearest him smashed his fist against his own face, imitating the staff. Others enjoyed that. They began to stir and call out until the male nurse moved towards them, his face comic-book serious, his own comic fist raised high. They did what they were told when he said so. 'No problem, Doctor,' he said. 'I'll settle them down.'

'*Let me know,*' *Doctor said. He pulled her hair back, and her scarf, so that the scar was covered. She hated it showing, that was the fact he liked to hang on to. Something was going on so long as she was concealing, wanting to conceal.*

The rain against the windows so heavy the staff had to raise their voices to talk. The car-lights outside mixed and egg-yolky and running into each other. Water pouring loud and rushing, the sky not even there.

She pulled the scarf right across her face. The wool smell was nice against her, the infirmary now muffled pinpoint of light.

Nurse Harris said, 'We'll have you back in your room in no time, won't we?' And she said quietly when the tall man passed her, 'Being a male I suppose you'd have queued up to give the enema yourself?'

'Nurse!' the man reprimanded. 'Not in front of the loonies!'

Jesus there was this commotion everywhere. He saw it happening before the racket came in on his ears. He knew whatever he should have done had gone badly wrong because Scully was in his corner waving his hands, his arms lifting and falling, his mouth open and bawling out at him, and it was then he realised everyone else was yelling too, because there was no sound coming from Scully's mouth, just this opening and closing and a chain of spit leaping from the pink hole in his face, his upper plate slipping so for a second his lips were clamped shut and then opened again. His hand came up and swept across his slavering chin and at that moment the racket in the hall broke on the fighter's ears. That was how he first knew. And then there was the Scotchman's blonde wife in the row closest to the ring, the woman standing and leaning forward and thumping with both fists on the edge of the canvas floor, within inches of the thick black hair that lay directly beneath the ropes. Her pounding as though to some compulsive sense of time while her face flooded with the effort of her scream. Her sound came to him in its high thin thread across the deeper roar. A vein stood out like a piece of rope in the strained reaching of her neck. But what he saw and wondered at was that while the woman's body was flung in such agitation she was not looking at her husband lying in front of her but her eyes were raised and gripping at his own, a force that he felt almost with the impact of a blow. And when her eyes left his they went to the referee's stooping body, his weight supported on his knee where his palm was spread, and an island of sweat across the stretched back of his white shirt beneath the searing lights. And then came the third thing apart from Scully and the Scotchman's wife. The referee had raised himself upright and grabbed at his shoulder, even as he was in the act of turning to walk towards Scully, and spun him back. He saw the froth of grey hair above the neck of the referee's shirt and bow tie, and the stained armpit as the fat arm was raised level with his own shoulder. The man's extended fingers were then pointing as though beyond the ring and beyond the hall itself, further than the tiered rows of shouting and abuse and hysteria in the blue air beyond the solid fall of light above the ring. He saw anger in the ref's eyes as well. His weight turned with the pressure from the hand gripping at his shoulder, and his glance spun from the judgement of Scully and the Scotchman's wife to take in the Scotchman himself. The man had now half raised his body so that he was on his knees for several seconds, then his weight heaved forward and was taken by his gloved fists against the floor of the ring. His ear was cut, a bright small flag of blood unfurling across his cheek. He shook his head and raised it, focusing on the rabid movement of his wife. His head swung from side to side, the heavy bewildered movement of a pained animal.

Collins stood confused. His own gloves he held still in the stance he took to fight, his awkward southpaw's right higher and in advance of his left. The Scotchman's trainer had slipped between the ropes and was now stooping forward, his hands tucked beneath his boxer's armpits, attempting to drag him to his feet. His movements were crab-like and parodic. The trainer raised one fist towards the referee, a useless but dramatic gesture that brought a different roar, a higher and sustained pitch from the hall. Another of the seconds was clambering through the ropes. The referee shoved at Collins's chest with his opened palms, the action of a man who presses against a weight that burdens and infuriates him. 'Back! Back!' he shouted, until they were in the corner of the ring where Scully gripped the top rope. The trainer's blood-shot eyes widened at the men who shuffled towards him. The referee still pushed at him, although. Collins leaned deep into the ropes, and the heavy panting man whose sweat the boxer now realised was the stink that oddly troubled him said, 'For Christ's sake Scully, get him out of here.'

What was it, Collins tried to think, where was the centre of the confusion? He had hit the Scotchman hard when inexplicably the bigger fighter's guard had dropped, and his body had smacked headlong across the canvas with the sound of a falling bag of wheat dropped from several feet. And now the referee stepped out in front of Collins with both arms extended, fending off the other boxer's second who had grabbed at one arm as though at a bar, attempting to wrench it from his way. The Scotchman himself was sagged in his corner, his trainer rubbing at his temples, draping his gown across the shoulders, on one of which the dripping blood from his cut ear had begun to spread. Scully's hands were through the ropes and dragging at Collins. He pulled hard at the forearm above the puff of the gloved wrist, so that the younger man was drawn off balance as he slipped between the strands of the ropes. He fell from the edge of the ring to the floor several feet beneath, landing on one knee. 'Keep moving,' Scully was shouting at him even as he fell, 'just keep fucking moving!'

Collins gave a grunt of pain as his knee jolted against the boards. He turned his head to see only the outline of Scully's squat frame above him, the low round head against the brilliant flare of the lights above the ring. Outside the glare there was nothing but haze, the core of falling yellow light now a solid smoky wedge on the empty ring. Then Scully was at him again, dragging him up, his shoe sharp and rapid against his leg, the same low intense urging that he fucking get a move on while he herded him along between the flanking seconds and the tall Islander in front of them who flung out to left and right with the slow definite movements of a swimmer, ensuring a way was cleared for them between the pressing crowd. The same man gathered up Collins's shoes and clothes when they passed through the dressing room, and Scully ordering him now, 'Stay where you fucken are.' The close-cropped grey head jabbed in front of him to pull the door shut. The Islander then urged him from the side door, an exit onto the quiet tree-lined street behind the hall. There was shouting now and banging on the door into the dressing room. It then came to Collins with the dull urgency of a poisoned finger that had just begun to throb, that indeed he had done something seriously wrong, for which his friends now turned against him. He allowed himself to be thrust into a car drawn close against the pavement. In the back seat of the car he tugged with his teeth at the tapes that tied his gloves, then clamped the thick pads beneath his armpits, easing his hands free. He pulled over his head the black jersey that the Islander handed to him from the front seat. Scully was panting beside him. The bandaged fists he began to unwind as the car lurched from the footpath. The driver hunched as he watched the rear-vision mirror and swung out in a wide turn.

Jesus, Collins said. His first spoken word since the bell at the beginning of that last round when he rose from the corner and Scully flicked the towel from across his shoulders. He heard his trainer's warning, 'That prick's got a right like a mule, Colly, just ride back and let him chase you.' And he said back to him before the mouth-guard eased from his trainer's hand and packed his mouth, 'Reckon I'll go for him, Scull.' And he saw his trainer shake his bristled head. 'Ride him out,' he ordered him again, 'make him use his fucken legs.' He felt the older man tap his shoulder as he rose with the bell. It was round four and the fight had been his so far, all the way. Then instead of listening to Scully he had gone at the Scotchman and pounded him back, advancing on him while the fancy weaving of the early rounds desisted and the other man blocked as he could, moving always back, away, his own trainer bawling to him not to get near the ropes, for Christ's sake use his right, stop the bastard with that. But Collins knew by then that the Scotchman with his great record and the rest of it simply could never move as fast as himself. He nudged him with several rights, teasing him to step in closer, goading with the contempt of his flicking jabs that only the other man would know were deliberately light, dismissive. His left hand curled waiting at the middle of his chest. Then twice with extraordinary speed it leaped and jarred against the Scotchman's head, a third time smacking under the defending forearm to raise an instant pink blotch on his ribs. Collins felt the satisfaction of control, the pleasure of again holding back his left, of biding his time. (At the small bag in the gym when his right flickered against the leather and the shape blurred with the speed of the successive impacts, Scully would holler at him, did he even have a left, did he, was it tied against him with fucken rope?) Then the Scotchman tried to turn the fight his way in the few minutes that he knew remained. Twice Collins felt his head sharply snapped back. But that was all. He bore in on the other fighter, again jabbing lightly and rapidly until his left uncoiled two, three times, while the Scotchman's guard floundered in front of him. Collins watched the red smear he had opened on his ear. He set himself to work on that. His gloves wove between the weakening thrusts of the Scotchman's defence, regularly and easily as a machine slipping to where it was meant to impact. He could see the amazed recognition of loss in his opponent's eyes before he tamped at him finally, almost delicately, his right glove indicating as it were against the side of the man's head where he intended to belt out with his left hand, the long sweeping arc from the level of his waist that lifted the Scotchman from his feet and tilted him, suspended him, so it seemed, like that moment when a falling plank resists the momentum that then drags it horizontal.

Collins's bandages at last came free from his hands as the car dipped down to the road beside the park, passing the brick walls and the looming bulk of the gasworks. Scully's head was turned to watch through the window behind him, his face obscured as it tilted, his voice breathily urging the driver to keep his fucking boot down, not to shag about.

The car was turning left from the top of College Hill, but the confusion from the hall remained undiminished in the fighter's mind. The square black Ford passed the hotel on the corner and drew in against the kerb twenty yards further on. Once inside the house Collins took his bundled clothes and his shoes into a bedroom off the passageway. He came back to the kitchen fully dressed. Scully sat at the table, his hand rubbing against the back of his neck, while the Islander poured whisky into four stubby glasses. There was a moment in which the lap of liquor was the one sound in the room. The driver of the car had not come in. One of the seconds, a nervous sallow man who tutted continually to himself, stood with the blind slightly eased back between his fingers. He turned to look blankly at Collins as the boxer came into the room.

'Leave that blind will you,' Scully told him. 'We'll know soon enough if anyone's trailed us.' The third man, whom Collins had never seen until he stepped into the car, said, 'I'm off then. You won't get me hanging round for them.' He shook his head when the Islander held out a glass. They heard him click down the wooden steps at the back of the house. After he had gone the Islander locked the door and drew across a bolt. And only then, after a long pause in which the men raised their glasses and drank, did Scully turn to accuse. He emptied his glass in one rapid tilt and held it out again towards the Islander. 'And you,' he said to Collins. 'You've buggered things good and proper this time.'

'For himself?' the second laughed.

'For all of us,' Scully said. And so Collins clicked that the Scotchman was going to throw the fight in the sixth, that his trainer had a packet with the Sydney bookies and Scully was in on that too, there was money in it all round. There was loads for the picking even over here, because Collins had never been given a show.

'I was good,' he said suddenly. 'I was better than he was, Scull.'

Scully coughed and spat his scotch back into his glass. 'You were a fucking sight deafer anyway.' He exposed the stained rack of his teeth.

'Was that it?' Collins said. And then by way of excuse, his voice raised like a child's close to tears, 'You know I don't hear on that bad side. You should have said.'

'You're all fucking bad sides as far as I'm concerned,' Scully shouted back. 'Am I saying that loud enough for you?'

'Jesus,' Collins said, and Scully told him, 'Are you ever going to need him, sport!'

Collins said, 'We should have had a signal or something. You should have let me know you fixed it. Why didn't you do that?'

The older man rubbed again at the back of his neck. He rolled the scotch round in his glass and looked down into it. 'Because you're too thick to even guess what we were up to. Because you fancied yourself as some kind of bloody Jack Dempsey and you wouldn't have gone along with it. Too bloody thick to even take the bell in, bugger me', and he knocked at the side of his own head with his opened palm. 'Bone-headed at just about fucken everything except ballsing things up.'

And Collins looked at him and said, 'The Scotchman was really going to throw it?'

'Christ!' Scully laughed at him. 'You didn't really think you were in his class?'

Collins felt the sensation of slipping from his chair. In fact he did not move, although the walls seemed to him to slide, and he knew that shame was opening a pit beneath him, 'But that wasn't true, Scull,' he called out. He could tell by the look in the Scotchman's eyes, across his defending gloves, that he was shit scared, that none of this was what he had expected or so much as thought possible. He hadn't slackened off, that other joker, he hadn't stopped there taking those final lefts because the bell had signalled him to stop but because he was fair rooted, he had come to the end of all he had. Collins tried to find the words to tell them that, to say all right he hadn't heard the bell but had beat him fair and square for all that, and then he saw that they were laughing, mocking him.

'He's off his fucken swede,' Scully said. And then there was silence again. The second belched, and a man Collins had never seen before came in from another room. He spoke and took up the scotch and sucked at it straight from the bottle, but Collins missed what he said as he had missed the bell thirty minutes before. Scully's arms lay along the table while his fingers turned a matchbox over and over and the Islander remained standing near the blind. A car drove slowly up the street, changing gear when it turned and took the hill behind the bacon factory.

'Might be better with the lights out, eh?' the new man said. The Islander took a candle from a cupboard under the bench. The second he struck a match Scully leaned across the switch on the wall. Scully's face was like soft putty in the light from the candle. The new man said, 'No one's going to believe this.'

Scully kicked at the leg of the table. 'What sort of excuse is that, some bloody ox with a deaf lug didn't hear the bell?'

Collins had believed for almost two years what Scully had told him early on, that a fighter must look on his trainer as a kind of special friend. There were no secrets, there were no holds barred, there must be trust above everything else. When his trainer massaged his shoulders he used to close his eyes. It was the warmest feeling in his life. 'There's either total trust,' Scully had told him, 'or there is nothing. That's the way this game works.' He had fought for that feeling as much as for anything else. Six fights in this last year and only one he hadn't stopped within the first few rounds. That was the American nigger it seemed impossible to hurt. Yet even that one Collins had moved and weaved his way through as though he was enchanted, they all said afterwards. He made the bigger man lumber like an ape, he piled up the points as Scully said like a kid setting up his fucking blocks, you went like a champion, boy-o.

Scully had discovered him sparring in a gym. Ten bob, Collins had read in a notice, ten bob to work out three rounds with an Aussie pro. The pro hammered at the boys who stood against him while his own head was protected by a padded cage. But Collins had stood up to him and held him off not so much through skill as through sheer strength and the ignorance that he was not expected to fight back. He was there as the other kids were, simply to be a target. He had rocked the Aussie pro back and they'd stopped the round.

'You hurt them you know you're good,' Scully in time would tell him. 'A punch bag doesn't tell you how hard you hit it, but seeing a man go down's another story. Makes you want to hear them crack.' When Collins had looked puzzled, Scully laughed and slapped his oiled hands across the broad shoulders. 'You're not a killer, boy-o, that's your only trouble.'

'Teach me, then,' Collins had said to Scully's amusement. 'Everything else I can,' he said, 'I can't teach you that.' For Collins didn't give a damn for the fighting itself. It mattered only because Scully rubbed him down and talked to him like his best friend and said to him, 'Son, I'll teach you everything I know, there's no stopping where we can go together, right?' His closed fist smacked in play against his protegé's shoulder, his opened hand ruffled the brown curly hair. Then when Scully saw the room where he lived in Parnell he said that no boy of his was going to live in a dump like that, there was an old woman in Franklin Road who cared and cooked for her boarders with the attention of an aunt rather than a landlady, Scully would fix it for him. Old Scull would take care of everything.

Collins did what he could in return. He longed for Scully's orders and the chance to carry them through in the way other young men might hanker for freedom. Until tonight. Until his trainer instructed him to stand back from the Scotchman for another round or two and he had thought no, he would go it alone. He would fight better than his trainer had ever expected, he would give him that. So now it was not only Scully's abuse but his own treachery which had taken him beyond return. In his confusion he saw at least that one fact with clarity, that things were now too bad for him ever to mend.

The Islander standing at the blind cleared his throat into his handkerchief. There was a sudden flicker in the candle flame and again the shadows swayed and rocked, altering the men's faces. Then it was Scully who spoke. He was suddenly subdued. 'We've pissed on our chips good and proper this time.' Then he came and stood in front of his boy, his foster-son, the champ he was going to make. As quietly as if he were talking of the most casual things, he said, 'Take your bloody snivelling somewhere else, will you? You're not the one in the gun, are you?' He turned, raising his voice in interrogation, asking the Islander and the second and the man who had come in, 'No one's going to chase him just to kick his arse round for a bit, are they?' He stood in front of his boxer and waited. Until Collins said, 'Do you want me to go then, do you?'

Another car turned into the street. There was quiet and immobility as though the men in the room were held in a frieze. They heard doors slam further along the street. The older man watched his fighter. Then there came a crack from Scully's hand, and he turned to open his fist above the table, setting down the glass that fell into two clean halves as his hand relaxed. Collins looked at the face that had now come to within a few inches of his own, at the squat cropped head. The older man began to shout, a gravelled sound that dragged from inside him, that passed into a thick aggressive sob. This was the last chance ever going to come his way, Scully was shouting, the one chance to get anything out of this racket after forty fucking years and a half fucking wit just screwed it up, he could kill him for that. The Islander stepped across and laid both his arms round Scully in what looked an almost gentle embrace, drawing him back towards his chair as if he thought that any moment he would lash out at Collins. 'For Christ's sake,' the second hissed at him, 'why not open the door and invite them in if they're looking for us, doing your block like that?' And Collins said quietly, 'I could have won for you straight if you'd done it that way.'

Scully sounded now like an enraged and weeping boy. 'I took you from nothing and gave you everything and now where are we, eh?'

'Stow it, can't you?' the other man warned him again.

'A thousand fucking smackers off this one, that's all you cost me, Collins. A thousand!'

Collins looked down at the glazed cheeks, the shine of spit and tears on Scully's chin. He thought how people go saying one thing and doing another and unless you're smart you never know, you think you understand something and then it ends up something else. He felt his head blur with anger. He swung his right fist heavily against the door beside him and a split leaped along the wooden panel. Crockery in a cupboard somewhere rattled after the blow. The other men stood still, watching him, none of them game to restrain him. Why had they told him he was good then if he wasn't? Eh, why had they? Hadn't there been those other fights – they weren't all punks, were they? Kid Tapai and Billy Welch and the Yank nigger and all? He'd made a job of the lot of them. The newspapers said he was the best for years. Not everyone could have been lying, putting it across him.

'I can win again,' he said. 'I can be good as I ever was, Scull.'

This time Scully only sighed. He said as he reached again to the bottle across the table from him, 'Just fuck off will you, eh?'

Collins left the kitchen and went down the short flight of steps. He heard the key turn in the lock behind him. The street was empty, a tram crossed away to the right in College Hill. What were they waiting inside for, then? Was someone coming to sort them out? Were they going to shoot through themselves? No one had explained anything. He turned left and took the sloping net of back streets. He must keep away from the main road up in Ponsonby where he did his running and where people knew him. At least he knew that, to lie low as he could. They used to call to him from doorways and the side of the kerb as he ran past in his black jersey and his training shorts, 'Ready to knock them down again, eh mate? Ready to clout that nigger, are we?' He liked it when they spoke to him like that. He didn't know who they were, but they were friends all right, the old codgers and the kids and the ladies even who sometimes smiled at him. There were some kids lived near the fire station who had a sugarbag stuffed with grass they'd rigged up on their front verandah. They sparred and pranced in front of it, they'd wait for him to run past and they'd stand with towels round their necks. He would jump the picket fence in front of their house and tap at the bag. He feinted swiftly with each of the kids then jumped the fence again to keep on with his run. The kids blew and snorted as they supposed real fighters did and they were all great cobbers. He liked it when they chanted at each other in their make-believe contests, 'I'm Collins! I'm Collins!' Only now that was over too. He wouldn't be the champ any more but the mug who couldn't even hear when the bell was struck, the champ who was so fucken thick he was a dead loss, they'd be saying. 'You won't see him haul his arse into the ring again.' And not one of them would know how the Scotchman in his tartan shorts and his blonde wife screaming out for him and a piper leading him into the hall like Scully said Christ's knows what, that he was jacked up to throw the fight anyway. If there was a crook bastard in the fight then he was the one, wasn't he? He bloody was. Not Colly. But none of them would ever know that. He thought of the write-ups and the talk round town and how he would come out of it, disqualified and dumb as they come. No one would defend him. No one would say how Scully himself had answered when he told him right at the beginning, when he said, 'I've got this bit of a crook ear the same side as my mark is', the trainer laughed like he was having him on. 'Takes more than that to stop talent.' And now Scully never wanted to see him again. There was no one now who gave a stuff.

Collins hurried along Russell Street and into Wood Street, keeping himself close against the hedges and the fences and waiting at the corners to check that there was no one coming towards him. There'd be no one back at the boarding house yet, not if he was quick about it. The other men had been going down to the fight then on to a buffs' club one of them belonged to. They were going to make a night of it.

He opened the back door and went through to his room without switching on a light. He went on tip-toes like a creeping child, past the yellow thread of light from under the sitting-room door. He took his suitcase from beneath his bed and folded his few clothes inside it. Then his spare pair of shoes. There were some pictures pinned to the walls, magazine photos of Johnson and Georges Carpenter and a small shiny photo of Billy Murphy that the champ had signed for him one afternoon in the gym. On the back he had written 'For the up and coming boy'. Billy Murphy had told him he had another picture at home that he'd like to bring in and show him, 'Me and Bob Fitzimmons,' he had said. 'I'm not up to his shoulder, you know the size he was, don't you?'

'And it's true about his arms, is it?', Collins had asked him. 'You know, about his reach?'

Billy had laughed. He said, 'His fists came to below his knees. They weren't a man's arms on him, they were an orang-utan's.' And then to cover himself, to show he meant no disrespect for the greatest fighter maybe of them all, Billy Murphy had said, 'He was a gentleman, mind, first and last.'

Collins took the signed photo from the wall and put it inside his wallet. He took the five pounds he had beneath the newspaper in the tall-boy drawer. There was only his overcoat to take now from its hook behind the door. There was nothing else he couldn't afford to leave. He remembered the cloth cap that had been hanging in the hallway since he first rented the room. There was no question of pinching anything from anyone, he knew no one had claimed it for years. He could do with it now all right. He would wear it with the collar of his coat turned up. And later on he would grow a beard or at least a moustache, and he wouldn't need his hair so short as it was now. Scully had told him his first week as his trainer that he couldn't stand seeing a fighter with more than an inch of hair to his head. 'If a man worries about how he looks in this game,' he had said, 'dolls himself up and that, he's as good as fucked. I've seen them come and go, Collins, you take my word for it.' But now he would let it grow again. He would become what he was before Scully took him under his wing.

He stood on the back steps again, only minutes after he had entered. He tugged on the cap that was slightly too small for him. He closed the door, turning the handle so there would be no click.

Mrs Murfitt as they all said could hear like a cat. He walked down
the path beside the house, beneath her window with its frill of lace
curtain showing beneath the blind. He heard her move something
on the table as he passed. At the gate he looked up at the plane tree
in front of the house, the lines of the telephone wires stretched
against the sky. The clouds were low and pink, burning with the
city's lights. He considered now why hadn't he tapped at the
landlady's door and told her he had to leave at once. His board was
paid in advance, there was no question of him skipping off. He
knew how he always liked to do things straight. And it would have
been easy enough, wouldn't it? To say goodbye to the old thing?
Because she had been kind to him, and now here he was shooting
through like the punk Scully had said he had been all along, and
Jesus that wasn't true. That's what she would think too. Again he
felt the confusion come over him, a swirling in his brain as he felt
inept and stupid. But if he rang the bell now and Mrs Murfitt came
out and saw him there with his case and the stolen cap, she
wouldn't know what was going on and he wouldn't be able to tell
her. There would never be the words to explain all that. He would
just look dumb at her. He picked up his suitcase and began to
walk. He kept to the shadows under the line of trees.

He experienced, as he often did, that awful feeling of how
nothing is ever quite fixed, how there is always this flow of one
person's mind over things and then another person's, time moving
on and everyone sort of grasping at this thing or that thing, trying
to hold it back. It was always there, he thought, just over the edge
of what we say or do or look at, that sense of melting away.
Sometimes he only needed to close his eyes to hear the dynamo,
the thrum underneath everything else. Often at night he switched
his light on so the things outside himself could come back and take
control. Because somehow it was light that made things true. Only
the other night when he felt the panic coming close, he had picked
up the sports paper from beside the bed and read again the story of
Georges Carpenter who was more like a film star than a boxer. He
went over the details of his fights that then became the story of
his throat cut and the champagne living and the sheilas who went
for him, they wouldn't leave him alone. Carpenter didn't fight his
way into the title, Scully had said, he rooted himself out of it.

And now as Collins walked up the road he remembered that the paper was still folded as he had left it under the bed, and it came home to him that he would never see Franklin Road or the boarding house again. It was a door that had shut behind him for ever. He began to walk more quickly. Before the police station near the reservoir he stopped in a doorway to tug up the collar of his coat, to settle the cap and slant its brim across his face. Then he walked again without for the moment being sure of where he would go. If it weren't for the fine rain he might have kipped under Grafton Bridge – he had known enough blokes who said there were places down there behind the graves you could make comfy as a bedroom. Only it wasn't just the rain either, he thought. He'd only need to run into somebody and they'd know him in a flash. That was what he had to get away from. From anybody knowing anything.

At the corner of Pitt Street he stood in a doorway near the Naval and Family while a tram swung round and rattled past him. He saw the reflecting light slide over the doctor's brass plate level with his head. He then crossed to the road at the side of John Courts. He ducked down past the small wooden houses in the gully and came up to the mick church and the stonemason's on the corner. Symonds Street was almost empty. The tram tracks under the rain stretched out in shiny webs. He felt tired now. His jaw hurt where the Scotchman had landed him one in the first round. 'That's always your trouble,' Scully used to warn him, 'you're too slow off the fucken mark.' The first real punch after the bell could be the beginning of the end.

He touched the side of his face, just below the eye. It was swollen all right, a soft painful cushion above the bone. It was the one time mind you the Scotchman had got through to him, a lunging awkward jab that set him back and brought the first growl from the crowd. They were always strange, those first few minutes of a fight. Just the shuffling of their feet across the canvas, the cautious early slapping of the gloves, the solitary yells of abuse or encouragement until the first real contact, the first real belt in the sequence of sorting each other out. The bellow then when the crowd half stood, the smell of blood as Scully called it, what most of the bastards had come for. You're fighting them as well, he used to say, until you're on top it's not just the man in front of you, the whole fucken hall's got his gloves on, see? You got to knock all of them into shape as well. You got to get them wanting *his* blood and not yours. That blonde sheila the bitch the Scotchman's wife, hers was the first yell Collins had heard, it was that pulled him round so quick after the heavy jab that rocked him back. Every time he landed one on the Scotchman he was teaching her as well, her cry piercing through by itself and then the racket from the whole crowd. Maybe his crook ear cut even that noise down a bit too. But it made him think now of the noise walking beside the river ages ago near the small rocky stretch where the current lifted and buckled white across the stones, the one place you heard the river before you saw it. If you walked along that stretch the sound surged beside you, yet after a bit you weren't aware of it until you'd walked further on and the sound was no longer there. The pouring of the crowd on its feet. He heard the crowd and saw the river.

I must be tired, Collins thought, I'm muddling things. He rubbed his eyes with his finger and thumb, then shifted his suitcase across into his other hand. He hadn't really thought of that stream for ages, not clearly as he was thinking of it now. The track he used to walk beside it, his first job when he was just fourteen, the best place he had been. The sound from the crowd always came when the punches hurt, only you could tell the other bloke was stinging too. And it's all the same whoever it is. The same flecking and twisting of the river whoever walks there, the noise burling out from the crowd. That roar as it came to him in his first big fight, the poor flat-footed blighter with his jaw suddenly swinging loose, his eyes dead as a fish, the pain and hopelessness as he waited to be finished off. 'Old Macready' he was known as, he was so far over the hill, Scully said, it's a wonder he remembered what his fucken name was. He had broken Macready's jaw. Collins thought even now, walking with his case rubbing against one leg, I didn't have to do that, did I? I shouldn't have done that. When the man's gloves dropped as though suddenly weighted with lead, Collins had stepped back and waited. And he could see without looking directly that his trainer's fist was pounding the canvas in his corner, he was calling up at him to go in for Christ's sake, to make a job of it. He had waited because he was confused. Why hit him now, he had thought. Then that man who was sixteen years older than he was, who the *8 O'Clock* said shouldn't have been in the ring at all he was in such bad shape, fell without his being touched, toppled with the slow accumulation of pain and weariness, and just before he fell, raised his left glove and tamped softly at his own jaw, at the grotesque unhinged lop-sidedness Collins was appalled by.

Collins thought of that now as he touched the swelling beneath his eye. Then he heard the heavy singing of the tram coming up the incline towards him. He stepped out onto the safety zone, the only passenger to board. He stood on the back platform and slid the case behind his legs. He held out half a crown in his opened palm and watched the man's fingers tear off the ticket from its stub, then root about in his leather pouch for change. 'All the way?' the conductor said, 'Harp of Erin?'

As the tram leaned at the turn into Newmarket, Collins tightened his legs against his case. He stood stiffly with his right hand holding the grill of the safety gate. 'Warmer inside,' the conductor told him. The man jingled in his hand a clutch of loose change. It was cold out on the platform all right. But inside the tram was brilliant with yellow light. What if anyone recognised him? People were piling on at the stop above the picture theatre. People who looked at you the way they do when they enter a tram, a room, look you over, size you up. 'Feel like a bit of air,' Collins said. He breathed in deeply through his mouth to prove it. The conductor told him, 'Please yourself then. Brass monkeys out here before long, mind.'

His fingers threaded through the grill. His body rocked with the swaying of the tram. At the terminus he took the main road south. He now walked through the night and felt the flatness of everything surrounding him. He thought of Franklin Road and the city he had crossed as places he would never go back to again. A tooth at the back of his mouth began to beat. It continued to rain. His left hand gripped together the raised collar of his coat, his right held the suitcase at his side. He thought, I'm running away like a pet or something that's been kicked out of a house. Hadn't Scully said once to a journalist while his boy skipped in the blurred oval of the spinning rope, 'He's pure instinct, that boy. You can't plan a fight for him any more than you can for a cat.' He had liked hearing that. The journalist stayed on and watched him while he lunged in at the heavy bag and the tightly padded training gloves smacked cleanly on the canvas. He moved back and then towards it again as attentively as if it were a man. He trained always with that same meticulous care. And he stepped into the ring without either swagger or make-believe ease, which sometimes disappointed Scully who loved a boxer first, he said, but a showman second. But there would be no more of that now, none of those work-outs with Scully's breath hot against his ear between rounds, his hands working over him, easing the elastic waistband as Collins flopped into his corner, holding the rinse out for him, talking to him quietly, telling him you're good son, just watch his left a bit then beat the shit from him, let him have it in the slats. Have it from us both. Scully had always said that. *Us.*

The street lights were further spaced now, with greater blocks of darkness between the houses. He had to get well out of the town. He had left his watch in the dressing room at the Town Hall, the Islander hadn't thought to pick that up with his clothes and his shoes when they scarpered. He supposed it might be near twelve. And he walked on for several hours, past the glassworks and the holding yards for the freezing works and the diminishing ribbon of lights beyond Otahuhu. The rain had eased off. The sky cleared enough for a few hard stars and a weak moon. An hour further on he went into a shed a few yards behind a hedge. There was a house behind a belt of trees a hundred yards further back. The shed smelled of oil and manure and at the far end, beyond cans that in the dark he kicked against, there was a kind of platform. After knocking the cans, he had stood quite still for several minutes until the night noises came in on him again, the snuffling outside which must have been a hedgehog near the wall, a late car further along the south road, the slow pitting of its engine against the silence. He stooped to brush his opened hands about in front of him. He felt the corner of a folded tarpaulin and ran his fingers along its length. He raised one of its flaps and slid his body between that and the thick folds beneath him. He took the towel from his suitcase and folded it under his head. Within minutes he was asleep, the almost instant comforting fall of a child away from consciousness.

As he turned on his side beneath the canvas, Collins heard the far whinnying of a horse. In the old house near the Pottery the horses came up sometimes from the paddocks and trotted along the street.

The boy lay in bed one night and heard the horses outside, their hooves ringing out on the sealed surface of the road. There were the voices of men calling from further down near the paddocks, the high whooping sound of trying to round the horses up, to turn them back from their canter towards Jervois Road and their shying at the traffic. Then it was quiet for a moment, an absolute hush like God had put his hand over everybody's mouth. The boy sat up in bed and pulled back the thick curtain. His mother stood there quiet on the verandah. Her thin back was only a little in front of him, then out beyond her was the great space of the sky above the houses on the other side of the road. There was this piece of silence as though it was in the middle of the night instead of only early, because he had hardly gone to bed. Quiet except the man was in the kitchen eating, making his fork scrape along his plate. When he stopped, it will be like everyone slept, that's how quiet it will be, the boy kept thinking. And why is Mumma still standing there, why is she still watching? Then he jumped with the suddenness of the noise outside, the unfolding bursting clatter as the horses flung in different directions, the three sets of hooves breaking from where they had stood, arcing out in such awful noise. He heard someone shouting very loudly just outside their house, the percussion of hooves that must have been so close to the fence. A tall man stood there, just near their gate, the bridle shining in his hands. The horse flowed past him, so big and slippery under the street light from the corner. The boy climbed on the small table at the foot of his bed. He held up handfuls of the heavy curtain, he saw the smear of street light melt along the horse's flanks as it turned at the corner then trotted with its legs very high, like it was pretending somehow, like he did himself when he played moving like a horse.

Mumma had been startled too because she came back from the verandah rail and leaned against the wall. The man with the bridle ran down the little street towards the factory. The bridle hung and slapped against his back, and the boy could hear it leaping. As the horse went down the street in front of the man the light had slipped off its haunches like it was a blanket. For a moment he had seen the tail trailing out behind it, the flopping of its mane up and down. There was an echo from down in the shadows, the exploding nervous hooves that came through between the houses when he could no longer see the horse but thought of it running on and on, the big dark animal with the man trailing it, the jangle in the man's hand that he would never tie it with. Down that little street now and past the factory and into the further streets where the boy had never been. Once down in the paddock near the Pottery a man had lifted him onto a horse and his legs had spread nearly straight out. It was like sitting on a wide piece of board except there was this tough brown hair that felt prickly when you ran your hand along it one way and smooth as the cloth on the sitting-room table when you stroked it back the other way. He had touched the mane which hardly had the feel of hair at all, it was like the unravelled end of a rope he had felt down at the factory.

Through the window he saw Mumma stand at the rail. She rested one hand on the edge. Her hand was so white beneath the dark material of her dress and so still while it lay there on the wooden ledge. The boy liked looking at her hands when they rested together on the table. When she said goodnight to him they stroked against his face, they smelled nearly always of special soap. It was soap, she told him, and a garden mixed together. Her hands were never hot like some people's hands. Like the nun's at school who all the time whether she was talking or just standing there she was touching that stiff cardboard stuff at her throat and the sides of her head as though it was too tight, as though her head was inside a white paper cage. When she touched you, her hands were warm and sticky and bossed you in the lines when the bell rang. She even took the pencil right out of your hand if she thought you weren't holding it properly. There was a silver ring on one of her fingers that pushed the skin right in like a cushion. The ring meant she didn't have a house like everyone else did but that she was married to the school. It meant other ladies went home and cooked for their families but she sat in the classroom by herself and thought about Jesus. He was their friend too, she said, their best friend who loved them and cared for each and every one of them, even for the ones who were only primers. But it was wrong to say his name when you didn't have to. You only have to think of him and he knows.

Then the boy standing on the low table at the window, the curtain dragged up and bunched in both his hands, was knocked sideways and so hard by the man's opened hand his feet were lifted from the table before he began to fall. The man whom the boy never thought of by his name but only as that, *the man*, who towered above his mother as he did above the boy himself. He had come into the bedroom and seen the child at the window. The sight of the boy with the bunched curtains in his hand like the stem of a large broadening fan angered him as all things did that declared he was not obeyed, even a six-year-old standing beside his bed in the excitement of running horses through the early night. So that he called out *Jesus, boy*!, stepping towards him from the door. His hand raised and struck out, then fell again after the clear impact against the child's head, fell back like a heavy knotted rope against his side. The boy saw the street light blur like a whirling sun, the burning haze behind his closed lids when he lay on the floor.

He did not know until after Mumma dabbled at his face and his hurt ear that the side of his head had caught against the table's edge and the hearing on that side was smashed for ever. He tried to crawl to the dark cave beneath his bed. There was no pain in his head, none in the arm that had banged against the end of the bed and that tomorrow would be too sore to bend. For the boy was feeling only the pressure of the sound that he knew must come from him like a spat-out stone. He waited for the cry from his guts that would summon his mother. The man's face was in shadow as he looked down into the room. The boy saw the light from the hallway behind him catch in his hair like a kind of yellow froth, the head itself round and heavy like the great concrete balls on the pillars either side of the convent gates. The man had one arm raised and his opened hand was pressed against the door jamb. The boy saw the same illuminated froth along the length of the arm and right up onto the naked shoulders. 'That'll do you,' the man told him. 'That'll keep you in bed when you're told to stay there, right?' Then his mother was standing beside the man. She ducked her head beneath the raised arm and ran across the room. And it was she who was saying *Jesus* now for her fear and distress. And she called at the same instant as she drew the boy from beneath the bed but looked away from him, looked back over her shoulder at the man standing there in the yellow square of the doorway, 'What have you done this time, you swine?' And the man had laughed shortly at her, 'Fuck you both, then.' He stepped back into the other room and the light poured unimpeded across the bedroom. The boy could now see Mumma's face, the thin features, the dark hair drawn back so smoothly against the sides of her head he sometimes thought it must be varnished there, the same little shiny lines as when the man down the factory ran his brush across smooth wood. She grabbed him up and pressed him hard against her. Then his cry came at last, a long rasping bellow, while his mother said into his shoulder, 'I'll kill him sure as God.'

They heard the man slam out of the house. Mr Schwartz was his name whenever anyone else spoke to him but Paul when Mumma called him for tea or said it softly sometimes when he sat for a night without shouting or swearing or breaking something because of the boy. But in the moment of the door's slamming the man no longer mattered. Not his body that filled the doorway when he stood there nor his voice that could make the plates rattle and the table jump when his hand fell on it, or when he put his arms round Mumma and she would laugh and push him away and look across at the boy, at his solemn uncomprehending scrutiny of the man's possession. The boy clung with his arms so tight about his mother's neck that a broken dome at the back of her dress cut into his forearm. It left the smallest wound there which next day he would look at closely, a small crescent-shaped cut like a piece of the moon.

His mother said, 'Hold your sore arm like a soldier, there's the boy.' She dabbed at it with the stinging brown iodine and said one of her grown-up words, she said *infection* as she patted the soft wet cottonwool on his arm. Then she lifted him up and carried him through to the sofa where she lay him down and touched the side of his head. And the big man did not come back as he sometimes did when he crashed the door shut like that. This time he had kicked the rubbish tin too as he walked down the narrow path between their place and the people next door. And next morning because the boy's head was sore and he stayed home instead of going to school, he and Mumma picked up the spilled rubbish and put it back in the tin. 'I like being home just us,' he told her. Then for a special thing at lunchtime his mother made them pancakes and he squeezed the lemon on the sprinkled white sugar that changed to the colour of water nearly. Then you rolled up your pancake and leaned right across your plate before you bit it, otherwise it sloshed over the cloth or sometimes down your wrist – that was the stickiest feeling you could think of. But after lunch he said about the little bell that kept ringing inside his head, like. He tapped with the tips of his fingers just in front of his ear. He shook his head but the distant tinny buzz kept on like a little insect was in there too, it was that as well as a bell. 'Lie down for a bit then, shall we?' Mumma said. They lay in the big bed where the man would never let him climb up. He lay rubbing his hand on the smooth black stuff his mother's blouse was made of, and when he looked up her eyes were closed and her eyelids were fluttering, like when you tried to hold a piece of paper very still by the corner and it shook so very gently. The boy lay and looked at her and at her hands that were so thin the little bones made him think of wires and there was a big bony lump on each of her wrists.

The boy liked to remember before the man was there. But that was so long ago it was like one of those pictures in their reading books at school, very clear and simple but not like ordinary at all, it was a story in another place. A picture of an older lady standing beside him and in a house that was in the country – it must have been, because there were animals in the picture too. He was sitting on the grass. There was a very high hedge in front of him. Something was moving that seemed huge and slow and breathed heavily on the other side. The old lady picked him up because he was scared. She carried him to a white gate between the high wings of the hedge and sat him on top of a post. Both her arms were around him. She showed him the thing behind the hedge was no more than a cow. It was dribbling while it ate. And the old lady had a handkerchief she kept folded, a white square tucked into her belt. If she put it close to her face his head went back suddenly from the smell of it, it prickled inside his nose. Whenever the boy tried to think back as very far as he could to what it was like at the beginning, it was a clear sky and only those three things, the lady with her hankie and the white gate between the hedges and the dribbling noisy cow. And after that always there had been the man sitting in the kitchen, the newspaper spread right across the table. While he read his hand moved inside his singlet, his fingernails scratching against his skin, and the boy thought it was like somebody rubbing with sandpaper a long way off. He had never called the man anything, although Mumma said he was Uncle Paul. The man lies here every night, the boy thought. This close to Mumma. He shut his own eyes but he was not asleep. He could see the red inside his head like looking into those shells he picked up at Point Erin Park and liked to hold against the light. If you turned the other way, away from the window, the pink flowed away and it became a sort of flecky grey.

Then his mother's hands were on his shoulders, shaking him. She asked him, 'You all right, love? Can't you hear me?' He saw her leaning above him, there was a piece of hair hanging loose from the side of her head as it did when she first got up in the mornings, before it was smoothed back so flat, so shining. 'But I was talking to you, love, couldn't you hear I was talking to you?' She took him to a doctor who looked in his ear with a light and a cold piece of tin that made his ears feel choked. The doctor rubbed his fingers together with a dry papery sound and asked him, 'Hear that, can you?' 'Yes, I can hear that.' But at the other side the boy shook his head because he had not heard the doctor's fingers nor even the questions. Mumma had guessed his ear had broken when he hit the table, guessed it that day when he moved his head from side to side, watching the grey and then the pink come and go behind his eyes. Moving his head as he must have been doing now and he felt the ache along his cheek before he opened his eyes, and the memory hung there so vivid for the moment, before the day poured in on him.

His mouth was thick with thirst. He saw there were broken panes of glass above him in the garage wall, a piece of tacked scrim that bellied out then flattened back in the gusts of wind. His body was stiff and cold on the tarpaulin. He looked at the clutter of the shed, the drums and a wheelless chassis and the tangle of wire and dumped lengths of timber that the night before he had felt and scrambled his way across. There was a grey cat watching him from a shelf above his head. When he raised himself on one arm, grunting with the effort, the cat arched then moved towards the window. It slipped through the one frame where the broken glass had been removed. Then the clarity of last night came complete to his mind. That dreadful mess-up at the Town Hall and Scully throwing him out and the long walk until he had flopped here in his exhaustion.

He got up from where he had spent the night. He folded back the tarpaulin as neatly as if he had been making a bed. Then he looked through one of the panes, at a jagged star of pure morning between the filthy glass. There was a house obscured behind its trees. The trees flailed in the slap of wind. It must be nine o'clock at least, he thought. They would have to get a bloke in from the yard to do the clearing up round the saws, tossing the ends and the off-cuts into the bins as he usually did himself. Collins worked at the factory three days a week. The boss sat above the despatch in a tiny office like a glass cage and he came to every fight. 'You needn't ever worry about a job,' he had told him. 'When you stop fighting it makes no difference, there's always a place for you here.' But the job and the yards and the furniture factory and the boss peering through his thick glasses that made his eyes like kind of dirty pebbles, who liked to tap him on the arm with a pretend jab whenever he walked past him, they were even in one day too distant to seem quite real.

He found a can at the side of the shed half filled with rainwater. He leaned forward as though across a basin and poured the water over his head. He gasped at the cold and clenched his eyes. He rubbed his face and neck and his stubbled hair with the towel that had been his pillow, then folded it inside his case. From the pocket of his coat he took a dark-red tie that he slipped beneath the flap of his collar and knotted carefully. He didn't want to look like just some hobo once he began walking on the road. He would have to thumb for lifts and perhaps later in the day ask some place for a job. He had heard it a hundred times in the home in those years after Mumma died, how if you looked respectable there was nothing more anyone could ask for, if you were clean and tidy that was half the battle won in a world that didn't like mess or squalor or being reminded that there was dirt and the poor. He rubbed at his shoes with a rag from inside the shed and while he was about it ran the rag across his suitcase until the leather shone. He thought that if only the rain held off he could make a reasonable pace. The walking wouldn't worry him. He would walk until something turned up.

Much later he would say to the girl, 'Once a long time ago, before your mother and that, I walked for over a week. I had blisters on my feet that were bigger than two-bob pieces.'

He told her that the first week on the farm at Pukeroro, an evening when the girl was perched on a kitchen chair and peeled back her white sock. There was a blister where her new shoe had bitten into her heel. He had driven into Cambridge on the tractor to get the shoes for her. She mustn't look anything but the best from the very start.

'You'll have to fix this,' she told him. He was leaning across the kitchen table with a small pig pinned under his weight. The animal threshed at the sheets of newspaper covering the table as he tugged with a pair of pliers at a rogue tooth that pierced through the animal's cheek. The creature squealed but was unable to move. He dabbed with a disinfected cloth at where the flesh was torn. When he placed the pig on the floor it yelped more shrilly. It raced across the lino and skidded as it made for the door. It smacked against the cupboards beneath the sink before it righted itself and scampered from the room. They heard it trip again as it crossed the verandah. He stood with the pliers still in his hand, laughing at the panic and escape that left a sliver of greenish pig-shit across the lino and ribboned against the wall. The girl smiled too, partly at the scuttling pig but in surprise as well at hearing the man laugh aloud, a kind of boyish pleasure that came oddly from him. He ran a cloth along the fouled lino and threw it into the porch. He then took the shoe she handed him. He tapped it softly with the snub nose of his pliers before he said, 'I think I can stretch this okay.' He looked at her directly, as he seldom did. As though it were easier now because his mind was on something else. 'How soon?' she asked him. 'Tonight,' he said. 'Tomorrow.'

There was little casual talk between them. She had said, 'Thank you for the shoes', the night before. Then today she had shown him the blister. He said he would stuff wet paper in them overnight. The girl raised one leg on the chair and touched again the sore watery paleness on her heel.

'Why for over a week?' she asked him. 'Why walk for that long?' And then another question. 'Was that on the way to Mum's?'

'No,' he said. 'It was a bit before that.'

He did not tell her because the calculation did not occur to him, but he had not crossed to the South Island for another couple of winters. The third July, in fact, from when he left Franklin Road. Because the fight with the Scotchman was in May and a year later exactly he had been working on the rail lines. He remembered that anniversary more easily than he did his birthday. Then the second year on that day he was clearing scrub in the Wairarapa in spite of the rain that pissed down on them for the best part of a fortnight. There was one bloke in the gang got pneumonia from it. But if you said you weren't going out in weather like that, if you jibbed at standing like cattle up to your hocks in mud, then it was, 'Right, if you don't like it sport you can bloody shoot through.' That was what the foreman told them if he thought they were slacking. There'd be a tap on a man's shoulder and when he looked up from the dripping brim of his hat the foreman would be there above him on his horse. 'You,' he'd call out. His thumb was lifted level with his shoulder and jerking back downhill towards the camp. He was a bastard and a half that foreman, as if the sole purpose of his life was to see the scraggy steep hillside shorn of its growth and its clay side exposed. Then the dismissed man would nod to those working beside him and begin the trek down towards the huts. He would collect his bundle of possessions and head out south, as Collins himself had done, asking for work along the way as a beggar asks for alms.

'Yeah. Well before your mum,' he told the girl. He watched her tear an old singlet and slip the strip between her skin and her sock. As she leaned forward the curtain of hair swayed slightly and the light from the opened door leaped across it. He stood watching her, wondering at it. He asked her, 'Do you want me to do that?'

The girl tossed her head at him. Again her words were brusque, dismissive, as they usually were. She then began to make their tea while he went out to the shed nearest the house and came back with an iron last. 'Give it a go stretching it on this,' he said. He worked the shoe onto one of the black flanges, tugging it towards him then easing it away. The pan of sausages spat on the stove and the girl moved about at the bench while he handled the new leather, making it softer for her, taking the bite from its heel. Then he screwed up newspaper and wet it, folding the grey damp mould and cramming into the shoe. 'So,' he said. He placed them at the doorway that led through to the bedrooms. He then sat in a cane chair with unravelling arms and waited until she served their tea. Neither of them spoke. He was thinking, she is not just a girl any more. He had no inkling of what she thought, or of what might happen when she tired of living here at the new place. He refused to think of that. Just get to tonight, he used to say to himself in the bad days, just get through to tonight. He thought, we needn't think of that now.

When he left the shed that morning seven years before, the surface of the road was black with its new seal. There was no rain, but there was wetness in the air, a watery greyness of sky and quickly skimming clouds that headed south with him. He felt the oppressive openness in which he was a figure moving slowly on a long road, alone among stretched-out farms and swirling skies. The cattle raised their heads to look at him, then lowered them again to the boggy growth of the paddocks. A few vehicles passed him. He made no attempt to ask for a lift. He knew he must walk until things fell into place.

Later in the morning he came to a long belt of pines that followed the road. He rested there for twenty minutes. The black trees were stacked above him, their roots extruded and buckled from the yellowish bank level with his head. There was the feeling he was among the roots of life, yet what he looked at was dry and scabbed and dreary. He felt the presence of an awful stillness, a cap of silence that pressed down on him. A grey light fell beneath the trees. There was a red crust of needles close against the bank that broke his footsteps like a carpet. But as he walked back to the road from beneath the stretch of pines, a truck blared its horn and stopped to pick him up.

Thus he began his real journey, in which he was to walk far more than he rode, a succession of hills and plains then hills again, and country that was faded and tawny like rubbed chamois, and across it, raising themselves as if to meet him, were the mountains. Later in the journey, after the railway gang and the scrub camp, he would come across more men like himself on the road, most of them with sugarsacks slung across their shoulders. Sometimes they would be travelling in pairs, but mostly each walked by himself those long stretches of open country between town and town. It became harder then to get lifts, as though the number of them made up some kind of fraternity that drivers became more wary of. But that lift the first morning took him thirty miles on his way.

There quickly developed a pattern to his travelling. At most small towns he made some attempt to ask about work, a query that might lead him along a back road for half a day before he was told no, he had been misinformed, and he turned back down the drive to the road. Sometimes he was fed bacon and fried bread, which gave the trek some purpose. In those first days the weather improved and he had money for his food. He walked beneath the clear skies that followed on the morning frosts. Occasionally another man would stop him and ask if he had the makings for a smoke, or hold out to him his own packet of tobacco. 'Roll yourself one, cobber.' But from the start he tried to avoid having to speak. If it could be managed he walked past the odd group, never more than three or four men, who might be chewing the fat at the edge of a town, swapping the information that could save another mate a pointless trek to a job already gone, to a district that held out nothing. They liked to yarn, to hear what luck the others had been striking, to tell where there were decent places to kip for the night. Who were the easy touches. The real bastards to keep away from. But he always tried to get past such encounters. He simply waved back if he was spoken to, jerking his head sideways in brief laconic greeting. 'Yeah, she's going all right.' As the days went by he grew more cautious, more certain that sooner or later a voice would hail him by his name.

In his second week on the road he threw his suitcase away because a sugarsack was more comfortable to walk with. By now as well his beard had grown enough for the reddish fuzz to cover half his face – even his mark was almost lost beneath it. He began to feel safer. Then he was struck with flu. It came on him as quickly as a sudden turning in the direction of the wind, a warm gust that flushed him, and at once he began to shake. The heat alternated with shivering cold. He lay in a barn on a high hill twenty miles from Taihape, certainly for two days but possibly for four. He would not remember. He had with him half a loaf of bread and a small parcel of cheese, and a bottle of soft drink which he felt no desire to touch. He drank rainwater from a tank at the side of a nearby shack that had slumped over to one side, possessed by tangles of blackberry and gorse and the stink of something that had died inside it. No one could have lived in the place for years, although the dead thing was perhaps there no longer than a week. He did not go inside to see. But the barn twenty yards further on was sound and dry. It must have been used over the summer for storing hay. He curled himself in one corner, on a heap of straw he scuffed together. He had taken an old cocoa tin from beside the tank and set it, spilling half its water, beside what would be his bed. Then he slept and woke and slept again and woke, aware only of his weakness and a lack of concern. He could see the sky in long irregular scraps above the loose-hinged door he pulled to before he settled. He lost count of how many times the slivers of sky lightened and darkened beyond the door which itself was so distant from him, endlessly far from him at times, as if in a dream that was another's life rather than his own. Then he woke one morning with the illness past and a hunger that came on him savagely. He took from his bag the cheese and half loaf that had speckled with mould, the bottle of sweet orange stuff that he drank off without lowering the bottle from his lips. He tore at the bread in hunks and stuffed its bitterness into his mouth. He unwrapped the cheese with delight, talking to himself as to a child, telling himself of his luck.

Within minutes of his scoffing a wave of nausea lifted him. It drove him outside where he vomited orange mush against the faded red boards at the side of the barn, the convulsive spasms doubling him over as though he had been struck. Then he leaned back from his kneeling crouch, taking his weight on his heels. The stink of his own stomach came up to him. He walked across to the tank and swilled the bitterness from his mouth. He felt scoured, oddly purified, empty as a husk. Then there came an elation seemingly poured to fill that hollowness. He heard his voice give a sharp cry as he looked up at the early washed sky, at the edge of the hills about him clear as cut tin, the vividness of colour and shape coming in on him in one delighting rush so that he was pressed, possessed, to call out, to salute it. He raised his hands and looked at them, the light catching on their sparse reddish hairs, the lines defined and intricate and marvellous as he turned his palms. He held them out in the shape of a shallow bowl, balancing all this, he thought, holding up the morning's presence. He was the cup that light and distance and his own immersion in this irrefutable stream of exhilaration had chosen as their centre. He was ringed with the purity of his standing, of his simply being. Then the feeling played from him slowly as light might lose intensity by such subtle gradation that the picking out of single rocks, of even favoured blades of grass, recedes, drifts back to usual sightings, the normal flow of common things. The moment – minutes – ebbed from him as easily, as accepted, as a breath slowly expelled. And what came on him then was an intimation, but absolute. It was the certainty once and for all of his isolation, that his walking down in a few minutes' time from his place here on the hill, from the derelict fallen shack and the unused barn which now was so much smaller than his fever had dimensioned it, down beneath the washed expanse of sky and against the chilling gusts of wind that plucked against the flaps of his coat until he came again to the main road and, an hour further on, to the huddle of untidy shops – such travelling could only be a kind of diversion between one loneliness and another, a space between empty barns. His meetings with other men would mean even less because he cherished his distance from them, because he had been to the hilltop and the brightness had come down on him, the morning balanced on his hands. 'This is how it should be,' he said aloud.

He went in and fetched his sack from the dark enclosure of the barn. He walked down the rutted track to the loose metal road, then after half an hour to the main road itself. On the first morning of his madness. For he now knew as well that words and talk were chips from the great block of deceit that people circled as the people in the Bible had moved about their golden calf, before Moses who stood in light had come down and called it false. He now knew that words were the pellets that humans feed to each other as a vet prises up a muzzle and pushes with his finger those things that slow the hearts of animals and beasts, stop the thin flowing of their blood so that soon it lies still for ever like a dropped scarlet skein. And against the violation and the lies he would pit his own cunning, his alertness that would elude them. So that twice in the next few days when he was given lifts he denied that he had ever been near Auckland. When the talk had turned to sport he lied against the driver's craft; he said no, he had never played any game in his life. He said he knew that God had larger things for us to do. The driver then became silent until he dropped his passenger at the end of a straight road running down the floor of a valley. Often when he thought of a word it was both its sides at once that he saw, the way it turned for those who heard it, how it streaked with different colours for the mouth that said it. He liked to think of the great hollowness there was in a word like God, the depth and space of it to be filled. He walked on for another two days to where he had been told there was a camp that took on labourers for clearing scrub. As he walked he thought of it. Inside that word like a massive vault there was room for each of those who used it. For the man in his black singlet with his flailing arms, for the nun who wore his ring, who knew the echoes of the word, its splintering into daggers that came as light. For Scully's tongue, dirty as a piece of stamped-on shit, as a spat-out piece of food. Even to think the word, not even to say it, was to stand in its enormous arch. Your spread-out arms could never touch its sides.

At the camp a bloke younger than Collins sat behind a length of timber supported by two wooden cases. He said, 'Been on the road a while, have you?'

'Ten days,' Collins said. 'Ten days or more. Just wanted to keep walking.' The bloke looked at him, his question on his face as much as in his words. '*Wanted* to?'

He thought of his face obscured by its beard, the torn cuff on one leg of his trousers, the raincoat that had picked up oil stains and the marks of spilled tea since he left Franklin Road. He shifted his sugarsack to between his feet. He said, 'I heard there was work going here, like.'

Then the young rooster said, 'If you're fit, there is.' On his plank of wood there were papers and a black tin box and a wire spike that he could stab other bits of paper on. He looked at the man in front of him and knew he was in good shape. But he warned him, 'Any bolshy talk and you're out on your arse, right? There's only one reason you're here and that's to work.' He tore a chit of paper from a block. He thought, this bloke's not too bright by the looks of him, and softened enough to say to Collins, 'You'll be right, eh?' He laughed across at him. 'Some of these buggers,' he said, 'some of them turn up here coughing their guts out, you have to ask them was it a hospital they were looking for.'

Collins said, 'You needn't worry about that.'

'Course I needn't,' the other man said. He stood up then and walked to the door, pointing down to the huts. And he said, 'I'm Pike.' He stood in the doorway with a clip-board in his hands. He was big and beginning to run to fat. He said, 'You're not on the run or nothing?'

The bearded man stepped closer to him. 'What?'

So he asked him again, and Collins told him, 'Christ no, I'm all right.'

He leaped so unexpectedly from where he stood, the foreman ducked sideways as if from a blow. But he had simply leaped to the rafter that spanned the roof. He raised himself by one arm until his chin was level with the beam, lowered himself until his arm was at full stretch, then raised himself again. He said, looking down on the foreman's head, 'I can stay like this as long as you want.'

The foreman grinned like he thought the dangling man was a fool. 'You can come down,' he said, 'I'll sign you on.' He saw the strained bearded face turn from side to side for a moment, one hand meet the other and rub across it. He guessed that whatever he heard would be a lie, but that was none of his business. It took all sorts, everyone knew that, and half of them seemed to land up here one time or another.

The foreman waited and looked at the form in front of him until this new fellow said his name. Said it several times. Because words in any case were not the same as the truth. *Schwartz*, he was saying. His other name had slipped from him, he needn't bother with that again. The man he hated most, who first took Mumma from him, who knocked him into the wall of half-deafness, he had his name at last, he ruled him now with his own word. From now on he walked inside its shell, he showed the lie of it. He was safe because of it. He leaned to sign it on the form when he was handed the scratchy pen.

After several months he again took up his journey south. He left the scrub-cutting and the dirty weather and the pointless hours swinging with his reap-hook not because he shirked the work nor because he had ever expected the job to be anything but boring but because one afternoon, as simply as if deciding to stop for a drink, he decided to chuck it in before things turned bad. He took his slasher and carried it down from the hill to the camp and handed it to the new man who sat behind the foreman's desk. He asked for the money owed to him and watched while the man ruled a line through the name he had given and that he now thought of himself by, because it was what the other men called him. In ten minutes he was walking the wet yellow clay and sprinkled loose metal towards the town. He put off thinking of where he would go. It was good enough to be on the road again. He picked up a stick which he swung beside him as he walked. That evening he ate in a cafeteria instead of the long hut where he had sat with the men for a hundred meals. He enjoyed the quietness, the woman reading behind the counter, the absence of banter and obscenity and temper that filled the camp. He touched the milk jug and turned it for the pleasure of its smoothness, until the woman came across and asked him, did he need more milk or something?

He drank two more cups of tea. He considered how he was here because two mates in the same gang had broken into a scuffle. Their bodies had interlocked, their weight pitted at each other. He had stepped between them and lifted them from each other as effortlessly as he might have separated boys. The men standing round, who at first had called out in support of one or other of the fighters, watched that part of it in silence. Then the strength of what they had seen came in on them. 'Christ,' one of them said, 'you a bouncer or something, Schwartz?' And he knew the word would be put around. Every man in the camp would hear as surely as he had heard about the pansies who were caught with each other the week before, the Aussie queen who was turfed out in the middle of the night because the foreman said he would turn a blind eye to most things but he wasn't having bum-scuttlers in any camp he ran, not on his bloody life. This too would go round. How this mild joker who lay on his bunk almost all the time he wasn't working, his hands locked behind his head as he stared up at the roof, moved in and broke up the brawl like he was slicing cake.

For half an hour after the incident they had all gone back to work. He heard and felt only the falling jar of his blade against the stems of gorse and the easy swishing sound as he cleared it with one long swing and turned it behind him. There was the scraping from further along the hill when someone stopped to run a whetstone against his blade. Schwartz turned the event over and over in his mind. It was an effort to push his thinking too far ahead. But he knew it was now impossible for him to stay. The men would ask each other about him and one of them for certain would come up with the answer, would know the other name behind the one he wore. They would ask at least where he was from, where he had learned to handle himself so that he was a man among boys. There is always someone who knows things and will say them. But he could not think past that into other words that might be said. He saw only the blankness of a wall. Between Mumma's house and the place next door. The fence of Mrs Murfitt's. The high grey concrete in the yard at the gym when you went out to have a pee. They were in front of him again as he swung the blade in low against the ground, then eased it loose and drew back to swing again. And then it hung there behind him momentarily as though his wrist had been seized, as though the wall indeed was there before him and he did not want to swing the grey half-moon of metal from the sky to clang against it. That was when he had turned, nodded to the men he worked with, began his walk downhill.

The woman watched him eating from her perch beside the till. She was heavily built, perhaps his own age. When she had leaned above him, placing the butter at the centre of the table and the plate of thick-sliced bread beside his fork, he had eased back in his chair, away from the female smell that pushed against him. It was the smell of Mumma's bedroom, and the man whose name he now carried as his own was raising himself from where his mother lay, calling at him, what the shag was he gawping at then, eh? Mumma hushed, Mumma said, 'Go back to bed, there's nothing the matter, love, Uncle's just getting changed.' She was dragging the sheet up high about herself because she must have just got out of the bath, he could see her shoulders and her side where the sheet had not pulled tight. And later she had come and sat with him. She had pressed his head close against her dressing-gown and the powdery sweetness. But now he drew back when the woman leaned so close to him that the plumpness of her arm almost brushed against his face. She would have touched me, he thought, if I hadn't just leaned back in time. She wore a chain around her wrist and there were tiny trinkets hanging from it.

She came back twice while he was eating. She asked him was there nothing that he needed? He watched only the plate in front of him, the few things on the table that concerned him. He piled the sausages and the fried potatoes onto his fork. The light in the square of wall where the plates were pushed through from the kitchen darkened from time to time. He knew without looking up that she was stooping there as well, watching him from the other side. She wanted him to talk, he knew she wanted that. She kept him at the counter even when he paid, putting down the coins of his change one by one while she talked to him about the weather, about where he was going, what was he going for? The words, he thought, she is putting them down as well, in lines, in piles, pushing them towards me. The last coin she held in her fingers above his opened palm. She held it there longer than she needed, but at least her words now stopped. She held the last coin in silence. He took it from her, his sugarsack already hung in his other hand. He left the place without speaking to her and he heard her laugh, call something to him that he didn't catch as the door behind him scraped across the rubber mat. He flung the handful of change so the few pennies and the threepenny bit turned and winked the merest second then clattered, spilled across the road. Throwing away the money everyone had touched, the words everyone had used, their spittle on them, the words they swill them round like lollies in their gobs, the coins warm from her skin as she put them in his hand.

(Then that day so much later Schwartz would see them run together yet again, the currency of words, the speaking out of lucre. The day when he found that the girl had taken the money from where he kept it folded in a saltbag in the roof of the barn and he spoke to no one again after that until his death. But before that when he would first see her talking to the boy after school, this kid who biked along the road, who walked beside her even in the drive, even towards the house, *Jesus*, and Schwartz seeing him instinctively raising his head, expecting some distant scent, some expected fear. He would whistle down to her at the end of the drive. And that night at tea her warning to him, 'Don't do that when I'm talking to someone. You make me seem like a dog.' And with calculation altering the word she had used. A bitch, she said. Other days he would stand in the shadow of the deep garage or behind the dirty scrap of curtain in the kitchen so he could see them as they saw him too, knowing his eye was steady on them wherever they moved. She would walk through the house and around the farm, more and more she would not acknowledge that Schwartz was there. Standing behind him on the tractor, her white dress against his back, her hand on his shoulder while he took her down to school and brought her home. He told her, 'It's only for a while like this, we'll have that car in a couple of weeks.' When the boy was out of sight he would take the balaclava from his head. He would stand in the garage doorway or beneath the black cliff of the macrocarpas until she had walked into the house. He would wait for her to tell him. To pass him the name like a coin across a counter. Or they could go whole days without speech, only the very simple words whose edges were clean, the ones for things they ate, for what they held in their hands, the good unrotting words for the farm. Not the kind that were pieces of the people who said them, the fragments from their mouths. The communion words. He took the bread in his hands, Sister used to tell them, his words made the bread his body, the words that Jesus said. Schwartz would come to sit in the barn one summer afternoon, the sick pig shuffling in its pen beside him while he spread the molasses and then the sulphur across the rag he had torn in strips. The animal's neck set with its row of boils neatly together as a necklace, Schwartz with the poulticed rag between his hands, the collar he would tie on the pig and cure. He hears the girl say from outside, 'He's watching us from somewhere, you know, he always is.' Says it to the tall skinny boy who walks across the farm with her in service to her voice, her will. Through a gap in the boards only yards off, in the paddock's blaze of brilliant light. She swears, smiling at the boy. Says one of the words of filth. And the boy's look, the uneasy smile as he stops his idle kicking at a clump of thistle and looks directly at her. She begins then to move her hands on him. Schwartz sees she moves him with her fingers and her words. He sees the shine on her lips where she has passed her tongue, and the boy's sandshoe stumps against the soft stalk of the thistle. 'Tell me what he is, sneaking after us,' she commands him, '*you* tell me what he is.' The boy looks at her then. He takes the words she has passed across to him, and he gives her them back. 'He's a fucking mad man,' he tells her.)

Schwartz stepped from the train and stood on an empty platform. It was August, almost twelve months later. It was late afternoon. Already the frost was setting in the shadow at the side of the station. He dumped his sack on the ground and took a piece of paper from the pocket of his coat. He had folded and put it there the night before, when the stranger gave it to him on the deck of the ferry. The man who had worn a soft felt hat with a feather in the ribbon. He had talked to Schwartz with a voice that made him think of someone consoling people outside a church. How long since he had worked?, the man asked. How long since he had left home? Was it true, the man said, that he had seen others sleeping under hedges, walking the roads in the rain?

The questions were put to him quietly while the man stood at the rail of the slowly heaving ship. He had torn a page from a small black book and written rapidly on it, turning to face the side of the funnel while the wind riffled at the opened pages. Schwartz unfolded the paper now and held it to the uniformed man inside a small office.

'Is that far?' he asked. 'Can I get that far tonight?'

The man put on a pair of silver-framed glasses. 'Not even if you run,' he said. 'It's a good thirty miles back from here.'

He began to walk along the road behind the station, towards the lift of the foothills. He supposed that the coat he wore, and the blanket he had lifted from the camp the afternoon he left, would hardly be adequate in a few hours time. When the dark came down. His hands and his face now ached in the hardening frost. The air he walked in was like moving inside a very thin cold glass. He had never walked so lightly. He thought how the mountains in front of him were like the white serrations on a saw, so clipped, so brilliantly distinct. He looked at them with the early wonder of a man who had never seen them before, who thinks first of beauty and silence and elevation before he has heard from those who live with them daily, who know the steep immaculate slopes for what they are. With Schwartz that first broad surprise was never quite to be changed, although he heard soon enough of a local climber who was brought down with his frostbitten foot and in a week its rotten bloom was lopped from him to save his life; and soon enough too he would live through the rising of the river fed by those snows, the snarling elaborate rope surrounding the town. Yet that child's delicious stir at a brilliantly lit shop window that exceeds expectation stayed with him each time he looked across the foreshortening of the plain to the yellow foothills, the blue and white wall of the alps. It remained with him as indeed did the admiration and then the fear with which he first saw Jess next morning. The handsome woman smiling at him in the store, then coming across to him, asking, 'You slept in a haystack or something, did you?' She raised her hand to take something from his shoulder.

He told her, 'In a warehouse sort of thing. It wasn't as cold as I thought it would be.'

'Looks like you're still wearing the floor of it,' she said.

He looked at her dark hair drawn back from her forehead. The back of her neck, her throat, were clear and pale and exposed. He saw how her blouse swelled with her breasts. He looked down where the top button had fallen loose and only the thread remained. He raised his own hand, then as if to touch that thread in the way she was taking wisps from his own coat. For those moments he never understood, moments without his own direction, he was much as a stick moves without will on the forces of a stream. He opened his hand and laid the width of his palm on the soft cream flannel of her blouse, the pliant rise of her breast.

The woman said, 'That hand's so cold it's like it's been holding ice.'

In the next twelve months, however bad it was, he remembered that time the best of all, when his hands first took her tits, when she closed the shop door and then came back to stand in front of him and his hands rose again to enclose her and her arms reached round to snap the hooks to let her breasts swing free. There was no other part in what they ever did as intimate as close as comforting as sudden as that. Those moments at the very beginning, with her breasts weighed and rising in his hands, his head sinking towards them. Before her tongue was inside his mouth and she began to say those love things, before those other things she would tell him later, what he had to do to her, what she would do to him. She tried to say her words so they were inside his mouth when they were said. Like the wine she once held in her mouth and then gushed into his. But there at the start on that first morning she put her fingers and thumbs round his wrists and tightened them until her knuckles were pale as her throat. She lifted his hands with her grip and carried them back to his own chest. She then turned from him and walked back to where she had first stood behind her counter. She wore loose-fitting shoes; her heels rode up at every step she took. Without turning or speaking again to Schwartz she walked through a curtain of clicking wooden beads and he followed her. She made him breakfast and told him she could give him work if he wanted it. She told him how much she could pay him. 'Keep walking though if you want to,' she said, 'go up to where that man has written out for you. You'll find it a damn sight easier than here.' And he said to her because he thought she should know from the start, 'I don't always hear proper. Does that matter?'

When she laughed he saw how her teeth sloped slightly back, a fleck of gold in one of them that made him want to get up from the chair and touch her again, draw her to him. Her wet laughing mouth excited him. She said, 'Not what I want you for it doesn't.'

Later she told him he must make the deliveries from the shop and that much of it would be by horseback, she hoped that didn't worry him? It was a shambling gelding that nevertheless in his mind would be one of those trotting, resonant marvels his mother watched from the verandah. And picking up the child after school, she said, that was part of it too. The girl's name was Barbara. She wasn't any trouble. She wasn't one of those brats you couldn't do anything with. And of course there would be helping out in the storeroom, sometimes maybe in the shop. 'General dog's-body,' Jess laughed at him. The gold scrap in her tooth winked out as she told him, 'There's no time like now to start.'

Then Jess had taken him into the storeroom. She told him, 'Start on this.' And so he weighed out flour for her, dipping a tin scoop into the gaping sack, shaking the scoop carefully over the small brown paper bags until the scale weighed one pound. Or three pounds for the bigger bags. 'Make it exact,' she instructed him. 'If any spills, scoop it back up even if it's on the floor.' Later again she came to the storeroom to watch him work. She stood beside him so he could smell her. She told him again he would like it there. Then they ate German sausage and bread that he dipped into a dish of tomato sauce. Afterwards he measured tea from a large three-ply box with strips of tin along the edges, and she was in the shop. Sometimes the phone rang in the little passageway behind the bead curtain, between the kitchen and the shop. Late in the afternoon a girl in a white dress stood there in the doorway. She looked at him with eyes as grey and steady as her mother's. Schwartz lifted the small pile of weights from the scale before he said to her, 'You're Barbara, are you?' The girl let her bag bang down on the floor. He asked her again if that was who she was. Her lips moved and he thought perhaps she had said something that he hadn't heard. He walked from behind the bench where the bags of tea were stacked in a pyramid beside him. He would get closer to her, he would ask her what she had said. But as he moved the girl stepped back and gave an odd high cry, a call perhaps, because her mother was there at once behind her, putting her hands on the girl's shoulders, pulling her in against the strained fabric of her blouse so that Schwartz no longer thought of the child but looked once more at the woman's tits, the nipples standing in small hard cones. She looked at him across her daughter's head. Her tongue moved slowly and rested between her lips. He knew that it was a signal for him. Then she explained to the girl that he was the man who was staying a while to work for them, he was there to help Mummy with the shop.

When the girl took up her school bag and went through the wooden rustle of the curtain, the woman said, 'Don't mind her. She has bugger all to say for herself the best of times.'

(Much later he would watch while she talked to the schoolboy who was her friend. The boy was leaned across his bike as though he was looking for something in the grass and the girl stood with her foot bearing down on the loose wire of the fence. The man thought, she is like her mother. When he raises his head the boy is *enamoured* – that strange word her mother used – his cock is angry for her. While in fact the boy was merely thinking how he had no idea of the feeling she was talking about, that he could not imagine such hate for someone as Barbara had for the man with the balaclava who drove her to school on the tractor like a princess and waited in the afternoons to pick her up, who spied on her, she said, who watched her like he was guarding her. 'From the minute I saw him,' she said. 'When my mother was with us and we were down south. I came in one afternoon and looked in this storeroom place behind the shop. I saw this tall man looking down on me. You could tell first sight he wasn't all there. That he was a loony or something, though *she* couldn't see that of course, that bitch, not for ages. I screamed or something and she came and held me against her, telling me it was all right, he wasn't a burglar. He was simply there to help.'

'What was so bad about him?' the boy said.

And she told him, 'All I looked at were his hands, the reddish hair on them, it made me sick just looking at them.'

Alex said, 'She must have liked him though to make him stay?'

'Like him! She couldn't stand him after a bit, don't worry. She hated him worse than I did!')

For over two years he stayed on as the woman's lover. From that first night. After the shop was closed she had shown him the shed where he would sleep. The girl trailed close behind them. The woman explained as she lifted the hurricane lamp from the table and showed him the trick with the wick, the dressing table he could put his things in, the little wash-house at the back where he could shave or whatever and do his washing there as well. 'Better to see it properly in the daylight,' she said, 'you won't be breaking your neck then in the dark.'

Already the shed was gloomy like a cave. Then they went back into the kitchen for their tea. The woman turned on a wireless. A green eye dwindled and expanded while she moved the knob to find the station. The meals were eaten under its domain, the tinny pieces of music, the faintly echoing voices that seemed to hold such charm for her. By chance and in time he would come to carving bits of wood as they listened. While the woman hummed with the wireless on its shelf level with her head, while the girl sat at the table after tea and did her homework, he worked with a pocketknife on whatever wood came to hand, shaping walking sticks and crudely ornamented boxes, chains linking hearts together that he whittled from unbroken curves of wood. Peelings from the side of his knife fell in small heaps beside his hand. But that was in the months ahead. On this first night when the girl had gone to bed the woman who was his boss now, wasn't she, she led him to his room as though he too were a child. She held his hand across the few yards from the back porch to the shed. 'Just stay put,' she said, 'just do as I tell you.' She stood him against the closed door, both his hands behind his back. She undressed him, watching his face, raising her hand to lay it palm down across his mouth when she thought he intended to speak. She moved the lamp on the table beside him, then knelt on the floor in front of him. Their shadows flung and shook enormously across the room. When the flame steadied he saw her head moving on the wall, his own shadow thrown up until it was taken into the dark nets above them. 'This can't be the first time?' she said.

'Oh no,' he said, his fingers pressing hard against her neck.

The other word the one true unchanging word *oh Jesus* he had almost said, then held it back to himself. She clasped her hands behind his knees, his legs pressed against her flattening breasts, and from his throat now the inarticulate animal sob, until her smeared mouth drew back.

She came to him almost every night in his room. She trained him until his demands were as strong as hers but subservient always to her will. He learned to serve and kneel and cover her by command like a smart dog reared to tricks. Through the day he watched her moving about in the shop, listened to her daughter after school taking down the orders over the phone. He thought how in daylight it seemed so far off, that shared enmity and performance in the small shed out the back. The yellow well of lantern-light where she sinks him until he is bewildered, unable to set himself free. She spoke to him with words that were instruments, she lashed him with them at times so he rutted at her more by revenge than even lust, attacking the imprecations, the abuse from her as she grunted at him *you fucking donkey, you fool, you bloody thing.*

Through the days they spoke as remotely as people who had only met, as though shyness on Schwartz's part and indifference on hers allowed them to work within yards of each other and not impinge with tenderness or speech. Once in two or three days she would have him take her in the storeroom, approaching him, unbuttoning him without speaking. Then his belting into her while her buttocks rode against the edge of the bench, his broad hands spread across her thighs, the bell on one occasion ringing from the shop so that he faltered and she bit into his cheek, demanding him to keep on. Then at the bead curtain into the shop she turned to say so the woman would hear as he did himself, a light quick laugh before her words, 'And clean that mess up there, will you? This is supposed to be a shop.'

At times he tried to speak to her more closely, to draw from her some fragment of affection that moved outside their butting flesh. That she cared for him maybe as well as using him as she said like her horse, her load, her bastard rut. They lay one night before she sat to reach out for the dressing-gown beside his bed. He continued to kiss her neck, the smoothness of her shoulder, the pale shadowed side below her breast. He had been there now for several months. He said for the first time to any woman, *love.* He said the word again, took it close beside her ear, held back the mane of dark hair that he had lowered for her, taking the clips out for her, before they had begun. But she rolled herself away to sit upright on the side of the bed. Schwartz began now to kiss her back, his tongue tracing the curve of her spine, then took the soft weight of her breast in the hand he moved beneath her arm. A kind of reverence to her. As she began to rise from the bed he manouvered her so she sat across his chest. He eased her up towards his mouth, he would do that for her now, she had told him he could kill her doing that. Her closeness blocked the light, there was only her smothering, her darkness. But one of her knees she lowered not beside his head but brought down into his waiting mouth. She felt the crushed wetness of his gob as it slobbered on her leg. He turned his weight to one side, forcing her from him. Then for a time neither moved. They heard the corrugated iron of the roof snapping in the cold. Until Jess slid herself back across him. She began to speak to him quietly. She took his head in her hands and drew it gently towards her. He allowed his head to swing as she directed, as though she led him by a rope. She put her head close against his own and told him, 'When *I* say so, see?' She moved her lips slowly across his. 'When *I* want it. Yes?' She waited and said to him again, 'Yes?'

'Yes,' Schwartz said.

His feelings turned at times to actual fear, when she laughed and threatened him that she would turn him out. He put off speaking to her as though he were muddled in some rising private tide. He sat in silence when he ate with her and the girl. I will go next week, he began to think. As soon as summer is really here. When I can get back to the road. But by the evening, by the time they had finished eating and the girl was bent over her work on the kitchen table, he knew that what he wanted most was for her mother to come to the shed that night. He would lie waiting for her, for the click at the door, the woman stepping into the pool of gentle light and the dressing-gown falling from her so that she stood there naked. Whatever she asked he would answer yes to her. Their tongues sucked at the same words as he laboured towards the drifting gasping seconds. And after she had gone and his body at times lay stinging from her demands, Schwartz opened the door into the wash-house and went through to the tiny porch on the other side. He stood naked in the cool air, the stars on a good night strewn broad and deep towards the mountains he could not see but knew were there, the unattainable spaces and pure falls. Or in rain he sometimes stood there too under the heavy sky. He looked to the mountains during the day. He kept his eyes on them as he drove in the light cart behind the horse, delivering the groceries in the mornings then picking up the girl in the afternoons. In the clear sharp weather you could see the detail of the escarpments, the deep-cut valleys slanted into delicate and timeless planes. They became the furniture of his mind. At times they vanished for a week or even longer beneath cloud, then again they would stand there. He thought, a week, a thousand years. He would watch them from the porch before he went into the house for tea.

At mealtimes he sat in the chair assigned to him from his first night, its back towards the door and the square of window, the yellow wall in front of him with a large calendar with the months and days picked out in blue against the grey paper. Round the edges of the calendar there were pictures the girl had cut from magazines and pinned there. An American eagle sitting on the bone-like branch of a dead tree, a foreign temple with its dome pointed like an onion; pictures too of people dancing, a black man standing on one leg, resting on a spear. Always while they ate the wireless played from its shelf beside the bench. When the girl was eating her head seemed always bent over homework, over books. Once a week she ruled the lines in the big ledger and did sums for her mother. The down along the nape of her neck was gold when she bent her head. She was calm and certain as her mother was restless. Jess veered between her joking with customers in the shop and banging cupboards in the kitchen as she cooked. Each night she slapped the knives and forks in the centre of the table and the girl took them up, quietly set them out. The girl made him think of a still centre, an enchanted place like there must be in the mountains, surely, where storms circled but held off, a pool in a river where the current seemed to cease. He watched her, puzzled at how she seemed untouched, even at those times when her mother turned on her, accusing her of laziness, of being a slut the way she never helped, living off other people's sweat then sitting there like she owned the bloody world. The girl's eyes followed her mother while she raged. But then other days Jess would hug the girl to her, ask her how things went at school or chat to her as one friend to another. The girl would take that too, offer back her own smile, her own gossip, but cool, Schwartz thought, remote; there is always something there her mother does not guess at, can never touch. The images in the man's mind were confused and laced with worry when he thought of her. 'Don't stare at me,' the girl sometimes told him.

The mother too, he tried not to look at her. But in the first seconds of her sitting down beside him, at tea, her leg brushing against his beneath the table, he knew he would be ready for her, that he would lie in the room with its soft lamp and its packed heavy shadows, afraid that it might be a night she chose not to use him. The wireless loud and crackling above them, their knives and forks chinking on their plates, then the girl taking the things away, her arm moving close against him, in front of him, until she drew back the blue-checked cloth and flicked it at the door and folded it and came back to sit opposite him with her books. Schwartz fetched from his room the piece of wood he was working on. He took his penknife from his pocket. His nail caught beneath the slotted edge of the blade to lift it out. Three or four times he drew the blade across the front of his shirt then tilted it so the light ran along its edge before he began at the incising, the whittling, from where he had left off the night before. There was the sound of his blade drawn against the wood, a slow curling sliver at its side. Most nights Jess wrote in one of her ledgers, setting down the details of her stock, the columns of expenditure and profit. Schwartz wondered at how she did this from memory, for she never referred to dockets or notes of any kind. Or when that was done she would sit with her eyes closed and her head resting on the wall beneath the calendar and the coloured pictures. Sometimes she baked. Then at nine o'clock the girl closed her schoolbooks. Her work was not disturbed by the serials her mother listened to, the stories that Schwartz found intricate and pointless, uncoiling from the wireless. Jess's face tilted towards the voices in their adventures and romance. He thought how she is like someone waiting for something special to happen to her. He thought how the noises that came through, the sobbing or the laughing from behind the shiny cloth in front of the speaker, were things so utterly far off, uninteresting as the shadow lives in books. He watched the moving point of his blade, the loveliness of the wood so smooth then bitten into then giving up its pure lines, its circles and overlapping angles as the designs spread over the surface of a tray, as a block in his hands was changed to hearts and linking chains. When the iron-framed clock on the mantelpiece gave its single flat note at nine o'clock the girl drew her books together and pushed her chair back from the table. Schwartz too gathered together the pieces of wood he was working at. He wrapped them in a length of cheesecloth from the storeroom, and overnight left them in the heater cupboard, on the slatted boards above the califont. He would take the bundle back to his room next morning after breakfast. 'You can't risk wood getting damp,' he told Jess. 'You let it get wet like even between here and out in the shed, it can ruin what you're working on. That's why I have to leave it here.' He said good night to the girl as she left the kitchen for her own room, and said it again to her mother from the door. When she followed after him, perhaps in an hour's time, the flame in the lamp burned so steady that the lines of shadow across the roof and walls were firm as though drawn by the man's own hankering for fixity. In winter the walls snapped and creaked with frost, and his breath was visible as he breathed above the lamp. He placed the small kerosene heater a few feet from the bed.

'It's warm for you,' he liked to tell her when he heard the soft closing of the house door and he waited there behind his own to swing it open for her, and the swishing of her dressing-gown against the doorway and her hair loosed down across her shoulders. He could not imagine anything so lovely as her standing close against the red flare, the rising of the light across her flanks, her shoulders, her hair. Then the spill of her words commanding him, flowing across her loveliness their runnels of abuse, excess. Begging her. Her nipples hard small grapes, the hair between her legs glinting as she turned at him. He was humbled by the flow of light across her body, kneeling on the rough floor in front of her, his head tilted as though he waited for some kind of halter, for her to lead him, labour him. *Ah*, and the girl now would be doing that! The boy from the school came after her, their flouting across the paddocks near the pines above the river where the boy had gripped her arms and she had turned, knowing Schwartz was standing at the corner of the sties before she faced him again, before her hand touched him. There can only be that. She is ready for that. He thought of the distant planes of snow the escarpments the pure heights, *not shit like that*, the running dribble of their tongues, Jess's wetness jammed against him.

'Don't fancy yourself,' she used to warn the girl. 'Don't strut round here like your father did, thinking you're something God-almighty special.' Even then the girl was untouched by her mother's words, swirling the long red gown behind her, rehearsing for a play at school, practising in front of the mirror until her mother flared at her.

Schwartz watched the females confront each other. Inside the tangle of words he saw the mother's envy of her daughter, the child's invincible certainty that she had won. The girl had only to raise her young arms and place the cardboard tiara on her head. 'Swanning round,' Jess said, 'thinking you can bend down and pick up jewels or bloody something.'

'And so I can,' the girl told her. 'That's what you don't like. I can call things by any names I like.'

Her mother slammed the door of the safe, shouting at her. 'You're mad,' she said, 'you're crazy as your bloody father!' The man who had brought her pregnant to the shop a hundred miles from any decent town and left her there for ever with no way of getting out. 'Dead!' she screamed, 'That's the only way of getting out!'

Then in September a year further on, when the big white daisies were thick in the grass at the sides of the roads, the woman told him to harness up the cart. Weather like this made her want to take a drive. 'To the cemetery,' she said.

The sky was a scoured and deep blue, the long grass between the graves pale as the girl's hair. The wind moved across it and the grass combed out.

'I don't come out here for grief,' Jess told him, 'don't think that.'

They lay on a slope beside a row of stones, below the raised arms of the flower-dropping angels and the rounded glass containers of artificial wreaths, domes like divers' helmets. He had thought of asking why did she come then? Knowing the answer as they lay there, his certainty for the first time that the woman whose hands worked between his legs was madder than ever he might be. He knew without the encumbrance of actual speech that they were there to punish. She dragged him on top of her. She called at him loudly enough for her words to reach up to the incised stones, to the avenues of the never-fucking dead.

At first they had stood by the grey stone while the girl crouched down to push the few scrappy flowers she had brought from home through the netting across the top of a vase. He had read the words picked out in white lettering. Then the girl had gone off by herself, hopping between grave and grave. She carried an empty sack and made for the row of pines beyond the cemetery's enclosing fence. When the girl had reached the pines, Jess said quietly, as if what she proposed was no more than sitting down, 'There's time for it now.' She drew him down into the yellow grass.

The girl had come back to them with the bag half filled with cones. At home she arranged them in the wicker basket near the stove. She took each one and set it as though piling eggs in careful layers. 'These eggs,' she would say later in the other place, the other island. 'There's more of them each day. I don't know where the extra chooks are coming from.' She held each egg she took from the colander and rubbed a wet cloth across it. 'We found half a dozen on the bank above the river there.' *We.* Schwartz thought, she is saying that deliberately. She is saying those words more and more, *we* and *us* and *Alex* even, she likes to say them to me. She watches me while she says them. She put the eggs into a carton with separate cardboard squares for every egg. Then she said, 'Shall I get you lunch?' She fried bacon for him and two of the eggs the boy would have stooped and handed up to her. He had seen them doing that the other day, her own hands held out like a wide cup where he placed them and smiled at her. Schwartz ran his bread across the streaming orange yolk. He said to her, 'I thought you would go to the funeral, eh?' She had finished eating first. She stood at the bench and ran water over her plate. She said, 'I didn't know her. I've never even seen her.'

'Not that you know of,' Schwartz said. 'You might of and not known it was her.'

'I don't think so,' she said.

And he told her, 'I could of driven you down.'

He watched her lean at the sink. Her dress came only to her knees. He saw the swelling of her calves, the gold colour of her arms. She said, looking through the window, watching across the paddocks and the stirring watery shiver of the heat above them, 'I know you would have.' She went through to the corridor to her room. Schwartz stood to look through the window as she had done, although his own attention was on the pigs at the side of the barn, the cluttered pack of them lolling in the sun. He watched one that was troubled with lice rubbing itself against the fence where he had hammered sacking soaked in sump oil. The young sow's sides gleamed with the smears. Schwartz turned and saw the girl down the corridor come from her room. Her arms were crossed and she grasped the end of the old shirt she was wearing. She lifted it above her head. He saw the silhouetting of her body against the silverish light of the pane. It reminded him of Jess taking her own things off. The same quickened beating of his pulse. He was not ready for the images that poured together into his mind. The girl he had always feared who was pure while the rest were rotten now ran together with her mother whose lubricity had shaken him as easily as a kid, say, picks up a puppy and shakes it for the fun of it. He saw in his mind as clearly as though watching other figures in that clear bright light of the corridor, his own mouth across those pure tits, his rutting at the girl's smooth thighs. He felt the sweat moving suddenly beneath his eyes, the feeling that comes before a man throws up, the rising of his guts heaved against himself. She stepped back into her room and called something to him. Her words came to him slurred, his own mouth too filled with the coppery taste of rising nausea for him to call back, only the rasping of his breath, the guttural animal catching of his throat. Before she came back to the kitchen he had walked from the house and across to the barn. He leaned there against the broad doorway, the brooding fetid darkness with its slivers and chinks of light slashing the walls in front of him. The sky was bundling with clouds across the river. Before the hour was out the paddocks would soak with the summer downpour. There was the hot smell of hay hanging across the air from the neighbouring farms. A tractor chirred remotely from down past Larsens'. With a gesture that sometimes came to him when the effort of speech had become too great, he raised his head, his throat stretched so the sinews of his neck stood rigid with the strain. He lifted his left arm to brush at the runnel of spit that moved on his chin. He saw the distant tractor move for a moment into a clearing beyond the trees. It shimmered in haze as though dipped in water. He turned back towards the house and saw the same heat waves rising from the bonnet of the car. At the side of the house and beneath the car and below the line of macrocarpas he saw the shadows lie so darkly vivid he thought of the girl at the table after their tea was over down south, doing one of her drawings on her yellow pad, the heavy hatching blackness of her shadows. The black crayon working over and over itself, the paper stiffening with it. The bitch her mother, those evenings before she scarpered off. Shot through and left him with the girl – he could be responsible for her, the note said, or send her to a home. When she was young and pure, before she met the boy or stood in the silver light pouring over her body. Even if she hadn't meant to. He spat a gob of yellow phlegm into the sink. Then he took the few steps from the January sun into the darkness of the barn. He climbed above the thick reek of the sties, balancing himself on the edge of a barrier he had built the month before. His hand edged along behind a board until it touched the tin he lifted down. The top he expected to find on it was gone, the tin itself was empty. The crammed saltsack was gone. He held the tin in his hand as he walked back into the sunlight. It was as though he had expected its emptiness and yet the discovery seemed to stun him. One of the last litter ran to him and rubbed against his dungarees. As if in reflex his leg wheeled against it, tumbling the animal in a squealing arc.

Schwartz took up a solid wooden crate from just inside the door. He carried it a few paces and set it where the mud had

hardened firmly as a solid floor. He sat and the tin in his hand
rested against his knee. From a little distance it would have
seemed that he was holding a drink, that he sat enjoying the sun.
He turned the tin, the torn name of the baking powder passing
beneath his hand. Aloud, he said, 'She must of pinched it, then.'
He placed the tin upside down on the ground beside the box. He
then walked away from both it and the box towards the shed
where the car was parked with its bonnet protruding into the sun,
the metal too hot for his hand to rest on. He moved between the
car and the garage wall until he stood before the tools and the
petrol cans and that other odour he picked up, the musty smell of
possum. He squatted before the workbench and reached beneath
it to a shelf, groping for the handle of a gladstone bag he then
drew towards him. He pressed hard against the metal clasps before
their stiffness gave. C.R. was stamped on the leather, almost too
faint to read. It was a bag he had taken from Jess's before he left.
The initials were those of the man whose grave they had fucked
beside. He had put in it some of the things packed into his suitcase
so long before in Franklin Road, things transferred in time to the
sugarsack he carried on the road. Schwartz now lifted from it the
frayed boxing magazine and laid it on the top of the bench. On the
cover was a picture of Jack Johnson, his head round and shaved,
his grin that they said he never lost, especially if he was fighting a
whiteman. That bloody cheeky nigger, Scully used to call him. It
had stood propped against the bedroom lamp the night he left
Mrs Murfitt's and he had lain it smooth in the bottom of the
suitcase with Billy Murphy's signed photograph. There were
other magazines, a few tools, a tin of camphor ice he had used on
his chilblains in the south. His hand again entered the bag, his
knuckles for a fraction brushing the smooth lining that made him
think of Scully coming up to him that first day in the gym, the
man's hat held in the trainer's hands, the stained satin lining
moving there in front of him while the stranger put it to him, 'I'll
make a champ of you, son, give me two months and see what you
think.' His fingers now touched the wooden handle and then the
rope itself which he had taken that same night from the hook
behind the door. He drew out its smooth length, winding it round
one handle until he came to the wooden grip on the other end.

The wound rope was now like a fat bandaged fist. He walked back to the kitchen and took his balaclava from the shelf above the bench. The girl had left the wireless playing although she was no longer in the house. He turned the knob until it clicked, the green eye going dead. Then he stepped again across the shadow of the porch and back to the hard brightness of the afternoon. Within minutes the bank of clouds drew across the sky like a blanket. Schwartz stepped over the wooden gate into the first paddock, and the dog which kept step with him flattened itself beneath the bottom rung. The man stopped at the patch he had wired off and planted with cabbages. Countless grey moths seethed and fluttered above the pale clumps, the earth seeming to palpitate with their flickering drift over the blown vegetable life. There was a different heat here too. Schwartz felt it rise towards his face, the smell that mingled growth and decay together. Already some of the cabbages had declined into browning heaps. A few lay withered like huge ears. The simmering life, the rise and fall and agitation of the countless moths, touched him with a puzzled grief – so many unquenchable scraps of life. Then across the paddock he turned into a smaller shed he had also converted for the pigs. This was a kind of sick-bay for the runts. Barbara joked to him about it, she called it the Ward. Two of the animals he held here now had eye infections. They set up when they heard him walk towards them, a grunting snuffle as he went about the usual routine of hosing out, feeding them from a bin of grain that he kept especially for the sick. Other pigs in the paddock streamed across towards him, snapping at each other's ears and sides and arses, shrieking at the beating of the tin jug he used to scoop out the grain. Today he flung them more than their share. With the crook he had made from a forked piece of matai he hooked one of the smaller sows towards him. There was a seeping wound at the side of her neck. 'I've got to do that first,' he said. He sank down, straddling her, smearing the ointment he tugged from the pocket of his dungarees. His fingers smoothed across the wound, the animal went limp, content to lie beneath his hand. When he opened his knees she scuttled from him, taking up the racket of the others around the grain. He rested there on his knees. A sow with its belly huge and distended moved to him and nuzzled at his back. Three days from now and she would farrow. Three days, but the girl would make sure of all that, wouldn't she? She would feed them. He now hung the crook on a loose board and walked the twenty yards back to the main barn. Those others he thought, those neighbours with their cows, they thought they knew it all but no one had ever seen pigs this good round here before, they said he was off his swede, that he didn't know farming from a kick in the arse, he knew they said that. But they didn't know who he was either, none of them had seen him without the balaclava, he had taken every one of them in. The pigs. The pigs were what showed them. He grabbed the rim of an empty forty-four gallon drum and spun it towards the opened door of the barn, guiding the drum's movement until he stopped before the pregnant sow that had trailed him across the paddock. He stooped to scratch in the blonde bristles and the caked dirt behind her lug. Then he shoved her back with his boot and drew the door towards him. He heard the dog barking off somewhere near the river. She would be raising ducks from the reeds beneath the bank. For a moment both his hands rested on the rim of the drum, while his eyes adjusted to the darkened high space. The daggers of light through the gaps were no longer blue but grey. He could smell the hay mingled with pig-shit. He saw that the sow was against the wall outside, watching him through the slats. Then from where he had tucked it at the back of his belt, he took the neatly folded rope. From his pocket he fetched out the knife he had carried for years, and raised the narrow blade. He cut one of the wooden handles from the rope, placed it on the edge of the pens, and returned the knife to his pocket. Schwartz then lifted one knee to the flat surface of the drum, which he balanced with both hands. Slowly he raised the other knee towards the first. He rested there on all fours as though poising himself for some trick, making sure of his balance before he stood carefully upright on the yellow circle. His right hand lifted and touched the wooden beam above him. His left hand he brought up until it lay beside the other, then he slid the remaining handle of the rope across the beam, dragging down on it once it had crossed the wood. He knotted it quickly, the smooth pegshape wedged hard in against the beam. His hand had brushed for a moment against the frail prickly sides of a nest. He nudged the rope a few inches further along so as not to disturb it. And as quickly as he had tied the first knot he now tied another, shaping a loop at the further end of the rope. There was only a short length between the beam and the loop, so that he raised himself slightly on his toes to reach it comfortably, then again stood flat, his heels on the top of the drum. His fingers played at the knot to ensure that it flowed. He remembered, last of all, that he should have brought the balaclava that still lay on the fence across at the other shed. He wished he had it now to put on. Then he flicked his boots back sharply against the drum that fell and rolled and rocked against the door, the sow eager and grunting at the other side. He had won he had kept her back he had not allowed her to take his mind like the other the girl's long reaching back her silvered tits there was a flare like a lamp had been picked up and dashed against his eyes there was tapping rocking the sound like hooves against a pavement *Jesus*. He tried to turn his head against the dragging tearing weight the pouring gush of light as though at last the mountains close as *O Jesus! Jesus!*

Nurse Smithers held up her wrist, to read the time on the tiny gold figures of her birthday watch. She then held it against her ear. 'Hardly hear its ticking, know that?'

The young man who had given it to her earlier that evening, who had seen her first eight months ago as she walked into the ward where he visited his father and he could scarcely believe it, this girl who came and held his father's wrist and looked down at him and smiled slightly as she took the old man's pulse, he said to her now, 'I asked for the quietest one they had.'

'They won't let us have ones with too loud a tick.'

'I know. That's why I asked for one like that.'

'It looks lovely anyway,' she said. She ran her cheek against his. She let him put his hand again on her breast, now that they were engaged. As long as it was only there. Sometimes he said in the nicest way that it seemed an awful long time to wait, like — eighteen months. And she made a little pout that she knew he liked and told him, but think of how long they would have after that, he'd get tired of it, wait and see. It was good being able to say things as direct as that to a man. We'll wait and see all right, her fiancé said.

When she read the time in the light from the street lamp at the edge of the bridge, Nurse Smithers said again she would have to go earlier than usual, remember, it was the big exam in two days' time. When her fiancé's fingers worked deeper and scooped her up by the handful, and he ran his rough dark handsome jaw along her throat and licked behind her ear, and breathed more quickly than usual, she raised her arms and let them meet across his shoulder and she saw the stone in her engagement ring flash out like a distant bright signal. She liked it, of course, when her fiancé became so ardent and she felt the strength of his embrace, and the fact too that he was better-looking than almost any of the men who took out girls from the nurses' home. But the exam was in two days' time after all, and as her fiancé turned her and leaned her back so her hair as she could imagine it flowed over his sleeve and the street light reflected glinting strands in it, she still couldn't put it out of her mind, not even then. She would spend an hour at her desk when he dropped her off at the home and then get up for another hour's study before she was on duty in the morning. There were always the tricky questions you couldn't quite prepare for, though the case studies part she knew she could do almost perfectly. She liked getting those by heart. They were easier too, because she liked the patients and even that old battle-axe Sister Harris said she had a natural calling. When she learned the cold facts from her notes it was the people she also saw and tried to understand. The woman, say, whose hair she enjoyed brushing, it was not such a different colour to her own, but so much longer, finer. Some of the staff thought it was sheer favouritism that it wasn't cut like other patients'. Nurse Smithers was very glad it wasn't. And she wondered sometimes what on earth the real story about her was. Behind the other story, she meant, the story of the runaway, the river, the man who scarpered off. Her chart was not even certain about her birthday. It had '1920' and then a question mark.

Her fiancé released his hand and she helped him button her blouse and they drove in silence along the Te Awamutu Road. There was no moon and no stars either that she could make out, only the yellow tunnel from the car lights that drew them through the dark. Her fiancé asked her just before the Otorohanga turn-off, 'What are you thinking about, then?', and she fibbed to him. She said, 'Oh, one thing and another. Like next weekend at home and that.' But she had really been going over her notes, seeing how much of them she knew. But when he kissed her the last time just before she left the car and he told her he would be thinking of her all Thursday until he knew how the exam had gone, she felt with a rush what a good man her fiancé was. She pushed her tongue against his and took his hand, placed it on her knee and let his fingers stroke just as far as the top of her stockings.

When she sat at her small desk five minutes later and turned the desk lamp lower and took a sip from her cocoa, that woman across the lawn there in her white bed, her white dream, was the last thing on earth Nurse Smithers wanted to have to think about. She looked up from her notepad and recited. Post-traumatic head injury. Expressive aphasia. Intermittent focal seizure (Jacksonian epilepsy). Medication barbiturates and bromide syrup. Recent years obesity, occasional constipation (Epsom salts). Self-feeding and toileting. Early arthritis left hand and joints.

She let her own hand lie at the edge of the paper directly under the bright circle of the desk lamp, so that the ring showed very clear and bright.

'S_{pain?}'

'Spain,' Rory said. Beneath the fruit trees, the dapple across his pale face and his thin arms, as the two boys took their lunches from the paper wrappings. He has lived in these long hot days, this one place, all his life, Alex thought, and he is pale as I am in winter. Already his own arms were tanned; his forehead that at first had peeled and reburned was bronzed and smooth. You'd have thought I was the one who lived here always and Rory who came from that cooler place, the winter fogs, the February humid days that never burned like this, never ruled you the way the blaze of sunlight rules you here.

His cousin was not as tall as he was, nor as strong. Alex with his height and his spareness that made them joke his first few days in the orchard as he bent to hook his fingers beneath the laden cases, 'Don't break yourself in half there, sport, we don't need kindling.' Not as strong yet more compact, the sense of a spring held down, ready to throw its pent energy when the pressure that held it was taken off.

Rory. Alex had heard the name, seen it in the notes his aunt wrote twice a year, once at his mother's birthday, the other at Christmas. The half dozen or so lines in her hooped untidy hand that stretched across the card like broken fences. I'd love to see him one day, his mother said. He's just about your age. She wondered if he was a little chap and took after his father.

'I don't know the first thing about Spain.'

'It's where it's going to end,' Rory said. 'The struggle that decides us all, I mean. The truth hammered out.' He bit into a sandwich. Before he chewed he raised the bottle of orange cordial so his mouth was full of mush. 'These bloody teeth,' he had said another day to Alex. 'Must have got them from my old man.'

He made Alex think of church. Of the taste of varnish when he was really small and put his mouth against the rounded back of the pew in front. When they knelt on the little cushions once or twice a year. When the family met at church. When someone died. The light through the high slender windows behind the altar, the windows curving in and pointed at the top, the light poured in bars. The light and the varnish taste that between them made him think of something else, of the pale waxy feeling of lightest shoe polish that came off yellow on a rag. And Rory like the voice in church, the voice with the prayers or not even the prayers themselves so much as the pictures the words built up. When Rory spoke the feeling at times was like that. Clear and sharp yet distant, what he spoke of. It was amusing, that, Alex thought. Because there was nothing Rory hated more than church. Than God. Than whatever made things as they were.

His cousin put his hand inside his checked shirt. He ran his palm over his chest and over his shoulder, letting his fingers rest there, moving gently while he talked. His fingers moving beneath the material of his shirt. Alex thought, you could imagine it was some small animal under there.

'That old bastard,' Rory said. 'His books all round the walls and talking to the workers like his only begotten bloody sons and lapping it up when they call him by his first name.' His cheek bulged as his tongue scooped along his teeth. 'The master in fancy dress.'

Alex liked it when his cousin raged. At times he wondered how everything could still seem so new to him, the view looking down through the orchard, up there along the slope of the mountain. Two months he had been here now. Nearly three. That newness, he supposed, that's what fills the gap. His aunt had said the phrase – *this will fill in time.* Simply by keeping his eyes open he supposed was what she meant, his heart ticking, his mind merely being there. The gap filled in any case. Nothing can stay empty. His cousin talked of Spain and Alex thought how it did not seem quite real, not even yet. The sparser rising of the trees than he was used to, the simpler stretching out of the land, the expanse that took you with it. Making him feel the green, the tightness, the manageable hills at home were somehow small, too easy. A cheek that had just been shaved, say. Those hills behind Cambridge. Most of the Waikato.

'Christ,' Rory asked him, 'can you imagine anything more condescending than that? To say to a man who works for you, *pretend* we face each others as equals.'

Alex raised the apple he had rolled for several minutes across his knees. When he bit into it the taste was cool. The feeling of a vault. '*Sir*, then,' he said. 'Better, is it, if they call him that?'

'Of course it's better,' Rory said. 'You're not having anybody on. You're not singing hymns to stop people thinking how God kicks them in the arse.'

'You don't believe in God.'

Rory's tongue moved again inside his cheek. It was not worth answering that. His hand taken now from his shirt, from his skin smoothly pale as a girl's. Rubbing instead behind his neck. He looked directly at his cousin, Alex's face in moving segments, light broken into coins as it sifted down through the trees. In rings, circles, leprous spots across both their hands. He said, 'He gets all the papers. All the stuff about it. He subscribes to everything.'

'That's how you know about it, then?'

Rory's bad teeth showed. Of course it was how he knew. 'He sits with his port in one hand and all the stuff about Spain in the other. Reads it all, the old bugger. Tuts away. "The day is coming," he says.'

'What day?'

Rory laughed. 'The day without his expensive drinks. Without his matey workers.'

'But he's made you what you are!' Alex smiling, knowing his cousin's irritation.

'The argument isn't weakened because of that.'

The spinning shifting coins of light, the patterning between the shadows slipped across them both, each of them leaning back against a trunk. Inside a shimmering tent. Alex flicked his wrist, his applecore propelled against a stone ten yards distant. Down the slope of the orchard, through the aisles of the trees, the hooter sounded from the sheds. Rory folded the paper from their lunches and laid it inside one of the tins. Before Alex arrived he had spent his lunchtimes reading up here. The best time of the day. Down in the sheds the others sat at the long table, the huge enamel teapot at one end, the cups passed down by Madge whose job it had been for years to mother the table. The workers drifting in and out, the pickers who came for the late summer months, even these days when so much of the industry was on bad times. They slept in the old stables, eating the same food as they ate across in the house. Rory said, 'Share your tucker with the itinerants and it's next best thing to pulling the loaves and fishes.'

'His books, though,' Alex kept on. 'His house. His food. You're close as Siamese twins.' Saying it from mischief. To see his cousin's cool distaste, to hear the steel certainty of his voice.

'Then there'll have to be some blood-letting, won't there? Sooner or later?'

Alex thought how he could see his father in Rory, from that one small snap in his mother's album. He had some vague idea of the family ructions years and years back, the disgrace of Frances going off with a jockey. He remembered from the photo the man's jaunty stance, his arm actually raised to reach across the shoulders of the woman, the girl, who stood beside him. A checked cap tilted back, the narrow face. Vulpine, Alex's mother had said, explaining to him what the word meant. Handsome in its way. You could understand it all right. Or she could anyway, his mother could. Although as she said her parents saw only the depravity, their own faces being spat in by the girl who was given everything, who could have the pick of the field for God's sake. So her father had shouted with that way of his, slapping his opened hand on the dark polished wood, the cutlery as Alex's mother remembered it leaping right up from the table, clattering down again, crooked and askew, and his wife, their grandmother, leaning across, setting them parallel again, the world in its place.

Rory took up the tin lunch-box. He slipped its handle along a twig and then took Alex's from his cousin's hand, setting that close beside his own. He hung them there to keep them from the ants. Inchmen, Rory called them, the big ones that moved wherever one happened to look. The ones that were supposed to nip like hell. Alex thought how his cousin's movements seemed always so precise, so in control. Even the way he stood on the ladder, his swaying with the swing and movement of the tree, not trying to work against it as Alex felt himself doing. He liked to watch him move. That must be his father in him, that natural sporting grace. Certainly not his mother, not as she was now, Aunt Frances with her weight, with the effort it cost her to walk even as far as from the house to the sheds. The beads of sweat always there along her upper lip, the dampening smear at the back of her dress. He could charm a horse, his mother had said, what chance was there for the likes of me? About Rory's father.

'How are the feet?' Rory asked him now. He was moving the ladder from the last tree into the abundant springiness of the next. He jerked at the strap of the canvas bag that lay empty and loose against his side.

Alex took up his own bag from where he had left it before lunch across the rung of his ladder. 'They're okay,' he said, and flexed his toes inside his sandshoes. There was still a slight soreness in his soles from the narrow pressure of the rungs. 'That trick of yours must've worked all right.' The wedges of cork tied beneath his shoes had taken the bite from the rungs. He climbed his ladder and once again was in that grey mottled world, the heavy scent of the fruit, the constant brushing and scratching against his arms and face. Within a minute he was sweating, sweat Alex thought like the point of a knife run down very softly against your sides. Wet even in his eyes. He leaned his head sideways and rubbed against the cotton shoulder of his shirt.

They worked on in the dull heat of the afternoon, the apples swelling the canvas bags at their sides, the straps across their shoulders cutting harder with the weight. The tumble then as the fruit was emptied out into the bins, the boxes hoisted up between them when Reg drove down between the rows on his tractor. The flickering streaming arc of fruit into the bins. Further along another picker broke out into song. An Italian with a treacly kind of voice, high and wafting over the intervening trees. But a warmth in it, Alex thought, a solace even. When the Italian stopped singing, that other kind of silence then, and through it sounds coming back in so slowly, the creaking in the tree he leaned against, his buckle against the waist-level rungs, one or other of the tractors. Nearby there was Rory's pushing his breath between his teeth, not quite a whistle, a sustained level hiss.

Rory called across, 'I'm going to have to fill you in about Spain, Alex.'

Alex's first sight of his aunt and Mr Wallace was seeing them together. His aunt so grotesque and fat that he could not believe she was a relative of his, let alone his mother's sister. And the elderly man with a neatly trimmed white beard standing a little away from her, his weight leaning forward on the iron he pressed down on, the flowing tumble of a spread-out sheet on the ironing board in front of him. He sprinkled the sheet from a bottle of water with a silver cap just as Alex came into the room. The steam hissed from the sides of the iron, the man's hands in the quick warm mist as he said to the woman, but without turning to her, 'So he's here at last, then.' His aunt's hand raised to her cheek as the man spoke. A quick wet glitter on her finger as if a drop of water fell and shone there when light grazed the stone. 'Ah, so he is,' she said.

Mr Wallace tilted the iron back on its base. The sheet hung in front of him like a long crumpled skirt. Alex felt as if he walked across a stage to stand right up close beside the actors. He saw how the man's hand still held the handle of the iron. The window was opened behind them. Outside there was a blue shimmer and the sickle leaves of a gum. His aunt sat perfectly still. She waited for his stooping towards her, for the kiss she had demanded. In duty then he leaned towards her, repelled at the same time. Where the collar of her dress lay against her shoulders the material seemed to bite down, the flesh rising puffed above it. He thought of dough on the bench at home. His mother taking the thin gold band from her finger, setting it on the sideboard before her hands plunged. That smell coming up to him as he leaned. He saw on her neck the thin cord that held a sachet. He closed his eyes against the sweetness. The spread sheet over the ironing board smelled hot beside her. Then the drawn-out tableau snapped, the sense he had of stepping into a photograph, into some moment of performance he had arrived at but not understood. For his aunt's arms raised to clasp him about the neck, there was the quick intake of her breath wetly against his ear. Unexpectedly, his own eyes prickled, the floor across his aunt's shoulder, the legs of the table, wavering. His face then squashed softly as in a pillow, the pervading wash of lavender swamping him, drawing him in. She released him and she was laughing. He surprised himself by laughing back. He said, 'I just about lost my breath there.'

'Old Alex,' she said. She turned to the man who had not moved from the board. 'All over again, isn't he?' Then, 'Not so solemn, mind. Not the way your dad was.'

'Only in looks. My mother said we were chalk and cheese.'

The man said, 'He'd have got a good price for either, mind you. Whether you wanted to buy it or not.' Again he tilted the iron and brought it down on the sprinkled sheet. But briefly. Because then the strangest thing. Mr Wallace had walked from behind the ironing board and there was a composite embrace, the man bearing down his hand and then his arm on Alex's shoulder, his other hand on the woman, his fingers moving, kneading the soft dough. The smell when he opened his mouth was peppermint.

He had expected his aunt to ask him about it, but she had not said a word. He knew one of the other relatives must have written, Aunt Mary or Aunt Nan. Perhaps one of their husbands. Or more likely that cousin in Auckland. They were the only two, his mother had said, who really kept up the bonds over the years, only Lizzie and herself. But there was not a sign from her, or from the old man or Rory either that they had heard anything more than that Mum had died. Yet they watched him, didn't they? Glancing up at dinner sometimes he caught his aunt looking at him, her clear grey eyes placing him under scrutiny, setting him beneath a glass like the things in the lab at school had been set. The dry fur he remembered, the stretched-out scraggy wings, the spread pink interiors of life. But Alex had thought too, no, that's not fair on her. Aunt Frances isn't prying, she doesn't think like that. The other aunts would all right, but she wasn't part of that team, was she? She's the girl who ran off with a man the family hated because he didn't fit. His mother had said that too. Not out of the same drawer. Forgive him if he was a thief or a wife-beater but not forgive him that. His mother had smiled when she said, 'Nothing ever gave the others such a sense of moral victory as Francie gave them. Ran off for love then came a cropper. Mary would think a hundred years of boredom was a triumph over that.' So even if she knows, Alex thought, she won't be judging me. She won't be *feeling sorry*.

'I don't ride,' he told his cousin.

'Then you'll have to learn.'

'I don't even like horses.'

'Scared of them?' The pale head level with his own shoulder. Rory's eyes like his mother's, like Aunt Francie's.

'Yes,' Alex said.

'Good.' His cousin ducked beneath the horse, came back, bobbed again with the leather girth-strap in his hand. He said, 'In time we'll get so you can ride without one of these things too. Saddles. They take half the fun from it.' He buckled another strap then dragged back, straining at the leather. He slapped against the saddle, which was a mere fold of leather blanket.

'Why good?' Alex watched him. He thought how he had been on a farm all his life, yet he wouldn't know where to start making anything.

Rory went to the horse's other side, only his legs in filthy moleskins visible beneath the animal's barrelled sag. There was no answer until his cousin came round, took the reins in his fist and passed them across. 'Because if you're scared that's something to get over, see. Once you've got the best of that you'll ride better than if you started off all cocky.' He laughed, his teeth so small they made you think of a child's. The smoky smell from his hair as he passed in front of Alex. 'That's my theory.'

Alex at first so tall and angular, leaning forward so awkwardly, his weight was wrongly thrown when he mounted.

'Use your knees,' Rory ordered him. 'Your legs are part of you too, you know. Use your weight here to swing on, like.' He tapped at his own stomach, meaning to pivot from his pelvis, telling Alex how control was always balance, knowing how to sway, taking your rhythm from the moving horse beneath you. He said, 'Strength has bugger all to do with it.'

'She's got to know who's boss.'

'She'll know by the way you sit. Wrench too hard at those, for instance' – Rory was pointing at the reins – 'she'll know you're panicky, see. That you don't know what to do. Once a horse knows that, she's got you.'

Soon, as he woke each morning, Alex anticipated their ride in the late afternoon. His own horse was docile enough after the first few days, but Rory's roan was eager, prancing sideways as they walked the path from the stable past the sheds, then took the track through and beyond the orchard to the bushy scrub on the steeper slope. Rory leading always, riding bareback, the flicker of the gums and the tea-tree and those long confusing vistas when they slowed their pace and pulled up. The smoky blue depth into the bush. It struck Alex, every afternoon, how different this was from home. A dozen steps into the bush there and you'd lost everything except height, except looking up. Here you'd get lost in openness. Thirty yards off, fifty yards, you see the trees surrounding you and stretching out. There is hardly any undergrowth. You see where you're going and yet you still get lost, the distant trees turning, passing always faster than those close beside you, as though they're at the edges of a wheel and you're at the hardly moving centre. And always the sense of light, he noticed, nothing really green, the colours flaring off to ochres, pinks, a dozen flickering greys. Lost here, you'd die of fear, Alex supposed, as you would die anywhere, die of thirst and all the rest of it but always as if the light was taking you, drawing you closer to it than you wanted to go. It was quite the opposite at home. Lost there, you would die in gloom. The nearest trees would loom in on you. That's what you would feel, the pressing in, the cutting off. Not this awful opening out.

'What do you think of that, then?' Rory reining in at the side of a huge rock, its side shot through with glittering mica.

'The rock?'

'No, not that!' A few paces, and now Alex's horse panting beside his cousin's. Both of them suddenly looking down on the coast, the bush to within a few feet of the water, a low shelf of yellow rock between the trees and sea. The water so calm. Like rolled silver or something, Alex thought. He cantered ahead, raising his arm in a sweeping slow advance to ask, would they go on, up there to another ridge? The trees were sparse against the sky. And then their coming back in the almost dark, quietly, the horses ambling down, there was hardly a need to direct them. The lights from the floor of the valley when the track turned above the orchards, the sense of ordinary things returning. Sometimes, late, the Italian's voice coming up to them, the horsing-about laughter of the blokes in the quarters where the single pickers slept. The piping and shouting of kids racing round the barns. Alex liked that ride down best of all, that clicking of the lights behind and through the trees, the stars edging through, hardly there at first, then so quickly firm, glittering and flung across so much space when you leaned back and took the sky full-face. You could sometimes hear small animals turning from the horses, their brushing away against the bush.

Each day, like a drum behind a procession, insistent yes as that, Alex thought. Like each day is a parade the banners the exaggerated figures the blaring here of so much light. Of noise behind it always. Why do I think of it as sound? Absence and presence. Each day, *Barbara*.

Each day his aunt came down to the shed where the air churned a tunnel of smudged dust and the heavy smell of the apples seemed not an odour so much as a veil one pushed through, its weight slipping against one's face. The soft cushioned thunder when the hopper tilted, the rolling of the fruit in their hundreds down the rubber mats to the lanes where the hired women graded and selected, their hands poising, diving down, their arms bare and crossing each other's. And Beatrice Fordyce, the child of Madge the forewoman and Reg the driver, a different being among the older women. Her hair caught up beneath a scarf that she wore like a peasant's bandana. Rory said nothing to her although in the shed his eyes came back to her.
'That girl *exudes*,' Alex's aunt said. Saying it fatly, jokily. Her bulk laughing at the word she used. Exuded the welling of sap, she meant, an early ripeness in the hot packed atmosphere of per-vasive apple scent. The girl worked in the sheds from seven-thirty in the morning until the sky flared late behind the inked shadows of the orchards. The men hovered at her like the wasps above fruit that had fallen, that sank on itself in reeking sweetness or was tossed in the bins for cider. Aunt Frances was diverted by the excuses the men put up to hang about her while they ignored or

merely accepted the other women. The girl wore a loose blue smock, a garment that also amused Frances because of what it so clearly declared, her mother's desperate hope that somehow its shapeless fall would protect her daughter from the inevitable. Alex felt a flushing rise of disgust when he heard his aunt remark as casually as she might answer a request for the time, 'Nothing short of a miracle's going to keep that one off her back for long.' Giving out her opinion one afternoon when a drizzle fell outside, blurring the trees, steaming off the concrete. The work in the shed slowed down. Some of the women sat on upturned crates and lit cigarettes. His aunt stood at a trestle table, running the brush from a tray of glue across the backs of labels she then smoothed on the ends of empty boxes. Beatrice moved backwards and forwards, taking the labelled crates, setting them in neat stacks. At one turn her smock snagged against the bench, the blue material lifting and trailing back, her leg exposed to the middle of her thigh. A man passing her with petrol for one of the tractors, his body tugged to one side by the weight of the can, called out, 'God, I'll give you more than a hand there, Beatrice, give me time to drop me load.' The women sitting on the crates howled out at his joke. One of them called, 'Know what you'd give her, all right.' She put her cigarette on the edge of a beam beside her as her laugh grated into a cough, her leaning one arm against a neighbour's while she hawked in her amusement.

Alex was shocked that his aunt spoke so directly to those stale joking women. It was as though she sided there with them, and not with the girl who turned so her burning face was out of eyeshot. He saw her smile broadly across at them. He watched how that old bitch over there opened her mouth in a fresh spasm of coughing. Her tongue curled back, soft and grey and raw. Imagine his mother ever speaking as her sister did, throwing herself so easily into their dirty talk, so deliberately joining their rancour, their physical ugliness. The girl had snatched so quickly at her raised and trailing frock that the material parted in a jagged rip. And now she ran from the shed, adding to the store of fun.

'Put out, is she?' another woman said. Then in a higher make-believe voice, 'Lady Muck like, my!'

'Wouldn't say arse for a big red apple,' the cougher put in.

After that the women had to lean against the bench to support their amusement.

They used to talk like that at school too, didn't they, Alex thought. Calling her Princess when she walked out on them. Their talk and shit didn't even touch her. He said now, his voice not level enough to cover the anger or the nervousness brushing through it, 'Why can't you give her a break for a bit, you lot?' Then the man, at least, laughing directly at him. 'You wouldn't know the first bloody thing about it though, would you, dig? About her or anything else?'

One of the women looked over at him. She said, dismissing him, mocking any right he might have to an opinion among the locals, 'Listen to the blow-in, will you?'

His question had hardly touched them. That other one then with her fag back in her gob, turning again with relish against the girl, declaiming, 'She'll get what's coming to her one of these days.' And her mate telling them all, chuffed at putting her tongue to it, 'Asking for it a damned sight before then too, I'll give you even money on that one.' The laughter racketed out. A pity Rory's up the orchard, Alex thought. He would shut them up. Whether his mother was one of that mob or not.

She noticed how her nephew looked away from her. He was repelled by her bulk, by the threads of sweat gathered between the ridged folds of her neck. Frequently she paused from her labelling to dab under her chin, at the creases where the cushion of her upper arms folded against her forearms. The handkerchief she dabbed with was a damp discoloured ball. When she smiled he observed again how her teeth were perfect. But her laugh when it came was as raucous as the others', the bond they liked her for although she was the one who employed them, who fired them like a shot if she thought their work not up to scratch. She set them each morning at their tasks and watched, they supposed, on behalf of that stuck-up old bastard who once a day walked slowly through the shed, who tried to make small-talk with them and the moment he had passed they signalled behind his back, God Almighty, what a drongo! He killed the singing and the joking and the talk as surely, Madge said, as if he was a bloody undertaker or something, as if he'd come to bury them one by one.

Alex liked to see her smiling. Rory must have his father's teeth, then. Funny how you get one thing from one parent, something else from the other. Missing out, Alex thought, as likely as not missing out on what you'd choose to get. Like not being so tall, not looking so that everyone back home and even his aunt here sized you up and said, 'Old Ecky over again, don't you reckon? Dead ringer.' And how odd to think of her and his mother being sisters – that was what really got him. That was too grotesque to think of. There was always such composure with his mother. Her voice never raised, her hands set still in her lap while she talked. She had worried so much about giving people a fair deal, about doing what was right. Stressing to him even as a child, before the words could mean much to him at all, how it was important to balance what an argument was about. Weighing another person's right as deliberately as you did your own. 'Everyone counts as much in their world as you do in yours.' It was so easy to be back there, thinking about it. Their sitting together on winter nights in front of the range. In summer with the windows open, the white tulle curtains rising slowly, pausing, wafting back. Some nights the curtains hung there still as cliffs. She took up her needles, they clashed softly against each other, she raised her head to look at the time on the yellow clock. Their silence together, rather than their talk. Her stillness. Aunt Frances for all her bulk was never that.

They were supposed to sit and laze through summer – that was the story you always heard about fat people. From six in the morning she found things to do, even when the other women took a spell. And so it was always strange somehow, to see her sitting in the evenings sipping her sherry while Mr Wallace ironed or darned or read silently with his glasses tilted to two bright coins in the low-angled light. Yet if he read they would not go more than five minutes before one or other of them spoke. Mr Wallace removed his spectacles, crossed the metal arms so carefully you would think they were something precious. His aunt's talk was easy, chatty. While Mr Wallace was so precise it seemed every word was chosen from several that surrounded it, as if picking over stones, electing these.

In those weeks when the apples were picked in the long sloping orchards, and the sheds hived with their weighing and packing and shipping off, Mr Wallace was so much in his element Aunt Frances said you'd think he had grown every one of the damned things himself. He went among the workers doing his best to chat with them, to put them at their ease, although at least half of them continued to call him 'sir' even after he suggested they might drop such formality, telling them in curt phrases that they did not quite comprehend, 'There – that's all right then without that, isn't it? All workers together?' There was a certain level too at which they despised him, knowing as they did that for all this energetic working of the orchards he would not be covering his costs, that the market was so depressed there was bullshit in his stories about shipping them out from Hobart – he was probably dumping the cases somewhere without letting on. If there was really a market the ships would have been sailing up the Huon, the way they did before the slump. Still, if the old bugger's fantasy kept them in work, they weren't going to complain too loudly, although he needn't come that 'we're all cobbers together' stunt. He had the brass and they didn't, that was the guts of it.

Alex heard Mr Wallace one day telling Reg the foreman how some of these trees were from the seeds Admiral Franklin's wife had brought out with her from England.

'That a fact?' Reg said. Then Mr Wallace had turned to Alex. He altered the tone of his voice as he spoke to him, as if less deliberately aiming at matiness. 'Giving apples to the Antipodes then losing himself in endless packs of ice. Frozen himself somewhere to this moment like a tray of apples that will never rot.'

He reverted to it again that night at dinner. 'The irony of that, imagine, Alex. Imagine, Rory. The North-west Passage, indeed. *Per fretum per fretum febris, in these straits to die.* The undiscovered country etcetera with a vengeance, eh?'

The old man smiled at them. Rory winked across the table at his cousin. Across the silver and the glass. Alex remembered Rory saying to him soon after he arrived, 'Would you credit how a man can call himself a communist, eating the way we do every night?'

'Does he really think it though?' Alex had asked. 'I mean, he must *know*?'

Rory showed his bad teeth. 'He believes it up to the hilt. He believes he's got the red flag furled there in his pocket, he's just waiting for the signal to come through before he runs down to the sheds and the workers stream out behind him.' Then with utter dismissiveness, 'Absurd old goat.'

'Better than not trying, isn't it?' Alex asked.

His cousin looked at him coldly. 'Why? A Tory enjoying a pantomime?'

So the pretence went on, Alex himself being tutored in how to observe it with contempt. And the pretence as well that the business was taking care of itself. Mr Wallace asking each night as they sat at the table which, like Lady Franklin's apples, had been brought from England, 'How many bushels today, then, lads?' His figures scratched with a fork on the cloth beside his plate, his announcing, 'Up on last year. Almost fifteen per cent. Would you believe that, Francie?'

And Aunt Frances smiling down the table at him at first warmly and easily, as to someone she cared for. Gently teasing him. She spoke briefly to Alex, who sat between them at the table. His own glass of claret was barely touched, his aunt's already empty. She commanded her nephew simply, 'More.' His raising then the heavy decanter, the dark wine pouring into the reflecting glass. And then on some nights the teasing grew into something more, a baiting match between the grossly heavy woman and the man with hands that were so much whiter than hers, the middle finger with a silver ring and dull red stone leaned into his bearded cheek. He watched her like a man watching an impudent but fetching child, his eyes not taken from her face as she goaded and sometimes slanged him.

'God,' she would break out on him, 'what sort of life do you think you're living, tell me that?' Both young men, the pale son and the darker brooding nephew, sat silent. 'Primping up the house,' she said, 'drinking out of this stuff.' One fat finger tapping against her emptied glass, the room so quiet and demure beyond the crystal's small impatient ringing out. Mr Wallace's hand now closed to a fist on which his chin rested. His eyes puckered to mere slits. And in his turn, but far less flailingly, striking back at her. 'Don't pour any more of that for her, Alex. Tends to make your dear aunt rather skittish.'

While Alex thought, is she only drunk, is that all that's going on? Or a game I don't comprehend? Rory never mentioned that part of their lives. But after several weeks Alex took in something of how the moves were made. For one thing his aunt's drinking usually ended sooner than one expected, the woman choosing to stop after six glasses although Mr Wallace's attention was by then pressing her to take another, as courteously as he had said a little before, she had drunk enough for one night, surely?

Uneasily, Alex saw how that limit was what attracted them. There was even a bizarre flirting to it, he could detect that too. A charm the old man responded to when Aunt Frances abused him. And when Mr Wallace came back at her, so graciously it seemed, calling her 'my dear' as he reminded her she was out of her depth, was she not, trying to deal with thoughts that were too big for her? Offering opinions on life that she was not quite up to? *Old sod*, she had called at him once. Her eyes fixed on his, as though her son and her sister's boy were no longer at the table with them.

'We all have our vocations,' Mr Wallace answered her. 'Our calling.' The stem of his glass had broken with the pressure he put on it. Yet for Alex it was always a matter of obscure guessing as he watched his aunt and the man who had been his mother's friend as well. Rory surely must know what was going on. But Rory would speak of a thing only when he was ready, Alex quite knew that. It would be another time, months away from this. They would talk of back here, and the words would be like those in a story he had heard a long time ago. They would ride over time as the candle flames rode now across the dark polished wood of the table. Alex would think of that image among those other words they were growing used to. *España. Palabra. Muerte. Libertad.*

She said, 'You don't need to talk about it?'

'No.'

'Not her? Not the girl?'

'Not her either.'

'Mary wrote, you know, and told me. Something about it.'

'There's nothing more to tell you then, if you already know.' Not a matter of holding back. Neither of them thought that. One morning when his aunt observed him at the window in the kitchen, looking out into the yard, she came to stand beside him, the waft of lavender rising from between her flaccid breasts. She saw that from behind the fall of the curtain he was watching Mr Wallace. The old man was shaking out wet teatowels across a hedge.

'He likes making out he's a servant?'

She said simply, 'He'd like to be wearing a skirt.'

'What?' Her nephew thought she must mean something else.

He caught the mocking beneath her voice. 'He'd like to dress up more than anything else in the world, but the poor old blighter simply washes and sews and does the dishes.' Mr Wallace flapped out the cloths in front of him, then carefully unfolded a handkerchief from his pocket to wipe across his hands. He looked up into one of the gums, as though spotting something that interested him. Alex could see nothing but the small wavering of the sickle leaves.

His aunt took it up again. She said, 'Very much a second-best to frillies, Alex.'

'It's his business then.'

She picked up his irritation. Her mouth opened, showing her lovely teeth. 'Nonsense! That's just one of those clichés that peg our curiosity down. Like those tiny threads in the Gulliver story, remember?'

He said he hadn't read it.

'A grown man's tied down by hundreds of little threads. He could have snapped any one of them like cotton, only all together they held him fast.'

'Oh?' He smiled back at her. Why doesn't she ever say anything straight out? He thought how once she was laughing like this she somehow didn't seem so grotesque. The fatness didn't matter.

'Oh, indeed,' she said. The boy knew he was now being teased. But she was serious when she told him, 'Every cliché. Every old assumption. Every one of them ties us down a bit more.'

He watched her looking at him. He was thinking how it was only eight o'clock in the morning and already the sweat gathered along her neck.

Aunt Frances said, 'I was brought up to say thank you for

everything they tied you down with. That's the sort of family we were.'

His mother too, he supposed she meant. And then, surprising him, still smiling, she said, 'I know I disgust you.'

'A bit,' he told her.

'Good boy!' Her hand came down on his arm, the palm moist against his skin. He moved from her slightly, reaching out to tug at where the curtain had rucked up.

'My size?'

'A bit of that.'

'The way I talk?'

'Yes.' And now Alex actually laughing with her, mildly baiting her back while she dabbed with a wet cloth at the neckline of her dress and yet again shocking him, as it was so easy for her to do.

'Nothing more revolting than old female flesh, that right? Hundreds of pounds of it like here.' Her hand inside her dress, tugging at the strap of her brassiere which Alex thought must be like a couple of sacks.

He said, 'I still don't understand all this, mind.'

'The way we carry on?'

'I know that when you pretend to make something clear, that's just another way of covering up.'

This time his aunt's hand came down more firmly on his shoulder, turning them both from the window and Mr Wallace's finnicky housemaiding.

'You've got an eye for things,' Aunt Frances said. 'We can't put much across you now, can we?' Although even now her words confused him. Putting what across him? What was it that he was supposed to see? (Only so much later with this too, as they sipped the canned fish soup with its residue of discoloured rice beside a sluggish yellow river the same colour as the stuff that was supposed to nourish them. Talking about back home. His cousin telling him neither with shame nor quite indifference that if he hadn't realised *that* he would never understand a thing. About Wallace, about his aunt. 'She was on the game for years. In Sydney after my father cast her off and Wallace rescued her. That's the bit of the jig-saw you've got to know. It's the centre of the whole bloody farce back there.' Rory telling Alex that about

his mother, then tilting his tin mug high, draining the last
fragments of rice. His fair hair by then so much paler from the
constant sun. His eyes squinted against it now as his head strained
back, the mug balanced there on his face, a muzzle. And then to
Alex, 'Not a bad yarn, eh?' As if his mother like her aging saviour
and the house itself and all the rest, the long bright corridors of
the orchard and the slow lift of the land towards the striated
heights of the mountain, were things now so remote that to
mention them at all was simply to remember a story. And Alex so
obviously disconcerted that Rory, after crouching to dip his mug
in the discoloured pouring of the stream, walked across and stood
beside him. 'Jesus, Alex, when will you see the world for what it is?
The picnic's fucking over for all of us, mate. It always was.')

His aunt steered him to the table and sat him down. She said, 'I
always have a cup of lemon tea this time of day. You can join me
for once.'

Her long smock swirled as she turned to the bench, to the
board where she placed a lemon and sliced thin strips from it.
'They don't know what lemons are in this country. Wizened
things like this.'

His mother had always spoken of her as if she were a girl. The
child whose bedroom she used to share. Several times she had
mentioned what the family for years had called only 'her going
away.' She used to say, 'Dear Frances, so much brighter really than
any of us. Bright and kind and pretty in her slightly solid way.'
Francie sitting on Father's knee even when she was sixteen. And
then the rest of it. At first her riding out with Dinny Neville because
she said they were both mad on horses. Who else did she know who
knew about them as Dinny did? The year he won the Derby at
Ellerslie. And the square Ford with its white painted tyres and
collapsible hood, driving her back later and later, for the afternoons
with the horses had then become the evenings to themselves. Until
her father waited for her finally on the verandah, raging at the
dapper young man with his bow tie and his tweed cap jaunty across
his forehead. And Dinny Neville saying to Frances's father once, so
that the older man attempted to lean into the car and drag him out
to thrash him, 'There's nothing to worry about with her, sir. She's
all in one piece. You can take my word for it.'

Night after night for weeks, Alex's mother had said, just before the stroke, Father's hand slapping down on the table and her mother as usual in tears. But Frances was defiant and determined while her parent levelled at her his detestation of her friend so that she said at last, what about it then, yes all right then, supposing she was in love with him? A jockey, a corner-boy, her father called him, a cad who painted his tyres and wore a cloth cap, didn't she even have eyes? And this gross intelligent woman in front of him now, taking the cups and saucers down from their shelf, whose story indeed it was. It was impossible to bring those two together, that far beginning and where now it was. 'Eloped', as his mother would say, that strange word he did not quite understand, running away with a man five inches shorter than herself, his bow tie hardly level with her chest. And his mother tilting a photograph that had been included with the Christmas card, 'Her boy Rory. He's the living image.' Mother's favourite sister, lovely Frances. Only her teeth, Alex thought. There's no other way to tell what all those descriptions were about, what it was the jockey loved.

The tea steamed in front of them, the black cups with their frail handles, their curled and gilded rims. They were among the few things his aunt had taken from Cambridge when she left.

'I was thinking of those this minute.'

'About my cups? Good Lord!'

He ran his forefinger round the shiny rim of his cup. He asked her, 'Why were they so special?'

'Because they were already packed. One of Mary's wedding presents that she didn't like. I was twelve or so and said how pretty they were. She jumped at the chance to give them away. There used to be four of them at one time.' She picked up the saucer and turned it over, looking at the stamped name on its back. 'Shows what rotten taste I had, doesn't it?'

Alex waited for a moment, the bitter tang of the lemon too strong for his liking. Then he said, 'The others – the other aunts, I mean – they always bored me a bit.'

'And I didn't?'

'I didn't know you, did I?'

'Lord!' Aunt Frances said for a second time. Laughing again, heaping a teaspoon of sugar, letting it submerge slowly in the tea.

'Sharp today, aren't we?'

'That's why you were my favourite. That's what I meant.'

'Exotic?'

'Distant. Disobedient. Disapproved of by everyone except my mother.'

His aunt's spoon stirring, shrinking round and round against the delicate cup. 'Darling old Em!'

'I think she was the only one who didn't panic.'

'Panic?' His aunt held the fragment of lemon between her fingers and tapped it softly against the side of her cup. It made her nephew think of a small dead fish. She said, 'This was the obvious place to come, of course, when Wallace gave me that chance.'

'I'm glad I came here. She would have liked that.' Alex with his hands in his trousers pockets, slumped slightly in his chair. Looking not at his aunt now but at the bright white box of the windows. 'The other aunts were dead against it.'

'Of course they would be!' But that said not with irritation so much as an amused acceptance. And underneath the amusement, weariness. As if her nephew had remarked that boys kill flies, men go to war, women are always disappointed, one way or another.

'Uncle Frank advanced the money from the estate – for me coming over. On condition I wouldn't stay here more than six months.'

His aunt's tongue made a hollow tuck of contempt.

'Funny thing, none of them really wanted me anyway. Not when the chips were down.'

'I haven't heard anyone say that for years,' she said.

Alex moved forward, propping his elbows on the table. He said, 'They thought whatever was wrong about me being here with you, it couldn't be half as bad as being close enough to embarrass them by staying on.'

'Mary's letter more or less told me that.' Aunt Frances raised her hand with its balled cloth to dab the back of her neck. The wisps of her hair caught against the sweat. The lavender too was moist, sickly, so that her nephew turned, raising his own hand as he hoped without her noticing, laying it across his face against the rising herbal reek. A thing so simple and yet distasteful as that closed, for the moment, such intimacy as was almost there between them. So that when his aunt, speaking with her curved palm against the roundness of her neck, made him the offer, 'You don't need to talk about it then?', he told her, 'No.'

'I didn't mean your mother.'

'Not her either.'

Not Barbara. How talk of her? To anyone?

The rifle leaped back into the cushion of his shoulder. His left hand felt the lifting of the barrel as his finger eased against one of the white streaming cockatoos that for its second, its fraction of a second, focused as though some force were holding it there dead centre, the swinging barrel tied to its rising weight until Rory hollered, 'Now!' His first shot fired, the edge of utter silence after the ringing crack. Before the panicked flurry of the surviving wings, the pull upwards and back of the startled white flock, the thud beyond the fence no heavier than if a woman's purse, say, had been lofted a little into the air and landed in the yellow grass. Alex lowered his gun, and his cousin yelled at him to pick off another. But the birds had slanted away, skied out and dispersed and come down together again across the paddocks at a pepper tree too far to be considered. Their shrieks subsided in the safety of distance.

'You could have knocked off a couple. Two at least.'

Alex said, 'One'll do. To prove I could.'

Rory's mongrel, without the instincts of breeding or retrieval, snapped up the mutilated bird and made off into the scrub with its unexpected gift.

'You haven't got too bad an eye.'

Alex broke open the breech, fed in another bright green cartridge.

'Make a soldier of me yet, you reckon?'

'Someone will.'

Alex padded down the pack he had carried on their tramp and sat on its levelled top. 'You think there's no way of getting out of it, do you?'

'You've read the stuff I've shown you. All our so-called democratic countries letting a handful of mad bastards do what they like.'

It was already mid-autumn on this side of the world, placid and uninformed. But some of them knew, Rory said, by Christ they did. Some of them had heard the call go out for the young of the world to help bury the rotten old corpse of capitalism, to put it to ground once and for all.

'I know,' Aunt Frances said when they spoke of it more and more often at dinner. Across the candlelight which made them all seem on stage, on a set where time seemed to stop and briefly they lived in costume. Rory so contemptuous of it, so increasingly bitter of how they lived that he spoke of mealtime as the bloody pantomime, Wallace's Waxworks. When Alex said, 'Well it's harmless enough, isn't it?', his cousin flared back at him, '*Nothing's* harmless. Everything has implications. There is no such thing as an isolated act.'

And Alex's voice altering slightly, so that the mocking was obvious but also its concern, as he proposed, 'Those who are not with me are against me?'

So Rory, his face unsmiling, as pale as wax himself, declared, 'Bloody oath.' And Aunt Frances was saying across both of them, 'I know.'

When the two of them were alone together, Alex asked didn't it strike Rory, though, as at least a bit odd that it was privilege when one got down to it, it was old Wallace's money that subscribed to the magazines, bought the books, gave Rory the time to read them? The old codger's eagerness to have them talk of such things that put them precisely where they were? 'How could you even know of Spain if capitalism wasn't paying for it?' Alex was surprised at his own mischievousness in putting it like that.

'I'd know all right,' Rory countered. 'If we can use the old bugger we do. But don't think for a minute everything depends on him.' He meant his own mail, the papers that arrived once a fortnight with their postmark, *Cobar, N.S.W.* The information sent out free by the Miners Federation, or rather one enthusiast whose advertisement Rory had taken up. The man who wrote letters that began not even 'Dear Comrade', as did the typed notes with Mr Wallace's pamphlets, but less escapably, 'Brother'. In recent letters even that had moved into the plural. When he was shown the letters, Alex thought, so I am in this whether I want to be or not. Then they were sent photos when the first volunteers went off from Sydney, the men and the four nurses who sailed to join the Internationals.

'It's only a matter of time,' Rory said. 'We'll be in snaps like that.'

'I don't like shooting,' Alex told his cousin.

'You didn't like riding either. Now you can't get enough of it.'

Every day now, as they worked in the orchards or rode in the early evenings or lay in those first few minutes after the light on the table between them in the bedroom was switched off, the talk was of Spain. Or of what the flow of mail told them was taking place over there on the mainland, the rallies that were held, the union meetings, the government hacks condemning fascism with one mouth, keeping silent when Mussolini's primped and arrogant army sailed in to do its bit in kicking socialism to death. Both the rhetoric and the facts from Rory's unraised voice. From the distance, to someone merely observing the patience and the seriousness with which he talked and occasionally raised his hand, a slow rhythmic beating to what he said, he could have been a teacher instilling tables into a chanting class.

Mr Wallace frequently watched them from the window of his study, that room with its sloping gabled ceiling, its numerous books, its crudely coloured print of Lenin inside the door, and behind his desk the two large reproductions: Michelangelo's David in one dark wooden frame, The Winged Victory in another. The images he had once thought might be brought together. With his Italian friend Pietro, that summer before the Great War even, when they had read aloud to each other or passed drinks from hand to hand as they sat on the canvas deck chairs, the coast of Albania, the coast south of Corfu, slipping away in front of them. Pietro, ah! His head like a design from a Greek coin. The coin Mr Wallace had bought for a song in Alexandria, that he still wore on his watch-chain the few times in the year when there was occasion to visit Hobart.

He lit a cigar, which Frances would not allow elsewhere in the house. He watched the boys walk up and down the drive, Alex so gravely like his mother, young Rory doing the lion's share of the talking. Young Rory, whom he knew despised him. He must

blame Frances for that. Frances who took so little effort to keep
one's life as it should be, utterly private. He supposed the silly
girl's past had everything to do with that lack of discretion –
Andrea del Sarto's mistress for some odd reason popping into his
head. Then of course it came to him. The browned walls of the
Pitti Palace, the cluttered brilliant rooms with the worst-hung
pictures in the world. Andrea's woman in that marvellous Mother
and Child – what was it called? The virgin-whore, in any case, the
face not unlike young Francie's at fourteen, fifteen? The woman-
boy. That lovely stage when sex, as it were, seems to hold its
breath. The only time a woman's body holds something like
genuine fascination. Before the *function* side of it takes over, rules
them, utterly commands them. Yet the curious pleasure even so at
times, in evening light, across the nimbus of the candle flames.
She could still, as one might say, make one tick. And those two
quite ordinary, even unattractive boys. Their open honest
antipodean faces – what could they know of all that, he wondered,
the world of Pietro, the half-lit beds in Alexandria? But these lads,
bless them – their only conceivable charm was the fact of their
youth. Though Rory's mind was interesting in its way, and
surprisingly sharp considering the dreadful school he had dragged
himself to and his indifference now to everything except the
international commune. And the boy desired that not with his
mind so much as with his total being. His politics were as intrinsic,
as irrefutable as his height, his pale skin, his unfortunately
wretched teeth. Mr Wallace conceded the rightness of such
passion. He thought of his own kind of life, how that was hardly
possible any more.

The boys turned again in the drive, Alex whacking at tall
grasses with the stick he carried in his hand. His mother's thirst
for clarity, Mr Wallace remembered that. Wanting the truth at all
costs. 'The way things are,' she used to call it, 'giving things their
right names.' He had been so swept away by it once, the kind of
fire that burned in her, that he had kissed her. On the tennis court,
before dinner. Out of pure admiration. Poor dead ungainly Emily!
Did she ever come within a bull's roar of it, he wondered?

Mr Wallace poured himself another tot. Who can ever say
about another soul? Putting it to Frances once, years ago, an

evening after dinner when the boy was out after possums, their own sniping subdued to a weary closeness. Frances across the candlelight, morose as she remembered her sister. Then laughing, because her words were sentimental. 'Who knows anything about another?' she repeated. He had watched her across the bright cup of flame, the room blurring off into darkness at a point impossible to determine, like all shadings off, all boundaries. Middle age into something more, say. Sexual desire into what once you thought was the impossible state, the absence of desire. Yet it was not the loss after all that one feared. No sense of grief, as he had supposed, as he had read and heard older men say. Tears in Frank Harris's eyes – what was that story again? Seeing young girls in their springtime flouncing past him. But a sot, a *roué*, Harris. And Frances, dear girl, telling him *everything* quite early on, before they decided on Tasmania and apples. Apples! The lovely irony of that. 'Where the apple reddens, never pry' – old Browning, wasn't it? Rather a heavy harvest with it in her case, you might say. And poor drunken Lionel Johnson's line. *Hic sunt poma Sodomorum*. How's that for an epitaph? Tell me more, as he sometimes says to Frances, the bottle moving between them. The excesses, the tawdriness of what many men of course would consider normal. Her great nipples like bronzed half crowns. Frances's face seen across the candle flare, the lap or stillness of the light across her features, her hair, the unexpected massiveness of her arms. Inexhaustible, that fascination, the child's mouth, the perfect teeth. Her mouth when she leans over him, describing as he asks her, his interest almost morbid at times like that. Mr Wallace is willing to concede that too. At the table, sometimes, after dinner. The boy perhaps passing outside, a dead possum gripped in his fist, a white blur against the window while the filth came from her mouth. Child of a whore, if one used one's language precisely. And more recently that other boy, Frances's nephew, child of a woman Mr Wallace had for perhaps two days believed might be the 'salvation' of him. Frances had told him how simple it was, when she was working at the trade, to do anything required; how lubricity and vileness even, if you wanted to call it that, how these were no more than a garment one slipped on for a time to raise sagging flesh. And her pure anxious sister, walking beside him he remembered almost like a singer, her hands clasped in front of her, desperate to achieve what her younger sister now so easily dismissed. Emily had said, 'I must bring my words as close as they will come to whatever is truth.'

There was the sudden thrum of rain on the window Mr Wallace stood at. He saw the boys trot towards the hedge and shelter beneath the maple that spanned the drive. As unexpectedly as the weather had turned, he noticed his own eyes blur, the tears springing to them against his will. He disliked the easy luxury of that. How right young Rory would have been to sneer! Tears which he knew were for no particular memory – not Pietro, not a living soul – but for such a vast absurdity, he supposed, as Time. The hopeless endless ringing in the stellar spaces. Plato, Pascal, what did it matter who had said it? And against that, his own life like the rubbing of grass stalks, the blur of an insect at the corner of one's eye. Mr Wallace knew it was ridiculous to be so moved. Thank God, he thought, I am the last of a breed.

The boys had seen him watching from where they stood in the drive, under the tree's resonant creaking as the wind picked up. His shape there behind the smoky texture of the curtain.

'It's a mystery house, this one, Rory. Figures at windows. Candles at dinnertime. Everyone saying things that mean something different to each person. It's like the kind of stories my mother liked reading.'

Rory drew back from more disclosures than for the moment he was prepared to make. There would be time for all that. For the inessentials, as he thought them. His obsession with Spain made anything beyond it trivial, a luxury they had no right to. At least with Alex he was doing things. Talking to him, explaining, teaching him the things he would need to know. For he knew that when the time came, and he asked directly, Alex's answer would be the only one possible. Yet for the time being, that question could not be asked. Not until the autumn was quite over and his own obligations to the orchard out of the way. He had promised his mother that six months ago, when he told her, 'I can't stay here for ever.' Once, harshly, he had said to Alex, 'She understands this sort of thing, you know.' He had tapped the pamphlet on his knee, the crude drawing on cheap newsprint of a man holding a hammer above his head, a woman next to him with a child folded into the protection of her shawl. 'I mean she knows what I think about it. How you've got to stop all the shit of history because it's gone on long enough. She knows that means as much to me as jockeys did to her when she was my age.' Alex had said nothing while his cousin went on, 'I could say I wanted to do anything, come to that. She'd have no right even to an opinion.' He had rolled the pamphlet in his palm. 'She's got no more inkling of a political idea, mind, than I have of talking Greek.' And there was another silence broken only when Alex asked him, 'So?' Because the silence itself was clearly part of the message, of what Rory's tense leaning forward also conveyed. 'I've no more choice in the long run against all this,' – the rolled pamphlet for the moment raised as if in salutation to someone beyond Alex, perhaps to the man with his own raised hammer signalling him back, beckoning him on – 'against truth, if you want one of old Wallace's big words for it. No more choice than she had because some horny little two-timer in his flash clobber felt her up behind the silver teapots and the embroidery frames.' The anger behind his declaring that. The one ground of his certainty. And Alex shocked at someone speaking like that of his mother – of his father too, even one like that. The 'sexual tangle' was a phrase he had heard somewhere. He had used it once to Barbara. Barbara telling him with her contempt flashing hard and efficient against the man she said always watched her, who wanted to be her slave. Flinging her head back, her throat white and exposed. Tender beyond belief, he thought, watching his cousin and thinking back to her, the brown light as they lay in the row of pines above the river, Barbara going back to the time she told him of, the shop with the mountains leaning over them, the river she said like a knot of snakes thrown down on the flat bed of stones. His own thinking forward while she talked, *how shall we make this last?* He came back to Rory's words.

And that afternoon, strolling up the drive, the light rain standing in beads on their shirts, Rory took up the word his cousin had used of the house. 'Mystery? Nothing's too interesting once you know all about it, mate.'

They stood on the back verandah, beneath the sloping iron of the roof. They could see Aunt Frances at the doorway of the shed, talking with Beatrice and her mother. The two women and the girl were laughing. The voices came up to them through the still afternoon. Rory allowed himself a rare personal note. 'She's all right,' he said. 'Beatrice. About the one thing round here the rot hasn't got to yet.'

'You don't think much of them,' Alex said. Saying it lightly, wanting for the moment to keep his cousin's solemnity at bay.

Rory said, 'No, I don't.' His mouth moved to a slow grin. 'Not in theory. Day by day can be a different story, right?' He picked up the gun that leaned against the wall of the verandah. He snapped back the breech and looked along the barrel. He said, 'I love things when they're looked after. When they work to perfection.' Alex was on the point of teasing him, of saying, 'Not like people, then?' But what would have been the point of that? Thinking how his mother would have thought the same, that words were too precious to let loose without good reason, yet almost everyone did. Words flying all about, refined silver bullets like Mr Wallace's, the endless chattering streams ricocheting round the sheds when the workers broke for lunch or tea and hollered out across the bins and across the rows. Rory there so oddly calm in the swarm of his own speech, only his wanting it to scour, to pock the great oppressive wall of fact with cleansing patterns of his own. Rory now handed him the gun. He explained each step. He then took it back to demonstrate.

'You should think of being a teacher.'

His cousin was untouched by the irony. Alex leaned against one of the verandah posts. He watched how the movements were both rapid and patient. The same gift, the same naturalness, which later – only eight months later – he would use in competition against the giant quiet Swede who had survived Guadalajara. In that inevitable mixing that the Brigade did not encourage and yet took for granted, the giant blond had been with the Spaniards who flushed out the Italian divisions ranged against them. Men who had been in on that one were accorded respect. He squatted down a few feet away from Rory, who crouched almost like a parody of the larger man, with his own paleness, his slant of straw-coloured hair. Each of them had a Tukkurov mounted on a tripod in front of them. Alex had heard Rory sing the merits of the gun half a dozen times. He handled the weapon with a kind of love. Then the young Spaniard who openly wore a silver crucifix around his neck, who assumed on the company's behalf any office that was required by way of adjudicating or refereeing, stood a little behind the two crouched men. He took the watch from his wrist and held it with the strap dangling over the edge of his hand. (Only later again, after he had seen a stretcher-bearer bringing in the casualties, did Alex learn that the man was a law student from Salamanca. He would in due course receive a wound that was surprisingly neat, a shallow and almost bloodless trench above his ear. He was dead before they arrived back at the camp, and they dropped him quickly at the side of a rock. They ran back to pick up another whose luck might be a little better, who might last it to the tent where the Sanidad team were not concerned with corpses.) Several of the veterans stood in the semi-circle that faced the two men who knelt in a kind of worship at the side of their guns. Most of the men were laying bets. There seemed little doubt about how the contest would go, although they admired the brash youngster who thought he could make a go of it with the Swede. For the morose lean northener was better at this game than anyone else, his reputation was known in companies that had never even seen him. Deadly accurate at his job, that was his main glory. But by way of sport he could dismantle his gun and reassemble it faster than any challenger. His pride was unostentatious but certain. When he came in the night before, on his way to a legendary Falangist sniper who picked off men almost at will, he asked whether the outfit had anyone they would like to put up against him? It was offered seriously and with the broadest goodwill. An officer who looked the age of a school prefect said, 'No one's challenging you, Lars, just for the fun of being beaten.' No one was thinking of Rory until he spoke. The laconic Aussie who looked like a boy and for all the Spanish sun stayed almost as pale as when he stood on the deck watching Mt Wellington haze back, the low blue stretch of the coast slip away, the morning romantic Mr Wallace turned the hand-mirror to them as he said he would far down the peninsula, the quick tight diamond wink where the old fool and Rory's mother cried together at the passing ship.

A middle-aged man from the north of England wagged his head. He laughed outright when he heard Rory's taking up the challenge. 'Swede'll eat thee, lad,' he said. And turning to a friend who leaned against a short scraggy pine, 'E'll do for 'im proper.'

But the men were glad that he had offered. They liked him for that. There was something flinty in the little bugger. Simply thinking he was good enough to have a crack at the Swede! And so his crouching there ten minutes later, his face set with concentration. You did things well, you extended yourself to do them. You were an instrument, like the efficient shining weapon that waited there in front of him. You had to think like that in a war or you weren't any good. The time-keeper counted for them, ordering them to begin. '*Dos. Tres. Ya!*' He released them as though two thumbs had been removed from two pressed springs. The Swede moved with large-boned earnest rapidity, the dimensions of the machine-gun apparently diminished by the size of his hands. Opposite him, Rory's movements seemed almost casual, a process set to a certain pattern one could not imagine being tinkered with. The Swede had already placed several pieces on the ground while Rory seemed almost to fondle the machine beneath his hands. The crowd of men sportingly called encouragement, a paternal edge to their voices for a boy pitted against a man.

Of course the Swede was better at it. He had stood and was waiting for Rory to complete the cycle of dismantling then reassembling. But it occurred to some of those who watched that the youngster's competition was finally with himself, that what they watched and had bet on was not perhaps what most interested the boy. He was several seconds slower than the Swede, but faster than he had ever performed it before. The applause broke out for both of them, for the still unsmiling northerner, his palm running against the stubble of his close-cropped head, and for Rory who stood from his task with one side of his mouth raised slightly, taking the older man's hand as it stretched out towards him. Then he went across to the time-keeper who began speaking slowly, with wide gestures, to the Swede. The big man's Spanish was not much better than Alex's own, and he seemed not to understand. He was looking towards Rory, his broad face surprisingly like a child's. The best killer in his company. Then for the first time he smiled, and shook his head. He spoke directly to Rory, who took the watch from the Spaniard and lay it in the Swede's opened palm. Then he gave the scarf he wore about his neck to the other man to fold into a strip and tie behind his head. The men watched with fresh curiosity as the champion placed his hand on Rory's shoulder, leading him the few paces until he stood once more beside the gun. Again Rory crouched. He stretched out a hand to pat the barrel with the kind of affectionate firmness he would touch a horse. He brought his hand back so that both fists lay on his knees, before he called out *'Preparado'*, and the Swede, looking down at the watch, called back, *'Ya!'* Blindfolded, Rory moved with an identical precision, the same unusual method of dismantling so that the parts fell into either hand at the same instant, his placing them then on the hard earth, his hands returning with such seemingly unhurried casualness to uncouple the final bolts, until the ranged components lay side by side. His right hand fluttered across the separate metal shapes and at once he began to reassemble his weapon. The men who had called out and joked during the earlier contest now watched with fascination, their silence the acknowledgement that what they looked at was no longer a game but a kind of private rite. Its true meaning was somewhere else, in the space where Rory controlled his life with the severity of a monk.

Then Rory himself was again standing, the ceremony completed. The Swede was untying the knot in the red scarf, so that for the first seconds of exposure Rory blinked against the sun. The Spaniard called out the time. There was a shifting among the men, then they called out their applause. Rory had taken the same time for the dismantling, the reassembling, as when he had seen where his hands moved. Then the Swede stepped forward and pressed the younger man against his chest. *'Buono,'* he said. For the first time the two men smiled directly at each other. *'Muy listo.'* And Rory answered him, *'Luchamos tambien.'* The Spaniards seemed amused at the oddly accented exchange. The colonel who had watched with the others, indistinguishable in his dress from any of the lesser ranks, walked to the tents where supplies were kept. He ordered a soldier to bring them brandy.

That would be only eight months, almost to the day, since Alex took the gun on the back verandah, and handed it back to his cousin. Only three until they were in Spain, into the extreme heat that made the landscape shimmer, the flow of hills seem shifting and insubstantial, the rocks drifting in their cage of refractions. The long low horizon would seem a buckling length of heated metal when that action was repeated, a gun handed from Rory across to Alex but the barrel now so violently hot that the weapon was taken awkwardly by its stock. In the one street of a village with a dozen white cube houses, their shadows falling flat and dark as black sheets that gave out a kind of chill, for all the dazzle of the hardened mud road, the glare of the pure walls. The light itself gave an impression not so much of falling on the high facade of the church that faced them as smashing with suppressed detonation against the piled whitewash, the elaborate baroque whorls. Those who lived in the village had moved on as the Front approached and then engulfed their homes. In a few more days they would begin to drift back, down from the hills they had taken refuge in, back from other villages further from the action. They may hardly have spoken as they left or as they returned, Alex already had noticed that. Speech seemed a luxury to them, as was food. Or were they like that only now, in wartime? Or in front of foreigners? Sometimes when they came on a village deserted in the fighting, it amazed him how little those houses contained, yet nothing had been removed. He would tell his cousin as though going over an exercise, over phrases from a catechism, to keep himself politically honed. 'Not a thing, can you believe that? A few bowls. Straw mattresses on the floor. A table and a bench. That's about it.'

Rory said, 'It's a pleasure then, isn't it, knocking off bastards who make them live like that?' He passed his rifle to Alex in the empty street. Alex wore the armband of the Sanidad, he carried no weapon apart from the Swiss sheath-knife in his belt. He said, 'What am I supposed to do with this?'

His cousin pointed to the church's facade, to high in the centre where a white statue, perhaps the size of a man, stood in its shadowed niche. And Alex thought of something made from icing, a decoration of sweet Christ. The statue had one hand laid across its chest. The other was raised to shoulder height, the fingers crooked in benediction.

'See if you've kept your eye in,' Rory said.

'Why?' Alex said.

'Because it's him or us.'

Alex tucked the butt against his shoulder. The wood lay warm against his cheek. Then he squinted along the sights, running the crossed wires over the smooth face with its symmetrical beard. Like one schoolboy to another he said, 'This is vandalism, know that?'

Rory snorted, amused at Alex's warning from another world. 'No it's not,' he said, 'it's fucking war.'

The wire sights moved along the upraised arm, stopped at the exposed palm, the lifted fingers, the tucked-in thumb.

'Shooting without adequate cause?' Alex said. He was quoting from some manual he had almost forgotten. He noticed how crudely made the thing really was. The hand was far too large for the arm. The arm itself was shapeless, a plaster cylinder until the ruffled-back sleeve at the wrist.

'I'm the superior officer aren't I?' Rory said. 'I could have you up for refusing orders.'

'In that case, then.' Alex felt for the one time in his life how there was something almost – sort of tender, that was it. Stroking a target with the sights like this. Like running your hand along a neck, across a throat and breast, over a cheek.

The shot volleyed back at them. The hand leaped up, disintegrated in the air. The rattle of fragments on the earth a little way out from the church wall.

'What were you going for?'

'There,' Alex said. 'The hand.'

'You're wasted with that ambulance outfit, know that?'

The statue held up a clean stump at the wrist.

They went back across a field where the vines were higher than the men who walked between the rows. Their camp was on the other side, near another small group of houses that operational command had thought a better site because its well was deeper. It was Sunday afternoon. They exchanged passwords with the sentries who knew both of them as friends. One of them was the 'Madrid Scot', a man who had survived every action for two years. It was supposed to be unlucky to be near him once anything started. There was a superstition that you would draw fire away from him towards yourself.

Their friend Johnson was sitting on the running board of a supply truck. He leaned back against the door, his eyes closed, his finger holding his place in a book closed on his crossed knees. He opened one eye when he heard their voices.

'Been rabbiting, you blokes?' He asked it ironically. He supposed Alex there disliked guns or he wouldn't be in the medics. But that crazy young Australian, Christ, he was the real thing if ever anyone was. There were not many of them, surprisingly enough. The true killers. The steel traps. The ones driven only by an *idea* – that's what always made them, Johnson supposed. An idea, and every bullet refining it, every corpse polishing it up. So God's city would rise from the steaming flood.

'Hardly,' Alex said. But Rory did not answer at all. He went into his tent, where he sat cross-legged on the ground and began to clean his weapon.

Mr Wallace smoothed the letter out in front of him on the polished Huon pine. Already Rory had shown it to his mother, who had leaned forward for the decanter, filling their four glasses. She had said 'Thank you' as she handed it back to her son. She knew that he was going through the pretence of consulting them. She had thought, this will be one of the last little courtesies he can do me, I am grateful for that. For she knew as she passed the letter back that a decision had been made.

The old man read the letter, slanting it against the light. He said with an emotion that embarrassed Alex and more clearly irritated Rory, although the boy did no more than turn his glass's stem rapidly between his fingers, 'I'd have given anything to receive a letter like that, at one time.' He removed his spectacles by one of their thin wire arms, quite openly rubbing at his eyes with a finger that then crooked into a knuckle rubbing briskly at the side of his nose. He folded the letter before he passed it back. The red stone in his ring fired as his hand moved in the candlelight. He sighed and glanced at the ceiling, and said, 'You must grasp it with both hands.'

Rory rolled his table napkin and slipped it into its ring. He said, 'I don't think, Mr Wallace, that you're reading it properly.'

'Am I not?' The old man appeared startled.

Knowing how crudely he said it, Rory told him, 'Money. That's the important thing about that letter.'

Aunt Frances raised her glass. 'I'd propose a toast,' she said, 'only I can't wait.' And drained her wine. Another kind of crudeness, Alex realised, quite as deliberate as her son's. Alex drank with her, a bitterish early pick from the Clare. He knew that only because Mr Wallace said something at the beginning of each meal about what they were about to drink. The year, the grape, the quality they might expect. His 'socialist's grace', Aunt Frances called it. His first night at the table his aunt had turned to him saying with a quietness meant to be overheard by the old man by whose largesse they drank, 'There's the hope of course that some of this courtliness will rub off on Rory – and you too from now on.'

Mr Wallace held his hand towards the letter he had just returned. 'I've missed something, then?'

'It's not a letter of permission,' Rory explained. 'It's not an invitation either. It simply tells us where to go if we want to join. There's no more reason to get emotional over that than there is for a traffic sign.'

And Aunt Frances teased them both. She said, 'He's more like you than you think, Wal. Everything he wants is entirely because of qualities he possesses. He owes precisely nothing to anyone.'

It surprised Alex to see Rory glance across the table, smiling at his mother. But why isn't he annoyed at that, he wondered? Why put up with her mocking at everything? And again the thought came to him as it did so often, how can she and my mother have been sisters? Each of them living a life that contradicts the other.

Mr Wallace dabbed at his mouth. The sentiment had passed. He was the businessman, the steady arranging mind. 'Money,' he said. 'So you want your fares from me?'

Alex was the one who spoke. He said, 'Simply until the farm's sold up at home. I can pay it back then.' There was a silence which he mistakenly thought was his cue to strengthen his case. 'You saw the details I had from Uncle Frank. You know what's coming to me once the place is sold. Even if the price is rotten.'

Mr Wallace said, 'You may not know but the market signs are not all that bad. There's a turn for the better, as they say.'

Aunt Frances was already drunk. She cut across them, missing the point of where their interests stood, 'You'd know about the marketplace,' she said to Mr Wallace, 'it's your natural home.' Goading him to make the obvious reply, to throw the insult she so seldom could draw from him. The pleasure, as she had told him once, of occasionally talking like a bastard, then the pleasure of regretting it like a gentleman. But she saw he would not be drawn. Not tonight.

'Yes or no, then?' Rory said. He knew the absurdity of making it sound like a choice. Before dinner, as the cousins leaned on the supports of the verandah, looking out to the massed dark hills against the orange west, he had said, 'It's the closest the old prick will ever get to what he's gabbled about for fifty years. He can no more say he won't stake us than he could chop his own arm off.' And so again, with confidence, with insolence, 'Yes or no?'

But Mr Wallace anticipated him. He said, quite matter of factly, 'There's no question about it, is there?'

They spoke then for half an hour of the practical side. There was a sailing up to Sydney next Tuesday. There was a comrade in Redfern who would put them up while they sorted out the waterfront. He would help them find a ship. After that it was simple. London and then the Front.

'A hundred pounds, then?' Mr Wallace proposed.

'Each?'

'Of course,' he said. 'Each.'

They did the sums together. It would cost them thirty-eight pounds for a passage, on top of the Hobart fare. Allow a week, two weeks at the most, in England. Say thirty pounds left for Spain. Rory explained that they would hardly need that. According to his correspondent at Cobar they staked you out for everything. It was men they were after, not donations.

'And after?' Mr Wallace said. 'After that?'

Rory looked at him, puzzled. Then his face split with the amusement of it. His voice ran high as he answered, 'You've been waiting all your life for the revolution or what bloody ever, for a chance to do the right thing, and all you want to say now is *after*!'

The old man conceded the joke of that. 'I've been brought up as a lawyer,' he reminded them. 'I encourage people to write their wills when they talk about a marriage licence.'

Both the boys laughed good-humouredly. There was almost a rapport between the males at the table.

'I don't see how that's appropriate,' Aunt Frances put in. The wine in her glass swirling, drops leaping to the table.

'Tithes to Ares?' Mr Wallace said, the only one understanding what he meant. But the boys for the moment tolerated him, understanding his excitement, his skittishness. They were briefly at one with him against the woman who interrupted.

'You know the old saying,' she challenged them. 'Whores and wars and whatever. How's it go?' Thinking, why do they always imagine it's a game? That there's romance in kicking someone's guts about? The three faces blurred, oh already so very far, across the table.

They waited for her to settle, then went on without answering her. Mr Wallace saying now to Rory, 'You know you'll get all this, sooner or later? You must know that?' There was the slightest inclining of his head, by which he meant the room, the house, the extending acres of the orchards. 'Is it even borrowing?, is what I'm saying. Rather an anticipation?'

'I don't care what you call it.' Rory sounded amused at the lawyer's pickiness with language. Words with kid gloves.

Taking up the lightness, the sense almost of fun because what they spoke of round the gleaming table had drawn for once the three of them together, Alex provoked his cousin. 'Communist and landlord. The Tasmanian variation.'

Aunt Frances guffawed. Her gob gaping, red. Fat wetness. 'Wit!' she slurred across at him. 'Last thing we expect from you, Alex.' Her eyebrows raised to Mr Wallace. 'The gift of the fathers.' Meaning dour gangling Ecky with his stiff politeness all the girls had laughed at. Inventing his milking-machines or whatever, counting his shekels, about as much sap to the old bugger as a fence-post. Imagine *him* as a lover – couldn't you just!

But Rory, coldly as though he pronounced a sentence on them all, said so quietly that it could have been nostalgia moving him rather than the malice which it was, 'This will be the last week we ever sit at this table. All together.'

Mr Wallace said, 'I'll write a note to the bank in the morning. It's entirely over to you chaps now. When you want to go. When to sing out for more money. Cable across or whatever if you need it.'

'Thank you,' Alex said.

The man at the top of the table stood up. 'Port?'

Alex enjoyed the journey across. The days slipped by, it was impossible to do anything other than the limited rounds of the deck, to play a few games and read, to lie watching the tilt of the cabin, the line of the horizon slant against the ship's dip and rise. He could think of Barbara now without the tearing sense of being removed in some way from himself. He could think of her without hope, a dark final fact. Yet her presence was still a part of him, especially during several days when the decks were deserted and he took in the long slow unsettling slide of the sea, the slanting lift of water so vast that at times it seemed the ship voyaged on the side of a hill. She was only real because he was real. His mind made no effort to bring what he felt more precisely towards definition than that. *Not what I think. Barbara is what I am.* On other days it struck him as absurd to fall for such comfort. She was gone, that was the fact of it.

He found that it was easy enough to chat not only with Rory, but with the other passengers. He was surprised and pleased that he could explain his views quite clearly, without his cousin's help. He learned that he could think by himself. He was now quite certain that he was on his way to Spain for no one's sake except his own. Because in the enormous shambles of history there was perhaps never more than one point where your single and rational line crossed that great jumbled scribble. But he contrived to use Rory's word when he thought of it – the one point where you could *impinge*. Not be a fleck on the stream, a mere bubble, as his cousin orated, like bloody old Wallace, or a bag of self-satisfactions like Rory's mother. 'Go easy,' Alex sometimes asked him. 'Everyone's not evil because they don't agree.' There was a small nuggety bloke from Queensland who was also going across to join up. He had been over there for 'the big one' and was twice their age. He sat with them often while they talked, and told them the whole show would be different from what they expected. 'It'll be shit,' he said. 'After a while the theory and all that won't matter a dead shag. You'll just want it to be over.' They were standing at the rail, watching England come up like a long white cheese. Rory said without turning to him, 'It can be all the shit it wants to be. It won't make any difference to me.'

It took them a fortnight to get to the Front. They stayed, as a comrade in Sydney had advised them to, at the Sailors' Home in East India Dock Road. When Alex had wondered to the man that they were hardly sailors, he was told, 'Tell them what you're there for. They'll take you in with open arms.'

The long dormitory they were put into reeked of cheap clothes and too many bodies. At night they were woken by the hawking and coughing and the creaking beds as men turned. But there were free baths and yellow pieces of soap, and stews were served in the mess for sixpence. For the first few days Alex felt ill. Rory urged him to rest up, there wouldn't be Buckley's of them going on if he was crook. And so Rory went alone to make the contact with a bloke called Myers. Or Brown as he called himself over here, so his family in Melbourne wouldn't track him down. He was a droll dark-humoured type who sat behind a desk at the Jewish Refugee Organisation, a two-storey building opposite the Elephant and Castle.

Alex spent the day in the small room they called the library – a table, a few chairs, a glass case with about sixty books. The bluff custodian who clanked a bucket and mop along the corridors inspected the row of beds each morning at nine. With a benign roar he ordered those who kept to their beds to look sharp on it, this was no bleeding hospital, was it lads? Some of the older men sat on the edges of their beds for most of the day, or played cards in the public rooms downstairs. It seemed to Alex that at any time, night or day, there was someone shuffling past him, someone coughing or retching behind the bathroom doors. Yet there were younger men, well-built boilers and fit deckhands who spent their daylight hours at the docks, waiting for a berth to turn up. A young fellow in the next bed to Alex had gone off elated. He had heard there was a tramp unloading wheat at Port of Avonmouth and several of the crew, 'diggers like you two chums', had skipped ship for this Spanish lark. So there was a bit of graft, he said, going there for one trip at least. The fellow had taken his hand just before he left. He said, 'Don't let yourself rot for too long in this country, will you?'

Rory came back from the city with instructions that they were to stay put for the next few days, but everything was underway. And when Alex asked him about the city itself, the places he had seen in magazines and read about aloud to his mother and sometimes to Bet from next door as well, his cousin said, 'It's like one great rotten tooth, if you want to know. Grey and black and everything you look at's had its day.' But there might be time, he admitted, for them to look round a bit on Thursday, if Alex felt up to coming in. He might have a decker at St Paul's and the rest of it, but only if they went together.

The Embassy in Paris was a high grey building in a row of what looked like mansions. The sky behind it, above the red and black flag, was the same drab colour as its frontage. The trees in the street had begun to come into leaf.

A man looked at them with professional coolness as they stepped through the ornately handled doors. When they asked him where did you go to enlist, he held out a hand to each of them and said simply, 'Passports?' He looked at them, checking the likenesses.

There was a leaden sky and yet a feeling that it should have been spring. But unlike London, there was a gabble of foreign speech which Alex more than Rory found distressing. It worried him that they were not able to make anything clear.

'We know what we're here for,' his cousin insisted to him. 'The rest doesn't matter.'

Alex looked at the river and thought of the black current beneath the cliff leaping to their tossed stones and the fragments of drifting pumice, of their touching on the way back across the paddocks to the house where the curtain moved and the mad man tried to vanish back without their seeing him. And those other curtains, white and drifting in the kitchen at home while they ate and his mother moved the tea things with her unhurried neatness. They were there in his mind so suddenly, so clear, set with a kind of surety like the glinting piece of glass in the necklace his mother had given to her sister and which Aunt Frances sometimes wore, tapping it, saying to him once while she held it between her fingers that there, Alex, bits of time did stand still, didn't they? Smiling, teasing him, for no one believed more than she that the past is not only dead but goes rotten if it lies unburied. (On one of the famous bridges while the water spread in a rippling fan behind a long dark barge, he felt that curious certainty that all you watched, or even all you took part in, was on a stage, in a play, a picture he had already seen. The minute you began to think of things like that, then you looked at surfaces and knew they were the depths as well, that everything becomes the kind of cloth that shimmers and moves when you hold it to the light, that reality more than anything else is how the light falls, now.)

A man, this time in uniform, gave them back their papers. 'In there,' he said. Into a room where, naked, they were examined by a doctor who called out to an aging woman who sat behind a desk and she wrote on a card each time he called. Then, dressed again, they were directed across a marble floor into a larger room. There were perhaps two dozen of them. The ceiling was ornate with gilded scrolls and patterns in the plastering. A map hung against a wall behind a table with thin curved legs. Most of the men sat with their arms folded, strangely shy of each other. Two other men came in, both of them in uniforms so simple that they told you nothing about rank. They sat on two chairs that matched the table, one on either side of the map. One of them spoke in French, and sometimes in Spanish. Occasionally he touched the map. Then he smiled and must have asked a question, because half the room raised their hands. Then the other stood, a thin red-haired man who spoke to them in English. He sounded as though a scarf was tied too tightly around his throat. 'I gather some of you chaps are from up home then?'

'Australia,' Rory said.

The man gave a slightly buck-toothed grin. He said, 'That's close enough for the time being.'

Later they heard he was something of a legend. He had been

with the Republicans since before the Brigade was formed. His father was some kind of consul, and he had grown up speaking the lingo as naturally as a native. They said if it hadn't been for his hair he would have made a marvellous spy. But he began to speak to them now with a passionate precision that made the men forget his gangling appearance and his overposh voice. He seemed able to draw the idealism that was there in one form or another in all the men who listened to him, and direct it to the lines and names and positions on the map. He told them how the situation stood, and where they were likely to be used. As he spoke, Alex felt for the first time in his life the sense of solidarity and trust that arises in a group of men with the same degree of commitment. There was almost a tenderness between them by the time they filed from the room an hour later. They were now indeed inducted to a world where man spoke to man without servility or privilege. And they had been told how they would be brought into the line. They would leave tomorrow morning, not as a group by train, as they had assumed, but in different batches, transported by motorcars towards the border. On the night of the second day they would march twelve hours, more or less, then be sent to where they were needed most.

The figures that Rory knew by heart, the details and the statistics that he never tired of passing on to Alex, would then stand with the purity of rock against the first light. As would those other facts which were indeed such objects of hate – the illiteracy of almost ten million peasants, the hunger of at least half that number; the forty men who owned a million acres for breeding bulls; no schools or hospitals in towns where the black beetles of the Church rolled the country's wealth like balls of dung into their treasuries. At last those facts would lie along one's barrel, the arrogance and the ignorance tangle in the cross-wires of one's sights. The pressure of one's finger against the vileness of their breath. Rory knew that at last it would come to that. Alex, less passionately, only hoped that it might.

There was a festive spirit as the cars crossed France towards the border. The shyness that in Paris had prevented the men from saying much beyond an exchange of names had thawed by the time they ate together the first night. There was a man called Bob

from Oxford who at first embarrassed them with his manner and
with his laugh, a girlish whinny when he found almost any remark
hilarious. But he knew the languages, and Rory quizzed him on
military terms which he wrote in his small black notebook. It was
the kind that Mr Wallace carried with him as he jotted down
figures in the shed or took his readings from the brass-rimmed
barometer on the back verandah. Rory made one of his few jokes
when he took three such notebooks from his suitcase the first
evening on board ship. He held them up towards Alex on the top
bunk. He said, 'The first act of pillage.' The Englishman spoke
slowly while he now took down the words. Alex was struck with
how quickly his cousin picked up whole phrases as well. 'A couple
of months and you'll be chattering like one of them.' The
Englishman neighed at the thought of it.

In the same car with them was a Welshman, who surprised the
Oxford man by not being a gabbler, and a Finn who spoke not a
word of any language that any of them knew. His face was oval,
the features slightly flattened as though beneath a cloth, his hair
dark and very short. He looked the most professional of any of
them, even more than the driver who was back from the Front
recovering from lung infection. The driver told them there was no
certainty that they would be posted to the same position. He told
them how you might meet fifty men in your first week, as they
were doing now, and then never sight any of them again. It
depended what your skill was, where you could be most useful. He
himself was an expert in mines. It was simply better to have no
expectations one way or the other, he advised. When he several
times used the words 'les cons' for the Germans, the Englishman
turned awkwardly from the front seat to those in the back. 'He
says the Huns really are a dreadful mob.' Then they drove on in
silence for a long time. They passed vineyards and wooded slopes
and compact villages that were like flipping the pages of a book.
Rory and the Welshman went to sleep. The Finn, Alex noticed,
looked out at everything with a slight smile on his face.

The second day they spent at Pau. They were told by the
driver, as he left them outside a *pension*, to catch as much sleep as
they could. It was some walk they were in for. The high spirits of
the night before, when the men from the different cars had eaten

at the same restaurant, and drunk wine enough to horse about as though on some football excursion, had taken another turn. Now that they were on the brink of what they had enlisted for, the men turned in upon themselves. They preferred to sit quietly, smoking, sipping at small cups of coffee or glasses of cognac. They shared rooms in the same groups as they travelled in. Only the Welshman became separated, moving in with two coal miners from the north. The miners wore white shirts and dark suits, as though they had set off for a wedding and simply removed their ties. The Finn slept the entire day, as though the driver's advice had been a military order. Rory sat at the window of the same room, filling pages in his notebook, writing over and over the Spanish words he would not forget.

The Oxford man was out looking for some church. He had stood at the bedroom door and laughed when he told them where he was going. Then he explained himself. 'I've got this sort of, you know, interest in the Romanesque. In case you're wondering.'

Rory had looked at him coldly. 'Why should we?'

Then the man at the door, rolling back one of his cuffs against his thin forearm, said, 'Ideologically. In case you thought I wasn't sound.' They heard him move down the stairs, then his footsteps coming up to them from the street. Rory snorted above his writing. 'What sort of bloody dingo's that?'

Alex dozed off. He woke when Rory's chair moved sharply against the tiled floor. He watched his cousin walk to the jacket hanging behind the door, open his wallet and take out some stamps, which he licked and fixed to an envelope as he went back across the room.

Alex said, 'You're organised.'

'We still have to find somewhere to post the thing.'

The shops were beginning to open again as they set out along the streets. Men were raising with long poles the canvas hoods that stretched out above their stalls, or rattling up the doorways in front of the shops. A woman hosed the pavement in front of a window where bread a yard long lay stacked. It was half-past four in the afternoon, yet it was like a new day starting. The water deflected off a wall and sprayed across them. The old lady shouted out to them, showing her few teeth when she saw they were not irate with her. She seemed to know where they were going, for she raised her closed fist and held it towards them.

'That to your mother?' Alex said. He nodded to the letter in Rory's hand. The water had splashed the back of it and he was rubbing the envelope against his shirt.

'No. Beatrice.' The one time her name had come up, or ever would.

They turned into the next street, moving from the pavement as two nuns, with a trail of children in blue school smocks, eased past them. How strange it was that he wrote to her, Alex thought. The girl he remembered blushing as she turned from the women shiyacking her with their dirty meanings, her skirt caught up on the nail, her legs and thigh exposed. For him she was merely part of all that back there, the hanging odour of apples always in the sheds, the smoky blueness from the dust, the rumble as the fruit poured down from the bins to the rubber mats. And that other sweetish scent when he stood beside his aunt. And now almost tasting it in the air, the memory of it coming back so strongly. The clothes Beatrice wore always too large for her, too coarse. The top of her breasts when she leaned forward across the flow of passing fruit. His cousin had never spoken of her and yet now, in their last day, you might say, in their old accustomed world of peace, he had written to the girl who tried to separate herself from the clamour and the crudeness of the rest of them. It had never occurred to him that those two lives could touch. As if each of us is in a room alone, he thought. We hear taps from the other side, and we tap back, when it should be so easy all the time to *see*. Was that the story with everyone, he wondered. Missing always as much as one took in?

'She said she wanted to hear what it was like over here. Over this side.'

They found the post office in a square. The windows were opened in adjoining buildings, the blue shutters laid back along the whitewashed walls. A child practised a piano in one of the upper-floor rooms. The same few bars played over and over. Rory asked, 'Did your ever learn?'

'No. My mother knew but hardly ever played.'

'Be good to know what different tunes were, wouldn't it?'

'I suppose your mother must have too.' Remembering how his own had explained the notes but he had scarcely taken them in, and Bet's frizzy head bent low over her opened music, thirsty with her need to learn.

'They had nothing else to do, that family. It was other people's kids who had to work.' His own mother, he meant, Alex's mother too. He was good at hating the closest thing to hand.

They faced the church which Bob had gone off to inspect. He was sitting there now at a table outside a café, looking across at its facade. He was tapping at the edge of the table with a spoon. He saw them and called out, 'Coffee, you chaps?' He ordered for them before they crossed the square. He drew out a chair at either side of him. When he grinned his teeth hung at them like a rabbit's. 'Worth taking a squint at.' He raised his spoon to the church, to the curved meeting lines above the huge doorway. 'Not one you'd go out of your way for, but seeing it's here, as it were.' Then the fluted jumpy laugh.

'You mightn't see so much of churches over there.' Rory's voice so flat beside the other man's.

'Don't expect to,' Bob said. 'But we're not across there yet, are we?' His hand moved slightly, meaning across *there*, beyond the buildings surrounding them, the life any of them knew, behind the vast curtain of the Alps.

They sat at the table for half an hour. It would have seemed to anyone observing them that they were as leisurely as tourists. Bob was the one who talked the most. Behind the high-pitched hesitancy, the frequent awkward yelps of his laughter, there was a confidence that drew from the other two the acknowledgement that words were much more the Englishman's line of country than their own. But they liked him, and listened to what he said. He told them of a New Zealander at Cambridge he had known. Not known so much, he corrected himself, but heard about. Met him once or twice at meetings before the chap had left. He had come down with the very first of them, before most of us, he said, really knew what the score was. This chap had been on to it like a shot. 'You lot over there seem to be born with socialism in your veins or something. Oh brave new world!' His curiosity about them was open. They were quite another breed. He took in how these two now, they sort of sat inside themselves. As suspicious of themselves as of everyone else. They used talk as a fence instead of a road, he thought. Was that being too fancy? And he asked, 'You've had your share of meetings out there, then? Whipping up support?' Rory told him there were marches and the rest of it on the mainland, but not down where they were. But they got the papers and a friend had kept them in touch.

'Your people?' Bob said. 'At home, I mean. *Simpatico*, were they?'

'They couldn't have been more so.'

The Englishman was delighted. He said, 'I didn't get a pat on the back from mine, I can tell you that. Cut off without a *peso* kind of thing.' It amused him to tell them what his family had threatened. Alex smiled back at him. He was thinking of his mother's saying how when it came to the push there was only one point ever to consider, and it was always very simple: did you think a thing was right to do? Saying that as she died with a disease he now knew was like an infinitely slow fragmenting bomb inside her guts. With her he supposed the belief had been so much more important than ever putting it to the test. A belief threw out lines like a net, didn't it, crossing everything, moving out this way and that? His mother below the yellow clock, saying 'Free will' across the click of her needles. And his saying it to himself this very minute, in the booming out from the tower across the square, from the high black Roman figures, the five banging strokes so loud that the young men paused in their talk and waited, the pigeons slapping up against the sky, wheeling out above the square then back again, settling before the reverberation of the final stroke had ended.

'So your mother gave you all that, then? Support? Money?' Bob was fascinated. He waited to hear more. But Rory was not to be drawn further than to say, 'The only other thing she ever gave me, mind, was a jockey's body.' Winking at Alex as he said it. But the Englishman thought that the funniest thing he had heard. He slapped the table and his bray set the nearest pigeons scuttling beneath another table. But he said shrewdly, 'She must have given you enough anger too. To get this far.' He then proposed they have a cognac for the road. 'Luxuries might run out pretty quickly over there.' His teeth adding to the absurdity of what he said.

The liquor tasted like warm metal. It was hard to swallow the first mouthful. Then the warmth took over. Rory's face twisted against its strength. He said to Alex, 'Go a Cascade now, couldn't you?' Both of them laughing at that. Back, each of them, to the party for Rory before they left, the kegs on the tables out the back, the supper the women had prepared. It had been at Madge's house, down on the broad flat beside the river. The Italian singing for them a farewell song in his own language and the women looked far off into the trees as they listened, the men kept quiet and clapped awkwardly when it ended. It had been too sad for them to know quite what to do with. Then an accordion came out, and the raucous singing of the songs they all knew. 'Don't start those bloody war ones,' someone called. Rory seemed a favourite with them all. They gave him a glass vase brimming to the top, and he knocked it back at one go. 'You'll do,' Madge's husband told him. He had his arm round his shoulder. Then the man turned to Alex, calling to him from where he crouched at the keg, carefully keeping the froth down as he refilled the vase. 'You a starter, are you?' He had shaken his head, raising the glass that he had in his hand, meaning this would do him all right, thanks. He supposed it must have been because this was his last night here, the feeling that came over him then for the people who moved about the party, their warm easiness, their quick crude wit. Dancers started on the back verandah. Above them the insects whirred and slapped against the lamps. A cry went up when someone stumbled into the shallow river. Alex slipped away through the orchards. No one would mind that he sloped off.

He had walked back slowly. The music came up the hill behind him, there was a quick clattering through the branches as he startled some animal. The party would go on down there for hours yet. He had seen Madge's husband before, sitting on a crate in the sheds, holding his head, telling anyone who passed, 'Bugger me, that was a right one last night!' A bird creaked in its flight above him, disturbed by the shouting down the valley.

He removed his boots at the back door in case the old ones were asleep. Once through the kitchen and across the hallway there were the stairs that creaked if you stood on the centre of the boards. He mounted close against the wall, the twisty vines of the wallpaper brushing at his shirt. The door to Mr Wallace's library several inches open. The sounds of quiet movement so that as he passed Alex was about to tap, to say good night. His aunt in the broad dark leather chair, her dress slipped from her shoulders, her enormous and naked breasts dragging down. Her cheek leaned into one folded fist, her forefinger raised and lying beside her ear. Mr Wallace was on the leather footstool in front of her, his mouth at the brown slobber of her nipple, his naked arms like something dead, like chicken flesh, the skin sagged loose at the upper arms. In a shiny dark-blue gown. At its opened front the hair was white and dense. His guzzling and pawing at the flaccid breast, Aunt Frances's other hand moving softly across the back of his neck. But her face turned so that her nephew saw in its profile the indifference and habit at what she did, and what she permitted to be done. The expression of a woman baking a cake, leaning over a sink, no more than that. Something that must be done. Mr Wallace moved a hand that seemed absorbed in her flesh, sliding it deeper between her breasts. And Aunt Frances looked above the old man's bobbing head, across the room to the slightly opened window in whose pane she could catch the grey reflection of her face. She brought up briefly the hand from the back of Mr Wallace's neck and straightened a piece of loosened hair, her joined fingers then running across it, smoothing it, before returning to their work of comfort, titillation. Alex felt the pelting rock inside his chest. He stepped away, his back against the wall, his palms hot against it. He gritted his teeth against the cry he felt forcing at his throat. The half-lit corridor wheeled in darting spokes, his own tears revolting him.

'Right then are we, comrades?' Bob saying the words ironically, as he expected his antipodean friends to take them. Alex followed the Englishman and Rory across the square, towards the street where outside their pension a group of men stood on the pavement chatting, smoking, looking towards the sky to estimate the weather for that night. There was a gaiety among them now that the beginning was so close.

Alex thought, 'Thank Christ, something must happen soon.'

The air-raids came at precisely the same times each day. At nine in the mornings, the heat already setting in with its fury, the Stukas skidded in low above the hills. They flashed across again at four, when the shadows from the rocks were flung the other way. It was eight weeks since the night when the group of volunteers climbed for eight hours then descended for two. Sixty days of 'action', as the newspapers always put it. And as the men who had never been there also said, that short time had 'hardened' them. Already it was as if this were normal life, those alert ten minutes before nine in the morning or four in the afternoon, the impetus to get whatever one was doing completed. And done so methodically, after the first few days, it seemed as though it were merely a train, say, about to pass through and not the line of black squat aircraft slamming down above them, their wings shuddering with fire before turning off to the east. The men were settled in their dugouts by the time the attacks began. There was even something inane about their clockwork precision. Their sheer regularity robbed the scudding attacks, the whining snip from the rocks, the pattering lift of earth as the bullets struck harmlessly, of any fear. To cope with death was a matter, after all, of common sense, like stepping back from a railtrack when an express hurtled through on time. At eight-forty in the mornings then three-forty in the afternoons, Alex went out with others from the First Aid to pick up scraps of paper, cigarette packets, the occasional towel left lying against a rock on the days when they were close to the river. Even a book had to be retrieved and hidden. That was one of Sanidad's special duties. For it was said the pilots could spot a scrap of paper, anything isolated and pale, no matter how small it was. They were the clues that told them they were near a camp, and the bullets would ring off the rocks and churn the ground for a hundred yards each side. Without such certain clues, they could fly over two hundred men, dropping their bombs, playing their necessary rounds of fire, on land where the nearest life might be a good half mile's distance.

Between the bursts of ground action when their services were called for, their retrieving the wounded, bringing in the dead, the First Aid mucked in wherever the commander thought they might be used. In his couple of months since coming down, Alex had helped out with digging latrines, with laundry, mostly with bringing up the metal containers of food from a dozen miles behind the lines. When they were not actually fighting, the men mostly thought of food. Alex's outfit had come across at just the wrong time. They heard stories of how only a few months before the Brigade had been eating ham and fried fish, there had been butter and honey. But in each successive month after the Fascists blocked the ports, the marvellous tucker sent down by the Soviet trade unions slackened off then stopped altogether. Most of the larger docks were lost. There was only Barcelona and Valencia left, and then a handful of small loyalist ports. So there was now a dreary regularity in the rations they received, the half-pint measure of beans, the occasional scrap of meat for dinner, the bean soup and the coffee substitute that the men took for no other reason than they craved food from the time they woke.

Alex accepted from the start that the business of manoeuvres, the finer points of tactics, were not his gift. He had realised that the first morning as they faced the officers who questioned them on their aptitudes. 'How', one of them put to him, 'can you best serve the cause?' Until then it had not occurred to him that a preference might be made. So he said, 'I don't mind killing if that's all there is.' His answer was translated for those in the room who could not quite fathom it, and he was taken for something of a wit. Bob was in the line in front of the second desk. He gave his usual bray, a delight that his friend amused not only the new chums but the die-hards as well. An older man who leaned against the wall behind the questioning officer smiled as he threw down his cigarette and turned his boot on the butt. He waited until Alex had been given his card with his photograph and the official stamp. Then he followed him out into the bright well of sunlight in the building's courtyard and asked him more precisely where he was from. When Alex mentioned the Waikato the stranger said, 'I reckon we might have been neighbours maybe one time back there.' He held out his hand. They were standing beside a triton who blew an empty horn against a dry fountain. He said his name was Johnson. He had to run for it, actually, he joked, but that was hardly going to bother them at this distance, was it? 'I might even feel homesick if you talk nicely about it.'

The man offered a cigarette that Alex refused. A few minutes later he was introduced to Rory, and the three of them became friends. Johnson was almost avuncular in the way he spoke to Alex. But when he spoke with Rory it was always of the war. The passion that the Tasmanian brought to what he was there for made Johnson give him the nickname 'Monk'. The name took on among the other men. Most of them would put their lives on the line several times a week, but the Aussie Monk became a touchstone even among themselves. As much so it seemed by instinct as by deliberate study, he became expert in the terrain they fought on. An even greater gift, touched enough with the inexplicable to make him a figure of superstition with some of the Spaniards, was his ability to anticipate the enemy's mind. On that first morning in the queue before the questioning officer, he had volunteered for a machine-gun. The turnover of men was higher there than anywhere else.

More often now, the Brigade took over positions that the Italians had held until the day before. Booby traps had become the expected thing, crudely wired tins, a crate that would explode in the hands of the man who picked it up, trip-wires wherever there were stands of pine, and rifles positioned in branches set off by walking past. Because the advancing line was wary of them, the casualties were few. The demo people knew precisely what to look for. Later they were aided by a prisoner who understood that his life would run out on the day he failed to uncover one of the traps. He believed the threat, as well he might. There were stories that no one believed, but liked to pass on, that he was now setting them up himself, almost having himself killed for the sake of proving his goodwill. Once he was hit in the leg. He had sat in the Sanidad tent grinning like a kid with a toy he had always been after. '*Buono, si?*' he kept saying. Alex did what he could with the wound until the doctor showed up. But the next day Rory compelled him to hobble along when he went out on his reccy. He pumped the Italian for information that no one else could see the point of. He wanted to know what sort of men the Italian snipers were – did they volunteer, for example? Were they simply detailed because they were good shots? There was one in particular he wanted to know everything about. The prisoner swore he had never so much as clapped eyes on him. He was *famoso*, yes, but he himself had not seen him. Rory became obsessed with him, the smart-arse gunner who played snatches of tunes each day when he opened up, spacing out his fire at intervals that tocked the rhythm of Neopolitan songs for twenty seconds before he swung in seriously on his target. Did he joke much, Rory demanded, was he a clown or was he a master, as he suspected? Did he do it coldly, spicing himself up to kill? And the Italian prisoner began to follow Rory without being compelled to, as though the Aussie Monk had become a kind of charm. He told him directly he felt safer if he was there. *Compadre*, he began to call him. The fair-headed man's sharp features made him think of puppets in a town square on feast-days.

When they went out together, the Italian always went in front. Sometimes he sang quietly under his breath. Rory would tell him if he liked the tune. They shared their lunch together. He looked at the photographs in the prisoner's wallet and quickly learned a range of words they used when they were together. They worked closely for a fortnight before they came to a circle of stones at the edge of a bluff. They were a hundred feet above a ravine, and as far forward as the Brigade's territory went. The Republicans had been advancing for several days. On a map their position was at the point of two converging lines, the tip of an arrowhead. Across the shallow river the rock rose up again, slightly higher than where they now crouched. There were trees on the shelving rock. One could see a bird lift up a half mile or so off in the clear quiet air. Across the gully, on a level with themselves, there was a small white shrine. 'All gone,' the Italian gestured, '*tutti son partido.*' Rory set his tripod in the cover of the pines. The Italian helped him balance the gun. Then he gave the prisoner a cigarette and his own hat. He asked him to wander over to a group of stones, to pace it out as though the precise distance were important. The cigarette was in the Italian's mouth twenty seconds later when a stream of fire from across the valley kicked him sideways to the yellow ground. Immediately Rory opened up at the white shrine. The plaster tufts sprayed out until the sniper's arm was revealed. Another two passing sweeps from the Tukkurov and the shrine crumbled like a biscuit. He picked his man off as easily as a target at a fairground.

Rory waited for his gun to cool. He dragged the Italian the few yards back into the pines and put his own handerchief over his face. There was no time for more than that. He took up his hat and thwacked it several times against his knee, freeing it of dust. He then sat for long enough to have a smoke, watching the heat waves daze across the opposite shelf of rock. He then took the prisoner's belt to lash more firmly the dismantled gun, and placed it on his shoulder. He jogged back to camp. He said to one of the men, 'You always looked like you fancied this.' He gave him the gold medal that had swung on a cord around the Italian's neck. The soldier bit the disc and laughed and tossed it with his thumb, like a coin. In return he offered a wineskin he took from his pack. 'Never mind that, cobber,' Rory told him, 'it wasn't any effort.' But he took the skin and thanked the Spaniard for it. He swung it by its neck until he reached the shelter where he and Johnson and Alex had their palliasses. He threw it on the end of his friend's bed.

Two days later, he and Johnson volunteered to cross the river.

There was the rumour that the Ities were leading them towards some manoeuvre they did not expect, that their pulling back in these last few days was a ploy to lead them on. The men remembered what they had heard of how they surrounded the 57th, the retreat the Italians had then driven before them like dogs snapping at the heels of exhausted sheep. 'Never let anyone tell you those dagoes can't fight,' Johnson said.

'We need more observers up front,' the English intelligence officer said in the evening while they sat on the cooling ground, the daily swill of brandy in the bottom of their mugs drawing them together as it always did, to chat of home, of politics, of what the brass had up their sleeve. He said it directly to Rory and to Johnson. He thought as he looked at them how they might almost pass for father and son. The two men were now almost always in each other's company. They knew when the chips were down they would be a good team together. For the sense of inevitability that falls on some men when an army engages in action, the way a few are picked out by their fellows as the ones who are inexplicably 'charmed', and on whom the luck of the rest somehow depends, was centred on the two of them. They never actually said they would go across the river. Yet no one doubted that they would.

For one entire day Johnson sat at a small folding table. Almost always one earphone was clapped against the side of his head while his fingers moved delicately among the nest of wires and connections. Rory with equal precision attended to their packs. He chose the food they would take. He sharpened their knives until a cigarette paper divided smoothly against their edges. They would carry pistols, but there was no intention of getting themselves into combat. They would wear black peasant clothes and black shirts. Rory carefully wrapped the matches they would carry in squares of oilcloth. He broke a small mirror cleanly in two, setting one half aside for each of them. Lives before now had been saved or lost, because of mirrors. He got hold of two rosaries. He said, when one of the Spaniards laughed at him, that those beads might carry more weight with a Sicilian officer than a battery of guns. He concealed razor blades between the heels and uppers of their boots. That night he and Johnson were excused their two-hour stint on guard. At two o'clock in the morning they were woken by a sentry, and dressed in silence. Each of them touched Alex's shoulder as they passed from beneath the canvas into the night. For a few seconds they were outlined against the welter of stars. They joked quietly with the sentry as they passed him and slipped down towards the river. As if they were coming back, they gave the day's password. '*A la Victoria,*' Rory said.

The sentry, whose face was blackened like their own, said quietly, '*Paseremos.*' They would be gone three days.

The weather was stinking hot, and becoming worse. Alex's time was spent working on the 'drives', those twenty-foot tunnels sloping into the sides of the hill towards the small chambers that served as armoury stores. The work was exhausting. Wooden supports were raised, the rock and dirt from the drives were carried sometimes for over a mile, to be spread unostentatiously and become part of the lie of the land. If you were lucky, or skilled, then you worked at carpentry, at planing and sawing and fitting the struts for the first few yards inside the tunnel. If you were not, then like Alex you took your turn swinging the picks, lugging out the bags of soil. The men moved towards each other, swearing in their irritation, moved apart, dropping in exhaustion when the officer blew his whistle for a break. Bob worked in the line beside him, skinny and pink in his khaki shorts. He said, 'Trade places with our *dos amigos* any day, wouldn't you?' And in case his friend thought he took it too lightly, he said, 'Don't worry about them, mate. They can look after themselves.' He sounded a little awkward saying 'mate'.

The next afternoon Alex and Bob were detailed to 'river duty'. This meant they were spelled from the bags of dirt and stones and between them dragged up cans of water for the men who mixed mortar. They were half way though one trip when the planes flew in on them, early. Two squat shapes coming from opposite directions. The bastards opened fire from five hundred feet. Most of the men began to run. A few threw themselves to the ground. One seemed to leap, as though avoiding something in his path, and then fell, buckling from the knees. It reminded Alex of a boy going down in a tackle. The bucket between himself and Bob, which they had lowered slowly as if reluctant to spill what it carried, rang with the impact of the bullet striking it. In the terror and slowness of those moments, Alex saw with the same precision as if observing such detail were his only concern, how the water leaped in a bright stream through the sudden rent in the tin. And raising his eyes from the clear spurt of water he saw Bob kneeling a few yards to his left, his hand raised to his jaw, his bare arms reddened with the splash of his blood. Alex supported him under the arm, drawing him up and directing him, shoving him, towards the trees. He heard the beginnings of that high-pitched familiar voice, but the speech, whatever it intended, was lost in a sound like an emptying sink.

Several men had been hit. Bob was handed to a group at the entrance to one of the tents in the shelter of the pines. Alex grabbed at the folded stretcher handed to him, and at once ran back, down the slope towards the river. Another medic helped him fling the stretcher open and raise an unconscious man. It was one of the miners who had travelled down from Paris in their convoy of cars. There was a stain on his shirt the size of a large plate. They carried him quickly towards the tent, where a French medical student already worked in his white gown. Already, too, there was the buzz of flies.

Alex and his companion ran back again. There was a man

sitting upright on the ground, both his hands clamped above one knee. He looked at them as though quite unconcerned. Then Alex saw the buckling rush of the plane's returning shadow down the opposite slope, and heard the heavy rattle of the guns. The river sheaved briefly with the standing impact of bullets. A blaze of light racketed through his body as his boot ripped apart. Yet there was little pain as he lay watching the canvas roof of the tent, the bright dappling where the sun found gaps between the trees. Until the French student touched his leg, and his voice came from him in a coughing sob.

Two days later, Bob the Englishman died.

No word came through of Rory, nor of Johnson.

Alex was loaded on the same truck he had ridden dozens of times in bringing the cooked meals from the kitchens up to the Front, and was taken to a hospital three hours behind the lines. Three other stretchers were loaded onto the hooded back of the truck beside him. He thought how it stank like a butcher's van in the heat.

At the hospital, three of his toes were removed. But while his foot healed normally, he showed the familiar enough signs of nervous distress, the sleeplessness and the tears he was ashamed of. He was taken a short journey by sea, the coast always in view to his left, and then across France by train. There was a nurse with them who wore a long blue cape. She talked to him sometimes while he looked from the deck, but he could think of no reason to answer her. At an institution a little way from Oxford, set on a hillside in tidy country like a picture book, he found that he cried when he sat alone in the gardens or, on cold days, in the glassed-in verandah from which the weather moved across the vast green space below the hospital. A doctor said to him, 'You know we can see three counties from here?' Alex lit cigarettes that burned down before he raised them to his mouth. He could not recall the next day, whether or not he had slept during the night. Much of the time he thought about food, as he had at the Front. Very often he walked from the ward to the hallway, to look at the clock above the entrance. One day when he walked in the garden, along the gravel drive with its now dry hydrangeas and cut-back rose stumps, he picked up a kitten and took it to the kitchen for the staff to feed. His hands were almost grey with the cold. He watched the small rapid tongue lap at the milk. He laughed and began to talk to the girl with the strange voice who stood watching beside him. She held a huge chromium jug in her hands. She told him she was Welsh. He said, 'I knew a Welshman not long ago.' It surprised him that he wanted to tell her. He said, 'His name was Morgan. He was in Spain.'

'That's a good name for the puss there, isn't it?' The girl laughing with him. Smiling at him. The trees bare through the windows behind her, snow beginning to fall in big thick flakes. 'Here, Morgan,' she was saying, 'lick up, lad.'

Three days later, Alex signed himself out. The next week he would turn nineteen.

Minutes after the injured were taken from the car, the restraining willow snapped and the vehicle slipped into the water. It entered smoothly, slowly. The river then lay inches above the hood. From the road it looked as much a submerged box as a car. By the time the ropes were attached, the injured were already in the hospital. Late in the morning the girl was operated on, the sheared metal strip taken from her head, the long scar sutured. The boy was concussed and bruised. Within twenty hours he was given soup and a thin stew. He asked for two helpings of each.

When the winch on Miller's Service Truck grated into movement and the rope ran round the turning drum, the river ran in thick pale braids from the emerging car.

'If it hadn't been for that tree there in the first place,' the apprentice said. 'Talk about lucky.' He was still excited by his first month on accidents.

'You see all sorts,' the boss told him.

It had taken the town only minutes to hear about those two mad young bastards who were making a run for it. Neither of them could even drive, apart from fooling about in a paddock. You couldn't credit it.

Pulling cars from under water never failed to give Fred Miller the creeps. As though with their streaming bonnets and the massive pouring from their wrenched doors they had been far further than those few feet below the surface, as though they were being drawn from distances so much deeper than you'd guess. Although he did them up and as often as not had the business of selling them for the insurance people, you wouldn't catch him riding in one of them. Not on your life.

'Ever seen one with the people still in it, have you?' the apprentice asked.

'Just worry about this one, that's all you've got to do,' Fred Miller said. He stopped the winch and told the lad to clear those sticks and muck

251

clogging the back axle. And that weed stuff trailing along the side.

One of the headlights had been forced back and snapped from its stand, and the mudguard crumpled where it had taken the weight of the car against the tree. Both the windows on the driver's side were smashed, the windscreen buckled in. A piece of metal like a dagger was pointing towards the wheel.

To watch the car come up was like seeing a film run backwards almost. The wheels slithered on the bank as it rose back towards the road, then with expert precision, so that the final moments seemed accomplished merely by resting his hand against the car's flank, Fred Miller eased it across the lip of grass. 'They don't come easier than that,' he said.

The apprentice scrambled up the bank, carrying a white shoe. 'This is satin or something, know that?' he said. The small discovery entranced him. 'Satin, shit! Who'd she think she was?'

'Never mind the bleeding shoe,' the boss shouted down to him. 'Get behind the wheel there and try to turn her. And slowly,' he added. 'It's buggered enough without adding to it.'

The sogged white shoe, the resurrected car, less than twenty hours after Alex and that crazy girl had made a run for it. Princess who could not drive but insisted that she could, Alex in his sweating funeral suit beside her. And their night as it was later pieced together in the broken-into school at Gordonton on the tumbled costumes of the school's Christmas play, the tossed assorted colours and Princess in the crown of Balthazar or Melchior, standing before him at dawn, naked, jewelled. Alex laughing with her, drawing her back down to him, saying, *Now Barbara there is only us.* Saying love, and then demanding, *Say it. Say it back to me.* And the girl has decided already the day will last for ever. She will make it last.

Dick hunched into his overcoat on the bench beneath the oaks. Across the road, the white arches of the hotel began to glimmer in the early light. There was a stretch of narrow lawn between there and where he sat, the memorial statue at one end, the clock tower at the other. The clock had been silenced during the war, in the fear that Japanese invaders should be helped in some way by its striking through the night. The war had been over for years, but the town still waited on the expert from Auckland who sooner or later would come to reconnect the chimes, to do something too about the minute hand which had broken off on the evening of VJ Day when one of the Larsen boys, having climbed a pyramid of inebriated friends, leaped and tried to swing from it. His leg was fractured in the fall and a local erratic solicitor still prosecuted a claim that the disabling injury might be construed as an accident of war. Until the claim was finally argued out, the clock could not be fixed.

The small man, older-looking than his years, watched the high dead face of the clock glimmer into his vision. His shoulder was giving him jip. This rheumatism or whatever, he thought, his old cobber Alex's foot. We're crocks and we're not past thirty, either of us! Yet Jeez, he thought, there's a lot worse off than we are. Like the dead, for starters. Like Princess who's as good as. When you think of her, Christ it doesn't bear thinking on. And poor bloody O'Brien having his hand stamped on for her that day, his head blown off in North Africa somewhere. Dying under fire or whatever the phrase was. His wife with the medal and its bit of rainbowy ribbon and stuff-all else to show for it. And Tai Weston lying out there now with his hori outfit at Matangi. They said he wouldn't last the summer out. They said his lungs were thin as tissue paper, one of them sliced to hell with a wound he'd picked up over there. Alex was spot on about that one all right. The bullshit about war and glory and dying for the flag. Look at that monument over there against the lightening sky, a great fucken concrete coffin on its end. Blow your bugles to buggery, it wouldn't make a jot of difference to those jokers. Whether Tai there got his punctured lung running single-handed at Rommel or copped it in the back scared shitless as he scarpered, still the same lung that had a hole in it.

There was a sheet of mist lying at knee height across the park. It was grey when the dark first slackened and now it stretched out in a thick skein of brilliant white. The birds had started up above Dick's head, a regular throbbing brawl. Funny how his friend knew the name for any bird you pointed out to him. The names too for trees and shrubs and for God's sake the stars even – Alex often remarked on those if they were strolling down to the bridge. Aldebaran, he'd say, Sagittarius, and the Pleiades, see those ones up there, those small seven ones, see?

Alex told him one morning after they had been down to the river, trying their luck for trout fifty yards up from the bridge, 'It's only the names of things make them real.' Dick must have looked lost with that one because his friend tried to explain. He said if you couldn't name something then you had no right to say you had ever known it. 'Like when I was over there,' he said. He had tapped the side of his trousers with his opened hand. He meant when he was in Spain. 'I'd see something quite ordinary, say. A tin mug or a sack or some piece of equipment. And I'd want to say something about it to the bloke next to me and I wasn't able to.' Dick said, 'Because he was a wop? Then of course you couldn't.' Alex looped in the line and wound it round a stick. They still fished with the same gear as when they were kids. 'Because his words were different to mine, see. So in a way the mug or whatever wasn't really there for both of us, I mean unless we had the same word for talking about it.' Which puzzled Dick even more. He said, 'You only had to point, didn't you?' But Alex seemed not to hear that. 'Like if he'd said *watch out* and I didn't click and a sniper did me. It was knowing a *word* that kept me alive or left me dead. See that?'

He had wound the line right in. He untied the hook and slipped it into a matchbox. He caught his friend's small contorted face. 'Never mind about my rambling on.' He laughed in his tall awkward way, drawing his breath in suddenly before he said something serious. 'Words are like colours, that's what I'm getting at. Don't know what things are called, then it's like seeing everything grey all the time.' Dick thought his friend meant Princess, in some obscure way.

The rolled-up line made a gross bulge in Alex's pocket. They had to go slow on the steep bank because of his foot. Once Dick grabbed at a branch with his left hand and leaned back, holding out his right. Alex grasped it, and hauled himself up. Back at road level, the dry stalks of cocksfoot brushing against their legs, Dick put to him, 'Do you really think about that kind of thing, Alex? Names for things and what not?' They paused while Alex took out the blue Capstan packet and Dick held a match they both leaned towards. Alex picked a trace of tobacco from his tongue. 'All the time,' he said. 'That's what most of us are doing all the time.' They headed for the bridge again, Dick adapting his pace to the stiff swinging progress of his friend. 'Bugger me then,' he said.

The first stock truck went past just before six, pulling up at the public lavatories on the far side of the park. The driver left the engine running while he jumped from the cab. The exhaust feathered out in the chill morning air. Dick knew how Bet'd give him what-for if she ever found out he'd been over here on the bench since five in the morning. But you couldn't wake people at that hour. She'd insist on rustling up something for him to eat then and there. That had happened once before and the next day she'd taken sick. She said she would have been sick anyway, don't go imagining a knock in the night could make that much difference. Still he would lie to her and say that he caught the *Herald* bus through from Auckland. She need never know that he had taken a lift at midnight that two hours later dropped him six miles along the road at the Brunton turnoff, across from Corbies' farm. He had walked the rest of the way, arrived there dog tired and just flopped on the bench. It was the soaking cold that woke him, his bad shoulder so cramped it had taken him minutes to turn and sit up. But you didn't put people out more than you could help, that was one thing Dick stood by. And they would put him up as long as he wanted to stay, he knew that. He knew they were dead level when they said it too. But what with all they'd done for the old lady, not even a relative but treating her like one, for Christ's sake.

The driver came out from the square concrete lavatories. He looked out briefly across the park before heaving himself back behind the wheel. The door slammed like a gunshot. Dick noticed how he wore only a black singlet even at this time of day. They said fat kept the cold out, but that one there, he was no bigger than Dick himself. And he could hear his own teeth going nineteen to the dozen. It couldn't be long before Bet got up now. He stood and took the brown suitcase from the grass beside the bench. The skeins of fog were thinning out. The trees looked heavy with the damp. He would walk down there to the dunnies himself. Round the footpath though. He didn't want wet shoes into the bargain. He walked deliberately and quietly, as though he feared his steps would set off the town and wake the hotel across the street. By the time he walked down there, then back round the full square of the park, it would be after six, surely? The light shot through between two of the trees and he was looking into the direct dazzle of the sun. At the same instant as it gleamed on the metal rim of the clock in the bedroom upstairs, above the whitewashed roughcast arches, Bet stretched out her hand, stopping the alarm before its clamour began.

She saw the small man with his cheap suitcase against the blur of trees. She understood at once what must have happened. Dear Dick, she thought, he's apologised for breathing since the day he was born. And his crazy bitch of a mother now so terrified of death that she jangled in her holy medals like a suit of armour. Bet let the long white curtain fall back from her hand. Beyond the main street and the slope towards the river, across the farmland on the other side, she saw the hills hard and bright against the early sky. That meant the day would be fine, thank God. She so disliked that drive when it rained, although she'd never yet used bad weather as an excuse not to go. But the trip made her feel nervous even now. She hated saying goodbye to Alex as he stood on the step beneath the central arch and waved her off. She hated the walk once she had arrived, the distance she would have to cover from the car to the low grey pre-fab that made her think vaguely of something stretched out, dead. Vaguely, because no image ever hardened in her mind of precisely what it was. But the grey asphalt of the carpark, the ribbon of grating clinkers between the building and the patch of earth where a few sparse geraniums made a bid for colour – she thought of these first thing on the days when she knew she must drive across. And as she dressed she wished that she had baked the cakes last night. That was one more chore for this morning.

Alex turned heavily in the bed behind her. The springs creaked, the newspaper he had been reading the night before crackled as he drew the covers closer around him. Bet fixed them more firmly at his back. He muttered at her a phrase she did not pick up. 'There,' she said to him, her hand briefly touching his shoulder, 'I'll let you know when it's seven.' On the broad landing of the stairs her hand ran over the smooth bumpy head of the elephant that had stood there since the hotel opened fifty years before. Her fingers made the same slow caressing sweep every morning since she and Alex had taken over. The dark wood shone as though it had been oiled.

Bet liked entering the clean bare kitchen. The light streamed across one wall, and the others were cool in their early shadows. The long table and its cane-seated chairs, the scoured yellow wooden bench and the new aluminium sink, the racks of pots on their nails above the bench, all struck her agreeably. She was glad to be back among them. She believed that by doing the small things well, life added up to something that mattered. As Alex's mum had told her years back on the farm, if you hate what you do each day, the routine of the kitchen or running the bars and attending to the business of the hotel, then you find you are hating the greater part of your life. But there's not a plate you pick up, Bet thought, not a reflection on a cup, that you can't feel your own pulse by. That you can't take into yourself and so the smallest things become doors, don't they, opening out, leading you through?

'I'll crown that bloody girl when I see her,' Bet declared to the empty kitchen. She took the dirty dishcloth that lay curled in the sink and let the tap run across it while she went to the door to the back verandah. 'No one's forgetting you either,' she called. She picked up the wire crate of milk bottles and carried them through to the table. She placed the bottles inside the fridge then slipped the crate into the space between it and the wall. 'I'm coming, I'm coming,' she said quietly. She turned off the tap and wrung the cloth in both her hands, spreading it across the two taps. 'That girl, Clive,' she confided, 'if they make them any dumber than her I'd like to hear about it.' She went back to the verandah and lifted the canvas hood from a cage balanced on an iron stand. The large white bird let out a run of shrill squawks. Its sulphur crest jerked against the wire mesh as its beak stropped Bet's poking knuckle. She touched the soft wad of feathers at its throat. The bird's claws moved with a dry rasp along his perch, backing off from her. 'Don't fancy that then, don't we?' She took a packet of seed from the top of an outdoor safe, and the funnel whose snout she slipped between the wires to the small china dish tied to the cage's side. The bird nudged at it sharply, the black eyes flickering at her as the head turned. 'My God, Clive,' she told him, 'if I was as ugly as you are I wouldn't expect attention like this every day. And you pong rotten into the bargain.' She pointed at the mess on the cage's tray. 'Time old Alex there did a bit of work for his keep, wouldn't you say?' And she thought how the bird's scaled eyes always reminded her of Dick. She walked down the few steps to where the thistle grew in a patch that Alex told her was a God-awful eyesore but she defended by saying it couldn't conceivably be that, it was useful and it was beautiful as well if you bothered to look at it properly. She took handfuls of the rich green stuff that left its stickiness on her fingers. She folded it and slid the wedges between the wires. 'There. Just like slipping a smoke to a friend who's inside.' The bird stabbed at it rapidly. Bet's finger was at the yellow crest. She told the bird, 'She had just better like you, that's all I can say. If she doesn't think you're the cat's whiskers she can just go back with her Polacks or whatever. I'm going to tell her that straight out.' She felt such a happiness welling in her when she said that. She brought her hands together in a quick clap, leaving them joined as though she walked back into the kitchen in some kind of prayer. She stopped to look at the *Herald* calendar on the wall beside the fridge. A blue cross for each day since she and Alex had known it was going to come off. Three months, they had said. Three months and already it was a fortnight past that. There would be a phone call, she supposed, or a brown envelope with OHMS across the corner or even a car turning up one morning – she had heard of them being delivered like that. Beyond the pouring sunlight across the wall of the kitchen she saw those other fractured walls and the piled bodies they were always showing a while ago in the newsreels. The tanks in those streets where the people ran out cheering and threw flowers at the soldiers. The faces sometimes close up to the camera, the faces that could have been cut from paper and the eyes burning in them like holes. She imagined a town she herself had never seen nor so much as heard of but must be as real as her own hands were. From the broken town a girl was walking, she carried a small bag in her hand and wore a scarf you could never tell the colour of because those films were always flickering grey. And she would open the door there and come into the kitchen and colour would pour into her then, like a thousand candles lit suddenly in front of you. A room quivering back to light after years like in the newsreels, black shapes against the sky, people running to doorways. She saw the girl standing on the stairway in front of the elephant and then Bet was telling her that was her room, over there, with the new chintz curtains, the new wallpaper and bedspread, the room next to Alex's and her own. Next to Daddy's, would she say? No, that didn't sound right. And what would she call herself? Everyone else might think it mad of course, but why not Bet, simply? All other words were a lie that neither of them would believe. It must all be *new* for her, wasn't that the whole point of it? There must be no pretending about anything. That would be their only rule. A girl and a woman just being as straight as they could be with each other. And she'd not have any of those old crows from round the district trying to tell the girl how lucky she was, how she was one of the chosen in this marvellous land while millions back there were not so fortunate, not like her and themselves the apple of God's eye. Bet could hear the old fools coming at that one. You might as well tell her, *Hasn't God been a right bastard then to all the others?* You – everybody – simply had to stop thinking in ways like that. It was keeping yourself in chains. Alex understood that. Oh but she would be her own being, this one. That is what they would be able to give her. 'All chains isn't it, Clive? Wherever you look it's chains. But this girl will walk away from them like that.'

'How's the warren?' Dick called to her from the door. Speaking before he knocked.

Bet was at the bench, greasing a sheet of paper with a dollop of butter. She turned, wiping her hands on her apron. She took her ring up from the windowsill and slipped it onto her hand as she walked across to her cousin.

'Come in. Come in. You don't stand at the door when you come home.' She embraced him warmly. Dick's hand still awkwardly hanging onto his suitcase as he stepped inside to her opened arms. She felt his frailness through the gaberdine. His dry skin was cold against her own. 'Like ice,' she said. She took his case and led him over to the range. 'There's some warmth there that should heat your bones.' She opened the iron door and threw in pinecones from the big basket by the hearth. 'These take like nobody's business.'

'Don't fuss,' Dick told her. He looked at her while she placed his coat on one of the hooks behind the door. He rubbed with his knuckle at the wetness the cold air had brought to one of his eyes.

'Not crying to see me again, are you?' She stood in front of him with her hands held together like a singer's. They were smiling at each other. 'By the time you've warmed your skinny backside I'll have some tea to pour into you.'

She moved quickly, speaking to him across her shoulder, touching him lightly as she leaned past him to place the kettle on the range. It must be six or seven months, she was saying. And Dick confirming, 'Six.' By God, he said, it was good to get out of that city up there, he never liked the place. 'The element you get up there these days. You wouldn't want to walk round in Auckland, Bet.'

'Look like me, you can walk anywhere,' she said to him. She pulled a wry face, touching the hair that was as frizzed as it had been at school. She disliked it quite as much now as she did then. Then she told him, 'You should have stayed here all along. We've missed you not being round.' She could see him lifting the crates out in the yard, mopping out the bars, watering the patch of earth for her because he knew what pleasure she took in whatever happened to grow there. His dear comic self-importance, liking to think himself Alex's right-hand man.

'You know how it is, Bet. I was never a great one for staying put.'

'Well I'm glad you're back,' she told him. 'Both of us are.' She gave him his cup of tea to go on with until his fry and bacon were cooked.

'I could have waited till Alex had his, you know.'

There were several minutes while the only sound was his knife and fork against the plate. Bet opened the oven door to assess her baking. She then went through to look at the grandfather clock in the hallway. She said as she came back, 'Say what you like, they don't half worry themselves some of these kids, do they? Supposed to start at seven and here it is twenty past already.'

She knew she had told Alex she would call him at seven but the longer he slept the better. He tended to be edgy on these days when she drove across. It would be on his mind every minute of the day until she arrived back and he would limp out to the car and open the door for her. She would tell him then the words he wanted to hear, the same ones said so often they had become a ritual between them, *Much as ever, love*. He would relax then like a man reprieved. He would bring in two brandies from the bar once she was seated in the kitchen.

Dick directed at her his serious lizard gaze. He was waiting for her to go on.

'Miles away,' she excused herself.

'Who's the maid you've got here now, then?'

'Lucky to have any, Dick. Last year every girl in town who wasn't a hunchback got herself knocked up by one of the returned soldiers. This year even the hunchbacks have lit off for Auckland on the lookout for it.'

Dick laughed at her explanation. 'You don't find many girls anywhere want to do housemaids' work any more. That's another thing the war's done.'

'Can't blame them, mind,' Bet said. Then she was off on another tack. 'I never answered you about the warren though, did I?' She gestured to the low building that ran along one side of the yard in which Lilian was now leaning her bicycle against piled empty crates. There were four doors that led into four small rooms. The quarters had been built early in the century for men who couldn't afford more than a couple of bob a night for a bed. The same iron bedsteads were still there, the rough bedside tables, the windows divided into four small panes. But the rooms were clean and warm and Bet still let them out on weekends when a crowd was in town for a match. They'd lost one of the rooms in the main building, of course, the one she'd been doing up with the new blue curtains and the kidney-chest with the same material gathered round, it was so pretty when you opened the door and looked into it, any young girl surely would fall for it? If you'd never had a room of your own, if there was only charred Europe to remember. God, when she thought of the first time she and the girl would walk up the stairs together. That was always how she saw it, whenever her mind leaped ahead to the arrival. Alex standing there on the landing and the girl going up just ahead of herself. Those long white socks they wore because she had seen pictures of them standing in their pleated skirts and their pullovers and those socks. Nearly all of them with fair hair. Standing outside an army hut in the Wairarapa where they had to be 'inducted' – the word the official letter used – before they were delivered to their foster parents.

Lilian came into the kitchen unwinding a long red and black knitted scarf. She went to lay it across a chair, caught Bet's eye, and draped it across the coat already there behind the door. Bet as ever couldn't help her tongue. 'If there were trophies for being late you'd have run out of mantelpieces to put them on in your house, Kate,' she said. She knew that was what her family called her at home and that the girl hated it. It was in fact only a year ago that the tall heavy eighteen-year-old decided with all the inventiveness that she owed to *Movie Parade* that 'Lilian' was so obviously the name she was made for. Because it went with lovely skin and nice chestnut hair and almost everyone she knew remarked sooner or later how she certainly had those. And breasts that often made her worry that she was being smiled at only because of them. She wanted her new name to mean sensitivity and a nice disposition among other things. Yet she suspected tits, as Rex always called them, were somehow more interesting than those, at least to some men. And now if you please this midget she worked for trying sarcasm out on her first thing when she arrived.

'I got a puncture,' she said. 'I had to push the bike here most of the way, that's the trouble.' Bet watched the smear of colour mounting up the girl's throat and into her cheeks. There's no need to take it out on her, she thought. So she said, 'Lilian, this is Mr Norwood. He'll be living here from now on and I've told him you wouldn't mind making him lunch when you get Mr McLeod's.' And to Dick she said, 'If it wasn't for Lilian I hate to think what this place would look like sometimes.'

'I'm only here four days a week,' Lilian said. She half turned to look at the man who must be Madam's brother, she wouldn't mind betting on that. You could just about slip him through a serviette ring. She smiled at the little bloke and said if he ever wanted a cup of tea through the day or anything he mustn't hesitate to ask her. Only her ladyship was down on her properly over that one. She said very slowly as though it needed that to make it sink in, 'Oh, he's not a guest, Mr Norwood. He's living here because he's family. So don't worry if you see him raiding the cupboards. Don't think you need to report him.'

And there the girl went blushing again! You wouldn't be able to say good morning to her soon without a little nervous collapse. But here was Alex at the doorway, his hair sleeked back as it always was first thing in the morning, his black strides and his white shirt with the sleeves always rolled down, never mind what the weather was like. And he hadn't put on an ounce of weight Bet supposed since those years ago on the farm when she'd watched him walk across the paddock. He smiled at her and she nodded towards the table. 'Return of the prodigal,' she said.

It amused her the way men were so formal when they met, shaking hands, standing up if one of them was sitting. She could tell from Dick's eyes how much it meant to him, Alex making it so clear he was glad to see him back.

Dick rubbed his hand against his jaw. He said he had just been asking Bet whether the old room out there still had a bed in it. 'Wondering if I might stay over for a while, like.'

'It's been like a morgue out there,' Bet said. 'So long since

263

we've had people using it, the place is probably haunted by now.'

Haunted! Lilian thought at the sink. She watched her hands go down through the suds that left cuffs round her wrists when she drew them out. Honest to God that woman was off her rocker, some of the things she come out with.

Alex took a chair beside his friend. He said, 'You know we had your old lady staying with us for a bit?'

Dick said, 'I heard she was over this way.'

'When she had that trouble with her leg.'

Dick felt uncomfortable when they talked about his mother. He thought of her taking up God when bloody old Larsen died the way other people take to the piss or whatever. Alex was saying quietly, tapping the end of his cigarette on the table before raising it to his lips, 'Your sister could hardly bring her across every day to that clinic place. Made sense for her to stay here.'

So that's where he fits in, Lilian was thinking. She dried the dishes and slid them into the wooden racks. She moved quietly so Madam might think she was being polite and not just doing a bit of ear-wigging. That crazy old biddy that she remembered her Dad telling her about, rooting like a rattlesnake half her life with Jerry Larsen the chemist's father and the minute he pegs out she's into religion like the Pope's her uncle – she just became a proper fanatic, that's what happened. Rex said to her once when they saw her coming out of the church leaning on the arm of that priest bloke, 'If religion's that good to round off years of shagging, there might be something in it.' He said it just to embarrass her, of course, to see her blush at words like that. She'd simply told him she had more to worry about than old ladies and Roman Catholics thank you very much.

'She's doing all right then, is she?' Dick asked. His mother seemed even further from him now than she had been when he was a boy, that large intense woman he used to stare at sometimes and wonder why there was nothing he could feel for her. Those awful rows there used to be, Mum picking up the meat knife and saying one of these days she'd plunge it in herself, and Dad saying go ahead then, there's no petition to stop you doing it, none he'd heard of anyway. The door slamming like it was the last sound they would ever hear.

'She brought her suitcase full of statues,' Bet laughed. 'She could have opened a shop with all the stuff she had.'

'If she gets something out of it,' Alex said. He thought of the white fingers blooming out, the spurt from the opened palm when he had pressed the trigger.

'Oh, I know,' Bet said. 'If something works for someone they don't have to justify a thing. Not to anyone.' She still thought it was damned crazy, mind.

Lilian stood in the little alcove that served as a pantry. There was only one guest breakfast to worry about this morning. That commercial traveller with the wig in the side bedroom had already left. He was beating the road as he liked to say before the rest of the town even knew the day had arrived. She thought how it made her want to throw up, Madam going on there about religion being all right when you need it and the rest of it! Talk about putting on a turn. You'd only have to ask the first person out there in the street why half the town went down to the Masonic and the Empire rather than drinking in here and they'd tell you soon enough. Rex said to her another day when he tried to touch her close and she wasn't coming at that, not just when he wanted it anyway and she wasn't in the mood, he had turned on her and said, 'La-di-dah like that bloody scarecrow you work for, are we?' And then he said the really offensive bit. 'Probably a communist too, if you were on the level about it.' She said back, 'Well at least she knows what she thinks about things.' Which was a lot more than Rex did, apart from one thing of course and you don't get a prize for guessing what that is.

Dick wanted to say how decent it was to let the old woman stay there with them for those weeks, to say there was hardly anyone you can rely on in the long run who gave a gippo's stuff about her. His sister had written to him at Christmas and when he opened the red card with Santa smiling on it like the world was one good happy place her untidy writing was there saying to him, 'I don't know how much longer I can put up with that old bitch and her carrying-on. If it wasn't for Bet and Alex taking her off my hands for a bit I'd be the next one queueing up at the Leamington bridge.' Why should it shock him to see in the hard permanence of writing what his sister had said to him often enough over recent years? He thought again now of his mother who was not, he supposed, that old but seemed to long for age and illness as a suffering she required. Her body that had always made him feel uncomfortable to be near, whose smell between soap and flour and disinfectant had made him want to move from her as an adolescent, the flesh that she pampered and reviled together now that she grew older, that soon enough would be rot and fire and the rest of those things he knew she thought of always, in terror and remorse for the same body's delights. The sins of the flesh and the sins you commit against others, the catalogue he remembered from his scattered attendances at church as a child, and knew later from his mother's warnings of what the world and the devil between them put in each soul's way, envy malice deceit sloth concupiscence jealousy despair, the last and vilest, despair. What goes on in your head, Dick thought, that is what lasts for ever. Acts in the long run have so little to do with it.

There was the quick tick of Bet's fork against the bowl she cradled on her lap. She took a knife and spread the mix onto the cakes cooling in their paper cups on the table. She edged the tray towards her cousin. 'They're pretty good,' she tempted him. He peeled back the ridged paper and bit into the smoothness. Alex smiled and said no, he would enjoy his more at morning tea.

Lilian stood beside the shorter woman. Both men took in the girl's handsome fullness. She said, 'Shall I wake that casual up in number four yet, missus?' She nodded vaguely towards a room somewhere above them, to the engineer who was here for a week from Wellington. He had told Alex he preferred to stay at the hotel, where at least he could get to bed early, rather than having to hit the grog out at the hydro camp every night.

Bet said, 'If he didn't read till all hours he wouldn't need to be given a knock this late.'

'God,' Dick laughed at her, 'you still don't let anyone get away with much, do you?'

His cousin waved her knife at him, the strawberry icing smeared along its edge. Alex said, 'You look like you've been stabbing cakes, not icing them.'

'I simply can't make people like that out. Who sleep their lives away.'

There were eight dull strokes from the clock in the hallway. Before it had finished there was also the heavy flap of the dining room door. 'Spoke too soon,' Dick said.

Bet watched the girl take the plate of bacon from the warmer. She said, 'Leave it there till we've made the poor man's toast for him. He doesn't want it in bits and pieces, you know. Breakfast isn't a jig-saw.'

Alex stood and took one of the dining-room teapots from the rack. He measured out the teaspoons of tea and poured water from the large black kettle on the range. He knew when the chips were down that Bet was the kindest woman in the world. But he had seen how the girl was flustered when she thought Bet was getting at her. Putting one across you, Lilian had in fact explained to Rex, that's what Madam's always on about.

Alex set the teapot on the tray with its white starched square.

'We women can manage,' Bet said. 'Not as if we need help, is it, Lilian?'

Alex said, 'If the man doesn't like his tea then I'll blame one of you.'

Ten minutes later Lilian swept through from the dining room so savagely the swing door chugged back and forth several times. She held a plate out in front of Bet. 'Will you look at that?' A corner had been sliced from one of the rashers, the rest were untouched. Half of one of the eggs had been eaten. All the engineer had bothered with was toast and marmalade, Lilian said. 'There's something wrong with a man like that.' It irritated her when people did things that didn't make sense.

Bet rested her hand on the girl's back. 'That's only one plate of waste in the whole world you're seeing there, love. Imagine that multiplied by millions and millions. Men like that one in there not only pushing his own plate away but taking them from other men as well. From those who are hungry.'

Lilian knew this must be it, the commo stuff people said she went on with. Talking the way she did just to make you feel uncomfortable. The older woman had taken the plate from the tray and scraped what the world would never eat into the bin that was collected twice a week for a pig farm. 'Those who have and those who haven't,' she was explaining now. 'Everything comes down to that. To how we'll ever arrange things so a few don't pile up everything for themselves. So a person gets their share simply because they're alive.' She was trying to pick her words with care, to make sure she didn't turn the girl away from her. While Lilian was thinking she wasn't such a tartar after all. Because it rang so true when she was talking like that about some starving and others wasting, and then suddenly the yard through the window began to blur and the doors along that shed out there wobbled like water was pouring over them. Lilian had no idea why on earth she wanted to cry because of commo talk for goodness sake! So she said as she moved away, 'I don't know what good it does thinking of that, mind.'

Bet spoke very quietly. She was glad the men had moved out onto the verandah for a smoke. She said, 'Lilian, *everything* is worth thinking about. Otherwise you'll never know one thing from another.'

Lilian ran the hot tap over the oven tray. She turned the tap on so hard that the water rocketed up to her, splashing above her apron and across her blouse. 'God,' she said, 'I hope this doesn't stain, that's all. It's the one I have to wear out after work.' And as suddenly again she just wished Madam there would shut up. If she had it all worked out, why couldn't she convince other people then? Why did the whole town think she was off centre?

Bet dabbed at the girl with a folded teatowel. She said, 'But you see what I'm getting at, don't you?'

'I know,' Lilian said shortly. Even Madam should click that she didn't want to keep talking about it.

Bet took in the girl's fine looks. She thought, this is talking to a brick wall. She is thinking of men and what a bore I am and that what I'm trying to say embarrasses her. She remembered a sentence from one of the Party pamphlets. *A happy animal is most unlikely to fight.* For a moment she glanced from the girl's lovely bare arms to her own, from their ripe firmness to her own flesh that made her think of parchment as much as anything. She couldn't even blame the girl. As if I gave a stuff, she thought, when I first took up with Burkie. Older and all than me as he was, God if I'd been able to save the world on condition I forgot about him, then the world could go hang. But at least you had to try. You saw what you were up against and yet you still believed. That was why she could understand Dick's mother perhaps better than the rest of them. The old woman was a pain in the neck but that didn't alter facts. And the fact was that God was her centre as surely as the sun was the earth's, the way mine is the hope that some day people will know what I'm on about. She knew that beyond her own love for Alex or for the hotel itself there was a level to her being that nothing could subvert. It was not just the Party either that she had in mind, although the Party stood for it more strongly than anything she herself was likely to do.

And now the girl was humouring her, and being impertinent as well. She was stroking her hands this way and that on her apron, looking down at the woman she worked for but actually disliked apart from a few moments like just now, only even those moments went wrong, Lilian thought, she always had to go and muck them up. She said, 'Oh I might give time to thinking all that one day, Mrs MacLeod, but for the moment I've got my work cut out.'

'Hardly a painful condition for some people,' Bet answered sharply. And was sorry at once that she said it. For the girl was wheeling from her, rejecting her finally.

Lilian took the duster from its shelf in the pantry and went through towards the hall. She would take it out on the bannisters and that bloody hideous old elephant that should have been tossed out years ago.

Alex had come in from the verandah. He sat at the table and said, 'She's not up with you, Bet. She doesn't understand you and then you take her the wrong way.'

Dick looked at them apprehensively, the same puzzlement on his face as when he was a boy sitting at the kitchen table, hearing the first light exchange between his parents before the racket began. But there was no reprimand in Alex's voice. Bet rested her hand for a moment on her husband's arm. 'I'm the good Samaritan the afflicated keep telling to bugger off.' She smiled at both of them. 'It's a gift I have to live with.' And directly to Dick she asked, 'Has he told you yet? Has Alex told you?'

Her cousin's small face turned at her quickly.

'Come on,' she said, 'he must have.'

'Not a word,' Alex said.

'So.' Bet sat again at the table. She folded her hands in front of her as though she knelt in church and rested her wrists on the back of a pew. 'He hasn't told you that we've got our names in for a girl?'

Dick wondered what in hell she was on about.

The bird started up a racket from outside the back door. Alex slid back his chair and moved across the kitchen, taking up a pebble from a dish on top of the wooden safe. His arm flicked out smoothly, there was a quick high howl. A black cat flowed across the yard and under the fence.

'Not that Clive couldn't look after himself,' Bet said. 'Once when a tom got his paw into the cage he nipped it just about through.' Then when Alex was seated again she took his hand and continued to explain to her cousin. 'We're adopting one of those kids you must have read about in the paper. Those Polish kids the government's bringing over?'

Alex watched his wife while she spoke. He felt the same quiet excitement. A child they could give all this to after the starvation and the hopelessness that he couldn't visualise so vividly as Bet did but that came into his mind when he thought of that phrase, 'a displaced person'. He thought of children and bullets flicking the earth up around them, quick small blooms of dust. One of the children was walking through them quite calmly, although she could not know it herself that she was walking towards here, to them.

Alex said, 'You probably knew we couldn't have kids?'

'You told me that,' Dick said.

'Then you'll know what we're talking about,' Bet told him. She would stand there in a white frock and a ribbon tied in her hair and those white socks almost to her knees. And that would only be the beginning. For beyond that first and lovely image another life took over from the one she would have known. And how much better a world she would grow into than even the one they had known themselves. Brotherhood and peace would be as natural a thing as wars had always been until now. Bet knew how even Alex teased her about her optimism. The Party won't do everything overnight, he sometimes told her. But it will *begin* overnight, she used to tell him, even that's more than has been done before. But she saw that the two men were now looking at her as though waiting for an answer to something she had missed.

'I said, will you call her something different,' Dick said. 'Like if she's got some outlandish foreign name or something?'

Bet laughed at his solemn stare. 'We'll call her whatever she calls herself.' The official in his dark suit and with his folder of papers had asked her precisely that as well. As if you'd change a child's name! He had said, this bloke she hadn't warmed to, 'But you must remember for all intents and purposes she won't be a Pole any longer, shall she? She'll be a New Zealander like the rest of us.' And Bet had answered with deliberate wryness, 'Does the child know she'll be that lucky to be an Anglo-Saxon like us?' The man had looked at her across the plate of meringues she'd made for his visit. Alex had spoken then. He had said surely we ought to give them something *as well as* their own race? Not try to take that away from them? The man had brushed the white crumbs from his lapel. Quite, he had said to them, exactly. Alex had come in just as she was saying that to offer someone Christianity and democracy or whatever we called it just wasn't enough any longer, was it, we had to start from scratch all over again? If history was to make sense this time round? And Alex must have seen she was saying too much. That evening as they undressed and he stood in front of her and took the hem of her petticoat and lifted it above her head, raising his arms far higher than they needed to go, so that then as so often there was joking there too in the middle of their loving, she had said, 'Thank you, my love, for today.' He knew of course what she meant. He had begun to stoop, to take her small breast in his mouth, to put his arm between her legs and carry her across to the bed in what they laughingly called his animal rush. But he paused. He sat on the edge of the bed, his long legs stretched out each side of her as she stood in front of him. His hands ran along the smoothness of her thighs, across her naked buttocks. He said, 'You can't say too much to fools like that, Bet. You have to remember that.' And she apologised to him, telling him she regretted what she had said to the man as she regretted almost everything she said to anyone. She lay on the bed beside him. He said to her, 'I hate bastards like that just about enough to kill them.'

She put her own hand on his as it lay across her thigh. 'Because he's a fool?'

He shook his head at her. She closed her legs against his knuckles. 'Because it's little pricks like that, Bet, who stand between us and everything we want. It isn't even the big things like governments and armies or whatever in the long run. It's the ordinary ones who can't conceive of either good or bad. Who don't even know there is something bigger than what they know about themselves.' He brought his face close against her, then drew back. 'You know the Bible bit,' he said. 'It's the luke-warm Christ said he would vomit out.'

Bet said, 'I've never heard you quote the Bible before, Alex.'

He told her not to give him credit for it. He must have heard Rory quote it a dozen times.

'Who did *he* mean?' she asked him.

Her husband was drawing her across him, his mouth against her shoulder, along her neck. 'He was like all you commies,' he teased her, 'he meant everyone who didn't see things the way he did himself.'

She grabbed his hand as it spread beneath her. 'You're not going to get anywhere talking like that.'

He grunted in exaggeration against her. 'I've got where I'm going anyway.'

His skin was so white, she always thought when they made love. So white and young. His hand was rubbing against her neck, his fingers moved through her hair. She hooked her arms beneath his as they rocked against each other.

Dick asked her now, 'You don't know when though?'

'About the girl?'

'Any day,' Alex said. 'Surely we have to hear from them any day?'

Lilian carried an armful of crumpled linen to the wash-house off the verandah. She glanced at Madam and the two men lolling there like there was nothing more to running a hotel than drinking cups of tea and patting each other's hands as if they weren't even married!

When Bet had heard about the tragedy, as it was always referred to in the district, she thought life could never again resume its normal ways, its expected shapes and habits. On that afternoon of the funeral she had seen Alex in his dark suit and his black tie walking across the paddock from where her Dad had dropped him at the gate. She had never seen him dressed like that before. He made her think of people in the stories he read out loud to his mother. He was tall and black and darling, walking in the front paddock where the hay had not yet been cut. A flurry of sparrows shook up from the middle of the field. The cattle in the next paddock raised their heads and silently watched him. There was a feeling of great stillness after the storm that must have pelted down while his mother was being buried. All day she had turned from whatever she was doing to look up at the clock. The thick ticking on the shelf above the fireplace made her think of something locked up, scratching to be let out. She hated the idea of death. She had lain the night before, long after the lights were out in the rest of the house, and tried to think of it, testing its enormity. At one point she had knelt on her bed and moved aside the holland blind. There was enough moonlight for the house across the paddock to seem a pale distant box. She thought how she knew exactly where everything was inside that house, not just in the kitchen but in *her* room too, the big jug in its sprig-patterned basin that was never used but stood there like in the old days. The bed there would be smoothed out and the white crocheted cover stretched across it. If the blind was up and you stood at the doorway, you would see it across the room the way you could see the house now across the distance, here. And in that building in town in the side street, the one high window with bars across it that she had looked at sometimes and thought, why is it so hard to believe in it, to think there are dead people in there lying on marble tables? Because that is what she had heard. The tables were of solid marble to keep the bodies cool. And the men so she heard lay in their suits like they were dressed for someone else's funeral and the women in white gowns. Or like people getting married. For some of them must be young as well, it was not only the old who died. When she lay back again in her bed she wondered how their hands were, she supposed they were crossed as she had seen in one of the drawings in the novels. 'At Peace' was what they always said. Which was what they called emptiness. She crossed her own arms across her body and felt a sudden terror excite her, a tightness at her throat. She touched the sweat that gathered on her neck. They tied their chins up so their mouths wouldn't sag. Sometimes they had to put things on their eyes. She saw Mrs MacLeod's eyes glittering like two pieces of cold glass.

Oh no! the girl said loudly. What was death that it even turned your friends into something you were scared of, took your breath away with the fear of it? She closed her fists until she felt the nails bite into her palms. She said so that her own words seemed like someone else talking quietly to her, I am not going to let it take her away from me, not like that. Nor would she get up to switch on the light. She would not let it win over her like that either. Yet it had come so close in those few minutes of speechless fear. She knew that death had been there in the room with her, a darkness that was corrosive and everlasting, a thing on a chain that pawed to lie across her. Then she had felt an anger she could not explain. It moved over her physically, along her arms and chest and mounted to her face in a thick warm rush. It was the anger of life turning the shadow back. She heard herself call out, *you can bloody wait*! The girl realised with a hard intense perception that life was exactly this, it was having to call out alone to whatever wanted to take you over, to use you for something other than what you wanted yourself. She heard her own blood pushing silkily in her ears. Then the day was showing at the edges of the blind. She saw the small bedroom rise in a cold greyness before she turned and pulled the blankets about her. She slept then until her father's heavy movements in the kitchen. As she dressed she thought calmly about her dead friend, the morning of her first day in the earth where she would lie for ever. But Bet thought too how their closeness had grown out of life as heat comes from a fire, that warmth would last and last and so her friend's life would last as well, that was how she must think of it. How Mrs MacLeod would want her to. And she understood for the first time how it was not only that awful breaking down of your body that waited to possess you. There were other things, she thought, pieces of the same dark-centred threat that wanted to take fragments of your life in advance, to throw its smear across you as a kind of token, coming between the fire and yourself. Like other people ruling you when they had no right – that was a piece of the darkness. Like all those things you heard about in history, the beliefs and orders and rules that were flung across people like nets. Those nets were made from the darkness too, fine wires of it to hold you still.

For several days, Bet's thoughts had poured in on her in a rush of images. At one point she felt her body shaking with the excitement of them, her voice saying softly *yes*, as her mind accepted. Years later she would say to Alex as they walked in the early evening and stood above the river, 'What some kids seem to get quite suddenly from God or what you got, say, from Princess came to me in those days just after your mother died, only my angel was about as ordinary as you could get. It was simply knowing with that same sort of certainty that I would never let anyone, *ever*, use my life for theirs.' Her telling him that perhaps a month after they had come back to this town, to the hotel she had wanted since she was a child. Since she had stood there beside her father while he spoke to another man behind the green-topped desk and the polished hallway with its gleams and refractions enchanted her. She told him, 'Of course that went for you as much as for anyone else. If it hadn't, you would have used me too, although you might not have meant to.'

Alex asked her, 'How would I?'

She told him, 'You would have made me a ghost. I had to be quite free first or we could never have been like this. I would never have been able to choose about it.'

He asked her then what until that night he had deliberately tried to avoid. He asked her, 'Does she worry you? You know? Barbara?'

'No,' Bet told him. She guessed that might even disappoint him. She knew how men enjoyed those pockets of power, those fragments that told them, *there, I am stronger than she is*. Even good men like Alex. She said, 'She never mattered to me that much.'

And when Alex murmured, 'No, I suppose not', she had said, 'I mean, I never liked her but I never hated her either. That's why I say she doesn't matter.' The river curved slowly beneath them, dark with overhanging bush. She told her husband how his mother meant far more to her than the tragedy did, his mother dying, she meant. 'Most of my feeling went into that. That was the thing that changed me. The other was quite a different thing.' Which was not the final truth. She did not tell him, not even her own Alex, who turned towards her there in the middle of the bridge and kissed her while a car from the power station derisively honked and bellowed past, that she had thought for a time how nothing worse could happen.

Her father had come into the house chalk white, his good hand moving across the stump of his other arm. He told them the car had been found in the river and Schwartz had hanged himself, and the police were investigating. They were over there now, moving through the house. As if snooping through empty rooms would help. And when she had gone to stand on the back porch, looking across to the house and the uniformed man walking through the orchard at the side, she heard her father's voice sound strangely from the kitchen, telling her mother, 'That poor bastard's legs. The pigs got at him while he was hanging there. They reckon it was like he stood on a mine.'

Bet had gone out past the dunny and beyond the hen-coop to where she sat on the stump of what once must have been a great tree. It was large enough for kids to play on and pretend they were at either end of a posh table. But she sat there then and deliberately bit into the soft flesh below her thumb until the pain was intense, until she felt the sudden taste of her own blood sticky in her mouth. She knew that whatever happened she would not see Alex again. All the rest of it, the hanged man and the car in the river and for the moment too even Mrs MacLeod's death, were distant things. There was only the space where Alex had been. And she said, 'If he's killed her I'm glad. If Barbara's dead it's the best thing I've ever heard.'

Later she did not remember the words she had said. Only that she had bitten herself badly and that several days later the hand puffed out with infection. But in those few days they heard at least that it was an accident and that the mad bastard who hanged himself in his pig sty had nothing to do with anyone else. They said Alex would leave the district anyway as soon as the inquiry was over. Until then he would stay with his uncle in Hamilton. In time it would be his aunt who came out to settle the house. She supervised a truck that was loaded with the furniture, and out the back she told Bet's father to light a bonfire of books and rubbish and papers that did not burn completely, because pages from a notebook skittered across the paddocks when a wind rose and the scraps lay under the hawthorn until the rain mulched them into nothing. But that would be winter. That was still several months off.

So Bet was right in thinking she would not see him again. And he had gone away. Different people told her different places, to Queensland and Tasmania and Western Australia. Then the truck and bonfire must have been about Easter. Because next thing it was August, the cows were almost completely dried off, and Dad announced that they would have to go. The place had been sold up. There was a farm up north he might be able to get work at. There was no need for everyone blubbering about it, they weren't going to starve. There was years of work in him yet, he said, Christ knows he was lucky to get anything at all. And for one of the few times she saw her father lose his temper. Her mother kept on crying and the twins became upset and he shouted that if they didn't like it then how did they fancy going on the streets, because that was the only other place there was. For the whole bloody lot of you. Yet even as Dad was saying it, and then explaining to her mother about when and how they would make the move, Bet knew she would not be going with them. They were part of the darkness they wanted to cast across her.

When Alex asked her once, 'Was it Burke who got you out of it?' she had to put her hand across his, speaking to him as she might when explaining something to a child.

'Burke was only part of it. Not even the biggest part either.' She thought perhaps Alex would never believe that.

'It isn't jealousy,' he said, 'my wanting to know that.'

And she said, 'It mustn't be Burke with me versus you with Princess. Never believe that.' She knew to prevent that must be the secret effort of their lives together.

'He was a fanatic, old Burke,' Bet said. 'He wanted to swing history round like going up to a man you don't like and just ordering him to be something different. You can't do it like that.'

Alex asked her, 'You'd do it by preaching then, would you? By good example?' He said it tenderly enough, but mocking her too. That was on another of their evening walks. Bet said, 'I love the look of our arches, don't you, through the trees like that?' There was the sound of a piano from behind the yellow windows.

Bet liked the feeling in the front bar, the men who nicknamed her Madam behind her back, their greetings when she walked through. Most of them were shy if she actually stopped to speak to them. They were polite and laughed too much when she joked, but they were glad once she had shouted them a round and moved away. She envied Alex the way he could get on with them, the comradeship it would be so nice to have with other women, she sometimes thought, although that seemed like asking for the moon. He could stand there with a man and say scarcely a word, and at the end of twenty minutes know as much as if the fellow had been talking to a priest. He drew them out without trying. They knew he would not pass anything on, not even to her. That, she supposed, was the secret of it. But when they had gone in that evening from the cold autumn air to the warmth of the bar, into the bitterish smell of beer and the blue haze of cigarette smoke, Bet felt there was nowhere else she could possibly wish to be. Yet for a moment the talk had stopped.

'Killed the party, have I?' she said. She took the cloth from beneath the bar and ran it along the top. She emptied the ashtrays into a bucket. 'We were making a move anyway,' one of the men said. Another said, 'Mum'll have mine for yo-yos if I'm this late again.' Dick made a thing of looking at the clock with feigned surprise. Bet told them not to worry, that Lonergan had gone to Auckland because his son was playing up there the next day. 'His constable wouldn't dare walk in without the boss being with him.'

'Never trust them, missus,' one of the group advised her, 'never go that far.'

Bet asked one of the Maoris about his kids who had been down with chickenpox. She passed a packet of sweets across the bar. 'Give them those,' she said. 'It's even money they'll be well enough to eat that.'

Alex picked up the glance of two farmers who were playing darts. It told him everything that Bet herself would never see. While Dick in turn was observing his friend, the movement of his head from the customers towards his wife. What would you call that look, he thought – sad? Tender? That crazy midget pinko, that's what some of them thought about Bet. Madam who fancies she's got the answers no one else has. Alex must know that as well as he did, Dick was certain of that. And now a couple of years further on he was taking in that look again while Bet told him about the kid they were going to have sent up from Wellington, the kid whose parents were bombed or shot or in any case simply disappeared, and Alex watching her while she spoke, smiling. Until he himself said, 'So next thing you know, cobber, there'll be a third one in the family. Neither of us can hardly wait for that.' The girl Alex could see as clearly as Bet could. Only with him she was walking down towards the river. Her hair ribbon was moving in the breeze while they walked. She held his hand and he told her what things were called.

'I've got to slip down town,' Bet invited Dick, 'come down with me for the walk.'

She was ready for the street. A red chiffon scarf was knotted at her throat, a silver crescent brooch that Burke had given her sat in the centre. Over a silk blouse she wore a jacket that matched her navy skirt. The collar was cut high. It made her look competent, uniformed. Both wrists rattled with the bangles she wore when she went out. You could hear them from the kitchen when she walked down the stairs. Alex told her she sounded like a get-away from a bank robbery. He had bought most of the bangles for her himself. There was a small Victorian cabinet on her dressing-table piled with the things. A few were solid silver, the rest an assortment of glittering Indian hoops with worked-in scraps of mirror, tortoise shell, bakelite, carved wood, cheap metals. The ivory one she wore every day. She had a habit of touching that one as she spoke, turning it about, smoothing over the years the tiny figures, the string of animals, following each other round and round.

Alex looked at his watch. 'The tanker from the brewery should be here any minute.'

'You don't need a hand?' Dick said. Although he wouldn't say so, he'd rather have stayed here with Alex than gone down town with Bet.

'That Scott youngster should be here by then. He can do the heavy stuff.'

'Scott?'

'That music woman we used to have at school. Her grandson.'

'You've never seen anything like it,' Bet said. She was at a drawer in the large wooden dresser against the wall. 'Energy. Will to work. You've no idea the bargain we've got in young Scott.' There was no mistaking her irony.

Lilian banged the flyscreen on the back door as she came in from the clothesline.

Alex said, 'If you can't find the money you stashed in there it's because I put it in the office.' And to Dick he explained, 'She still rolls up fivers and tenners like rolling a cigarette or something and tucks them away in corners. We'd be rich if we could find it all.'

Lilian dropped the cane basket deliberately so it clattered against the wall. As if she didn't click to who they were really talking about when they said Timmy Scott! Changing the subject and thinking she was dumb enough not to notice. At least Tim Scott's got two legs to call his own and doesn't limp round like old Alex there. And his wife had a bit more to hold onto, what's more, than that clothespeg there ever had. With all her jingles and jangles and rolled-up fivers.

'I thought the war was over,' Bet observed. 'I didn't know we were using baskets for bomb practice.'

'Give it a break, love,' Alex said. He told the girl, 'You've been sweating out there in that wash-house for so long you've missed your cup of tea.' He noticed how she smelled of the yellow soap that she sliced like pieces of peel and dropped into the copper. Of that and of wet sheets and her own young freshness. He said, 'You'd better take a break hadn't you, Lil?' She didn't actually mind that he called her that for short. At least he got marks for trying. She smiled at him and said, 'All right then.' He pushed the recently warmed pot towards her. And because it was just too hard not to flirt, she told him, 'Seeing you're the one who made it, I will.'

It was too warm for Dick to take his coat. The sky was clear above the oaks across there in the park and the white stone of the war memorial almost dazzled you in the late morning light. Bet said, 'I don't know why you don't wear glasses. Those dark ones.'

'You can't see properly with those things. They make all the colours wrong.'

'You can hardly see anyway,' Bet said. 'What's the odds?' She thought how Dick didn't miss out on being an albino by that much, if you asked her. You could hardly tell from the other side of the road whether his hair was white or pale yellow. His skin looked pinker now than it did even a few years ago. Dermatitis or whatever. She had noticed the backs of his hands were itchy much of the time. After he had been here for a week or so she would make an appointment for him. But she wouldn't mention it yet. He would think that it was irritating her as well.

'So you're still liking it here then?' her cousin asked her. They had walked to the line of shops along the town's one central street.

'The hotel? You know what I've always thought about that.' But it was impossible to talk walking like this. Bet was always stopping for a word with someone, tugging his arm to lead him to a window that caught her eye. 'There's that stuff I must get for the room,' she said now. Dick waited in the chemist's doorway, watching reflections from the street as they streaked and flowed in the two huge bottles in the window. One red and the other a brilliant blue, they had been there since he was a child. There was a time, perhaps even before he started school, when they had been the best thing about coming to town. To press against the glass then look up at yourself, strung out and altered, in the huge magic bottles. He thought now that the colours alone were enough to make you sick.

Bet bought a cake of soap in fancy wrapping and talcum powder and a sachet filled with dried violet that she put against her cheek as she came from the shop. Out again in the street she said, 'I hope it's not true what they say about old Walton. That he does abortions.'

'Oh?' Had Bet taken that up as a cause now, he wondered? There was always something that she threw herself at, some fresh banner she felt obliged to carry.

'He's got a black thumb from hitting it with a hammer, that's all,' she said. 'It wouldn't inspire a girl with confidence seeing that, would it?'

At the post office Dick read the noticeboard about missing persons, and the new peace bonds, and how to make rehab claims if you were in doubt about what to do. In the picture on the wall above the counter the King still wore his Navy uniform. He had so many ribbons he looked as though he was bandaged in them.

Bet came back and stood beside Dick. She folded the postal notes and slipped them into a brown envelope that she took from her purse. It was already addressed. She stuck a stamp in the corner and dropped the letter into the pillarbox on the pavement. Then she said, 'Oh damn. I suppose I'll have to.' She had spotted the cake stall set up a few yards further along the footpath, beneath the land agent's verandah. It was a trestle table with white newsprint laid along the top, and an arrangement of tarts, leamingtons, fruit squares. Two women were watching her silently until she came across.

Bet's hands came together and the bangles shuffled on her arms. '*Anglican* cakes!' she said. She chose a halved madeira and called back across her shoulder, 'You'll eat this kind, won't you Dick?'

Both the women who watched her were middle-aged and plump. One smiled slightly while Bet spoke to her. The other wrapped the cake in greaseproof. Before she moved from the table Bet asked after the minister, 'Mr Keenan well, is he?'

'Quite comfortable, thank you.' There was a briefly awkward moment. Then Bet said, 'Well he won't have far to go for prayers, I suppose, will he?' Then she turned and beckoned to her cousin to follow her across the street.

'I thought you did some baking this morning?' he said.

Bet brushed dismissively at the bag she handed to Dick. 'The guests can eat this lot. You wouldn't catch me touching their stuff.' She explained that Mr Keenan, she knew for a fact, had warned the St Michael's Ladies Guild against having truck with the MacLeods. He told them to carry the same advice home to their menfolk. Bet was talking quickly, brightly, trying to turn to a joke what Dick knew had wounded her. 'You see the whole town knows we're politically suspect. That communists corrupt the young and set the brand of discord to decent family life.' But her voice was louder now, so that a couple turned to look at her as she passed. 'The word that he used was *sympathise*. The MacLeods sympathise. That means we are worse than perverts or whatever, naturally.'

Dick felt, as he always did, embarrassed at her emotion. It was what made others shy off too, he knew that. Her insisting that she call things by what she at any rate thought were the right names. He remembered the problem when he had been staying down here before, that local committee the do-gooders tried to get up to help returned servicemen who had run into one kind of trouble or another. Booze or the missus cleared out or not getting work. Some of the churches thought they should club together. They would forget the usual boundaries between them and simply help where they could. Bet had offered the lounge at the hotel for their meetings. She would act as secretary herself, it was obvious she was good at management. They could use the hotel phone for toll calls; she was offering them time and money and space and conviction. Dick had gone with her to that initial meeting at the RSA where the details were to be worked out. But the vote went very clearly against her. It was decided that the Catholic hall would be the place for the meetings and that Mrs Hislop be appointed secretary. Her husband was a big wheel in the Masons and she had never kept minutes in her life. If she was any thicker, Bet said, the timber mill would have started logging her. Alex knew how the town was seeing her as it always had, the girl no one wanted to play with. He remembered the skinny girl alone in the playground, the kids calling out in excitement from the windows, calling out as well to the dog. Her face had paled that same way, her eyes made him think simply of holes torn in white paper. Her hands had gripped tightly in her lap. He had tried to say to her afterwards that she should not bother herself so much, that if she wanted to help and they knocked her back, then bugger the lot of them. And she had said, 'Even if they don't want you, you have to try.'

They crossed the street at the war memorial and went in through the hotel's front door. Dick was thinking of the figure she cut in the bar, the curiosity that was always there as the locals watched her at her work. 'You'll never fathom them' – he had heard that a dozen times. Meaning Alex as well. The tall bloke with his limp that none of them had ever heard the exact details of. It wasn't there after the tragedy and he hadn't even gone to the war, he couldn't have copped it there. And the frail-looking woman with her hair sprung out like a bloody kanaka's. 'You'll never fathom them. That Burke business and the rest of it.' And someone had said once across the bar to Dick, 'First bloke works those two out deserves a fucken medal.'

Burke. When she first saw him at the door she thought that he was a blackman. There were men like him in one of the few books she had as a child. Their lips were like bits of red sausage, they wore pants that were black with yellow spots. Two of them jigged between them a black baby who had hair just like her own. Her father made a joke of it, touching the man in the book then ruffling her hair.

He wasn't sure of it himself even, but Burke said he was forty-five when he met her. The day when he came to the door. He stood there with the November sky bright and blue behind him and said, 'I've heard, sir, you might have a spot of work going, is that right?' He wore a pink singlet and black trousers with patches and boots without socks. Her father had asked him in for a cup of tea. When he stirred the sugar into his tea and leaned forward, smiling at her mother, his legs were crossed and the girl could see the stretch of white skin. It was puffed out above the boot and reminded her of the putty her father used to fix a window after last year's storm. He caught the girl looking at it and said, 'Don't let mortality frighten you, lass.' But he laughed towards her parents and explained, 'It's only a sting I have there. It's nowhere as deadly as it looks.' He pushed at his ankle with his finger and the skin looked shiny. With his mouth stretched back she saw that his teeth were neat brown squares. She thought they must be very bad until the day a little later when she watched him take the top from a beer bottle by grabbing it between those teeth. When he lit a cigarette he picked shreds of tobacco from the end of his tongue. And over the top of his singlet there was a grey froth like suds, it was more like wool than hair. She could not keep her eyes off him. Because on his arms, even up on his shoulders and right down across his wrists, was the thickest hair she had ever seen. As if he was wearing another skin over his own, something cut from an animal. It was the hair that at first made her think he must be a blackman. It was across his face as well, a week's growth of beard. And he spoke like no one else she had heard.

For several years the man came and went to and from the farm. Her dad would give him work for a week, a month, whatever he could. The stranger used to talk of 'going north' and 'heading south' and 'packing his traps'. And he used to 'go on the bash'. That was another thing she heard said about him, and about no one else. She had thought for a long time that this must mean he went and beat people up, so that when he came to work on the stumps in the far paddock, or to do the fencing that of course Dad couldn't take on with his bad arm, the girl kept her distance. Her mother advised her to, in any case. But he would wave to her as she stood in the back porch and roar out that by gosh he'd get her one of these days, and roar with pleasure when she slunk back through the kitchen door. He wouldn't hurt a fly, her father used to tell her. But Mum picked about him being there at all.

'I don't know why you're taken in. All he's interested in is the nearest bar.'

He lived in a house that was really only a shed. Bet liked looking at it on the way into town. There was a squitty window at the side that faced the road, and the door was always a little bit open whether Burke was there or not. And he had a dog whose eyes were different colours, its tongue hanging out like a bit of pink felt. The dog would start to run up to you and Burke would bawl out at it, and it stood there then like it didn't know what to do. Her mother insisted that he tie it to a fence as she didn't want it causing havoc with the chooks. But her father said if it hadn't a tooth in its head it couldn't be more useless. And across the paddock sometimes the girl saw Burke talking with Mrs MacLeod. They must make jokes together because they would laugh at the same time. Mrs MacLeod gave him bags of things to take home. But mostly over there he worked in the orchard. Bet watched him swing his axe and the sun winked on the head of it when it flew up behind him. She wondered why you only ever heard the axe after it had already stopped chopping.

When she was thirteen or fourteen and by then so used to him that she told him they were friends, he said indeed they were, he'd like to see someone who dared to say they weren't. That was when she told him as well how at first she had believed he was a blackman. 'Ah,' he had said, pushing his fingers through her tight clump of hair, 'you're not the first to go thinking that now.' She had thought, what exactly does that mean? Why does even Burke say things I don't understand?

Once several years later in a caravan outside Hastings, Burke drank a flagon of sherry that an Italian had sold him. But she knew by then that he never raised his voice when he drank. But it was only then that he liked to talk about the past. So he told her that night while she leaned against him and fingered the medal that he wore on a cord around his neck, how he wanted nothing more when he was her age than to turn his back on everything in his own country. He meant the fighting, but not only that. There was the endless talk of fighting too, the songs and the music and the weather even, he told her, that drove a man in on himself so that the violence started there, before you had so much as opened the door. He had grown to hate the endless talk that was stretched across the loneliness, the patriotism that deludes a man with its bribery that you are part of community. 'If two of you decide on shooting a man, then you believe you must be friends. That the ground is firmer beneath your feet if another man is stretched out on it.'

Bet listened, and understood only slowly, when he had spoken like this several times. All this dying for your country, he said. And so he had come to hate dispute and argument more than anything else. He had settled on New Zealand only because a bachelor uncle had owned a menswear shop in Timaru. Burke laughed and explained how he had disappointed the poor man utterly. 'He thought we would sit at nights and talk endlessly of what he was missing at home. He had no inkling of history but all the passions of a clan.' He loved the older man, he said, and pitied him, but what choice did he have but to move on? 'It was like having a dead person roped to you, you know what I mean?' Well, after that then, he said, he had put in time at shearing and worked on coastal shipping and come very much to stick with himself. There was a woman at one stage he had been keen on but it came to nothing. Though God, he said, who could go blaming her for that? An Irishman of no means or abode, no skill but his brawn? An accent that made most people suspicious of you as a mick, a stirrer, the first words you spoke? So for years then he worked on a station in the middle of the island, beneath the grey sheer cliffs and among these strange chalky peaks. He said it was a remote and eerie world that you wouldn't want to dream of even, given the choice, you know that? But it had suited him fine for the time he was there. It was a time when he believed that for a man to hold his peace, to put in an honest day's work, was as much as one could reasonably do. Then he began to realise he was wrong even about that. It began to matter to him that a man who owned property must always, when the chips were down, be stronger than the man who merely worked and received his wage. He began to think that decency in a man was not enough. He would walk for hours at a time to attend political meeting. He watched the men standing on platforms in their dark suits, their watch-chains across their waistcoats, their grey felt hats on the floor beside their chairs. He knew when he heard those clever fellers who came down from Auckland, or up from Wellington, that he was hearing men who believed, who saw a new kind of world that it was possible to possess, that they invited him to share. When others in the audience cheered and rose to their feet, Burke did so as well. By God, he had thought, it was round the corner and as close as that. Yet how could he put it, he said to Bet, it still did not work on him as he wanted it to do. There was like this pip of ice he felt where in other men it was entirely flame. Bet nodded and listened carefully and waited for what he said to become more clear. He said how he knew too that the Church was full of good men, ones who would die of fever in a jungle to baptise a single infant, who spent a lifetime changing the bandages of lepers. Yet what he felt with the socialists as much as with the priests was that he was the kind of man who would never be at home with any of them. To admire and almost to believe even, but never quite the whole way, did she understand? 'It means you never move very far from yourself. There's a great weariness in that.'

One evening Bet tapped the medal on the cord around his neck.

'Why's that then, Burke?' she asked him. They were lying in the caravan the night before the A & P Show at Waipuk. They had made love, a man in his fifties and a girl not yet seventeen. There was probably not a man within miles who would not have wanted to thrash him. He knew how the men on the platforms in the cold wooden halls would have detested him as much as the priests behind their dark screens, hearing and deploring but at least obliged to forgive. 'You don't believe it do you, Burkie?' she demanded. He told her, 'It's not a question of that.' Her young lovely head was against his shoulder. She said nothing after her question. He knew her silence was a politeness to himself, that she did not wish to press him however much she might wait on his answer. So he tried to explain to her that talk of belief or disbelief was not the point. He told her simply, 'I feel myself when I wear it. I wouldn't if I took it off.' And he thought as he heard his own words, how to Christ can I expect a daft notion like that to mean a thing to the child? While the girl in fact thought yes, she could quite see that. They lay there and the rain began. It drummed on the caravan's roof and they each supposed that would mean bad business for tomorrow. The rain and the girl's quiet breathing and her arm lying across his chest. He thought she must have slept. Then she said to him, 'It's like Alex with me, you know that? What you mean about the medal?' He touched her hair. He thought he had never heard anything so sad in his life, a girl saying that, lying there with an old geezer like himself, talking of what she loved and had lost entirely.

It was very simple for her to decide to go with Burke. When her father announced to them one night during tea, that they would have to move off the farm within a month. It was eight months after the old lady had died, after the accident and Alex shooting through. Her father said it was all right, they had another place to go to. It began with K and was further north than the girl could imagine. She knew before her father had stopped explaining that she must leave them now or be with them still in ten years' time. One of the twins knocked a cup to the floor.

'Can't you do something with them, Bet?' And it was then her mother began to whimper, softly.

'You'll be closer to your own family,' her husband said. With a weary dutifulness he put his arm across her shoulder. 'You'll see your sisters a damned sight more than you ever could down here.'

'No,' Bet said, butting across her parents. 'I can't do anything with them.'

It surprised the girl herself how clearly she knew what she wanted to do, and how decisively she acted. She remembered Mrs MacLeod telling her about that relative of hers in Auckland, and her husband who was now in Parliament. So she wrote him a letter, saying she had been a friend of the woman who had died. She said she was sixteen and intelligent, and could he arrange work for her in the city? She gave as her address the post office in town. Each Friday for three weeks she went in with her father. On the third there was a typed envelope for her, and on the letter the printed address of Parliament itself. The man had written, *you must of course understand my position. If your request however was supported by the full consent of your parents, I shall do, in these very difficult times, whatever I can* . . . She folded the letter and tore it into small squares before she left the post office, and walked to meet her father at the grain store. He was a long time discussing what he owed, and when it must be paid. She knew if the manager had not been his friend there would be no credit at all. She sat on a wooden bench and looked uptown towards the white-arched hotel. There must be other ways, she thought. There had to be other ways.

Eight months since the only talk for weeks was the death of Alex's mother, and the hanging, and the stolen car, and the accident. No one knew how they quite interlocked. Bet had listened and watched and guessed more than came through the talk she heard. Her schoolmates offered theories as wild as those their parents threw up. But she hungered only for the facts, the actual details that the district circulated with a rabid delight that obligatory words of sorrow or pity could not conceal. About the hanged man's eaten feet. About Alex gone from his mother's funeral in his black suit and Princess as usual in white when someone who saw them drive awkwardly and at speed through Hautapu thought they must have been married that afternoon. There was the hall that had been broken into at Gordonton, and a sort of bed made so it was said from the costumes from the Christmas pantomime, and the cardboard crown that one of the Wise Men had worn was in the car when they dragged it out. The unconscious girl wore a brass ring that was off a curtain rod, and another with a stone in it that they said Alex must have taken from his mother before the coffin was sealed. Bet knew but did not bother to say that the ring with the blue stone had in fact lain beside the yellow tea-caddy for as long as she could remember. But she believed the rings were on Princess's hand because it was Burke who told her that, and Burke's friend had driven the ambulance when the car was turned the right way up and the injured taken from it before that other extraordinary thing happened, before the brake released itself and the empty car slid down into the river. His friend told him also that there was a wad of money. It was as thick as a man's wrist and tied with a piece of twine.

That was a day when Bet's mother did not mind speaking to Burke, and even invited him inside for a cup of tea because he knew details she had not yet heard. He was asked to sit at the kitchen table, where he drank from a briar-design teacup instead of the enamel mug he was given when he worked at the fencing. 'Mr Burke', her mother called him. She pushed the sugar bowl towards him so he would not have to reach. 'No ma'am,' he said when she thought he might care for another of her afghans. Bet had watched how his cheek bulged as his tongue worked back along his teeth. 'Thank you kindly now, I won't.' And the girl noticed how in fact he was nervous, even with a woman like her mother. She liked that strange way he said 'th' as though it were a d. Later on her mother said, 'He's still got the bogs all over him.' Her father had looked up sharply at that. 'At least he's got something,' he told her. 'At least he knows who the hell he is.' Which was his getting at Mum because God knows where *her* father had come from, he had shot through before his daughter was even born. She said nothing and turned back to the twins, spreading dripping for them across slices of bread. And then her father said, 'He was a dark horse, that Alex.'

Bet asked Burke before he left the kitchen if he knew who had been driving, did anyone know that?

'Oh it was the girl all right,' he said. 'It was the splinter on the driver's side that went into her head.'

The August storm wore itself out in the stand of pines beside the house. The corrugated iron moaned and cracked on the roof. One of the twins called briefly in its sleep. When the dog moved in the yard she heard the rustle of its chain above the wind. She tried to remember exactly what it was Burke had told her father when they left the kitchen and she had walked outside with them, carrying a few scraps for Burke's mutt. Burke had rolled two cigarettes and handed one across to her dad. He said, 'I'll be moving on any day now.'

'For a while, you mean?'

Burke said, 'No, for good I'm thinking. You know what work's like round here now, don't you?'

'So you're out of a job yourself then?' Bet's father said.

Burke laughed good-humouredly. 'I've a job of sorts,' he went on. 'I'm in the next thing to a circus, would you credit that?'

'Get away with you,' her father said.

Burke answered, 'But I am, Stan. At least it's a job.' He told him of the travelling caravans, the simple stalls, the few tricks from a few horses and dogs. 'They charge next to nothing and people flock to it. It's times like this they need fun.' Burke said he was there to do the hard yacker, to put up the tent, to manage the stalls. The husband and wife did all the tricks or whatever. Bet's father said once Burke had gone that he thought the man was mad. 'Circuses!' he said. 'Christ almighty.'

It was a joy how matter of factly Burke took her proposal. He spoke to the husband and wife and told them the girl was good with animals. They took one look at her and knew she wasn't the type to make trouble. They said nothing about why a man of that age was pressing them to take along a young girl. And when Burke asked them to speak to her parents, to make the proposal seem to come from *them*, they agreed because after all the girl was to cost them next to nothing. He told them that at the end of the summer season Bet would join her parents in the north. She would have twenty quid from the job, and that could help on the new farm. In fact she never joined them again, and there was not to be one day in her life when she regretted breaking up the family at just that time.

'It's enough to make you believe in Providence again,' Burke joked to her weeks later on the road, in the caravan with the sacks of bunnies and knitted golliwogs and wooden ducks, the invariable choice of prizes whether at rifle shooting or coconut shies, piled behind their bed. By then of course they knew that it was going to work out all right, their chumming up together. They had known that after their first few days, when he said that she had better stop calling him Mister didn't she think? It mightn't look too good.

'It isn't,' Bet said to him, laughing, touching his hand. Those first couple of months became memories of mud and disgruntled crowds huddled under wet canvas, and hardly enough from the shooting gallery to make it worth the effort. But the weather picked up and so did the crowds. Out of sheer boredom, she later thought, for it was the most God-awful show on earth. But that didn't bother her, nor Burkie either. They were good mates, he said.

They were free together, Bet told him.

As Bet and her cousin came back into the hotel lobby the tall clock whirred, clicked in that way that always made her think of old men preparing for a spit, and donged out its solemn notes.

'We'll need lunch spot on twelve,' she called through to Lilian. The girl was rolling out pastry for that night's steak and kidney pie. Rex had phoned thank goodness when Madam and her gnome of a cousin were down the shops and Mr Alex was with the driver from the brewery truck. For the last twenty minutes there had been that rumbling sound of the barrels along the back of the truck, the grunting of the men when they eased them down the ramp. She was taken with how graceful the boss could look as he spun the barrels at the bottom of the ramp, turning them on their metal rims towards the opened doors of the cellar, directing the movement of the heavy weights. There he was strong and quick in spite of that limp, and she thought my, no wonder *she* thinks she's on to such a good thing. She heard Madam calling out to her now. The girl turned from the table, her forearms white with flour, and called back that she'd get on with lunch the minute the pastry was out of the way. She had said to Rex that as soon as the coast was clear she would phone him back. She knew Mr Alex would be in the bar all afternoon and the little joker probably in there with him. Of course it would be okay, she said to Rex, as if she was the one doing the chasing! As long as he was away again by four o'clock. It wasn't even any great effort to smile at them while she served them lunch. You couldn't help but be amused by them either, the little pink one scratching at his hands and his neck, that dry flaky skin that gave you the creeps to look at, and her ladyship of course, having to have the serviettes in their silver rings even in the kitchen at lunchtime. The girl made a joke with Mr Alex that the other two laughed at as well. She had taken the starched folded cylinder from its ring, flicked it out with a snap, and put it across his knees for him. The way she had seen them do it in the pictures. Myrna Loy or Charles Boyer leaning back slightly from their table in some posh restaurant but gazing only at each other while snap, the white square appeared there in front of them.

'Been practising, have you?' Alex asked her.

'Don't know for what,' the girl said. She felt rather silly now that she had done it.

The frizzy head beside him bobbed up and Madam was smiling at her too. 'Nothing's ever wasted if it's done just for fun,' she said.

Lilian thought, she's not so bad when she's nice like that, is she? She's got lovely teeth anyway.

At one o'clock Bet got into the navy Austin parked in the yard. Alex carried the paper bags and laid them on the back seat. His arm was across her shoulder as they crossed from the back porch.

She had changed after lunch. She wore a skirt and a cut-away jacket and a blouse that matched, all in light grey, with a pink scarf and a brooch she had kept since those days on the road, a pink toucan on a branch. Several silver bangles slipped loosely on her right arm.

Alex stood with both hands rested on the car door across the wound-down window. He ducked his head low for his lips to meet his wife's. Their faces touched for several seconds. He drew back from the car and neither spoke. For it was like this three times a year, those three days which each of them marked off in their minds but seldom talked about directly other than to say 'before or after the next visit'. There was no such thing as a bargain about it, no playing off one tolerance with another. Yet both Bet and Alex knew that there was a considered agreement between them, that on the birthday in April, in the week before Christmas, and once in the winter months between, she would go where he himself had never been, and would not have gone under any duress. She would drive across the damp green landscape, beneath the usually bundling drift of the clouds, to sit in a room with a woman who did not speak, nor listen, nor show interest in anything but the cakes and the presents brought to enliven her. For forty minutes exactly Bet would sit there. She would pour the tea from its blue enamel pot into two hospital cups, and tear open one of the paper bags. The flowers she always took would be set in the same glass vase she had brought with her, years back, on the first of her visits. Christmas lilies in December and a mass of roses for the birthday in April, and near the end of winter a bunch of copper beech leaves and hot-house chrysanthemums, tawny and rust-coloured. The present, unopened, was set beside the vase. This time it was a nightdress. Bet said how through the war you had to make do with wincyette until you were sick of it, luckily the shops were full again now with pretty things, with satins and pastel colours. It made no difference of course what she said, what news she rattled on with. But Bet found that if she talked, if she arranged the flowers and fiddled with the tea things, the drag of the minutes was easier to cope with. She would look past the immobile and silent woman to the bed that was made so smoothly it always made her imagine a warm knife must have passed over it, the way you smooth the icing of a cake. There was a rowan tree outside the window, its branches naked and stark, the clusters of red berries shiny as china beads, or in other months a mass of shifting light and movement.

The nurses always left them alone. And to have sat there in silence would have been morbid. So a story was told over the years which no one heard, the story of both Alex's life and Bet's, the details of the hotel and its customers and its guests and its staff, the district weddings and scandals and bereavements, the political changes and the plots of books. If nothing else, Bet thought, it was a place to give her ideas an airing, to hear herself say what she thought! While Princess sometimes would look at her, and at other times gaze from the window, or watch the cakes until she had consumed them all and shaken the bag of its crumbs. Bet liked to tell her how international fellowship must win, that the problems, the excesses of the moment, would quite naturally be left behind as logic and experience brought clarity closer to all their lives. Communism would win because it was common sense, because its bottom line was decency towards each woman and man. 'The phoenix from the ashes of the old world,' Bet said, 'it's what keeps me going, that certainty. Why I don't get too annoyed when I know the men in the bar are thinking I'm some kind of freak, this believing that anyone who runs a hotel should be a Tory or the natural world is at risk. They think I should be in here with you lot. I doubt if any Catholics come into the hotel any more. I know the Anglicans don't, and none of the farmers. But the place is paying. The place will always pay.' When she said 'the place' Bet always saw the hotel from the outside, or the polished hallway from where she had stood as a girl beside her father and looked into the gleam and shadow towards the marvellous elephant at the bend of the stairs. 'Even if it didn't we'd never give it up. Not with the kid coming and the rest of it.'

The woman facing her began to pick the enamel from the side of the teapot. Bet said, 'You won't get me telling you about anything else except her next time I'm over.'

It began to rain, the drops sharp against the window. And the room suddenly darkened. The polished surfaces were strangely luminous, the chromium legs of the trolley, the darkly glittering taps above the basin. Bet knew it must be time to leave as the last of the cakes were eaten. The other two bags she had handed over to one of the nurses before she came into the room. They would be put in Princess's tin and then doled out at one or two a day. As soon as the light altered like that funny how your voice seemed to alter too. People talking in the almost dark – to you, to someone else – it always sounded so different. As though it was the light that made things seem so normal, so matter of fact. The other woman's leg jerked as it sometimes did, so that the things on the table shook. Bet supposed that they'd never clear up those curious twitches, any more than they'd fetch the words back from whatever well it was they had fallen down and shattered. She looked at the long hair as it flowed across Princess's dress. At least that was as lovely as it ever was. It covered the scar as well, there was something good about that. She talked on and told her exactly, how she hardly seemed to age, that all of them weren't that much more than thirty anyway but it was only Princess who really was no older than those days at school, she never would be. 'All that pain and the rest of it. All the hate even, I suppose, I had for you.' Not a word of it gets through, yet not a word of it is wasted. It does not make sense, Bet thought, to believe both of those things can be true. But I still believe it.

Then for the last minutes of the visit the two women sat in silence. Bet saw how the other woman's crossed leg ticked with the rhythm of her pulse. Once Princess raised her hand and held it in front of her and turned it slowly, then replaced it beside the other on her lap. The smock she wore did not conceal the firmness of her bust.

From outside the window there came the crunching of a wheelbarrow pushed slowly along a scoria path. A voice called from the block across the strip of lawn and its clumped hydrangeas. Bet watched how the other woman raised her head briefly, then lowered it. She thought how from this angle her profile remained perfect. She must have looked good like that for Alex as he sat in the passenger's seat, the rush of trees beyond her, the glimmer of the river. His hand on her knee. His hand on her naked leg. His hand between her legs.

The light was switched on suddenly, a pouring of ugly yellow clarity across the room. The folded quilt on the stool beside the bed leaped garishly purple, the low table with its dirtied cups and crumbs. The nurse asked, 'Not interrupting am I?'

Bet turned at the inane remark. 'No,' she said. She stood, taking up the handbag from the side of her chair. 'We'd more or less finished all we had to say.'

'She ate all that herself?' the nurse then said. She looked with heavy attention at the eight screwed paper pellets.

'No. It was cake for cake, you might say.'

The nurse explained, 'Just that it puts them off their meals rather.'

'What about her, though?'

The nurse hesitated, surprised at how she was misunderstood. 'Oh, any of them,' she said. 'They'd eat tar, half of them, just because it was something different.'

Bet handed the nurse a sealed envelope. 'Give that to the sister, will you? She knows what it's to buy.'

Later Sister Harris would take the envelope without saying a word. She would think, as she did after every visit, that they couldn't go on looking after that long yellow hair for ever, not with staff shortages the way they were. It was hardly fair on the other patients anyway, there were regulation cuts for everyone else. But her friend kept paying for shampoos and the rest of it. Like the fancy underwear and the nightdresses and the delicate handkerchiefs. It was morbid, Sister Harris in fact thought. It was dressing up a doll.

Bet had no secrets from Alex, except that. Not a thing that she had done with Burke, for example – there was no secret about any of that. She had begun to tell him the day after that afternoon when she came into the raw red country of the mine and stepped down from the bus. And when the bus had driven off she felt as though she was abandoned in the centre of a desert. Herself and the aboriginal pointing with a hand that had only two fingers, telling her when she asked him, yeah, missus, that tall one that way, every feller that way.

'In the morning,' Alex had said to her. His first words. He spoke to her from the bunk where he lay in a pair of shorts, lean and pale for all the weather he had been living in. She had let the fly-door swing back, its tinny rattle turning his head towards her. She spoke first.

'About time I came to get you, Alex.'

Her voice controlled and quiet, echoing slightly in the long bunkroom with this one man lying there, his face darkened by his short beard. She had stood there like a schoolgirl, the small suitcase held in front of her skirt, both hands gripping the handle. She was thinking should she put it down, or wait until he had spoken. She waited for what seemed a long time. She could smell the heavy tang of sweat inside the hut. There was a cat on one of the other bunks that looked at her slowly, then screwed its eyes closed. On the wall at the end of the hut a woman was sketched crudely in chalk, her fat breasts far too big for the rest of her, a pot-mit tacked between her legs. *Ha Ha Jocko* was written in big letters beside the drawing, a series of arrows pointed at different parts of the drawing. She had waited and looked at the drawing and back at the man whom she could tell was sick, although she was not to know for days that it was simply a kind of food poisoning that had forced him to lie there on the bunk, it was not a fever or something he carried with him from his time in other countries. There was the sawing of blowflies across the still afternoon. From the distance there came a regular muffled thud, like someone hammering felt. But she noticed that only after she had stood there for several minutes. It was the battery at the mine.

At last he spoke. He said, 'In the morning. I'll see you in the morning at the bus.' He spoke without looking at her directly. She saw the sweat shining on his chest, on his throat.

'All right.'

She had then walked up from the hut and past the aboriginal who was sitting under the tree. She said 'Thank you' when she walked by him, not noticing if he acknowledged her or not. She went back to the corner where the bus had let her down, in front of the gas station and across from the wooden hotel where she would stay for the night. She felt the sweat running inside her blouse, her feet swollen with heat in her canvas shoes. She went to a room on the second floor and washed in the warm water from the one tap above the basin. Then she sat at the window, her hands resting on the sill. Before her, stretching out interminably, the red scrawny country shook under the heat. The scraps of vegetation made her think of herbs floating in soup. Even the flesh around her eyes was wet with the heat. When the sun went down, the late brightness flared across the sky. There was utter stillness. Then the clatter came up from the dining room, there were the shouts of men calling through the dark, flags of light spread across the yard from the windows of the bar. Bet put on a fresh white blouse and went down to the dining room. She picked without interest at the mutton, the peaches in cold custard, but drank two cups of the pale tea. Then back in her room she stood in darkness at the window. Through the scrub she saw pinpricks of light from the camp a mile down the track. She said aloud, while her body seemed to vibrate with her certainty of what would happen, 'We'll make this one work all right, Alex.' She thought of the tin figures on the wires at the stall, and how if the pellets clipped them without knocking them flat, they quivered for several seconds. She laughed that they came into her mind. As she lay in bed, under the spread netting between herself and the dark, her hands moved on the smallness of her body. For once, she did not dislike the way she was.

Next morning at nine o'clock she saw Alex walk to her out of the scrub. It was the first time she had seen the drag of his left foot. He wore dark trousers and a white shirt. He carried a suitcase no larger than her own, and by one finger he held a jacket draped across his shoulder. There was no time to talk before the green bus eased at the side of the road to take them up.

For the next ten hours, in a heat that made it seem they were drawn across a stove in a gradually heated tin, she began the things that she must tell him. They came from her so easily she was surprised. 'You remember Burke?' She said how she had been with him for those years, since the family had been forced to move off the farm. She spoke simply, keeping her feelings beyond the details that she offered him. She knew that when people meet again like this it is facts that must first be handed across, it was facts that would begin the bridges where later they might walk in greater intimacy, but it was here she must start. And so she told Alex even of the prizes they used to give away, the cheap glass vases and the felt toys and the two cuckoo clocks that no one would ever win because of the scores required, how she unpacked and packed them at each country show, while Burke erected and took down the canvas stalls, attended to the air-guns. When Alex asked her, 'What else was there?' she told him rubber masks and dart boards and painted velvet cushions. And the circus that was a horse and a monkey and not much else. She said how it was hard not to win something if you were a reasonable shot, yet there was nothing that you would really want to win. Not once you'd got home with your prize, in any case. But she had liked the way they made a living. She came to trust the sly couple who ran the little circus and the older woman who could throw her voice so you were taken in even after knowing her for years. Burkie sometimes cheated and gave prizes to people who hadn't won them. It was exciting with the big lamps outside the stalls, everyone was more or less handsome in light like that, the women looking as though they were on stage. And you saw the country, the places that were empty between the places with the people. 'And I'd do these finicky clothes for the celluloid dolls while we listened to the wireless at night time. In the caravan. They went like wildfire because the shops were so boring then, weren't they?' Bet laughed, bringing her hand down on Alex's. 'I charged them for it, mind you. The whole point of those years was to save as much money as I could.'

Alex then slept on the bus. Bet ceased her talking only when his weight slewed against her. Once when he woke he stared at her, then past her to the unchanging stretch of the country, as though it surprised him to find that he was there. Then for long minutes he looked at her carefully, for the first time since she had called for him. He asked her, at last, 'Who told you how to find me?'

'Burkie,' she said. 'He heard from someone you were over here and by yourself. Then he found out exactly. It took him months. And when he knew for certain he told me.'

'Did you tell him you wanted to know?'

'I hardly ever mentioned you.'

That night and the next Alex was ill again. They slept on single beds but in the same room, each wearing the clothes they had travelled in. Each night Bet listened to his breathing until very late. When she woke on the second morning he was standing there beside her, offering her a cup of tea. Alex had shaved. For the merest moment she did not recognise him, seeing him as he had been on the day of the funeral.

'Is it time to go?' she asked him.

'There's a while yet.'

On the train, she told him she had their tickets for going home. 'By sea?'

'By flying-boat.' Burkie had put the rolled money into her hand only ten days before. His saying to her quietly, without either fuss or embarrassment, *See how it goes lass, anyway.* He too had shaved, and wore a tie. *Give it a go.*

After the unevenness of the first hour out, the flight was calm and level. The sea far beneath them made Bet think of blue ticking on a mattress, the flecks of white so fixed and tiny. She took from her purse the half page of the *Waikato Times*, the properties for sale, the real estate. There was a bad photograph of a building, the dark spaces beneath the arches like the entrances to caves. 'What do you think of that, then?'

Alex smoothed the paper across his knees. He read it several times. He then folded it along the original creases and handed it back. This time Bet left her hand resting on his. She had known he would come back with her from the moment she set out. Because when Burkie told her he worked in a mine in stinking heat and remoteness, at a place where men would go for one of two reasons, to make money quickly or to escape, she knew with the clarity of blinds being snapped open in a room sealed up for years that Alex was there because he waited. As she knew absolutely when he could have said *Go away*, the tin door into the bunk room clattering behind her, the reek of stale sweat and the chalked woman on the wall. There was no compulsion that he come limping towards her from the scrub next morning, yet no surprise to her that he did. It was what she had expected and waited for in one form or another since the afternoon when her friend had stopped the van in Victoria Street and she had stepped down from the cab for the last time and taken the rolled notes that he handed her, when she had said simply, as she closed the door, 'Thank you, Burkie.' From then there was only time and space and courage between herself and Alex.

Now she asked him again placing the paper back into her handbag, what did he think of that, then?

Auckland and the Waikato seemed full of men who had recently left the forces, who came back from a broken world to the peace they had left in greater numbers than ever returned. The euphoria lasted for perhaps a year. There was so much talk about the future, the promises ahead. Bet and Alex were touched with that optimism. 'You're children still,' Lizzie told them at the lunch she bought them after the marriage, in a teashop round the corner from the registry office in Kitchener Street.

'We hardly feel it,' Alex said. Dick too had been a witness. He watched them like a story he was watching on a screen.

Dick travelled down a few days later and moved in for six months. He was general rouseabout, part-time barman, oldest of their friends. He left and came back in a pattern that would continue. And a year later Burkie, whose health was packing up, came to live in the warren. For several months he ate his meals in the dining room. It was the time when Bet exulted still in every detail of the hotel, when she supervised with such precision, such watchful eagerness that the staff used her nickname for the first time, *Madam*. It caught the paradox they saw in her, the small fiery woman whose tongue was a thing to fear, who could never quite get across her dream of the brotherhood of man. Then when Burkie was so clearly for the high jump, as he put it himself, losing weight rapidly and – as he said – going off his oats, he moved from the verandah to one of the bedrooms in the hotel. There was a period for several weeks when Alex or Bet sat with him all the time, talking, laughing, taking a cumbersome gramophone into his room so that songs poured along the corridor several hours a day. 'You'd think it was the time of their lives they were having,' Dick sometimes said across the bar, the town puzzled at what rumours it heard but could not comprehend. Dick did not say what he suspected, that this too was part of the deal. But it was clear to anyone that Burke would die among friends, the aging man who had screwed Madam for God knows how many years and then brought her and Alex together, so that when the last days came it was as much a hospital as a hotel and it was one of the family who was leaving them. There was no question, Bet said, of his dying anywhere else, except in that room which in time would be decorated in blue for the Polish girl who never came, the child from that broken world whom the Authorities finally decided would be tainted by Bet's suspect ideals. In time. But at the moment, as Dick knew, the dying man was there because Alex accepted him; yet Bet too would concede her pride. Three times each year she would make that trip across green and changing country in her suits and her coloured scarves, and with the tight springing curls that she never got over regretting. She would then walk down the polished corridor to stand at the doorway in front of the silent woman in her tent of shining pale hair. Each time she visited she hoped it would be the last. Even as she stretched out her hand, the bangles shuffling on her arm, their rattle as though from further off as her hand reaches, touches the other's shoulder, draws back without lingering or warmth. The circle slinging light in bright thin bands, in watery loops.

*P*rincess's arm bare beneath its short sleeve, the small hairs reflecting in the light. Along the lowered window of the stolen car so it feels as well as heat the tearing air, the first kicking then of the wheel, the spinning away from the humped centre of the road, his hands' sudden grasping towards her own, taking the dragging of the wheel himself and through the rushed crammed seconds the river's flashing from down the bank, the quick coinings between the trees, keeping level with the speeding car's acceleration as the tyres lose their purchase on the gravel, the slewed tug towards the slope. The long grass now flicking at the car's side, her hand gripped hard with his.

The bangles gravelly, quick, beside her ear. His watching her wetted lips, her calm resisting face; his voice beginning in its shouting to her, at her, his realising her hands are working towards the river, not away, the river uncoiling into a protracted smear behind, beneath her head. The nearer branches whack the rocking side, the willows' rapid bars, the first swing and belting of their bodies inside the rolling car, towards the tree.

The bangles drawing back, the images receding, the river lying flat again as tin as Princess thought it. The river as her hand flows softly across her neck, along her throat, the quick tocking of the woman walking down the corridor's polished lino, river-flat, reflecting. The room then quiet in its yellow glare, its rafting now above the cooling silence, the always drifting flow.

Tara Pammi can't rememb
when she wasn't lost in a bc
romance, which was much more exciting than a
mathematics textbook at school. Years later, Tara's
wild imagination and love for the written word
revealed what she really wanted to do. Now she
pairs alpha males who think they know everything
with strong women who knock that theory *and*
them off their feet!

Michelle Smart's love affair with books started
when she was a baby and would cuddle them
in her cot. A voracious reader of all genres, she
found her love of romance established when she
stumbled across her first Mills & Boon book at
the age of twelve. She's been reading them—
and writing them—ever since. Michelle lives in
Northamptonshire, England, with her husband and
two young Smarties.

DEFIANT BRIDES

TARA PAMMI

MICHELLE SMART

MILLS & BOON

First published in Great Britain 2025
by Mills & Boon, an imprint of HarperCollins*Publishers* Ltd,
1 London Bridge Street, London, SE1 9GF

www.harpercollins.co.uk

HarperCollins*Publishers*, Macken House, 39/40 Mayor Street Upper, Dublin 1, D01 C9W8, Ireland

Defiant Brides © 2025 Harlequin Enterprises ULC

Vows to a King © 2025 Tara Pammi

Forgotten Greek Proposal © 2025 Michelle Smart

ISBN: 978-0-263-34464-6

05/25

This book contains FSC™ certified paper
and other controlled sources to ensure responsible forest management.

For more information visit www.harpercollins.co.uk/green.

Printed and Bound in the UK using 100% Renewable Electricity
at CPI Group (UK) Ltd, Croydon, CR0 4YY

VOWS TO A KING

TARA PAMMI

MILLS & BOON

CHAPTER ONE

"YOU SHOULD BE out there. Not hiding in the dark pockets of the palace, Jemima."

Jemima Nasar jerked up from the secluded spot on the parapet of the Thalassan palace—a hidden alcove nestled within the ancient stone walls, and quickly signaled to her maid.

Having witnessed Jemima's father—and the powerful Chief of crown council—Aziz Nasar's affinity for cutting words, the maid hurried away with her charge.

Feeling bereft without the weight of her brother in her arms, Jemima took a deep breath.

Vines of jasmine and bougainvillea draped delicately over the walls, their vibrant blooms releasing a sweet, heady fragrance that mingled with the salty tang of the Aegean breeze.

While he'd never been an affectionate father, the sight of her younger brother, Zayn—the product of her mother's indiscretion before she passed away in childbirth—was sure to provoke her father's temper. He barely tolerated the young boy he'd given his name to. Being a master strategist though, he'd soon discovered that Zayn served as an effective tool for controlling Jemima.

"I'm not hiding, Papa, but mourning," Jemima said,

smoothing her expression of the fear and confusion that
had been dogging her for days now.

Below them, the courtyard, sprawled out in solemn
grandeur, matched her mood. A sea of black-clad mourners assembled to pay their respects to their fallen Crown
Prince—and Jemima's fiancé—Adamos Vasilikos.

From her vantage point, Jemima could see rows of vel-
vet-covered benches full of state dignitaries, the grand
funeral altar adorned with candles and flowers, and the
towering marble statues that stood sentinel over the pro-
ceedings. Beyond the palace gate stood hundreds of members of the public who'd come from corners of the kingdom
to pay final respects to their Crown Prince.

The late afternoon cast a golden hue that reflected off
the polished mahogany of Adamos's casket. After five
years of relentless, exhausting training, in one evening,
she had gone from Queen-to-be to…nothing.

"The public should see you standing by Queen Isadora,"
her father said. "They need to remember that your association with the royal family doesn't end with the Crown
Prince."

Jemima bit her lip to hold back her retort. Provoking
her father only resulted in life becoming difficult for her.
Not that he wasn't right in this instance.

She and Queen Isadora had developed a mutual fondness, and she hoped respect, for each other.

The Queen's grief at this moment was too raw though,
and real. Jemima refused to sully it by pretending to feel
the same.

"You're right, Papa," she said, keeping her tone steady,
"but I didn't want to embarrass our family by losing my
composure in public. I feel too…raw." There, that claim
to weakness should appease him.

In the distance, the sparkling waters of the Aegean stretched out to the horizon, their azure depths shimmering under the May sun. Seagulls wheeled and cried overhead, their mournful calls adding to the solemnity of the occasion. And beyond the palace walls, the bustling streets of Thalassos lay silent and still, the city holding its breath as it mourned.

She was as devastated by the sudden death of Adamos in a plane crash as all of Thalassos was. He would have made a good king. But her grief and her sense of loss were not personal, like the world and her father assumed.

If anything, her mourning of him was diluted by a very real, selfish sense of dread about her own future. While Adamos had showed no more interest in her than his bed or a chair, she had been guaranteed distant politeness and comfort in their upcoming marriage.

Now, she once again had to face the fact that her usefulness to her father was in the alliances she brought him in marriage.

If she didn't figure out how to keep herself relevant to him, he would banish Zayn to some Godforsaken corner of the country and force her to marry some old crony of his.

She shuddered at the thought.

"Do not think me foolish, Jemima. I'm aware that Adamos had been growing increasingly restless in the last year. If you had done your job of keeping him happy with your company and other abilities, he wouldn't have looked for entertainment in other places."

Even having braced herself for some version of this conversation, his censure hit Jemima like a lash against her skin. All the more hurtful because there was truth to it.

Despite knowing her fate since she'd turned twenty, Jemima hadn't felt any special attraction toward Adamos.

Even at that young age, she hadn't wanted love or even the pretensions to it.

They'd gotten engaged when she'd turned twenty-one. In five years of their engagement, Adamos had been reserved, dutiful and unflinchingly polite. He hadn't even kissed her. The polite, chaste arrangement had suited her perfectly. But now...the seed of doubt had been sown.

Was her father right? Would Adamos have been less... restless if she had let him closer? If she knew how to flirt and play romantic games and how to seduce? Had she been too bookish and severe and lacking warmth as the palace gossip sometimes said?

As always, when she was cornered, logic came to her rescue. "You're the one who drilled into me that to be Queen, I should control my wild impulses and behave beyond reproach. I could hardly pursue Adamos through the palace corridors and seduce him when he barely made eye contact with me."

The words reverberated like cannonballs around the parapet, crass and brazen. Dread filled her at her daring. "I'm sorry, Papa," she said, the words rushing out of her. "I'm upset at losing Adamos and cannot control myself enough for the crowd or the cameras. One public appearance this morning was too much."

Whether her father believed her fear-fueled apology or not, she never found out. A hushed murmur pierced the crowd below, drawing their attention.

Beyond the palace gate, a ripple appeared in the sea of black as if a great wave was approaching to drown them. Suddenly, the sea parted and a large black motorcycle appeared.

On it, clad in black leathers, was the Devil Prince of Thalassos.

A shiver pulsed down her back as memories gripped her.

Memories of the one evening in her life where she had tasted unprecedented freedom and reveled in her femininity.

One forbidden evening at a masquerade ball.

On a dare, she'd stolen a kiss from the Devil Prince under a star-studded sky.

Her first kiss, full of a fiery passion she didn't even know to dream about.

It had been the best evening of her life.

Here he was now, a larger-than-life figure, breaking any number of palace protocols with his brazen, disrespectful arrival. And with no regard to security whatsoever.

Dressed, not in the dark navy Thalassan uniform as befitting the occasion and his rank as air force commander, but in a black leather jacket and white shirt open at the chest. Dark trousers molded to his long legs. His dark blond hair, tousled and unruly, framed his stunningly gorgeous face.

Even from a distance, Jemima could note the high forehead, the large beak of a nose, and the wide, sensual lips that women all over the world gushed over. Framed by the thick dark slashes of his brows, his blue eyes appeared startlingly bright. Everything about him was a stunning contrast, ending with his near-angelic beauty and devilish nature.

His arrival confirmed his fiendish reputation, even as his name broke out among the crowd like some kind of chant. *A benediction even*, Jemima thought, awestruck by the sudden uproar of gaiety.

His expression remained somber as he stepped off the bike and reached out hands to touch the animated crowd. Around him, security staff ran around like little rats trying to corral the elephant into place.

Adonis Vasilikos, the Devil Prince of Thalassos and adventure sports billionaire, cut a striking figure as he strode confidently through the courtyard and reached the Queen standing alone.

For just a second, Queen Isadora's iron-tight composure broke at the sight of him. The Prince shielded her tiny frame with his powerful one—a protective gesture that made something twist in Jemima's chest—before the cameras or the state guests could catch her fracture.

Jemima stared at the unfolding scene, shocked. Even after seven years of his absence—his rift with King Aristos was popular knowledge, though the reason was not—Thalassans were clearly…overjoyed by the sight of Prince Adonis. She couldn't think of one occasion when Adamos had received half the overjoyed greetings or the wild energy that the Devil Prince commanded now.

Once upon a time, as a teenager whose every hour and day and life were planned out by an autocratic father, as a girl who'd constantly toed the line in the hope of being rewarded with affection and kindness, Adonis Vasilikos had become the object of extreme fascination to her.

It wasn't simply his fearlessness or his daring feats or his irreverent bucking of the very traditions and rules that had been poured down her throat even as a child, but that he had never let anyone, not even the King, contort him into a box he didn't fit into. Even as a rowdy, rebellious teenager, Adonis had been completely his own creation.

Of course, throw in his godlike looks, and she'd been as gaga over him as the rest of Thalassos.

Growing up, she'd had very little interaction with him— except for the kiss, but she had collected every little tidbit she could about him like a magpie collecting treasure. In the past few years, she'd become aware of how highly the

Queen thought of her younger son. Even Adamos had always praised his brother.

And yet, what kind of a man stayed away from his family and his adoring country for seven years without a single visit? What had kept him away? More importantly, what would Adonis Vasilikos choose now—his adventure sports empire and playboy lifestyle or Thalassos in its hour of need?

"Finally, he returns," her father said, bringing her out of her trance.

"What?" she said inanely, eager for any information about the mysterious prince.

"The Queen summoned him months ago. But, of course, Adonis Vasilikos only does as he pleases. It will be highly amusing to see her fail to leash him."

"Leash him?" Jemima said, her gaze tracing the powerful breadth of the Prince's shoulders as he stood by the diminutive queen. "You make him sound like a wild animal, Papa."

"That is what he is, for all intents and purposes," her father said, his mouth twisted in distaste.

"Leashing him is," Jemima said, following the strange urge to defend the Prince, "akin to bottling lighting." Below them on the ground, the energy of the somber occasion was shifting, Adonis's name whispered, over and over again, sprinkling joy and hope amidst a mourning populace. "But if anyone can, it will be Queen Isadora," she added, her admiration for the older woman bleeding into her words.

She knew how much the Queen worried about the future of Thalassos and somewhere during the years of being trained as queen, Jemima had begun to care just as much. That same urgency beat at her. "With Adamos gone and the King declining, she needs Adonis at the helm. Now."

Her father scoffed. "He won't give up his freedom. Or his daredevil adventure sports or his fast cars or his...disgusting lifestyle. Prince Adonis lives for the next high," he said, as if Jemima hadn't said a word.

"His rift is with King Aristos. Not Thalassos or his mother," she pointed out.

Hands clasped behind his back, her father cast her an assessing glance. "With that much faith in the Queen, you better prepare yourself then."

Jemima turned her head so fast that it was a wonder there wasn't a loud click. "Prepare myself for what?"

"To join the Queen in persuading Adonis to wed you and take the crown."

"No!" The word escaped her like the loud gong of the monastery up in the hills she'd once planned to run away to. "That's preposterous. I can't marry...the Devil Prince. We don't even know each other and I'm sure I'm the last woman he would glance at."

Except for a scorching, stolen kiss they'd shared once and the fairy tales she'd woven as a young girl with him as the charming hero who would rescue her from her boring, miserable life.

The Devil Prince falling in love with her was as possible as her father turning into a caring man overnight.

"Of what use are you then, Jemima?" her father said with a silken smoothness that made it sound like he was actually interested in her answer. "Don't pretend to silly romantic aspirations now. It's not like Prince Adamos cared for you either. No man is impressed with that face and body of yours and either Prince should do to become Queen."

Her belly rolled on itself at the casual cruelty of his comments. "Do you hear how...awful that sounds? I can't just replace one brother with the other. Adamos has been hardly dead for a week."

"You can and you will. If anything, our family will have even more bargaining power in this alliance now. Queen Isadora needs to bring the Devil Prince to heel and she knows what she has in you."

"What do you mean?"

"Prince Adonis has been gone for seven years. With the best of intentions to rule, he needs someone who understands the palace and its politics. You would be an asset to him. As for you suiting him…the man has a reputation for *chasing any woman* and the face of an angel. So it should not be a hardship for you to produce children with him, *ne*?"

Jemima raised shocked eyes to her father's face. "That's…disgusting."

Her father shrugged. "The point is, nothing holds his interest for too long. So you can be assured he will return to his daredevil ways, while leaving you behind. As the Queen, you will have a host of powers. With me and the council bearing the burden of important decisions, you can devote yourself fully to your brother and any children the Prince will give you. *And* have full control of your life. It is not such a bad deal then, is it?"

So that was his brilliant plan. He was counting on Adonis to be bored—of his responsibilities, of her, and the kingdom. Then, with her as a placeholder, her father and his cronies would have unprecedented power.

As for her, she *would have* full control of her life and Zayn for the first time… Even as she abhorred his plan and the idea of marrying the Devil Prince gave her chills, Jemima was sorely tempted.

"I can't, Papa. Please—"

"It is not up for discussion, Jemima. Present yourself for

dinner with him tonight. Remember that you get to keep your bastard brother around only if you convince Prince Adonis that you are his best bet at ruling Thalassos."

Jemima stood there on the parapet for long minutes after her father left. The sun began its fiery trek down, leaving the courtyard and the parapet and her painted in bold orange and pink slashes.

A cold breeze flew in from the Aegean, making her shiver.

As if she'd screamed his name from the highest tower, Prince Adonis looked up. His alert gaze scanned the myriad parapets and terraces before settling on her. And just like that, the world fell away, leaving the two of them locked together in their own battle.

Eventually, Jemima broke away from his gaze, but not before those penetrating blue eyes swept over her features with a thorough scrutiny. Then his mouth curved in pure mockery, as if he could read her and her father's grubby intentions, as if he knew how much of a pull he still held over her.

It hadn't been more than half a day since Adonis Vasilikos had arrived back in Thalassos and he was already enraged by the machinations of those who ran the palace.

Yes, he'd been gone for seven years but the staff was as ancient as the palace and knew of his utter hatred for protocol. But of course, they still insisted on it. And the last thing he wanted to do was throw a prissy tantrum and play into their hands. Which had been his default once upon a time.

He'd barely gotten a word in with his mother and he had yet to catch a glimpse of his father. Who, he'd been informed, was too unwell to attend his favorite son's burial.

Once the funeral procession had been complete, a host of admin staff had descended on him like vultures circling carrion. Already, he'd been given a schedule of events for the next three days, the final draft of a speech—written without any input from him—he was to deliver in two days, a list of public appearances for him to show his face at.

All the while the truth barely settled inside his gut, like a lump of oily sludge, making it hard to breathe.

Adamos was gone.

His older brother, his first and sometimes only friend in the entire world...gone in a puff of smoke.

His serious, silent and endlessly supportive brother, the man destined to be King, the man Adonis had adored... now out of reach forever.

Frustration, and something darker, fueled him as he strode through the opulent corridors of the palace, the familiar scent of beeswax and lavender polish mingling with the faint aroma of old books and aged wood.

As a boy, he'd loved running around the endless maze, laughing, shrieking, and generally creating mayhem. Unless his father was near and ready with his cold disapproval.

His heart pounded now—turning him into that eager, needy child—as he approached the King's chambers, a place he'd once been forbidden to enter as punishment.

The pattern of the heavy oak door was as familiar to him as his own face in the mirror. He had spent hours staring at it, while their father regaled his firstborn and favorite son with war stories, taught him to play chess, and loved him with all his heart.

The cruelty had been unbearable on his young heart for he hadn't known then why his father would love Adamos so much and yet so thoroughly neglect him.

Gritting his teeth against the memory, Adonis pushed the double doors. The room was dimly lit by late afternoon sun filtering through the heavy drapes, casting long shadows on the rich, intricately woven tapestries depicting the glorious history of Thalassos. The scent of medicinal herbs and a hint of stale air lingered.

His gaze fell upon the large, canopied bed where King Aristos lay. The once formidable monarch appeared frail and diminished, his hair silvered with age, his eyes clouded with confusion. Gnarled hands twitched on the embroidered bedspread.

"Father," Adonis said softly, nearing the bed. His voice, steady yet tinged with emotion, seemed to drift into the stillness of the room.

The King's eyes flickered toward him, a bright spark of recognition making them shine. "Adamos," he whispered, a tremor in his voice. "My wonderful boy, you've come back. I told them nothing could hurt you. Nothing."

The words hit Adonis in his gut, a physical blow that knocked his breath out. "It's Adonis, Father," he corrected gently, bending and taking the King's trembling hand in his own.

The older man's skin felt paper-thin and cold, a stark contrast to the strength he had prided himself on.

"Adamos, my son. I knew you would return," the King murmured again, reaching out to touch Adonis's face, his eyes lost in a distant memory. "Nothing could take my mighty son. Not the wind, not the mountains, not the sky."

Adonis felt the sharp sting of heartbreak as his father kept repeating his brother's name, each utterance a knife twisting deeper into his heart. Apparently, nothing had changed. He swallowed hard, fighting back tears that threatened to spill over.

Tears that spoke to his weakness after all these years. How could he still crave this man's acknowledgment, a kind word, even a chance to offer a moment's respite from the horrendous loss they had suffered when it had never been offered before? Hadn't he hardened his heart enough?

As always, his father didn't see him, much less need him.

But his refusal to even acknowledge Adonis's presence—even with festering resentment that the wrong son had died—felt...wrong on a deeper level. Like, his father was present in his body, but in his mind, he was not fully there.

Adonis patted his father's hand and stormed out of the chamber, confusion warring with anger. Questions pounded at him. How ill was the King? Why hadn't he been informed?

The nearly half-mile walk did nothing to grant him control of the whirlwind of his roiling emotions. He turned the corner when a woman stepped out of his mother's chambers, closed the doors behind her, and turned.

Jemima Nasar.

His dead brother's fiancée. The Almost Queen of Thalassos. The only woman he'd ever wanted with a blazing honesty and burning desire—not to bury his own demons or escape into gluttonous pleasure—but because she fascinated him.

The only woman he had realized soon he shouldn't touch and couldn't have.

The smoldering kiss she'd demanded of him before she'd been engaged to his brother had only poured fuel on their connection. The memory of her lush body wrapped around him sent echoes of longing through him even now.

Your freedom and adventure and unfettered spirit, Adonis, she'd boldly claimed when he'd asked her why she'd picked him for her first kiss, using his name before he had given her permission to. Her amber eyes glittering with desire under the mask she wore. *In that interview, you said the moment before you dive is when you're the most afraid and yet you do it. I...can't imagine being that willing to face life at its scariest.*

And he had known then that approaching him had been her most defiant act and he had pulled her to him and sealed their lips. The second kiss had blazed hotter than the first, deepened into a soul-drenching one in mere seconds, the sweet eagerness of her passion stoking his own.

He'd learned only at the end of the masquerade ball when her father came to stand by her that she was Aziz Nasar's daughter. The dutiful mouse who never put one step out of line, a brainy bookworm whose poise and smarts been praised even by his father the King.

In two minutes, she'd stripped him of all the things that had weighed him down, that had given him a false sense of belonging in the damned world.

Seeing him only as he was.

It was the first, and only, time a woman had wanted him simply for who he was at his core. The only time he'd allowed one actually close, even though he'd glutted himself on women all the time.

That she had been chosen as his brother's bride, by the King no less, mere days later had only entrenched the memory deeper inside him.

In his mind, she'd become another thing he'd been denied, another chance he'd been robbed of, because he hadn't been found worthy.

At the sight of him now, Jemima froze, her fingers pressing into the heavy oak doors. Her brown eyes widened, then swept over his features with a swift and greedy curiosity he'd known since he had shot up during adolescence.

A black silk dress with a high collar clung to her breasts and the thick outline of her thighs. Her cheeks had filled out, giving her a round face, and her smooth honey-gold skin glowed like the facet of some rare metal. Her mouth—so wide and so plush that it had once filled him with the filthiest of thoughts, was the only hint toward passion that wasn't buried beneath steely reserve.

Her presence hit him like the last in a series of punches, knocking his breath out of him.

With her dark hair falling in unruly strands from the sophisticated knot and skin damp with a sweaty sheen, she looked…achingly real and stunningly beautiful for it. Having surrounded himself with fake and cheap things for so long, Adonis recognized raw beauty when he saw it.

At twenty-six, her beauty had sunk deeper into her skin, aided by her bright, whip-smart eyes and resolved chin. And then there were her rosebud thick lips that he knew the taste of…she was a decadent invitation to sin.

Had her innate composure unraveled in his brother's bed? Had he devoured the blazing hot passion she had let Adonis taste? Had she loved Adamos enough to…

He gritted his teeth and arrested the torrent of questions, both disgusted and infuriated. Too late, he noted the stirrings of that old fiery attraction claw through his gut. It was bad enough to covet her when Adamos had been alive but now…it felt like it made every nasty thing that his father had said about his "dirty" blood was right.

"Prince Adonis," she said, her voice fracturing. "What are you doing here?" Color streaked her round cheeks and she swallowed. "I mean…" Her slim fingers played with the pendant at her throat, betraying her nervousness. Perversely, her reaction to him calmed him.

"Should I be flattered or insulted by your shock at finding me still here?" he said, defaulting to mocking her. "Did you and your dear papa wish for me to disappear already?"

"Of course not." Breaking their tethered gazes, she took in a deep breath and forced a smile to her lips. "Welcome home," she said softly. "The Queen will be overjoyed to see you."

"I want to see her. Now," he said, moving past her.

Arms spread wide across the dark oak, she blocked him. "She just settled to a nap after a brutal day. Let her rest for now." When he raised a brow at her imperious tone, she added, "Please."

He stepped closer, unable to stop himself from reveling in her sudden, shallow breaths. The idea of his proximity affecting her...appealed to his perverse nature, to the bubbling that wanted to unleash destruction to morph his own pain.

"Still playing the role of the future Queen?" he said, curling his mouth into a sneer.

Amber eyes flashed with a mix of anger and hurt. She chased away both, donning equanimity as if it were armor, as if it were the bloody crown itself. "I understand today has been hard for you, Your Highness, but none of us have recovered from it either."

"You cannot know what or how I feel right now, Ms. Nasar," he said, biting the words out. "And I'm too old to be lectured about good behavior."

"No, I can't even begin to imagine how you must be feeling," she said, even as her honey-gold skin turned pale. Her voice held steady and damned if he didn't envy her steely hold on her composure. "But coming in here like an angry bull and unleashing your temper on everyone around you only makes a bad situation worse. Please get a grip on yourself before you...meet with the crown council."

So the news of his frustration with the palace media had already spread. And yet the more she tried to appeal to his better nature, the more Adonis felt riled up. "You're not the Queen-to-be anymore. Drop the Goody Two-Shoes act."

She didn't bat an eyelid at his name-calling. "Other than Queen Isadora, I might be your only ally here. So, if I were you, I would not burn the last bridge you have."

"I don't need you or your conniving father."

"You do," she said with the kind of conviction that he found both intoxicating and infuriating. "You *do* need me, Prince Adonis. And I'm willing to be realistic about a difficult situation, about what's coming for both of us. About the fate of Thalassos itself."

That...stopped him in his tracks. She wasn't faking the urgency in her tone or the very real worry in her eyes.

With the new and excruciating awareness that something was wrong with his father's mind, the vacuum left by Adamos's sudden death, and the new trade agreement renewal with their war-hungry neighbor dead on its feet, even he could see things had reached a boiling point. Could nearly feel the cold, metal shackles binding him to the crown, to the palace, to the place he hated.

And being pushed toward a decision he didn't want to make turned him as tame as a caged lion. "Ahh...looks like the little mouse has finally grown claws."

CHAPTER TWO

"Only someone who has had every privilege served up to them since birth would be threatened by a simple offer of help." A self-deprecating sound left her lips. "That you see me as a threat speaks volumes."

Damn it, but she was right, again. Though it wasn't her reach in the palace that threatened him as much as her composure, her conviction, that she belonged here.

In the seven years since he had left Thalassos, he had made a name for himself in the world. Built an adventure sports empire through nothing but his daring and sheer resolve to carve out his own destiny, separate from the crown and the royal family of Thalassos.

He thrust a hand through his hair, the restless energy that had always plagued him as a child clinging to him now. "You cannot blame me for resenting you for your closeness to my family."

"And whose fault is that?" she retorted. "As for me, I'm as consequential as I've ever been, Your Highness." She pushed off from the door, resignation coloring her every move. "Forgive me for my foolish naiveté in believing your mother and brother that there's more to you than your reputation."

For the first time since he'd heard of Adamos's death,

the haze of grief and rage that had clouded his head fractured.

When she tried to move past him—dismissing him as if she were the damned queen—he stepped into her path. "Tell me then."

She regarded him with her cool gaze, as if he were an annoying fly. "No, you want to take out your powerlessness on me. Believe it or not, I'm so very..." her throat moved up and down in a hard swallow, "exhausted. I will not be your punching bag, Your Highness."

Suddenly, he could see past his own emotional haze to the dark shadows under her eyes and the lines carved around her mouth. She'd just lost her fiancé and her entire future with it. If he couldn't show her compassion, he could at least be civil, couldn't he?

"No attacks or punches, Princess." He raised his hands, palms facing out. "You're right that I need someone to give me the status quo. Who better than the woman who's trusted by my entire family? At least you're not hiding under a mask anymore to approach me," he said, curiosity a sudden flame inside him.

Color streaked her cheeks at his mention of that one forbidden evening but she didn't let it stop her. "Everyone around the palace has an agenda for you, to push you toward their own ends. I'm, however, aware that you'll respond to honesty better than anything else."

Some wild thing in him calmed at her faith. Though he couldn't help asking, "And how have you arrived at that?"

"Adamos spoke of you frequently as does the Queen. I have faith in their judgment."

His heart gave a little spasm at the thought of Adamos talking about him even as he wondered if the knot of grief would ever loosen. "So you're about to tell me that you're pure as snow?"

"No. I'm admitting that I have an agenda too. One that's least harmful to Thalassos and therefore you."

Adonis searched her eyes, intrigued like he'd never been before. Suddenly, he could see why she had been his father's choice for his favored son. Had Adamos known what he had had in this woman? Had he loved her? "You have successfully captured my full attention, Princess. Don't hold out on me any longer."

"The last thing either of us needs is the staff relaying our petty argument to my...to the crown council," she said, catching herself at the last second.

"I see that you're still a very..." when she raised a brow, he tempered his words, "obedient daughter."

Her smile became richer, deeper, bringing out the burnished amber flecks in her eyes. "Oof, that was probably six months' worth of diplomacy you just used up on me, huh?"

She looked so incandescently beautiful that he almost missed her neat sidestep.

"Are you afraid that your father will call you out on wasting your time with the useless prince? He must be cursing my brother for foiling his life's work."

"Not here please," she whispered.

She grabbed his arm as if he was a recalcitrant child she didn't trust to behave and tugged him. Her touch sent shock waves through him as she pulled him into a suite before she dropped his hand.

Adonis looked around the dimly lit suite and its ornate furniture. The air was thick with the scent of polished wood and old books and...a thread of lush roses he had smelled on her.

This was *her...suite.*

He blinked when the lights came on, the suite unlike any in the palace.

Books—old and dog-eared, some with new glossy covers, some falling apart at the spine, were strewn across every available surface. Along with piles of folders, maps of Thalassos, and little ceramic jars bursting with colorful pens.

A cozy window seat tucked into an arched alcove was also littered with books and chocolate wrappers and leather-bound journals. Stationery and sweets, it seemed, were her drugs of choice.

In the sterile perfection of the palace with its polished marble floors and winding staircases and imposing paintings of ancestors he'd rather not look at, her suite was a streak of brilliant sunshine. It seemed like the politics, power plays, and palace intrigue her father involved her in hadn't erased all of her.

He kept his gaze pointedly away from the large, intricate four-poster bed that sat in the back recess of the large room. The last thing he needed in his head was an image of her and his brother in it. Not that the ghost of his perfect brother was ever going to be far behind amidst these walls.

"The palace team let you move in before you and Adamos married?" he said, walking toward the window seat. From here, there was a perfect view of the courtyard and the wing he'd once burned down, nearly trapping Adamos inside by accident. "How positively… scandalous."

A dusting of pink streaked her honey-gold cheeks. She pursed her lips, her hands going to her updo with a sigh. Thick, light brown waves cascaded onto her shoulders in a silky shower. Her hand lingered at the back of her neck, the lush globes of her chest pushing out in a stretch.

Adonis looked away—five seconds too late, heat streaking through him. Did she have any idea how sensuous she looked?

She didn't, he decided with a perverse anger.

Jemima had always been too busy honing her mind, her head buried in history and art, busy being trained at the finest finishing schools to be Queen, to have much use for her unconventional beauty.

"I moved in to be close to the Queen. Not... Adamos." Her gaze shied away from his, making him wonder what she was hiding. "She personally requested me."

He nodded and tucked his hands into his pockets. "Mama did always have a sweet spot for you. Good to see you've kept it well buttered."

She frowned. "You promised to behave. And I thought you were smart enough to understand that I'm not your enemy."

"You're definitely not an ally."

Her hands fisted by her side and she jerked into sudden motion. An angry flush spread up her neck. "I was foolish to think I could—"

"You could what?" he said, snagging an arm around her waist. Their legs tangled and her hands clutched his arm. The scent of her coiled around him.

Her shocked huff warmed the edges of his cold, frosted heart. He was aware that he was behaving disgracefully— like the very *devil* his father used to call him. But then, he'd always found it impossible to resist throwing himself against the barricaded armor of her propriety. Especially after she'd given him a forbidden taste of what lay beneath.

"Tell me."

Her amber eyes held his. "I thought I could take control of my life for once. That I could be of use to you, to the crown, to the Queen. To Thalassos even. Instead of just being a pawn," she added the last to herself, her lips curving down.

"And what does that mean? Is there a coup your dear papa is planning before my brother is cold in his grave?"

"No. But they're going to pressure you into marriage and coronation per the original schedule. They know they have the Queen's support."

"What original schedule?"

"Adamos and I were to marry in three weeks, right before the coronation. The way I see it, you don't have much of a choice. But with my help, you can twist this situation around to your advantage."

His mind whirred, hitched on one word. "With *your* help? Pray, tell me, what does that entail?"

She pushed at his chest and he released her, almost reluctantly. A long breath left her. As if he were a wild beast that might turn on her any moment. "I'm your best bet at controlling the crown council, at ruling Thalassos with its well-being at heart."

"You're talking in riddles."

"Your father's dementia has been progressing rapidly. Getting worse each week. Only the Queen and Adamos and… I knew how bad it is. Now, with Adamos gone, if his condition gets out… Thalassos will plunge into political chaos. The talks for the renewal of the trade agreement are in bad shape. If you don't agree to be crowned immediately…"

"Then what?" Adonis demanded.

She paled and licked her lower lip.

"Come, Princess. Who's withholding trust now?"

"I trust that you want the best for Thalassos," she said,

granting him a conviction he wasn't sure he deserved. "Adamos always spoke of how much you adore the kingdom."

He didn't bother to correct her or tell her that Adamos had tried to appeal to something in him that had long ago died. "Then what is it you don't trust?"

"Your opinion of me," she said, sighing. "But you're the lesser evil so I must throw myself on your mercy."

Despite the urgency of their discussion, his mouth twitched. "I would like to see that, Princess."

She shook her head and started pacing around him. "If I tell you this...will you promise to at least consider my proposition?"

"Having you at my mercy begins to sound better and better."

"Please, Your Highness. This is...my life I'm trusting you with."

"You have my word," he said. "And enough of that greeting."

"My father and his cronies," she said, stalling again, "not all of crown council though, have located some far-flung cousin of your father's in the US. The man has a son who's...barely fourteen. If you don't fall in with their dictates, they plan to crown him King and rule Thalassos through him. The only option left is for you to be crowned immediately."

"If I'm to be crowned..." he said, refusing to betray the tension that suddenly swamped him. He wasn't sure he trusted her yet. But he could feel the noose tightening around his neck. "I need a wife."

Something flashed in her eyes and was gone before he could pin it down. "And I'm your best candidate."

"You want to marry me," Adonis said, the words swimming through his veins like thick honey. "That's what your agenda is all about." For just a second, the prospect of finally unraveling all of Jemima was…intoxicating.

Until reality crashed into him, filling him with self-disgust. "My brother is hardly cold in the grave and you have already found a new way to reach your goal? Is there no end to your ambition, Princess?"

If he thought her dignity would crack at his direct attack, he'd have been disappointed. If anything, her spine straightened, her eyes flat with resolve. "I've spent the last five years learning the ins and outs of this kingdom's politics. Learning who is to be trusted, who is playacting, and who has grudges they're nurturing against the royal family. I have the kingdom and the crown's best interests at heart. As for Adamos…"

His breath hung suspended in his throat as something danced in her eyes. "What about him?"

She hesitated, her hand going to her temple. "I… I don't wish to sully his memory."

"Contrary to popular opinion, I know that my brother wasn't a saint. Adamos was a man with his own set of desires and flaws, despite my father calling him perfect." Somehow, he kept his own bitterness out of his voice. "It's a disservice to the man he was to turn him into some kind of god."

Jemima's head came up in a jerk. "I see now why Adamos loved you so much." Something lingered in her words. Instead of probing, he waited.

"Clearly, you feel the same about him." Her eyes swam with sudden tears. "I'm so sorry, Prince Adonis, for your loss."

He nodded, feeling the chokehold of his grief loosen just a little bit. For the first time in days, he felt…seen.

Understood. To hell with the kingdom and politics, he had lost a brother and his friend.

"If you want me to consider your proposition, nothing but the truth will do, Jemima," he said, testing her name on his lips.

"I'm confiding in you only because I expect our partnership," she said, without acknowledging his apology, as if she didn't dare trust it, "to be at least courteous, Adonis. You will respect me, even if you despise me."

Admiration filled him at the steely core she hid beneath the reserve and he gave her a swift nod. Realizing he had always respected her.

Turning toward the window seat, she gave him her profile. He had a feeling she didn't want to meet his eyes for this part. "Adamos and I had a purely political, perfectly polite relationship. The palace media of course painted it as a fairy tale for the masses. He has—" grief and something else burned in her eyes "—he had barely even kissed me in five years of our engagement." She roughly swiped at the lone tear that dared fall on her cheek. "Like you, your brother thought me a necessary nuisance, if not evil, that he should keep close. To appease my father and have his support, he agreed to the engagement. But he…never tried to learn who I was."

The last she added almost to herself but Adonis heard it. And he heard the oceans-deep pain in it too.

"Jemima…"

She shook her head, forestalling him. "I no more want your pity than I deserve your disgust. My grief for your brother is…like any other Thalassan's. Great, yes, but completely impersonal. Adamos would have been a good king and his loss…might fracture the very fabric of peace in Thalassos. And so," she turned and met his eyes, hers clear of any emotion, "yes, I can easily swap one Vasilikos brother for another. And yes, I'm prepared to be Queen and help you rule Thalassos, outside of the crown council's immense pressure. It's all I know how to do. As for my loyalties, they were with my father when I was forced on this path. But the last few years, they have shifted toward Thalassos, and now to myself."

"Why?" The question burst out of Adonis, his mind whirling on so much new information. He had not an inkling of doubt that she was telling the truth. In fact, Jemima was one of those rare people, especially among the palace, who wore truth like some kind of armor.

"Why what?" she said, bristling at his alleged disbelief.

He cupped her shoulder when she'd have turned away. "My brother was devoted to his duty, yes, and far too rigid and reserved to believe in love and passion but he…he must have developed some affection for you."

She moved, to throw off his hand, and began piling up the books spread around on the window seat. "I believe his affections, and passions, were engaged elsewhere."

Her answer stunned him, for he hadn't expected one. Much less one ringing with absolute conviction. "What do you mean?"

"I heard…rumors." Her cheeks flushed as she kneeled at the window, picking up chocolate wrappers and loose paper. "I confronted him."

He went to his haunches to join her. "And?"

She stilled, her fingers twitching around the spines of well-worn books. "He admitted that he had a lover tucked away somewhere. And that he wouldn't be giving her up anytime soon." A broken smile danced across her face. "He even gave me the heir and spare speech and said that I was welcome to take a lover after we had both. As long as I was discreet, of course." Laughter fell from her mouth, devoid of warmth. "Honestly, I don't think he'd have given a damn even if I fell pregnant by another man. I...didn't matter to him at all as a woman. Or as a person."

"That doesn't sound like my brother," he bit out more to alleviate her pain than to defend his brother. "I mean, yes, Adamos isn't emotional or hotheaded or...prone to fickle rages." Like him. "But he isn't, *wasn't* cruel. He must have known how much he was hurting you."

She shrugged. "I told you the truth as I know it. Whether you believe me or not is up to you."

He shot to his feet and reached out a hand. She didn't take it and got to her feet on her own.

Anger drummed through him at her small defiance, at his brother's behavior, at all the secrets pulsing within the damned walls. The same straining tension that he had left behind once. He wasn't sure how much more he could take this time either.

"What?" he said, when her gaze danced over his face. "What else is left, Jemima?"

She sighed and then seemed to come to some kind of decision. "Adamos...changed in the last year. He was always polite and reserved. But the last year, he was angry and...struggling. With what, I don't know. He'd barely see your mother even. When I brought it up, begging him to seek help or advice, he snarled at me. For what it's worth, I even asked him to reach out to you."

"What did he say?" Adonis asked, eager for some small thread of light in the darkness that seemed to surround him from all sides.

"He said the last thing he could do is pull you back into this...pit of vipers. That after everything you went through to break away, you had earned your freedom."

Finally, his knees gave way and Adonis half stumbled and half fell into the window seat. Leaning his head against the wall, he looked out into the courtyard, tears filling his eyes.

There was the palace wing he had once set fire to, then the highest parapet where he'd hidden after smashing some incestuous ancestor's marble bust, and there was the room up in the most desolate wing of the palace in which he had been locked after he'd been caught debauching the wife of a crown council member when he'd been eighteen—and where Adamos had brought him food four times a day and kept him company.

Every time Adonis had enraged their father, Adamos had come to his rescue. Protected him from their father's wrath, either by owning up to the mischief himself or by begging for leniency on Adonis's behalf.

And then six years ago, during the mighty row between Adonis and his father, Adamos had tried his best to keep the peace. While he hadn't been happy about Adonis's decision to leave Thalassos, he hadn't stopped him.

Now, he would never have a chance to tell his brother how much he had appreciated him, how much he had adored him for loving him just as he was. And he wished Adamos had reached out to him, had let him for once be the one to offer support.

Adonis blinked and darkness descended onto the courtyard, blurring and smudging all the memories fraught with ache and joy. Without his brother, there was only the former now.

When he left the past and came back to the present, Jemima was sitting at the opposite end of the window seat, her knees tucked up against her chest and her arms wrapped around them. Her amber eyes held sympathy and regret and...something more. Like she saw his grief and his loss and despite their strange relationship, could hold space for it.

She silently extended him a bottle, the amber glass nothing against the color of her eyes.

He cocked an eyebrow and took it. When he took a sip, the smooth whiskey burned his throat and lit a fire in his empty stomach. It also loosened the band of tightness that had been constricting his chest for days.

He rubbed a hand over his mouth, and her gaze followed the movement before it skidded away.

"You drink whiskey incognito. What is this? Perfect Jemima's dirty secret?"

"One of my two vices," she said, reaching a hand between them for the bottle. With the sun fully set, the light in the room shifted, draping her in shadows and light.

"I didn't know what Adamos had become in the last few years. I'm sorry that he treated you with—"

"*Don't.* My relationship with Adamos is not your burden. I made my peace with it a long time ago as I shall with ours, if we have one."

"I don't want to marry you," he bit out. When she flinched at his abrupt tone, shame burned in his chest. Christos, was there any emotion that hadn't touched him today? The innate fairness his mother had taught him reminded him that he was taking his frustration out on the wrong person. Whether she was as innocent as she claimed or not, Jemima Nasar owed him nothing. And yet, once again, she had seen his pain, his confusion and shown him kindness.

He clarified. "I don't want to marry anyone."

She snorted, spraying them both with the whiskey. "And you think I wish to marry you? You...you...think I wish to saddle myself with a man who's so hauntingly beautiful that the world will make *Beauty and the Beast* memes of us? You think I wish to be trapped in marriage with a man who thinks I'm a grubby social climber? Who has never committed to a woman for more than a weekend?"

He laughed then and it was the first liberating emotion he'd felt in days. It burst free from deep in his stomach, burning up through his chest, filling his throat with a cleansing fire.

Jemima shot to her feet, her movements as ungainly as a duckling flapping in its mother's wake. Hand on one hip, looking thoroughly un-queen-like, she rolled her eyes.

And that strict, schoolmarm expression set him off a little more.

He grinned up at her. "You're something else, Ms. Nasar."

"I can appreciate your ability to find humor in a horrible situation, Prince Adonis," she said with a long sigh. "Except I have a feeling you're laughing at me. As will the world when it learns of this…new partnership."

"I'm laughing at *us*," Adonis corrected, wiping the combination of tears and whiskey from his mouth. "At how fate catches us all in the end. Although I must admit that only you could make me laugh at a time like this."

"I can get a T-shirt made that says *King's Jester* then," she quipped, warmth filling her eyes. And just like that, Adonis could see the beauty in her, making her glow from inside.

Then there was the realization that he was thoroughly enjoying sparring with her. Just enjoying himself in the very place that he had always been so very unhappy.

He didn't trust that this lightness she brought out in him would last forever but it would make the next few months at least interesting.

"I think you'll be too busy keeping me in line and being my queen, *ne*?" he said, accepting the inevitable.

A kingdom and a bride—that both should have been his brother's. And yet, Adonis didn't feel the bitterness he'd have thought he would. And he knew it was because of the woman staring at him with her eyes going impossibly wide in her face.

She stilled, like a deer caught in the sights of a predator. "You're not joking?"

He shot to his feet and stared down at her. "No, I'm not. Whether I can actually rule Thalassos as my brother would have is a different matter. But I'm not a man who can't admit to needing help. Especially when it's offered in such a delightful package."

CHAPTER THREE

JEMIMA CAUGHT HER passing reflection in an immensely large framed portrait of Adamos in full regalia as she followed the Queen and bit her lip self-consciously.

She'd dressed in a hurry this morning and was now regretting the choice of the dark navy, nearly black sheath dress she'd chosen for the meeting Prince Adonis had summoned with the crown council present.

Bad enough that she'd barely slept last night reliving the confusing encounter with him.

This morning, she'd alternately worried that the whole thing had been a bizarre dream or that she didn't look good enough to marry the most beautiful man on the planet.

She scoffed at herself just as they arrived at the large doors to the summit room. Vanity had never been one of her flaws and she couldn't begin now. If anything, she needed to toughen herself up even more in this marriage.

With Adamos, there had been no attraction, no zings, no awareness of any kind. But something about Prince Adonis—other than his blond god looks, had always piqued her interest. Had urged her to cross the lines that had always been drawn around her.

After all these years, it was the same again last night. The man both fascinated her and attracted her, all smoke and shadows, roiling emotions and sudden fairness. Every inch of her had been drawn to him like a magnet to true north.

Giving in to the ridiculous fantasies that had plagued her last night about him, about them…only heartbreak and humiliation lay that way.

She couldn't, wouldn't, become one of the multitude of women over the world who lost their hearts over him, who thought they could tame and leash the Devil Prince. Even if he was legally bound to her.

That brought her back to how she should approach the upcoming partnership with him and the terms she needed to lay out for their convenient marriage. Her belly twisted into more knots as they stopped in front of the doors to the summit room.

Prince Adonis and crown council in one room was not a peaceful combination in any way.

"Be yourself with him, Jemima," the Queen whispered at her ear.

Jemima drew back to study the older woman, glad to be out of earshot of anyone. Shock made her words stutter. "What…do you mean, Your Highness?"

Grief clung to the Queen's drawn features, but there was a new brightness to her eyes. "Adonis apprised me of your…talk last night. I'm glad you made him see sense in a partnership with you."

Jemima flushed, both with pleasure and embarrassment. She clutched the Queen's bony hands in hers, desperate to explain. "Please believe me that I'm not doing this for power or ambition. I do grieve for Adamos."

"Hush, child," the Queen said, patting her hand. "You'll be a great queen, Jemima, precisely because you've never sought this for your selfish needs. I know I have no right to ask this of you but be patient with my younger son, *ne*?

Adonis has a heart of gold if only you can excavate it. And I believe with my whole heart that you're the woman for the job."

The Queen smiled at her own joke but it was strange how the conviction lit her up from inside out. Curiosity about the man flooded Jemima but she couldn't betray herself, not even to his mother. Couldn't make a habit of indulging either that curiosity or her fascination with him.

"All I aspire for are respect and the means to live my own life, Your Highness."

"Do not sell yourself short. Believe me when I say that Adonis is unlike any man you've known." The Queen's brows drew into a fierce scowl. "Demand what you want of him and more. Remind him of what he owes Thalassos like you did last night, of what he owes you as his queen and wife. That's the only way Adonis will respect you or give you anything."

"I thought you would be angry with me," Jemima said, relief making her tongue loose. "Or see it as an insult to Adamos's memory." Her heart ached at losing this gentle but fierce woman's regard.

Jemima's mother had loved her but she'd lived in her father's shadow, never questioning his autocratic orders, never stating her opinion. In the end, her obedience had made her resentful enough to drive her into another man's arms.

Queen Isadora, though, had taken Jemima under her wing in the last few years and Jemima had come to adore the woman for both the easy kindness she had shown her and the valuable lessons she had taught her. That her mind was a weapon she should wield with full awareness, especially since she was always going to be underestimated, and that she could be both soft and strong. Not one or the other, as her father had made her believe all these years.

"Only you could have convinced Adonis to walk toward the altar," the Queen said with a mischievous smile. "As for Adamos, nothing would have made him happier than to see his brother find his place in Thalassos. I'm happy to gain one son back while I must grieve the loss of the other."

Jemima squeezed the Queen's hand back just as the doors opened.

Shivers of apprehension gripped her as she caught sight of the full contingent of the crown council—including her father—in formal regalia, their old, withered faces already radiating grave disapproval.

Prince Adonis's absence, on the other hand, was highly conspicuous.

Was their displeasure simply because the Devil Prince dared summon them, first thing in the morning, for a meeting, like mere children? Or because they were realizing that he could ruin their greedy plans for ruling Thalassos?

Even having attended these meetings for nearly three years, Jemima didn't dare do anything but stand at the back of the room like another ornamental decoration. Adamos had neither invited her nor discouraged her from being present for the meetings. It was because of the Queen's command that Jemima learn everything about how Thalassos was run that Jemima had been included at all.

Now, she settled into the seat at the back and waited with bated breath. Her quick conversation with the Queen settled inside her like the gnarled roots of a majestic tree sinking deep into the ground, making her lightheaded with relief.

A large part of her had worried that the Prince had been mocking her, or that he would think better of the whole plan in the light of the morning. But he had already shared it with the Queen.

Which meant she was about to marry the Devil Prince.

All that one impending arrangement constituted ran through her mind like a torrent drowning a bank.

What would he be like as a partner, a lover? Christos, what if he laughed at her inexperience? How long before he got bored with her? What could she do to hold the attention of a man who looked like some mythical warrior from one of her art history texts and behaved with the wild abandon of the very devil?

She was pulled out of her reverie by the hard scrape of a chair. A restless anger began to fill the room as the old men of crown council shifted in their seats. Some of them, like her father, dared cast doubtful glances at the Queen, both in pity and bloated arrogance.

Anger on Queen Isadora's behalf flushed through Jemima. Just as she was about to get to her feet to request the Queen to leave, *he* strode in.

Looking as casual and devilish as he had done yesterday, in a white linen shirt that spanned his broad chest, open to below his chest to reveal taut olive-toned skin and delineated pecs. For a second, she wondered if he'd even gone to bed and that led to wondering whose bed he'd tumbled into eventually.

There were any number of his exes that would have waited at the doorstep of his palace wing, willing to restart their wild associations.

Hadn't the Queen's aide whispered that Prince Adonis had had an inordinate number of guests waiting for him last night when she'd inquired of his whereabouts this morning?

Had one of those beautiful exes given him an escape from his grief and the tightening shackles of the palace? Hadn't she sensed the restlessness in him even as he'd agreed to her proposal last night?

She sighed. They weren't even officially engaged and

she was already tying herself in petty knots. The reminder that she had no real claim on the man, even if their agreement last night stood, didn't help though.

There was something so primal about Prince Adonis that his presence had always been like a hook under her belly button, tugging her. Her gratitude at his continued absence in the kingdom—even as his mother and brother bitterly missed him, had filled her with constant shame.

Now, she gripped her seat with one hand, trying to resist the crazy impulse of running toward him.

His dark blond curls lay stylishly haphazard at the top of his head, making him look like he had just rolled out of bed after a night of debauchery. Thick bristles dotted across his sculpted cheeks. She wondered if he meant to make a statement with his disheveled, disrespectful appearance, or if he had simply treated this meeting as another boring, mundane task he had to deal with.

If not for his bright, penetrating blue gaze, Jemima would have thought him hungover. Those eyes now roamed the expansive room without landing on anyone, even his mother.

Until they found her and stayed.

Warmth bloomed under her skin as he skimmed her from head to toe. Something like displeasure flashed across that gaze before he shut it down.

Jemima couldn't help rubbing a hand over her belly in self-consciousness. Clearly, something about her appearance had already disgruntled him.

He sauntered past the watching crown council toward her with all the grace and power of an untamed lion. And she, despite her best effort to control her raging heartbeat, felt like wanton prey, foolishly excited to be devoured whole.

His large hand, with its long, elegant fingers, landed in front of her face, upturned. Calluses and raised rope burns danced on his palm, reminding her that despite his appearance of dissipation and life of excess, the truth was something else.

This was a man whose physicality was the stuff of legends. The same physicality that seemed to press up against her like a warm blanket on a chilly night.

She stared at his hand, stunned beyond belief that he was seeking her out while dismissing the waiting council in the same breath. Beneath the sudden sticky tension that swamped her at his nearness, she was aware that he was creating a spectacle, making a statement from the get-go that they would not control him but still…fear and excitement twin punched her.

She hadn't even informed her father of their discussion last night, worried that it had all been a fantastical dream. Surely, he would punish her in some way after this public statement the Prince was making, would only see it as blatant disloyalty.

"Princess?"

Her gaze trailed up his arm to collide with his.

Blue eyes danced with devilish amusement before they sobered at her expression. Could he see the fear and trepidation that kept her rooted to the seat?

In another move that sent shock waves rippling through the room, he went to his knees in front of her. His stunningly beautiful face swam into view and she got lost in the pure, poetic symmetry of his features, in the lush sweep of his lips and the sharp up-tilt of his cheekbones. A soft, slow heat drizzled down her spine as his blue gaze swept over her features with leisurely scrutiny. Pausing at her lips for way too long.

"What are you doing?" she whispered, the dark, delicious oceans and forest scent of him coiling around her like a sensuous leash. God, the man was a master at upending her hard-fought-for composure. Even knowing that this was an act for the benefit of their eager audience, she felt like a giddy teenager meeting her celebrity boy band crush.

That lush lower lip of his stretched in a smile she wanted to touch and smudge with her finger. Stamp it with her touch. "Going to my knees for you, Princess. Something I forgot to do yesterday evening."

A thousand butterflies flapped their wings in her belly. Not grinning like a silly fool was the hardest thing she'd ever accomplished. "There are no cameras here, Prince Adonis. All this playacting amounts to nothing."

"You know better than me," he said, as one shoulder rose in a fluid movement to gesture behind him, "that in all of Thalassos, no one gossips more than the bunch of old men behind me. In two hours, the whole world will know that you're to be mine."

A grin she didn't want to give up danced on her lips. "Why do I have a feeling you're creating a spectacle out of this, mocking me even?"

The harsh slashes of his brows met. "Mocking you? No, Princess. I simply wish to ensure the world, starting with these power-hungry vultures, knows that you're my choice. Not a hand-me-down from my brother. I thought you would appreciate that too."

Some dark, hungry thing inside her that she had stifled for so long found solace in his words.

Jemima searched his eyes, but the bitter edge she heard in his words didn't taint them. The more he infused that laid-back charm into his words, the more she was beginning to realize the topic mattered to him.

He didn't like that Adamos had had a prior claim on her, as trivial as it had been. The realization made her heart stutter in her chest. Why did it matter when it was nothing but a convenient arrangement between them?

"Come, Princess." A cajoling note entered his tone, but something hungrier dwelled there too. Or she was already going mad, imagining things that didn't exist. "Don't back out on me now."

She laid her hand in his and his fingers closed in a tight grip. Every inch of her being hovered hungrily at that place of contact. Giving in to the wanton urging of her flesh, she leaned in and rested her forehead against his shoulder. Her heart felt too big for her chest at her daring.

And for all his disheveled appearance, he smelled like fresh soap and…clean male sweat that she wanted to drown in.

If the sudden intimacy she took shocked him, he didn't show it. If anything, he pressed into the contact, his broad shoulders both a shield and a cocoon. His fingers tightened with a possessiveness she desperately wanted to believe in.

For the first time in weeks, or was it years, Jemima felt a moment's pure, utter peace. With hot, honeyed longings pulsing beneath.

"I don't want to have this conversation in front of so many curious eyes and prying ears," she said, looking up into his stunning face. This close, the tiny scar near his upper lip was visible—a tiny imperfection in a landscape of perfection. "Most of whom wish for us to fail in a spectacular fashion."

A ferocious emotion dawned in his eyes, making them glitter. "I will not stand for any of them cowing you, Jemima. You should know that if you're to be my wife."

Her heart thumped against her rib cage.

Mine. My wife...

He made their association sound so much more than purely political and convenient. If he continued to talk about her like that, she was going to melt into a puddle of goo at his feet soon. And her poor, naive heart would surely take a beating too.

She pulled back and stared into the blue depths. "I'm more than glad to accept your support, Adonis. But I refuse to perform any part of our relationship that's already going to be for public consumption, for anyone. And definitely not the damned crown council or my father."

His answering grin was the very definition of delight. Because her little statement of rebellion pleased him?

She squealed like a scared bunny when he went from stillness to motion like a sudden flash of thunder. A spurt of childish—and utterly flippant laughter escaped her as he pulled her to her feet and dragged her along, past so many pairs of scandalized eyes, into a landing that cut off into corridors leading to different wings of the palace.

Her chest was still heaving when he pushed her against the wall, caging her with his lean body, but not quite touching. "Thank the lord there's no dreary, draconic Vasilikos ancestor scowling down at us here," he murmured lazily.

Far above her, the generous May sun cast a warm, golden glow that filtered through intricately designed stained-glass windows, scattering into vibrant patterns of reds, blues, and greens.

She stared up in awe as the brilliant light created a kaleidoscope effect around the Prince's head, as if anointing him with its rich blessing. As if this was how it was supposed to be.

Adonis returned her stare, his gaze lingering on her smile. "You are not reconsidering this, are you?"

"No." Something about interacting with this man made her feel like she was splayed open under a microscope. Like things she didn't know she wanted were being drawn out of her by some secret sorcery he wielded. "But I have some conditions for this…marriage. That we have to agree on," she added.

He nodded. "I do too." His hand came up to her face, his knuckles grazing her cheek in a feathery caress. "And I had the best time dreaming them up last night."

Molten heat uncoiled low in her belly at his teasing tone. "This is serious, Prince Adonis," she said, sounding like a strict schoolteacher. It was the only defense she had against how easily he unraveled her.

"Of course, it's serious." He pulled back and air rushed into her lungs. "I would never think of producing the next heir to the mighty kingdom of Thalassos as a joking matter."

Heat poured up her neck and into her cheeks. She fought against the sudden shaking in her knees and forged on. "That heir you talk so casually about producing is first and foremost an innocent child. It's the most important issue in all this."

"Explain," he said, for once very much the arrogant prince and not the scandalous devil.

"There is nothing in the world—no man or crown or kingdom, for which I'll let my child be used as a political prize or pawn. If you have other ideas about the matter, we can call off this sham now."

His eyes gleamed with something she thought might be sheer, giddy joy. Or was she imagining what she wanted to see? The man was like a chameleon, shedding and donning new skins too fast for her to track. "We're in perfect agreement on that, Jemima. And it will be our child, not yours."

Surprise made her mouth slack. His blue eyes glittered with a conviction she hadn't expected. Especially of a man like him, who'd made an art out of escaping duty and commitment.

"And it should not be a sham either," he said with a steely edge to his tone.

"What…do you mean?" she whispered.

He shrugged and even as her stomach twisted, Jemima couldn't help admiring the sheer beauty of how he moved. "If we're committed to doing this for Thalassos and we agree on not turning our child into a sacrificial lamb, then it should be as real as we can make it, *ne*?"

It was as if he'd already read her most secret desire and decided to use it to manipulate her. Just like her father had done for years. "No. It shouldn't," she bit out.

He raised a brow and studied her.

She tried her best to not flush under his scrutiny.

"Illuminate me, Princess."

For once, there was no thread of mockery in his words and that made it so much harder to speak the truth. "Real means respect and understanding and fidelity and…" *Love*, though she didn't say it—the mirage of everything that word constituted scared her. For she had never seen it being real.

And suddenly, she could see past the haze of desire and foolish longings clouding her usually clear head.

"You have decided that these are qualities I'm incapable of?" The silky thrust of his question pulsed with anger and…something more.

"No." She folded her arms at her middle as a defense against her own stupid need to touch him. "What you're suggesting means committing to each other before anything else. It means…love."

He scoffed, though there was no mockery in it. His lack of conviction in the concept sounded as oceans deep as her own. "You think I'm that desperate to be loved by you, Princess? Or that I set much store by the concept?"

Jemima knew she was making a mess of things, but faced with her pull toward him, even as he mocked her, she couldn't stop herself. "I simply think that the palace and the politics surrounding it and Thalassos itself doesn't allow for *real* marriages. Fairy tales are for tricking the populace into thinking everything is well with their betters. It is better to keep oneself on the ground than to imagine flying and come crashing to earth."

"With such diplomacy at your fingers, no wonder you're in quite the demand around this place." A smile bloomed on his lips, of a different shape than his mocking ones, swirling with a darker emotion. "You sound less eager this morning than you were last night, Princess."

That he could read her so well was…surprising to say the least. She frowned, trying to corral a thousand thoughts into some semblance of sense. Hard enough to do without the magnetism of the man pulling at her. For a man who was reputed to know nothing but his own pleasure, he was…proving to be far too perceptive.

"Yesterday it seemed impossible that another prince of Thalassos would agree to wed me."

"And this morning?"

"This morning is for reality," she said without hesitating. "You're marrying me under the influence of twisted guilt and a belated sense of duty, Adonis. While I believe that you want to thwart my father and crown council and do the best for Thalassos at a critical time, you and I both know this won't be any more than a temporary arrangement. I'm more than happy to be your representative here in Thalassos when the choking grip of those emotions fades and you want to return to your...exciting life."

"Your arrogance, thinking that you know me, is astounding, Princess." His tone cooled and yet, she could feel the sharp blade of his anger. Feel his retreat in the distance he put between them, as if she was some vile, stinky thing. "Maybe I should shop around a little more for a more suitable bride then. All this cynicism is extremely off-putting."

The idea of him with some stunning, sophisticated creature made an unnamed ache pulse through her. Which only struck her—with sharp clarity, how tangled her feelings were already about him. Not one day since his return and he affected her more than Adamos had in years. She'd already given up on the why of it.

"I didn't realize your fragile ego needed a bride that would cling to you with limpid eyes and adoring delusions, even in marriage," she said, hating the taste of the acerbic words on her lips. "After all, you're not a stranger to that kind of devotion everywhere else in your life."

"Ahh..." he said, a plasticky smile rising to his lips. "Using my reputation to attack my character...how original of you, Princess."

"I'm not...doing that." But her protest was both weak and false.

"And here I hoped for a peaceful, stable marriage, given I'm told what an amenable, practical creature you are." The words dug deep under her skin and stung. "There are any number of pretty, willing, desperate daughters among the men of the crown council for me to choose from, *ne*?"

CHAPTER FOUR

WITH ONE SILKY remark Prince Adonis reminded Jemima that it was she who needed this marriage. Desperation stole her composure and the comportment she'd been taught at the finishing school her father had banished her to for years.

He radiated distaste as if he were a melting glacier and she dared not touch him. As much as a part of her wanted to soothe him. And that too, she told herself, was an impulse left over from a lifetime of pretending subservience. One that she needed to break with him. "I vow to give you everything I can, Prince Adonis. My unflinching loyalty whether you're in Thalassos or not, my political expertise, my knowledge of the inner workings of the palace. Every little bit of cunning information my father has secretly amassed about the power players. But I cannot pretend that this marriage is…anything but an arrangement and temporary at that. In fact, except to produce the required two children, I think we should refrain from any physical association."

From behind her, the light shifted, suddenly leaving his features in shadows, as if it were in cahoots with him. As if it too wanted to please him.

When he remained stubbornly silent, she huffed in frustration. What did the man want of her? "You can't honestly tell me that you'll be faithful to me beyond the few minutes you'll spend in my bed," she bit out. "At least Adamos was honest about what we were getting into."

And she knew, the moment those words landed on her own ears, something precious and pure had been stripped from her by her father's constant criticism and relentless demands over the years. When had she become so unwilling to give life a chance, begun to think so little of herself? When had she become so judgmental and self-righteous that she would spit on an offer made in good faith?

Also, it was the worst thing she could have said to the man she'd nearly begged to marry. No, bringing the dead brother he hadn't fully grieved yet into the discussion was the worst.

But she was beginning to see that the Devil Prince was unlike his brother. Or any man she'd known. Even the moniker seemed like nothing but a mask. One of several he used to hide his true self from the world.

He didn't betray anything, even at her direct insult. Whatever else he pretended to be for the rest of the world, Adonis Vasilikos exercised his control as though it were the jaws of a steely vise.

No shadow, no mockery, not a sliver of anger showed across his features. Only a slick smile coasted over those sinful lips, as if she had been relegated to the rubbish heap in his head. "I have a better idea, Princess," he said, using the mocking address she was beginning to hate. "How about we do not produce these required two children the fun, traditional way at all?"

"What do you mean?" Jemima whispered, her heart hammering in her chest.

"It is clear that you're willing to wear the crown and sacrifice yourself at the altar of Thalassos's well-being for reasons of your own. But I find it extremely distasteful, not to mention downright disgusting, to touch a woman who will bear it under sufferance. As you cleverly reminded me, I've never been deprived of the sources of infinite pleasure."

Jemima stared, with no apology to offer in return, for she had dug the hole to bury their tentative truce with her own hands. Still, she said, "I'm not sure I understand."

"I'm a very possessive sort of man, Princess, for all that I don't get possessive about most things in life. The idea of my wife, the mother of my children, cavorting with some lover...fills me with distaste. I'd rather we stay strangers to create these children. Science has come up with all kinds of neat little tricks, *ne*?"

That the last thing she wanted was a lover when she'd be bound to him rose to her lips but she pushed it away. She'd ruined any chance of truce between them already. "And you, Adonis?" she demanded, provoked by both distrust and a gnawing sense of loss. "Would you promise to not look at another woman in this marriage of ours?"

"You have lost the chance to find out, Princess," he added, without a trace of bitterness. As if he had already overcome the insult she had dealt him.

To her utter dismay, their little heart-to-heart apparently wasn't over yet. For one miserable moment, she thought it would be better if he rejected her and her stupid, desperate proposal, even at this last minute.

But, as she was beginning to learn, Adonis Vasilikos was a man of his word, of integrity, of kindness even. The last an impossible quality to find in men of power.

With smooth movements, he opened a dark blue velvet box that looked tiny and fragile within his fingers. "I asked Mama to have this brought out this morning from the crown treasury."

In his hands, the emerald and sapphire ring shone brilliantly, the simplicity of its cut emphasizing the regal beauty of the stones. It was as different as could be possible from the diamond monstrosity Adamos had pushed onto her finger with such alacrity that she had felt utterly humiliated.

"This comes from Mama's line," Prince Adonis said, a strange grief dancing in his eyes. "I'm told it has been worn by strong, selfless women through centuries."

Her breath punched out of her lungs so painfully that Jemima would have slid to the floor if not for the wall at her back.

She knew, as surely as the loud clamoring of her heart, that Adonis had picked the ring for her specifically. That he had meant to honor their arrangement as much as was possible given the strange circumstances surrounding it.

That, despite his mockery of protocol, and grief over his brother, and anger at being shackled to her and the kingdom, he had appreciated her, like no one else ever had.

Adonis Vasilikos, the Devil Prince, the man who could have anything and anyone in the world, had seen something of note in her. Had *seen* her, period.

If there was a moment in her life where Jemima would have given up all pretense of strength and bawled her eyes out, it was that. All through her life, she had lost countless precious things—friendships and opportunities and freedom and something as fundamental as a sense of self—thanks to her father's autocratic nature. But this loss of the… tentative trust between her and this man, hit harder than anything else, for she had wrought it with her own hands.

"Adonis—"

"You might think it all the same," he said, reaching for her hand, "but I find it tacky to marry you with my brother's ring on your finger. Even if it's the renowned Pink Diamond ring worn by every Queen of Thalassos." Blue eyes, of the shade of arctic frost, held hers. "But I'm also not a man who forces his views or his touch on a woman. So choose for yourself, Princess."

Her fingers shook in his grasp even as soft heat pooled where he touched her. Her pulse went haywire under the pad of his thumb, as if rushing to say the words she couldn't form.

The tips of his fingers lingered over her empty ring finger, his surprise evident in the sudden tightness of his jaw.

"I removed the ring as soon as I heard of his death," she said, not mentioning his brother by name. "And I want the one you picked. For me."

He didn't look remotely mollified by her obvious and pathetic attempt to make up for her words. Neither did he shove the ring onto her finger with tasteless hurry or distasteful apathy. Even in his anger, Adonis Vasilikos remained in utter control.

He slid the ring onto her finger with extreme care, as if the moment was precious and…real.

And suddenly, Jemima realized that for him, it was real. That it was his greatest duty and commitment to Thalassos, and therefore automatically extended to her.

Because while she had made arrogant claims about it, he truly saw this as an equal partnership between them, if nothing else.

Adonis wasn't sure why he was fuming with anger and some darker emotion that he couldn't even pin down as he stormed back into the summit room.

His betrothed was apparently both practical and cynical, which only increased her value as a perfect candidate for the role of his wife. She demanded nothing from him, even as she gazed at him with a hunger he recognized within himself. And more than just a carnal one too.

Knowing her father's reputation for cruelty and his exacting demands of her over the years—the extent of which Mama had revealed to him only last night—meant this morning, he could see the same shadows of self-doubt and distrust mirrored in her wide amber eyes. Even in that, she was a perfect match for him, for he had lived with the same for years. Neither did she want the performative pretensions to love.

Mistakenly, he had assumed that it would make them grounded partners who could have a real marriage with trust and respect and fidelity, who could focus on the well-being of their children and that of Thalassos.

Instead, her utter lack of belief in him before they had even gotten started, grated like a thorn stuck under his skin. Like the wound that had continued to fester for years.

It was the same casual distrust that his father had shown him for nearly three decades, eroding his self-confidence from within like some great disease. Until he had realized that he was his father's shame, a weapon used by Mama in her own rebellion against him. The harm had been done by the time she had realized that.

Now, the last thing he wanted was another relationship where he constantly had to prove himself or was measured against Adamos. But for all his threats to her, it was too late to find another candidate, as much as he itched to do so.

And the fact was that no other woman would do as well

as Jemima Nasar. His talk with Mama last night had confirmed his own instincts.

Jemima's refusal to committing to making their marriage a half-decent thing was one thing. That he had made her the offer was in itself a shock.

Not once in his life had he considered marriage before last night. But, apparently now that he'd agreed to enter the institution, a part of him wanted stability he hadn't known as a child for his own children, a solid foundation from which to rule Thalassos.

Her blatant honesty had appealed to him so much that he had realized he wanted something as close to a true partner as he could achieve.

Then there was the attraction between them. Something about Jemima Nasar had always provoked fiery desire in him.

Contrary to how the media painted him and that he allowed—to build his reputation as a daredevil—he didn't go around sleeping with every available woman.

At least not in the last decade, when he had stepped away from the toxic cloud of his father's presence. If it wasn't the imaginary crown on his head that drew women—especially of the shallow, superficial variety—it was the genetic lottery he had won.

The fact that women were drawn to the specific arrangement of his features—the very same his father had passed on but hated looking upon—had nothing to do with who he was beneath.

It worked fine when he had mistaken lust and covetousness for approval and affection and nearly drowned himself in it. But now, he knew better. And he had to admit, he wanted better for himself. He wanted a fulfilling life that challenged him to be a better man and a good king, and he wanted it with a family.

For months, he had been aware of his growing restlessness, of falling into a rut, that even chasing the most dangerous high couldn't cure him of. For the first few moments when he'd heard of Adamos's accident, he'd felt an overwhelming relief, because it meant he could return home under the pretext of caring for his brother.

He had missed his brother and mother, and even though it galled him to admit it, Thalassos itself. Without his family around him, he had felt…alone.

As hollow as the halls felt without the commanding presence of his brother, the challenge of ruling Thalassos with a capable, strong woman like Jemima by his side… last night, it had felt like destiny. Like the very fate he had been trying to outrun for so long. Like, finally, he could spin some kind of meaning out of his life.

Maybe he was a fool to think that it could be a real marriage based on trust and respect. Maybe she was right to question him about his commitment to her, because, when had he truly devoted himself to anything before? Maybe he was what his father had always called him…

A crow in the cuckoo's nest, a man who would never be his brother's equal, or good enough—smart enough or strong enough—to take on the mantle of Thalassos in any way.

And yet, the duty had come to him. He didn't know whether to laugh or cry at fate for giving him what he'd always wished for, but in the worst way possible.

"As pleased as I am to serve the royal family and Thalassos in every capacity, I am disturbed by this…inappropriate conduct in public, Your Highness." A deep voice disturbed the fraught silence. "Am I to assume that you've decided to take pity on my daughter after the grievous loss of your brother?"

Adonis looked up to find Aziz Nasar staring up at him with that oily smile on his lips. All the members of the crown council watched him and Jemima with the same expressions, following the top dog. He sensed Jemima's presence behind him and moved a step back so that she stood by him. Whatever their personal differences and his anger with her at her supposition of his character, he knew that she was his one true ally. And neither did he forget that he had made her the target of her father's ire by declaring their...association so publicly.

Adonis clasped Jemima's hand in his and felt her stiffen. Donning a completely besotted smile, he lifted her hand to his mouth and kissed the back of it. She trembled from head to toe, and this, he knew, was her honest reaction to him. The hungry beast in him calmed.

When he felt her gaze caress his cheek as if it were touch, he found himself smiling.

"If I'm to be the bloody King, I think I'm afforded a few indulgences." He wrapped an arm around her shoulders and pulled her closer, making a clear statement to her father and the rest. "And if you dare point out that I'm not, then we'll have to change more things than Jemima tells me need changing over here."

The silence was instant and deafening, Jemima's hitch of breath the only sound. Her gaze met his, absolute shock swirling through the amber depths. In answer, he squeezed her fingers harder.

Gratitude flooded those amber depths.

Looking away, Adonis made sure to meet every pair of eyes in the room until they understood that each word he uttered had the power of his might behind it.

One pair, a warm brown, filled with utter joy and full tears. He gave his mother a quick nod, buoyed by the conviction he saw there.

"You're speaking in riddles and threats, Your Highness," Aziz Nasar said, with a cutting look Adonis didn't miss in Jemima's direction.

Adonis could feel her fear as clearly as if she had been dealt a sudden slap.

"Crown Prince Adamos—"

"Is not here anymore. As much as I respected my brother's vision and ideas, I'm not him. I will rule Thalassos my way, with Jemima by my side. Is that clear enough for everyone assembled?" A vow Adonis made to himself too—it was the least he could do for the woman who had raised him as his own.

He had no doubt that he would stumble and stutter, but it was better than the alternative—which was this pack of jackals who would bleed Thalassos dry to build their personal fortunes.

A temporary arrangement, Jemima had called his fulfilling of his duty, narrowing on his own doubts perfectly.

But, bored or stifled or challenged, he knew there was no turning back for him.

While he didn't expect enthusiastic nods and approving pats, he did expect more than the glacial anger he received in return from the council members.

He reined his temper in, for he knew he needed these men to rule well. "The wedding and coronation will go on as planned before. In the meantime, Jemima and I will review the trade treaty documents and see why it stumbled so badly on the last attempt."

Shock rippled through the room, ending in frenzied whispers.

"Your Majesty," Aziz said, appealing to his mother. Adonis gritted his teeth against the clear disrespect, even as Jemima squeezed his fingers, as if urging him to practice patience. "The public must be allowed the formal mourning period, to grieve Crown Prince Adamos in the proper way. This…" he gestured toward Adonis and Jemima in a slashing motion, as if it were tacky to even look upon, "will give rise to terrible rumors about the royal family, add fuel to the talk of rift between the brothers, make a mockery of the most sacred institutions that form the basis of the crown."

An irreverent snort escaped Adonis's mouth and he instantly regretted it. For he could sense his mother stiffen at Aziz Nasar's words. His father, the great King Aristos, had committed the sin of mocking their marriage, even though the knowledge wasn't public.

"It is true," Adonis said, his mother on one side and Jemima on the other, "that the palace PR team has done a shoddy job of representing the royal family. I'm bringing in my entire team here, along with new assistants for my mother and Jemima. Any messaging about this engagement and the upcoming wedding will be handled by them."

Aziz instantly changed tack. "Better to paint it that you're taking pity on my daughter in her hour of loss, Prince Adonis. It would go a long way toward pacifying the Thalassan public instead of provoking them into thinking that you're stealing their beloved Prince's bride along with his kingdom."

"Thalassans love Adonis as much as they loved Adamos, Aziz, if not more. That has been made clear by the welcome he received from them," his mother said, pure steel to her tone.

Adonis met Jemima's eyes and saw the simmering anger

there. He tightened his fingers over her hip, urging her to speak out. Her fear of the hateful man had his insides burning with fury. He hated bullies of any kind and Aziz Nasar was one.

Jemima's chest rose and fell on shallow breaths before she said, "Prince Adonis and I are making the best out of a hard situation, Papa. While I loathe the idea of painting it as some fairy-tale romance, I would also hate being portrayed as the recipient of pity or to be seen as a sacrifice he's making. This is and will be a partnership. Neither should anyone forget that Prince Adonis is giving up his personal life to take up the mantle of the royal family.

"The Prince's teams will have the final say but I would like to state that we're starting from a basis of friendship and trust and well-being of Thalassos as the foundation for this marriage."

She said the whole thing holding his gaze.

The same admiration he felt for her burned there too, giving rise to fresh curiosity.

For all the stuff she'd told him about her relationship with Adamos, did she still hold affection for him? Or was her rejection of his idea because of who Adonis himself was?

"I should think your doubts put to rest, Aziz," his mother said, satisfaction ringing in her words. "And that you and the rest of the council will extend Prince Adonis every support that you have offered my husband and my older son."

Deafening silence greeted him.

Adonis knew even the Queen's command wasn't enough for them. Christos, what had Adamos been up to, letting these old vultures puff up with their inflated sense of arrogance? Why hadn't he shown them their place? How dare they challenge the Queen's direct command?

It was time to flex his claws. Men like Jemima's father only understood a show of power. "One more thing," he said, infusing a silky undertone. "I do hope that any more attempts at finding long-lost cousins from broken branches of the Vasilikos family will end today. Or I will treat any such efforts as treason toward the royal family and the crown."

With his mother on one arm and Jemima on the other, he walked out of the summit room. But not before he caught the pale, horrified faces of the members of the crown council.

And if he felt a well of conviction rise up at Jemima's whispered "Well done," he tucked it away in the farthest corners of his heart like a giddy child.

CHAPTER FIVE

IF JEMIMA HAD thought she was wholly prepared to be the wife of a Prince of Thalassos—which *she had* assumed because she had prepared for years for the same role, she was proved completely wrong.

The fact that Prince Adonis was nothing like his brother had become apparent after the public declaration in front of the crown council, making it clear that Jemima was, as his queen-to-be, not just his wife but his political advisor, and his equal partner in all things.

While performative plays and provoking crusty old rich men by bucking tradition were Adonis's tools, he had proved that he also very much stood by his words.

He hadn't let her go the entire afternoon, keeping her by his side and busy for hours, knowing her father was dying to take out his volcanic temper on her. By the time Adonis had dismissed her, two armed guards had flanked her wherever she went, having been ordered to never leave her alone. Then there was the relief that her brother was out of her father's hands literally, for Queen Isadora—with brilliant foresight—had demanded that Jemima send Zayn to a trusted friend's place in the city for a couple of weeks.

By the same evening, her stuff had been moved to a suite in a different wing, connected to Adonis's chambers through a small private hallway. The new suite not only denoted a clear upgrade—spacious with high ceilings and large arched windows that overlooked the sapphire waters of the Aegean, but had been done up in cream and light gold walls, adorned with intricate frescoes depicting the mythology and rich art history of Thalassos.

She'd learned later, by probing some of the staff and even Queen Isadora who had supplied the information about Jemima's interests, that the order from Prince Adonis had been to make the space worthy of not just the Thalassan queen, but Jemima Nasar too. As if he were acknowledging that she wasn't just a placeholder as everyone in her life had always thought her. As if she was an actual person.

So many of her favorite elements had been braided into her new space and every time Jemima walked in, she felt a wellspring of…gratitude and a prickle of shame.

He was giving her everything that came with his word—status, influence, and freedom. Every step she took on the cool marble floors with the gorgeous inlaid patterns of olive branches reminded her that she had thrown the olive branch he had offered her back in his face.

The fact that he had traveled to Monaco the next evening—to take care of his business affairs before the coronation—only made the man and their upcoming wedding even more mythical in her head. All of it felt too good to be true.

Now, as she sat at the vanity table staring at her reflection in a gilded, ornate mirror, readying herself for their first public appearance as a couple, nerves twanged through her as if she had been tuned too tight. Even the gentle breeze from the sea caressing her skin, filling her nostrils with the scent of salt and blooming jasmine, couldn't calm her restlessness.

And she knew the reason was her appearance. To begin with, at least.

The afternoon sun bathing the suite in a golden hue couldn't transform her high-necked, shapeless dress in a muddy brown color into anything better. Even her sensible, low-heeled pumps seemed to scream how boring and predictable and dull she had become.

It was as if she'd allowed all the lines her father had drawn around her to become solid walls, boxing her in.

Shooting to her feet, she did a dance kick she'd once been forced to perform as part of some ghastly weight-loss program, and the shoe flew in the direction of the veranda.

The door connecting the hallway between their suites opened just as she raised her other leg.

Dressed impeccably in a hand-tailored dark navy suit, Adonis exuded effortless command and power. Having only seen him in casual clothes so far, Jemima's breath hitched in her throat.

God, the man looked…magnificent.

Her knees buckled beneath her—forcing her to pull her quivering thigh down, as he casually leaned against the doorframe, biting into an apple. As if he didn't tempt her entire being into wickedly decadent thoughts just by existing. His lush lips glistened with the juice of the fruit and she so desperately wanted a taste.

"Were you aiming for my door, Princess?"

She shook her head, stupefied into muteness by the twinkle in his eyes.

"I thought maybe after three days, you were missing me and throwing things around to express the displeasure. A great improvement over the placid little smile you show the world, I promise."

"No, not missing you," Jemima said, even as she fought

the tendril of pleasure that wound around her heart. How was the damned man so perceptive? Did anything she, and the world, assumed about him hold even a whisper of the truth? "But I would like a little notice in the future before you up and leave the country."

Straightening, he ventured into the vast sitting space, immediately reducing it, sucking all the air out. She huffed through her lips, as if she had been running nonstop, as he continued coming at her.

"Noted," he said, reaching her. This close, she could see the small cut under his right jaw from the shave and smell that unique woodsy scent of him. God, how did he manage to smell as if he had rolled around in the lush jungles and roaring river rapids of Thalassos? How did he make her want to roll and writhe against him in turn?

"If this king thing fails," she said, determined to start over, determined to punch through those stupid walls one word and action at a time. She refused to become that cynical creature completely. "You could simply bottle that unique scent you create and sell it for millions. It's...sure to melt the panties off any woman."

"Is it melting yours?" the devil shot back at her.

Her core gave a spasm at the silky taunt, not that she would ever admit it. "I thought you weren't interested in touching me," she said, hoping he wouldn't notice the stiff peaks of her nipples. The barest contact of his chest and they were all attention.

"I'm not interested. But it doesn't mean I don't want to tease and torment you, Jemima. Doesn't mean I won't make you melt and writhe and beg for me. After all, I have to feed my monstrous, kingly ego and my wicked reputation." He snuck his finger under the ruffled collar of her dress, until the tip landed on her fluttering pulse. Distaste speared itself across his lush lips. "Why is it that you hide yourself in these bag-like dresses?"

"I'm not hiding."

He must have heard the conviction in her voice for he nodded. Though one thick brow raised with lordly majesty, as if to say *I'm waiting...elucidate.*

"I'm in half-mourning."

"Not anymore," he bit out. "You're my fiancée and I find it insulting that you continue to act as if you're being led to the sacrificial altar."

Jemima swallowed at the thin thread of anger in his voice. And beneath it pulsed something more. It was the same shadow that came over his eyes when his father was mentioned. Neither had she missed the fact that he had refused her offer to accompany him during his visits to the King, nor that Queen Isadora actively encouraged him to abstain from visiting his father too often.

Whatever the rift was between them, it hurt this man still. And that in itself was a major puzzle piece to him.

"I did not mean to insult you, Prince Adonis."

"Then prove it. This is our first public appearance and I refuse to show up with you looking like...that."

She smacked his arm, pricked by his poking. Which she had a feeling he was doing on purpose. "What is that you would have me do?"

"Open your wardrobe, put on something else."

She frowned. "My wardrobe only has..."

"Go, Princess. Look inside that antique piece." His fingers landing on her shoulder and turning her around left her with no choice.

She felt his eyes on every inch of her as she made the trek to the hand-carved wardrobe that she had fawned over ages ago in some wing of the palace. On her shoulder blades, the cinch of her waist, and then lower, on the swells of her bottom.

Heat seared her as if he were tracing a finger over the highs and dips of her flesh.

She opened the antique wardrobe doors with their filigreed handles to find a rack of glittering new outfits. A soft gasp escaped her as she fingered the soft silks and bright colors.

Nothing this man did anymore should surprise her but it did. And she was beginning to think it had to do with her and her low expectations—of him *and* herself, rather than him.

Over her shoulder, she cast a look at him. "When did you arrange for these?"

"Try one and show me. Hopefully, we'll get to see more of that smooth, silky honey-gold skin."

Her core fluttered at the compliment, as if now in tune with his every word and touch. "Is it that important that I should look glamorous next to you?"

"I think it's important to you too, Jemima, but you don't want to admit it. Nor do you want to look like you care about it. Intellectual snobbery is also snobbery."

"I was raised to not make a splash," she added, her throat tight suddenly. How had he known something she was only now discovering—that she had hidden her true self under layers of camouflage?

"And this is a gentle nudge to remind you that that time is over. If we're to make a success of this whole stopping the kingdom from burning down into ashes, you need to stop hiding and step up." Sudden steel entered his tone. "And if your father says or does anything remotely threatening, you will immediately bring it to my notice without hesitation."

Now, it was tears that clogged her throat.

"I mean it, Jemima. You're not just his daughter anymore. In fact, it is the most insignificant of your roles now."

She managed to say yes without letting the sniffle that threatened, out.

"You continue to surprise me," she said, once her breath was steady again, pulling out a seafoam-green dress in a soft linen blend that was perfect for the sunny day. The rich fabric had a slight sheen to it, elevating it from being too casual for their first outing.

Grabbing the dress and the thin, woven belt in gold that came with it, she ducked behind a hand-painted privacy screen.

His mocking laughter made honey drizzle down her spine as she shrugged off the heavy dress. The lace of her bra felt far too tight against her nipples. It took her two tries to pull the dress over her head, as trembly as she felt.

"Such modesty, Princess? Or is it to hide those melting panties?"

"You wish you knew, Prince," she retorted, and his laughter deepened.

Her heart thundered with excitement as the dress fell into place, kissing her skin like a whisper of a caress from the man taunting her even now. Without even looking at her reflection, Jemima knew, with the flattering V neckline with a subtle scalloped edge and the tailored bodice highlighting her waist, the dress made the best of her curvy figure. That it had been made for her.

When she stepped out from behind the screen, it was to find Adonis within touching distance. And a pair of elegant gold sandals with intricate straps to wrap around her ankles.

For what felt like eternity, he stared at her, from her

hair to her bare feet, and then back up. His eyes gleamed. "You're beautiful, Princess. You should own it more."

And when he went to his knees—uncaring of ruining the creases of his trousers or the cut of his jacket, Jemima's breath whooshed out of her. Her trembling legs would have taken her to the floor if she didn't lean down and balance herself on his shoulders. His hard thigh muscles clenched under her digging toes.

Every inch of the skin he touched with his nimble fingers sizzled. He made a quick, efficient job of wrapping the gold straps around her ankles.

Something she'd never thought possible released inside of Jemima, breaking all barriers. She pushed her fingers into his thick, stylish waves, giving in to the urge to touch him, to claim some small part of him for herself.

The line of his shoulders stiffened under the jacket, but he said nothing.

"Am I imagining it? Please, Adonis, I need to know."

His hands moved from her ankles, one to her knee, and one to her thigh, steadying her. "What, Princess?"

She licked her lips, pressing her fingers into his scalp. It was so much easier to ask without those penetrating blue eyes peeling layers off her. "This thing I feel between us, this attraction, do you feel it too? Or am I just projecting my silly fantasies onto you again?"

"I did not realize you had fantasies about me," he said, pushing back against her hold and meeting her eyes. If she was indulging any ideas that he would simply let her live in delusion land, he told her no with those eyes. Nothing with this man would be easy. Not even her own surrender. "That is the sort of thing you should put in your famous memos for me."

"Please, can I have the truth for once? Just between you and me."

Whatever languid humor had been swimming in his eyes seconds ago disappeared in an instant. "And what do I get in return?"

"I've already admitted that I'm beyond attracted to you. If your hand sneaks up my thigh any further, you will find the evidence that I'm melting for you."

For just a second, a feral kind of satisfaction glittered in his eyes, making them sparkle like rare sapphires. In the next second, it was gone. "What is the guarantee that you will believe me if I tell you the truth, Princess?"

With one push and swoop, he was on his feet, his gaze clashing with hers. But he didn't let go of her, for a second.

His large hands spanned her hips, his thumbs digging into the sharp divot of her waist, as if he meant to leave fingerprints behind. Stamping her with his possession, but refusing to actually claim her.

Frustration gouged through her. "Is it so wrong if I can't believe in…this? In things being so different from before?"

He didn't even seem angry at her anymore. Not that he ever was. Instead, she saw the same exhaustion in his eyes that she'd complained of on that first night. "I tire of having to provide proof for everything I say, Princess."

When he tugged her, she went like a doll. Suddenly, she knew the hurt she had dealt him had been fathoms deep, building on an already festering wound.

"It is a curse I've lived with before and I find it extremely…boring," he said.

She stared at herself in the gilded full-length mirror, her cheeks full of lively color. Her eyes…the black eating out the amber in voracious desire. Even her skin felt different, tingly…as if an electric charge had been fed under it.

Her chest rose on quick breaths as Adonis framed her from behind. Tall and broad, he engulfed her, making her feel like the center of the universe.

The small hairs on her skin stood erect as his fingertips danced over her nape, and his breath coasted over her neck. She stared, fascinated, as his long, dark fingers collared her throat before he clasped a simple, elegant gold necklace with delicate platinum beading and flowers.

Arousal—sharp and sweet—flooded her entire being, and she had to clutch her thighs together for fear of betraying herself.

It's too late, you fool. You've already admitted it, her inner voice said. *And he's not treating it as a weapon, much as you worried that he would.*

He bent his head until his chin rested on her shoulder, the rough nap of his cheeks like velvet against her own. His chest against her back was a wall of warmth and hardness. "I think it could be real, this…heat between us. Pity you aren't that bold girl who could steal life-giving kisses anymore."

With that, he patted her on her shoulder, told her they were late, and left the chamber with a brisk efficiency she couldn't emulate.

And Jemima knew, whether she willed it or not, that more of her walls were coming down for this gorgeous man, whose outward beauty was the least interesting thing about him.

Adonis Vasilikos, she was realizing, was capable of feeling with more depth than she'd ever thought possible. More than he would ever allow his mask to betray.

Adonis looked at the documents on the tablet in his lap, the letters and numbers jumbling in front of him, as usual.

Stress only made matters worse and it was all he'd been drinking for more than two weeks now.

At least, the afternoon event at a luncheon auction for a charity that Jemima was on the board of—education for girls from underprivileged backgrounds of course, because his fiancée was a bloody saint—hadn't involved reading out the shitty draft of a speech someone had written for him, with no attention to his personality or principles.

Meeting the other board members who had been women from all walks of life, giving out awards and announcing scholarships for the new academic year, meeting teenage girls with stars in their eyes—it had been one of the few public outings as the King-to-be that he had thoroughly enjoyed. The afternoon had made him feel like there was a greater purpose to the roller coaster he'd willingly jumped on. Even made his constant doubts that he would not let his father be proved right, worth it.

And he knew most of it was due to the woman he found equally fascinating and frustrating. Fascinating because he had never met anyone so brutally honest with themselves—except himself perhaps, and frustrating because she so easily snuck under his skin.

He hadn't meant to exact some kind of petty revenge for the distrust she'd shown him. She, and her indirect insults, should fall off like water over rocks, for he had already decided that she meant nothing to him in the grand scheme of things.

And yet he had exacted revenge and thrust his own lance into her—especially when she'd made herself vulnerable to him by admitting to wanting him. She had sounded so adorably baffled by the whole thing even.

He could see too, how much it cost her, how hard she

was trying to emerge from the cocoon her father had forcibly wrapped around her.

He didn't know how to shut off the admiration, for in her case, it led him to feeling and wanting more.

"Thank you for picking the charity gala as our first outing together," Jemima said, from the opposite seat on the limo. Her fingers clasped in her lap, her face shining with damp sweat, her hair already falling apart from the knot, she looked...good enough to devour. Through the event, she had been in her true element, always ready with a kind word and a helping hand, calling forth a hundred details from that brain at a moment's notice.

She'd been like a butterfly, flitting from table to table, and all he'd wanted was to catch her for himself.

He could pull her into his lap now, lift that alluring dress, and test for himself what she'd so boldly declared earlier. And then he would plunge his fingers into her waiting sheath and let her see how real and bloody uncommon this kind of pull was.

"No need to thank me, Princess," he said, burying his fantasy under a bored tone.

"The board members couldn't believe they got to meet you." Jemima went on as if he hadn't sprayed cold water on her enthusiasm. "I think you charmed the pants off Mrs. Skyros, eighty-six years old as she is. Many of them told me it was the thrill of a lifetime to meet you."

"I didn't—" Adonis began.

"You did. I checked with both our secretaries and the palace PR team and the media team. They all said it was your choice to make this our first outing. That snooty aide Mr. Kairos even said that he informed you that this charity wasn't high-profile enough and that you shot them down."

Damned minx!

"If you want to give me a crown for it, Princess, join the queue."

A fierce frown pulled her brows together as she scooted forward on her seat, her eyes full of reproach. "I wish you didn't do that."

"Do what?" he said, coming to recognize the blood-thirsty glint.

"Make light of what is good about you." Her words were a soft whisper that nonetheless landed like harsh rocks against his flesh. "Make what you do for others sound like an afterthought or an excuse or a game."

"If you want relief from the wet panty problem, you could simply ask me, Jemima, and I might oblige. There's no need to sing my praises."

Dark pink streaked her high, round cheeks and the tip of her tongue swept over her lip. *As if,* for just a second, she was actually considering his filthy suggestion. His blood pumped with renewed lust, and something much deeper.

If he wasn't careful, the perceptive minx would get too close to the pulsing, resentful center of him and then there would be nothing to do but drown her in his pain too. And for some reason, when it came to her and only her, Adonis felt the least destructive he had in his entire life.

"I will admit, the offer is far too tempting." She gasped, as if the words had come out without her permission. The amber of her eyes glittered with naked want. A sigh lifted her lush breasts. And just like that, she was all serious-ness again. "I'm trying to understand you, Prince Adonis."

"Why?" The question came bursting from the depths of him, for no one had ever tried much less admitted to it.

"How else will I know you? I already made the mistake of thinking you were just your reputation. I won't make that mistake again."

"Maybe I'm not solely my reputation, but there isn't much else."

She settled back into her seat with a nod, but he knew that resolve in her eyes. "This must all feel dreary after... your exciting life."

"Not sure about excitement but definitely more dangerous," he said, pulled into the discussion despite his resolve to keep things either polite or sexual between them.

"I've always been curious about what pushes you to do all that you do, pitting yourself against nature's extremes." When he hesitated, she leaned forward again. "And how is the palace more dangerous than that?"

"Navigating the palace politics is like willingly wading into a lake full of piranhas desperate for a taste of your blood. You know that. While nature, whether jagged mountain cliffs or roaring river rapids, is hard and cruel but not calculating and cunning like people. It doesn't manipulate you or use you or conspire to harm you. It just stands there, showing neither pity nor mockery when you pit yourself against it. And it doesn't care whose blood you bear in your veins, or what civilized society considers your flaws. It is constant in its ruthlessness."

Her eyes wide, she stared at him with an intensity Adonis wasn't sure he could withstand for too long. And yet, somehow, her curiosity about him was a spark that added fuel to the constant hum of desire in his veins. He wanted to...consume her whole when she looked at him like this. "You've never said anything remotely like that in all your interviews."

"How would you know?"

She colored. "I have watched every bit of media that has ever been released about you. My curiosity about you was a wildfire...even Adamos used to laugh about it."

A well of longing rose up within Adonis, and not even his brother's name could curb it. He wanted to tell her the number of times he'd thought of her since their kiss, how he'd been equally fascinated by her. How she had become the ideal woman in his head.

And how, he was realizing, she still could be—a mirage turning into lush curves and keen mind.

But no. He couldn't give up any more of his secrets to her. While she had wounded him by assuming he was nothing more than his reputation, it had also been a sharp reminder that he couldn't let anyone close. And definitely not the woman he'd have to live with for the next fifty or so years. He couldn't bear her disappointment if, no, when he inevitably crushed her hopes or God forbid, hurt her.

"I think you were right—"

"Will you not tell me the reason for the rift between you and the King, Adonis?"

Head jerking up, Adonis stared at her.

She looked half shocked, half startled herself at her daring.

"Do you have a questionnaire from that stuffy aide hidden somewhere, Princess? This is beginning to sound like an interview."

"Of course not. Like I said—"

This time, he cut her off. "No, Jemima. There is no big hidden secret about our rift. He wanted another perfect son like Adamos. And the last thing I am," he said, his throat burning as if he were a child again, and all the inadequacy and vulnerability he had felt scratching like thorns again now, "is perfect. By any standard."

"I want to help with this—"

He laughed and if it was filled with a serrated ache, he didn't care. "There's nothing to help me with in this,

Jemima. Nothing you can help me see in a new way. But yes, it is a twisted fate that determined that I'm all he and you and Thalassos have now. And if you wish to truly be of use to me, then start working on the things plaguing Thalassos now, instead of worrying that pretty head about my past."

It was a weight that had become almost unbearable since he returned, this burden of determination and fear, equally driving him. Even reminding himself that only a selfish, power-bloated man like King Aristos could blame an innocent boy for his own mistake, didn't help rid him of that feeling of unworthiness that was his father's gift to him.

But damn the whole world if Adonis wouldn't prove him wrong.

CHAPTER SIX

TWO WEEKS AFTER his return from Monaco—and two days away from coronation, Adonis sat back in his chair and looked out into the expanse of his study that stretched into an open courtyard.

Beyond it was the sparkling blue waters of the Aegean, meeting the sky in a seamless blend of colors.

In the distance, the rugged cliffs of Thalassos rose majestically, dotted with ancient olive groves that swayed gently in the breeze.

Unlike the large, luxurious study that had been occupied by his father for decades and lately Adamos—an overdecorated oval hall that boxed him in from all sides, with haughty ancestors looking down from every wall— this view calmed Adonis.

White marble columns with intricate carvings of vines and mythical creatures framed the courtyard, creating a sense of both openness and whimsy, with a dash of history thrown in.

The space was the perfect blend of Thalassos's rich, natural history and its advent into modern times. If he could drag it.

Like his personal suite in a newly renovated wing of the palace, and his set of public office rooms, that he use this space as his private study had been Jemima's suggestion.

He was nothing like his brother or father, and the idea of being constrained by the same solid walls that had once felt like a prison, made him utterly restless. Even with his own team's arrival, it had taken him a few days to get used to the constant barrage of demands and details coming straight at him.

For so long, he'd been alone, whether in personal life or business, and had done as he pleased.

It had been Jemima who had assembled his own team and the palace teams together, sketching out a daily and weekly agenda for him with the aggression and authority of a clever military general. Then she had instituted several checks and balances to protect his time, cutting off everyone's access to him but for the most important matters.

Despite her attempts, the crown council had already brought up several pending issues that awaited his decision, some of them truly critical. The matters betrayed the truth of her words about Adamos being distracted in the last few months.

It was only with her insider knowledge and pertinent but exhaustive information on those issues that he had been able to make a decision. Neither had he hidden the fact that she had enabled him to make it. He wanted the crown council and Thalassos to know that she was his partner.

The fact that she was so much more equipped—better than anyone else to rule Thalassos—hadn't stopped her from attending to his needs first, from the most trivial to the important. She seemed to possess some kind of sensor that told her of not only his moods but also how to handle him. Despite the fact that he had pushed her away when she'd made the mistake of trying to understand him.

The woman confounded him, in more than one way. She rejected the one real offer he had made for their future and then made herself indispensable to him. He had thought her a partner, but now he was left to wonder whether she didn't trust that they could make this work or if she was still her father's pawn, her actions dictated by his cunning motives.

Shooting to his feet in frustration, Adonis stared down at the summary notes of the trade agreement renewal with their neighboring country that he'd been reading for the last two hours without a word sinking in.

Frustration rattled through him at his inability to parse the simplest of legalese. All he had to show for the two hours was a pounding headache behind his right eye that reminded him how ill-fitted he was for this role.

Something he spied in the depths of King Aristos's exact blue eyes. In a cruel twist of fate, his father kept calling him by his brother's name when Adonis visited him every night. Why he insisted on putting himself through the torment, he didn't know. But a part of him wanted his father to know that the son he had never wanted, the boy he'd shamed and ignored and neglected with such casual cruelty, was about to be crowned King.

Once, it would have been Adonis's wildest dream to have the right to rule Thalassos, to continue the legacy of the Vasilikos dynasty in service to it. But now that the hour was upon him, he...wasn't sure he was equipped for it.

A part of him, he thought, would forever remain that child who didn't quite belong anywhere.

Giving in to one vice, he was pouring himself fine Thalassan wine into a cut crystal glass when he sensed *her* presence.

Comfort and desire prickled through him instantly, and he felt annoyance at how easily she was sinking under his skin.

Jemima Nasar, it seemed, was a creature of habit, for she visited him every night since she had installed him here. Even though they spent several hours together going about their duties together during the interminable day. And every night, her approach was wary and calculated, as if he were a barely restrained predator that somehow happened to be her responsibility.

He sipped the wine and walked around the serene fountain at the center of the courtyard. Its water cascaded gently over smooth stones, flowing into a shallow reflecting pool. Lily pads floated on the surface of the pool, their delicate flowers adding a burst of color, along with koi fish darting below.

"Was adding the pool to this courtyard your idea?" he said. There was something extremely arousing about the efficiency and expediency with which the woman was stitching herself into his life.

He saw her startled reflection in the pool and smiled to himself. Today, she was dressed in a peach-toned silk dress. The severe cut did wonders for her hourglass figure. While it didn't bare any skin—which he would have preferred infinitely, despite his pettiness that he wouldn't touch her—it was a huge improvement on the dark, somber colors she wore to mourn his brother.

This was her Let's-Try-to-Pacify-the-Devil-Prince outfit, he knew.

Giddy anticipation swirled through him at the thought of her clad in a towel or a robe, shuffling through her wardrobe, wondering how far she should venture in dressing to please him. Not that she would admit to it.

A chunky emerald necklace—one of his engagement presents to her—glinted at her throat, almost like a collar. He loved that idea even more. Although the fact that she would be outraged at the idea of being collared by someone like him only added to his perverse satisfaction.

"Why…do you ask that?" she said, straightening her stance, as if readying for battle.

"You're already an expert at managing me and my moods, Princess. Installing some kind of serenity pool in the hopes of calming me, or even better taming me, though, seems a little naive of you. What I have seen of you so far suggests eminent practicality."

She scrunched her little button nose at that. So she didn't like being called practical, did she? "I wish I could claim the credit for the idea but it goes to the architect who designed the courtyard." She walked around the pool in the opposite direction from him, but slowly heading toward him. He had a feeling she was bracing herself for the collision. "Although, yes, the Queen insisted that I give him my input. Studying interior design and architecture was one of my dreams from a different life."

The wistfulness she buried under the casual words tugged at him. What else had she dreamed of and given up on because of her father's greed for power?

In the two weeks since he'd returned, he'd not seen her resentful of her duties even for a moment. While she might not have wanted the crown, the woman was a born queen—something his father had recognized and obtained for his golden son.

"I'm sure Thalassos has benefited from your lost dreams," he added, more to provoke her than anything else.

Her laughter boomed in the cavernous courtyard, as majestic and real as the peaks of the snow-laden hills he could see in the distance. It swept through him like a river, charging up every cell into primal desire. "If only you could employ a pinch of that diplomacy with the crown council, Your Highness."

"I'm not interested in seducing the crown council," he said. "I'm sure my tastes run too scandalous for them even if I could get them to bend over."

Pink bloomed on her cheeks and he drank it up like it was nectar. Pursing her lips in that way he was coming to recognize as her wrestling herself under control, she made a tsking sound. "Beware, Prince. Say such things and I might think them true."

"About the pool, Princess?" he said, annoyed by her refusal to accept the pull between them.

"I have no intention of taming you. Or even thinking that you need to be tamed. Whatever the crown council might whine about, King Aristos, and in his absence Prince Adamos, have brought us to the current crisis with the trade renewal treaty. Two men who have been constantly lauded would be great kings, that is. It is important to remind them and our dear neighbor that you're dealing with a major loss and these are inherited problems."

The imaginary anvil that seemed to constantly press down on his chest lifted just a little. He knew, firsthand, that Jemima wouldn't offer him empty platitudes. "I didn't see it that way."

"How can you with the entire palace laying the problem at your feet without letting you breathe?"

"I'm not sure I deserve such a fierce champion, Princess," he said, fighting the feeling of having someone in his corner. Which was a novelty in itself, but he couldn't get used to it.

She was an ally, yes, but not a friend, he reminded himself with a cynicism that was all too familiar. He had been friendless for a long time—his father and his face had seen to that.

"I think everyone deserves a champion. Even moody, brooding kings who are as volatile as the volcano that made Thalassos so fertile."

Two more steps and they would be upon each other. Adonis thought he might burst from the pulsing need he felt to taste her and touch her and consume her whole.

Would the constant inner conflict he felt at being in the palace be soothed by it, by her? Was that why he felt so drawn to her? "I'm curious, Princess. Do you visit me every evening to see my cranky, threadbare temper or to remind me that soon-to-be kings shouldn't so easily lose it?"

"If I told you the truth, Your Highness, you would not believe it."

"Enough with that address," he snapped, just as he reached her.

She looked up, and once again, he was hit by the allure of her simple beauty which came from utter acceptance of herself, he thought. Like the Aegean that surrounded the tiny island kingdom he called home, like the hills dotting its perimeter...there was something timeless and earthy and utterly enchanting about Jemima Nasar.

"As soon as you stop calling me Princess in that infuriatingly mocking tone then. I've never been princess of anything."

"And if I stop it, will you grant me the truth behind your visits, Jemima?"

She smiled then and it touched her eyes. And he thought it was her first real smile of today and that it was his. "I come here because I want to be of help. I know how over-whelming the constant demands of people dancing attendance on you can get. But I also come because I'm curious about you. I always have been."

"Because I'm the most beautiful man in the world?" he said, a bitter edge to his tone. "Or because I'm the most devilish and you would like a taste of the scandalous and the forbidden?"

"Are you forbidden to me still, Prince Adonis?" Jemima asked, her breath hovering in her throat.

It felt like one of those moments in life where one leapt off the cliff into the unknown or was forever left behind thinking what-ifs.

And Jemima was finally ready to leap.

For two weeks, she'd made this same trek from her far-off wing in the palace—Adonis had ordered that his fiancée move closer to him, out of reach of her father—to this courtyard which had morphed into his study. She had known, instinctively, how he would chafe at being cloistered inside solid walls for hours and days on end.

His escapades, as a rambunctious child and then as a teenager, were legends among the palace staff, often repeated with fondness and amusement. Yet, she hadn't seen that spark in him, that devilish humor much, since his return.

A part of her also resented that she only got this close to this stunning, intriguing man under these extreme conditions. And she wanted to change that. She wanted to know him.

Her father's autocratic commands ever since he had realized she had a working brain had turned her into a coward. But now, enough of her dithering, of not shooting the best shot she had been given after years of subservience.

She covered the last step and placed her palm on his

chest. Clad in a fitted button-down shirt, he was warm and solid under her wandering fingers. "Does my question scare the man whom nothing scares?"

His fingers steepled her wrist in a firm grip but he didn't push her touch away. "No, *pethi mou*. I'm not forbidden to you. But that's not the same as having me, is it?"

The taunt landed with silky smooth precision, taking a chip off of her courage. "No, it's not." She sighed. "You were right that I judged you and your decisions based on nothing but your reputation. On reflection though, half of that is because of my own hang-ups. It's easy to lose oneself in the games and politics that abound within these walls."

"And what is it that you want of me, Jemima?"

"Another chance. A fresh start. For just you and me."

"To begin what?"

"I meant what I said to my father and his cronies. I want friendship and trust and whatever else we can muster up between us. Especially the last for ourselves, for everything else will be tested and devoured by Thalassos. Including our ability to be parents."

A soft, utterly beautiful smile hovered on his lips. He released her wrist and she opened her mouth in protest.

Jemima felt his fingers land on her hips like she was the main character in some slow-moving, live action film. With a searing burn that should leave deep fingerprints on her willing flesh. Tilting onto her toes, she tipped forward, eager for more contact, more of his hands on her flesh, more of him.

She'd been granted a feast and she wasn't going to simply stand on the sidelines and salivate.

The tips of her breasts brushed his hard chest and breath whooshed out of her, as if she were a child's balloon deflating during the festivities of the National Day Parade.

"I'm not the brightest when it comes to words, Princess. My headache after two hours of reading those legal documents confirms it. So please clarify your intentions for me. Also, 'whatever else we can muster up between us' sounds…" he scrunched that blade of a nose in distaste and Jemima wondered if she could get away with calling him adorable, "…tedious and dry and uninspired. You should know that I thrive on challenge."

"I want to see if there's passion between us, Adonis," she said, grabbing the bull by the horns. "And if that can be the thing that adds another brick to our foundation. Because that cannot be dictated by the crown or the council or the cynical media. It would be all ours. Only ours. And honestly, the idea of owning some small part of this arrangement makes me—"

His mouth sealed over hers, stealing her breath, her thoughts, and her conflicting emotions. In those first moments, Jemima clung to him like a limpet. And perhaps sensing her stiffness, the Prince softened the press of his lips immediately.

Slowly, she relaxed and her other senses rushed into focus, bringing more awareness and keener yearnings.

For a hard, leanly muscled man, he had the softest lips. The taste of wine and something darker he had indulged in dribbled down from him to her lips, into her throat and further below to her chest, to pool into liquid sensation at her center.

One touch of his lips and she could feel her entire world tilt and shake, rearranging itself into one with more color and light and sensation.

No wonder she hadn't forgotten that first kiss, and her only kiss, all these years later. Even as a naive, utterly inexperienced eighteen-year-old, she had sensed the pull between them. Not that she had any more experience now, she thought, as he moved those sinuous lips over hers in a slow dance. But she had the bone-deep conviction that this was right.

One of the few right things in a life full of nasty twists and turns.

His fingers edged around her waist, claiming more and more ground, but Jemima sensed him withholding, treating her as if she were a porcelain figurine. As if he wasn't sure she wanted this.

If she was doing this, she was going all in.

Sinking her fingers into the nape of his neck, she dragged her breasts against his rock-hard chest. Their raw groans rent the air. "Kiss me properly, please. As you want, Adonis. Not this tedious, dry version you have decided is my worth," she said, meeting his gaze.

His smile was a delight when she tasted it with her tongue and that was the last coherent thought she had.

Adonis sipped at her lips like she tasted better than the finest Thalassan wine, nibbled like she was his favorite treat, and when she dug her teeth into the lush sweep of his lower lip, he devoured her as if she were a feast to a starving man.

Even the shattering of his wine flute on the tiles couldn't fracture the urgency that beat at them.

Jemima gasped when he lifted her and brought her to the chaise longue where she'd found him fast asleep one night. As if she were a sweet, light feminine thing made of feathers instead of the sturdy, dependable accessory she had turned herself into for her father and his brother.

The burgundy leather was soft against her fingers as she gripped it while Adonis knelt over her, caging her.

For just a second, as she read the naked hunger pull-

ing at his features, she felt a sudden attack of bashfulness
about her body. Round and plump, she was no man's fantasy of a woman but she had always loved her body for all
that it had given her.

"No," Adonis said, pressing a finger between her brows.
"Do not let the world intrude on this moment, Princess.
Like you said, this is for us." He leaned down and touched
his forehead to hers, his warm, wine-scented breath coast-
ing over her lips. "And I need this, need to see you unravel so badly."

"It's not the world interfering, Prince," she said, clasping
his cheek. He leaned into the touch like some great cat, willing to be petted, and more than desire lashed through her.

"Touch me. Wherever and however, you want. All the
madness that's swirling around me right now, and the grief
that haunts me…" Blue eyes searched hers. "I need escape, Jemima."

His whispered command filled her with liquid longing to the brim.

She'd never counted it as such but her father first and
then Adamos at his turn, had deprived her of even the
simple comfort of touch.

That Adonis not only needed it, but demanded it openly
felt like her most secret yearning given color and shape
and the wings to fly.

Without curbing her greed or worrying about betraying it, she ran her hand over his shoulders, neck and back,
finally settling them over his chest. The buttons popped
open on his shirt when she tugged. A sigh escaped her
when she discovered warm, taut skin. Christos, the man
was hewn in rock, every inch of him cut and lean, as if a
master sculptor had removed all the excess.

Jemima explored the planes of his chest and back with

increasing fervor, eager to feel it against her own body. Already, the idea of rubbing her curves against all that muscle filled her with unbearable heat.

The whole time, Adonis bent his head as if he were being granted a benediction.

"Tell me what interferes with the need I sense in you and I will banish it to the ends of the earth."

"I think you're getting the hang of this whole king thing, Prince."

He grinned but the solemnity didn't leave his gaze. "I want no doubts between us, Jemima. Not when it comes to this."

She looked into his electric blue eyes and made another leap. Being forced to be vulnerable had made her grow an abundance of prickles but being asked to bare it so that he could soothe it away…was a new experience. And she had a feeling this man would never mock her for her own short-comings—real or imagined or forced on her by the world.

Feeling more than possessive, she grazed her nails over one flat nipple and then lower. The rippling contractions of his abdominal muscles, the soft graze of the sparse chest hair…everything about him was a study in sensu-ality. "You're perfection, Your Highness. A Greek god among us mortals. And I'm not beautiful or sophisticated or experienced, measured by any standard or scale."

He leaned further down and Jemima felt cool air brush her bare skin before she heard the rip of her flimsy silk dress.

She could feel her heavy breasts rise and fall, the nip-ples eagerly peaking under the nude lace bra. Her belly was soft and round, like the rest of her, a testament to her snacking late at night and comfort eating.

Of course when she had first been engaged to Adamos,

the palace team had added a nutritionist and a trainer and a weight loss expert to her team. Jemima had never been so angry in her whole life. "I like my body just as it is," she said now, feeling compelled to defend herself. "But the world is tiresome, constantly telling me that I could and should look thinner and better. Whiskey and chocolates... I'll never give them up."

She heard his soft laugh at the end.

"Open your eyes, Jemima."

Her eyes flew open to find him studying her with naked desire etched on his face. Spine arching into his touch, she eagerly followed the lazy trails his fingers drew over her belly and lower. Her flesh quivered under his nakedly admiring gaze.

"Give me your hand."

She did.

"Do you trust me in this?"

She nodded and added, "I do. In the end, it has been that easy." If she sounded baffled, he seemed to understand that too. For he gave her a swift nod. The same sense of awe she felt was reflected in his expression.

Her breath came in sharp pants as he brought her hand to move down his chest, past that concrete slab of his abdomen and then to rest against his...crotch.

His length was hard and throbbing already. She gasped as it grew impossibly harder under her curious fingers. Desire pooled at her core, making her lace panties damp. Emboldened by his sharp exhale, she clasped him fully and squeezed.

A pained grunt fell from his luscious mouth. "You cannot doubt my body's reaction to you, Princess. You rendered me so even all those years ago with one kiss." Something flashed in his eyes and she sensed his reluctance and then resolve. "Remember that time when I came to meet Adamos in Paris two, three years ago?"

It was the one trip where she'd been allowed to accompany the Crown Prince, not that Adamos had liked the idea. But the Queen had insisted that they start presenting a united front to the world.

"At that charity gala," Adonis continued, his gaze far off, "you wore a rust-colored dress that hugged your curves. I was so jealous of Adamos and disgusted by myself. I turned hard as stone when you slipped on the steps and I had to catch you. One brush against you and I was nothing but pure want. It was another nail in the coffin of not returning to Thalassos." A sound that was nearly beastly emanated from his throat, snatching him from her in this moment. "I coveted the relationship he had with my father, maybe even his crown, and then his fiancée."

"No, come back to me, Adonis," she whispered, pushing onto her elbow and kissing his jaw. The blond scruff on his cheeks tickled her lips. "Adamos's death has nothing to do with you. Surely you know that."

When he didn't respond, her chest ached and her courage flared. With her breasts rubbing against his arm in a wanton gesture, she captured his lips with hers. Then swept her tongue inside the warm cavern of his mouth.

His fingers tightened on her flesh. And in a matter of breaths, she got the hungry Adonis back.

She arched deeper into his touch when he pushed her bra down and cupped her breasts. "You're gorgeous, Princess." The hard nipples prodded and poked at his palm, eager for attention.

Then it was his tongue dancing and swiping and licking at the peak before he sucked her breast into his mouth.

Pleasure shot through every nerve ending as if she had

been electrocuted and she was nothing but spiraling sensations and cavernous need. The more he stroked and nipped and licked, the more the flames grew and the emptier her core felt. She wanted the climb to the peak but God, she craved the free fall at his hands desperately.

The rasp of a zipper barely registered and soon, she had his shaft in her hands. Her eyes widened and an unbearable ache unspooled in her pelvis as she ran her fingers over the thick, veiny length of him. Then there was the perfect V of muscles leading to the throbbing length. Her throat worked as she tried to form the words. "I've never been allowed to explore a simple want or desire or my sexuality in any way. Which means I don't have the expertise I like to have in everything I do, Prince."

His answer was a quick nip of her lower lip. "All that matters is that you want this as much as I do, Princess."

She nodded vigorously. "And you do?"

"Everything about my reputation is not true, Jemima," he said, tweaking her nose. "Being a daredevil is my brand, yes, and that attracts a certain kind of attention. I don't push it away when it gives me free publicity. Like the expectations placed on you, the media fuels as much as it feeds the public."

"And they have always been extra interested in you because you were always a rebel."

The smooth, olive-toned skin of his shoulders glinted in the soft lighting when he shrugged. "The myth becomes bigger and juicier than the man. But enough of me, Princess," he said, whispering the words into the arch of her neck where her pulse was begging to explode. "And just a kiss won't do if you want to explore this."

"I want more, Adonis. All of it."

His grin this time was all Devil Prince, his perfect white

teeth flashing at her. With his designer cut ruffled by her possessive fingers, his sinuous lips dark pink and glistening wet, he looked utterly debauched. That it was at her hands...added an extra zing.

"We should wait to be married for all of it, Princess. I don't want the damned crown council questioning our child's legitimacy."

She nodded, thankful for his common sense when she had none. "I...went off birth control that night you agreed to my proposal."

"We need a better story to tell our children and grandchildren than that, *ne*?"

Dear God, was the man a closet romantic? Was anything the world knew about the Devil Prince actually true? "Why? Does it hurt the Devil Prince's masculinity if it is said that he was rescued by his wife and queen-to-be from an untenable solution?"

His laughter was genuine and breathtaking for that. "No, *yineka mou*. I have a feeling my masculinity will be thriving in your hands."

She laughed then, a strange sort of awe filling her. A grasping greed filled her. The more he gave her, the more she wanted of him. "Did you know that it is customary that Thalassan princes give their brides-to-be an engagement present of their choice? There's a story about how Queen Isadora didn't use hers for a long time."

A sudden flash of anguish shone in his eyes before he chased it off with a slow smile. His fingers danced on her belly. "I love the greed I see in your eyes. Clearly, there's something you want from me, Princess."

Jemima didn't miss the thread of mockery that entered the last few words. But she forged on, refusing to let his mistrust of her ruin the moment. "Give me one thing the world doesn't know about you. Anything. Even as trivial as your favorite dessert."

He looked thunderstruck for so long that Jemima felt foolish. When he shook it off, he searched her eyes. "You're a strange woman, Jemima Nasar," he finally quipped. His defined chest rose and fell with his decision. "I have been celibate for six years. Which is why all this rubbing and writhing is driving me crazy."

Shock robbed her of thought or speech for long moments. "But...they...the tabloids..." Meeting his eyes, she pushed the doubts away. "May I know the reason?"

"Some other time. Right now, I want us both to have one gloriously high point amidst the circus we've been thrust into."

"That sounds perfect," she said, backing off. He'd already given her so much more than she'd expected in this relationship, and she didn't mean just the drugging kisses. She trailed her fingers down his stomach, and then traced the veins on his shaft. "Tell me how to give you what you need. I... I want to satisfy you."

"Oh, Princess." He pulled her fingers over his thick shaft, the tendons in his neck showing taut when she rubbed her thumb pad over the soft head. "Keep stroking me, *ne*?"

She nodded and applied herself like a diligent student eager to please her master. Touching him, stroking his hard length, hearing grunts and groans fall from his lips only pushed her up to the edge.

Slowly, his fingers pushed past the hem of her dress, mapping and tracing her thick thighs and finally landing on her pulsing and wet and agonizingly needy core.

"All that uptight efficiency and beneath it," his whisper

was a gravelly torment as he traced her folds with reverence, "you're melting for me, Princess?"

Jemima had no answer.

A very deliberate swipe of his fingers from her clit to her slit had her jerking her spine and squeezing his cock harder. He half groaned and half laughed, a serrated sound that tore through the thin threads of her frayed control.

"I'm reminded of my science lessons, Jemima," he whispered at her temple, his lean body somehow half prostrate over hers and yet, not giving her any of his weight. "Something about equal and opposite reactions."

Then he, with excruciating slowness that threatened to spin her out of her own skin, fed one long finger into her channel. Every nerve ending she possessed flared with a brilliant light when he added another finger and then went exploring inside her until he found the perfect spot.

Electric sensation made her lift her hips.

When he plunged his fingers in and out, hitting and pressing at that spot, she followed the rhythm, her entire body dancing at the edge of that cliff. All the while he told her what a good girl she was to take him like that and how wet and tight she was and how incredibly hard the sight and sound and feel of her wanton response made him. The rogue even said she was a damn queen already, the way her body sang for him.

And the proof was in her hands, she noted with a feral satisfaction.

Even with her wrist cramping, she kept stroking his shaft, determined to bring him over with her.

Moans and groans and unintelligible sounds rushed from her mouth and her pulsing flesh, adding to the lilting cadence of the fountain. She protested when he pulled her hand off his cock. Laughing, he replaced it with her other, and then covered it with his own free hand.

They stroked and caressed each other, to the background of their rasping breaths and hitching moans.

Jemima spiraled first, thrown into a maelstrom of pleasure, shattered and broken, her muscles contracting and milking his fingers in rhythmic pulls that made her eyes roll back in her head. A bone-deep satisfaction and languor suffused her but she couldn't let it keep her from watching him.

As if he was thinking the exact thing, Adonis said in a gravelly voice, "Give me your eyes, Jemima. Stay with me."

The black of his eyes ate the blue, and taut lines pulled at his mouth. His fingers covering hers pulled at his shaft in fast, brutal strokes. Then he roared, throwing his head back, his olive skin shining with sweat, his lips slackening, his tapered hips pumping greedily. It was a stunning sight. And would remain only hers for the rest of their lives, Jemima decided with a possessive instinct she'd never known before.

Hot spurts of his release coated her skin. She spread her fingers over his panting chest, loving the hard thud of his heart under her fingers. "You look exquisite, Princess, painted in shades of me," he said, rubbing his release into the curve of her breast.

Jemima felt branded, owned, possessed.

In the dark gleam of his eyes, she saw the same intense instincts that flowed through her at how hotly they had exploded together.

Reaching down, his mouth found hers in a fast, hungry kiss and Jemima knew that the Devil Prince was already carving a place for himself in her life, her thoughts, and maybe even her untried heart.

CHAPTER SEVEN

ADONIS DIDN'T REMEMBER when or if ever he had held a lover like he was holding Jemima, or if he had even stayed with one after satiating his base impulses.

But then, before he had decided on proving to himself that he would stop the path of self-destruction just to spite his father, he had been an angry, aggressive, reactive animal with little common sense.

Only when he had stopped sleeping around with anything that moved, and stopped drinking, and doing foolish stunts just to feel something, and fully focused on building his career, had he, for the first time in his life, known his true self. Until then, he had been nothing but a construct, like some horror hall of mirrors, reflecting nothing but reactive, destructive behaviors, designed to court his father's approval, then his attention, and then to provoke shame and anger in him.

All of which he had succeeded at enormously.

Honing self-discipline and control and focus had become another daredevil stunt, another way to test himself, because without it, he would have imploded.

And when control had slowly become a growing muscle and he had begun rebuilding himself from all the twisted pieces of his self-worth, he'd been filled with disgust and pity at his previous behaviors.

He had been no better than a child, even at twenty-five, desperate for his father's affection and approval. While he knew he hadn't fully cured himself of the disease, he'd gotten rid of most of the symptoms through distance and by hardening his heart.

He had been at his healthiest—physically and mentally—when he'd been thousands of miles from his father and Thalassos. Still, it had been the life of an ascetic, because his mind operated in binaries, in all or nothing. He had no deep connections to anyone.

The last thing he'd expected when he'd returned, especially without the comforting buffer his brother provided between him and his father—was this kind of respite amidst the chaos.

And yet... Jemima was here, in his arms, soft and sated and real. More real and giving than any relationship he had had in his life.

The unhealed part of him still didn't trust her fully and neither could it come up with some devious reasoning behind her actions.

"You're off somewhere again, Prince. Not that I'm complaining."

Her whisper was thready against his forearm, though she didn't try to move out of the cradle of his thighs. When a cool breeze flew in, carrying the night's chill with it, she shivered. Adonis rubbed his palms over her bare arms and pulled her tighter against him.

"But since you aren't restless or frothing at the mouth as you were at this morning's meeting, I shall happily take credit for it."

The minx was damned good at reading him right and then provoking him. "If you have a question, Princess, I'd always prefer you ask it than speculate on my motives. The entire world already paints a picture of me that pleases itself and had no basis in truth."

She scooted up on the chaise longue, rubbing that delightfully round ass against his groin. A groan rumbled up through his chest, his cock all too ready for action again. He gripped her ample hips none too gently and bent his mouth to her ear. "Two more days, Jemima. Try teasing me like that then."

Her breath came in raspy huffs as she said, "How will you punish me?"

"I will simply lift you and impale you on my sword, Princess. And then I'll make you ride me, as I intend to be a lazy, arrogant king. Maybe I'll have a mirror installed against the opposite wall and watch those luscious breasts bounce as you make yourself come."

Tilting her head into an awkward position against his neck, she looked at him upside down, the thick curves of her lips damp and trembling. The amber of her eyes glinted brilliantly, desire shining through like a flame inside her. "You think you scandalize me?" she said, digging her teeth into his chin with a casual intimacy that floored him. "All it does is fill me with eagerness for our wedding night." Her hands swept over his body, stroking, pinching, constantly touching.

As a child, as a teenager, as an adult, touch had always been his primary need. And he'd always been denied it or had sought it in the worst ways possible.

That this woman who had come into his life through a cruel twist of fate would grant him the thing he had always craved…felt too good to be true, or real, or permanent.

Christos, he couldn't let her entangle him into believing that this was anything more than passion and partnership at best. He had been her choice under the worst kind of duress just as he was Thalassos's. She had only wanted him when he was a challenge, as a stolen memory for one kiss. Not two weeks later, she'd bowed her head, accepting her betrothal to his brother.

He couldn't forget that he had been nothing but excitement and fun for one evening to her, couldn't let this forced connection dig its claws deeper into him. Couldn't forget that he was the Prince of Thalassos for her. Nothing more.

When she'd have moved up and kissed him, he shifted his head away from the touch and slowly untangled her from him. The bastard he was, he didn't even try to make it look casual or as if he weren't rejecting her touch. "I think playtime is over, Princess," he said, infusing easy lethargy into his tone.

"What?" she whispered.

Steadying her shoulders against the lounger, he threw his legs to the side and stood up. "I still have to finish reading those damned summary notes and come to some sort of conclusion," he said, without meeting her gaze. "You should go back to your wing and rest. No doubt your calendar is as packed as mine is for the next couple of days."

His skin, warm moments ago with her lush curves bare and pressed up against him, instantly chilled as he walked to his desk. He tightened his jaw against the soft sounds of her straightening her dress and hair, fighting the urge to wrap his arms around her.

What he didn't expect was that she would precede him to the neatly tucked away bar at the rustic wall and pour a finger of whiskey into a tumbler. She drank it in one long gulp, giving him the perfect view of the elegant arch of her neck.

Just like that, heated longing filled him. It had taken every ounce of willpower he had to resist her innocent demand that she wanted everything now and wait for their wedding night. A primal, near-animal part of him wanted to fill her with his seed and get her pregnant as soon as possible. It was the first time in his life that fate or the universe or whatever higher power was out there had granted him a boon. He wasn't going to lose it.

Jemima was the sort of woman who would upend the world for her children, would give her undying loyalty to every commitment she made. Having children with her, he knew would create a bond between them that he didn't know how to create, or want to create, in any other way. It felt like a cheat, a shortcut for binding her to him, without giving her anything of value in return. Getting her emotionally tangled in him, in them, without investing his own emotions.

But he didn't care.

Her true loyalty, her clever mind, everything she had to give would be his then. The one gift Thalassos was giving him as its king, and he would claim as his due.

"I won't be able to wind down for a while," she said, pinning her hair into a tight knot. He couldn't look away from her breasts thrust up by the action. "Why not talk through the sticky points of the treaty with me?"

"How, if you aren't aware of its contents?" he snapped. "It's a stupid rule that you shouldn't be allowed into the meetings until the coronation. I too was an outsider until two weeks ago. Even with all their conniving heads put together, those old men don't have your common sense."

Whatever she might have thought of his sudden cold treatment of her, his praise made her eyes light up with humor. And he remembered how she had gushed damp when he'd called her a good girl.

Could his regal, efficient, damned smart queen-to-be

have a praise kink? "Careful, Your Highness. Or your subjects might call you whipped."

"If that's what I get for listening to the smartest person in the palace, then so be it."

"So use that intelligence, Adonis," she said, urgency seeping into her words. "It's at your disposal. Just imagine if you can solve this problem and pass a new treaty as your first act as King of Thalassos. It not only sets up your regime spectacularly but it cements your place among the people. No one can question your—"

"I don't like seeing you scared, Jemima," he said, despite his resolve to keep her at a distance. Something about the innocent being bullied had always riled him up.

Her throat worked as she tried to smooth her features. "I don't trust my father. You're the answer to so many wishes and the target of such ill wills, Adonis. And not just because you're Queen Isadora's son but because you've seen the world outside and are not bogged down by outdated traditions. Just in two weeks, you have earned my trust."

The weight of her faith sat like a boulder on his chest while his own behavior of moments ago shamed him. And he knew that he had to extend that very same faith at some point. That he had to trust that she wanted the best for the kingdom, even if their relationship couldn't be more than duty.

Clasping her hand with his, he brought her to his enormous desk. "I don't have a list of sticking points because I didn't understand the legalese." He smoothed out his tone, refused to dress up his words with either pity or importance. It had taken him a long while to see himself as whole, as not deficient, and he wouldn't change that for anyone.

"I have a host of learning disabilities that I have addressed with therapy and such. But that bloody tome is too dense for me to get through without professional help."

Shock made Jemima still, flushing her with a cold chill. His admission was matter-of-fact, if tinged at the end with frustration.

Suddenly, a lot of tiny tidbits she'd heard about him around the palace made perfect sense. Admiration and worry filled her chest. She spoke with care, managing to make her tone free of either. "And you don't want to betray your condition to even your team?"

"I have two assistants I would trust with my life. One is off on maternity leave and the other is unable to travel long distances due to his chronic illness."

"And yet you told me about…it," she said, disbelief ringing through her.

"You're right that either we trust each other or we don't." His gaze held hers. "It can't be doled out through some calculated process."

"Am I allowed to ask any questions about it or why you—"

"It's a set of disabilities I've lived with for thirty-four years. The last thing I want now is to make this about me when Thalassos stands at the line of debt or war. Let's focus on how to find a solution to this trade problem. Our excessive, extravagant wedding is only going to push us deeper into the debt hole."

Jemima nodded, burying the million questions that wanted to spring out of her mouth, her heart suddenly heavy with ache for this Prince who was unlike any man she'd ever known.

It took them three hours to figure out how to listen to each other, how to get their ideas across and then how to understand the problem that was bogging down the trade treaty that should have been signed eighteen months ago.

At the end of it, Jemima sat sprawled in the armchair in the most un-queenly manner, her fingers wrapped around a whiskey tumbler that she was precariously balancing on her belly.

Adonis, for his part, had taken to the floor thirty minutes into their discussion, clad only in linen pants that highlighted the tight cut of his hips and deliciously taut ass, claiming that he thought better when he performed his grounding exercises. When he was moving and interacting with the world around him.

Halfway through his stretches, she had muttered that while the routine might be grounding him, it distracted her like hell.

In response, he'd kneeled in front of her—this tall, gorgeous stud of a man, buried his hands in her hair and kissed the hell out of her.

It struck her suddenly that Queen Isadora had been exactly right. Apparently, the more honestly she gave of herself and demanded from him, the more Adonis would give her.

After that detour, Jemima finally finished reading the dense summary and highlighted the crux of the problem for him. His anger and frustration at bureaucratic red tape that bogged down the matter were as hypnotic to watch as when he grabbed a pen and started doodling.

It hadn't taken him long to understand that Ephyra was struggling with the worst economic crisis in decades, with a young queen leading it, and was therefore digging its heels in.

And finally, the brilliance of his unique approach when he'd come up with the suggestion for creating a joint adventure tourism company with their neighbor Ephyra, using its natural beauty and Thalassos's technical advances.

A new partnership, he declared, pooling resources and technology rather than constantly being at each other's necks.

Exhausted and yet somehow wired, Jemima stared at the man who clearly was still tormented by the rift with his father, who didn't see himself as the right man to rule the nation, who spoke of Thalassos with such deep love and loyalty...and marveled at how he was an even better fit than Adamos to be the King of Thalassos.

A chill enveloped her as she wondered how close Prince Adonis was to the man she'd always imagined would come into her life and sweep her off her feet, despite the fact that even dreaming had been forbidden to her.

It terrified her that her fairy-tale fantasy had somehow turned real and that it might all disappear in a puff of smoke if she didn't hold onto it with both hands and her heart.

CHAPTER EIGHT

ADONIS STARTLED AT the sudden strength in the older man's clasp as he knelt in front of his father and took his hand.

In front of his eyes, the gold-veined marble floor blurred, making his knees quake. His coronation day had dawned bright and clear, with the capital city dressed like a bride. That he and Jemima, after two days of intense discussions with their teams, had a solution for the trade treaty problem and he was about to meet Ephyra's ambassador soon—without the crown council's permission—set the right note. Still, something in him resisted fully giving in to the day.

What had begun as a hazy headache between the royal procession and the anointing by the high priestess had turned into a viselike clamp by the time he had been required to recite the Oath of Kingship with his hand on the Scroll of Kings.

Adonis couldn't admit it to another soul, not even Jemima maybe, but the fact was that he was overwhelmed by the sanctity of the rituals and could feel the shadow of his brother Adamos press down upon him with each step of the long, laborious ceremony. His brother's absence felt like a void in his heart and yet, he wouldn't be standing here if Adamos were present.

And nothing in his life, no extravagantly lethal stunt

that he had performed, had readied him for this moment. For this responsibility.

"Give me your blessing, Father," he whispered, having been ordered to kneel in front of the King by the high priestess.

"Adonis…" King Aristos said, with such sudden urgency that Adonis looked up, warmth a flickering kennel inside him. Finally, would his father give him one measly moment of recognition, if not approval?

With the sun at its zenith, bright golden light streamed through the large stained-glass windows of the Grand Sanctuary Hall within the palace. But only darkness and confusion dwelled in his father's eyes.

Until the moment he suddenly wasn't confused. His blue eyes turned shrewd, almost calculating.

"Adonis," he repeated, his hands reaching for his son's shoulders. "What are you doing here? Why are we here in the Grand Sanctuary?"

Out of the corner of his eye, Adonis saw his mother and Jemima move in closer. More to protect the King's sudden confusion from prying eyes than to listen to Adonis's whispered attempt at a conversation.

"I'm to be crowned King, Father. I come to seek your blessing and words of wisdom." The words felt like ashes on his tongue and still, a tiny flame of hope flickered.

The King's head reared back, a sudden glint in his eyes. "King? You?" Harsh laughter escaped his mouth. "The Crown of Thalassos is not for you, Adonis. It would have been better if you had perished in the crash instead of Adamos. You're nothing but my taint, my shame, a crow in the cuckoo's nest, for all that Isadora tried to hide it. A maid's son and no more."

It was the first time Adonis heard the words straight

from the King's mouth. Of course, he had known the truth of his birth, having heard it during a heated discussion between his parents, hiding himself behind one of those bloody columns that littered the palace.

He had been nineteen, already a captain in the air force, and more than anything in the world, wanted to be his father's son, to be loved and appreciated like Adamos had been.

Instead, the bitter truth was that he was the son of a maid his father had either forced himself on, or black-mailed, or simply commanded with his bloody royal authority to submit, when his mother had been heavily pregnant with Adamos. The great King Aristos was nothing but another predictably powerful man who preyed on those that depended on him for their livelihood.

Of course, Queen Isadora, being principled and refusing to compromise and wanting to teach her cheating, conniving, power-bloated husband a lesson, had brought Adonis to the palace as an infant, to be raised alongside her own son. As her own son.

His mother had been careful enough to make it look like Adonis had been born during the time she had spent in Paris, during a temporary separation from King Aristos, persuading him by threatening a scandal of disastrous proportions. Knowing full well that King Aristos would have to see his mistake grow up in his own household, in the palace, as his younger son, as another contender to the throne.

She had also, whatever her feeling toward her husband, loved Adonis as if he were truly her own, trying her best to protect him from the King's fury. But neglect and apathy were much harder to fight than direct cruelty, for his father had never made even eye contact with Adonis.

He had never forgiven Adonis for existing, for being the walking, talking symbol of his weakness. And when a host of learning disabilities had plagued him as a growing boy, the King's satisfaction had been cruel and prevalent, for he had started calling Adonis a crow in the nest.

"Hush, my love," his mother said, bringing a glass of water to King Aristos's mouth, her eyes filled with anguish and anger. Like a puppet whose strings were pulled, the King sat back in his seat, his eyes panicking like a child's.

Drawing back her shoulders, his mother pinned Adonis with the same intensity that she had used to talk to him as a confused, desperate-to-please boy. "You're my son, Adonis and the Prince of this realm. Do your duty by Thalassos. Make me and your brother and all the Thalassans that love and trust you justice."

Adonis nodded, tried to swallow past the hard rock lodged in his throat and got to his feet. And when his gaze clashed with Jemima's shocked amber one, he pretended to not see the fat tears that his new queen didn't let fall.

A part of him was suddenly glad that he had bucked tradition and married Jemima in a quiet, private ceremony at dawn that morning with no one but his mother present. Still the obedient daughter, she hadn't liked going through it without her father present. But he had insisted on it and the Queen's request that it was better that way, with Adamos's death so recent, had finally convinced her.

Even as he felt Jemima's inquiring gaze on his face, Adonis refused to meet hers. He didn't want to see her shock or her disgust or her distaste at the dirty secret of his birth. Her pity would be both the best he could hope for and the worst to bear.

Hardening himself against the tumult, he proceeded toward the royal balcony that overlooked the courtyard where thousands of Thalassans waited to bestow their cheer and trust and blessing on him.

But everything inside him craved freedom from the pain, craved a challenge, craved something that would take him so close to the edge that all the conflicting emotions pummeling him from all sides would burn out in flames.

She was married.

To Adonis Vasilikos, possibly the most beautiful man in the world.

She, Jemima Nasar, of cunning mind and round body and far too ambitious bones, as one tabloid magazine had called her after their engagement had become public, was now not only the Devil Prince's convenient wife but Thalassan Queen.

She was married to the man she'd spun fantasies around as a teenage girl, the man she'd stolen a kiss from on one bold, daring evening of her life, the man who now held her entire future in the palm of his hands.

The man she'd just learned carried a torment no boy should have had to shoulder, who had bent but not buckled at the casual cruelty with which the King had greeted him at the most important moment of his life. The man who was a bloody legend and a billionaire in his own right, who had always marched to his own drum and forged his own path.

In the infinitesimal moment that their eyes had met, he hadn't let the strain seep through into his expression.

Suddenly, she realized what a sacrifice it was that Adonis Vasilikos was making by returning and agreeing to be crowned King of Thalassos. And that she was part of the sacrifice that he was making out of some blind loyalty to the mother who had raised him as her own, to the kingdom he had once called home.

Another horrifying thought struck her as her royal attendants stripped her out of the heavy velvet gown she'd worn for the coronation, to ready her for the public tribute Adonis had planned to honor Adamos's memory.

Was that why he had insisted on the quiet ceremony for the wedding? Had he taken stock after the endless rituals and meetings of the last two days and decided he'd had enough of the pathetic pomp that he didn't even want?

Jemima met her own gaze in the full-length mirror, automatically lifting her legs and arms as the attendants pulled a burnt-copper-colored dress over her head. The color instantly made her golden skin shimmer and she made a note to thank the new stylist that had come on board with Adonis's team.

She tugged at a couple of pins and her silky waves tumbled out of the complicated knot they'd been set into. In the reflection, her gaze fell on her engagement ring and the plain platinum and gold band, an inexplicable ache making her chest heavy.

Was she anything but a part of the sacrifice he was taking on for the greater good? Had she been deluding herself that they could have a meaningful relationship?

He had barely made eye contact with her as they had made vows to each other, after he had insisted on a secret, dawn wedding that was nothing like what she had imagined.

Even the Grand Hall of the Palace, with its opulent high ceilings adorned with intricate frescoes depicting the history of Thalassos, only seemed to mock her. The arched windows and the stained-glass panes, filled with dawn's pink light, couldn't banish the solemnity of the occasion.

Jemima, surprising herself, had resented the hell out of the whole damn thing. She hadn't wanted a grand celebration or extravagant festivities but she had wanted a ceremony that was meaningful to both of them. She'd wanted to choose a beautiful dress, wear her mother's jewelry, have her brother present for the occasion.

She'd wanted to honor the tenuous but real connection between her and Adonis and she wanted to nurture it without guilt or grief or any of the million constraints that seemed to surround them.

And now that she had learned of the final piece of the puzzle that made up her mysterious husband, Jemima understood why he had pulled away, why he had turned their wedding into nothing but a somber ceremony he had to go through. She had a feeling she was nothing but another piece of duty he had tacked on for the good of his country. And having come to know the honorable, kind man he was under all the suffocating masks, she detested being no more than a placeholder for him.

The sky was a brilliant blue, the May sun casting a golden glow over the capital city as Jemima arrived at the main plaza—a sprawling open space surrounded by ancient buildings, with the palace looming majestically in the background. Banners and flags waved in the gentle breeze, adding color and movement to the scene. A large crowd had gathered, filling the air with a buzz of anticipation and excitement.

She took her place on the roof of the plaza, her eyes scanning the sea of faces below. The entire kingdom seemed to have turned out for the air show, a tribute by Adonis to Adamos. The plaza was alive with noise—children laughing, vendors calling out their wares, and the buzzing hum of conversations. Yet, amidst the clamor, a sense of solemnity lingered.

When the crowd's attention shifted to her, Jemima wore her practiced smile and waved, feeling wholly like a fake.

She was their Queen now.

But first in her mind, she was Adonis's wife. He hadn't even kissed her at the hurried wedding, and whatever real foundation she'd imagined between them suddenly felt like a pipe dream.

The sound of engines roaring to life pulled her from her thoughts. She looked up, her breath catching in her throat as she spotted the sleek fighter jets cutting through the sky.

Adonis had planned this air show himself, a gesture of remembrance for his brother. She knew how much Adamos had meant to him, despite the fact that they hadn't seen each other in so long.

The crowd's excitement peaked as the jets climbed higher, their silver bodies glinting in the sunlight.

Jemima's heart raced with a mix of awe and fear.

Adonis was up there, leading the formation. She had heard stories of his daring feats as a fighter pilot, but seeing him in action was an entirely different experience.

The jets performed a series of breathtaking maneuvers, looping and twisting in perfect synchrony. The crowd gasped and cheered with each daring stunt. Jemima's eyes never left Adonis's jet, admiration and anxiety knotting in her chest. He was so close to the edge, pushing the limits of what seemed possible. She feared for his safety, yet couldn't help but be captivated by his skill and courage.

As the jets flew in a tight formation, drawing a heart in the sky with their contrails, Jemima felt a pang of sorrow. She wondered if he would ever open to her truly, about his grief over Adamos, about the wound his father fueled even now.

The final stunt was the most daring of all—a verti-

cal climb followed by a sudden nosedive, pulling up just
before hitting the ground. The crowd held its breath as
Adonis executed the maneuver flawlessly.

The plaza erupted in applause and cheers, a thunder-
ous tribute to the fallen prince and the skill of his brother.

When it was time for her to leave the plaza and greet
him in public for the first time since his coronation,
Jemima found her hands were trembling, her emotions
a tangled mess. Her heart seemed to have permanently
lodged in her throat, cutting off her breath.

She was proud of Adonis, awed by his bravery, yet terrified by the risks he took. Their marriage was nothing
but a partnership born out of necessity. He kept reminding
her of that through his actions, and yet, she couldn't keep
her heart from weaving around his magnetic presence.

Clearly, the man was going to make zero changes to his
lifestyle, just because he was married or because he was
the damned King upon whom millions depended. Maybe
she could ask him for lessons on how to harden herself.

As the jets returned to the ground and Adonis climbed
out of his cockpit, the crowd surged forward, eager to con-
gratulate their new king.

Jemima watched him, her heart aching with confusion
and longing. He was a hero to the people of Thalassos, a
symbol of strength and resilience. But to her, he was an
enigma, a man she barely understood.

Adonis made his way through the crowd, his eyes
searching for her. When their gazes finally met, Jemima
felt a flicker of connection, a reminder of the bond they
had been braiding in the past two weeks. But today—the
somber wedding, the coronation and now this stunt of
his—proved that it was tenuous at best.

As he approached, she forced a smile, determined to

play her part, especially in front of his adoring public. "That was incredible, Your Majesty," she said, her voice steady despite the turmoil inside.

His thigh pressed against hers, as security created a tight bubble around them, keeping the screaming public at bay behind steel barricades.

Jemima jerked at the contact, feeling as if burned. How foolish had she been to think she would become at least a factor he would consider in his life…

Nothing and no one would tame him, remember?

Adonis quirked a brow at her plastic politeness and her panic to put distance between them. "Thank you, Jemima. Although I must say I'm used to much more effusive welcomes after such an exhilarating stunt."

"I'm not your groupie, Your Majesty, but your queen. It is possible you might have forgotten the little fact since you would barely meet my eyes during the ceremony."

"Is that a complaint I hear, Jem? Did you want a week of festivities, a princess's ball gown, and an enchanted ball?"

"You will not shame me for expecting the minimum out of this life, Adonis. As for the stunt—"

"It was for Adamos," he said, interrupting her.

She placed a hand on his arm as they reached the dais from where they would watch the rest of the coronation day festivities. "Is that what you tell yourself?"

Adonis stared at her, his eyes dark and intense. "Why do I have a feeling you're dying to have a go at me, Princess?" The moment stretched, ripe with tension and unsaid things.

A cue from one of their aides had them standing up and waving. And then came the next cue—for a chaste, polite kiss, perfect for the public's consumption.

When Adonis dutifully reached for her, Jemima stiffened. "I'd rather kiss a frog right now than kiss you."

"And here I thought you didn't lie to yourself, Jem. Come, let's see how much of a lie that is."

And then, without warning, he sealed his lips over hers. Breaking convention, breaking protocol, breaking every boundary she drew around herself, Adonis deepened the kiss. He licked and nipped at her, his tongue sweeping over the cavern of her mouth as if he were looking for treasure.

The kiss rivaled his stunt in how dizzy it made her.

When he released her, her chest was heaving, her head was off floating in the clouds and her heart…her foolish heart was ready to get on the roller coaster of wanting to know the real Adonis all over again.

She flushed to the roots of her hair at the applause that broke out and pretended to not hear when he whispered at her ear, "Now, who's the liar, Your Majesty?"

CHAPTER NINE

WHEN ADONIS STUMBLED into his palace wing past midnight, it was to find his private suite, *their private suite*, and the extremely large kingly bed, disappointingly empty. Like the city itself, some interfering busybody, apparently also incurably romantic, had decorated the room like a bride itself.

The air was thick with the scent of jasmines and roses, arranged in lavish bouquets through the room. Through the large, open French doors, the sound of the waves endlessly crashing against the cliffs matched his hungry mood.

Where the hell was his new bride?

You didn't pay attention to her all day. And yet you stomp about like a child now, that innately fair voice whispered inside his head.

It had been necessary, he reminded himself yet again, to keep her at a distance, to snuff out the very real thread beginning to weave between them. She had been so incandescent—her passion so achingly honest, that he'd forgotten he didn't do emotional intimacy. That the deepest wound he'd been dealt still pulsed with pain. And given a chance, she too would find him not enough someday, she too would only cause him pain.

But now that the endless day was over and the inky darkness of night had surrounded him, he wanted her under him. Away from his father and the crowds and without the crown on his head, he wanted her, as a man would want the most thrilling woman he'd ever met.

He wanted her unraveled for him, wanted to spend himself on her lush curves so badly that he would forget that he was nothing but a poser, a fake.

How like a bloody king to seek her out when it pleased him, he thought, but even the voice calling out his hypocrisy couldn't stop him.

He continued stomping through the endless, expansive rooms, even searched behind those stupid marble columns and thick velvet curtains as if she could be playing queenly hide-and-seek with him on their wedding night.

Their wedding night...

He pushed a hand through his hair as the phrase brought on memories of her expressions from the day. There had been anger, relief, pain, and disappointment in her gaze. That he had been the author of all of them didn't sit well with him.

Not that the day had been the least bit about either of them. For a man who had thought he would never marry though, he did feel a sort of disappointment that it had been so utterly somber. Nor was he completely sure why he felt this sudden urgency to seek her out now.

Of course there was the ever-present lust pounding through him, urging him to plant himself deep inside her. Made even more potent by the adrenaline running through his veins since the air show. Not that it had satisfied the dark urges roiling through him. Only one thing, he knew, would at this point. Touch and connection and losing himself in the voluptuous valleys of his new queen.

And this, he knew, she needed it too.

Pushing the heavy double doors that felt like sentinels

silently ordering him to stay out of her private space, he entered the pretty decorated salon. It was a replica of the smaller suite he had stood in on that first night. Some tight constriction in his chest that he had been walking around with eased to find the familiar sight of piles of books and discarded chocolate wrappers strewn about.

He maneuvered through a host of sofas and footstools and walls covered in breathtaking local art, instead of the heavy paintings of ancestors he didn't want to think about, to reach the recessed part of the room.

With the flick of his hand, Adonis dismissed the young maid who had been half-asleep on the armchair.

Was the young woman to have acted as buffer between him and Jemima? Was his peace-loving queen pissed off that he had neglected her all day?

With every step he took toward the bed, her shape took form and something else with it. Jemima was half sitting, half lying down on the bed in a baby-pink wrapper that fell off one shoulder. Baring gleaming golden skin for his eyes.

The thick reading glasses she wore dangled precariously at the edge of her cute button nose. But even in exhausted slumber he could see the dark circles etched under her eyes, and her left hand was stretched to rest on the head of a boy child of about four or five.

Shock punched through Adonis, leaving him sweaty and cold. In the boy's sleeping face with its thick lashes and button nose, he could see the resemblances to the woman who couldn't let go of him even in sleep.

Horrifying speculations abounded in his head, causing a sudden frightening buzz. He rubbed his temple and was about to shake her awake when her amber eyes came alert.

She jerked up into a seating position as if someone had poked her and rubbed her knuckles under her eyes.

At whatever she saw in his face, she suddenly pulled the sleeping boy toward her until his head lay in her lap. The protectiveness in the gesture, as if he were a monster, infuriated Adonis and filled his head with wilder theories about the boy's parentage that made his blood run cold.

"Your Majesty, what did you need of me?" she said, her voice husky with sleep.

Even in his horrified state, it pinged over his skin, filling him with heart-pounding awareness of what he did want with her, of her.

"The child..." he said, not even glancing down at the small face. He had a feeling it would haunt him for nights to come if his speculations were true. "Who is he?"

Jemima frowned and then sighed, as if it were no big deal for her to have a child in her bed. "I will answer that question if you didn't ask it as if I were in an inquisition. After you so rudely disrupted my sleep."

He gritted his jaw. "This is not the time to test me, Princess. Just answer the question."

"I'm not one of your subjects to be dazzled by everything you say and do, Your Majesty. And I've had enough of you and your stunts and your..."

With gentle movements, she lay the child back against the pillows and tucked him under the duvet. She threw her legs off the bed with sudden vigor, drawing his gaze to the rucked hem of her nightgown that bared thick, toned thighs.

Adonis could no more look away from the sight of her heaving breasts and the golden cleavage they made than he could stop breathing. All he wanted was to bury his face there and not come up for air.

Coming to her feet, making sure to walk far toward the door, away from the sleeping child, she folded her arms at her middle. "Please...leave. I'm not myself."

"Is he your son, Jemima?" Adonis whispered, feeling like a drunk fool. "Is that why you went through the elaborate plan of beseeching me to make you my queen? Is he yours and my brother's son?"

Her head jerked toward him with such alacrity that he wouldn't be surprised if it hurt her in the morning.

"What?" She looked horrified. Taking his face in, she sobered. "No, of course not. I told you. Adamos and I didn't have that kind of relationship. Wow, you really think I would trick you like that?"

Air rushed into his lungs as if he had been pulled out of a drowning flood. He rubbed the heel of his palm over his eyes, relief shaking him from inside out.

A confrontation with his father had always made him needy and weak, and today had been the highlight of their miserable, nonexistent relationship. The last thing he could do was to take it out on the one innocent in all this. He turned to leave, only to be blocked by a five-foot-two queen, her arms thrown about in a dramatic fashion, her chest rising and falling. With a splash of pink washing up her ample chest and cheeks, she could drive any man to the edge and he...already dwelled there.

"Leaving without answering my question, Your Majesty?" Jemima said, the softness of sleep gone from her eyes.

"Who is he then?" Adonis asked, the blankness of relief giving way to new questions. Although, whatever her answer, it would only take another shot to bring him to his knees. Because, clearly, his freshly minted queen was attached to the boy.

Jealousy scoured his insides with its sharp, green nails, and this too was new and strange.

"My brother, Zayn. My half brother, to be precise. Apparently, my mother, beaten down by my father, took a secret lover." She said it all by rote, as if any emotion on the topic had already been bled through. "That he isn't my father's son became apparent to me when he started saying he would banish Zayn to some far-off boarding school. He tries to behave like he doesn't exist. Until he realized that I adore my brother and that he can be used as a weapon to control me. If not for Zayn," she said, lifting her chin, resolve blazing across her face, and Adonis braced himself for free fall, for the thud and the splat of his poor heart, "I would not have begged you to marry me. I'd have run far away from you, the palace, the damned kingdom, and my father. But in the law's eyes and the world's, Zayn is my father's child and he threatened to take him away from me any moment."

Understanding dawned in Adonis, but he couldn't find it in himself to be angry with her for hiding her true purpose. Especially when he knew the kind of neglect the boy could suffer at her father's hands. Neglect, which would be the best he could hope for.

"He could still send your brother away if you didn't follow his commands, couldn't he? If you didn't finesse me or control me or manipulate me per his wishes?"

She blanched but didn't deny it. "I hoped as the King of Thalassos, you could order him to keep the boy with me to be brought up in the royal household, as part of this family. *Our family.*"

Adonis had to admire her strategic thinking. "You're counting on the fact that your father would love the idea of having that continued extra connection to the royal family?"

She nodded. "Once I got to know you, it became clear

that you wouldn't begrudge an innocent boy your love and protection."

He snorted. "Managing me yet again, Princess?"

"I dare not even think that, Your Majesty. Self-delusion isn't my favorite vice."

"And what is the meaning of bringing him to your suite tonight, Princess?" He cocked his head when she blushed, although certain other parts of him also started saluting her. "I imagine there's a statement you're trying to make but I'm not sure I see it. Given you have kept a huge secret from me."

"I am angry with you," she stated easily, shedding the reserved entreaty for blazing fury. And Adonis wondered, yet again, how easily she gave him her trust, the intimacy of sharing her emotions. "For a host of things I couldn't even begin to talk about. And I have no wish to share a bed with you tonight."

"You do know that producing a child does not require a bed, don't you?"

She gasped. "Of course, I know that…" She closed her mouth and opened it again. "I simply refuse to be thrown about like a child's toy by your stunts."

"My stunts?" he said, even as understanding began to dawn.

"You might call it a tribute to your brother, and Thalassos might foolishly rejoice in seeing their new king splash about in the sky, making a spectacle of his anger, of his pain, and even of its promised golden future." Eyes bright with unshed tears, an inferno of emotions crossing her face, his wife looked like the very volcano that had made Thalassos rich with fertile soil that could nurture and grow the wildest of weeds. And that was how he had always felt amidst the carefully manicured garden that was his family—a wild, robust weed that wasn't of use to anyone.

"But I will not take part in your self-destruction, Your Majesty. I did not find it moving at all."

As if to mock her defiant assertion, her tears fell one by one, onto smooth, round cheeks.

Adonis decided he didn't like the sight of her tears at all. No, he actively hated them and he vowed to be rid of them, as much as possible.

This whole…caring about someone else and accommodating his actions toward that end felt…both strange and alluring to him, like a new challenge. Even, a purpose.

It terrified him, this purpose, as much as it lured him. After all, he was a man who thrived on pushing his body to its extreme limits. And now, a part of him wanted to try it with his heart, even as his head blared warnings. Wanted to grab everything that stood before him with both hands and full heart, even as the young boy inside him raged in protest, begging to protect himself from that pain again.

In the end, the pull she had on him won out, at least for the moment. After all, he had treated her horribly on what should have been a special day.

Covering the distance between them, he wiped her tears with his knuckles and sensed the great volcano of tension she held inside. The fact that she had sought solace in that little boy's body made his chest tight. As if she had known that she couldn't get it from him.

Acting on an impulse that he didn't understand or was ready for, he pressed his mouth to her temple. The scent of sweet vanilla filled his nostrils, his lungs, and all the cold, far-off reaches of his body, replacing the chill he had felt earlier with silken warmth.

He wrapped his arms around her and instantly, she fell into him, her silent, hiccupping sobs bathing him. "Jemima…" He didn't even care that her name sounded like an entreaty on his lips. "I did not do it to cause you pain. I do it to ease mine." Even speaking the words was cathartic, but then, he had never verbalized the urge to scream at what destiny had landed him into. Of how hard it was to fight such brutal cruelty. "I was in a rage and when one of those rages takes me, the only way to wrestle control over myself is to challenge the upper edges of what my body can do, to drown myself deep into the adrenaline released by an act of tremendous risk. When the fear and the excitement and the gratitude from it floods me, I'm centered again. I am also unused to thinking that some-one would worry over me so."

Hands on his chest, she pushed at him so suddenly that he nearly stumbled to the floor. Only the fact that she was small and he was all muscle stopped him from landing on his ass. A sight he was sure his fierce queen would have thoroughly enjoyed.

Her tears were gone and the anger was back. "I did not think the Devil Prince Adonis Vasilikos could suffer from self-pity and victimizing himself. How dare you say that no one would worry about you, Adonis? Your mother loves you," she said. "And your foolishly impressed sub-jects love you. Even the stubborn, relentlessly proper staff at this damned palace have begun to love you. To risk so much in a fit of anger…you should be ashamed of your-self. I refuse to tie myself, my future, my children to a man who thinks so little of his life."

"It might look risky to you, but I was in control the en-tire time," Adonis said, surprised by the fact that he was offering an explanation at all. Untried as he was in relationships, her concern stole under his skin like a small worm digging its way in. "I have made billions out of what I do in the form of outrageous, spine-tingling, death-defying stunts, Princess. However reckless I feel, I'd never risk my life in such a wasteful way. Not when the Queen risked so much to raise me as her own."

The roiling confusion in her eyes didn't abate as she muttered to herself. "I can't compete with that kind of excitement. A flesh and blood woman would have been better."

"Don't be ridiculous," he said, anger edging into his own words now. "I do not expect you to somehow provide me with that kind of adrenaline." Even as he said it, a new kind of anticipation thrummed through his veins. "Unless you're offering to try?" he said, grabbing her hips.

Her tearstained eyes rose to his and her throat worked. Another thing he was beginning to adore about his new queen—she did not back down from a challenge, just like him.

"What are you suggesting? If I do something for you…" She licked her lower lip and he suppressed a groan. "Will you stay away from such risky stunts in the future?"

"Why does it bother you so?" he said, clasping her shoulders, genuinely curious. "If you want, I can have my team prepare a report that shows you the risk statistics of every stunt I have ever done. It is as much a part of me as the hills are a part of Thalassos."

Something softened in her eyes but she pushed back out of his hold and walked around him, her steps both halting and urgent. "When my father decreed that I should somehow persuade you into this marriage, I did so with the least amount of hope. And yet, with each minute that I talked with you, each endless hour we pored over those trade documents, each time you gave me credit for every small thing I did, you gave me hope, Adonis, when I didn't have any in so many years. Hope for a good relationship. Hope for a loving father for my children, for *our* children. I even dared hope that you might take on an active role in my brother's life, for I have seen the kindness in you. Then you treat me like a dummy, a stand-in, at the wedding ceremony."

"Jemima—"

"I could still forgive the last, knowing how hard this... day must have been for you. Knowing what I know now. But I don't know if I can forgive you for snatching away that hope by taking these risks."

Anguish swirled in her eyes. "It's the cruelest thing you could ever do to me and if you touch me, if you kiss me, if you give me a baby," she said, a bitter laugh falling from her lips, "I cannot keep myself separate from you. I cannot remain my own. And then if something happened to you and I was back under my father's thumb..." that the idea terrified her was clear from her expression, "I won't have the strength to look after the innocents around me. All these years of bracing myself for the next calamity and you've already rendered me weak."

He felt as if she had pushed him into a burning building. He had the memory to supply the fear that came with it. His breath tightened like a vise in his throat, and with only one step toward her, there could be salvation or utter destruction. "Love was not a part of our agreement, Princess," he said, filling his words with cold steel.

"I'm not talking about falling in love with you. Even I am not that foolish. But I could still get attached to you, to this relationship, to the father of my children. And I can't bear it if..."

It was exactly what he had hoped she'd feel for him, manipulative bastard that he was. That she could actually see facets of his true nature...only made her words sweeter.

Her honesty demanded he give her something in return. "And if I promise to give this matter serious thought? You have to understand," he said, clasping her cheek, "that these...actions have been a part of me for so long. I do not know what I am without them, Jemima. But I see that my life now has much more value than it ever had before, whatever my father's ramblings."

"Is that a vow you're making me?" she said, her eyes so bright that they gleamed like precious jewels. "That you will consider it?" she added, as if she knew that he would offer up that correction.

He nodded.

"And about these ramblings of the King that I overheard this morning and how they—"

Adonis cut her off with a hand over her mouth, not all surprised at her smooth segue. The woman was as cunning as she was generous. "The last thing I want to discuss at the end of this bloody long day is my father, wife. How about we get back to the topic of you offering me something in return for me giving up an essential part of my life?"

Her shoulders straightened, her spine arced. Pushing her luscious breasts up into his chest, she looked like a princess of the tribe her ancestors were from, readying herself for battle. She took his hand, cast a glance over her shoulder at her sleeping brother, and tugged him from the suite.

Anticipation and excitement and such naked desire fueled Adonis's limbs that he didn't remember the adrenaline that had coursed through him as he had made the vertical leap through the sky just that morning.

And he wondered, if maybe, this day was the beginning of something new, something good in his cursed life.

They had barely reached his cavernous room when the overhead chandeliers, three of them, flicked on and Adonis's gravelly command filled the room. "On your knees then, Princess."

Challenge rippled through the room, hitting Jemima in waves that threatened to bring her under. Behind her, the large bed with its dark navy sheets loomed.

Standing at the foot of it, she could smell the earthy, cedar scent of him that made her want to strip every piece of clothing from her flesh and roll around in it.

Liquid yearning gave her the courage to want more though. And why roll around in sheets scented with his musk rather than taste it on her tongue?

This was her life now, abundant with a man, a bloody king, who made it clear that he wanted her.

She'd long been curious about every kind of sexual act, but nothing more than this one he was suggesting.

The power dynamic in the act had always made her tingly with pleasure when she'd read erotic novels. But nothing, not even the most salacious tome, could come close to experiencing it live with this man.

All her adolescent longings and naive wishes morphed into something else when it came to her new husband. Oh, what she wouldn't give to bring this man to his knees, this man who had known every high and chased every challenge, with her mouth?

Keeping her gaze twined with his, she sank to her knees in what was hopefully a smooth gesture. She shrugged off the wrapper she had on and instantly her nipples peaked against her silky negligee, goose bumps rising on every inch of her skin. Though it had nothing to do with the fact that her husband apparently liked his room quite cold.

It stuck her then that the man lived like an ascetic, a monk, even. Constantly testing his willpower and his self-control, and flooding himself in adrenaline only when he dictated it.

A new thirst formed in her, of building a future where he did not have to conduct himself with such iron-clad control, where she could be his landing place, his place of comfort.

For now, she would begin with being the one who made him lose a fraction of that control.

"If you do not want to do this, wife," he said, coming close enough that she could lean her forehead against his muscled thigh, "you could just say so. I could make this easier on both of us. I could simply spread your thighs and plunge into you without any of this drama or foreplay or challenge. Especially since you've already claimed that your inexperience bothers you and makes this uneven between us."

She looked up at him, at the flaring nostrils, the dark pupils pushing out the gleaming blue. A savage satisfaction filled her.

He was desperate for this, not that he would ever betray it. She licked her lips, her mouth as dry as the desert. "I am the Devil Prince's wife. I do not back down from a challenge. The world might call this relationship whatever it pleases, but between you and me, this will be a relationship of equals, my king. So enough of distracting me and give me that majestic weapon you keep under those pants."

He threw his head back and laughed. The open V of his shirt made the corded tendons in his neck something to watch. Before her courage left her, Jemima busied her hands with his trousers.

Instant tension tightened his muscles as she unzipped his trousers, loosening them around his tapered hips, and his hard, throbbing length fell into her hands. Her hungry core clenched and spasmed as she traced one thick vein on the underside. When she gave him a firm stroke, pre-cum beaded at the tip.

Mouth falling open, he grunted when she gave him a couple more squeezes and then bent and licked the drop. He hissed and cursed and sank his fingers into her hair. "Take me deeper, wife. I need to brand your throat."

Jemima's fascination for him increased a thousandfold at the rough need in his voice. He'd been right when he said he would not coddle her for anything in the world.

As he talked her through, in deep, rumbling tones, how to keep breathing, while his shaft slowly inched deeper and deeper, hitting the back of her throat, Jemima thought she might love him just a little for that.

On and on, she sucked him and his own commands increased in both need and intensity. His fingers tightened in her hair while her nails dug into the hair-roughened columns of his thighs. And he used her mouth the way he wanted. The way she wanted him to, to fuel his ravaging need.

She braced herself for whatever he would give her when abruptly, he pulled himself out of her mouth. The world barely made sense until she was on her back in the large bed and lavishly frescoed ceilings with dancing cherubs greeted her gaze.

"What are you doing?" Jemima whispered, the sheets cool against her heated skin. Every inch of her tingled, as if she were the capital city on Christmas Eve.

Climbing onto the bed, Adonis planted his large, calloused hands on her inner thighs and pushed them apart as indecently as possible, making a place for his impossibly wide shoulders between them.

Eyes gleaming, he pushed up the hem of her negligee. Her core wept with fresh damp desire as he gazed at the small landing strip the palace beautician had left on her sex. One fingertip traced her endlessly. He licked his sensuous lips, as if she had been readied just for him.

"Saving my seed for where it belongs," he said, putting a large hand on top of her pelvis. Her belly rolled in delight.

She faked a pout to cover the nerves tightening up inside her.

Christos, she wanted his mouth on her there, and him inside her, but the eagerness with which she wanted this, with which she wanted this whole life with him, scared her. "I would've swallowed every drop of what you gave me, you know," she said, adding a teasing tone to her words. Who said Jemima Vasilikos could not do coy? "Now you'll complain that I didn't see it through all the way."

His mouth split into a rakish grin that made her heartbeat stutter. The fact that his breath coasted over her lower lips had nothing on what his smile could do to her. Especially when it touched those blazing blue eyes of his.

Suddenly, she knew she could get addicted to wanting to make this man smile like that, just for her. For the world, he could be the Devil Prince but for her, he would be just a man.

"Since I plan to use you every which way tonight, Princess, you will be sore in the next couple of days. Then you'll have more chance to apply yourself. You can practice swallowing as much as you like. Now," he nipped at her inner thigh with his teeth and Jemima jerked at the pain providing a sweet contrast to the pleasure she wanted, "let me taste you and ready you for my mighty sword."

His eyes crinkled at the corners and Jemima, pushing herself upon onto her elbows, watched him.

His dark hair ruffled, blond scruff on his jaw, his lips damp, he looked like her most feverish fantasy come true. "I didn't think kings could prostrate themselves in such a way, Your Majesty."

"This king does, for his queen," he quipped, before rubbing the scruff against the sensitive skin of her inner thigh. "Now stop distracting me from my honey pot."

Jemima laughed and within seconds, that sound transformed into a serrated groan as he rested the flat head of his tongue against her center and then swiped down like a cat.

He played with her clit for barely a breath before he swept his clever finger over her folds inside and out. And then finally, thrust it into her tight channel. Her elbows were shaky as a newborn calf's legs, and Jemima fell back into the bed and gave in to her other senses.

With her eyes closed, every pinch and twist and lick of his lips over her core hit her like a tsunami. Sensation built and built as if she were nothing but a flood of water rising up and hitting itself against a dam. And she so desperately wanted to break the dam and fall over.

"Put your hands in my hair and steer my head whichever way you need," he said, his words reverberating through her core to touch some deep, forbidden place inside of her that she didn't know existed. "I'm yours to use as you wish, Jemima. Only yours."

His blue eyes met her and she melted. Digging her fingers into his thick hair, she did as he said. She tugged and pulled, pressed and arched her hips up, chasing the rhythm he set, amplifying it to what she needed, on and on. Pain teased and sizzled at the edge of the aching fullness when he added a fourth finger and rocked them inside her.

"I have to get you ready for me," he said, almost sounding sorry.

Fisting her hands into the sheets, Jemima licked her sweat-drenched lips and said, "Please, Adonis. Send me over. Whatever you give me, I take it willingly."

And then there was no need for words. His mouth was on her clit, making the most scandalous sounds she had ever heard.

When he drew that bundle of nerves into his mouth and sucked at it with his lips, she exploded. More colorfully and brightly than the Parade Day fireworks in the sky.

Pleasure rippled and spread through her and outward in concentric circles, making her core contract and expand in hungry spasms. On and on her orgasm went as he continued licking at her, and Jemima knew she would never be the same again.

CHAPTER TEN

IT FELT LIKE she barely got air back into her lungs when Jemima felt the delicious weight of his whipcord body pressing her into the bed.

Every inch of her soft, plush curves was dimpled and smudged by his spectacularly muscled planes.

His mouth found hers for a slow, deep kiss and filled her with her own tart taste, spinning her anew into another plane. "You unravel at my hands with such abandon, Jemima. I want to do it all over just so I can watch again."

The sudden drag of his hair-roughened chest against the sensitive tips of her breast made her gasp. "I didn't know it could be that…heavenly. Or is it the mortal man I should be thankful for?"

He grinned. "I'm glad to have satisfied my queen."

She colored at his teasing. His steely shaft poked at her thigh and she rubbed at it, anticipation making her tremble again. "I want my prize."

"Shall I take you now, Princess, when you're all sated and boneless like this? Or should I drive you to the edge again?"

"I want to come again," she said, nipping at his lower lip. "But I want to do it with you inside me. Shall we be ambitious, my king, and try for that? I've heard that you have an inordinate amount of liking for impossible feats."

Such delight bloomed in his eyes that her heart spasmed in her chest. "How well you understand your husband already," he said, nipping a line of kisses down her throat.

His tongue swirled around her breast, finally licking the engorged peak. Fresh sensations assailed her as he sucked at her nipple and then applied the same ministrations to her other breast. The deep pulls of his mouth sent twangs of sensation to her sex.

There was not a square inch of her that he didn't kiss or taste or nip. And soon, Jemima was panting again, starting that inexorable climb toward another ecstatic shattering.

Her skin tingled, tears flew down her cheeks as he teased and teased, building her up all over again. Until she was so incredibly sensitive down there that even a breath of air made her sizzle.

Only when she dragged her nails over the taut skin of his shoulders, pulled at his head and begged him to take her, did he run the head of his shaft down her folds and thrust into her in one smooth stroke.

Pain spiked like a live flame for an instant and then slowly faded out as new sensations clamored to be felt. The heavy, aching fullness that came after was unlike anything Jemima had ever known and yet she wouldn't trade her crown for it. They lay chest to chest and their hearts thumped in unison.

"Adonis," she whispered, feeling an absurdly desperate need for more connection in that intimacy. A new kind of vulnerability seemed to fill her from inside out, just as he did.

His weight on one elbow, her husband stared down at her. Sweat pearled over his olive skin and in his eyes, a cavernous hunger lurked. For just a second, Jemima found herself utterly unequal to it and blinked rapidly to shy away from it.

The man didn't miss anything. "There's no way I could avoid hurting you that first time," he said, mistaking her panic for pain. His thumb traced the fold of her hip and thigh, as if to soothe her. "I promise I won't, ever again."

"I know that," she said, not hiding the awe in her voice. "I can't believe you didn't do this for so long."

"What do you mean?" he rasped, shifting around her, rotating his hips in such a way that honeyed shivers sizzled down her spine. An earthy moan escaped her. Suddenly, she was desperate for him to move. Desperate to claim him as he had her.

"I cannot fathom the amount of control it would take to deny yourself. Especially when such temptation dogs your every step." When he didn't answer, she fidgeted under his heavy, drugged gaze. "I guess what I'm asking is why."

A silky shoulder rose and fell and along with it came a slight but masterful thrust of his hips. As if to remind her she was pinned under him in every way.

Jemima writhed under him, needing friction at that place, and his eyes nearly blanked with pleasure before he said, "You ask too many questions and dictate too many conditions, wife."

Laughing at his exaggerated tone, she licked at the seam of his mouth and when his tongue came to play, she tangled hers with it. The kiss deepened in mere breaths. His rough groan and rougher thrust had her nearly jumping out of her skin. "Please," she said, panting now. "All I'm doing is trying to understand you."

His gaze searched hers. "My excesses led me to despise myself, more than *he* despised me. One morning, when I woke up with a sour taste in my mouth, a pounding in my head and couldn't remember how I ended up on the floor, I realized I was making everything he said about me true. I realized why Mama decided to punish him so and that I *was* his son, in the worst way possible. And that was…unbearable."

Tears prickled behind her eyes for the torment and burden he still carried, but she knew instinctively that he would loathe her sympathy. Neither did she like it that she would never be able to take this pain from him. And she desperately wanted to, fool that she was.

With a forceful laugh, Jemima shook the useless tears off. "No more denying yourself then," she said, nipping at his chin playfully. "Or me, rather. You have unleashed a wanton creature. I want this pleasure, this claiming over and over again."

Utter glee transformed his face from godlike looks to boyish beauty. "I vow, Your Majesty—" he whispered the words into the skin over her breast, that tantalizing, teasing swivel of his clever hips, never entering fully or deeply, paving the steps to her unraveling "—to please you as and when you want. I'm utterly at your service."

Jemima laced her fingers with his. "Tell me how it feels for you. Please."

"You take me so well and clasp me so tight, Jem. As if you were the prize for my penance," he said, nuzzling his nose at the arch of her neck. "So good that I don't want this to end."

Her shortened name sounded so sweet to her ears that she stroked her hands down his back with a greed she couldn't hide.

"Oh, but I want the destination you promised me, again." With that, she lifted her hips in an experimental thrust.

His shaft lodged deeper inside her, nudging at that very spot where heaven seemed to linger. With a moan, she did it, again and again, seeking friction. It sent them both arcing and shaking into each other, setting off a new explosion.

Jemima tried her best to keep her eyes open as Adonis moved over and inside her with a precise, calculating rhythm that was designed to maximize her pleasure.

But she no more wanted his finesse than she wanted his masks.

Clasping her feet around his bottom and meeting his thrusts, she urged him deeper and faster. He gave in with a curse, pistoning into her, his flesh slapping against hers and when it felt like he might carve a path to her very heart with his hard thrusts, Jemima's climax drew her into another vortex. She spiraled and shattered into so many fragments and over her, Adonis let out a feral groan.

And then, with his mouth buried at her neck, his teeth grazing her skin none too gently, the Devil Prince unraveled. And a small part of him had become hers, Jemima decided, pressing her cheek against his.

May tumbled into June, stuttered into July, bringing with it the glorious but sticky splendor of summer to Thalassos. To escape the heat, Thalassans and visitors to the kingdom alike swarmed to the beaches for swimming and sailing and simply lounging on the golden sands.

The more daring ones, like His Majesty King Adonis Vasilikos, opted for cliff diving, or exploring the dangerous coves and caves that dotted the coastline. Apparently, when her husband had promised her that he would consider giving up his…dangerous addictions, he meant that he would pull back his stunts to the less dangerous tier first.

Shocking both the crown council and the rapacious

media, he had settled into his duties as the King surprisingly well. Not that it surprised Jemima at all.

Despite how he had been taught to view himself at an early age, her husband was a man of great thinking and daring. He also understood human nature well, better than any politician Jemima had ever encountered, and employed it to guide his negotiations strategically.

In just six weeks of his reign, not only had he signed a new trade treaty with Ephyra—dictating better terms than the previous one for Thalassos—but was already in talks for new business ventures for both countries. Despite most of his naysayers commenting on the fact that Thalassos and Ephyra had shared a contentious relationship for centuries, which King Aristos had tried to settle—in the worst way possible, by arranging a match between Adonis and the current queen years ago.

Like Adonis, Queen Calista hadn't been for the match at all, knowing that King Aristos planned to absorb Ephyra into Thalassos gradually, with his spare son as its new king. That Adonis had defied the King who had commanded him to make the match had been public knowledge. But now, knowing the basis of the rift between him and his father, she couldn't believe how he had withstood the offer of gaining his father's approval and affection, in addition to the keys to a bloody kingdom. When it was the very thing her husband wanted, despite the mask he presented the world.

One night, when they both lay panting after he'd taken her hard and fast after a day of stressful negotiations with Ephyra's own cabinet, the words had tumbled out of her mouth. "Why did you refuse Queen Calista's hand? It would have given you everything you ever wanted—your own kingdom to rule, a beautiful consort, and... King Aristos's approval."

He had stilled so suddenly that every nerve in her sated body had tightened painfully. Burying her face in the soft cotton, she bit her tongue. Even braced for his retreat and an empty, cold bed for the rest of the night.

Her new husband indulged her every whim and desire—he even spent an hour every day with her brother, Zayn, playing and talking with the boy who had started calling him Ado, but his deepest wound was still forbidden grounds to her.

And it ate at her, that she couldn't heal it for him, or at least, take the pain away for a while.

"You don't have to answer that," she whispered, trying to roll out from under his delicious weight. Years of trying to not anger her father had left her with an instinctive fear that she had crossed the line.

"No?" he said, throwing one muscled leg over her and arresting her retreat.

She shook her head and stared at this beautiful man who was slowly becoming the foundation of every truth and joy in her life. "I'm curious as to why you said no to the royal command, yes. But I won't pay the price for it with your pain."

A flicker of shock widened his gorgeous eyes. Gripping her hips, he pulled her closer and took her mouth in a kiss that spun dizzying joy into her senses. Was it reward or simply a need for deeper connection with her, she wondered. Would he admit it if it were the latter?

When she opened her eyes again, it was to discover that he had sat up on the bed and pulled her up with him.

Relief flooded her as she realized he wasn't putting distance between them.

His gaze swept over her face with a curious expression. "I...knew, even before Adamos understood it, what my father's plan was for Ephyra. I heard him say enough times, in outraged tones, that the tiny nation was no more a thorn in mighty Thalassos's side. He meant to swallow it whole. And after his rejection of me all my life, I refused to follow his dictates and put that plan into motion. Even if that meant he would never accept me, as he declared minutes later. I had no choice then but to leave Thalassos because he actually banished me."

Jemima pressed her cheek to his chest, clasping her hands around his waist. She wasn't sure if she was comforting him or herself. "No wonder Queen Calista was looking at you like you were her favorite man in the entire world at the summit yesterday," she said, managing to sound extra jealous. Not that she wasn't.

"You are jealous," he said, sounding...wary.

"Of any woman's covetous gaze on my husband, yes. But it doesn't mean I don't know that I'm the only woman who has his gaze."

Some of his tension deflated at her words and Jemima realized how much he needed to be trusted, to be seen as who he was—a man of integrity and principles, a man worthy of the crown. Not that he would ever ask for what he needed.

Although she was beginning to wonder if she and the crown of Thalassos were worthy of him.

"I think," Adonis said, sifting his fingers through her tangled waves, "back then, Queen Calista appreciated the fact that she didn't have to be the one to do the rejection. Neither was she unaware of my father's devious plans from the start."

Now, years later, Adonis had once again maneuvered

the land mine with Ephyra—which had been brought to the cusp of war by the power-hungry crown council, with diplomacy and sheer honesty.

Weeks later, Jemima was still filled with admiration at not just his innovative approach but his plain decency toward a young queen.

Then there was the fact that even as he settled into the mantle of the crown better and better with each passing day, Adonis hadn't once dismissed her opinions as extraneous or unnecessary. Hadn't viewed her as an accessory.

A part of Jemima kept waiting for the other shoe to drop on their relationship, for him to render himself like any other man she had known—made of fragile ego and more than willing to punch down.

While the other part of her knew that she was already forging down a path from which there was no return.

A week later, having discharged Zayn to his young nurse and dismissed her own aides, Jemima was studying her schedule for the next two weeks and trying to not fall asleep when someone grabbed the papers from her and pulled her to her feet.

"I'm going to pass a new law soon," her husband whispered at her temple, laughter dancing in his tone. "You look like a delicious dessert in that pink dress, my lady. And your king is hungry."

Jemima had hoped he would notice how the pink complemented her coloring. And Adonis always delivered. "What law?" she said past the breathy anticipation that inflated inside of her.

The familiar scent of cedar and rain enveloped her and she gave herself over—body and mind, into his capable hands, wrapping her arms around his neck like tentacles.

Clinging to him like Zayn did when it was time to bid good-night.

His broad palm spread over her lower back, the tips reaching her buttocks. "No overworking for my queen. And if she continues in this way, I'll say off with the heads of the staff that supply her with it."

When she scoffed and refused to meet his eyes, his words turned stern. "I'm not joking, Jemima. The reports I receive from your aides every evening of how much paperwork you've gone through that day, making notes for me...even the puffed-up staff is awed by you. You work too much."

"I like working. I like being useful and...proving my worth to you," she said, the words flying off her lips. Still, she refused to meet his eyes. Pressing her cheek to his chest, she reveled in the steady beat of his heart.

A sudden realization—one that she had been fighting for days now, burst into her awareness, flooding her with a sudden onslaught of emotion. Burrowing closer, she shuddered in its wake.

Instantly, Adonis's arm tightened around her waist while the other tipped her chin up to study her. His blue eyes dug into hers, as if he meant to see to her soul. And what would he find there but her growing...regard for him, she thought tremulously. "You have nothing to prove to me or Thalassos or your bloody father, Jem. I wish..." Frustration rippled through his lean body. "I could make you see yourself through my eyes."

She opened her eyes and met his then, desperate to see a fraction of what she felt for him reflected in the blue depths.

"What?" he said, aware of the tiniest shifts in her mood.

"You look...happy today," she said, pulling out of his

arms. Not knowing why she was pushing aside the confession she needed to make.

Suddenly, she had a feeling that everything he had given her, everything she had with him wasn't enough. She was the bloody Queen of Thalassos, wife to the Devil Prince and yet she wanted more. She wanted the one thing she might not get...his undying love. The deep care and connection that she was beginning to see he was capable of.

She wanted to be his most dangerous risk and his most fulfilling reward. And she wanted this gorgeous, wonderful man to be hers, completely.

"I do have some good news," he said, pulling her toward the private terrace.

Summer nights in Thalassos were near-magical, with gentle breezes blowing in from the ocean, providing a welcome relief from the heat of the day. At this particular terrace which was her favorite relaxing spot at the end of a long day, the intoxicating scents of jasmine and lavender rose up from the palace garden, heavily scenting the air, while the view of the city with its whitewashed buildings and open-air markets rooted her to the place.

It was only now, with this man beside her changing her very outlook, that Jemima realized how much her father's dictates, and Adamos's apathy, had turned this paradise into prison. And with the foundation Adonis provided, how much she loved Thalassos.

"I have some news too," she said, jumping into the fray.

His eyes flared in anticipation.

Clasping his jaw, she said, "But you go first."

"I don't have the documents in hand to give this moment the dramatics it deserves," he said, pulling her into his lap on the chaise longue. Enveloped by his muscled warmth and masculine scent, she sank into him.

His tongue traced the shell of her ear, revving her up like a virtuoso tuning his instrument for a masterful performance. "I have a feeling you're going to want to show your gratitude in a very effusive way, Princess."

Her heart twisted in her chest, spewing words she couldn't say. She settled for what was clear between them. "I think you know, Adonis," she said, burying her face in the warm cavern of his neck, every cell in her wanting to burrow into him, creating a nest for herself deep in his heart, "that I would do anything to satisfy you in that arena. You only have to command me."

Under her thighs, he rolled forward and back with a groan. His shaft turned rock-hard and her core pulsed emptily. "I don't like the caveat 'in that arena', Jem." Pure arrogance filled his tone before he let out a self-deprecating laugh. "But we will deal with that later. This afternoon, I met with your father and asked him to sign over Zayn's custody to you."

Jemima shot up so fast in his lap that she bumped her head hard against his chin. "You shouldn't have." Tears piled in her eyes, fueled by panic. "What...what did he say?"

"He insisted that I take custody of Zayn and he had a price for it." Utter disgust filled Adonis's voice. "And I paid it."

"Was it..." Jemima had to swallow past the hard lump in her throat. Only being caught between the solid strength of his thighs stopped her knees from buckling completely. "I'm afraid to ask what it is."

As if he knew where her fear dwelled, he patted her belly in soothing strokes. "It's between him and me. You don't need to worry about it, Jem. Remember that Zayn is ours now. And believe me when I say I have plans to strip everything from him."

"No, Adonis," she said, gripping his chin. "Don't—"

"I didn't think you weak enough to hold affection for a bully, Jem." There was not an inch of give in his words and she wondered if he was talking about his father too. If he finally gave up on King Aristos and cut the last thread of bond connecting them, would he be stronger and healthier for it? Or would that part of him that loved his father forever be cauterized, leaving him unable to love anyone again?

The conundrum made fear spike through her.

"Jemima?"

"I don't have lingering affection for him," she said without hesitation. "He's a spiteful man who tormented my mother. I just don't want him to come for us. Especially when our family is growing."

Adonis stilled, as if he'd been suddenly rendered into one of those marble busts littered about the palace. When Jemima looked into his eyes, it was to find disbelief and an ache flashing there.

"What are you..." he turned her to face him fully, his fingers gripping her arms painfully, "do you mean..."

It seemed he couldn't finish the thought.

Jemima nodded. "My period is late by almost three weeks."

He shot to his feet, nearly tumbling her to the cold marble floor in the process as he muttered, "And why the hell haven't you consulted the palace physician for that long?" His hands instantly steadied her as she wobbled.

She tried for a shrug that didn't quite materialize. "I..."

"Jem? Talk to me."

Whatever he sensed in her, he gathered her to him in an

embrace that brought tears to her eyes. "The first week, I just waited because you never know with my period."

"And after that?" he prompted.

"After that, I was scared that it might not be what I thought. Then about how desperately I wanted it to be true."

Jemima could feel his tension in the way his sinewed strength tightened against her, could see his confusion in how he tightened his jaw, as if he couldn't betray himself in front of her.

"I...want this, Adonis," she said, whispering the words into his chest. "So badly. I want this child, our child. I want this family we're building. I want this more than anything I've ever wanted. And I'm afraid that it might all crumble into...dust." Just speaking of it made her shiver.

"Don't be afraid, *yineka mou*. I promise you, Jem, nothing will touch you or Zayn or us. Ever." When she sniffled, his words turned stern again. "Be happy, *agapi*. That's an order from your king, Jemima."

What if it was you that ruined this? she wanted to say. *You who won't share your pain or your torment with me? You who took this kingdom on to prove that you belonged? You who cannot fully love me as I do you?*

The unsaid words twisted her from inside out.

And when she couldn't calm her thundering heart or the anxiety that surged up through her body, making her break out in shivers, he gave her the thing she needed.

His mouth. His kiss. His utter possession of her where no fear or worry or anticipatory tension for the future could touch her.

As he pushed her back into the lounge, pushing her thighs wide and burying his face between them, Jemima wondered if her king would always know what she needed.

And if he would so readily offer it to her if he knew it was his heart she craved, with a scary intensity.

Bracing himself on his elbow, Adonis shifted to his side and studied the woman who had, in a bare seven weeks, transformed his life.

His queen. His wife. And now the mother of his growing child.

A sudden, overpowering emotion choked him with a forceful intensity as he planted his palm on her belly. He wanted to run away, escape the sheer overwhelming intensity of it.

He wanted to wake her up from her peaceful slumber and have her tell him, for the hundredth time, that it was true.

Instead, he pulled away from the yoke of her lush arms and the easy lure she cast and made his way to his private offices.

He might resist the urge to submerge the emotion that surged through him in some outrageous stunt, but he couldn't let it own him either.

CHAPTER ELEVEN

THE CALL FROM Queen Calista came in the last week of August when dawn's deep clutches had Adonis peacefully asleep.

The call was routed to his private cell phone, the number which only four people in the world had in their possession. The shrill ringing had woken Jemima first and her soft, sleep-husky voice, laced with confused urgency, had woken him.

With the French doors open, the midnight air was warm and tinged with the briny scent of the Aegean. Even the view of the moonlit ocean, its surface shimmering like silver, couldn't ground his worry.

His first instinct had been to splay his palm over her belly while holding her tight to him. Only when she assured him that she was fine and sulkily complained that the shrill tone of the cell phone had woken her had he let her go.

He felt no shame in the fact that his first thought, and worry, had been for his wife.

Especially when the day had been particularly fraught with emotions.

Thalassos had celebrated his three-month regime, which had included a weeklong tour of the big cities with Jemima—his pregnant and nauseous but determined-to-do-her-duty wife, a summer fete in the royal gardens and a ball to celebrate the new and flourishing trade agreement with Ephyra, and the ousting of certain crown council members who'd had their fingers in too many powerful pies.

In the last three days, he had been so busy with media interviews that he had barely seen Jemima outside of a meeting.

That morning, in the middle of a meeting with the cabinet ministry that had gone over its limits by a whole two hours, he had been reminded by his personal aide that his queen had a medical appointment. He'd rushed to the state-of-the-art women's clinic—that Jemima had inaugurated only two weeks ago, in his armored car, his heart thudding in his chest.

Like him, his wife never asked for anything and he desperately wanted to cure her of that. He wanted to be a good king for Thalassos, but for that, he first desperately needed to be a great husband to his wife.

He knew, with each passing minute, that he had married a woman who was not only smart and brave but extremely generous with her affection. A woman that made him dream like he had as a boy again. Which felt both right and dangerous.

Maybe this was his prize after everything he'd been through—attraction and companionship and even friendship in marriage. Not tainted by the crushing expectations of love, but defined by simpler, easier terms like fidelity and respect. Because that was a price he could easily pay.

After a half hour of worries circling him like vultures, he'd rushed in through the private entrance into a large expansive waiting room at the private clinic to discover his wife lying prostrate on the examination table with tears streaming down her cheeks.

His heart had nearly torn out of his chest with worry.

Rushing to her, he'd clutched her hand in his, demanding to know why his queen was crying and why someone wasn't treating her. It was as if a deafening roar had filled his ears.

It had taken Jemima pushing up to sit and gathering him to her with soft kisses along his jawline before his heart settled into place again. Then she'd told him in a tremulous voice that her tears were happy tears because he was to be the father of twins.

Stunned into wonder, Adonis had glanced at the large ultrasound screen and the two little beanlike images that were his children. The entire axis of his life had tilted at the beautiful future shining in front of him in black and white.

He'd banished the doctor, her attendants, and his own staff with one imperious command. Then like a beast in fear, he had tackled her into the bed, brought her to her knees and hands, and used her to ride the treacherous edge of the expansive, nearly choking feeling that had filled him.

Two children...of his own, of his blood, and finally, his family irrevocably. A dream he had nurtured for so long, without even whispering it to himself.

Not even the old King could take this away from him.

Happiness, he realized only later, could be as devastating as pain and he wasn't sure he could trust it. He couldn't take it. And so, he had worked it out on her. Sending his wife over the edge, again and again, until she begged for him to come inside her.

Only when he had collapsed on top of her, her limbs shaking like they were made of some airy dessert, had he realized how roughly he had taken her.

Skin damp and flushed pink, breaths coming in shallow pants, Jemima had convinced him that she had needed it just as much he had. That she needed to know that the dream was reality.

When they had returned to the palace—Adonis having canceled all his appointments for the day, she had wrapped herself around him, begged him to stay with her, and promptly fallen asleep.

Now, as he slipped on a robe over his shoulders, Jemima's vanilla scent clinging to him, and marched into his private office, a strange, dreamlike quality dogged his steps. Rubbing at the tightness in his chest, he switched his phone on and found a request from Queen Calista to contact her through a video call. And to make sure he had utter privacy.

Fully awake and tense enough that he considered waking Jemima for a moment and then discarded it, he switched on his laptop and made the call.

The young Queen greeted him with the usual serene greeting that he returned.

Feeling impatient to get back to his bed and his wife, he said, "Clearly, it is an emergency that you should contact me like this, Queen Calista. How may I be of service to Ephyra?"

A soft smile split Calista's lips even as her expression remained somber. "It is a wonder every time I speak with you, Adonis," she said, disregarding protocol and using his name. "It gives me hope for myself. If a rebel like you could learn the intricate intrigues of the palace and rule with such fairness, I feel like I could do right by Ephyra too."

It was a sign of the trust they had developed that she would admit to having doubts about her rule. "Most of the credit for this transformation goes to my queen," he said, the words rolling off of his lips, coming straight from his heart. The truth of it rooted deep inside him like some immovable tree sinking its roots deep inside the fertile soil of Thalassos. "Without Jemima, I would only be half the King I am now."

A curious light dawned in the young Queen's eyes. "This generosity and this ability to give credit where it's due...do I dare hope are qualities shared by your brother too?"

Adonis felt as if she had punched him straight in the throat. He scowled. "May I ask why you're bringing my dead brother into this discussion? Especially, when it is my understanding that Adamos and you did not see eye to eye."

"We did not," she accepted easily. "Because your brother refused to even honor the meeting that had been scheduled for months with his presence. And broke every line of protocol when it came to dealing with Ephyra. In some moments, I wondered if I had the Princes of Thalassos crossed. If not for the fact that he disappeared and you took his role, I would not be surprised if our nations had plunged into war."

The shock of the events she relayed made Adonis still in his armchair. Not for a second did he doubt the veracity of what she said. Queen Calista had proved herself to be a true ally.

Rubbing his hand over his face, he tried to keep his irritation out of his voice. "And this midnight chat was to reminisce about my brother?"

The little humor disappeared from her eyes. "I know this is going to come as a shock but bear with me, Adonis. I have yours and Thalassos's best interests at heart. A month ago, a land scouting team discovered your brother in the jungles of Ephyra. He was hurt pretty badly, but he's alive. My physicians insisted that he must be induced into a coma for his internal organs to heal. He has been under my care for the last month."

Adonis shot to his feet, the heavy armchair he had been sitting on, toppling upside down. "Adamos is alive? And you hid this for a month, Calista?" A growl emanated from his throat and he gave it full rein. "What could your motive be in hiding this big truth from me for a whole month? And here I thought I could trust you."

"Please," Calista whispered, her expression of calm serenity unbroken. "He was in a coma, Adonis. And for the first time in years, I was meeting a man who understood what I needed to do as a queen. A man who came to the table willing to negotiate a deal that did not actively harm Ephyra. I wanted to see if you were a better ally than your brother. And you proved to be. But now that Prince Adamos has come out of the coma, I made contact instantly. Please know that I have kept this secret from most of my own council. Only my trusted physician, two attendants, and two bodyguards know of his existence."

Straightening the chair he had toppled, Adonis sank into it, seconds before his knees gave out.

Adamos was alive... His brother was alive. Which meant he was nothing but a fake monarch, taking what wasn't his.

Immediately, all the consequences of that rammed at him from all directions. "You are sure it is him?"

Calista nodded. "Your brother is a six-foot-four giant of a man of commanding presence. Even hurt, it is impossible to mistake his innate royal arrogance for anything else."

When Adonis remained silent, Calista continued. "I understand all the political ramifications that this has for you and Thalassos, Adonis. And I am willing to keep him in my care for as long as needed."

His head jerked up as Adonis considered what the young Queen was saying. "I could not hide Adamos's presence any more than I could cheat Thalassos."

"Come, Your Majesty," she said, infusing the address with gravity. "Thalassos is thriving under your rule. Do not let some misguided loyalty to your brother undermine all that you have undertaken as King. Especially when he's having problems with his sight and his memories."

Adonis refused to give her his assent. "I will be in touch with you, probably as soon as tomorrow morning. Guard him well, Calista. And my gratitude to you for looking after him with such care and discretion."

The Queen shrugged off his thanks and ended the call.

Adonis had no idea how long he sat in the darkness of the room, his head in his hands. A part of was overjoyed at the fact that Adamos was alive and well. And another darker part of him resented the hell out of the fact that he would give up the throne he had a taste of, already.

"Adonis?"

Jemima's breathy whisper from the threshold of the vast room made Adonis jump from numb stillness to exploding action. With a curse, he closed the video call browser, switched the laptop off, and took a long, deep breath before he turned. "You shouldn't have gotten out of bed, Jem," he said, keeping his tone steady through sheer willpower.

Whatever he thought he could hide from her, it was too late. "Was that…" She rubbed under her eyes with her knuckles like a child, but there was nothing childlike about the fear and something else that flashed in her eyes. "Did I hear that right? Calista said Adamos is…alive."

Adonis cursed, feeling itchy and restless under his skin. But the last thing he could do right now was to take to the skies or push himself off the cliff of a mountain. Not when his brother needed him and… Jemima needed him. For just a second, he regretted everything he had become part of in the last three months. And then, he hated himself for the thought.

"We will discuss it later," he said, knowing that he sounded dismissive and imperious. He had never aimed that tone at her but right now, he felt raw and reduced to his lowest denominator and didn't want to be examined with her brand of brutal honesty.

She ventured into the room, like the storm suddenly raging outside, and closed the doors behind her. A mesmerizing sort of resolve etched across her face when she reached him.

"Queen Calista called you to let you know that Adamos is alive. Clearly, he survived the plane crash. Why is he not here then?" With each sentence that she gave voice to, anger surged through her. "Why is he playing this cat-and-mouse game with us?"

Adonis thrust a hand through his hair. "He is not well. There's something wrong with his sight and apparently his memories come and go. Calista told me he only woke last night from a coma that he's been in for the last month."

"He does not remember who he is?" Jemima's question rang out like a missile, ricocheting against the silent walls of the room.

"I don't know," Adonis said, his own frustration bleeding into his words. "I need to consult my mother and the crown council and the high priestess immediately. This calls everything into question."

Shock nearly distorted the aching loveliness of Jemima's features. She grabbed his hand, urgent desperation radiating from her. "Are you mad? There is no need to bring this to the crown council or your mother even. It's cruel to give her hope when we don't know what is happening with him. There's a reason he has chosen to hide himself from her and Thalassos. You should continue to do the same."

He pushed away from her, a riot of conflicting emotions swirling through him, making his head dizzy with confusion. "I have no right to the crown of Thalassos, Jemima. It belongs to Adamos. It has always belonged to him. As long as he's alive, all of this…" He waved a hand between them, gesturing to the hall they stood in, to the bloody palace itself, "is a lie and I am nothing but a pretender to the throne."

"That's not true," she said, conviction bleeding from her every pore. "In a mere three months, you have made welcome changes to Thalassos that even the crown council couldn't deny. You were born for this, Adonis, even if it took a circuitous detour for you to get here. I refuse to let you walk away from this. If we told Queen Isadora, I am sure she will say the same."

"But I'm not even legitimate. You heard his ramblings that day. Knowing the truth, knowing that I was born of a palace maid, knowing that now the true heir is alive, you still think I should keep myself on the throne?"

"Please, Adonis—"

"Or is it that," he said, spewing all the poison that had festered since he'd been a boy, "the idea of not being the

Queen of Thalassos anymore, the idea of being married to only Adonis Vasilikos, does not suit you?"

Jemima felt as if she had been slapped across the face.

Her flesh had the memory to supply her because her father had once slapped her out of nowhere and Jemima, back then, hadn't known to duck.

The same metallic tang of fear flooded her mouth now, while the rest of her body shook, as if it couldn't understand what her mind had already perceived. As if it couldn't understand the source of the sudden shivers that overtook her.

Still, she tried to leash her own roiling emotions, knowing that her husband needed her now. After all, her vows to the King had long transformed into love for the man. "You know that is not true," she said, her throat full of tears turning her words into a soft whisper, instead of the mighty roar that they should've been. Beneath the shock came hurt, twisting her insides with its vicious fingers. "Please don't make this about me."

"Make this about you?" Adonis thundered, anguish and rage and hurt ravaging his beautiful features. He looked like a painting by some great master caught in the minute of acute torment. Frozen in that state forever. No, she would not stand for that. "Of course, this becomes about you and me and the family we are growing. You're naive to think it doesn't touch our lives."

She planted a palm across her belly and his gaze instantly zeroed in on the gesture. If she thought the subtle reminder would calm him, though, she was proved wrong. Tension radiated from him in buffeting waves. And she tried to stand still and steady in the middle of it. Knowing that this moment could make or break them.

"Our children will do fine even if they're not the heirs to Thalassos, Adonis. You know that there's no bigger present to these boys than us loving them. In fact, I would even go so far as to say that they might thrive more being your children rather than heirs to the kingdom. So, what is it that bothers you about this?"

"And what about Zayn?" She didn't doubt that it was his affection and attachment to her young brother that reverberated in his words. "You think your father would allow me to have custody of his son if he learns that I'm nothing but a pretender to the throne? What then, Jemima? Would you be willing to lose him?"

Jemima knew a minefield when she saw one. Reaching him, she clasped his cheek, hoping that her touch would anchor him. "You know how much I love my brother and that I would do anything for him and that I have. But you forget the most important thing in all this, Adonis." She pressed her forehead into his chest and the scent of him fueled her on. "I trust you. I trust you more than anything in the world. I trust that you will find a way to keep Zayn with us, a way to keep my father away from him."

Her hopes were once again squashed when Adonis stiffened against her touch and moved back. Sudden desolation claimed her, followed by raging fury.

She loved this man so much and she had been sitting on that realization for so long that Jemima did not remember who she had been before this love for him had suffused her entire being.

And the very same love filled her with an inordinate amount of courage to speak the truth, to speak her truth.

"It is clear that Adamos does not wish to return to Thalassos, at least for now. It is also clear that the kingdom thrives with you as king. So, what is it that you cannot accept about all this?"

"I would not be able to forget, for a second, that all of this is not mine. I would not be able to forget—"

"One old, hateful man's spewing and twisting lies? You are his son, Adonis, whether you were born to a maid or a queen. Your mother raised you as her son. To my calculation, that makes you King. But if you want to continue your delusion, if you want to revel in the pain he caused you instead of your people, instead of everything you and I have built together, then yes, maybe you're not fit to be King."

It was his turn to blanch. Whatever anger and fury and anguish she had seen in him before disappeared, leaving a bleakness in his eyes.

And her heart thought it might shatter in her chest as he stood there alone. As he'd been his entire life. As he was choosing to be in this moment, even though he didn't need to be.

The words burst out of her, even though she knew they wouldn't land just then.

"I love you Adonis," she said, loudly enough that her words rivaled the raging of the storm outside. "I love you even though you are struggling in this moment. I love your sense of integrity, your command of a room, your hatred for diplomacy. I even love your madness for risks. I love that you put everyone else before you. I love that your respect and love for your mother and your homeland brought you back to all this. I love that you care about your brother and that you think you're stealing this from him. If only you could see yourself through my eyes, Adonis," she said, repeating his own words to him. "Then you would know that you're a king no matter who you were born to, no matter what one mad king says."

"And if I refuse to be king? If I give up all this, what would your love do then? Would you follow me anywhere, Jem? Would you leave this blasted kingdom and give up all this?"

She smiled but it lacked any warmth or humor or good feeling. He would still continue to test her love then? Or was it himself he didn't trust?

Her heart nearly shattered at the sadness of the thought.

"It is because I love you that I will not let you give up all this, because I see what is possible for Thalassos and its subjects and even Ephyra, that I should stop you from giving it all up. My love would not be what it is, if it shies away from the truth, Adonis, if it only tells you what you want to hear."

He rubbed a hand over his face, his lean chest rising and falling.

Seconds piled by and Jemima waited for him to cover the distance between them, to take her in his arms and tell her that she was right, to tell her that he loved her too.

With each passing tick of the giant clock on the wall, she also knew that she had lost him. She took a step back then, and it was the hardest thing she had ever done in her life. Harder than loving this man. Which came to her easily, for he was one of a kind.

He was a king truly, where it mattered.

When she reached the door that would cement their differences, she heard him call out her name. Head bowed, she stopped but refused to turn. "What?" she said, all of her disappointment turning into belligerence.

"I'm going to Ephyra to…bring him home. I have to do that, Jemima. I could not live with myself if I didn't—"

"You are the bloody king, Adonis. Do whatever you think you need to. But don't expect me to be an obedient queen. Don't expect me to stand by you quietly when you're intent on ruining a good thing. I've had a lifetime of obedience that I barely rid myself of, thanks to you. I'm not going to begin pandering to another man now, even if that is you."

"You made a vow to be my wife," he said, a thread of anger weaving through his tone. "You belong with me. Instead, you bandy about grand words like love."

"Tell me," she said, turning, "will you be the same man you are now far away from Thalassos and everything you love? With your heart trapped here, will you love me as I love you, Adonis?"

"The reason I returned is not love for Thalassos, but because it's what I owe to the woman who raised me as her own."

The self-isolation she heard in his words tore her up from inside out. "Wow, how did I not know how good you are at lying to yourself? I'm sorry he twisted you up so badly that you can't admit to what you love, Adonis, or reach for it. I can't imagine how scary it must feel. And I see now why you buried that pain in outrageous, risky stunts all your life. But this is me, your wife, and I won't play along. What I see in front of me is a coward who masquerades as the bravest man in the world."

"A coward?" he said, his chin rearing down.

"Yes. Whether it is you or Adamos that sits on the throne now, my place is here at the palace, with your mother, with Thalassos. This is where I will raise my children, teaching them to go after everything they love. If you want to run away at the first hurdle and ruin everything we're building, if you want to use this knowledge of Adamos being alive as reason to turn your back on all that you love, feel free to do so."

She didn't wait for him to reply to her grand statement. Laughter rose up within her, bitter and twisted, at her own pretension to nobility she didn't have.

Without him, she was nothing but a pawn again. But queen or pawn, she wasn't the same Jemima that had lived in fear, had borne apathy without a word, for so long.

He had changed her.

And she wouldn't settle for anything less than her king's utter devotion.

CHAPTER TWELVE

IT TOOK ADONIS nearly two days to clear his schedule of important matters so that he could travel to Ephyra.

That Jemima wasn't traveling with him—and more importantly, that she wasn't happy with his plan, had become clear to his and her aides and the palace staff. Not that she turned cold on him in front of so many prying eyes. She simply didn't have the effusive warmth that she radiated toward him so easily, anymore.

It was akin to sun's warmth and light not touching his skin for months.

Then there was the fact that the palace PR team hadn't made an official announcement of the pregnancy yet.

He knew how much the media, and Thalassans themselves who had been deprived of big celebrations, would be overjoyed at the announcement. But he couldn't postpone it until he figured out how to fix the mess they were in because his sweet wife had already begun showing.

In the end, he'd claimed it was a matter of national security that he travel to Ephyra immediately in front of the crown council, had been thankful that Jemima hadn't betrayed her misgivings in front of them or his mother, had kissed her soft cheek when she'd been in deep slumber like a thief stealing something that didn't belong to him.

The idea of her staying behind in Thalassos even if he

left…both confused and skewered him. How could she say that, when in the same breath, she claimed to love him?

It was only as he waited for Queen Calista's attendants to bring his brother into the stark, hospital-like room that Jemima's words struck him with the force of a hammer hitting the anvil.

A coward, she had called him.

Burying his face in his hands, he groaned. Because she was right and he realized that only now, when he was truly facing the prospect of losing everything he had.

The last three months of his life—ruling Thalassos with her by his side while building a bond together—had been his happiest, his best.

And yet, he had also lived it with the fear that Thalassos or Jem or his happiness weren't his own and might be snatched from him at any moment. So, being the coward he was, he had decided that he would give it up at the first obstacle instead of facing the pain of losing it all. Instead of fighting for it.

And she was also right that if he left Thalassos behind, he would only be a half man.

But even that wasn't as ghastly as the idea of returning to his old life without her.

His queen, his wife, his…*love*.

The quiet acknowledgment flooded him with a rush the likes of which he'd never known. He felt like he was diving from the highest cliff, his heart thundering with life in his throat, his entire body abuzz with the thrill of being alive.

His hands shook as he ran them through his hair, every cell and sinew and bone in him purring with the need to go to her.

Abruptly, he shot to his feet just as Adamos, leaning heavily on a walking stick, walked into the room.

Shock pummeled Adonis at the sight of his older brother, his love for him a suffocating anvil on his chest.

His brother looked...*wrecked*. Inside out.

Dark bruises shone on his rugged face, each bigger and more colorful than the last. Then there were all the stitches for numerous cuts. One arm in a sling, his stride crooked, his hip bent, he looked like he'd barely survived the crash.

Only his dark eyes—as gray as the stormy sky Adonis had left behind in Thalassos, shone with a forceful intensity that Adonis remembered.

Reaching him, Adonis gingerly hugged his brother.

With a harsh laugh that didn't sound quite normal, Adamos wrapped a thick, corded arm around his back. "I might look fragile. But I will not break, Adonis, if you squeeze me too tight."

Fighting the sudden onslaught of prickling tears, Adonis pulled back. "I've come with the intention of taking you back to Thalassos. To give you your throne back."

"Has that intention changed now?" Adamos asked, his thick brows tugging together. Ever the shrewd prince their father had molded him to be. And he knew his younger brother well.

"I have second thoughts now, yes," Adonis said honestly.

Jemima's words tickled at the back of his mind, like a song constantly unspooling wonder in him. So many things falling into place finally. All because she'd had the courage to speak the truth for him, to him.

You're a king no matter who you were born to...

She had seen so clearly, so well. And in return, he hadn't even acknowledged her admission.

Christos, he wasn't just a coward but a cruel one at that...

"Also, I realized I should take your wishes into consideration," Adonis said. He took a deep breath and searched for the right words. "I do not want anything that is rightfully yours, Adamos."

"You think I don't know that?" Adamos replied with an impatient huff. "Although it seems you have married the woman who should have been my queen."

"She is mine," Adonis said hotly.

Adamos, the cunning bastard, let out laughter that sounded like the boom of a cannon.

"The throne might be yours but you don't deserve her."

A flicker of shame danced in his brother's eyes. "No. I never did."

Adonis gave voice to the deepest desire he had hidden away. "But I will not leave Thalassos if you come back either. Until you recover fully, we can keep you and your condition under wraps. When you're ready to take back the throne, I'll help the transition and stay. Whatever role you give me, I'd like to continue to serve the crown and Thalassos to my best."

"I've been awake only a few hours but Her Highness of Ephyra," his brother said, a snappy anger touching his words at the mention of Queen Calista, "has made sure I understood all the things you've achieved already in three months." His brother's gray gaze pinned Adonis's, as if they were still boys. As if it were he seeking protection now instead of the other way around. "It is clear, for all of our father's ramblings, that you're a far better king that I ever could be, Adonis. And I'm not sure if I have the right to ask this of you but…keep the throne, won't you? And grant me freedom from the shackles of it."

Adonis stared at his brother, shock suffusing every inch. "I don't understand, Adamos."

"I can't explain now," his brother said, massaging his

right hip. Pain etched onto his features, distorting them with its cruel fingers. "I'm of no use to myself in my current condition, much less Thalassos. And even before the crash, I began to hate the palace and the crown for all that it stole from me. I...didn't want it then, and I definitely don't want it now, Adonis."

"Is that why Mama summoned me?"

"Yes. She knows her sons well, it seems. She knew you would take up the mantle if I gave it up. She even told me you would make a better king than I ever could."

"That's not true," Adonis said, even as his heart thrummed with joy at the conviction his mother showed him.

"She's right," Adamos said, without a flicker of doubt. "I know I have no right to ask this of you, but, Adonis, give me my life back. Even when I make myself known to the world again, there are any number of clauses that we can use to declare me incompetent for the crown."

"I don't understand," Adonis began but Adamos cut him off.

"I will share when I'm ready, *ne*? Please, grant me this."

Adonis wrapped his arms around his brother and squeezed him tight. "Mama... I need to tell her. Please, Adamos, it is cruel to let her think—"

"Only on the condition that she doesn't ask to see me," his brother retorted, steel in his tone. Whatever demons haunted his brother, it was clear that he'd rather not share them with his family.

Adonis nodded. "Fine. If you change your mind, know that—"

"Don't be so ready to give up what is in your heart, Adonis. And what is so right. Thalassos needs your competence, your devotion, you."

His brother's words—so similar to what his queen had said, reverberated through Adonis's mind all through the short flight back to Thalassos.

Regret pricked at him like a thousand needles stuck in his skin as he remembered how casually he had walked away from her, how much pain he might have caused her.

He knew, as he jumped off the chopper onto the terrace of the highest wings of the palace, that laying his heart out for his queen was the biggest risk he could ever take.

And that the pain that would come for him if she didn't forgive him would be the worst he had ever known.

As she'd so boldly and bravely declared, he would only be half a man without the woman he loved by his side.

"He is up to something in Ephyra. And if you know what is good for you, you will share it with me, Jemima."

Her father's whispered threat reached Jemima on the wings of high winds that played about with the elaborate folds of her evening dress. That he had discovered her hiding spot on one of the highest terraces of the palace—with devastatingly beautiful views of the Aegean and the hills and Thalassos itself, wasn't a surprise.

While she hadn't admitted it to Adonis—seemed foolish in retrospect now, she'd been aware that her father's spies had been watching both her and her husband, for any chinks in their personal armor or their tenuous faith in each other.

"Jemima? You think you're too good to respond to your father because you're Queen?"

She sighed and gathered her wits and queenly graces and weapons to herself. This was a confrontation she'd wished wouldn't come about. For she had no stomach to present her father with the disgusting truth of who he was and worse, what he was becoming.

Also, she was plumb out of truths and wishes and foolish delusions. But whether he was here or not, she would do her duty by her king. It was only the thought of the man she so adored that gave the energy to turn around and face her father.

With a flick of one brow, she dismissed the two personal bodyguards Adonis insisted follow her everywhere. The mess she was about to sort didn't need any kind of audience.

"I heard you, Papa," she said, turning around. "I was simply organizing my response to you for there is so much to say."

"What is he doing in Ephyra?" Her father's teeth bared in a tacky facsimile of a sneer. "Do you not worry why he visits the young, beautiful queen the moment she summons him? Do you not care that he's already broken every vow he's made to you?"

"Enough, Papa," she said, more tired than angry. "Your cheap tricks to make me doubt myself and my king will not work on me. You aren't half the man my husband is." Frost coated her words as she fixed the fracture in her composure. "The King is in Ephyra because there's an emergency matter he must deal with, himself. You, and the rest of the crown council, have already been notified at his discretion."

"It was clear to everyone present that whatever little connection was there between you two has already gone up in smoke, Jemima. If you had any sense, you would throw your lot in with me and the crown council, before he publicly humiliates you with a scandal."

"And if you had any sense," Jemima snarled, all attempts at courtesy and control disappearing, "you would think twice before engaging in treasonous speech against your king and crown."

"How dare you speak to me that way?" he said, taking a menacing step in her direction.

Even as fear flooded her—mostly for the babies in her belly, Jemima refused to pull back or step away from him. Never again was she going to be bullied by him. "Careful, Papa, or my bodyguards will throw you in jail for something as silly as encroaching on their queen's personal space. My husband is a possessive, protective man that doesn't like even the hair on my head ruffled."

"You foolish girl! Don't you see—?"

"She sees better than you or me, old man," came the voice before the shape of him revealed itself in the darkness. "Only foolish, egotistical men need to be schooled twice on the same matter. For my part, I have learned the lesson to not trifle with Jemima Vasilikos. Not if I don't want to be pushed into a dark prison."

Relief and agony came at Jemima like twin gales pulling at her in opposite directions. She wanted to throw her arms around him and cling to him and beg him to never leave her alone again.

Resisting the urge, she donned a cool mask that she'd learned from him. "Good evening, Your Majesty."

He, it seemed, had no such reservations. Wrapping an arm around her shoulders, Adonis pulled her to him. In such close quarters, with his delicious scent filling every corner and crevice of her soul, Jemima couldn't hide the shivers that overtook her.

Uncaring of their avidly watching audience, he pressed his mouth to her temple. When her own shivers abated, she recognized the stiffness in his lean body.

Thoughts pummeled her. What had happened with Adamos? What did it mean that Adonis had arrived alone? And when push came to shove, could she really walk away from the man she loved with every breath?

"Jemima might still hold some misguided affection for you, Aziz, but I do not have the slightest bit of tolerance for you or any man who would threaten her." Pure steel reverberated in Adonis's voice. "This is my last official warning to you. If you care at all about the power and wealth you have amassed at Thalassos's feet, you will respect my queen and my rule. Or I will make sure you're locked up in some dank, dark prison for treason."

Her father left, without even a glance in her direction.

The moment he was out of earshot, Jemima jerked away from the man whose arms would bind her, despite her best resistance. Neither did she have the energy to engage in another heartbreaking argument with him. "I'm tired," she said, walking away from him.

"Not curious about why I return without him, Jem?"

"No," Jemima said, hardening her heart against the naked want she spied in his eyes. "You left for Ephyra against my wishes, against my advice. Why you return now, alone or otherwise, is not my concern either."

Hurt reverberated through each word she said but she seemed to have no control over that. It seemed that, after decades of constantly suppressing her every emotion and wish and desire, that particular ability was not in her toolkit anymore.

Neither could she will herself to stop loving him, to stop seeing him as who he truly was.

Walking around her, Adonis planted himself in front of her, his arms coming to clasp her shoulders. While he kept his grip loose, the tension that radiated from him was nearly painful to bear. "Not even if I were to tell you that you were right about everything?" he said. "I do know how much you pride yourself on your wisdom, Jem."

She raised her gaze to his and begged her composure to stay intact. "At what time during our short relationship have I ever given you the impression that I cared about being right?"

"You were also right that I was being a coward, that I have loved Thalassos with all my heart for so long. But I denied the truth to myself. It was easier that way than to wish for things to be different."

"And I understand your pain better than anyone, Adonis. But it seems foolish to me to continue the delusion when it doesn't have to be true, to keep giving yourself that pain when it's not necessary anymore. When instead, you could choose happiness."

"Call it a stubborn fool clinging to the past, Jemima. Until now, until you pushed me to see it, I didn't even recognize the taste of my own happiness. I didn't recognize the fact that everything I had never wished for, not even in my wildest dreams, was already mine. You are right that if I left Thalassos, I would leave my heart here. But even more than the kingdom, it is you who owns me, Jemima. You own my heart. You claimed it without even asking. Maybe even on that first night when you asked me with such honesty to save Thalassos."

Tears filled her eyes and flowed down her cheeks. "I was only saving myself. Do not attribute nobility to me that I don't possess, Adonis. It is only through you and your eyes and your vision that I have come to love Thalassos too." A hiccup escaped her, all her composure a thing of the past. "When I told you that I loved you, it made no difference to you. You simply walked away, crushing me in the process."

He pulled her to him then, and her sobs broke through the dam of her control.

She was aware that he had lifted her, again as if she were nothing but a feather made of dreams and wishes, that he was going down a steep set of steps, to a small tower that was used for stargazing, but she couldn't stop her tears.

By the time he settled down onto a settee with her in his lap, she had soaked his shirt through.

His rough hands clasped her cheeks, forcing her to meet his eyes. "Shh...*agapi mou*. That's enough. I told you; your tears unman me like nothing else could. And that they come because of my cowardice, because of my own refusal to see what was right in front of me...it wrecks me through and through. Jemima, please, will you not forgive me? Will you not give me another chance?"

With a gasping breath, Jemima sought control over her tears. "You should not have doubted me or yourself for an instant. When have I ever told you anything but the truth?"

He smiled, but it lacked warmth. "My foolishness had nothing to do with you, Jem. It was all me. I suffused my entire being with rejection and pain, and when happiness danced in front of me, I was blind to it. But now... I will never again make that mistake."

Sliding her off his lap to the couch, to which she gave a loud protest, he went to his knees in front of her, just like he had done once in front of his mother and the crown council.

He took her hands in his, and kissed each knuckle with such thorough leisure that each press of his lips battered away the fear that had filled her for the last few days. Only his tender touch made her believe this was real, that he was real. And he seemed to know that too.

When he raised his face to her, his blue, blue eyes glittered with emotion that she finally recognized, and craved like air itself.

"I love you with all my heart, my queen. And there is no one I'd rather rule with by my side than you. Your trust, your honesty, your expertise, everything you give me," he raised her knuckles to his eyes, and Jemima felt her heart flutter about her chest like a bird finally free, "is a benediction that I didn't know I needed. Be my wife, the mother of my children and my queen, Jem, and I will worship at your feet for the rest of our lives."

She laughed through the tears blurring her vision again. Smacking him on the shoulder, she slid off the settee into his waiting arms. Ignored his warning growl to be careful. Needing to be enveloped by his warm, muscled strength.

Nothing could stop her from reaching him and touching him to her heart's content.

"I only wish to be loved by you, Adonis. I want nothing more; you know that, right? Not the crown, not the queendom, not all the riches in the palace. Only you."

He pulled her close and took her mouth finally. The kiss was slow, even tentative, for a man who punched headlong into deep canyons and terrifying river gorges with nary a thought.

Pushing him onto the thick rug, Jemima straddled his lean hips and stared down at him. "Adamos…how is he?"

Cupping her hips, Adonis stared up at her. "In pain. He begged to be free of the crown, Jem. Insisted that I was the better option for Thalassos."

"Then Adamos is a better man than I gave him credit

for," she said with a bold imperiousness she had learned from him.

Adonis grinned, his palm stroking her from her neck to her thighs in mesmerizing touches. "Such a harsh queen you are, *agapi mou*! I'm afraid to see how I will fare with you."

Leaning down, she rubbed her breasts against his chest, and kissed his lower lip. "I'm sure you will come up to scratch, Your Majesty, since you have the rest of our lives to prove yourself to me."

"I will never again give you reason to doubt my love for you, *yineka mou*. That is a vow this king makes to his queen."

There was no more to be said after that. Nor did she have enough sense left to. For her king ordered her to impale herself on his thick shaft and Jemima was nothing if not an obedient queen.

Raising the billowing skirts of her dress, she did as he ordered her to. Fingers laced, eyes held, they moved together to a desperate, wanton rhythm, the shimmering future laid out ahead of them imbuing the moment with a rich depth. Head thrown back, Jemima gave herself over to the climb, knowing that she would never be alone ever again.

"Come for me, Queen," Adonis murmured huskily, his hands stroking every inch of her, his hips pumping away at her as if their connection was the very air he needed.

And soon, he took her to the heights of passion and tumbled her from it. Making sure he caught her in his arms. Over and over again.

EPILOGUE

ILEANA AND AJAX VASILIKOS were born healthy and hale and screaming their hearts out a few months later, but far earlier than either the Queen or King of Thalassos had accounted for.

Breaking their papa's tender heart, as only their mother knew, because His Majesty Adonis Vasilikos was out of Thalassos at the time, on a scheduled trip to their neighbor Ephyra. To check up on his brother, Adamos, whose progressive blindness had completely spread over one eye.

I don't want to leave your side for a few months after that, Adonis had said, worry etching deep lines into his face. *If I check on him now, then I won't have to feel guilty that I'm abandoning him later.*

So he'd gone with Jemima's blessing and urging, despite his brother's protests that he *"didn't need to be coddled like a child"* by either him or *"the blasted queen."*

But of course, fate had other plans, as it always seemed to have where she and her husband were concerned. And she didn't much protest it, given labor pains had consumed her. Though Adonis couldn't muster up the same level of equanimity.

He railed and cursed at the fact that he would miss the birth of his children. Only his mother's soft entreaty that he might upset his queen further with his own outburst had eventually calmed him.

Jemima was eternally thankful for Queen Isadora's constant attendance, and for the fast labor and easy births at the private clinic, even as a part of her—the one that wasn't out of its mind with pain and agony, wished it had taken longer so that Adonis could return.

Of course, the fact that her children—as temperamental as their father, had chosen a stormy night to make their sudden appearance into the world meant Adonis's return had been delayed further.

In the end, it was two whole days before he appeared at the entrance of the large, bright room, looking as ravaged as she'd felt only two days earlier. Although it seemed he was less recovered from the ordeal than she.

Jemima scooted up on the lavish bed, hiding the grimace of pain so that she could better look at him.

Not that her wonderful husband missed it. "Are you in pain?" he whispered, his words coming as if he was speaking them through a heavy, clogged throat.

"A bit," she said, drinking him in.

Dark shadows cradled his brilliant blue eyes, making them pop even more. His hair looked like he had taken out all his frustration and urgency at it, the thick, short waves standing up every which way.

Then there was the thick blond stubble on his jaw. He looked thoroughly disreputable and utterly gorgeous.

"Are you going to stand there forever, Your Majesty?" Jemima teased, her own stomach twisting into fresh knots. She had known, all through the pregnancy, that the birth of their children was going to affect him more emotionally than her. Now, she could see that her fears had been right.

Anguish and affection and so much more swirled in

the blue depths, disbelief stretched those sculpted lips, and his nostrils flared.

"I thought you would be dying to meet them, Adonis," she said, emotion coating her own words. She'd been so worried about his feelings and how he would process them that she hadn't let herself acknowledge her own. "And me..." she said, speaking her heart now. A wet gurgle, not unlike her infant daughter's, escaped her throat. "I missed you."

"I'm angry still, *agapi*, that I missed it. I feel cheated." He rubbed a hand over his face, seemed to realize he had to shave, and grimaced. "I'm not sure I should touch them with that emotion pulsing through me. I want them to know me, need me, love me so much..."

Jemima's heart gave such a hard spasm that she had to open her mouth to draw in a breath. Tenderness and love engulfed her throat, making it several minutes before she could speak again. "Darling, one look at your face, one whisper of your heart, one touch of your rough hands, and they will know that. One glimpse into those blue eyes and they will never doubt your love, Adonis, just as I never doubt it. Ever."

"You think?" he said, and Jemima nodded.

A long exhale left him, making his shoulders straighten out. His blue gaze swept over her and the bed. "Where are they?"

Jemima pointed to the two bassinets that were out of sight from where he stood. "Shall I call the nurses?" she asked, giving him a choice.

"No," he bit out. Then marching to the small sink tucked into an alcove, he washed his hands, wiped them on a fresh napkin.

Jemima blinked back tears as he bent and picked up

their daughter first, his movements incredibly gentle. The sight of that tiny babe in his arms made her heart thud and her ovaries—already strained to the limit, melt. At least that's what that sensation felt like.

"She has your eyes," he said, lifting one tiny fist to his mouth. His eyes were wide, full of awe as he took her in, a feeling Jemima knew very well. "All sharp and wide and drilling into one's soul."

Jemima laughed, her heart expanding to a dangerous size in her chest. It felt impossible to contain the happiness that inflated her from within. "And she has your nose, the great Vasilikos beak."

"Remind me to tell Adamos that. He promises," Adonis choked a little, "to be the best uncle he can be."

"Whenever he's ready," Jemima said, meeting her husband's eyes. The fact that Prince Adamos wasn't adjusting very well to his half-blindness wasn't altogether a surprise. Although, Jemima had a feeling it was Queen Calista that prodded and poked at him as if he were a grouchy bear. Time would only tell if Adamos would see that the young queen was exactly what he needed.

"I told him the same," Adonis said, his smile touching his eyes.

Their baby girl cooed, and stretched and pressed her chubby fists into her papa's angular cheeks as he brought her over. "Papa loves you, Ileana, so much." His very heart seemed to reverberate in his words.

As if she could understand the sentiment, Ileana gave her papa a rare, toothless grin that disappeared as fast as it had come.

Adonis looked as if he had conquered the range of mountains that dotted Thalassos's perimeter.

Leaning down, he transferred her, ever so gently, into

Jemima's waiting arms. Then when she had their beautiful little girl all secure, he captured her lips in a tender,
soul-stripping kiss. The taste of him, minty and male and
devastatingly familiar, flew through Jemima, bolstering
her faith in them all over.

Clasping his cheek with her free hand, she leaned into
his kiss, needing it as much as he did. When the kiss
turned salty, Jemima realized her husband was crying.
Her own eyes filled up suddenly.

"She's perfect," Adonis said, pulling away, one long
finger grazing against the tiny head. "Just like her mama."

Their daughter watched with saucer-like eyes while he
kissed her mama again.

A wail—loud and clanging, erupted into the fraught silence, making Adonis jerk away from her. Jemima laughed
at the horrified expression on his face.

"That, my darling, is your son, letting the entire palace
know of his displeasure."

"What does he need?" Adonis said, straightening with
a sudden urgency.

"Either his nappy is wet or he's hungry or he's just generally displeased with the world," Jemima said, still smiling. "Sometimes he'll smile at one nurse while he glares
at the other. He gets cranky with hunger but won't drink
properly. He has neither the patience nor the happy nature
of his sister. Your son is going to be quite the handful, and I
believe is going to need all the discipline we can manage."

Adonis covered the ground to their son's bassinet in
quick strides. He checked Ajax's nappy, scrunched his
face, and changed it easily, as if he had done it a thousand times before.

Jemima's breath caught in her throat. "I wish I had my
phone to record it. The King changing a dirty nappy."

Adonis lifted the infant to his chest, pride shimmering in his eyes. "I did say I would be a hands-on father, didn't I?"

Even from the distance, Jemima could see her son's blue gaze study his papa with the same wonder as his papa showed him. "Many men apparently make those kinds of claims." Then before he could protest, she raised her hand. "I do agree that you're unlike any man I've known, Your Majesty."

"Exactly," Adonis said, pressing his mouth to their son's temple.

Ajax clearly didn't like the stubble on his papa's jaw for he squirmed and screamed and generally made his displeasure known. Uncowed by it, Adonis tucked him up against his chest. "And there will be no disciplining either of them, Jemima."

"You can't mean that?"

"I do," Adonis said, reaching her. With easy grace, he tucked himself into the bed, by her side. "My children, even this one with his temper," he said, kissing their son's forehead, "are going to grow up untethered like free birds. No one is going to stop them from exploring the world, the skies, the mountains itself if they wish."

"And if they fall?" Jemima said, heart in her throat at the wonder that was her husband, her king.

"If they fall, we will catch, Jem. But whatever they do or want, they will never doubt my love for them."

"So I'm going to have three devils to contend with instead of one," she said, grinning.

"Ahh…but you're so good at leashing us, *agapi mou*," he said, leaning toward her. "I do not believe for one second that you will struggle with us three."

There was no need to reply because Adonis took her

mouth in a soft, blisteringly slow kiss that drenched her in his love.

Not that their children gave them more than two minutes to indulge in it.

* * * * *

If you couldn't get enough of
Vows to a King
then you're sure to adore these other spicy stories
by Tara Pammi!

Saying "I Do" to the Wrong Greek
Twins to Tame Him
Fiancée for the Cameras
Contractually Wed
Her Twin Secret

Available now!

FORGOTTEN GREEK PROPOSAL

MICHELLE SMART

MILLS & BOON

CHAPTER ONE

THE PAIN THAT shot through Lucie Burton's eyes when she peered between her lids was so great it momentarily distracted her from the pneumatic drill boring into her head. It also stopped her registering the man sitting beside her, engrossed on his phone. But only initially. One painful blink and he swam to the surface of her vision, the registering of exactly who he was such a shock to her system that she blinked again.

He was still there.

Her heart made the most enormous thump. Thanasis Antoniadis was sitting by her bedside.

Too confused to be frightened, she lifted her head. Well, tried. Another shooting pain stopped her lifting it more than a couple of inches.

Pale green eyes with lashes as dark as the pupils and rings encircling the irises suddenly locked onto hers.

She swallowed, a reflex that had nothing to do with the dryness of her throat. 'Where am I?' Whatever bed she was in, it wasn't her bed, and this was no room she'd been in before.

'Hospital.'

Her next blink was slightly less painful and she became aware that she had things stuck to her chest and that something had been injected into her hand…a medical drip?

'You were in a car accident.'

So that was what his voice sounded like. Honeyed coffee. A thought that struck her confused mind as absurd even as her hazy, confused mind wondered why she was fixating on Thanasis's voice rather than asking what the hell she was doing in hospital with her family's greatest enemy at her bedside. Or, rather, her stepfamily's greatest enemy.

Lucie had been only three years old when her mother left her father for the Greek shipping tycoon Georgios Tsaliki, and so her childhood and adolescence had been split between her father and his new family, and her mother, Georgios and his varying offspring. Varying because Lucie's mother was wife number four. To everyone's surprise, over two decades later, the marriage was still going strong. Lucie suspected this was because her mother maintained an extremely well-developed blind eye to Georgios's many infidelities, infidelities she must have factored in when marrying him seeing as she was wife number three's replacement.

As a result, Lucie had grown up in two wildly differing households. Stability and order had come from her real father. Chaos and fun had come from her stepfather, whose gregarious nature had him on excellent terms with all his ex-wives and the nine children they'd collectively popped out for him. Life for Georgios and his extended family had been one great big holiday, right until the money had run out earlier that year and his eldest son, Alexis, wrested control of the company.

Because the converse to Georgios's generous heart

was also true—when he took against someone, they remained his enemy for life, and Georgios Tsaliki had no greater enemy than rival shipping tycoon Petros Antoniadis, and it was this mutual enmity to blame for the near destruction of both families' fortunes.

The original cause of the enmity between the two men was something Lucie knew only the bare bones of; a business partnership between two great friends turned sour. If there were more details than that she suspected both men had forgotten them, and now their mutual loathing and feud was simply one of those things, like the fact she barely touched five foot in height and had unmanageable black curls. One of those things like the fact Thanasis Antoniadis smelt as flipping wonderful as he looked.

She'd seen him in the flesh only once before. She'd been eighteen at the time and enjoying her last long Greek summer holiday. Athena, Lucie's sometime favourite Tsaliki offspring—Athena blew hot and cold—had invited her along to what she'd promised would be the party of the decade. They'd barely stepped into the apartment when Lucie had spotted the best-looking man in the entire world pouring himself a drink at the bar and had actually felt her jaw drop. There had been something familiar about him, which had made her think he must be a famous actor or model or something. Whatever he did for a living, he was the most gorgeous man she'd ever laid eyes on and she'd been unable to tear her gaze away, until Athena had grabbed her hand and in a high-pitched voice whispered, 'What's *he* doing here?'

Lucie had stared at her blankly.

'Thanasis Antoniadis,' she'd explained, panicking. 'If

I'd known he was going to be here, I would never have come. Papa will *kill* me if he hears about this.'

Lucie had looked again at the man causing the usually unflappable Athena to have a semi-meltdown at the exact moment Thanasis had looked across the busy room… and fixed his gaze right on *her*. The frisson she'd felt snake up her spine was like nothing she'd experienced before, or since for that matter. She might very well still be there gawping at him if Athena hadn't dragged her away, hissing, 'Stop looking at him like that! We need to get out of here.'

And that had been that. Less than two minutes under a roof with him.

He'd been familiar because he was the spitting image of his father. Georgios regularly refreshed the photo of Petros Antoniadis he kept on his dartboard.

The man who'd captured her attention so vividly six years ago was now scrutinising her with a strained intensity she felt like a touch to her skin.

'How are you feeling?' he asked.

'My head hurts and I feel sick,' she croaked, scrutinising him in turn with an increasing wariness as the drilling in her head settled enough for her brain to start vaguely functioning properly. There was something about the room that made her think she must be in Greece, but that was impossible. She'd gone to sleep in her shared north London flat…hadn't she?

She couldn't remember going to bed.

He grimaced. 'That is to be expected. You took quite the knock.'

'What happened to me? What's going on? Why are you here?'

His neck extended, the nostrils of his long, pointed nose flaring. 'Your mouth sounds dry. Water?'

'Please. But tell me what's happened and why you're here.'

He poured water from a jug into a beaker and placed a straw in it, then stretched an arm to place the straw close to her mouth. 'You don't remember?'

She inched her face to the straw. Before taking a much-needed drink, she said, 'I know you're Thanasis Antoniadis but I don't know why I'm in hospital, seemingly in Greece, or why you of all people are with me.'

Something flickered in his eyes. 'Me of all people? And drink slowly or you will make yourself sick. Take sips.'

His heavily accented English was excellent, she thought absently as she savoured the crisp coolness of fresh water in her mouth and hoped it didn't react to the nausea swirling in her stomach. Lucie's Greek was fluent but nowhere near as good as Thanasis's English. 'Thank you.'

He gave a tight nod of acknowledgement and put the beaker back on the table without his stare leaving her face. 'Me of all people?' he repeated.

'Why would you be here? Where's my family?' The more pertinent question, she dimly supposed, was why she wasn't terrified to have woken with the son of her stepfather's enemy by her bed; a brooding near-stranger who had to tower over her by well over a foot in height and probably weighed twice as much to boot. All that weight would be muscle, something she knew by the way his light blue shirt stretched across his chest. This man was in prime physical fitness. If he wanted, he could snap her bones with the ease of a cruel child snapping a bug's wings.

Instead of quailing at the thought, she had an absurd sense of certainty that Thanasis Antoniadis would never lay a hand on her, not in malice nor in anger. Absurd because she didn't know this man at all, only knew of him, and yet her certainty went hand in hand with the sense coming to life inside her that she *did* know him, as if they'd met before in a different life or a different world.

That must be some potent cocktail of drugs being pumped through her system, she thought. Her aching brain was being *wild*.

After a long pause, he said, 'Your mother is here and has gone to get something to eat, but tell me, why would I not be here?'

'Because we're strangers?' But there was uncertainty, the whisper of a memory floating in her aching head that could have been a dream. A busy restaurant. Alexis, Georgios and her mother.

There was another flickering in his eyes. 'What is the last thing you remember?'

'Getting back from work…' She blinked as the specific memory refused to form. 'No. Making myself a frittata.' She'd loaded it with feta—to Lucie's mind, there was no such thing as too much cheese—but try as she might, she couldn't conjure the memory of eating it, nor the mound of sweet potato fries she'd made to accompany it.

A sliver of fear snaked into her bloodstream. 'What date is it?'

The intensity of his stare increased, his full, sensuous lips tightening along with the skin around his fabulously high cheekbones. 'The twenty-eighth of July.'

She jolted in shock, the fear tightening its grip. How could it be the end of July?

'What date did you think it was?'

Lucie thought hard, remembered adding a meeting into her work planner. 'The twentieth of May.'

She blinked again. She hadn't eaten the frittata because her mother had called. She'd been in London and wanted to take Lucie out to dinner to discuss something…

The busy restaurant floated in her vision again. Her mother. Georgios. Alexis.

'They want me to marry you,' she blurted out, the words forming a beat before the memory. She met Thanasis's stare again. 'My family want me to marry you to save Tsaliki Shipping.'

His green eyes didn't blink. 'What else? What else do you remember?'

She shook her head in fear and frustration. 'Nothing. There's nothing else.'

The next pause stretched for an age. When he finally spoke, Thanasis's voice had lost the taut edge she'd only been barely aware it contained. 'Lucie, look at your wedding finger.'

Her heart seemed to go into stasis as she unclenched her hand and carefully lifted it, mindful of the medical line running through it. And then every atom in her body contracted with shock to see the sparkling diamond ring on it.

'This isn't possible,' Lucie whispered.

'You agreed to marry me,' he said quietly. 'Our wedding is in nine days.'

She could only gape at him.

'In nine days our two families will come together to celebrate the marital union of an Antoniadis and a Tsaliki, and the war that has caused so much destruction to both our families and businesses will be officially over.'

All she could think to say to this was, 'But Athena's a Tsaliki, not me. I'm a Burton.'

'To the world at large, Georgios considers you his own. You're a Tsaliki daughter and sister in all but blood and name.'

Wasn't that along the lines of what Alexis had said during the meal when he'd thrown the bombshell that, to save Tsaliki Shipping, the family needed her to marry Thanasis? She had only had vague snippets of memory of that evening and everything that followed was a complete blank, but she remembered enough to feel what she'd felt then—a bloom in her heart to be considered a real Tsaliki.

A tight-knit group despite being born from varying wives, the Tsaliki siblings had always welcomed Lucie into the gang during the long school holidays she'd spent with them, and always made sure to include her in everything, but she'd always had the underlying sense they never truly saw her as one of them, a feeling that extended to her half-brother Loukas, the only child her mother had borne Georgios. She'd always had the same underlying sense at her father's home too, a cuckoo in the nest who never fitted in, especially once her half-sisters were born.

Of all Lucie's half-siblings and stepsiblings, the only one she'd felt a real sense of kinship with had been Athena, Georgios's only daughter and the Tsaliki closest to Lucie in age, and even that sense of kinship had been dependent on Athena's varying moods. If Athena was to swish into the hospital room now, she would come armed either with flowers and chocolate or with a syringe to needle at Lucie with. She often reminded Lucie of a cat imperviously swiping its claws at some unfortunate rodent for no other reason than that it was bored.

Smothering a yawn, Lucie gazed again into Thanasis's eyes, wishing she could find in them the answers for everything her injured brain was refusing to reveal. She had to fight her closing throat to say, 'Are you telling the truth? Did I really agree to marry you?'

He didn't blink. 'I do not lie.'

'As any good liar would say,' she pointed out. Thanasis was an Antoniadis, and, if Georgios was to be believed, all Antoniadises were born with forked tongues.

There was the slightest loosening of his full lips but before he could respond, the door opened and a nurse entered the room. When she saw Lucie's eyes were open, she shot an accusatory glare at Thanasis, which she then quickly tried to cover by making effusive noises about Lucie being awake.

While the nurse checked the machine the things stuck to Lucie's chest were attached to, Thanasis got smoothly to his feet, his phone gripped in his large hand. 'I will let your mother know you're awake.'

Utterly dazed, not entirely convinced she wasn't dreaming, Lucie watched the man who'd once haunted her dreams leave the room.

'She's awake,' Thanasis said curtly.

The reply was reverential. 'Thank God for that.'

'She remembers nothing.'

A silence that went on too long and then a slow, 'Nothing?'

'Her memories of the last two months appear to have been wiped out.'

More silence. 'Have you filled her in?'

'She knows only that she agreed to the marriage.'

'Nothing else?'

'Nothing else,' he confirmed.

Another long, long silence. 'Then let us hope her memories stay wiped until after the wedding.'

Lucie's mother ended the call.

'He must be very much in love with you,' the nurse confided as she shone a torchlight into Lucie's eyes. 'It is the first time he has voluntarily left your side.'

Of all the revelations that had been thrown at her in the short time she'd been awake, that one came as the biggest shock.

Thanasis Antoniadis was *in love* with her?

'Do you think?' she asked doubtfully. Nothing in his body language had made that kind of impression on her, although, with the fuzziness of her mind and the gaping void in it, she couldn't really be sure about anything. If anything, she'd had a vague impression of being scrutinised with a watchful wariness, as if she were some kind of unpredictable wild animal with Thanasis tasked as her handler.

The nurse turned the medical torch off and slipped it into her top pocket. 'You have been here two days.'

This was certainly the day for shocks and revelations.

'Seriously?' That long?

'We had to keep you sedated.' A misty look came in the nurse's eyes. 'He has kept watch over you.'

Wow. He'd been sitting in that hard armchair the whole time?

And then Lucie remembered Thanasis had told her

she'd been in a car accident. Funny how she'd been too engrossed in listening to his voice to bother listening to his words. And then she'd been too engrossed in discovering she was supposed to be marrying him to worry about the fact she was lying in a hospital bed feeling as sick as a parrot and with a seeming head injury.

'Am I very badly hurt?'

The nurse gently squeezed her hand. 'There are concerns but all your vital signs are looking good. I have paged the doctor—it is for her to explain what has happened to you.'

'My head?' she guessed, a guess greatly aided by Thanasis's earlier observation that her head hurting *was to be expected*. And also aided by her memories being wiped. She wondered if it accounted for the dreamlike state she was in or if that was the result of whatever drugs were being fed into her.

But maybe this wasn't just a dreamlike state but an actual dream, she wondered again, and as she thought this, Thanasis came back into the room, all tall, dark and brooding, accompanied by a woman whose demeanour immediately identified her as a doctor, and Lucie's mother.

One whiff of her mother's overpowering perfume was all the proof Lucie needed to know that this was no dream.

Lucie had to wait until Thanasis left the room to make some business calls before she could speak to her mother privately. She was exhausted, her stomach still unsettled, and all she really wanted to do was sleep, but this was too important to wait.

'Is it true?' she asked. 'Did I really agree to marry him?'

Her mother's perfectly painted lips smiled. 'Yes, my darling, you did, and I cannot begin to tell you how proud and grateful we all are for the sacrifices you're making for us.'

But Lucie's head was too fuzzy to think about sacrifices, even when her mother airily mentioned Lucie resigning her job so she could move to Greece. The few short hours she'd been awake had been like waking in some kind of twilight zone where up was down and left was right. She had a diamond ring on her finger given to her by a man who when she'd last fallen asleep had been her stepfamily's enemy. And, she supposed, by extension, *her* enemy.

'Mum…how do Thanasis and I get on? The nurse seems to think…' But it was too incomprehensible to vocalise.

'Seems to think what?' her mother prompted.

She had to drop her voice to a whisper to actually say it. 'She thinks he's in love with me.'

The black eyes Lucie had inherited flickered. There was a long hesitation before her mother said, 'It has been obvious to us all that strong emotions have developed between you.'

'So he does love me?'

A shorter hesitation. 'I am certain of it.'

'And am I in love with him?'

This time there was no hesitation at all. 'Yes, my darling, I do believe you are.'

Thanasis strode to the end of the corridor by the fire exit, checked no one was within earshot, and made the call.

Alexis answered on the second ring. 'Is it true?'

'Yes. She has amnesia.'

'How long until her memories come back?'

'Unknown. Could be days. Could be months. They might never come back.'

'Who knows what happened between the two of you?'

'You, your father and Lucie's mother.'

'Not your parents?'

'Obviously they know about the accident but not what went on before. Have you told anyone else?'

'No.'

Thanasis thought hard and quickly. If it was only the four of them who knew the full truth, they could keep it contained. 'What about Athena?'

'She knows nothing.'

'Keep it that way. And keep her away from the hospital. She's a loose cannon.'

He heard Alexis suck in a breath at the slight to his only sister, but Thanasis didn't care. Of all the Tsalikis, Athena had proven herself to have the most poisonous sting. 'The press have been tipped off about the accident,' he said. 'The hospital's security team have moved them off the grounds but they are waiting to ambush her as soon as she's discharged.'

It went without saying that Lucie abhorred the press, and it was a mark of her affection and loyalty to the monster that was Georgios Tsaliki that she'd willingly put herself in the media's spotlight to save his fortune.

'When will that be?' Alexis asked.

'A couple of days at least. When she's released, I will take her to my island—no one can reach her there. In the meantime, I propose we put out a short statement confirming the accident and confirm that she is recovering well and that the wedding is going ahead as planned.'

'Is it?'

Thanasis closed his eyes, recalling the message Lucie's mother had sent him only a few minutes earlier.

She believes you were in love. Unless you want her to run again, play along with it until the wedding.

'If her memories stay lost and your sister keeps her mouth shut then yes, I am certain Lucie will honour the agreement.'

'Good.'

A figure stepped into the corridor. Rebecca Tsaliki. Lucie's mother.

Thanasis met her stare and felt a wave of loathing towards the Englishwoman. Bad enough that he and Alexis were planning to use Lucie's amnesia to their advantage, but this was her mother conspiring against her.

'I need to go,' he said curtly into the phone.

'Keep me updated.'

'Likewise.'

'And, Thanasis?'

'Yes?'

'I suggest you play things differently with her this time. For all our sakes.'

CHAPTER TWO

THANASIS ENDED THE CALL, rolled his tense neck and slowly filled his lungs with air.

Barely two days ago he'd thought his world on the brink of collapse.

'You're an immoral, lying bastard and I'd rather marry a plague-ridden rat than marry you!' Lucie had screamed before snatching the keys to his Porsche 911 from his hands.

'I never lied to you,' he'd retorted furiously. 'Now give them back.'

She'd delivered a curse of such uncouth viciousness that he'd recoiled. Never in his life had he been on the receiving end of such an insult, not even from Lucie.

If he hadn't recoiled, none of what followed would have happened. If he'd kept his wits he'd have been able to take his keys from her without any force—Lucie was easily half his size and weight—and she wouldn't have had time to storm out of his penthouse shouting, 'The wedding is *off* and I don't care what the world thinks. I never want to see you again. I hope you have a *horrible* life.'

He'd chased after her. Of course he had. Lucie had been like a human grenade whose pin had been released, and there had been no telling how far her explosion would spread. He'd stepped into his foyer as the elevator doors had closed and so had raced down the seven flights of stairs and reached the underground car park to find her reversing out of his space with the clunking of gears and the screeching of wheels, whereupon she'd spun the car towards the exit and put her foot down, flipping him the bird as she'd passed for good measure. He had no doubt that if he'd stood in front of the car in the hope of stopping her, she'd have hit the accelerator even harder.

She couldn't call the marriage off, he'd tried to assure himself even as he'd made the terse call to Alexis to inform him of what had happened. If the Antoniadises went down then so did the Tsalikis. Everyone would lose.

The decades-long feud between the patriarchs had escalated as they'd aged to the extent that the dirty tricks they'd employed had escalated too, dangerously so, dirty tricks the press had got wind of. What had been an infamous rivalry enjoyed by the public swirled into a maelstrom of relentless negative publicity that had led to investors threatening to pull out of Antoniadis Shipping. Thanasis's father had voluntarily stepped down his position as Chief Executive, the board of directors voting unanimously for Thanasis to step into his shoes, but this hadn't been enough to mollify the investors.

At the precise moment Thanasis had been wondering how the hell he was going to stop his company imploding, Alexis Tsaliki, who'd not long forced his own father from the board of Tsaliki Shipping, had called requesting a private meeting. 'Our fathers' actions caused all this,' he'd said. 'It is for us to end it.'

What had followed had started out like a scene from a

gangster film where the new heads of two families fighting over the same territory had faced off.

The deadlock had been broken when Alexis had said, 'The only way to stem the losses we are both suffering is to show we are serious about ending our fathers' feud. I propose a marriage.'

'An intriguing idea but you're not my type,' Thanasis had deadpanned, even as he'd immediately seen the sick logic behind the suggestion.

'A shame. We would make a beautiful couple. But no, I propose a marriage between myself and your sister.'

'Over my dead body,' he'd stated flatly. Alexis Tsaliki was poison like all Tsalikis, and an unscrupulous Lothario. Thanasis would sooner live bankrupt in a shed than countenance a marriage with his sister to him.

They'd eyeballed each other for a time that had seemed to suck all the air from the room, until Alexis had given a sharp nod. 'Then you will have to be the one to make the sacrifice.'

And that was how, eventually, Thanasis had come to be engaged to Lucie Burton, Georgios's so-called beloved stepdaughter and the so-called beloved daughter of Rebecca Tsaliki.

Rebecca stepped over to him. Voice low, she said, 'You got my message?'

He nodded curtly.

'Then you know what to do.'

He didn't bother hiding his disdain. Now he understood how this wife had succeeded where Georgios's other wives had failed—her ruthlessness. That this extended to her own daughter sickened him, even if he did despise the daughter as much as the mother.

'How could you let her believe we'd fallen in love?' he demanded.

'I didn't put the idea in her head, I just ran with it,' she answered, her own disdain as evident as his. 'What did you expect me to say? That she was mistaken and you hate each other's guts?'

'No, I would have expected you to correct her and tell her our relationship was cordial and businesslike.'

'If you'd kept it cordial and businesslike we wouldn't be standing here.'

That this observation was on the money only added to the burning angst pumping through him.

'You need to be nice to her for a week,' Rebecca said in the same acidic tone he'd heard her daughter use more times than were countable. 'That's it. Be nice, and get her to the damned church to make her vows. After that, you can do whatever you want with her.'

They both knew Lucie would never sell them out to the press. Even when she'd furiously screeched away in his Porsche, Thanasis had been certain her intense aversion to being public property would stop her taking that nuclear step. Whether she took that step or not though was irrelevant—her failure to marry him would set off a nuclear detonation of its own.

'I will go along with this pathetic charade until the wedding because you leave me no other choice, but you'd better pray her memories don't come back before it.'

'We should all pray for that.'

He shook his head in disbelief. 'When she learns the truth… She will hate you for facilitating the lies. You know that, yes? You could lose your daughter for this.'

Rebecca was unmoved. 'If that's the price I have to

pay then I can live with that. All that matters is that the wedding goes ahead. Anything that comes after can and will be managed. We'll pay her off if necessary—she pretended not to care but I know she was jealous of Georgios's brood having their own trust funds. Cold hard cash always makes injured feelings sting a little less.'

Sickened to his core, Thanasis turned without another word and strode with heavy footsteps back to Lucie's room.

Before entering, he took a moment to compose himself.

The path had been set and he had to follow it. The alternative would be devastation for everyone and everything.

Their engagement had stemmed much of the press negativity and calmed the investors, but there had been predicted cynicism too. If the wedding failed to go ahead the media would go into a frenzy, the becalmed investors likely pull their investments.

In only three weeks, Antoniadis Shipping would take delivery of fifty new container ships to add to their fleet at a cost of close to six billion euros. Two thirds of this still needed to be paid. If the investors pulled out, Thanasis would have to conjure four billion euros. Antoniadis Shipping was worth tens of billions but that money wasn't sitting in a bank account. It would take months to liquidate enough assets to cover it.

All these things had been going through his head as he'd tried to work out how the hell he was going to steer his company away from the impending disaster when he'd received the call that Lucie had been in an accident.

Thanasis's luck had turned one-eighty, but this luck was on a knife-edge. Lucie's amnesia was a blessing but he couldn't predict how long it would last, and now he was being forced into a risky game that upped the stakes considerably.

It was time to up the game to match the stakes and step into the shoes of the man Lucie thought him to be. If her memories returned before the wedding she'd run from his life all over again, and this time she really would destroy everything.

By the time night fell on Lucie's third day in hospital—technically her fifth but she didn't count the first two as she'd been sedated—she was seriously contemplating asking the medical team to sedate her mother. If she'd known it would take a traumatic head injury to make her do some actual mothering, she'd never have got behind a wheel because her mother's definition of actual mothering was doing Lucie's poorly head in. It was the non-stop chatter about the wedding, the constant emphasis about how wonderful it was all going to be, what a beautiful couple Lucie and Thanasis made and what a happy marriage they were going to have, how wonderful it was that the feud between the two families had come to an end because of it, plus the constant need to fill Lucie in on all the details about the wedding itself, the world-famous singers who'd be performing for them, the guest list, the catering, yada-yada-yada. All this while constantly watching Lucie with an anxious scrutiny she'd not shown a shred of when Lucie had caught the flu over the Christmas holidays a decade ago. The only Tsaliki to brave a visit had been Athena, who quite rightly assumed no germ would dare latch itself into her system. When Lucie had finally recovered from it, she'd been surprised to find her mother hadn't marked her bedroom door with a big red X.

All her mum's chattering meant she'd found herself grateful for all the sleep her body currently demanded. Lots and lots of sleep. So much sleep that she could feel herself coming out of the fog, becoming more lucid and less dreamlike. She didn't feel sick any more either, which was a blessing because Lucie hated feeling sick; hated feeling too ill to eat. Give her a headache over sickness any day of the week. And now she had neither, although she was certain her headache would be back with a vengeance at the rate her mother was talking. If she didn't know better, she'd assume her mother was deliberately distracting her from having to think.

For all that her mother was doing her head in, in one respect she was grateful for this late onset maternal blossoming—her mother's constant presence meant she'd only spent snatches of time alone with Thanasis.

Like her mother, he was a constant presence at Lucie's bedside. Unlike her mother, he rarely spoke, which in fairness was because her mum never stopped talking long enough for him to get a word in edgeways.

He rarely spoke but every time Lucie glanced at him she found his green gaze on her. Every time, a frisson would snake up her spine.

With no memories to fall back on it was impossible to know if she really had fallen in love with this man but her reactions were telling her she'd felt *something* for him. And, as incredible as it was to believe, something in the way he looked at her told her he'd felt something for her too, and she didn't know if it was relief or anxiety she felt when her mother finally announced she was going home to get some sleep. The other times her mother had left her alone with Thanasis, Lucie had been deep in sleep herself.

'I'll be back in the morning in time for the results of your scan, darling,' she said as she placed a kiss to Lucie's forehead. 'Let's hope they give you the all-clear to be discharged.'

Lucie smiled wanly. 'Fingers crossed.'

She watched her mother swish to the door, certain she wasn't imagining the significant look she threw at Thanasis before she disappeared through it. Lucie would have wondered what the look was about if she hadn't been so immediately aware that she was alone with the stranger she was shortly to marry.

A stranger she instinctively knew without her mother having to keep banging on about it that she shared something with, a short but significant history her brain refused to reveal.

It took an immense amount of courage to turn her face to him.

Their eyes locked.

'Is it just me or have you suddenly gone deaf too?' she asked, going into her default mode of cracking a joke to cover an awkward silence even though it wasn't awkward she was predominantly feeling but, inexplicably, shy. Lucie couldn't remember ever feeling shy, not once in her whole life.

Lines appeared around his eyes as his perfect teeth flashed before his expression softened and he hunched forward to gently cover her hand. 'How are you really feeling, *matia mou*?'

'Better. Much less fuzzy.' Although the sensation of

Thanasis's hand on hers made her glad the medical team had detached the sticky things on her chest that measured her heart rate, or the whole hospital staff would be kicking the door down to see what had caused the massive spike in it.

He was just so dreamily handsome, with his dark brown hair and thick stubble, and the deep olive hue of his skin and those mesmerising eyes and full lips. As hard as she looked, she couldn't find a single flaw, not unless you counted the lines that formed around his eyes when he gave one of his rare smiles, which she didn't because they gave perfection an extra dimension.

'That is good to hear.' Broad shoulders lifting, he rubbed his thumb over her palm sending sensation dancing through her skin. 'Do you feel well enough in yourself to go home if the scans show it's safe?'

She nodded, then hesitated before asking, 'Where is home for me now?'

'With me.' He bowed his head and gently brushed his lips to her fingers.

Warm breath danced fleetingly over her skin. The beats of her heart spiked again.

So it *was* true. They had fallen for each other, and as this thought swirled, she thought of the Montagues and Capulets…and then remembered how that particular story ended and quickly strove for a different comparison.

'Do we live in Athens?' she asked when no other comparison came to her.

'We have been, but when you are discharged I would like to take you to Sephone.' At her uncomprehending look, he smiled. It was like being doused in a ray of sunlight. 'Sephone is my island.'

'You have your own island? Seriously?'

'When we are married it will be *our* island. It is a secluded paradise. You will love it there, I promise.'

'You've not taken me before?'

'There hasn't been the time, but as you need peace to recover and we are due to marry there, it is the perfect setting for you to recuperate before our big day…that is if you still want to marry me?' He posed the question casually but there was a shadowy flickering in his eyes that made her pulses thump.

He was frightened her amnesia would make her change her mind, she realised.

'I know your mother has done her best to impress on you how far advanced our wedding preparations are, but I will understand if you want to postpone it and give your memories the chance to come back,' he said quietly, her hand now swallowed whole inside both of his. 'If you'd rather call the whole thing off…obviously it would make things difficult from a business perspective but that is the least of my concerns. You and your health are my primary concerns, so if you want to postpone or cancel altogether, do not be afraid to say. I only want what is best for you.'

A dizzying rush of blood filled Lucie's head.

He really did have feelings for her. Feelings enough to take the pressure of the wedding off her shoulders and give her brain the chance to heal even though the consequences for his business would likely be disastrous.

Close to being overwhelmed with the emotions being evoked by this man who was a stranger and yet with whom… Her heart skipped as her thoughts jumped.

If she already lived with this man then she was already sharing his bed…

Heat to power a small house suffused her from the inside out.

She'd shared a bed with Thanasis. Made love to him.

Concern creased his forehead. 'You are flush, *matia mou*. Are you in pain?'

But that only deepened the heat scorching her, and she gave a quick, frantic shake of her head. No way was she going to confess what was going on in her head, not to a stranger, especially not a male one. The embarrassment would kill her. Whatever intimacies they'd shared, she had no memories of them.

'You are sure?' he pressed.

She drew in a long breath as she practically pinned her thoughts into submission so she could think and speak coherently. 'Thanasis, I have no recollection of anything about our engagement or wedding plans but I know in my heart that I did promise to marry you. I've never broken a promise before and I'm not going to start now.'

The corners of his mouth twitched. 'I would understand if you wanted time to start over. You must feel at a great disadvantage.'

'It's frustrating more than anything,' she confessed. 'It must be frustrating for you too. You and I have a history together but my stupid brain is taking us back to step one in the getting-to-know-you stakes.'

He turned her hand and pressed his mouth to her palm. 'I would rather be on the first step with you than no step.'

The whole of her body sighed, and as his face inched closer to hers and the connection of the lock of their eyes deepened, anticipation pulsed into life and she held her breath...

He gently released her hand and gave a rueful twist

of his lips. 'It is getting late,' he said, inching his chair back. 'I will leave you to sleep.'

If there was one thing Thanasis had learned in the two months he'd spent getting to know Lucie Burton, it was that she was incapable of hiding her emotions, and he felt a flare of satisfaction mingled with guilt to see disappointment flash over her face.

'I will be back before you wake, but I haven't been home in five days.' He shook off the guilt. If Lucie had taken one damn minute to hear him out, none of this would have happened, but the pin on the grenade of her temper had spent weeks a hair trigger away from being pulled out. If it hadn't been Athena it would have been something or someone else. Lucie's mother had forced him into playing the role of loving fiancé but Lucie's actions had caused the necessity for it. 'You need to sleep and I need to make arrangements to get you safely to Sephone and ensure all your medical needs can be taken care of.'

'There's nothing wrong with my body, only my head.'

There was *everything* wrong with her body, and it took every ounce of self-control not to let his attentive fiancé mask drop and his revulsion show.

The revulsion was entirely for himself.

Thanasis had prepared himself to loathe Lucie. He could forgive Georgios's blood children for loving their father and being loyal to him but Lucie chose to love him. She'd voluntarily chosen to sacrifice her life in England to save his fortune. She'd freely given her love and loyalty to a monster, which to Thanasis's mind meant she condoned the monster and so made her equally despicable.

His first meeting with her had been after the terms of

the marriage had been negotiated and agreed between himself and Alexis. A marriage in name only, one that would last a few years before they quietly went their separate ways. Their fathers had been given no choice but to fall in line with their plan. With everything agreed, the only thing left to do…apart from arrange the wedding… was for Thanasis to meet his 'bride'.

The meet had taken place in the neutral territory of an exclusive hotel's bar. Alexis had made the call and minutes later a tiny waif with a mop of long black curls had appeared. Just one look had been enough for Thanasis's heart to explode.

Dear God in heaven, it was *her*.

His mind had flown back six years to Leander's party and the waif dressed all in black and with black hair piled on top of her head like a curly pineapple. A tiny, tiny creature with the most strikingly beautiful face he'd ever set eyes on.

It had been the only time in his life he'd experienced that 'eyes meeting across the room moment'. Before he'd had the chance to cross the floor to her and introduce himself, her friend, a blur to his eyes like every other face in the apartment had been in that moment, had dragged her away, not just from the room they'd entered but from the apartment itself. She'd vanished.

He'd asked Leander about her but Leander hadn't known who he was talking about. Neither had anyone else.

For months he'd been unable to drive or walk a street in Athens without casting an eye for a diminutive waif with black curly hair, but he'd never seen her again. In time, he'd convinced himself that he'd imagined her.

But she'd been real.

She'd strolled—although *bounced* would be a more accurate description—into the hotel bar wearing a loose-fitting, sleeveless black dress patterned with blood-red roses that fell to her knees. On her feet had been a pair of calf-length clumpy black boots. Her hair had been worn loose, cascades of curls springing in all directions. She'd looked like a cross between a modern-day Bride of Frankenstein and an ethereally beautiful elf. Except elves were supposed to have big, pointy ears and he'd been unable to see anything of her ears through the mass of curls.

Lucie, a beam on her face and expectation shining in eyes as black as her hair, had stepped to Thanasis with arms outstretched as if expecting an embrace.

Up close, her beauty had shone as much as the shine in her black eyes, and there had been a beat when he'd been powerless to do anything but soak in the oversized eyes and pretty little nose and full heart-shaped lips, all set on a flawless golden heart-shaped canvas.

His heart thumping hard enough to rattle his ribs, he'd pointedly held his hand out.

It was her hesitation before slipping her tiny hand into his that had confirmed in his mind that she too remembered that brief moment of connection from six years earlier, but it was the jolt of electricity that had powered through him at the connection of their skin that had made his jaw clench.

'Nice boots,' he'd said acidly, pulling his hand from her clasp.

The shine in her eyes had dimmed into confusion before her little heart-shaped chin had defiantly lifted. 'It's lovely to meet you too.'

If not hugely aware that time had been ticking to save his company, Thanasis would have called a halt to the agreement there and then.

He'd been fully prepared to marry someone he despised, prepared to spend a few years swallowing his loathing for the good of everything that mattered in his world: his mother, who'd always shaken her head at her husband's rivalry with Georgios Tsaliki, his father, who for all his faults had been a loving father and husband, his sister, who'd become increasingly gaunt and withdrawn since the extent of the rivalry between Antoniadis and Tsaliki had been made public, and the thousands and thousands of people Antoniadis Shipping employed.

What he'd not been prepared for was attraction. Not to someone who'd spent her life in the Tsaliki nest and who considered Georgios Tsaliki a father figure.

Attraction was the last thing he'd expected or wanted, and that he should feel it so powerfully for the captivatingly beautiful Lucie Burton had been additional nails in the coffin of his loathing for her.

By the time she'd screeched away in his Porsche, she'd hated him as much as he hated her, and now he had to remind himself of the expectant shine in her eyes when she'd bounced into that hotel bar all those long weeks ago. There had been hope in that shine too, a hope he'd scotched with his first words to her.

Lucie's amnesia had granted him a reset, a means to play things differently, and he had no intention of screwing it up again.

Speaking steadily, he captured a curl in a manner that could only be interpreted as affectionate. 'Every part of you is too precious for me to risk your health.'

She gave a sigh as soft as the curl in his fingers. 'I'll do everything I can to get the memories back.'

Exactly what he didn't want to hear.

'Just concentrate on healing, *matia mou*, and let the memories take care of themselves.' And then, because he knew he must, he bowed his head, held his breath, and pressed a kiss so chaste to Lucie's mouth he barely felt the pressure of it.

It wasn't chaste enough to stop his heart pumping harder and faster, and it took even more control not to recoil into retreat.

With unhurried movements, he got to his feet, but his escape was thwarted when she caught his hand.

Black eyes gazing up at him with a solemnity he'd never seen in them before, she quietly said, 'I was raised to despise your family. It was instilled in all of us that the Antoniadises were spawns of the devil. The loyalty and affection I feel towards Georgios means I would have agreed to marry you even if I had believed the indoctrination. I would have married the devil himself if it had meant saving Tsaliki Shipping. But I never did believe it, not really, and now you've proved I was right not to.' There was an almost imperceptible catch in her husky voice. 'Thank you for being here for me.'

Thanasis's throat had closed so tightly it was an effort to speak. *'Parakalo,'* he whispered hoarsely.

He left the room with his lips still abuzz from the barely-there pressure of Lucie's mouth, and with the skin of his hand burning as if her touch had marked it.

CHAPTER THREE

BACK HOME IN his Athens apartment, Thanasis set everything in motion so all Lucie's medical needs would be taken care of upon her discharge. That done, he checked in with the chief wedding planner, uncaring that the sleepiness in Griselda's voice meant he'd woken her. The extortionate price he was paying for her services meant she was on call twenty-four-seven.

The call finished with reassurances that Lucie was recovering well, and then Thanasis headed up to his room for a shower, passing Lucie's room as he went. He'd get a member of the staff to pack her belongings. He would need them to pack a smaller case with clothes for her to choose from for when she was discharged too. It was inconceivable that he'd bring Lucie back here to supervise the packing of her possessions. If anything was going to trigger her memories, it would be this apartment, home to virtually every bitter exchange between them.

As per the detailed plan drawn up between himself and Alexis, she'd moved in a couple of weeks after the announcement of their engagement.

He'd installed her in the guest room furthest from his own but it hadn't been far enough. The few public appearances they'd made together up to that point had been hell.

Holding her hand without flinching and forcing his features into something that resembled that of a loving fiancé had taken acting skills he hadn't known he possessed.

It had been Lucie who, off the cuff, had murmured to a cynical journalist that they'd fallen for each other during peace talks between the two families. A stroke of genius he hadn't wanted to admire her for. He didn't want to admire anything about her.

He could not bear to be enclosed in the same walls as her.

Being affectionate in public had taken acting skills on Lucie's part too. In public, she'd played her part perfectly, all doe eyes and soft smiles even though having the paparazzi's cameras aimed at her face was a form of torture for her. The moment they were alone, her black eyes would flash their loathing and her nose wrinkle its disdain. He'd lost count of the times she'd wiped her freed hand on her clothes as if wiping the feel of him off her skin, her back stiff and turned from him. Lost count of the times he'd done the same.

It had never worked, and that was what had made everything so much harder to endure. Every time their hands clasped, he felt the burn of her skin against his for hours after. Every time he slipped an arm around her waist as a show of affection for the cameras and she leaned into him for the same reason, he'd find himself breathing in the scent of her hair and find himself still inhaling it when alone in his bed. Still feeling the soft tickle of it against his neck. Still feeling the compression of her slight figure against his torso. Still feeling his heated blood coursing through his veins.

If they'd met under different circumstances, as genuine strangers with no entwined family histories and no bad blood, then things would be a whole lot different. He would bed her in a heartbeat and get this all-consuming ache for her out of his system.

It was the age-old conundrum of forbidden fruit, he acknowledged grimly as he stripped off his clothes. Being forbidden always made an object infinitely more tempting. As a child he'd been forbidden from using the swimming pool without adult supervision. The first time unsupervised opportunity had presented itself, he'd dive-bombed into the pool. If not for the racket his dive-bomb had made, the gardener would never have thought to look and would never have seen four-year-old Thanasis struggling to keep his head above water.

Lucie was more off limits than the swimming pool had been.

To Thanasis's mind, marriage was the ultimate commitment two people could make, and sacred for it. When he made that commitment in the future, it would be for love and it would be for ever, and he would not allow any aspect of his temporary marriage to feel real enough to taint that future. When he made his real vows, he wanted to join his real wife in his real marital bed knowing it was the first time for him to make love as a husband.

His anger rising, he stepped under the shower.

Why the hell hadn't he demanded a photo of Lucie before agreeing to marry her? Thanks to varying European privacy laws concerning minors, there were no pictures of her in the public domain, and the private life she'd lived in England since turning eighteen meant she'd escaped the paparazzi's attention. If he'd known it was her, the woman who'd captivated him with that one look across a room all those years ago, he'd have played hard ball and demanded Athena or no deal. There would be no temptation of forbidden fruit there. Athena was beautiful too, but it was a beauty that left him cold.

And now he had to spend the next week walking a tightrope playing the devoted fiancé to a woman who made him feel anything but cold.

'Wouldn't it be better for me to spend a few days in Athens before we go to Sephone?' Lucie said the next morning after the medical team left the room. Her latest scan results had been discussed, the doctor declaring her well enough to be discharged. This had resulted in her mother immediately diving into the carry-on case Thanasis had brought from the apartment for this eventuality and Thanasis getting straight onto the phone. It seemed her mother and fiancé were working in cahoots to get her out of this hospital room as soon as humanly possible.

'Why would you think that, darling?' her mother asked, shaking out a black summer dress with a wrinkle of her nose.

'Maybe because the doctor just said one of the best ways to aid the recovery of my memories is by going to familiar places,' Lucie pointed out drily. 'I've never been to Sephone.'

'The doctor also said you need to rest, and what better place than a peaceful island unless you *want* the paparazzi to stalk you?'

Lucie shuddered at the mere thought. If anything had tainted her childhood, it had been the paparazzi's near constant presence during her time spent in Greece. Her mother's love of the intrusive spotlight was but one of the many fundamental differences between them.

Her mother handed the dress to her. 'Do you still not own clothes that aren't black?'

Lucie looked at the tightly fitting, high-fashion, colourful attire her mother was wearing and chose not to answer. She was long past the rebellious teenage years when she'd adopted dressing from head to toe in black as a silent means of needling the woman who'd given birth to her, but old habits died hard. She'd added splashes of colour to her wardrobe in recent years but still felt most comfortable wearing black.

'Excuse me a moment,' Thanasis murmured, shifting from his position at the window where he'd been deep in conversation. 'I need to make a call that might involve shouting.'

Startled at the glimpse of humour from a man she'd assumed didn't possess one—in all their time in this hospital room, he'd been nothing but serious—Lucie grinned.

She'd woken with a clearer head than she'd had since coming round from the sedation and spent a blissful hour in peace and solitude with nothing but her thoughts to occupy her. But, instead of searching for her lost memories, she'd spent the time wondering what it was about Thanasis that had made her fall for him. Apart from his devastating dark good looks and perfect body that was. She'd had the odd date with good-looking men over the years but always something had put her off wanting a second date. Usually it was too much vanity or a lack of humour, often both—she found those two traits went hand in hand—and so she'd pondered what it was Thanasis had the others lacked and how she could fall for so serious a man, and now she knew. He *did* have a tiny, latent sense of humour behind the Mr Serious persona.

'Is my phone in the case?' she asked her mother once they were alone. It was the first time she'd even thought of it. She dreaded to think how many messages she'd have to reply to.

Sighing at the inconvenience, her mother had a quick rummage in Lucie's case. 'Not that I can see. Do you need help dressing?'

'I could do with a shower first.' Since being admitted into hospital she'd had to put up with the nurses giving her bed baths, which would have been the indignity from hell if she hadn't been so spaced out on the drugs, but now she was actually *compos mentis* she'd rather pluck each individual leg hair out than put up with that again. She wanted a shower. A long, lovely shower.

'There isn't time,' her mother dismissed. 'Another patient will need this room.'

'But the nurse said there was no rush.'

'She was being polite. Come on, get that dreadful plastic gown off you.'

It took an incredible effort not to go into sulky teenager mode. 'Underwear?'

Once everything had been placed on the armchair for Lucie to change into, she gave her mother a meaningful look. 'Some privacy?'

Her mother rolled her eyes. 'You always were a prudish little thing.' Magicking a bulging makeup bag from nowhere, she disappeared into the adjoining bathroom with mutters of 'touching up her face'.

Lucie glared at the closed bathroom door. She'd always hated it when her mother teased her for being a prude. Just because she'd made it to twenty-four with only one real boyfriend under her belt, and preferred wearing loose-fitting clothes that covered her breasts and backside rather than the tight miniskirts and low crop tops her mother favoured, did not mean she was prudish.

She stepped into her knickers, her grumpiness melting away as Thanasis filled her mind again. Had he seen her in these knickers? Stripped them from her?

What had it been like between them? Disappointing like her past experience? Or had it been good? Even pleasurable?

Thanasis knew his way around a woman's body enough to make it pleasurable, she decided as she removed the dreadful—her mother had been right about that—hospital gown. You could just tell. Although she didn't know how she could just tell.

Letting the gown fall to the floor, she reached for her bra, searching as hard as she could in the void of her brain for any memory of sleeping with him.

What had his touch felt like? Had she burned for him? Remembering how the touch of his hand had sent her heart rate spiking and how the gentle kiss he'd placed on her mouth the night before had turned her belly into mush, she thought she must have. Closing her eyes, she made a silent plea for those particular memories to come back. Even if all the other memories stayed lost for ever, please bring those ones back to her. Please, please.

'Lucie, we—'

Not having heard or even sensed the door opening, she whipped her head round and caught Thanasis frozen in mid-step at the door. Slamming her arms across her exposed breasts, she gripped her biceps, bra dangling from her fingers, embarrassment at being caught semi-naked scorching her in a white-hot flame.

A beat that seemed to last a lifetime passed between them, the dark pulse in his stare turning the flame of embarrassment into a different kind of burn, the kind of burn she'd been imagining only moments ago when wondering what it had felt like being made love to by him.

And then he blinked and the dark pulse vanished as he took a step back and a visible shutter came down in his eyes. 'I apologise—I should have knocked.'

Realising her reaction must make her seem like the prude her mum had just accused her of being, a fresh batch of mortification enflamed her skin, and she lifted her chin with a bravado she absolutely did not feel inside and went into default jocular mode. 'No, no, it's fine. Not your fault. Of course you didn't need to knock. I'm your fiancée and it's not like you haven't seen my boobs before... It's just that I don't remember the before.'

His jaw tightened a fraction before he gave a brief nod and took hold of the door handle. 'Understood. I'll leave you to dress.'

He closed the door with the same stealthy silence he'd opened it.

Her heart now threatening to explode out of her ribs, Lucie sank onto her bed and tried to catch her breath.

Thanasis stood beneath the air conditioning unit and blew out a long puff of air. A sheen of perspiration had broken out over his skin.

Closing his eyes, he clenched his fists and refilled his lungs.

Theos, that body.

It was perfect. That was the only word to describe it. Perfect. Perfection enhanced by the plainness of her black underwear, which created such a strong contrast with the lightness of her golden skin. Perfect gentle curves. Small but perfectly shaped breasts he knew with one look would sit perfectly cupped in the palm of his hands.

He expelled another long, tortured breath and pressed his head against the wall, closing his eyes even tighter to drive the image of semi-naked Lucie from his vision.

Theos, from the heavy thrumming in his veins, you would think it was the first time he'd seen a pair of naked breasts in the flesh.

What made the rush of arousal pulsing through him more intolerable was the beat that had passed between them before he'd found his voice to apologise.

In that beat, the filter had slipped off them both and the unwanted, unacknowledged desire that had always simmered between them had been a shimmering, living entity.

A violent blush crawled over Lucie's face the second she heard the tap on the door. She had no idea how she was able to call out, 'Come in,' in a voice that sounded in any way normal, and when Thanasis stepped into the room, she felt the blush deepen and spread.

To her immense gratitude, he gave not a single sign that he'd walked in on her practically naked only minutes earlier, and she was beyond grateful that he accepted and understood so well that everything they'd shared together was lost to her.

'My driver is here,' he said in that glorious deep, honeyed tone. 'Are you ready to go?'

She nodded, still unable to meet his stare. 'Before we leave, have you seen my phone?'

He cast his gaze around the room. 'It isn't here?'

'Not that we've found. Was it recovered from the accident?' The accident she still only knew the barest details of, namely that she'd borrowed one of Thanasis's cars and crashed it. She'd been too fuzzy of head to think of asking more questions about it, but one thing she didn't need to question was that she would have had it on her. Lucie never went anywhere without her phone.

'All the personal possessions you had at the time of the accident were put in the cupboard by your bed.'

'I've looked there.'

'I will ask the garage where the car's being repaired and see if they have found it.'

'Can you do that now, please? I need to check in with my dad, and Kelly and...' There was a pang in her chest to know she was no longer an employee of Kelly Holden Designs. Lucie had loved her job as an interior designer. Really loved it. Her resignation was another void in her brain. So too giving up her share of the flat tenancy. 'Check in with my whole life really.'

Thanasis gave a brief, tight smile. 'Of course.'

With everything that had been going on, he hadn't given Lucie's phone a second thought, but now he knew it was missing, he could only hope it stayed lost.

Thanasis's family and the Tsalikis would all keep their mouths shut about the animosity between them but he had no way of knowing what she'd confided to others. He was confident she'd not betrayed the pact they'd made before their final argument but Lucie's fury when she'd left his apartment that day was such that it was within the realm of possibility she would have called one of her many friends to vent about it.

The call to the garage was over within a minute.

'I'm afraid your phone wasn't in the car,' he told her, relief filling him.

Fate, it seemed, was determined to continue working in his favour.

'I have your father's number,' he added. 'You can use my phone to check in with him.' Thanasis had spoken to Charlie Burton numerous times since the accident and was confident Lucie had confided nothing in him.

'If we stop at a phone shop on our way to the harbour, I can buy myself a replacement,' she suggested.

He made a point of looking at his watch. 'It's a long sail to Sephone. The sooner we set off the better.' And the more isolated he kept her, the less likely something or someone would trigger her memories. 'I can have a phone helicoptered to you, if you wish.'

'Can't we take the helicopter ourselves?'

'No flying until you are back to full health,' he asserted firmly, and was rewarded with such a doe-eyed look that the guilt at his deception plunged a little deeper.

Damn Rebecca Tsaliki for letting her daughter believe they were lovers. And damn himself for going along with it.

Lying did not come naturally to Thanasis but what other choice did he have? Let his business be destroyed and his family face destitution?

And besides, if Lucie's memories came back before the wedding, they were all damned however they played it. The resulting explosion would lead to a scorched earth.

It was only for another week, he reminded himself grimly. Not even that. Six days. Just until they made their vows. The most pressing thing was getting her to the altar and the world's press witnessing Antoniadis and Tsaliki breaking bread together for the first time in forty years.

But as much as Thanasis needed to get Lucie swiftly away from Athens and to the solitude of his island, he would not disregard the doctor's advice. Flying the short distance—and by helicopter, it was a short distance— should be safe for her he'd been assured, but to his mind *should* was not cast-iron enough. His feelings for Lucie were a hot mess of lust and loathing but he would never wish physical harm on her or do anything to put her in danger.

He could still feel remnants of the ice his blood had temporarily frozen into when he'd been told of the accident.

She thought his basic human concern for another person's well-being was down to his 'love' for her, and he turned his face away so she wouldn't see his revulsion, at her and at himself, and dredged his parents and sister into his mind's eye. They were the people he needed to keep at the forefront of his thinking whenever the urge to rip off the mask of his deception became unbearable. Them and the thousands of Antoniadis Shipping employees. All those futures in his hands.

Turning his stare back to her, he smiled and held out one of the hands all those futures depended on.

There was only a small hesitation before her beautiful heart-shaped lips pulled into a shy smile and one of the tiny hands all those futures also depended on slipped into his and her fingers tentatively closed around his.

For the beat of a moment, he experienced the strangest sensation; the sensation of Lucie's fingers closing around his heart.

CHAPTER FOUR

FOR ALL THAT Lucie had said only her head hurt, there was a stiffness to her gait evident when they made the short walk along the harbour with the nurse who'd accompanied them from the hospital.

Keeping a supportive grip on her hand, like any supportive fiancé would, Thanasis shortened his usual stride to keep pace with her. There was something about her tentative but determined steps that highlighted her current fragility and tugged at his chest. For the first time since she'd walked into the hotel bar he was wholly aware of how tiny and delicate she really was. Only her determination hinted at the combative personality he'd spent two months sparring and clashing with.

The medics who'd attended the scene of the accident had said it was nothing short of a miracle that she'd escaped the wreckage with nothing more than a bleeding nose from the airbag. Those medics didn't know how tough Lucie was. Thanasis could well imagine his car crumpling around her and then having second thoughts. The injury to her head had come about, so witnesses had attested, when she'd caught her foot stumbling out of the car. She'd been too disoriented by the accident to put her hands out to break her fall. It was nothing but bad luck that her head had landed on the edge of the pavement kerb.

He couldn't bring himself to think of her head hitting the kerb as being his good luck, even if he was using her amnesia to his full advantage.

When they reached his yacht, she stared at it for a long time, silently taking it all in. '*Persephone*... Is she where your island gets its name?'

'Yes. My island was inhabited many millennia ago and all that's known of the islanders is that they worshipped Persephone—there are ruins of a monument to her on the south of the island—which is where the island's name comes from. It seemed fitting to name my yacht after her too.'

'Wasn't she Queen of the dead or something?' Lucie asked dubiously, thinking the last person she'd name a yacht after was someone who represented death.

'Queen of the underworld, but she was much more than that. Hades was the god of the underworld and stole Persephone from her mother to live as his wife there with him, breaking Demeter's heart. Demeter was the goddess of harvest and fertility,' he explained. 'After much bad blood, Zeus decided Persephone would spend six months each year living with Hades and six months living with Demeter. The months with Hades were months of desolation where the land became barren and nothing grew because Demeter's heart was so desolate, but the months Persephone returned to her mother were months where Demeter's happiness shone on the earth and blessed the land with an abundance of fertility, the months we know of as spring and summer.'

Her stare still glued to the yacht she was about to embark, a shiver ran up Lucie's spine. For a split moment certainty gripped her that this was all a trick and she was about to be stolen away just like Persephone had been.

And then she felt the comforting solidity of Thanasis's hand clasped around hers and shook the feeling away. Her mother would never win any parenting award but even she wouldn't send her daughter off to a remote island with a man to be stolen away. In any case, there would be other people on the island, household staff—she didn't imagine Thanasis had ever lifted a domestic finger in his life—along with all the people setting up for the wedding. And until they reached it, there was the crew of his yacht, a handful waiting patiently in identical uniforms of navy polo shirts and black shorts on the front deck for them to climb on board.

Most of all though, was Thanasis himself, and the intuition that had been in her since she'd first come round after the accident that he'd become a major part of her life. That they meant something to each other.

Thanasis's yacht, Lucie had to admit, was a lot classier than Georgios's. Georgios's yacht, a vessel she'd spent many of the long weeks of school summer holidays on, was a real party palace with everything geared around all ages having fun. Thanasis's, by contrast, brought to mind an ultra-luxurious spa with everything designed to aid relaxation, and she spent the six-hour journey to Sephone doing just that, mostly because she wasn't allowed to do anything else. In Lucie's case, relaxing meant sleeping, but that had nothing to do with the *Persephone*'s ambiance but was because of her jailers.

When Thanasis had said he wanted to ensure all her

medical needs were taken care of, she hadn't thought he'd meant turning a cabin of the *Persephone* into a hospital room with a doctor and two nurses in attendance for good measure. The cabin had a private balcony the strict medics grudgingly allowed her to sit out on, but she wasn't allowed to stray any further.

Being so restricted meant boredom kicked in quickly, and while she'd slept enough for England and Greece combined these last five days, she ended up sleeping because there was absolutely nothing else for her usually active brain to do. She had no phone, no books to read and, having never been one for sitting down to watch films and binge on boxsets, no interest in her cabin's television. Waking to be told by a nurse that they were minutes away from the island had her scrambling out of bed with an agility that was close to feeling normal. She was certain her earlier stiffness had come from her muscles not being used for days.

Released from her cabin, she was escorted by her jailers to a saloon with the same calming opulence that permeated the rest of what she'd seen of the yacht.

Thanasis, standing with his back turned at the far end of the saloon with a clear view of the nearing island, was discussing something with a member of his crew. There was something strange about his posture, but it wasn't until he sensed or heard her presence and turned his head and the animation on his face fell and his hands dropped to his sides that she realised what the strangeness was. He'd been gesticulating.

Gesticulations were nothing out of the ordinary for the Greeks—in Lucie's considerable experience, being expressive was part of the national DNA—but they were definitely out of the ordinary for the rigidly composed Thanasis.

There was a barely perceptible narrowing of his eyes and rising of his broad shoulders before his features relaxed and he headed towards her.

The same shiver of fear that had caught Lucie before she boarded the *Persephone* snaked freshly up her spine and stopped her feet moving forwards to him.

She didn't know this man.

Her bruised brain and Thanasis's ridiculously gorgeous face and wondrous scent had bamboozled her into believing that she knew him, but she didn't. He'd been hiding himself from her, and because of that, she couldn't read him. She didn't doubt her intuition that they meant something to each other but what was that *something* if he wouldn't let himself relax around her? How could she trust that *something* was a good something? It was absolutely in her mother's interest for the wedding to go ahead. It was absolutely in Thanasis's interest too. In fact, the only person in whose interest it wasn't was her. Or hadn't been. Lucie had led a fully independent life since finishing secondary school but the great job she'd adored and the funky flat she'd shared with three of her best friends were all gone. That all had to be the truth or why else would she be in Greece in July? No, make that August now.

He was only feet away from her.

Her heart thumped harder as his magnetic effect danced into her senses.

She was being irrational. What reason could Thanasis or her mother have to lie to her? She'd agreed to a marriage of convenience with him to save both families, so why embellish that?

He stopped before her and, his wondrous scent bamboozling her all over again, she suddenly realised just how big he really was, much more than she'd imagined from her hospital bed. He didn't just top her five foot nothing height but *towered* over it. The top of her head barely reached his shoulder and that included her untameable mass of hair.

'Good rest?' he asked, his stare as serious and intense as ever.

Matching his intensity, trying without any success to see into his head, she nodded. 'I think that was the most comfortable prison I've ever slept in.'

His forehead creased. 'Prison?'

'While you were having fun in the sun, my jailers refused to let me leave the cabin.'

'I asked them to watch you closely.'

'Did you impress upon them the need to watch me excessively closely?'

'Of course.' He folded his arms across his chest, biceps and pecs flexing with the movement. 'You have suffered a nasty head injury and I make no apologies for wanting your recovery to be as smooth as it can be. If it is any consolation, I was working, not having fun,' he added.

Trying very hard to concentrate on their conversation and not the swirl of dark hair visible through the opened throat of his black shirt, trying without any success to stop herself imagining those muscular arms enveloping her, Lucie lifted her chin and smiled sweetly. 'No consolation at all. I find my work immensely fun.'

'Then you, *matia mou*, are an anomaly. Work for me is work.'

'Poor you, but if you want my recovery to be smooth, I suggest you rethink any plans you might have dreamed up of locking me away until our wedding day while you get on with your non-exciting work, otherwise you'll find the wedding having to be postponed on account of me jumping out of a window and probably breaking my legs.'

There was another crease in his brow before his features loosened and he gave a short burst of laughter.

The only creases on his face now the lines around his eyes, he folded his arms and tilted his head. 'Consider your comment noted.'

Absurdly thrilled at the sound of his laughter, probably because if she'd had to put money on it she'd have said his vocal cords didn't stretch to laughing, Lucie mimicked his stance and riposted, 'Consider your consideration of my comment noted.'

The amusement on his face lasting longer than any of his previous smiles, he inclined his head towards a door leading outside. 'Now that we have noted each other's comments, shall we go on deck so you can see your home for the next few weeks?'

Lucie's home for the next few weeks—there were plans for them to stay on Sephone a week after the wedding too, for their honeymoon—was the most stunningly beautiful place she'd ever seen. Even before the yacht had moored she understood exactly why Thanasis had chosen this particular island as his private hideaway.

Sephone rose from the crystal-clear blue waters of the Aegean like the majestic goddess it was named after, the mountainous terrain thick with vineyards and olives groves, sheer drops creating coves where the sea lapped onto some of the palest, softest-looking sand she'd ever seen.

Travelling with Thanasis by golf buggy to the villa over a wide, snaking pathway that had to be manmade but seemed as natural as the sweet-smelling flowers lining it, Lucie breathed in the pure air with a sense of wonder she didn't think she'd ever experienced before, and then she caught her first glimpse of the villa and nearly overdosed on it.

Nestled above a hidden cove with waters of the palest blue, multiple white domes with blue-domed roofs of varying sizes connected to create one palatial wonder amassed with an abundance of arched and circular windows, all blending into something not only beautiful but sensual, as if the architect had eschewed anything that could be construed as a straight line. It was like nothing she'd seen before, a home any goddess would be proud to inhabit.

'Who designed *this*?' she asked, close to breathless with admiration.

'Thomas Breakwell.'

'No way. *Thomas* designed this?'

Although she was too busy gaping at the stunning villa, she felt Thanasis's stare fall on her. 'You know him?'

'He hired our company to do the interiors for the showrooms of his apartment complex in Canary Wharf. I would never have guessed this was one of his.'

'I put the tender out with the vision of what I wanted. He was the architect who most understood the feel of what I was seeking.'

'Good for him…although now I'm wondering how come I didn't know of it.' At Thanasis's questioning stare, she explained, 'When we were pitching for the Canary Wharf project, Kelly got me to trawl through his company website. There is no way I would have forgotten this…' Her spirits suddenly plummeted. 'Unless there's more holes we didn't know about in my memories?'

'You wouldn't have seen it on his website,' he assured her. 'The project was undertaken in secrecy.'

'How come?'

'I didn't want the world to know about the island. It only encourages tourists to try and find it.'

'Then why are we marrying here? From what Mum was saying, the whole world and their dogs are coming.'

'Sometimes it feels like that,' he admitted wryly. 'Sephone was chosen because it has the romantic feel we thought it necessary to portray when we marry. To work and soothe our business investors, our marriage needs to be believable.'

'So you're giving up your secret hideaway for the greater good?' The tourists he'd bought the island to escape from would soon be poring over maps trying to figure out where in the Aegean Sephone was located.

'Some sacrifices are worth making.'

'Is that what I said when I agreed to the marriage?'

'If I recall correctly, you said you expected a nomination to be given on your behalf to the Nobel Prize panel.'

Meeting his eye for the first time since they'd got into the golf buggy, she grinned even as her heart swelled. 'That definitely sounds like something I would say.'

Thanasis, knowing she wouldn't be smiling if she remembered the context of her comment, nonetheless curved his lips, and was saved from having to say anything further on the subject by their buggy coming to a stop in front of the huge semi-circular timber door.

Her Nobel Prize nomination comment had come at the end of their first meeting in the hotel bar. If he was remembering correctly—and his memory had never failed him before—her exact words, thrown at her stepbrother Alexis, had been, 'If I pull this off and convince the world I'm in love with that…' she'd glared at Thanasis '…*man*, and that everything between our two families is now all jolly hockey sticks and cream buns, then I'd better get a Nobel Prize nomination out of it.'

'Would you like a nomination for sainthood too?' Thanasis had asked acidly.

'Only if I manage not to kill you.'

There had been countless times after when a look alone from Lucie would have sufficed to kill him stone dead.

There was no look like that or any kind of glare on her face now. Colour had returned to the cheeks made pale by her injury and there was a lightness in her expression, as if this whole thing was one big adventure for her and he was the man joining her on it. It was much like the shine that had been in her eyes when she'd bounced into the hotel bar, before his coldness had wiped it clean away. Much like the shine he'd gleaned when their eyes had met across the room all those years ago, that long, unbidden moment that had captured them tightly enough that they'd both remembered it years later.

Lucie gazed around at the most stunning room she'd ever been in. It was like she'd stepped into an airy white cave carved into paradise. Light poured in from multiple angles, bathing the enormous bed in golden light. She let her stare linger on it only a second before her heart turned over and she hastily looked anywhere else.

She wasn't ready to think of sharing that bed with Thanasis, especially not when she could feel him watching her reaction to their room with that intensity she felt like a physical touch.

How were you supposed to behave around someone you were marrying in a week's time and who you'd already shared months of a life building a relationship with, but who you had no memories of? The few displays of affection Thanasis had shown while she'd been cocooned in hospital had felt natural and thrillingly wonderful, but she'd been doped up to her eyeballs on drugs. It all felt very different and real now she was back out in the real world with nothing in her system to pollute her feelings or reactions, and she wished there were an instruction manual available to help her navigate it all so it didn't feel quite so terrifying.

'Seriously, who was the interior designer for this? Because I want to kiss them,' she said brightly, going into jocular mode to cover the disquiet that felt like no disquiet she'd ever experienced before at being alone with Thanasis in a bedroom for the first time, even though she knew this wasn't the first time because he'd been at her hospital bedside all that time, but that had been completely different because it was a hospital room, and that was not forgetting—even though she *had* forgotten—that she'd been sharing a bedroom with him for weeks and weeks, and now even her thoughts were going haywire and were on the cusp of making her head explode. 'This is amazing.'

'Helena Tatopoulos.'

'Can you give me her number so I can ask for a job?' she said, only half in jest.

He gave the flash of a grin. 'After the wedding.'

'Invite her to it so I can badger her there.'

He adopted a stern expression. 'No business talk at the wedding.'

She made a pffting sound. 'But business is the whole *point* of the wedding.'

Laughing lowly, he reached out to smooth down one of her curls sticking up at the ceiling, and her heart went haywire to match her thoughts even though he wasn't really touching her, well, not any part of her that was living, because hair wasn't actually alive, was it?

'I am the last person to forget that.' He released the curl and stepped back. 'I will leave you to settle in. Does dinner in an hour work for you?'

'The sooner the better—I'm starving.' Or had been. Nerves had kicked in big time. Or what felt like nerves. Right behind Thanasis was the sprawling bed they'd be sharing and because her eyes were currently glued to his gorgeous face with a special focus on his full lips...oh, but the way they moved when he spoke sent her pulses as haywire as her heart and thoughts...the bed was in her peripheral vision, and with the way the falling sunlight shone through the multiple windows casting both Thanasis and the bed in its golden glow...

Soon, very soon, those full lips would press against hers in that very bed...

Oh, God, her efforts not to think of the bed she'd very soon be sharing with him had become a dismal failure because now it was all she could think of, and suddenly she realised that all the things she'd wondered about in her hospital bed would be wonders no more but her reality, that *this* was her reality, her and Thanasis, committed lovers, and as all these thoughts collided a glow began to build inside her, flutters of deep, pulsing warmth that had her clutching at the material of her dress around her stomach even though she didn't know what she was clutching it for.

'Good,' said the full lips containing such sensuous promise that she was now caught on a tightrope between yearning for them to just *kiss* her, and wanting to throw herself out of a window to escape a fear she didn't even understand. 'Make yourself comfortable. Everything's been unpacked for you but if anything's been forgotten or there's anything else you need, tell any member of staff. If they don't have it, they will get it couriered over. If you feel unwell, the medical team are based in the room to the right of yours—pressing the green switches by your bed and dressing table sends an alert directly to them. There is also a switch in your bathroom.'

Lucie nodded as if she'd been paying attention to his words and not lost in fascination and fear at the movement of his mouth, and then realised exactly what he'd said and blinked. 'Isn't this our room?'

The mouth she'd been lost in fascination with twitched. 'No, *matia mou*, this is your room. My room is to your left.'

Her heart and stomach shrank and plummeted as full comprehension hit her. 'Oh, I thought...assumed...'

Assumed this was *their* room, words that went unsaid but which still echoed between the walls and between them.

Although Thanasis didn't move—how could someone so big be so *still*?—she sensed a shift within him, sensed him again reining in his composure to give nothing of himself away, and yet somehow the intensity of his stare increased, giving the sensation that he was searching inside all the compartments in her brain and plucking out the files hidden from herself and reading them.

'I am thinking only of you,' he murmured. 'The reset between us that's come about because of your injury...' Exhaling through his nose, he closed the distance he'd created between them and gently captured her chin. The probing green eyes beginning to swirl. 'I know you feel obliged to marry me, *matia mou*, but the last thing I want is for you to feel any other kind of obligation. That would be unconscionable of me.'

Heart caught in her throat, trembling inside and out and captured in a stare she couldn't have pulled herself away from if she'd tried, Lucie held her breath as the mouth she ached to feel closed in on hers.

The warmth of his breath danced over her lips and then the soft and yet, oh, so firm mouth brushed over hers in a lingering featherlight caress that left her close to sagging with disappointment when he pulled away from it.

Catching a locket of her hair, he rubbed the tip of his nose against hers. 'Let us be on an equal footing and start over as if we were both strangers to each other, and take our time in getting to know each other without any pressure or expectation.' With a glimmering smile, he brushed another featherlight kiss to her mouth and huskily added, 'There is no need to rush anything. I can wait for as long as you need me to, and I know the wait will be worth it because we have our whole life together to look forward to.'

And then he released the curl and stepped back, stealing the warmth she'd been barely aware of bathing in, leaving Lucie gaping at him, the fleeting kiss having struck her dumb,

'Until dinner, *matia mou*,' he whispered.

By the time she came back to her senses, Thanasis had disappeared from the room leaving her with the sense that she'd just been hypnotised as effectively as a cobra would be by a master snake charmer.

CHAPTER FIVE

Sᴇᴘʜᴏɴᴇ ᴡᴀs ᴛʜᴇ one place Thanasis had ever felt a true sense of peace. Growing up, life had always been busy even during times of relaxation. Each evening, the family had congregated around the dining table to feast on the delicious food cooked fresh by the staff; grandparents, aunts, uncles and cousins frequent guests at the table along with numerous workers and business associates his generous parents would invite to break bread with them. The business had been central to Antoniadis life, an extension of their family, and it had always felt like Thanasis's family to him. He would never say it had been his destiny to one day run it, but it had never crossed his mind to do anything else.

It would never have crossed his mind to purchase his own island either, if he hadn't visited his friend Leander's island for a weekend of partying and found himself struck with the solitude one early morning while everyone else slept off the night before's excess. By the time the others started surfacing, he'd already determined to buy his own island and create a sanctuary for himself. Within two years, his sanctuary had been found and bought and the domed villa designed and built. It had been worth every cent of the vast sum spent on it, something his family and close friends agreed with as they all made liberal use of it too.

This was Thanasis's first visit to his sanctuary since the press had first splashed on just how toxic and dangerous the rivalry between his father and Georgios Tsaliki had become. He'd been in damage limitation mode ever since, barely coming up for air as he'd juggled investor concerns with stepping into his father's shoes and keeping an eye on his immediate family who were all suffering under the enormous strain of it all. And then there had been his need to be publicly visible with his new 'fiancée' to cement the idea of their 'love'.

It was the presence of his 'fiancée' that had stopped his lungs opening wide as he'd stepped off the *Persephone* and stopped the long exhalation that usually followed as all the pressures of his life lifted from his shoulders. The knowledge, too, that at the rear of the villa an army of people were transforming his landscaped garden into a wedding venue and that, dotted around the island, luxury yurts were being put up to accommodate the guests who wouldn't be travelling to the island on their own yachts and who there wasn't the room to accommodate in the villa.

But mostly it was Lucie herself. He'd never been able to breathe properly in her company. Always that cramped tightness in his chest, and as he did his best to compose himself in anticipation of her joining him at the poolside dining area, he took a long drink of his wine in another effort to wipe the taste of her from his mouth, and closed his eyes to wipe the image of her face as he'd last seen it.

She'd been as affected by those two barely-there kisses as he'd been.

Damn it.

Those two kisses had been too fleeting for any of Lucie's essence to seep into him but seep into him she had, a dark sweetness of breath that lingered, and he drained his wine, glancing at his watch. Two more minutes and she would be with him and he would have to pull himself together and carry on with the charade.

He'd had to kiss her. He'd read her surprise at their separate rooms. Read too her relief...and that flare of disappointment. He'd needed to placate her and stop doubts about their relationship fermenting, and he'd done it successfully. He should be in self-congratulatory mode because this was how it had to be, something he grimly reminded himself of as he refilled his glass. Whatever vulnerabilities Lucie might currently be suffering, that didn't change that this whole situation was of *her* making. She was the one who'd refused to listen, hadn't even let him explain. She'd seen what she'd wanted to see because it had suited her. She'd wanted out of their agreement and had run at the first opportunity, something else he needed to remind himself of if guilt at how he was playing her should bite a little too sharply.

She hadn't officially ended the engagement. That was yet another thing to remind himself of. As far as he knew—and he hoped like hell that his gut was correct on this—she had confided nothing about ending their engagement with anyone. For all he knew, if she hadn't crashed his car she might have let off all her steam thrashing it around and then come back home, thrown her Medusa glare at him, thrown some more choice insults at him and then carried on as if nothing had happened. God alone knew they'd had enough white-cold rages between them that had ended in that way. Always there had been the unspoken agreement that whatever their personal feelings for each other, their respective families and businesses were bigger than those feelings. It was the only thing apart from their mutual loathing of the press that they'd ever agreed on.

Some internal antennae lifted a moment before the bespoke French doors slid open and Lucie stepped out onto the patio.

The sun was giving its last goodbyes for the evening but even with little natural light to see by, he noted the slash of colour stain her cheeks as their eyes met.

She bit into her bottom lip and tentatively raised a hand. 'Hi.'

The beats of his heart strangely weighty, he exhaled slowly before rising to his feet. *Theos*, she looked stunning.

'Kalispera, matia mou.'

The beautiful smile she'd spent two months determinedly not bestowing on him lit her face, and she walked to the table, the stiffness of earlier much lessened. It wouldn't be long, he judged, before the bounce in Lucie's gait returned and she returned to full, glowing health.

She'd changed into another of her favoured black dresses, a strapless, floaty number that perfectly suited her tiny, slender frame. Her black, curly hair had been piled on top of her head in the style he so loathed because he was incapable of looking at it and not wanting to pull out the clip holding it together just to watch it all tumble down. When she slipped into the chair he held out for her, he wasn't quick enough to stop his face twisting in fresh loathing as the scent of her perfume engulfed his senses.

Thanasis despised all of Lucie's perfumes but this was the one he'd once considered stealing out of her bedroom and incinerating. Only his absolute refusal to enter her private space had stopped him acting on this urge.

This was the perfume, more than all the others, that amplified her natural scent and gave off a sensuous, musky aroma that made him want to bury his face into her neck to inhale it deep into his lungs. It was the scent that turned sexual awareness into a charge so strong that he became unable to stop all the heady fantasies hovering beneath his consciousness from rising up and tormenting him with their vividness.

It was the perfume that turned his hunger into a craving.

Lucie had barely taken her seat before two members of staff appeared with a variety of mezes for them to dive into. While they fussed over both her and the table, placing the dishes into a perfect diamond formation between her and Thanasis whilst pouring her water and offering her a variety of alcoholic drinks that she thought it best to refuse considering the current state of her head, Lucie took the opportunity to regain the composure that had come within a whisker of being blown to smithereens with one look at Thanasis.

Heavens help her, he *did* something to her, and in less than a week she was going to be married to him. In a life she had no memory of, they'd made plans to spend the rest of their lives together, and all she really knew about him was what he'd chosen to show her, and all she really knew for certain about *them* was that her pulses were still racing and lips still tingling from those fleeting kisses barely an hour before.

But she had learned something concrete about him that day. She'd learned he was a gentleman. You only had to look at him...although she wasn't quite certain how looking at him allowed her to determine this...to know he was a highly sexual being. Despite Thanasis practically oozing testosterone and sexuality, he'd guessed that she'd geared herself up for sharing his bed and guessed too how frightening a prospect it had been for her, what with him being a stranger to her, and so had reset things between them to put them on an equal footing. So that made him a gentleman, and it made him empathetic. More proof, not that it was needed, that he wasn't the monster she'd been raised to believe him to be.

Could that be the reason for his rigidity around her? she suddenly wondered. While he was understanding of the loss of her memories, he still had his own, and she took a moment to put herself in his shoes. If their roles were reversed and she was the one who had not only all the memories of their time together but all the feelings too...

To unexpectedly find mutual love with someone and then find that person's love for you had been wiped out as if it had never occurred? Oh, but it must be one of the most awful things in the world.

'Are you okay?'

Thanasis's voice pulled her out of her latest batch of rambling thoughts.

The intense green eyes were watching her closely.

'You looked lost in your thoughts,' he said with a half-smile.

She couldn't help but smile at how unerringly accurate this observation was, even as her chest filled with a fizzing emotion for this stranger who knew her so, so well.

'I was thinking about you,' she admitted.

He raised an eyebrow in question.

'I was thinking how hard this whole situation must be for you. I don't know how I'd cope if I were in your shoes.'

Pale green gaze boring into her, he said, 'All that matters is that you are here, and if having you here means you and me starting over then that is better than any alternative.'

The fizzing in her chest spread up and into her throat, and suddenly she recognised truth and sincerity in his stare, the first time she'd been able to accurately read him at all, and the relief that came with this reacted to the fizzing in her chest and throat, and shot out of her mouth as a burst of joyful laughter.

Bemusement playing on his dreamy face, now both of his dark eyebrows rose in question.

She leaned forwards. 'I know I've thanked you before, but I'm going to thank you again, for being there for me while I was in hospital and for being here for me now, and for all the accommodations you're making for me. Thank you.'

The guilt that lanced Thanasis's guts at this was so sharp and unexpected that it took him a moment to respond. 'It is nothing you wouldn't do for me,' he lied.

But he hadn't lied about Lucie being here being all that mattered. That was the greatest truth of all because the alternative was the destruction of everything and everyone he cared about, and the destruction of everything and everyone she cared about too. When the truth was revealed after the wedding, he would make her understand the lies were for both their benefit.

Her black eyes shining, her heart-shaped lips pulled into a smile softer than he'd ever have imagined Lucie Burton capable of pulling. 'I'm starting to believe that.'

Internal alarms ringing at the direction Lucie was steering the conversation—there were lies and then there were damned lies—Thanasis straightened his spine and pulled a smile of his own. 'Eat, *matia mou*. My chefs have been busy creating all your favourite dishes.'

One thing he had learned through all their torturous meals out together was that Lucie had a particular addiction to cheese. All cheeses. And so it came as no surprise at all when she loaded her plate with keftedes, Kalamata olives, sliced vine tomatoes and tzatziki, and sprinkled what had to be half a block of crumbled feta over the whole lot of it before happily diving in.

At her first bite of the keftedes, her already shining eyes shone even brighter. 'Wow,' she said once she'd swallowed it. 'These are amazing. Forget falling in love and all that business stuff—I'd marry you for your chef.'

He couldn't help but laugh, even as he remembered her once telling him the only worthwhile thing in his whole rotten life was his head chef. That had come off the back of Thanasis icily telling her when she'd unexpectedly joined him for dinner in his apartment, that he preferred to dine alone than have his meal spoilt by her presence. He would eat with her in public as part of the whole performance but in the privacy of his apartment, he wanted solitude. Unfortunately, solitude and Lucie did not go together. Her husky voice followed him everywhere, even when he was on the other side of the four thousand square metre space from her. The bounce of her footsteps echoed through the walls. There were nights when he swore he could hear her breaths of sleep.

'Let's play a game,' she said once she'd demolished her first course and was steadily working through their main course of spanakopita—another Lucie favourite—served with roasted vegetables.

'What kind of game?'

She stabbed her fork into a mound of roasted aubergines and peppers. 'Getting to Know You. We play it at work with all the newbies, but obviously, as it's just the two of us, we'll have to adapt it. It's literally a game of asking each other questions that allow you to get to know someone better.'

'What kind of questions?'

'Any kind. Favourite colour. Favourite film. First kiss. What car you learned to drive in. Anything, really. The only rule is no closed questions or answers—basically, nothing that can be answered with a yes or no, oh, and as you already know me and I'm the one with the big memory hole, I think it's only fair that I get to ask you three questions to each one of yours.' She popped the fork into her mouth.

That worked for him. He didn't want to get to know Lucie any better than he already did, and, watching her devouring her food, said, 'Where do you put it all?' It was one of the many questions that had built up during their two-month engagement. Their tortured public meals together had been spent with fake smiles, fake conversation, and Lucie eating everything put in front of her and more.

She caught his eye and grinned. 'Is that your first question?'

'I suppose it must be.' A nice, neutral question that would reveal little to nothing about her.

'I have a fast metabolism, but you must already know that.'

'I know you have more energy than the average person.'

'I just get bored sitting around and doing nothing, that's all. Maybe that does help with my metabolism, but seeing as I inherited it from my mum and she'd be happy spending her whole life on a sun bed, I don't think that's the full explanation for it. My turn—when's your birthday?'

'February the nineteenth.'

'Ah, so that must make you a Pisces.'

'I believe so… Do you believe in that stuff?' For all the dark, bohemian flow of the clothes she wore, this surprised him.

'Not in the slightest, but I went through a phase when I was fourteen of obsessing over it and wanting to know everyone's star sign, and the nosey part of me still likes to know. So, Pisces is a water sign… You like swimming?'

'No.'

'Closed answer.'

'It was a closed question.'

'Fair enough. I'll rephrase it—why don't you like swimming, and, seeing as you don't like it, why on earth do you have a swimming pool?'

'I don't like swimming because I nearly drowned as a child. I have a swimming pool because my friends and family like to make use of the island and they all like to swim.'

'Oh, blimey, that sounds terrible,' she said, clearly shocked. 'How old were you? What happened?'

'That is another two questions.'

'No, they're follow-ons because you didn't answer fully.'

He shook his head in mock disappointment. 'You didn't say that was in the rules.'

She fluttered her eyelashes. 'I forgot. I'm telling you it now.'

He laughed at her chutzpah. 'I dive-bombed into the pool when I was four. I couldn't swim and didn't realise the danger of what I was doing. One of the gardeners pulled me out—I was lucky that he was pruning the poolside flowers and heard the splash I made. I suffered no long-term trauma other than a dislike of my face being submerged. I did learn to swim, just to prove to myself that I could do it, but I've never taken any enjoyment in it. Is that a satisfactory answer for you?'

Her eyes narrowed. 'Hmm…' And then she gave a decisive nod. 'Yes, that'll do. Moving on, what—?'

'You've had your three questions,' he interrupted.

'No, I haven't.'

'Yes, you have. Birthday, whether I like swimming and why I have a swimming pool.'

She pouted in mock outrage. 'No fair—the two swimming ones were linked.'

'Linked but separate, which means it's now my turn.'

Her scowl was completely negated by the glee in her eyes.

'When was the first time you got drunk?' he asked as she dug into a thick slice of sticky walnut cake he couldn't even remember being put in front of her. There was a slice in front of him too. He had only the vaguest recollection of their main course being cleared away.

'When I was fifteen. I would like to point out that it was also the last time I got drunk.'

'Elaborate,' he commanded.

She spooned another huge mouthful of cake into her mouth. After swallowing it, she gave a dreamy sigh. 'Would you object to me snogging your chef? Because this is seriously good cake.'

'And you always "snog" people who make good cakes?'

'Never had the urge before, but this is seriously, seriously good. I bet they serve this on Mount Olympus... that is where the Greek gods live, isn't it?'

'Correct.'

'I'd lock your chef up in case Jupiter tries to nab him from you.'

'I think you mean Zeus—Jupiter was a Roman god.'

She shoved another spoonful of cake into her mouth with a this-cake-is-far-too-good-for-me-to-care shrug.

'But I will be sure to pass your compliments to Elias... and pass on your wish to "snog" him.'

Chewing contentedly, she stuck a thumb up.

'In the interests of employer and employee relations, I should warn you that if he objects to being objectified for his cake-making skills, then I will have to put the brakes on any form of "snog" or we run the risk of him leaving and never making another cake for you again.'

Eyes wide with alarm, she spooned in yet more of her rapidly disappearing cake and frantically shook her head.

'But if he agrees to your objectification, then a "snog" will be fine. Out of curiosity, will there be tongues involved?'

She frowned and shook her head again, turning her thumb down for good measure.

'*Kalos*. And now that that is resolved, you can elaborate on your one and only drunken escapade.'

She made him wait until she'd finished the last of her cake before answering. He didn't mind. Watching Lucie devour every last crumb had an erotic appeal that evoked fantasies about taking a masterclass in sticky walnut cake making and then spooning it into that delicious mouth himself.

Theos, the joy she took from food was something else. He could watch her eat all night. Watch those perfect heart-shaped lips...

'Athena stole a whole bottle of ouzo from her dad and the two of us thought it a brilliant idea to drink shots of it until the bottle was empty,' she finally said, cutting through his wayward fantasies. 'Alexis and Constantine found us in the garden and had to carry us to bed because neither of us was capable of walking...' Her voice trailed off, eyes narrowing again but this time with concern. 'What's wrong?'

Thanasis drained the last of his wine and shook his head. 'Nothing. Just trying to picture the scene.'

'It wasn't a pretty one,' she admitted, features loosening a touch, as if only half convinced by his explanation.

He could hardly tell her the truth, that the moment Athena's name had come out of Lucie's mouth, the erotically charged lightness of his mood had extinguished.

He'd forgotten who he was talking to. Forgotten why he was there. Why they were there.

For a few brief moments Lucie had stopped being Lucie Burton, stepdaughter of Georgios Tsaliki and daughter of Rebecca Tsaliki, and just been the beautiful, sexy, amusing woman sitting across the table from him sharing a delicious and increasingly flirtatious meal in the warm open air.

Their first meal alone together with no public watching them and he'd got caught in a moment he'd spent two months fighting tooth and nail to never be captured in.

He had to clear his tightened throat to ask the most natural follow-on question. 'You got into trouble for it?'

'Nope. It was put down to teenage high jinks, plus I think the general feeling was our hangovers were a worthy punishment—honestly, we were both as sick as dogs the next day.'

'I'm not surprised,' he murmured.

She grinned. 'I well and truly learned my lesson from it. Athena didn't though, but never mind, I'm sure she'll learn it one day. Anyway, my turn to ask a question.'

'Tomorrow.'

Her face fell.

Theos, he had to fight to make his voice sound normal. 'The medical team need to do all their checks on you.'

'But I feel fine,' she protested.

'I know, but for my peace of mind, I would like you to let them do their job. You've suffered a significant head wound, *matia mou*—you were only discharged this morning into my care on the promise that you would take things easy.'

She eyed him in silence for the longest time before giving a slow nod. 'Okay, I'll be a good girl and go to my room and let the medical team poke and prod me, but only for tonight. From tomorrow, I'm in charge of my own care.'

His heart nearly thumped out of his ribs when she reached across the table to cover his hand.

Her voice softening to match the softness in her black eyes, she said, 'I know your heart's in the right place and I can only imagine how hard these last few days have been for you, but I don't need or want you to make decisions for me. I've lived independently since I was eighteen, answerable to no one but myself. I'm not a child, Thanasis, so please don't treat me like one.'

He looked down at their joined hands with thick blood roaring in his ears. The sensation of Lucie's skin against his was like being marked by Aphrodite, the goddess whose seductive charms few men could resist, and it was taking all his strength not to twist his hand and wrap his fingers around hers.

Too much wine, he thought dimly. It had seeped through his system to dismantle the guard he kept fully raised around her, and only when he was confident that he could look at her without losing the last of his guard did he raise his gaze and hoarsely say, 'Message received and understood.'

She smiled tremulously and moved her hand away, pressed her fingers to her mouth and then leaned forwards to press them to his lips. '*Kalinychta*, Thanasis.'

He could do nothing to stop his lips kissing the delicate fingers. '*Kalinychta, matia mou.*'

CHAPTER SIX

ON HER FIRST morning in Sephone, Lucie woke to the rising sun and to the remnants of a dream where Athena had been cruelly laughing in a strange yet somehow familiar living room. The unsettled, almost sick feeling the dream had set off in her was countered by the lack of waking fuzziness in her head, and she climbed out of bed with the spring in her step that had been missing since the accident.

Making herself a coffee from the posh machine in her room, she was about to carry it through the arched glass door that led out to her balcony when a tap on her bedroom door stopped her in her tracks.

Her heart tripling the rate of its beats, a wide smile had formed before she opened the door, a smile that faltered when she found one of the nurses standing there and not the man who'd been lodged in her mind as she'd fallen asleep and still been firmly ensconced there when she'd woken. The nurse must have stayed awake all night with her ear to the adjoining wall listening out for movement.

After whispering refusals of painkillers and all the health checks that apparently were *still* completely necessary, and insisting she was completely fine, Lucie softly closed the door on the poor nurse and padded outside.

Just as the villa itself was uniquely beautiful, her balcony was too, gentle steps leading down to a comfortable seating area fronted by a narrow swimming pool that appeared to snake the entire upper perimeter in a touch of aesthetic genius, winding through the adjoining balcony to her left... Thanasis's sprawling balcony.

She only needed to think of his name for her pulses to go haywire.

Was he awake yet, an early riser like her, or was he like the majority of her step and half-siblings and a bear with a sore head if woken before midday? She'd caught a glimmer of the real Thanasis Antoniadis during the meal when he'd finally relaxed around her, and what she'd discovered had delighted her. He was on her wavelength! He hadn't taken her silly comment about wanting to snog his chef seriously but had played along with it and while this was just a silly, minor thing it meant so much because there was nothing worse than having to explain a throwaway jest, something Lucie had way too much experience with as her humour often went over people's heads, but Thanasis had got it and played along with it, and it had been wonderful.

Oh, but there were so many things to learn and discover about him, and she longed to knock on his door and continue all the learning and discovering, but it was too early for most humans to rise.

Close to giddy with anticipation for the day to begin, she decided to take a swim and hurried to her dressing room in search of a swimsuit, hoping whoever had packed for her had thought to pack beachwear.

Result!

Modest black one-piece squeezed into, she finished her

coffee, grabbed a towel from her bathroom and bounded back outside.

Lowering herself into the cool water, trying especially hard not to give her usual squeak when the water level reached between her legs so as not to wake the rest of the household, soon she was at the pool's edge gazing over the clear blue Aegean and the islands dotted in the distance.

Thanasis really had found paradise here. She'd never known such stillness before. Always there was noise in her life. Always. Here on Sephone, she could hear the birds singing their early morning chorus and the only sound to cut through it was the gently lapping sea rather than never ending traffic. The air felt cleaner, the sky crisper... She sighed with the pleasure of it all. Bliss.

Time to see if the pool really did snake the whole perimeter, but which direction to take? The route that took her past the bossy medical team's room or the one past Thanasis's? Decisions, decisions. She had the strong feeling that if either caught her, she'd meet disapproval, what with her 'condition' and all that. With at least one member of the medical team already awake and Thanasis likely still sleeping, her choice was made.

Swimming her preferred breaststroke, she set off with slow, lazy movements and made a studious effort not to turn her head to peek into Thanasis's room. Her peripheral vision showed that his balcony was vastly bigger than hers, the far end formed of its own half-dome with panoramic views that provided shelter from both the sun and the minimal rain the island was subjected to.

The pool wound round, intermittent narrow bridges to swim under and a new vista for her eyes to feast on of high rugged terrains and the undulating verdant greens of the island's olive groves and vineyards, and then she rounded yet another bend to the rear of the villa and hooked her arms over the pool's edge to take it all in.

Dinner had been eaten at the main poolside's dining area. She could just about make it out from her vantage point, but what she could see clearly now and had failed to notice the night before was the sensational sprawling grounds that had to be Thanasis's garden. He must have used a landscape gardener of equal renown to his architect, she thought, awed at what had been created out of nothing and so cleverly and sympathetically designed that unless you knew better you'd assume you'd fallen into the Garden of Eden. This Garden of Eden had a giant marquee in its centre and hiding just behind it—although she knew it was an illusion and really it was situated a long way behind it—a solitary domed white chapel, identifiable by the giant cross sticking out of its white roof.

Her airwaves suddenly tightened, white noise filling her ears in a rush.

That chapel had to be where she and Thanasis would marry. That marquee had to be where they would host their wedding reception. And those sleepy-looking workmen traipsing across the lawn carrying long poles over their shoulders had to be part of the crew tasked with transforming the garden into a fairy-tale wedding venue designed to convince the whole world that the bride and groom were destined to live happily ever after.

Their marriage was no abstract thing. It was real. In less than a week she would be a married woman and she had absolutely no idea if the sudden rabid fluttering in her stomach was an indication of excitement or terror.

'Please, tell me I am hallucinating.'

Still struggling to breathe, Lucie whipped her head round. Finding Thanasis by the side of the pool, all tousle-haired and stubble-faced and wearing a pair of baggy canvas shorts, made the struggle a whole lot worse.

He could have stepped off Mount Olympus for an early morning walk with the mortals.

Back off, Adonis, she thought dimly. *Your replacement has arrived.*

Adonis would take one look at Thanasis and retire on the spot.

She'd known he had a great body but even her vivid imagination had failed to paint it in all its glory. Thanasis had the broad muscularity gym bunnies around the world worked their socks off to sculpt their bodies into, but there was none of the bulging veins Lucie's nose always wrinkled at. Instead, it was as if Mother Nature herself had decided to bless him with perfection, from the deep olive hue of his skin to the smattering of fine dark hair that covered his defined chest and abdomen.

Dear heavens, had there ever been a finer specimen of manhood in the history of the world? This was the man who in a few short days she would exchange vows with and pledge to spend the rest of her life with, and as all these thoughts tumbled in her healing brain and her pulses throbbed just to look at him, she understood the fluttering in her stomach contained not an ounce of fear.

This gorgeous, sexy man was her fiancé and he was in love with her, and last night she'd finally understood for the first time since waking in her hospital bed why she'd fallen in love with him in turn.

The full lips she'd been dreaming of as she'd fallen into

her real dreams tightened. Folding his arms, he repeated in clipped tones, 'Tell me I am hallucinating.'

She swam as close as she could get and held on to the poolside to look up at him. '*Kalimera* to you too.'

'Are you insane?' he said in the same clipped tone that contained strong undertones of anger. 'You have suffered a major head injury.'

'So you keep reminding me.'

'I shouldn't have to keep reminding you. Swimming alone in your condition is the height of insanity. Anything could have happened.'

'Erm…you know I can stand up in it, right? And I'm barely five foot.'

'That is not the point,' he virtually snarled. 'You have recklessly endangered yourself.'

She was still filled with all the fizz she'd set off on her swim with, Thanasis's appearance having added extra zing to it, and her good mood refused to dampen despite his obvious anger. 'Are you always this overbearing or is it just an early morning thing?'

'Over—?' His mouth snapped shut and he took a visible deep breath.

'Look,' she said before he could open his mouth again. 'I appreciate your concern, I really do, although quite honestly I'd prefer it without the headmaster tone, but as I told you last night, I'm not a child. I don't just feel fine today, I feel normal, like properly normal. There was no danger at all in me taking a swim… By the way, how did you know I was out here? I swam past your room ages ago.'

'This is the other side of my room,' he said tightly.

'Your room must be humungous.'

'It's big enough.' He took another deep breath. 'I know you think you are recovered but I gave my word to the medical team at the hospital that I would make you take things easy until the wedding.'

She couldn't help but smile at how visibly he was trying to rid himself of his visible anger. 'Poor you, thinking you could make me do anything.'

His jaw clenched and he raised his gaze to the heavens. 'This isn't a joke. I know you hate being told what to do but for once will you please just do as you're asked and keep yourself safe?'

Absurdly, this pleased her, yet more unneeded evidence that Thanasis really did know her and more unneeded evidence that he really did care for her, even if he did need to work on how he expressed that caring. She got it though. If the shoe were on the other foot and she were in love with him and saw him doing something she considered reckless then she'd probably be all overprotective too.

Sidestepping on the tips of her toes to the nearest gently inclining steps, Lucie got out of the pool and gave a mock curtsey. 'There. I'm being a good girl again, and if it makes you happy, I'll make a good girl promise not to go swimming on my own without supervision or arm bands until our wedding.'

Even though his eyes were still raised and his body language all tight and controlled, to her delight, his lips twitched as a glimmer of amusement flashed on his gorgeous face.

'And now that's all cleared up, do you have a towel I can use please?'

His neck rolled before he gave a sharp nod and turned

to an inbuilt shelving unit stacked with towels and toiletries, and for the first time she noticed that this section of balcony didn't just have a long L-shaped sofa and coffee table but a Jacuzzi bath and an outside shower too.

Thanasis averted his eyes as he handed Lucie the towel. She was wearing what had to be the plainest, least revealing swimsuit he'd ever seen on a woman and yet his veins were as thick and heavy as they'd been when he'd caught that glimpse of her semi-naked in her hospital room.

He turned his face away so he wasn't subjected to the torture of watching her rub the towel over her delectable body. He needed to cool his core temperature, not raise it.

He should have bribed the doctors to keep her at the hospital a few more days.

After a night of restless sleep, which he'd given up on when the sun had risen, he'd thrown himself out of bed with a renewed determination to avoid Lucie's company as much as humanly possible... And then he'd glimpsed her swimming past his bedroom without a care in the world and clearly no care for the significant head trauma she'd suffered.

He'd come within a breath of bodily snatching her out of the water.

'Have you always been this rebellious?' he asked in a rougher tone than intended, but God help him he defied anyone in his shoes not to struggle containing their emotions when faced with someone who combined the beauty of Aphrodite with the discord strewn by Eris.

All the discord Lucie sowed lay entirely within him, and as Thanasis felt her stare fix on him and his awareness for her magnified, he thought she must have a touch of Hecate in her too. What else explained the growing sensation that he was being cast under a spell?

'I don't know about being rebellious,' she said musingly. 'I just know my own mind and have learned over the years how to assert it. I guess it was the whole growing up in two wildly different households thing.'

He made the mistake of looking at her.

She was bent forwards, drying her ankles, but those big black eyes were glued to his face. 'Sorry if you've already heard it all before—I'm guessing things are going to be like Groundhog Day for a while for you—but on the off chance I never shared my childhood with you, it was all pretty bonkers.'

She patted around her thighs... *Theos*, they were so exquisitely toned and slender...

'My dad's an accountant,' she explained, now drying her arms, 'and I spent the majority of my childhood living with him in a bog-standard ordinary house where everything was quiet and orderly and everything had its place and rules were strictly enforced, and then I'd spend the school holidays with Mum and Georgios and Athena and all the others, and life was just one big party and the only real rule was to *have fun*. Dad expected me to be dutiful and studious and grow up to be an accountant or a doctor, and Mum expected me to be glamorous—I distinctly remember her plucking my eyebrows when I was nine—and trade off my looks and attract a billionaire of my own like she'd done. I'd get off the plane in England and the first thing I'd have to do was wipe off the makeup Mum had trowelled on my face because Dad would have gone spare to see me wearing it. In their own ways, they both wanted to control me, but I guess I must have an inbuilt independent streak because I always knew I never wanted what either of them wanted for me.'

And this was why Thanasis had spent two months avoiding Lucie's company. He didn't want to know her, didn't want to have to think of his headstrong fiancée as anything but the woman she was today, most definitely didn't want to think of her as a child constantly yo-yoing between two households and countries, a square peg in a round hole in both of them, didn't want to hear anything from the husky voice that would knock at his defences and turn her into anything less than his enemy.

'What did you want?' he asked before he found the sense to end the conversation.

She shrugged and smiled and wrapped the towel around herself, and in the process wrapped the spell she was casting on him a little tighter too. 'To be free to live my own life and make my own choices. What about you? Did you ever want to do anything different from what your parents wanted for you…? I'm assuming your parents always wanted you to one day take over the running of Antoniadis Shipping?'

'They wanted it but they never put any pressure on me. If I'd chosen a different path, they would have been disappointed but they would have supported me.'

'Good for them. I got it in the neck from both my parents when I went straight into work from school. Dad wanted me to go to university and Mum wanted me to get a boob job. Oh, well, at least I've disappointed them equally so no one can accuse me of favouritism.'

'Your mother is a piece of work,' he said scathingly, an utterance and tone he regretted as soon as it left his mouth.

'She is who she is just as I am who I am,' Lucie said with a small lift of her shoulders that did nothing to hide the sadness flickering on her face. 'I will never be the daughter either of my parents wanted.'

Thanasis had to clench his jaw to stop himself placating her and pointing out that it was never a child's job to live up to parental expectations, that it was the parents' job to adjust those expectations to the individual child before them, just as his own parents had done with Lydia.

But none of this was any of his damned business. This was a conversation he should never have allowed to develop and he was damned if he was going to allow himself to feel empathy for a woman who'd given up the freedom she'd disappointed both parents by insisting on out of love and loyalty for the monster that was Georgios Tsaliki.

Time to extract himself from this situation.

Except there was no time to think of an excuse to rid himself of her, for Lucie, despite the towel wrapped around her hanging like a giant tent down to her feet, gracefully threw herself onto his outdoor sofa and with a smile said, 'Can we order some breakfast now, please? I'm starving.'

Why the hell had he gone along with this? Thanasis asked himself moodily as he watched yet another slice of *bougatsa* disappear into Lucie's delectable mouth. The wedding was only days away and there was no end of things that needed his approval, and that was without considering all the business stuff that needed his attention. A hundred ready-made excuses and he'd failed to conjure a single one.

'Do I get on with your family?' she asked, wiping her mouth with a finger and then licking the crumbs stuck to it.

He leaned across the coffee table to refill his coffee. It was getting to the stage where he'd rather dive into the main swimming pool than watch her eat. Anything than have to watch her eat. Each bite thickened the spell of awareness and the only way to break it was to escape her company altogether.

He needed to get out of here.

'It is too early to say,' he replied evasively.

'Ah, so they hate me.'

His gaze zipped back to her before he could stop himself.

She sighed and gave a rueful smile that shouldn't have tugged at his chest. 'Thank you for trying to spare my feelings but it really isn't necessary—I'd much rather have the truth even if it does hurt. I'm not a Tsaliki but I understand why they would see me as one, and I get why that would cloud their judgement of me.'

About to deny it, he closed his eyes briefly and nodded. Once they were married, Lucie would learn for herself the depth of his family's loathing of her and the entire clan of Tsalikis and hangers-on.

She gave another sigh and helped herself to what had to be her fourth slice of *bougatsa*. 'Oh, well, hopefully in time they'll see for themselves that I'm not the Antichrist and that the feud has nothing to do with me at all, and just accept me for myself like you did.'

He didn't want to hear this. He didn't want to hear or talk about *any* of this and put himself in a position where he had to tell the barefaced lies that were so necessary but that were becoming increasingly difficult to form.

Holding on to his loathing of Lucie had been a damn sight easier when the loathing had been mutual and she'd wanted to escape his presence as much as he'd wanted to escape hers. A damn sight easier when she wasn't half sprawled on his sofa with her pretty feet pointing at him, the towel having come loose and now lying half draped on the floor exposing her smooth legs, and with her beautiful face glued to his. Her hair drying in the rising sun was an untamed mass of curls pinging in all directions and damn if it didn't make her even sexier. Damn if the modesty of her swimsuit didn't make her sexier too, and it was taking everything he had not to let his eyes drift to the barest hint of cleavage on show.

It was like the forbidden fruit analogy but in flesh form, he thought, as he fought even harder against the awareness threading so heavily in his veins. The more flesh that was covered, the greater the desire to uncover it all. Most women's swimwear left so little to the imagination that you didn't need an imagination to know what lay beneath it. Not with Lucie. The bottom half of hers was more modest than the top half, wrapping around her skin like a pair of tight shorts and revealing not an inch of buttock…or anything else, and he could not stop himself from imagining what lay between those slender, succulent thighs. *Theos*, he kept inhaling that damned perfume even though he knew it was an impossibility and that not a trace of it remained on her golden flesh.

'What about you and my family?' his feminine temptation asked, bringing more *bougatsa* to her lips. 'I know

I wasn't fit for much when I was in hospital but I don't think I imagined the tension between you and my mother.'

'Until you were hospitalised, the only members of your family I'd had face-to-face contact with were Alexis and Athena.'

She chewed morosely before she brightened and sat up a little straighter while at the same time straightening her right leg.

Her toes were now barely an inch from his thigh. Sexy toes painted blood orange.

God help him, when had he ever found toes sexy? But Lucie's were. Pretty, sexy feet topped with pretty, sexy nails painted a colour filled with erotic imagery.

'Oh, well,' she said, clearly oblivious to the torture he was suffering, 'I suppose it's going to take time for the families to properly bury the hatchet.'

'There is not going to be any burying of any hatchet. Once we're married and the pictures of the two parties breaking bread together have been printed across the world, both families will return to their respective lives and go back to despising each other. The feud will be over on paper but not in hearts.' He said all this in as even a tone as he could manage, and then, using sheer force, wrenched his stare away from her sexy toes...

Only to land it straight onto her beautiful face at the same moment the tip of her moist, pink tongue darted out to catch a flaky crumb stuck in the corner of her exquisite mouth, and he found himself suppressing a groan as a wave of desire he could neither staunch nor deny to himself punched through him and his body twisted closer to her before he was even aware of what it was doing.

Theos, every inch of her was exquisite. Every damn

inch. She didn't need to wear sexy clothes to be sexy or to spray perfume onto her skin to smell heavenly. She was Aphrodite, the goddess not just of beauty but of pleasure…of desire.

The eyebrows first plucked by her mother at the age of nine—what kind of mother did something like that? he wondered dimly—drew together as her gaze dipped to his mouth. 'Do you really believe that?'

He leaned closer still. 'Do you mean that you don't?' he whispered.

The black eyes flickered back up to meet his stare and widened. How had he never seen the flecks of gold in her eyes before, and now that he saw them, they were all he could see, tiny flecks of gold fire burning…hypnotising him.

Colour heightened her exquisite cheeks, the flecks of gold swirling. Her lips parted and she hitched a small breath. 'I…' She shook her head slowly, her voice barely audible even though her face was craning towards his. 'I don't know…but if you and I can…'

Her words tailed away as another thick throb of desire pulsed through him, all his senses soaking in the flawless beauty of the goddess who was drinking him in with the same dazed intensity with which he was drinking her.

He could smell the heat of her skin and the sweetness of her breath.

Barely aware of what he was doing, Thanasis wrapped his fingers around the warm, silken calf of her leg. A groan rose up his throat.

Theos, even her skin was flawless.

Her lips parted and released a quiet gasp, her wide eyes pulsed and her knee made the lightest of jerks.

That lightest of jerks was strong enough to snap him back to his senses, and in an instant he snatched his hand away and, heart pounding like a jackhammer, pulled his face away from the flawless beauty he'd been barely an inch away from kissing.

CHAPTER SEVEN

LUCIE SHOOK HER head in a futile attempt to clear it of the blood rushing through it and sucked on lips that barely a moment ago had been alive with anticipation of Thanasis's kiss. She was trembling. Every part of her. Trembling and aching.

He rubbed a giant hand over his face and took a long breath.

Even through all the dazed sensations consuming her, Lucie had just enough wits left to recognise the torture Thanasis was putting himself through, and her ragged heart swelled at the control he must be continually exerting for her sake.

Pulling herself together as best she could, she shuffled over, closing the distance his sudden lurch away had created between them, and took hold of his hand. It stiffened at her touch.

The shutters were back in his eyes, his expression once again unreadable, and she gave a tremulous smile to see it…and to see the tic pulsing in his jaw.

On impulse, she scrambled unsteadily onto her knees and palmed his cheeks…her whole hands fitted on them, the thick stubble brushing deliciously into her skin…and brought her face even closer, dizzily breathing in the scent of coffee lacing his breath.

'You don't have to walk on eggshells or treat me like I'm breakable, Thanasis,' she whispered. 'My memories of us might be gone but something of what we shared must have imprinted in me because the feelings haven't.'

Something flashed in the green eyes before they closed and his strong throat moved. 'Lucie, I...'

She slid her fingers over his mouth and shook her head. 'You don't have to explain anything. I can see how hard this whole situation is for you.' And then, because she could do nothing else, she slipped her fingers away from his lips and replaced them with her mouth.

If Thanasis had been still before, every muscle in his powerful body now tensed, and as her eyes closed and she sank into the sensations dancing over her mouth and into her skin at the compression of the lips she couldn't stop fantasising about against hers, the control he was exerting made her swollen heart expand to fill every crevice inside her. Sighing into him, she slipped her hands round to clasp the back of his head and slowly dragged her fingers through hair softer than silk.

She sensed rather than heard the groan in his throat before the unyielding mouth flexed and his lips parted, only a fraction but fraction enough for his breath to fill her senses with a taste and heat so delicious that her brain shut down completely under the weight of sensation flooding her.

Thanasis could hear nothing above the roar in his head, could barely hear his own urgent commands to resist, to unclasp the hands clinging so tightly to his head and push

Lucie away before he gave in to the hunger and melted into her honeyed temptation.

He must not fall into it. He must resist. Resist, resist, resist, and with this one thought pushing through the growing cacophony in his brain, he lifted his hands with every intention of pushing her away but instead found his fingers cupping her face as his head tilted to fuse their mouths into one. The tips of their tongues collided and a burst of lust like he'd never experienced in the whole of his life smashed into him, its force so shocking that, with a hoarse groan, he buried his fingers into her mass of soft curls and opened his mouth to her.

Fire raging through his veins, his tongue swept into her hot, sweet temptation.

Theos, she tasted even better than their few fleeting kisses had promised, a potently dark sweetness that fed and stoked his hunger, the gentle softness of her mouth an aphrodisiac that punched straight into his heavy, aroused loins.

His senses consumed with a ravenous hunger he'd never felt before, Thanasis swept his hands down the curve of her back, and crushed her flush against him, holding her tight as he laid her down, the searing fusion of their mouths and tongues deepening into something primitive as he feasted on the beauty who had taunted and haunted him for so long.

Fingers dug tightly into his skull scraped lower, through the hairs of his neck and over the planes of his shoulders, and he shuddered at the sensations scorching his skin, shuddered again when her thighs parted and she wrapped her legs around him, and as he dragged his mouth over the delicate skin of her throat and felt the heavy thump of her pulse beneath his lips, he cupped a breast frustratingly covered in her tight swimsuit and felt the arousal of her hardened nipple against his palm at the same moment she circled her hips and his own arousal jutted into her pelvis.

God help him, he had never known desire could be this swift and this potent and this greedy, and he brushed his lips lower, his tongue sweeping over a collarbone that was as perfect as the rest of the body writhing beneath him…even her moans of pleasure were perfect, soaking into his ears like music, close to drowning out the voice in his head distantly shouting that he had to stop this, right now, before things went too far.

The voice cut through again, even louder.

Stop.

Summoning every ounce of his strength, Thanasis wrenched his mouth from the nectar of Lucie's flesh and pulled himself away from her.

The silence that followed was stark, the thumps of his weighty heart the only sound to cut through.

Theos, he could hardly breathe.

The sudden pleasure withdrawal of Thanasis's ravenous mouth and the glorious heat of his body left Lucie completely disoriented. Dazed, she blinked up at him, hand fluttering to her pounding heart, barely able to snatch the smallest of breaths. Her body was on fire. There was a deep, throbbing ache between her legs as though the very core of herself had turned into lava.

Dear heavens, so that was what a real kiss felt like. Like your bones were melting into liquid.

As she watched the rapid rise and fall of Thanasis's perfect chest and the pulse throbbing in his tight jaw, her other hand absently fluttered to her mouth, fingers exploring the delicate skin his lips had just ravaged. The trail his tongue had made against her neck burned deliciously.

'That should not have happened,' he stated heavily, breaking the stunned silence.

It was like he'd tipped a bucket of ice water over her head. All the heady, joyous zings careering through her blood froze in their tracks.

He twisted back to face her with a dark, forbidding expression. 'Your feelings for me are false.'

Utterly confused, she scrambled upright and swallowed. 'How can you say that?'

There was an implacability to the way he was looking at her. Only the heaviness of his breaths betrayed the effect their moment together had had on him.

'Listen to me,' he said roughly before taking her hands and placing them flat on top of his palms. 'You feel that, yes? The touch of our hands?'

She almost wanted to deny it. It felt like Thanasis had given her a glimpse of heaven and was now denying it even existed.

'You feel it because it is true and quantifiable. Whatever else you think you feel for me, it doesn't exist because it can't—without the memories, there are no feelings because there cannot be because there is nothing for the feelings to touch on.'

'But they're there. *I* feel them,' she protested, and wrapped her fingers tightly around his hands. 'I feel them the same way I can feel your skin against mine.'

He shook his head with that same implacable assurance. 'No. You feel them because that is what you want to feel, because you feel you must for my sake, but they are not true. In time your real feelings for me will develop organically and they will be true, but you cannot force them and I will not take advantage of their absence.'

'You can't tell me I didn't feel what I just felt then,' she said, searching his eyes with something close to desperation. Could he be right? *Was* she trying to force feelings on herself? Whether he was right or wrong, all the sensations she'd just experienced in his arms... She had never, *ever* experienced anything like that before, a kiss that had made her come close to spontaneously combusting. 'Or tell me you didn't feel it too.'

God damn that Thanasis wished he could. And God damn that he wished he could just tell her the truth, and it unnerved him to know how close he'd come to telling her exactly that in the moment before she'd blown his mind with a kiss. A whisker. He'd been a whisker away from telling her the truth and blowing up his life.

He couldn't tell her the truth but nor could he let her believe that any feelings she might have for him were ghosts of her past feelings, because those feelings had never existed.

A man had his limits and Thanasis had just found his.

'Of course I felt it too.' He groaned and tugged his hands away from hers, running them furiously through his hair.

He could still feel it, the entirety of his body alive to the flame that had just incinerated them both.

'The chemistry between us has always been strong.' So strong that they'd both fought it like warriors. 'But chemistry isn't what we're talking about. All you know of your missing memories is what you've been told—you have nothing tangible to pin them to and nothing real to pin your feelings to, and until you do, I cannot in good conscience allow anything to happen between us.' He fixed her with a stare. 'I won't.'

Never. Especially not under the weight of a lie.

God damn it, why had he let that happen? He'd known it would be hard keeping Lucie at arm's length whilst playing the role of devoted fiancé but hadn't guessed it would be impossible.

A noise too much like real life cut through the tension-filled silence, and it took a long moment for Thanasis to realise it was the sound of a reprieve.

With a silent prayer to whichever deity had taken pity on him, he reached into his back pocket and pulled out his private phone. 'I must answer this.'

Getting to his feet, painfully aware of the arousal still so tight in his loins and of the unsteadiness of his legs, Thanasis crossed the bridge of his pool.

'Thanasis.'

He turned his head to the sound of Lucie's voice.

Her eyes held his for a long breath before she gave a small smile. 'Thank you.'

A cloud of emotion filled and pushed against his chest, and he closed his eyes briefly before continuing to the balustrade.

His back to her, he put the phone to his ear. *'Yassou.'*

'How is she?' Alexis asked, getting straight to the point.

It took everything he had not to turn back round to look at her.

Theos, he could taste her as fresh as if her sweet tongue were still dancing against his. Feel the softness of her skin beneath his fingers. The hardness of her nipple against his palm.

He swallowed to answer. 'Doing well.'

'She is with you?'

This time he couldn't resist looking even as his hackles rose at the contemptuous tone Alexis used when referring to Lucie.

She was still sitting on the sofa. She'd pulled her knees up to her chest. Her stare was exactly where he'd known it would be. Even with the distance between them, he could see the concentration on her face, see her thinking with the same strength as the stare boring into him.

And then her lips curved into a smile. A real smile. Lucie's Aphrodite smile. A smile she'd bestowed him with only once in their previous incarnation, on their very first meet, right before his deliberately acerbic dig about her boots.

He blew out slowly and turned away. 'Yes.'

'Any signs of her memories returning?'

'No.' He almost—almost—wished they would.

'Good. Everything is contained this end.'

'And this end.' Dangerously contained.

'The paparazzi took pictures of you two walking Piraeus harbour. Holding her hand was a nice touch.'

His hackles rose even higher. His voice gained an edge. 'I'm glad you think so.'

'I've discussed things with my father and Rebecca, and we've agreed on a million-euro payment for her silence. You will match it?'

Outrage at this speared so deeply that if Alexis Tsaliki had been standing in front of him, Thanasis's fist would have connected with his nose without a second thought.

Breathing heavily to get a grip on his temper, entirely aware that Lucie was still watching him, Thanasis lowered his voice and growled, 'Twenty million each.'

Alexis laughed.

'One million is an *insult*.'

'It will be two million if you match it, more than she would earn in her lifetime.'

'Irrelevant,' he snarled. 'Your family might think her expendable but I will not see her paid off so cheaply when, without her, we would all have lost everything by now. Twenty each or I tell her the truth this minute and leave all our fates to the gods.'

He heard a sharp suck of air.

Good. Let Alexis think he meant it. He deserved it for his contempt and the cruelty of what all the Tsalikis were doing to her.

This wasn't a game. This was Lucie's life.

Bad enough that he was playing his part in it, but this was her mother and the people she regarded as family conspiring against her without any care for what the truth would do to her.

Thanasis had no control over what the truth would do but he could play his part in making it more palatable for her to live with.

After a long silence, Alexis finally said, 'Okay. Twenty each. But you are playing a dangerous game, my friend.'

'No, I am trying to save you from losing a sister.' Hadn't he warned Rebecca that she stood to lose Lucie? Clearly she'd not taken his warning on board or shared it with the rest of her family.

'She is not my sister.'

An image flashed in Thanasis's mind. Lucie's face in that early moment in her hospital bed when he'd told her the world at large considered her a Tsaliki daughter and sister in all but blood and name. The amazement and delight in her expression.

Alexis might not regard Lucie as his sister but she thought of him as her brother.

Responding with a voice cold enough to freeze the Aegean, Thanasis said, 'And you are not my friend. Goodbye.'

He disconnected the call then had to breathe all the way into his twisted guts to stop himself hurling his phone over the balustrade.

This was why he'd fought tooth and nail to keep Lucie at a strict arm's length.

One kiss. One goddam kiss. It had softened him up and humanised her in the way he'd always known he must never allow, not with someone he despised with such strong passion because how could he keep his future marriage pure living with such heady, twisted temptation?

He pulled more ragged air into his lungs.

He didn't know when his feelings for Lucie had first shifted but he was starting to understand that she'd never deserved his loathing any more than she deserved Alexis's contempt.

Shifted feelings and increasing guilt or not, there was too much at stake to confess the truth before the wedding, too many lives and livelihoods at stake to walk away.

He might have thought this whole charade wrong from the start, but he'd gone along with it and would continue playing along because there was still no better option. He needed Lucie to marry him. They all needed her to marry him. Even Lucie did, and he must never let the chemistry between them win before the truth could be told.

He sensed movement behind him and turned to find her crossing the narrow bridge.

Blood filled his head, all his senses whirring back

to life as she neared him. The taste of her in his mouth strengthened like a taunt.

She stopped before him like a proud goddess with her chin lifted and a hint of defiance ringing in the all-seeing eyes. 'What you just said before your phone call, about all my feelings for you being false...'

The blood in his head began to pound.

He held his breath.

'I don't believe they are,' she finished. And then she smiled her Aphrodite smile. 'But I get why it bothers you that they are and why you need me to be certain—'

'There can be no certainty until your memories come back,' he interrupted roughly. 'I could tell you anything and you have no way of knowing if it is the truth or not.'

Her Aphrodite smile didn't diminish an iota. 'You can tell me anything and I have no way of verifying it.'

'Exactly.' Now, at last, she was getting it. Thanasis might not be able to tell her the truth but he could damn well open her mind to the possibility that everything she'd been told about her missing memories could all be lies. Open her mind so when he revealed the truth on their wedding night, the shock would be absorbed.

'But if you keep putting me at arm's length, how am I ever going to get to know the real you and know if my feelings are true or not?' she said, a glint of stubborn knowing in her eyes. 'Because, let's face it, my memories might never come back.'

Lucie laughed to see the frustration flash on Thanasis's gorgeous face.

Once she'd got over her shock at his declaration that the most thrilling moment of her life was something that should never have happened, she'd realised nothing had changed and that he was still trying to protect her from both himself and herself.

Well, no more. She'd spent days trying to be compliant and behaving in a way she'd been told was for the best because of her head wound, and now it was time to take back control and narrate her own story rather than let others dictate it for her, and that included Adonis's sexier replacement.

Reaching for Thanasis's hand, marvelling at the power contained in it, she pulled it to her mouth and rubbed his fingers against her lips. 'See?' she said, gleefully gazing into a stare she could see fighting to put the shutters back down. 'Whatever my memory issues, I still have free will, and I had free will when I kissed you, just as you had free will when you kissed me back and free will when you pulled away. We both know I will marry you whatever happens, so stop treating me with kid gloves. I promise you, I'm unbreakable.'

Jaw clenched tightly, he pulled his hand away. 'No one is unbreakable.'

'I made it through my childhood in one piece and with a hide built of rhino skin. Trust me, there is nothing you or anyone can do to hurt me on anything more than a superficial level, so gloves off and mask off—I want to know the real Thanasis Antoniadis and make up my own mind about the man he is and let my feelings develop in the organic way he suggested just twenty minutes ago.'

That had him, she thought with yet more glee that *might* be an effect of the giddiness of his kisses still streaming in her veins or *might* be due to finally snookering him with his own words.

Not allowing him time to interject, Lucie pointed in

the distance to where the early morning sun was rising in an arc between the V created by two mountains directly in their line of vision. It was as if a straight line had been created from balcony to V, sweeping over the roof of the chapel for good measure. 'First question. Is it coincidence that this section of balcony is completely aligned with the rising sun?' She laughed at his disbelieving expression. 'I want to know *you*, Thanasis. Everything about you. So get talking.'

Sometimes, Thanasis thought, a man had to know when he was beaten, and there was no doubt in his mind that on this occasion Lucie had outplayed him with nothing more than a twisting of his words.

The quick brain that never missed a trick was back in full functioning order, but this wasn't the confrontational Lucie he'd spent two months despising. This was a different Lucie. This was the Lucie he'd spent all those long weeks determined not to know.

He hadn't wanted to know her.

For all that she'd given as good as she'd got, *he'd* been the instigator of the war that had erupted between them. It had all been him.

But that was then and now everything had changed.

He could do nothing to change what had already passed but he could play along and give Lucie the chance his determination to hate her had meant he'd refused to give her before. Get to know the real Lucie Burton and not the warped picture he'd pre-painted in his head, a painting made with all the wrong colours and strokes. Now it was time to allow her real colours to shine through.

As painful as it was to admit, he owed her that much.

His mind set, he filled his lungs with clean Sephone

air and met the expectant, sparkling black eyes. 'Even though you have presented me with a closed question, I will enter the spirit of the game as the game was intended and give a full answer.'

She gave a full wattage beam.

'The villa was designed with the rise and fall of the sun in mind. You have to get up early to see it, but when the sun first rises, the only light on the island comes from between those two mountains.'

'So my balcony and the balcony on the other side of your room must face west, then?'

He nodded. 'When the sun sets, our vantage point gives the illusion that it is melting into the sea.'

'Okay, but whose idea was it to capture both the sunrise and sunset in the villa's design? Yours or Thomas's?'

'Mine.'

'Now we're talking.'

He narrowed his eyes in question.

She rose onto her tiptoes and tapped the end of his nose. 'It means that you appreciate the wonders of the world.'

His chest filling at the teasing but affectionate gesture, Thanasis took a step back.

While he was willing to play along with Lucie's wish to get to know him better, and knew it was only fair that he should get to know the real Lucie better too, he could not in all good conscience allow himself to play along with the role of her lover. Not now. Not with the taste of her still alive on his tongue and the heavy weight of desire still so thick in his loins. It had taken more strength than he'd known he possessed to pull away from her, and he couldn't be certain he would find that same strength again, not when she was so warm and passionate and willing and…

He snatched a breath.

He needed to keep Lucie at a physical arm's length until they married. Just a few more days, that was all, and then the truth would be revealed.

It was even possible that she would forgive him.

'I can't say anyone has said that to me before,' he murmured.

'You must hide that part of your nature really well. Weren't you tempted to build your villa up there?' She indicated the slightly higher of the two mountains.

'That is where I originally wanted the villa built, yes. The only thing that stopped me was the terrain—it would have been too dangerous for the building crew. There is a particular spot up there where you can watch the sun rise and set. It is the only vantage point on the whole island better than what we have here.'

'Will you take me there?'

'When you are better.'

She pulled an unimpressed face.

'The golf buggies can't reach it so you have to walk, and it's a long, often steep walk,' he explained. 'Give yourself a few days to fully rebuild your strength.'

She eyed him for a moment and then grinned. 'Okay. But only if you get Elias to make me more of those delicious keftedes for me to build my strength with.'

He couldn't stop himself from grinning back. 'You have a deal.'

But a deal he absolutely would not seal with a kiss.

CHAPTER EIGHT

THE CHAPEL WAS much bigger than Lucie had anticipated from her vantage point on Thanasis's balcony, but it was too hot to goggle at it from the outside and she practically threw herself through the arched door.

It was every bit as cool inside as she'd hoped.

'Better?' the hulk who'd entered the chapel with slightly more decorum asked drily.

On this, Lucie's second full day in Sephone, she'd woken early again and had swum round to Thanasis's east-facing balcony. He'd been waiting for her by the pool steps.

She'd grinned up at him. After all, he hadn't actually made her give the promise not to swim unsupervised again.

He'd shaken his head in mock disappointment and handed her a towel to dry herself. And then they'd sat on his balcony sofa and watched the sun rise together over coffee and *bougatsa* as if it had all been pre-planned.

'Much.' She fanned herself with the back of her hand to rid her face of the last of the perspiration that had broken out on it during the short buggy ride from the villa. 'I spent every summer in Greece during my schooldays. You'd think I'd remember how hot it gets here.'

'When was your last summer spent here?'

'When I was eighteen. Full time work unfortunately does not allow for long, lazy summers.' Or didn't. She didn't have a job any more. Of all the things she'd given up to marry Thanasis and save their two families, her career was the only one she felt real pangs of regret over. Of all the memories lost, her resignation was the one she didn't want to come back. She had a feeling it would be a scene too distressing to want to relive. In her six years there, the Kelly Holden Design team had come to feel like family. It was a family she'd gate-crashed her way into but still a family. Or a version of one.

No point harking back to something that was already done, she told herself resolutely, and craned her head around at the vast space with its high, ornate pillars and frescoed ceiling in which she and Thanasis would soon marry. It really was the most incredible and awe-inspiring of spaces, like someone had Greek-ified the Duomo, shrunk it to vaguely manageable proportions, and transported it to Sephone.

A thought struck her and she whipped her stare to Thanasis. 'How can this be here if the island was abandoned millennia ago? I didn't think they had chapels back then?'

'I had it built alongside the villa.'

'Wow. So it's less than ten years old? It could have been standing for centuries.'

'That was the feel I was aspiring to.'

'You're religious?'

'Not particularly. It was for my mother. Church is a regular feature of her life. She always suffers guilt if she misses Sunday mass.'

'I think that has to be the most thoughtful gift I've ever heard of,' she said, astounded.

'She's my mother,' he said matter-of-factly before pulling a musing face. 'And it has come in handy for our purposes.'

'There is that,' she agreed. 'Did you imagine you would marry in here when you built it? Or did it just work out that way when we settled on marrying on the island?'

He took a while to answer, and when he spoke, his words were slow. 'When I saw it completed I knew it would be where I marry.'

'Bet you never imagined it would be with me,' she jested, and was rewarded with a short, non-committal laugh. 'So who's marrying us? Do you have a permanent priest here?'

'No. There is a semi-retired priest in Kos who travels over whenever my mother's here. He will be officiating.'

'I assume the ceremony will be conducted in Greek?'

'You assume correctly.'

'Good.'

He raised an eyebrow.

'It's fitting,' she said. 'It would be sacrilegious to have the service in English. This chapel, this whole island, it's Greek to its core... What time are we actually marrying?'

'Six p.m.'

'Is that to escape the worst of the heat?'

'Partly, but mostly because when the service is finished we will have the photos taken on the stretch of beach where the sun sets.'

'So we'll have the sunset as our background?'

'Precisely.'

'Sounds perfect and extremely romantic. The media will lap it up.'

He grimaced. 'That was the idea behind it.'

'Don't worry,' she assured him. 'First and foremost, this marriage is for business purposes and there's no point pretending otherwise. That anything else has come out of it is just sheer good luck—let's face it, it could have gone completely the other way. Can you imagine how awful it would have been if we'd hated each other?' She imagined it would have been unbearable. Lucie always felt awkward and prickly when in the company of people who disliked her. Whenever Athena had gone through her spates of being mean to her, Lucie had always coiled into herself and grown defensive spikes. Thank God Thanasis had been prepared to give her a chance and not park her in the camp of being his enemy.

But his family hadn't been prepared to do that. Strange how this hadn't bothered her when she'd first guessed it but now, just a day later, it made her chest tighten. She supposed it was the fact of their wedding no longer being an abstract thing. She was here, in the thick of all the preparations and glued to the side of the man who would soon be her husband... Well, glued as much as he would allow.

There had definitely been a shift for the better in the way Thanasis was around her. There was a greater sense of looseness about him, not just in his frame but in his speech, less of a sense that he was weighing each word carefully before allowing himself to speak, more gesticulation and more glimpses of the good-humoured man she'd dined with her first night on the island. She was growing to like a lot about him. She liked his patience, of course…that had already been established. Liked that he was happy to play Getting to Know You for hours even though he must already know so much about her and had probably relayed many of the stories she'd coaxed out of him before. Small, mostly insignificant stories that built a picture of a man from the loving, stable background she'd once longed for. A man for whom family was everything, and she had the strong sense that once this controlled bear of a man loved you, there would be nothing he would not do for you and nothing he would not do to protect you, and Lucie supposed it was a sign of his love for her that he was trying to protect her from herself.

Because what she didn't like was the physical distance he'd imposed between them. Even the small signs of affection had gone. If she stood or sat too close to him, he'd visibly stiffen and edge away. When she'd covered his hand over lunch he'd gently but firmly moved it away. When their ankles had brushed under the dining table he'd adjusted his position so his long legs were aimed in a different direction.

His control was impressive and infuriating because that heady, passionate kiss had unleashed something in her, an ache she carried everywhere, in every cell of her body. There was not a minute spent in his company when Lucie didn't long for him to just touch her, a longing made worse knowing it had unleashed something in him too. She could feel it like a vibration, the tempered desire beating beneath the powerful body, and she could see it too, a dark pulse in his eyes before he snapped it away with a blink.

She knew he'd imposed this physical distance for her sake, and while she appreciated his reasonings, she would look around his glorious garden and the romantic fairy tale it was being transformed into for their wedding day, and experience that thrilling rush of emotions, and it all felt so *real*. Her and Thanasis. And if they were real then it meant the fact that his family hated her was real too.

Another family she didn't fit in with.

She would make them like her, she decided resolutely. Well, try. After all, she'd had nothing to do with the war between the two families. In reality, only Georgios and Petros had. Everyone else was just a bystander. Collateral damage.

'What are you thinking about?' Thanasis asked, cutting through her ruminations.

'Everything.' She laughed and shook her head, wishing she could wrap her arms around him and breathe in his gorgeous scent. Wishing, if she did that, he would wrap his arms around her and not stiffen and then politely extract himself from her hold.

'I was thinking about your cynicism about our two families ever truly burying the hatchet. I think it could happen.'

'Our families have been at war for decades,' he reminded her. 'Too much has happened for it to be forgotten. The bad feelings run too deep.'

'I know, but if you and I were able to see past all that and build something together…' She lifted her shoulders. 'There has to be hope the rest of our families can build bridges too, because otherwise what's the point?'

'The point is saving our respective businesses and fortunes.'

'If that's the case, if the hatchet isn't actually buried, what's to stop your father or Georgios picking it up and

burying it into each other's backs again once the businesses are saved?' Saying this, Lucie knew not even a
written guarantee would stop Georgios from going after
his nemesis again if the mood struck him.

How the big-hearted man with an even bigger smile
could be so vengeful was beyond her understanding, and
that there were two elderly Greek men out there who'd
been unable to take a hard look at themselves in the mirror and say a firm *no* when the 'pranks' they'd played on
each other had turned so dangerous just blew her mind.

'They know what's at stake if they do,' he assured her.

'But there has to be more than that to stop them starting it all up again. Sure, with you and Alexis now in
charge there's not going to be the blatant sabotage of each
other's fleets—and I know I've probably said it before,
but I was horrified when I learned Georgios was behind
the fuel replacement in your ocean liners that destroyed
all those engines. I love him dearly but that was a terrible thing to do—but what's to stop them making it even
more personal if they hate each other so much?'

And how would that affect *them*? she suddenly thought
with what could only be described as panic. Would things
escalate to the extent she would be forced to choose between her new family and her stepfamily?

She might never have felt like a true Tsaliki but they'd
all been good to her. Georgios had doted on her as if she
were one of his own. The boys, all older except her half-
brother, Loukas, had teased and looked out for her in
the same way they'd teased and looked out for Athena.
As for Athena, with her being only two years older than
Lucie and the only girl in a household of boys, it was
natural that they should have gravitated together. Sure,

Athena could be a Grade A bitch and there were times Lucie would prefer to bury herself alive than be in her company, but when she was on form she was brilliant. When you knew and loved someone as much as Lucie knew and loved Athena, you forgave the less palatable sides of their nature.

How was she supposed to choose between all that and her new family who didn't even like her? They hated her!

'My father has given me his word, and Alexis has given his word to keep Georgios in line,' Thanasis told her steadily.

She pulled a sceptical face and tried her hardest to swallow back the growing angst.

He folded his arms across the gloriously broad chest she ached to bury her face in, and rested his back against a marble pillar. 'Trust me, *matia mou*. They both know how close they have come to losing everything. The hatchet might not be buried but, I promise you, the war is over.'

Loving and hating his endearment—loving how tender it sounded on his tongue but hating that it was the closest thing to affection he would currently allow between them—she expelled the last of her sudden panic with a sigh. 'I'm sorry. I forgot for a minute that you and Alexis put all the hard work in and dotted all the I's and crossed all the T's months ago. There would have been no point in you and I agreeing to marry in the first place if we didn't have those assurances from them.'

'Akrivos,' he said. Exactly.

But now the mentions of her stepbrother had stirred something else in her brain. 'Were Alexis and Athena really the only members of my family you had contact with before my accident?'

'In a face-to-face capacity, yes. Why do you ask?'

'I don't know.' And she didn't, not really, more that her brain was trying to take hold of something in her memory bank, the whisper of a recent conversation… with her mother? It had to be. Who else had she spoken to that she cared for since being hospitalised other than Thanasis and her mother? She had no phone so hadn't been able to make any calls since arriving on Sephone, and it occurred to her that she'd not given a single thought since her arrival of Thanasis's offer to have a replacement phone flown over for her.

To her surprise, she found she didn't want a replacement. Not yet. There was something quite freeing about being uncontactable here on this island paradise, and besides, everyone she loved and cared for would be part of the five hundred strong party that would be descending on Sephone in a few days' time for the wedding.

For the first time since their kiss, Thanasis's stare captured hers with the intensity of old. 'Do you have a memory coming back?'

Returning to the whispers in her memory bank, Lucie shook her head in frustration. 'I don't think so. Whatever I'm searching for is recent but I think the drugs I was fed in hospital have blurred things for me.' She shook her head again and tried to be philosophical about it. She had two months of her life missing and was fixating on one little nebulous thing? Sometimes she really needed to give her head a good wobble. 'Oh, well, what's another lost memory between friends…? Does that sound like a helicopter to you?'

She was quite sure she could hear a rotor.

Thanasis, his watchful eyes still on her, craned his ear and nodded. 'That must be your wedding dress.'

'Clever dress to fly a helicopter,' she deadpanned, and was rewarded with a loosening of his features and that glorious spark that always zinged between them whenever he hopped onto her wavelength.

Wryly, he said, 'For the amount it's costing, I'm hoping it can cook steak too.'

Almost giddy to have shaken off the disquiet that had sneaked up on her out of nowhere, she had to practically glue her feet to the intricately patterned cool flooring to stop herself from reaching for him. 'I guess that means it'll soon be dress-fitting time… What kind of dress is it?' Funny, she hadn't thought to ask that before.

'A wedding dress.'

'Very helpful. I meant what *kind* of wedding dress.'

'I do not have the faintest idea.' Pointedly, he added, 'I would assume it's white but if your wardrobe is anything to go by, it might very well be black.'

She curtsied in her short, black, strapless playsuit and flat black sandals.

He laughed loudly, the deep sound bouncing off the chapel's walls, a glorious sound that didn't just soak into her ears but soaked into her skin and veins, feeding the longing for him it felt like she'd been carrying for ever, and meeting his eyes, the lines around them creased with his amusement, she could do nothing to stop the sigh of her longing from seeping out…

His eyes flickered at the sound and in an instant the laughter died. The lines uncreased and the light on his face dimmed.

The air enveloping them thickened and suddenly the

chapel was filled with a silence more complete than anything Lucie had ever known. For one long, breathless moment, anticipation that he was going to unfold himself from his prop against the pillar and haul her into his arms held her hostage.

She didn't know if she wanted to cry or scream when she watched the shutters of his eyes come down with one forceful blink, and when he unfolded himself from his prop against the pillar, it was with his usual languidness.

'We should probably meet the design team so you can have your dress fitting, so shall we?' He indicated the door as if nothing had just passed between them.

Lucie summoned a smile. Or something she hoped resembled a smile. 'Sure, let's go and fight our way through the furnace just so I can be used as a human pin cushion.'

The lines around his eyes creased a touch. 'I'm sure that if you keep still and let the team do their job, Francois will be careful not to let them stab you too many times.'

'A cheering thought, and as a reward for the patience I'm going to have to display whilst being used as a pin cushion, you can take me up into the mountains later to watch the sunset.'

Not giving him the chance to argue with her, Lucie sauntered out of the chapel and into the oven that was the great outdoors. It actually felt quite cooling compared to the furnace inside her.

To Lucie's disappointment, she spent so long being used as a human mannequin that by the time she was released from the purgatory of the dress-fitting room, the sun was already starting to set. That wasn't to say it had been a nightmare—her dress was gorgeous and entirely in a style she adored, which was to be expected seeing as she'd had a say in its design even if she didn't remember having that say, and Francois and his team had all treated her as if she were a princess. As an added bonus, she hadn't been stabbed once—it was just that trying to hold a conversation for three hours when all she could see and think of was the expression in Thanasis's eyes before he'd pulled the shutters back down had been close to impossible. He was driving her crazy!

He continued to drive her crazy with his body language that night over dinner, all pulsing looks when she caught him unguarded combined with utter physical control of himself. They exchanged not so much as a touch of a finger between them. It was a torture that continued the next day, from the moment she swam to his balcony for breakfast right until the time came for them to head into the mountains to watch the sunset.

Changing, at Thanasis's insistence, out of the sparkly black flip flops he'd decreed unsuitable for trekking in, Lucie shoved her feet into her only vaguely suitable footwear, her chunky black calf-length boots, and met him at the front of the villa. He was in the driving seat of the golf buggy they would use to take them as far and as high as they could go before they had to walk. In the back seat, an enormous backpack filled with food for their adventure.

His gaze flicked to her as she stepped out of the door, then dropped to her feet. There was a long moment of stillness, as if someone had accidentally pressed pause on him, and Lucie had a sudden certainty that came from nowhere that he was going to comment with, 'Nice boots,' before he blinked himself back to life and welcomed her with a smile instead of words.

She walked over and showed him the tube of sunscreen in her hand. 'Can you put some on my back for me please? I can't reach.'

She watched his reaction, noted the tightening of his smile and the subtle flicker in his eyes, and knew applying sunscreen to her flesh was the very last thing he wanted to do.

She almost laughed.

It was the first time she'd needed to ask him. Daylight hours on Sephone had been spent avoiding the scorching heat of the sun but the climb they were going to embark on would leave her exposed.

Bad luck, Thanasis. Got you with this one, haven't I?

With a sharp nod, he held his hand out for the tube.

She passed it to him. For the first time since their legs had brushed two nights ago, skin met skin as the pads of their fingers touched. But it was no lingering touch. Thanasis practically snatched his hand away before climbing out of the buggy.

Turning her back to him, she lifted her hair with one hand and held her breath.

Thanasis gritted his teeth, squeezed some of the lotion onto his hand, and told himself to grow a pair. It was human skin, nothing more. So what if it happened to be Lucie's skin? There wasn't all that much flesh that needed to be covered, mostly the shoulders and down to the base of her shoulder blades. Her black vest with its thin straps covered the rest of it…the thin straps she lifted her free hand to tug down her shoulders so he could apply the lotion unimpeded, confirming what he'd spent the day determined not to notice. That Lucie wasn't wearing a bra.

He took a deep breath to clear his suddenly constricted throat and put his hands to the top of her back.

With brisk, wide strokes, he rubbed the lotion into the silken skin, fingers sliding over the nape of her neck, over the slender shoulders, and lower down until every centimetre of exposed flesh was protected.

He would never know what compelled his fingers to trace up her spine or why her shiver compelled his mouth to drop a kiss to her ear.

Breathing heavily, he stepped away from her and forced his thrumming body back into the buggy.

CHAPTER NINE

THE DRIVE TO the mountain and to the point where the buggy could go no further took only twenty minutes. They were twenty of the longest minutes of Lucie's life, and when Thanasis pulled the buggy to a stop in a natural clearing, her heart was still beating erratically.

Asking him to put the sunscreen on her had been necessary, but also a fun way to needle the man who'd developed a rigid determination to keep his hands to himself. She hadn't anticipated that the dial of her longing for him, carried in every fibre of her being, would turn even higher. From the tension vibrating from the powerful frame sitting so closely beside her, and the clipped way he spoke when describing features of the mountain they were about to climb and talking about the natural fauna they were driving through, Thanasis for once being the one to drive the conversation, it was a suffering that was shared.

She could still feel his lips on her ear.

First removing two bottles of water, one of which he passed to her, he shrugged the huge backpack onto his back with the same ease Lucie slung a handbag over a shoulder. 'Ready?'

Lucie looked up. The natural trail Thanasis was going

to lead her on to the top of the mountain didn't look too difficult to manage, at least not yet. The high trees surrounding them looked as if they would provide welcome shade from a sun still blazing its rays on the island. If they kept a steady pace, they'd reach the summit within the hour.

Feeling more able to breathe properly now she wasn't trapped on the buggy with his giant body so close to hers and his body language telling her loud and clear not to even think of breaching the tiny distance between them, she looked back at him and nodded.

'Then let's go. Stay close.'

She snorted. 'That's the last thing you want me to do.'

He fixed her with a stare. 'No, the last thing I want you to do is fall and hurt yourself. Or get bitten by a snake.'

'There's snakes?'

'If snakes frighten you, tell me now and we will go back to the villa.'

The last of the tight angst she'd been carrying inside her melted away. She grinned. 'You're not getting out of this that easily. I'm not scared of snakes, I was just surprised when you mentioned them. I've never seen a snake in all my years visiting Greece.'

'Snakes tend to avoid Athens and I can't see them sneaking onto your stepfather's yacht,' he commented drily. 'Here, in the mountains, it is different. Tread carefully, especially in non-shaded areas—they like to sunbathe.'

'Lazy so-and-sos.'

To her delight and relief, Thanasis's tight features relaxed into amusement and with a spring of happiness in her step, she set off beside him.

'Do you do much hiking?' she asked as they started up a shaded, gentle incline.

'I used to. Not so much now.'

'What kind of answer is that?'

He cast her with a swift glance. 'Are we playing your game again?'

'Too right. So proper answers, thank you.'

'When I was at university a group of us would go camping at weekends and holidays and find new places to explore.'

'You, camping?' Much as she tried, she could not imagine Thanasis squeezed inside a tent.

He laughed. 'I cannot say I enjoyed that aspect quite so much, but the camaraderie and adventure made it worth it.'

'And the beer?' she guessed.

'That was part of it,' he agreed. 'We still try to meet up a few times a year but I've not been able to join the others for the last two trips. I missed a week hiking in South California earlier this year.'

'All the stuff with the business?'

'Yes. It has taken every minute of my time.'

'Well, hopefully our marriage will go a long way to putting all your business troubles behind you, and you can start living your life properly again.'

'That is mine and everyone else's hope, and when we are all able to start living properly again, Antoniadis and Tsaliki, it will all be thanks to you.'

'You know me, here to help,' she jested.

He came to a sudden stop. 'No, *matia mou*, do not try to downplay what you are doing. If not for your agreement to marry me, both businesses would be lucky to still be clinging on. Your selflessness has ensured our survival.'

'Hardly selfless, and you agreed to it too.'

'I agreed because it was the only hope we had of clawing our way out of the mess. You agreed knowing you would gain nothing from it.'

'Other than my stepfamily's survival,' she pointed out.

'That is my point. You entered into our agreement for everyone else's sake when you didn't owe anybody anything.'

'Apart from a lifetime of being loved by them, that's absolutely spot on.'

Thanasis had to bite his tongue and swallow back his anger. If there was any love on the Tsalikis' part for Lucie, they had a strange way of showing it.

They set off again. 'How did your stepsiblings get on with your mother when you were growing up?'

He knew his question had him skirting dangerous territory but that was a risk he was willing to take. Lucie needed to be prepared in some small way for what was coming when the truth came out.

'They all got on fine. They'd had so many stepmums by the time she came along that I imagine they took her presence in their stride. She never tried to mother them so that probably helped. Saying that,' she added with a cackle of laughter, 'she never much tried to mother me, either.'

Another bite of the tongue and the swallow back of anger.

Thanasis had never imagined he could despise someone more than Georgios Tsaliki but his fourth wife roused a different, colder kind of loathing in him, and he had to bite his tongue another time to stop himself from pointing out that Athena and Stelios had never had another step-mother before Rebecca Tsaliki usurped their own mother.

They'd reached a steep incline that required concentration to navigate despite the rope he'd had put along its edge for support, and they didn't speak as they made their way up it. To reach the top of the incline you had to climb a sheer drop that was only six foot and which Thanasis could manage easily, but when you didn't quite reach five foot it meant you needed help.

'I will lift you,' he said with an impassiveness only his racing pulses would prove was a lie.

He shrugged off the backpack then stood behind her. 'Ready?'

'Yep.'

He put his hands securely to her waist and lifted her until her bottom, clad only in a pair of black denim shorts, was face high to him and Lucie was waist high to the ledge and able to swing herself over. The last he saw of her was the black boots that had earlier given him a cold case of *déjà vu* before her face peered over the edge and she grinned down at him. 'You coming up?'

Lucie thought she might just have discovered heaven on earth.

The top of the mountain was ruggedly sparse of vegetation but the thickness of the picnic blanket Thanasis had spread out stopped the rocks and prickly plants beneath them from jabbing into their skin and allowed her to do nothing but marvel at the scene unfolding before her. Oh, and eat the delicious spread of food Elias and his assistant had whipped up for them, of which she'd stuffed as much as she could manage into her belly. Stretched out on his back beside her, propping himself up on his elbows having eaten his fill too and playing the most major part in the heavenly scene, Thanasis.

'Thank you for bringing me here.' She turned her stare to him with a smile. She had never in her life seen such a spectacular vista, similar to the view from their balconies but so much, much more. The setting sun was not yet low enough to melt into the sea but its reflection had turned the Aegean's horizon a golden orange, the distant islands darkening and becoming all the more striking for it.

The man who outshone the vista in the beauty stakes responded with a smile that crinkled the lines around his eyes. *'Parakalo.'* After a beat, he added, 'I brought my sister here once. She spent more time complaining about the patchy phone signal than admiring the beauty nature has to offer.'

'I guess the world would be very boring if we all liked the same things.'

'I don't think Lydia and I have ever agreed on anything that we both like,' he commented drily. 'If she didn't have so much of both our parents in her, I would believe she was adopted.'

She laughed and studied the piece of pottery Thanasis had found when they'd reached the summit and he'd been deciding the perfect place to lay the blanket. Faded black paint with what could possibly be the tip of a pair of wings painted in faded gold on it, the relic measured roughly ten inches by five inches. Its concave shape suggested it had once been a pot and Thanasis's casual dating of it as 'probably being two, three thousand years old' would have blown her mind if she had any mind left to blow. With the benefit of hindsight, Lucie realised learning she was engaged to Thanasis Antoniadis had been peak blowing of her mind. Everything else would always be lesser in comparison.

She had yet to reach peak awe over his devastating good looks though, and she carefully laid the piece of pottery down and stretched herself onto her back beside him. Wriggling her bare toes—they'd both removed their footwear—she gave a contented sigh. Her feet were a bit sore from the trek and there were a few cuts on her thighs from where spiky plants had decided to scratch her, but she didn't care in the slightest. She thought this might just be the happiest she'd ever been.

'Are you okay?' he murmured, resting his head on the blanket next to hers.

She sighed again and turned her face to the glory of his. 'I'm just perfect.'

An assessment Thanasis found himself struggling to disagree with, although she hadn't meant it in the way his brain was interpreting it.

He didn't know if it was Lucie's goddess powers coming to the fore again and giving her the ability to read minds, but when she broke the comfortable silence by saying, 'What do you like about me?' he came close to laughing.

It was a laughter that would have died before it had formed for she rolled onto her side and tucked an arm under her head to cushion it, her face so close he could see the flecks of gold dancing in the black eyes now glued to his. Any comfort at being with her vanished as the awareness he'd been controlling with sheer brute force snaked its way back through his veins.

'Getting to Know You time again,' she said with a soft, spellbinding smile, 'so full and honest answers.'

Turning his stare to the darkening clear sky, Thanasis hooked an arm above his head but, such was the force of the spell she was casting on him, couldn't bring himself to move any further away from her. 'You want to know what I like about you?' he clarified carefully.

'I want to know what it was that turned your feelings for me from what I'm guessing is resignation at the situation we'd found ourselves in, into something more.'

'I don't know. It just happened.' He couldn't stop a quick turn of his face to her. 'Like magic.'

'I can believe that.' She lifted her chin onto her forearm and inched a little closer. Her smile had a dreamy quality to it. 'But there must be something specific you like about me. I mean, I really like catching your flashes of humour, and I really like that you love your mum enough to build a chapel for her, and love your family enough to build multiple swimming pools when you never swim, and I like that when you talk about your sister, you sound both proud and indulgent, like she's someone you really love and respect even if you don't particularly understand her.'

Thanasis only realised his quick turn of face towards her had become a full-blown roll of his body when he released the curl he'd taken hold of and pulled straight without any awareness of doing so. It pinged straight back into its original ringlet form in the same way his lust for Lucie could only be suppressed into a form of stasis until one look or word or inhalation sprang it back into its natural state.

'There are many things I like about you,' he said quietly, capturing another curl. 'I like your hair and the way the curls never look the same from one day to the next. I like the way you smile with your whole face. I like your addiction to cheese and I like that you treat all the food you eat with reverence. I like the way you stand up for yourself. I like your independence of thought and I like the way you always try to take other viewpoints on board. I like that I can bring you to a view like this and know you will appreciate it as much as I do.'

It came as a shock to realise that there was nothing about Lucie that he didn't like.

Nothing at all.

Lucie found she could no longer breathe. Her heart was thumping loudly in her ears.

The green eyes gazing at her were staring as if seeing her face for the very first time.

Silence more complete than any she'd ever known had enveloped them, the air charged with an electricity she felt in every cell of her body.

A trembling finger traced a line over her shoulder and down her arm, heated vibrations from the powerful body so close to hers the tips of her breasts were brushing against his chest, buzzing deep into her skin.

His breath swirled against her mouth and the ache she'd carried for days between her legs, so subtle she'd been barely conscious of it, throbbed like a pulse of fire.

Fingers wrapped tightly around her wrists and then the heat of his breath became the heat of his mouth, an unmoving, lingering, barely controlled fusion that ended with a deep groan and one hard sweep of his tongue into her mouth before he rolled onto his back and expelled a breath so long and so hard he could have been breathing out for her too.

Hoarsely, he said, 'You cannot know how badly I want you, but, Lucie, we can't.'

Frustration came close to making her scream. Lifting herself onto her elbow, her heart smashing so hard against her ribs it was as if it were trying to escape and cling to him, she pressed her hand to his cheek. 'Why not?'

Snatching hold of her hand, he inhaled as if breathing in for them both too, his green stare as intense as she'd ever seen it. 'You know why not. Believe me, I would give anything to make love to you but...'

He cut himself off with an oath and hoisted himself up, bowing his head and dragging his fingers through his hair with the same fury she'd witnessed before.

She couldn't just see the torture he was putting himself through, but feel it too, as deeply as she felt her own torture, and when she placed a hand to his back, could feel the heavy thuds of his heart. 'What if my memories never come back? We're getting married in three days, Thanasis. Are you really suggesting we could spend a whole life together in separate beds?'

'No.'

'Then what?'

He tilted his head and slowly rolled his neck. When he finally spoke, his voice was more moderate. 'We wait until the wedding. If on our wedding night you still want to make love to me, then, believe me, you will never find a more willing groom.'

Only the finality in his tone stopped her arguing further.

It was when Lucie was climbing into bed much later that night that her first concrete memory came back. It wasn't much, just a whisper, but it was something solid. Being in Thanasis's apartment. His back had had that rigidness to it that she recognised from her time in hospital and when she'd first been discharged.

They'd been arguing, although what the argument had been about remained a mystery, but he'd walked out of the living room without a backward glance at her.

It was the same room that had been in her dream when Athena had spoken so cruelly to her.

'Hi, Gracie, how are things?' Lucie asked the youngest of her two English half-sisters the next morning, and was rewarded with a grunt that might have been *Good, thank you*, but was probably just a grunt.

In seconds, her stepmother had taken the phone from her. Charlie, Vanessa said in reference to Lucie's father, was in the shower and would call her back if he had time before he left for work. After assuring Lucie that everything was all set for them to join her for the wedding, and that it was something they were all very much looking forward to, Vanessa disconnected the call. She must have forgotten to ask how Lucie's head injury was, so her pre-prepared airy, 'I'm absolutely fine' was entirely wasted.

'Your father is busy?' Thanasis guessed shrewdly.

'I knew he would be,' she admitted. 'It is a work day and he has his routine to keep.' Her father thrived on routine and order. Which was probably why he'd always found Lucie so trying. She dredged a bright smile so as not to show her dejection. 'I would call my mum but she's probably asleep in her coffin.'

He laughed and stretched his long legs out. 'She didn't

sleep in her coffin when she was watching over you in hospital.'

'Yeah, but I bet she got them to feed the donated blood to her.'

'She did disappear a number of times.'

'See, told you.' She passed his phone back and tried not to show her fresh dejection when he took care not to let their fingers touch.

They were eating breakfast on the balcony again, enjoying a few moments of peace. The wedding was only two days away now, and activity levels on the island had gone through the roof, the workers busy setting things up through the night so that any outdoor work could be avoided in the scorching heat of the day.

There was nothing enjoyable about this torture for Lucie that early morning. She'd slept badly, oscillating between sexual frustration, something she had never suffered from before in her life, and trying to force more memories, trying to at least expand the one concrete memory that had come to her.

'Are you okay?' he asked. 'You don't seem yourself.'

She shrugged and kept her moody gaze on the rising sun. If he could read her so well that he could see through her fake bright smiles, then he'd probably hear any lie in her voice.

Lucie had assumed she would tell Thanasis about the memory that had come back to her, but now found something holding her back.

Why couldn't her first real memory of those missing months have been a good one? Why couldn't it have been of them laughing or, even better, making love, not of the aftermath of an argument where he'd walked out on her and she'd been fighting back tears she would never let him see.

Why wouldn't she have wanted him to see her cry? She'd never been much of a crier but she'd never been ashamed of her tears the few times they'd leaked out over her life.

And why was she too frightened to ask him about it?

But she needed to say something. 'When we were living in your apartment... Did Athena visit much?'

There was only the slightest hesitation. 'A few times that I know of. What makes you ask?'

'A dream I had.' That much she could tell him, and now she did look at him.

He'd raised an eyebrow in question.

'The other night,' she explained. 'I thought it was a dream but now I think it might have been a memory.'

'And you think that because?'

She kept her stare on him, wanting to gauge his reaction although she didn't quite know why she wanted to gauge it. 'Do you have black leather sofas and a glass coffee table?'

His face moved a little closer to hers. There was the slightest flicker in his eye. 'You remember them?'

'Yes.'

'Anything else?'

She chose her words carefully. 'Nothing specific, but in my dream Athena was laughing at me, which is nothing unusual for her but the way it made me feel in the dream was unusual. Normally whatever she says to me rolls off—the only way to deal with her is to be Teflon coated—but whatever she said had really upset me.'

There was a tightness in his voice. 'Can you remember what she said? What she was laughing about?'

'No. Is it real, then, the dream? Did I discuss it with you?'

'No, but, Lucie…' His features loosened a touch. Slowly, he reached for her. Suddenly she found herself holding her breath as his thumb traced over her cheek. 'Athena has always been poisonous to you. She *is* poison. If you remember nothing else, remember that.'

The small, tender act of intimacy was over before she could take a breath. Before she could even open her mouth to speak, he expelled a short decisive breath and, with a rueful smile, got to his feet. 'I need to get changed. My helicopter will be landing shortly.'

She stared at him dumbly. 'You're going somewhere?'

'I have business in Athens.'

She stared even more dumbly. This was the first she'd heard of it. 'Can I come?'

'I'm afraid not.'

'Why not?'

'Because it's business and I need you here to supervise the wedding preparations.'

'That's what Griselda's paid to do.'

'We are marrying in two days, *matia mou*. One of us needs to be here, to be on hand if anything important crops up. You might be needed for another dress fitting too.'

Then, as if her morning for shocks wasn't already complete, Thanasis pressed a hand to the side of her head and swooped a kiss to her mouth. Green eyes glimmering, he said, 'I will be back before you have time to miss me.'

And then he kissed her again, a hard, almost possessive kiss that left her seeing stars long after he'd disappeared into his room.

It was as she was swimming back to her own room that another concrete memory hit Lucie. It had to be the day she'd met Thanasis for the first time because he'd been standing with Alexis by a dark hotel bar. Other than the bartender, they'd been the only people in there. Both had been watching the door, waiting for her arrival.

She remembered the smell of the bar. Wine. A subtle but significant difference from the scent of stale beer she'd grown used to during her nights out in her six years living permanently in London.

She'd been excited to meet him. She remembered that too. Could feel the fizzing anticipation that had filled her as she'd walked through the door to him.

And she remembered how their eyes had locked together and the stunned flare of recognition on his face. The fizzing joy had almost spilled out of her to realise he too remembered that chance brief encounter from six years before. That he remembered *her*.

CHAPTER TEN

THANASIS'S LUNGS WAITED until Sephone had disappeared on the horizon before opening fully. He was quite sure Lucie had watched the helicopter until it was nothing but a dot in the distant sky.

He put his head back and closed his eyes. He'd hated disappointing her by refusing to let her come with him, and it disturbed him just how *much* he'd hated disappointing her, but he couldn't risk having her in Athens until after the wedding. Couldn't risk her memories being triggered before he had the chance to explain everything to her.

The biggest truth though, another truth he could not share with her, was that he needed space away from her because he didn't know how much longer he could do this.

He wanted her with a desperation he'd never known it was possible to feel. He wanted all of her. Forget any future wife. No one could make him feel a fraction of what Lucie made him feel. That truth had hit him first in the chapel when he'd tried to picture the ideal wife of his future and then tried to picture marrying her in that same chapel. He'd failed to conjure any face but Lucie's. It was a truth that had solidified watching the sunset with her. Lucie was the only woman he wanted. The only wife he wanted.

Somehow he had to make it through to the wedding

and pray that her dream about Athena wasn't the start of her memories returning. If that dream expanded into a full-blown memory before he had the chance to explain everything to her...

The confession he'd known he must make since he'd agreed to this charade had changed since he'd first envisaged making it. Initially, he'd imagined himself laying all the facts on the table and, while not exactly relishing the shock that was bound to follow, being unmoved by any histrionics. It had been Lucie's own fault, after all, that the need to lie to her had been deemed necessary by any of them.

To envisage his confession now, to imagine her shock, to imagine her *hurt*...

It was enough to fill his guts with an acidic dread that spread into every inch of him.

Lucie sat on the soft sandy beach of the cove nearest the villa late that afternoon, binoculars she'd managed to pilfer from a member of Thanasis's staff glued to her face. She was watching the little white dot on the horizon grow bigger. It was a yacht, a very large yacht, and it was clearly headed towards Sephone.

Who could it be? she wondered. Thanasis had mentioned there would be around fifty yachts moored around the island for the wedding, but she'd assumed they'd all be arriving either Friday—tomorrow—or on the wedding day itself.

The yacht was coming closer. Could it be one of the singers who'd be performing for them? It looked like the kind of vessel a particular world-famous diva was often photographed sunning herself on surrounded by all her sycophants. Or maybe it was one of the tech billionaires named on the guest list she'd pored over earlier? Or any of the billionaires listed, she supposed. Owning a floating palace was pretty much part of the billionaire job description, and she was very grateful for it, having spent many wonderful months of her childhood partying and having fun on Georgios's. Mostly fun, in any case. If Athena was in an accepting mood then everything would be great. If she was in one of her bitchy moods then Lucie had known it was safer to stay in her cabin. The Tsaliki males, including her brother Loukas, had all been good company but without Athena by her side she'd never been able to properly relax, had always felt she had to try too hard to be a good sport about all the boyish pranks and japes.

A sudden thought struck her and made her stomach plummet. What if it was Athena with her current beau— Athena *always* had a current beau—on that yacht?

Something unpleasant had happened between her and Athena since Lucie's engagement to Thanasis. She was certain of it. Certain too, having thought about it incessantly since he'd flown off to Athens, that Thanasis knew it too and was trying to protect her from it.

The call of her name shook her out of her thoughts, and she turned her head to find the butler heading to her with a message from Thanasis. Friends of his were arriving early and had invited them to dine on their yacht that evening, and could she please be ready to leave at eight p.m.

Well, that explained the yacht, she thought, cheering right up, and with the same fizz in her veins that had filled her all those months ago when she'd walked through the door to meet her fiancé for the first time, Lucie danced back to the villa and up to her bedroom and through to her dressing room to find something to wear for their first real date since all her memories had been wiped.

Thanasis splashed off the foam from his neck and face and patted himself dry.

Towel hung loose around his waist, he strolled into his dressing room and soon he was dressed in smart dark chinos and a black shirt he left unbuttoned at the throat.

He could have kissed Leander for arriving early and for his invitation to join them that evening. It meant he got the pleasure of Lucie's company without the torture of being alone with her. He might even allow himself a drink, something he hadn't dared since her first night here when the wine had lowered his defences and set this whole damn ball of the Lucie rollercoaster rolling.

If he was being truthful, that ball had been rolling since she'd screeched away from him in his Porsche. Maybe even since she'd bounced into that hotel bar.

The coldness he'd experienced when told she'd been in an accident should have been the warning shot he'd needed that his feelings for her ran much deeper than basic lust.

Too late now, he thought grimly, and then shook the grimness off. His attitude had ruined too many evenings for Lucie before, even if she didn't remember them. This one he would make special for her. After all, come the morning, the wedding madness would start in earnest. Lucie's bridesmaids would arrive, as would Thanasis's groomsmen, and, as a sop to the old English tradition, he and Lucie would go their separate ways and avoid each other until the wedding itself, one of the many details planned to fool the world into believing that this marriage was real.

He would not allow himself to think tonight of how much he now wanted it to be real too. He didn't dare, not when the confession he must make hung like a dark cloud over him.

A little wax in his hair and a dab of his cologne and he was good to go.

He knocked on her door.

Within moments his senses were engulfed with the scent that most drove him wild…and then he saw her standing there.

A whistle he had no control of escaped through his teeth.

Her teeth grazed her bottom lip and she gave the shy smile he hadn't seen since her first night on his island. 'Well? Will I do?'

Do?

All the good his day away from her had done him had evaporated. All the fortifications he'd built in his mind to get through the next few days…vanquished.

Her usual black attire was gone. In its place, a sheer jade wrap dress with spaghetti straps that plunged between her breasts and tied at the waist, heavy jade embroidery threading in a leafy pattern from the breasts and down to the loose hemline below her knees. It was sexy and tantalising without being revealing, and had the touch of bohemian to it that only Lucie could pull off. Only Lucie could pull off the curly black pineapple on her head too, but even thinking of it as that was to do it an injustice when the soft curls framed her face and enhanced her beauty and the beauty of the deep red pear drop earrings in a way that was, to his eyes, a work of art. A tendril had come loose by her left ear, a long ringlet that brushed against her shoulder and filled him with envy that it wasn't his mouth brushing against that silken skin.

He fought the groan drawing up his throat and clenched his fists to stop them cupping those beautiful cheeks and pulling that beautiful face to him.

Thrumming in him was the deep certainty that should he kiss the delectable mouth painted a tantalising deep dusky colour that was neither pink nor red but, like everything else with this incredible woman, uniquely Lucie, he would never come up for air again.

'Well?' There was a touch of anxiety in her stare.

He blew out a long breath. 'You look beautiful. You *are* beautiful.'

Her smile would have blown out any air he had left in him.

Only when she stepped closer did he realise she was wearing red heels that lifted her height enough that she didn't have to crane her neck all the way back to look in his eyes.

The hand that touched his cheeks contained a tremor in it. 'You've shaved.'

He caught the hand and, fool that he was, pressed it tighter to his skin. 'Do you approve?'

Another smile. 'You always look gorgeous.'

Incapable of releasing her hand, he lowered it and threaded his fingers through hers, then brought it to his mouth to kiss the delicate tips. 'Truly, *matia mou*. You are ravishing.' He laughed to release the tension tight in his chest. 'I'd assumed you only owned black clothes.'

'I've not worn this for you before?'

'No.' He'd never seen her wear anything like it. For their public dates together she'd always looked beautiful—

hell, she always looked beautiful, whatever the time of day and whatever she was wearing—but this was the first time he'd ever felt that she'd dressed with him in mind.

'Good. Obviously I don't remember, but I didn't think I could have. I've no memory of buying it.'

When he thought of all the big memories her amnesia had taken from her, there was no reason why her failure to remember buying one dress should make him feel so wretched.

He gently fingered the loose ringlet and inhaled through his nose, filling his senses with the scent that was a manifestation of his addiction to her. 'Once the wedding is done with, I will do everything in my power to help your memories come back to you. I swear.'

The Aphrodite smile shone up at him.

Even with the sun having set, it was still hot outside, the breeze created in the buggy welcome as his driver zipped them to the harbour where a tender was waiting to sail them to Leander and Kate's yacht. Sephone had limited spots for large vessels and with Thanasis determined to leave as much of the island and its coastline untouched as he could, his refusal to dredge and create more space meant most sea-faring guests would be anchoring at sea.

He'd let go of Lucie's hand. To keep holding it was to torture himself.

From the way Lucie had pressed herself away from him, it was a suffering she shared. The airy way she was asking her questions—they were playing yet another round of Getting to Know You—betrayed it too. Her voice was too airy, like she was trying too hard to be carefree.

'Which of your family is the most likely to accept me?' she asked for her third question, the first two of which had been light and innocuous, and his heart sank to guess this was the question she had most wanted to ask and to know it must be playing on her mind. Worrying her.

'My sister.'

'How come?'

'My mother's loyalty is with my father. She will follow his lead. He's a good man—a great man—but he can be stubborn. Lydia is more open-minded, and, like a certain someone else I know, does not like being told how or what to think.' He thought of how subdued Lydia had been when the negative press had imploded their lives. He'd thought the news of the wedding and its real potential to save them all would bring some of her spark back but she'd only become more withdrawn, and he kicked himself for not having checked in on her since Lucie's accident. The truth was, his mind and his time had been entirely focused on Lucie.

Theos, give him the strength to make it through to the wedding.

'They will all accept you,' he vowed. 'Once they get to know you, they will learn to love you.' He would make damn sure of it.

They'd arrived at the harbour.

To Lucie's relief, Leander and Kate were two of the nicest and most welcoming people in the world. Unlike most of the uber-rich, they didn't start off their acquaintance by insisting on a tour of their yacht, something Lucie had found incredibly irksome as an adolescent whenever she'd joined the rest of the Tsaliki clan on one of Georgios's friends' vessels. Those tours were always, always designed to impress on guests just how much money and fabulous taste the host had. It would've been quicker for them to hand over their bank account statements and a listing of all expenses.

Mercifully, there was none of that with their hosts that evening. They greeted them with smiles and kisses and a bottle of champagne, and took them straight up to the sundeck without finding the need to wax lyrical about either the exact number of crystals in the chandeliers or the thread count of the thick carpet in the saloon.

The table had been set with high-class dining perfection but there was none of the formality Lucie had expected, the staff unobtrusive and polite without being fawning, Leander taking it on himself to be in charge of the drinks—Lucie quickly discovered he made a mean cocktail—and Kate, who was nearly as short as Lucie, taking it on herself to be chief taster of them.

With a variety of meze dishes to feast on and loud music playing and the stars above them twinkling, Lucie found herself relaxing in a way she hadn't expected, relaxing and laughing and generally having an excellent time.

'I hear you're an interior designer,' Kate said to Lucie after Leander had presented them each with a fresh cocktail.

Slightly embarrassed at what must seem a frivolous occupation considering Kate was a vet who'd studied for years to pursue her passion of working with orphaned orangutangs, she nodded and took a sip of her Espresso Martini.

But she really had loved her job. Loved how each job

was different but how the end result always gave the same sense of satisfaction, whether it was a subtle room design or the full-blown transformation of an entire house or apartment. Loved feeling she was contributing to Kelly Holden Design steadily taking more and more lucrative business from the bigger boys.

'Which university did you study it at?'

'I didn't.'

To her surprise, Kate grinned. 'Good for you. I swear I nearly gave myself an ulcer from the stress I put myself under at university. How did you manage to get your foot in the door?'

'I took a punt... Have you heard of Kelly Holden?'

Kate shook her head. 'Should I have?'

Lucie laughed. 'Of course not. She's a goddess to me though. I always knew I wanted to do something creative, but it wasn't until I read an interview with her after her firm won this really prestigious industry award no one thought she had a chance of winning as her firm was so small and new, that I thought, yep, I want to do that and I want to work for her.'

'Just like that?'

'Just like that.'

'That's amazing—it's really similar to why I decided I had to work with orangutangs, except mine was a TV documentary. So what came next—how did you get her to take you on? Was there a lot of competition for the job?'

'I collected my final exam results from school and went straight to her offices and parked myself in the reception room for three hours until she appeared, and then I ambushed her. God knows how I did it but I managed to convince her that what she really wanted to do was take on a green eighteen-year-old with zero experience and one A level in art as her apprentice.'

Leander lifted his glass. 'To always following your dreams.' His gaze darted to his wife, one of many secret, unspoken messages Lucie had noticed pass between them.

Theirs was the kind of relationship she longed for with Thanasis, a future she could feel them inching towards...

'Are you still working for her?' Kate asked, pulling Lucie back to the present.

'No, I had to resign... Not that I remember resigning,' she joked, even as her heart panged again at having had to walk away from the job she'd loved so much. Of all the expected guests at their wedding, Kelly was the one she was most looking forward to seeing. 'But Kelly's in London and I'm in Greece. It's just not feasible for me to stay, and interior design is not a job that lends itself to home working.' She glanced at Thanasis and, remembering his comment about no business talk at the wedding, gave a mischievous wink and said, 'I might just ask Kelly at the wedding if she'll consider expanding into Greece.'

He grinned, that gorgeous, gorgeous grin, and idly traced a finger around the rim of his glass. 'You don't need Kelly. You can set up on your own.'

'With what? I've got no money.' At the three identically shocked expressions, she laughed. 'I've supported myself since I was eighteen. I earned decent money but living in London is hugely expensive. I think I've managed to save about two hundred quid in the last six years.'

'I'll be your backer.'

She blinked, completely taken aback. It would never have occurred to her to ask Thanasis, just as she would never have thought of asking either of her parents or any of her ultra-wealthy stepfamily. 'I couldn't ask that of you, but thank you.'

'You're not asking, I'm offering.'

'And it's a lovely offer but I've always had an aversion to being in debt—I borrowed a hundred euros off Athena once and she harangued me until every last cent had been repaid, and then wouldn't let me forget how kind and generous she'd been to me.' Those one hundred euros had been to cover Lucie's share of the bill on a night out for her own birthday at an expensive club where Athena had insisted on taking her to celebrate it.

His smile and accompanying laughter didn't quite meet the serious hue in his eyes. 'We can discuss it after the wedding, but what I will point out now is that once we're married, everything I have is yours, so you can never be indebted to me.'

'No more boring work talk or I will get the baby photos out,' Leander interrupted with a grin. 'Now, who wants to try a Coquito?'

Was she drunk? Lucie wondered as she embraced Kate and Leander and thanked them again for a wonderful evening. She felt drunk, but not *drunk* drunk. Not like she had that night with Athena when she'd been fifteen. This was a different kind of drunkenness, one oiled a little by cocktails but fuelled by the joy of being alive.

In less than two days she would be married to this gorgeous man holding her with such secure rigidity to him as their tender sped them back to the harbour. He would be her husband and she would be his wife and the whole future would be theirs for the taking.

CHAPTER ELEVEN

THANASIS'S CHEST HAD never felt so tight.

Far from their evening with Leander and Kate giving him space to breathe whilst enjoying Lucie's company, all it had done was bind him closer to her. Bind him closer to the truth of her, which was that Lucie was the fiercest, funniest, most unique person in the entire world.

It was a truth that had been peeling away in slow increments since Lucie had screeched away from his house in utter distress, but he'd been too blind to see her anger for what it had really been. He'd seen what he'd wanted to see. Seen what he'd needed to see.

Too blind to accept the truth.

He'd been in love with her from the start.

He suspected she'd been in love with him from the start too.

They rode in silence back to the villa he already knew he could not imagine living in without her.

He needed to think and work out what the hell he was going to do. God damn it, they were marrying in two days.

Inside, she reached for his hand.

'Thanasis…'

The emotions spilled over. Clasping her cheeks, he

kissed her deeply, pouring into it all his passion and desire for her and selfishly helping himself to a taste of her
passion and desire for him.

He broke away and gazed intently into the stunned
black eyes. 'I love you, Lucie. Now get some sleep and
we will talk in the morning.'

He took the stairs two at a time, her dazed stare following his every step.

Lucie pressed her back to the nearest wall and her hand
to her heart.

Her legs felt like soggy noodles.

The butler appeared. Offered her a drink.

'Your smoothest Scotch,' she whispered. 'No ice.'

She swallowed it in one and then looked up the winding staircase.

The liquid medicine wound its way into her chest and
with it came the clarity she'd been searching for.

All her life Lucie had known that to get what she
wanted, she had to work at it and take it for herself because no one else was going to help her. She'd never
wanted anyone's help. Everything she'd achieved in her
life had come off her own hard work, so why was she still
letting Thanasis dictate all the terms when she'd resisted
being dictated to since hitting double digits?

Because deep down had been the fear that he was right
and none of her feelings were real.

But they *were* real. As real as the air she was breathing and as real as the cool tiles beneath her feet.

He wanted her. She wanted him. He loved her...

She laughed.

He'd never said those words before. Not to post-amnesia Lucie.

Kicking her shoes off, she ran up the stairs.

Thanasis stripped off his shirt in front of the mirror. He swore he could see the thrashing of his heart against his chest.

He unzipped his chinos and let them fall to the floor.

He felt sick. Sick with himself. Sick with what he had to do and what the ramifications could be.

He needed to press the nuclear button.

He couldn't marry her. Not like this. Lucie deserved to know the truth before they made their vows.

But not now. In the morning. First thing in the morning. Let her have peace for one more night before her peace of mind was shattered for ever. He owed her that much.

So caught up was he in his despairing thoughts that the first tap on his door didn't penetrate.

It was the hairs rising on the back of his neck that told him.

On legs that didn't feel like they belonged to him, he crossed the room.

He could smell her perfume before his hand touched the door.

Swallowing hard, he opened it, and then sucked in a breath.

It was the last breath he was capable of making for a long, long time.

Lucie was naked.

Heaven help him, she was fully, proudly naked and far more beautiful than his wildest imaginings, her chin lifted, her hair loose and as wild as the expression in her eyes.

She took a step towards him.

Oh, God help him.

'Lucie…' He lifted a hand to ward her off and tried to speak through his clenched teeth. *'Please.'*

She took the hand gently with both of hers and placed it flat on her left breast. Held it there.

His fingers reflexively tightened around it even as he fought harder than ever to hold on. *Theos*, he could feel the heavy thrum of her heart. Feel the jut of her nipple against his palm, not a whisper of barrier between them.

He closed his eyes and groaned. Blood was pounding in his head.

God help him, please.

Lucie drank Thanasis in with a greed she'd never known was possible. To see the rise and fall of his chest and the expression in the green eyes before he'd closed them to her…

She rose onto her toes and palmed his cheek.

His nostrils flared.

'Lucie…' His voice was ragged. Tortured. 'Please. Go back to your room. We *can't*.'

Thick stubble had sprung out on skin that only hours ago had been baby smooth from his shave, and the pads of her fingers tingled madly in reaction to the sharpness. Her longing for him intensified.

Slowly sliding her fingers across his jaw and down the strong throat, touching him as she'd done so many times in her fantasies, she whispered, 'I might not have past memories to pin my feelings on, but I do have my heart and my gut, and both have been telling me since I woke in that hospital bed that you mean something to me. Those feelings have only grown stronger.' She trailed her trembling fingers over his chest and tipped her nose into the base of his neck to breathe in the musky scent of his skin.

Other than the flexing of his fingers over her breast, he'd barely moved a muscle, but she could feel the internal battle he was waging against himself and it filled her thrashing heart with fresh tenderness for him.

Excitement building, she skimmed her fingers over the plane of his hard abdomen and thrilled over his latent power.

It felt like she'd been waiting her whole life for this moment.

His throat moved. She pressed a kiss to it before tilting her head back and cupping his cheeks, willing him to look at her.

Tremulously, she said, 'I saw you across that room all those years ago and something moved in me, and I have carried it in me all this time. I don't want to wait any more. I want *you*, Thanasis, the man I've got to know here, exactly as you are here with me right now.'

Thanasis's groan escaped his mouth before he could stop it and, before he could stop himself, his hand fell away from Lucie's breast to slide behind her back and his hungry lips fused hard against hers.

The relief at finally letting himself go was dizzying, and he held her even tighter to him and kissed her even harder, groaning as her breasts pressed against him and her arms slid around his neck, the passion in her response scorching him with a heat that melted the last of the mental shackles binding him and unleashed all his hunger in one long surge of passion.

He couldn't fight something this strong and this essential. God help him, he needed her, needed Lucie with a hunger he'd never believed existed.

Let her feel it all, all his passion and love for her. Let her feel everything she was and everything she meant to him.

Lucie sank into the ravenous kiss with a sob of pleasure, her lips parting as her senses overloaded with the dark, addictively intoxicating taste and scent of Thanasis. Flames erupted inside her, licking her into a furnace and liquefying her, and it was all she could do to bite her fingers into his neck to hold herself upright and sink even deeper into the possessive demands of his mouth.

Without a single word being uttered, he swept her into his arms and carried her to the bed. There, he laid her down and then, his hooded eyes fixed on her, removed his underwear...heavens, he was *huge*...and climbed on top of her.

For the longest time he just stared at her, breathing heavily, drinking her in as if she were the goddess of his dreams.

The swell of muscles in his shoulders bunching as he supported his weight to lower himself onto her gave another hint of his innate masculine power, and the most feminine part of her revelled to see it and thrilled to see the wonder in his stare. If there had been so much as a fleck of doubt that she was doing the right thing, it had vanished. This was exactly where she was supposed to be. In Thanasis's arms and in his bed.

And then their mouths fused back together, hot and greedy, a primitive hunger that burned through sense and logic and burned through the last of her thoughts.

Wrapping her arms around his neck, Lucie scratched her nails into the soft bristles at the nape, closing her eyes and her mind to everything but the sensory pleasure of Thanasis, keeping them closed when his mouth moved from hers and razed its way down her neck, would have cried her disappointment when he left her neck if he hadn't cupped her breast and sent a gasp flying from her lips, a gasp that turned into a sob when his mouth closed over the tip.

She was on fire, writhing with him and against him, her body gripped with such intense excitement it was impossible to still herself until he clasped hold of her wrists. Flames were licking her skin, heat bubbling deep within her, no longer some distant squirmy feeling between her legs but a pulse beating hard, and when his tongue licked and then suckled, rousing her nipples into hard peaks that had her whispering incoherently, the pulse tightened and she instinctively arched into his mouth.

The grip on her wrists didn't lessen as he snaked his way lower, and she spread her thighs for him without a moment of hesitation, surrendering herself to him in her entirety, desperate for the ache between her thighs to be relieved, and when his tongue found her swollen arousal, any sense she had left in her was lost in the thrills of what Thanasis was doing to her.

The flames were suffusing her, throbbing and pulsing, building into something entirely and solely within his control, and she cried out to him, pleading and begging until she spiralled over the edge and spasms of unrelenting pleasure flooded her with a force that sent white light flickering behind her eyes.

By the time the earth reclaimed her and she blinked

her eyes open, there was no time to recover before Thanasis crawled up her body to kiss her, and suddenly her mouth was filled with an exotic taste…her taste.

Fresh hunger filled her and suddenly she was consumed with the need to worship him with the same heady attention he'd just gifted her, and she pushed at his chest to roll him onto his back.

With the taste of Lucie's climax still on his tongue, Thanasis submitted to an assault of his senses that would have lost him his mind if it wasn't already gone. Every touch and mark of her mouth and tongue scorched him. Never had he been on the receiving end of such pleasure, but it was much more than that, more than a bodily experience, this transcended everything…

He groaned and had to grit his teeth when she took hold of his erection, then gritted them even harder when she took him in her mouth.

He lifted his head to look at her at the same moment her gaze lifted to his.

His heart punched through him to see the desire-laden wonder in her stare.

Closing his eyes, he gathered her hair lightly and let her take the lead, throwing his head back on the pillow as her movements, tentative at first, became emboldened. The fist she'd made around the base tightened and she took him deeper into her mouth, moaning her own pleasure at the pleasure she was giving him.

If heaven existed he'd just found it. This was like nothing…nothing…

The telltale tug of his orgasm began to pull at him, and with an exhale of air, he flipped her back round, pulling her up the bed to pin her back beneath him.

Throat too constricted to speak, he kissed her deeply, the tip of his erection jutting and straining against her slick heat.

Lucie felt possessed, that there was every chance she would go insane if Thanasis didn't take possession of her. She had never wanted anything as badly as she wanted this. Every inch of her body was alight with the flames he'd ignited, her senses consumed with him. His beautiful face was all she could see, his ragged breaths all she could hear, his musky skin all she could smell and all she could taste, the smoothness of his skin all she could feel.

Shivering with longing, she rocked her hips, encouraging his possession, her breathing rapid as he stilled himself to drive into her, and with a long, drawn-out groan he was deeply and fully inside her and it was the most incredible sensation she could have dreamed of.

Limbs and tongues entwined, he drove in and out of her, the burn in her core reigniting and deepening and then uncoiling like tendrils through her very being until she was nothing but a mass of nerve endings, and the burning pressure deep inside of her exploded.

With a long cry, she buried her mouth into his neck and held tight as rolling waves of bliss flooded her. Somewhere in the recesses of her mind, she heard Thanasis shout out, and then there was one last furious thrust that locked their groins together for one final time.

Buried as deep inside Lucie as he'd ever dreamed it was possible to be, Thanasis felt his climax roar through him. And still he tried to bury deeper, still she tried to pull him deeper, both of them desperately drawing out the pleasure for as long as they could until there was nothing left but stunned silence.

* * *

Thanasis, eyes closed, stroked the smooth back of the woman cuddled so tightly into him. Their legs were entwined, her soft curls tickling his throat and chin.

If not for the weight in his heart, this would be the deepest contentment he'd ever known.

He'd never experienced anything like that before. Nothing close. That had transcended *everything*.

He pressed a kiss into her hair and breathed her in, wishing they could just stay like this.

A little longer. Let them have this moment. Let all the feelings seep through them and work their magic long enough that when he made the confession that he must, Lucie would understand their lovemaking had been separate from everything else.

God, please make her understand.

She sighed and then lifted her head to rest her chin on his chest. 'I'm hungry.'

He ran a finger through a curl and smiled to watch it magically turn into three separate curls. 'You're always hungry... What did you eat while I was in Athens?'

'Not much. Elias made me a couple of flatbreads with that lovely feta and yogurt mousse.'

'Again?' They'd only had that for their lunch the day before. Each flatbread was the size of a dinner plate.

She gave him that mischievous grin but her eyes were still soft from their lovemaking. 'I asked him very nicely. Oh, and I had a bowl of pistachio ice cream too, which I think is the nicest ice cream I've ever had. I would seriously advise locking him away for the wedding or one of your guests is going to steal him.'

His throat constricted. He swallowed hard to clear it.

'I will give your advice the serious consideration it deserves.'

'Good. Because if you don't, you'll need a new wife as I'll be off tracking Elias down.'

Now his heart constricted too before expanding heavily, compressing him with its weight, a sluggish pulse beating in his head.

'Are you okay?'

Lucie's voice seemed to come from far away but her face had closed in, concerned black eyes hovering right before him.

'Earth to Thanasis.' Her concern was mirrored in her tone and it came to him with a sickening thud that he didn't deserve her concern.

Reverently tracing the line of her jaw, he gazed into the most beautiful eyes in the world and knew the moment he'd wanted to stretch for eternity was already over.

'There is something I need to tell you. Something you need to know.'

Her forehead creased.

'Lucie…' He closed his eyes briefly before fixing them back to hers. 'What I'm about to tell you… Know that I love you. Hold that thought. I love you.'

Apprehension written all over her face, she lifted herself up, hugging the sheets to her breasts. 'You're scaring me,' she whispered.

'I'm sorry.' Deep in the very pit of his being, the weight of dread was pulling at him. His next words would determine the remaining course of his life. 'I'm sorry, Lucie, but our past, what you've been told, it's all a lie. You and I were never in love.'

For the longest time she just sat there looking at him

blankly. And then she seemed to shrink, the colour draining from her face, eyes dulling with comprehension.

'Forgive me,' he said quietly, knowing as he said it that he didn't deserve her forgiveness, 'but we were never lovers. We were as far from lovers as it is possible for two people to be.'

CHAPTER TWELVE

LUCIE SAW THANASIS'S lips move but heard no sound above the roar in her head.

Time had faded away, the world spinning around her and then ebbing to a crawl, everything that had happened between them since she'd woken in her hospital bed flashing like picture stills in her vision.

Slowly, slowly, the present began to weave back into her consciousness, her eyes clearing to soak in the dark stubble on Thanasis's jawline, and the dark hairs of his chest which were so soft in stark contrast to the hardness of the muscle and bone beneath them, the nerves of her hand registering the tenderness of the giant hands holding hers... She had no recollection of him taking them or even of him sitting up to face her. She heard, too, the tenderness in his voice.

'Lucie, say something, please.'

Her head was pounding.

Slowly, she forced herself to meet his stare.

His green eyes were stark with torment.

She tugged her hands free and whispered, 'I need to use the bathroom.'

Twisting to the edge of the bed, she groped with her foot for the floor then fought to keep her legs upright as she staggered away from him, suddenly aware that she was cold. Cold and naked.

Naked from their lovemaking.

A whimper rose up her throat but she smothered it, dragging her legs to the door he'd silently indicated, suddenly desperate to cover her nakedness.

Oh, dear God help her, had it *all* been a lie?

There was a grey robe on the door but she couldn't bring herself to touch it, and she wrapped a bath towel around herself before splashing water on her clammy face.

She was shaking. Her whole body.

The memory she'd been searching for finally flashed before her. Lucie and her mother alone in her hospital room.

'Mum, how do Thanasis and I get on? The nurse seems to think...'

'Seems to think what?'

'She thinks he's in love with me.'

'It has been obvious to us all that strong emotions have developed between you.'

But her mum hadn't met Thanasis before Lucie's accident. It had been a lie. One of many, many lies.

She rammed her fist into her mouth to smother the scream fighting to break free.

Oh, God, how could she face seeing him again?

She *had* to face him. There was no other choice.

When she finally left the bathroom, he'd thrown on a pair of shorts and was sitting at the end of the bed rubbing his head.

She sank her weak legs onto an armchair facing him

and forced herself to meet his gaze. 'Was any of it true? You and me? The great unexpected romance?'

There was a bleakness in his stare. 'No. None of it was true. It was a lie we fed you to stop you leaving me again.'

She gripped hold of her knees and hung her head in an effort to fight against a world trying to spin itself off its axis around her again. 'Again?'

He gave a taut nod. 'I hated you. I made your life a misery.'

She turned her face away, his blunt admittance slicing like a knife through her heart.

The spasm of pain on Lucie's face lanced him. Drawing in a long breath, Thanasis filled himself with resolve.

She deserved the truth.

And he deserved whatever retribution came from it.

Especially now.

God forgive him.

'I hated your entire family. I agreed to the marriage because it was the only viable way of saving my business and saving my family from destitution, but I hated you before I even set eyes on you and when I did set eyes on you and realised you were the woman from the party I'd searched the streets of Athens for, I made damned sure that you hated me too.'

Her gaze turned back to him, her distressed black eyes wide.

'Oh, yes,' Thanasis said grimly. 'I was deliberate about it. I had mentally allocated two years of my life to our marriage, and then it would be dissolved and I would find myself a real wife to build my real future with. Georgios Tsaliki's stepdaughter was never going to be that woman.'

God that he could take it all back. Rewind to when

he'd opened his bedroom door to find her naked and tell her the truth then, before he'd lost himself to the heat of his passion for her and shared the most incredible and fulfilling emotional and physical experience of his life with the woman whose heart had connected to his and which he now needed to break.

He could only pray that Lucie could find it in herself to forgive him. He would never forgive himself.

'In my wildest, most secret dreams, the woman I would build my future with was the tiny waif with a mass of black curly hair who'd captured a piece of my heart all those years ago…'

Her chin wobbled. She made the smallest of whimpers.

God that he could lift all her pain from her. He would not close his eyes or his ears to it.

'And then I found she was you.' His mouth twisted in self-loathing. 'I cannot tell you how much I hated you for being her, or how much I hated myself for still wanting you. I even hated you for your selflessness—you were giving up your life and independence to save the fortunes of a monster and getting nothing in return. You asked for nothing in return. Nothing.

'You and I spent two months in a war I instigated and fed. I treated you despicably and in turn you treated me with loathing and contempt, but to reiterate—it all came from me. You'd been prepared to give me a chance… I'd seen it in your eyes and I hated that about you too. This was all on me. Everything that was toxic about our relationship came from me, and I will regret my behaviour and the way I treated you for the rest of my life.'

She closed her eyes.

Theos, she looked so small. So lost. The towel she'd wrapped around herself was swallowing her up.

If only she would let him reach across...

Her eyes opened and clamped onto his. 'What happened at the end?'

His stomach lurched. He pulled his lips together.

'What else?' she said, her voice hardening. 'I know there's something else and I know it involves Athena.'

Of all the things he'd never wanted Lucie to relive, this had been at the top of his list.

To relive it meant she would have to relive her pain and distress.

But he couldn't hide it from her or try and sweeten it. The truth he owed her was the full truth.

If he'd been a better man, he'd have said to hell with consequences and told her the full truth a week ago.

But a week ago he hadn't known he loved her. Hadn't known Lucie's happiness and peace of mind would come to mean more to him than anything.

'Did you sleep with her?'

He didn't drop his stare. 'No, but she led you to believe that I did.'

Whatever little colour that had returned to her cheeks vanished.

'When we first discussed marriage between the two families, it was agreed, at my suggestion, that I would marry Athena—she was Georgios's only blood daughter so it made sense to me. But just as I wouldn't entertain Alexis marrying Lydia, Georgios refused to let Athena marry me. Marrying you was at his suggestion. The fact the world has always regarded you as his daughter meant our marriage would have the same effect. At some point

Athena learned she'd been first choice.' Now he did close his eyes. 'She came to me.'

'Came to you?' she croaked. 'What does that mean?'

'She came to my offices.' He forced himself to look back at her. 'After everything about the marriage was agreed and you moved to Greece, you spent a lot of time with her. She knew you and I hated each other and seemed to think my suggestion of marriage to her meant that I must want her. She tried to seduce me.'

A pulse was throbbing in the base of her throat. 'Tried?'

'Yes. Tried. She kissed my neck, I pushed her away and told her to leave. She left. The first I knew that she'd gone straight to the apartment to see you was when I got home. You were waiting for me. You checked the collar of my shirt, saw the lipstick mark she'd left on it and that was it. You hit the roof. You refused to let me explain myself. You stole my car keys out of my hand and told me the wedding was off.'

'I didn't believe you?'

'You wouldn't let me speak to explain. You were in a terrible state.' He took a deep breath. 'I thought then that it was anger but it was distress. I think Athena hurt you very much. The things she said to you. She told you about Georgios insisting that you be the one to make the sacrifice of marriage for the sake of the family. Told you why.'

Her pretty eyebrows had drawn together. 'Why would Athena do that to me? Our relationship has always been fractious but I never thought she hated me.'

'She is poisonous.'

'She's been a sister to me since I was three years old.'

'Sisters because your mother stole her father from her mother.'

Her eyes squeezed shut.

'In Athena's eyes, it is the truth,' he said.

'But I was a *child*.'

'Her mother is poison. The whole Tsaliki family and anyone who marries into them is poison or becomes contaminated by it. They are all selfish and out for themselves—it is why our fathers fell out and separated the business into two. My father learned Georgios was taking bribes. Athena saw a chance to hurt you and she took it. To her, it was a bit of mindless entertainment to ease the boredom of her life. She had no care for your feelings because she is incapable of caring for anyone but herself.'

'Then you should have taken what she was offering because you have no care for my feelings either,' she whispered.

'Your feelings matter more to me than anything.'

Her gaze levelled back on him. 'Oh, I think I'm as expendable to you as I so clearly am to everyone else.'

'Don't say that.'

'Why not? We're speaking truths, aren't we? You let me believe you were holding back from me because you didn't want to take advantage of my missing memories…' Lucie closed her eyes, fighting with everything she had to hold on to her composure.

She'd instigated their lovemaking. *She* had. Not Thanasis. Right until the very end, he'd fought away from it.

Oh, God, she couldn't bear to remember how beautiful it had been. How beautiful he had made her feel. How *loved* he'd made her feel.

She'd given him everything she had to give and all along…

She'd thought she'd been taking control but she was

the one who'd been controlled, right from the moment she'd woken up in that hospital bed.

She snapped her gaze back to him. 'I'm sure you can soothe your conscience by telling yourself that you *tried* to resist the chemistry between us, and, quite honestly, I can imagine living with you *was* like living in a form of war zone. I'm a prickly bear when people are mean to me—you lash out at me and if I've got nowhere to hide then I lash right back, and I know perfectly well that if you of all people had been cruel to me then my self-defence mechanism would have kicked in, and when I say you of all people I mean it's because I spent six years painting you in my head as this romantic hero, luckily not to the extent where I fancied myself in love with you or anything, but enough that it would have hurt to learn you really were the unmitigated bastard the Tsalikis always painted you as being, and I am trying so hard right now not to lash out at you and call you every vile name under the sun for what you've done to me and for all the lies you've been feeding me...'

'I've tried very hard not to tell you outright lies.'

'Oh, aren't you a regular saint?' she scorned bitterly, needing to *be* scornful, needing to keep speaking because something was swelling inside her, pushing into her chest and throat, something hot and ugly and dripping with the pain that every word uttered by Thanasis had made her bleed with.

'Everything apart from our past has been the truth, I swear.'

'Quick, polish your halo. But as I was saying, I'm trying very hard not to call you all the vile names that are lining up on my tongue, and trying even harder not to imagine breaking your nose and, and…and…' She couldn't contain the agony a second longer. Before she could stop them, tears were pouring down her face and Lucie was on her feet and charging at him, pushing as hard as she could into Thanasis's chest to send him falling back onto the mattress, climbing on top of him, straddling him as she screamed obscenities and pounded her fists at his chest.

'How could you?' she sobbed when all her obscenities had dried up but not an ounce of the agony had been purged. 'How could you, how could you, how *could* you? How could you do that to me? I did nothing to any of you except love you and you all lied, and you, you bastard, you pretended that you loved me and cared for me when all along you hated me…'

Finally, he grabbed her wrists to control her and flipped her over, pinning her down. 'No, Lucie, I have *never* hated you, never believe that. I only thought I did, and it's only now that I look back and can see it was a lie I fed myself.'

She shook her head wildly. 'Every word out of your mouth has been a lie!'

'No.'

'You made me fall in love with you, and all so you could save your bastard business when you didn't even need to tell me the lie!'

'I know, but once the lie had been fed I had no choice but to go along with it.'

'You're Thanasis Antoniadis,' she screamed. 'Of course you had a choice! The only person in this whole sordid affair not given a choice is me because all the choices I made were choices based on lies because I'm the expendable one, the one who never fits in anywhere so who bloody well cares about Lucie?'

'I care, more than anything.'

'Well, I don't. I don't care about you and I don't care about the Tsalikis. You can all rot in hell together—you deserve each other, now get off me, get off me, get *off* me!'

Breathing heavily, he let go of her wrists and moved off her.

In a flash, she'd scrambled off the bed and was out of the door before Thanasis had managed to haul himself off the mattress to chase after her.

He slammed her bedroom door open. The room was empty but he could hear her throwing things around in her dressing room and snatched a tiny breath of relief that she hadn't run off naked into the night.

He stood by the door. 'Lucie, please, I know you're hurting, but please don't do anything rash. Hate me, hit me, punch me, do all the things you want, just don't go. Not like this. Stay with me. Please. Just give me a chance to put things right.'

She appeared in front of him hugging her overnight case to her chest, a broken Aphrodite with bloodshot eyes and hair like a nest and a thin black dress she'd put on back to front. 'Put things right so I'll marry you and keep the public lie going?'

'I don't care about the wedding,' he roared. 'All I care about is you, and right now I'm terrified you're going to go off and do something stupid like you did the last time.'

There was a moment of complete stillness before Lucie slowly straightened, seeming to grow and magnify before his eyes, as proud and as powerful as Hera herself.

'The only stupid thing I've done other than believe your lies is fall in love with you,' she said with deadly, ice-cold precision. 'But, believe me, I'm over that now, and if you think I'm going to do something rash that puts me in danger then you're the stupid one because you're the last person in the world I'd hurt myself over. Do not follow me, do not ever make contact with me again. I have nothing left to say to you.'

This time, Thanasis let her go.

Lucie sat on a rock by the harbour watching the sun rise. She would never now have the chance to watch it rise on the mountain's summit. Never mind. There were lots of things in life she would never get her chance at. Getting married was but one of them, and it was with that philosophical thought in mind that she got to her feet at the sight of the boat approaching the harbour with supplies for the wedding that would never take place.

An hour later she was sailing away from Sephone.

She didn't look back.

Thanasis watched the boat containing the woman he loved disappear on the horizon.

The world swayed beneath his feet and he had to squeeze his eyes shut to ground himself.

Heading in the other direction, sailing towards him, the first of the many yachts sailing to Sephone for the wedding of the century.

He rubbed at his raw, gritty eyes.

So much to do. A wedding to cancel. All the people who needed to be notified. The press, who needed to be managed.

He didn't have the heart or energy to do any of it.

It no longer mattered what he lost. He'd already lost the only thing that mattered.

This time, there would be no reprieve. No third chance.

Lucie was gone for ever.

CHAPTER THIRTEEN

THE KINDNESS OF strangers was something Lucie would never take for granted again. After docking in Kos, the captain of the supply boat, who must have thought she was some kind of castaway who'd ended up on Sephone by accident, had given her his phone and been happy for her to search the business number for Kelly Holden Design and then make a call to England. Four hours later, she had the last available ticket for a flight to London.

Her father, stepmother and half-sisters, all laden with luggage, all failed to spot her when she passed them outside the airport.

The package that had been couriered was nondescript. Just the ordinary white plastic packaging of a particular courier service. The only thing out of the ordinary was that the sender had known to send it to Kelly's house. No one other than Kelly and her husband knew Lucie had taken refuge with them. If the press found out, they would descend on the Holden home like bees around a honeypot but with a much nastier sting.

They'd been stalking Thanasis for five days. She wished she didn't know this but Kelly had loaned her a spare laptop and, like the masochist she was, Lucie couldn't stop herself stalking his name.

He deserved everything he had coming to him, she told herself with regularly needed fortitude as she read article after article detailing the mysterious circumstances of the bride's disappearance from Sephone, and article after article about the future of Antoniadis Shipping and the severe peril it had been plunged into.

Thanasis's refusal to discuss the cancelled wedding only added fuel to a fire keeping the Internet alive with gossip and rumour. The few paparazzi shots of him showed a dishevelled man who'd stopped sleeping. Well, he wasn't going to get any sympathy from her, not when she held him responsible for the purple hollows that had appeared beneath her own eyes.

Tsaliki Shipping wasn't faring much better in the publicity stakes, and now there were rumours circulating that the missing bride had been forced by her evil stepfamily into marrying their enemy, and that she'd run away to escape her fate and was refusing to return to the Tsaliki family bosom. Her mum, Lucie thought, played the part of distressed mother quite well but she really needed to get some stronger onions to provoke better tears. As for Athena…

Athena's actions had broken her heart, more so even than her mother's had. Her mother had always been selfish and single-minded, but Athena's cruelty cut deep.

Had she always resented her? Had her sporadic mood swings and bitchiness been symptoms of something that ran deeper than Lucie had known?

It was unlikely she'd ever know. She never wanted to see any of the Tsalikis again. None of them loved her. That was the truth. You didn't treat someone the way they'd collectively conspired to treat her if you loved them. Lucie was expendable to them. She was expendable to everyone.

The package was still in her hands.

Some kind of sixth sense told Lucie what it contained and who'd sent it: the person whose very name it destroyed her to think of. And it was because of this sixth sense that she held off opening it until night fell and she was alone in the guest room with her ninth cup of tea of the day. It was the only form of sustenance her belly could cope with. Coffee turned her stomach. All foods tightened it into a ball.

At least she wasn't pregnant. She supposed that should be considered a mercy. Certainly not something to feel wretched about. Hadn't even been something she'd given two thoughts about until her period had started that morning.

Why hadn't Thanasis used protection? It was the first time she'd dared ask herself that question. She knew why she hadn't—because she'd believed herself in love with him. Love, marriage and babies.

None of these were things she would ever have now. To love, you had to trust and she would never trust again. When she was back on her feet—Kelly had given Lucie her old job back without having to be ambushed into it— she would rent herself a small place and get herself a cat. At least cats never pretended to be anything other than what they were. Yes. A cat. Maybe a new cat each year, create a collection of them, and then when she was an old lady and her hair all wild and grey, she would morph into the local cat lady and let that be her legacy.

She couldn't put it off any longer. Lucie ripped into the packaging. Inside was a box as nondescript as the packaging. Wrapped around the box was an envelope with her name on it written in a penmanship she didn't recognise but which still made her tremble.

She closed her eyes.

Box or envelope first?

Box.

And there it was. Her phone.

She turned it on and waited for it to power up.

Moments later and it was beeping and chirping like an aviary at feeding time.

Ninety-seven missed calls. Two hundred and nineteen text messages…

She turned it upside down so she didn't have to see them and could ignore a little longer her friends' entreaties for her to get in touch.

She would ignore any entreaties from her family for ever. Except for her dad. None of this was his fault. His only crime was to like order more than he liked his daughter, and she didn't even think it was that he didn't like her, it was more that he didn't understand her. In his own way, he did love her, and she should message and let him know she was safe.

Duty to her father done, she held the envelope in her hand.

Now she really was shaking. The palms of her hands had gone clammy.

She ripped it open and pulled out the letter contained in it.

Dear Lucie,

Forgive me for going against your wishes in communicating with you, but this was recently found in my apartment's car park. I admit, returning it to you is the excuse I have been seeking to reach out to you.

I know that much of what I'm going to write now

is not what you want to hear so I can only hope you can bring yourself to read it, but will understand if it is too much for you.

I have been thinking a lot about our time together on Sephone, and, Lucie, they were the best days of my life. There is something inherently joyful in your nature that sings to something in me that is usually so serious, and I pray my actions haven't destroyed this essential part of you.

You were right in saying I had a choice over whether to lie to you. I did have a choice and I made the wrong one. It is a choice I will regret until my dying day, and I will regret it not for what it's done to me but for what it's done to you. You didn't deserve any of this.

I don't know if you realised it when we were dining with them, but Leander was the host of the party I first saw you at all those years ago. Seeing you at that party changed something in me. I don't believe there is such a thing as love at first sight but I have carried your image with me ever since, and now I carry you fully in my heart. You are beautiful, Lucie, inside and out, and you deserve the world. I just wish I could be the one to give it to you.

I'm sorry for the pain I caused you. I hope one day you find the courage to love again and I hope the man you find that courage with treats you with the respect and devotion you deserve.

I meant every word I said to you on the mountain.
I will love you for ever,
Thanasis

By the time Lucie had read the letter a fifth time, the paper was soaked with her tears, her face burrowed in a pillow as all the pain and anguish she'd tried so hard to contain purged from her.

Lucie lay like a starfish, unseeing wet eyes fixed on the ceiling, the ruined letter still clutched in her hand. All those precious words dissolved. All his precious words. All dissolved as if they'd never existed...

No, that couldn't be true because they'd etched into her heart, just as the man who'd written them had, and the world turned itself back to the moment she'd first opened her eyes to find him there, and then it speeded up, reeling her through their time together until that final beautiful night, before he'd confessed the truth...

But what was the truth? That she should listen to her head and forget him? Or that she should listen to her heart, which knew she could live a thousand years and would still carry him inside its broken walls?

The only truth she knew for certain was the truth about how Thanasis made her feel, and the pain of his absence hurt a thousand times more than the pain of the loss of her mother and the entirety of her stepfamily combined.

As memories of their lovemaking danced through her mind Lucie lifted herself off the bed and opened the guest room curtains. The sun would soon be rising in Greece. Thanasis would watch it rise under a different sky from hers. And he would watch it, she knew it. He'd watch the sun rise and he would think of her. Every sunrise and sunset he saw for the rest of his life would come with memories of her because he loved her. That was another truth.

And there was one more truth. Unless she could bring

herself to forgive him, she would have to endure a lifetime of sunrises and sunsets without him. She would be destined to live in perpetual winter like Demeter without Persephone, desolate and barren of heart and soul.

Thanasis showered, shaved, brushed his teeth, dressed, and styled his hair without any recollection of doing any of it. He fed muesli into his mouth. There was no point eating anything worth tasting. He couldn't taste anything. Food had become fuel, nothing more. Most aromas turned his stomach.

In the back of his car, he stretched out his legs and flicked through his notes. He'd been up until the early hours preparing. Antoniadis Shipping's major investors had demanded a meeting. In just two days, the fleet of ships would be delivered and the four billion would have to be paid. There was no guarantee that money would be available, not when the major investors were talking behind backs and working to their own agendas. He had a feeling today's meeting was nothing but a courtesy. He'd warned his parents to start looking for a smaller home. A much smaller home. His sister was refusing to take his calls. One more headache he didn't need.

The car pulled up outside his headquarters.

He rolled his neck.

Flanked by his lawyer and PA, Thanasis swept through the door and took the elevator to the top floor. Every employee he came across he greeted with his usual courtesy. He would not have anyone think he was concerned his world was about to be destroyed.

Besides, you couldn't destroy something that was already wrecked, and Thanasis's life was as wrecked as wrecked could be. If not for his family and thousands of employees, he would tell the investors to do whatever the hell they wanted to his business and then walk away from it all. There was nothing left for him. There was no life for him without Lucie. Only existence. All a man needed to exist were a roof over his head and three square meals a day.

But he would play the game one last time for his family and employees' sakes.

The walls of the boardroom were glass and he could see them already in there, plotting over good coffee and fresh pastries *he'd* provided.

He shook their hands and took his seat.

The moment Craig opened his mouth, Thanasis knew it was game over.

Words were bandied around. English word salads. Corporate jargon to justify the cowardice. He tuned most of the words out, only the odd ones floating into his consciousness. Reputational Management were his favourites. Especially coming from a man Thanasis knew for a fact was cheating on his wife with their children's nanny.

He made a half-hearted attempt to fight his corner but it was like a boxer already down on points in the final round with his opponent still fresh and bouncing in the ring.

He wondered if Lucie had found her bounce again yet. He hoped so. He prayed for her to have found her bounce again. The Lucie bounce…

The investors had stopped talking, their necks craned to a commotion occurring outside the boardroom.

Thanasis might be dead inside but he could still manage to raise one eyebrow as a sop to curiosity.

He started. Sat up straighter.

He could have sworn he'd just seen a curly black pineapple…

Just as he was blinking to clear his eyes, a tiny waif in a long flowing black dress, black jacket with crystals studded into it and chunky black boots ducked out from the crowd and, before anyone could stop her, flung the boardroom door wide open.

'Apologies, gentlemen…lady.' She smiled widely around the room. 'I just need a quick word with my fiancé.' Then, to Thanasis, she said, 'Can you believe I forgot my security pass again? I'm so sorry. Honestly, I swear I'd forget my head if it wasn't screwed on.' Attention back on the investors, she tapped the side of her head. 'Brain injury. I do *not* recommend. But on the mend now, so all good.'

Everyone's mouth had fallen open, none wider than Thanasis's. He'd lost control of his body. He couldn't even raise his hands to rub his eyes.

Was he hallucinating?

At a speed that threatened to give everyone in the room whiplash, she turned back to Thanasis. 'The medical team have just declared me fit to travel again, so can I borrow a helicopter to meet Griselda and get the wedding rebooked?'

'Excuse me, miss,' Craig, the Canadian investor, said, 'but you're Thanasis's *fiancée*?'

'Yes, for my sins. I'm so sorry we had to postpone the wedding but I'm sure Thanasis told you all about my relapse. Thank you all so much for not tipping the press off about it—he's been under enough pressure as it is without having to answer constant questions about whether the woman he loves is going to live or die. I really hope you'll all be able to make the rebooked date—I promise we won't make you wait too long. If I had my way we'd sneak off now and marry but my fiancé's a traditionalist and insists on marrying me properly. Anyway, I've taken enough of all your time, so is it okay for me to borrow a helicopter, my love?'

But Thanasis was incapable of speaking. He was watching Lucie bounce around his boardroom, charming and amusing his investors, and was almost completely certain he was dreaming.

He was still almost completely certain he was dreaming when the meeting came to an abrupt halt, files were shuffled together, laptops closed, hands shaken, murmured awkward apologies for all his 'troubles' and then, in what felt like the time it took to blink, the boardroom was empty of everyone but himself and Lucie.

She glided past him.

He caught a waft of her perfume.

She must have pressed the button for all the wall blinds lowered. A lock clicked.

'That's better,' she said happily, perching herself on the table beside him. 'Some privacy.'

He just stared at her.

She slid her bottom over so she was facing him, and reached down to loosen his tie. 'I think the words you're looking for are *thank you*.'

But still he couldn't speak.

'I don't know if you noticed or not, but I've just saved your business.' She smiled and pulled his tie off with a swish. 'You're welcome.'

Suddenly, she slid off the table and onto his lap, straddling him, arms hooked around his neck. The black eyes he'd never believed would look at him again were gazing into his. 'If you ever lie to me again, I'll rip your heart out before I leave you.'

'My heart's already been ripped out,' he said hoarsely.

'Good.' She slid her hands over his throat and opened the top button of his shirt. 'You deserve it.' More buttons were opened in quick succession until she spread his shirt apart and pressed her palm to his chest, right above his pounding heart.

He closed his eyes to the sensation, still struggling to believe what every one of his senses was telling him, that his Aphrodite had appeared before him on her pearl shell and that the warmth starting to unfreeze the coldness of his blood was the warmth from her light.

The warmth of her hands palmed his cheeks. The warmth of her breath danced over his mouth.

He opened his eyes and suddenly she was there, solid, real, his love, shining a love he didn't deserve into him.

She was *here*…

'Did I ever tell you how my parents met?' she said quietly, bringing the tip of her nose to his. 'Mum was a receptionist at Dad's accountancy firm. I think her glamour temporarily blinded him. And that's how I came to be made.

'Dad was Georgios's UK accountant. He did some clever accounting that saved Georgios millions in taxes. To thank him and to celebrate, Georgios insisted on taking the whole firm and their partners out to dinner.'

'He stole your mother from him whilst thanking him?' he whispered, finally bringing his hand to her face.

'If I know my mum, she played an active part in this

stealing and, I'm quite sure Dad was secretly glad when she went—I honestly cannot think of two people less compatible.' Her beautiful mouth brushed against his, hands winding round to bury into his hair before she pulled her face back enough to look at him. 'I didn't fit in with either of them or their new families. I tried. I think they tried. But ultimately, my existence has been spent being pulled by fundamentally different parents from fundamentally different worlds. Neither of them wanted to see me as my own person but as an extension of themselves. You, my love, see me exactly as I am and you love me for it, and I fit in with *you*. I belong with you, Thanasis, and if I don't give us the chance we deserve to build something true with all our cards on the table and complete honesty between us, then I will spend the rest of my life regretting it. You are mine and I am yours. The lies you told, they weren't selfish lies. Mum told me those lies for wicked, selfish reasons, because she'd rather destroy her own daughter than lose her life-style, but you didn't—you did it for your family. Because you love them. And your guilt over it...' She pressed another gentle kiss to his mouth and sighed. 'I know you felt guilt. I've relived every minute of our time together and I know the lies were eating you up.'

There was a burning sensation in the backs of his eyes. 'I love you, Lucie, and I am so sorry for everything.'

'I know you do and I know you are, and I know in my heart that we both deserve another chance to find that happiness we were just beginning to create together. When I saw how close you were to losing everything... I couldn't have lived with myself if I hadn't done something. I wanted to save you, just as you've been trying to save everything for your family, because I love *you*.'

She did. He could see it so clearly. A love worth more than all the stars in the sky and all the billions in the world.

He gathered a bunch of soft black curls in his hand and shuddered at how close he'd come to never having touched them again. 'I will never hurt you again. I swear. You are everything to me, Lucie. My whole world.'

Her smile was the sweetest, softest smile in the world. 'I know. And you're my world too.'

'Never leave me.'

'Never.'

And then her mouth fused to his in a kiss that sealed their hearts together for ever.

EPILOGUE

'WHAT DO YOU THINK?' Lucie asked, closely watching her husband and business partner's reaction. Of all the interior designs she'd created since setting up her own business four years ago, this was the one she was most proud of, the one that made her heart sing nearly as loudly as the man holding her hand so possessively did.

'It is incredible,' he said, awe in his voice as well as his eyes before he cupped her chin and kissed her with the same passion he'd been kissing her for the past six years. 'Your designs just get better and better. Our child will love it,' he murmured when they came up for air, and as he said that, their baby tucked safely in her belly kicked its agreement, hard enough for Thanasis to feel it in his abdomen pressed against hers.

He smiled and then laughed. 'It never feels less than miraculous, does it?'

She beamed, knowing exactly what he meant. The conception of their third child had the same magical feeling to it as her first two pregnancies. 'Never.'

Lucie often felt their entire marriage was built on magic, and thought it was the same magic that had stopped her memories fully returning. She was happy for them to stay lost for ever, but if they ever did return then it didn't matter. She had six years and counting of being loved and cherished to counter it. Six years and counting of utter bliss.

He kissed her again. 'Shall we?'

'Ready when you are.'

'Then let's go.'

They left their unborn child's nursery and quietly checked on their sleeping daughter, Ellie, and their not-quite-sleeping-yet son, Lea, and then, satisfied all was well, left them under the supervision of the nanny and slipped out of the villa.

The golf buggy had been parked out front for them, a huge backpack filled with goodies placed on the back seat.

And then they were off, heading to the mountain to watch the sun set, the route to the summit having long been made safe for a heavily pregnant woman to manage. It was a private journey they never tired of making and a scene they never tired of witnessing, and one they would take together for the rest of their lives.

* * * * *

MILLS & BOON ®

Coming next month

HER ACCIDENTAL SPANISH HEIR
Caitlin Crews

Something else occurs to me. Like a concrete block falling on me.

Something that should have occurred to me a long time ago.

I count back, one month, another. All the way back to that night in Cap Ferrat.

I stand up abruptly, gather my things and stride toward the front office.

My mind is whirling on the elevator down and I practically sprint out the front of the building then down a few blocks until I find a drugstore. I give thanks for the total disinterest of cashiers in New York City, purchase the test and then make myself walk all the way home to see if that calms me.

It does not.

I throw my bag on the counter in my kitchen and tear open the box, scowling at the instructions.

Then I wait through the longest few minutes of my entire life.

Then I stare down at the two blue lines that blaze there on my test.

Unmistakably.

I simply stand there. Maybe breathing, maybe not.

The truth is as unmistakable as those two blue lines.

I'm pregnant.

With *his* child.

With the *Marquess of Patrias's* baby.

Continue reading

HER ACCIDENTAL SPANISH HEIR
Caitlin Crews

Available next month
millsandboon.co.uk

COMING SOON!

We really hope you enjoyed reading this book.
If you're looking for more romance
be sure to head to the shops when
new books are available on

Thursday 19th June

To see which titles are coming soon, please visit
millsandboon.co.uk/nextmonth

MILLS & BOON

afterglow BOOKS

Afterglow Books is a trend-led, trope-filled list of books with diverse, authentic and relatable characters, a wide array of voices and representations, plus real world trials and tribulations. Featuring all the tropes you could possibly want (think small-town settings, fake relationships, grumpy vs sunshine, enemies to lovers) and all with a generous dose of spice in every story.

♪ @millsandboonuk
📷 @millsandboonuk
afterglowbooks.co.uk

#AfterglowBooks

For all the latest book news, exclusive content and giveaways scan the QR code below to sign up to the Afterglow newsletter:

SCAN ME

LET'S TALK
Romance

For exclusive extracts, competitions and special offers, find us online:

f MillsandBoon

X @MillsandBoon

⊙ @MillsandBoonUK

♪ @MillsandBoonUK

Get in touch on 01413 063 232

For all the latest titles coming soon, visit
millsandboon.co.uk/nextmonth

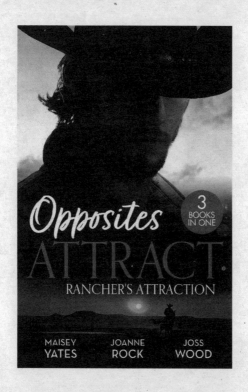

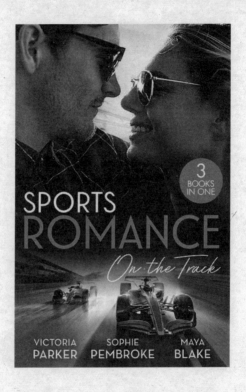